LOUISVILLE SALUTATIONS

A novel

By

MICHAEL DAVID COCHRAN

Modification Media
ModificationMedia1@gmail.com

Michael David Cochran: usmichael888@yahoo.com

Also by Michael David Cochran

Paying Allegiance

Oblivion Arteries

The Project

Utterly Unleashed

Utterly Unhinged

Utility Players

c u Tuesday

Dedicated to TYLER GERTH:

Someone we should all try to emulate in our own way.

Torts and Just Desserts from the mind of Alexander Arrington

An animated owl appeared and began speaking:

"Hello. My name is Alexander Arrington. As you can see, an owl has appeared before you on your screen and is speaking. It's a computer program, or 'app' as they call it. I am not actually an animated owl or proficient with computers. But this is relatively simple, even for me. I record my peace of mind, tap a couple keys and presto, it speaks for me. The icon or avatar is the Antithetical Owl and his name is Alexander, so I picked him.

In this space I, as Alexander the Antithetical Owl, hope to show you another side of what's been going on that may not always pop up on your radar screen. A different perspective that perhaps you may or may not agree with all the time, or ever. We'll see. Starting off, just to get some things straight, 'TORTs,' of course, means The Ohio River Ticks, a catchy blues-rock-country band from Louisville that really gets under your skin. I'll be keeping you up to date on this group as I occasionally bribe them to let me bring my guitar and sit in with my 'talent.'

'Tortes' are multilayered cakes filled with whipped cream, buttercreams, mousses, jams or fruits. I love this dessert.

'Torts' in Tort Law are misdeeds, frequently multilayered by one against another. Such as: negligence, breaking a contract, defaming someone, invasion of privacy, wrongful death and causing emotional distress. The areas where I earn my daily bread.

'Just Deserts' is derived from an ancient term that means one gets what they deserve, good or bad.

'Just Desserts' because these are the only edibles I'm reviewing in this blog."

~~~

"I confess, I seriously love Bourbon Balls. A delicious round chocolate shell filled with soft bourbon cream and chopped pecans. They are Heavenly. When I'm in NuLu I go to Muth's Candy and get a one-pound order, 28 pieces. I take a couple and give out the rest as little delights during the day."

The owl faded out.
~~~

Table of Contents

1

Amy Arrington was good at details and very well organized. Her work was accurate and fast. Ask anyone in the know at P3 – Padmore, Pearce and Payne, a behemoth even in the BigLaw arena of NYC law firms. They weren't technically the biggest, but were arguably the most influential. They only hired the cream of the crop. P3 understood they had a talented document reviewer in this associate. It was a marathon that she ran at a sprinter's pace. Amy also knew case law and could quote chapter and verse on legal decisions, learned from her father Alexander, also an attorney. He made it a game for her: legal battles, precedents, state and federal codes, along with the landmines and legal hurdles one must adhere to and will encounter in the law.

But Amy was quite sure she didn't inherit Alexander's save the world gene. The law was a tool, a vehicle that could take her where she wanted to be. She laughed at a law professor who suggested she would benefit from doing a year as a public defender. Amy couldn't understand lawyers who worked for little or no money. It didn't make sense. No other business did this.

Amy always wanted to be in the action. The main stage. New York and Washington. That's what sent the tingles down her spine.

The firm also deployed Amy in meetings with clients, especially the fussy ones, which seemed to be more than a few.

Ambrosia, 'Amy' Arrington, had pretty much grown up in Louisville, Kentucky, where, besides her father, she had been trained and molded by the ultimate modern southern belle—her mother—April Arrington.

With all of this it was thought that Amy Arrington, at 27, was on the fast-track to partnership at P3. Everything about her said corporate: she dressed conservatively, but quite stylishly. Her long dark hair was always pulled back, secured, only to be deployed when needed. Her golf and tennis games were good, but not too good as to show up the clients or senior partners. The American Lawyer Magazine had profiled Amy as 'an associate to watch, with a superior skill-set.' Amy too believed that the brass ring was close and within reach. Which was why she put up with the amount of time she put in creating billable hours for the firm: 9-9-6.

Amy worked in litigation support, reviewing those documents, maintaining databases and preparing trial presentation materials. However, Padmore also knew they had a rising star of a litigator. Amy was a national semifinalist in the ultra-competitive Herbert Wechsler National Criminal Moot Court Competition. It was a talent well-honed over the years of growing up debating both of her parents.

It was in the month of June, a Thursday afternoon. Amy thought, *8 days away...* And it made her happy. She then got an encrypted personal email from the Stableton Group Talent Agency in Los Angeles. She opened it, scanned the contents and grinned.

Amy sent a text: Lan, can you meet me at the clubhouse tonight at 10?

****

At 9:05pm a ride was waiting in front of her office building. Amy entered the vehicle and opened her tablet. Not wanting to give her legal overlords anything to ding her with, Amy didn't use company time and only now began to study the document from the Stableton Agency. She noted several amendments she requested and the film production company agreed to.

The car traveled up to the Lenox Hill neighborhood on the Upper East Side. Amy eyed several of the apartments perched high in the sky and pictured herself in one with the view they afforded, down to the furniture and drapes she preferred.

Years ago, her mother, April Arrington, had purchased a four-story townhouse on 69th. It was in her favorite part of town: four blocks over to Central Park, four blocks to the Frick Museum, right around the corner from Park Avenue, close to several Off-Broadway theaters and straight up Lexington to Lenox Hill Hospital. The bases were covered. It was her big five: dining, art, theater, luxury and preservation.

The clubhouse had 4,580 square feet of mostly hardwood floors, with four baths and was quite tastefully decorated with contemporary works of art.

Amy printed out three copies of the email from L.A. and continued to study the documents closely. The food arrived and she tipped the delivery guy.

Fifteen minutes later Lannie Telfair, in sneaks, t-shirt and a leather coat, was right on time and noticed the ton of Chinese food laid out.

"Are you feeding an army?"

"I'm having an early business dinner with you and later a social dinner with Tiago, he has a big appetite."

"The guy we went to see in the play?"

"Yep." Amy was corralling a wonton in her soup.

Lannie cleared her throat, "That guy is...hot."

Amy scrunched her nose, "You think? I haven't really noticed."

Lannie laughed, "Shut up."

Amy had a sly grin, "It's casual… He's coming over after his show is done."

"I'm guessing you don't discuss shop with him."

"The last thing I want to discuss after a day of wrangling with the law is the law. Tiago is a tortured soul that lives for his craft. When we're together, I transition to my artistic side."

"Ah… Oh?" Lannie snickered.

"All lawyers are actors. Our bad reviews can cost people millions of dollars and years of their life, or even their existence."

"I see."

"Are you ready to deal with Zabéla Z?"

"Definitely."

"Let's review the offer."

They both studied their own copies.

Amy finally looked up, "The terms are favorable. $25,000 option for the rights to your magazine article."

"$50,000 option for the screenplay I'll deliver."

Lannie and Amy eyed each other and shouted, "And $5 million paid on the first day of principal photography!"

After they settled back down, Amy went over the deal points.

"Delivery of original treatment, first and second draft of screenplay, rewrites and polishes are all well above minimums. Payment will be within 48 hours of delivery. They're covering you on the Errors & Omissions insurance and a passive payment for any sequels, 10% bump on your original. 50% if you don't write it, but someone else does and it's produced. I've negotiated a 10% cut of all ancillary revenues."

"Meaning if any John Hawkwood action figures are sold."

"Precisely."

"Not likely."

"You already missed out on the video game."

"The D.C. Massacre? That's okay."

"And I'm not sending you down the rabbit hole of figuring out what's the gross and net profit. You'll never find it. But there is something you can nail down. I've had them include a $15,000 bonus when producers gross exceeds 2 times the budget. Another 15K when they triple and $25,000 when they hit 4 times the budget."

"Nice."

"I've negotiated your ability to be on the set, so behave."

"Will do."

"And the rights revert back to you after four years, if they don't make it."

"All right."

"You need to fill out the I-9 and W-4, plus a certificate of authorship. That can be done tomorrow with a notary."

"Fine."

"And you authorize me to send a copy of the contract to the Writer's Guild?"

"Yes."

"As the first writer you get the opportunity to do a rewrite, which they'll most likely call for."

"Okay."

"And if they do make it, you'll be invited to view the director's cut within 48 hours of the company's viewing."

"Where do I sign?"

Amy pointed to the spot and Lannie signed. Amy signed at her place and then pulled out a bottle of Dead Rabbit Irish whiskey. She poured each of them a shot. They held it up.

"To your project." They drank up.

"Tasty."

"Irish single malt," stated Amy.

Lannie observed the bottle, "Dead Rabbit. I did an article about these guys."

"I read it. It came out after *Gangs Of New York* was released."

"Right. An editor of the magazine saw the movie and wanted more. He put me on it. Daniel Day Lewis was amazing. But it was all fictionalized."

"You were correct when you wrote that Scorsese got the spirit right with the anti-immigration sentiment. Trying to keep the Irish out," Amy said, lost in a deep thought.

Lannie saw how this subject was consuming her, "History rotating through its cycles."

Amy remembered the stories she was told, "A lot of struggles...against the Bowery Boys, who didn't like the Irish moving in. So many fights with a lot of bloody noses and blackened eyes, the Mulberry Boys, aka the Dead Rabbits, were successful."

"Some of your Irish roots there, Aim?"

"Somewhere in there."

"In my research for the article, I learned that the leader of the Irish mob in the 60's and early 70's was Mickey Spillane, not the writer. He controlled Hell's Kitchen. He was called the Gentleman Gangster."

"Mickey was good looking," Amy agreed. "And dapper, cheerful and respectful. There was order—but he was a thug."

"However," argued Lannie, "compare that to what came with the Westies gang in the late 70s and the reign of terror. Jimmy Coonan was their twisted leader. Even the Italian mafia was repulsed by their dismembering and tossing around of body parts."

Amy reflected on that, "Jimmy Coonan... You're staying in Hell's Kitchen. You know Hellcat Annie's on 10th?"

"And 45th? Sure."

"That used to be called The White House Bar. That's where Spillane, the Gentleman Gangster, had his headquarters."

"Interesting."

"It gets really interesting," said Amy. "One of Micky's revenue streams was kidnapping regular folk and ransoming them back to the family. It was a business deal, nothing personal. And then it became very personal when one of these transactions went sideways with John Coonan, an accountant. He was tied to a chair and pistol whipped. John's son was Jimmy, Jimmy Coonan, a kid in the neighborhood. Instead of following in his dad's footsteps in the financial world, he swore retribution."

Lannie understood, "Jimmy Coonan. Payback. And the hounds of hell were unleashed."

****

Lannie had left and Amy took a shower. She came out to find a text from Tiago that he was sick with the flu and was going home to Long Island to recuperate. Although he really was 'hot,' he only stimulated her one way.

Amy had become tired and Tiago would have put her right out as other than entertainment gossip, he was clueless on most everything else.

Amy got dressed, bagged up the food and tossed it down the garbage chute. She booked a ride, exited the clubhouse and stepped over a homeless person begging on the sidewalk.

****

It was after midnight when she returned to her official residence. The 'Microscope.' It was company housing. The associates of Padmore, Pearce and Payne were highly encouraged to live here. A building close by the office, with very reasonable rents and within shouting distance. It allowed employees to be on call at all times for their labors. It was 9-9-6: 9am to 9pm 6 days a week and a couple 9-9-7s or even 7-12-7 when a deadline approached. The work hours could be nonstop, crashing through 120 hours logged a week. But who was counting? Nobody that wanted to move forward.

Amy dreamed of the day she made partner and could leave the Microscope. She felt like she needed a permission slip to be out so late. She never entertained guests here. One's entire essence would be analyzed by the firm before being let into one of the world's most exclusive clubs.

She was bolstered by her upcoming holiday. After two years she put in to be free for a weekend, several weeks in advance, and got permission.

She tapped her residence keycard on the scanner and the door clicked open. Amy entered, smiled at the security guard and pushed the button for the 11th floor. She wondered when the biometric eye-scans were coming.

The elevator whisked her upwards in the modern, sterile high-rise the firm acquired some years ago at rock bottom prices in bankruptcy court. The story went that the building was remodeled and retrofitted. Amy heard East German Stasi jokes about the place and assumed recording devices were sprinkled about.

On the 11th floor, at the end of a quiet hallway with neutral displays of digital art on the walls, Amy again scanned her keycard and entered a code on the keypad. The door to her place clicked open.

Amy entered, brewed herself some chamomile tea, got into some sweats and wooly socks and read Lannie's screenplay adaptation of her article on John Hawkwood and Sovereign Operational Solutions.

2

It was early the next day. Amy had fueled up on a protein shake and was doing yoga while she endured the morning newscasts. This was another practice that she learned early as Alexander's daughter, always being aware of events, how they could impact things and considering ways to turn them in your favor. It was also how the mercenary John Hawkwood and his ancestor of the same profession operated and how they both became so successful, until they weren't. Amy hoped Lannie could push this project over the finish line and get it made. Odds seemed to be gaining in her favor. There was a definite buzz. Several Hollywood gossip websites were already talking about the project and speculating on who would get cast opposite Zabéla Z, the star who was controlling the project.

Amy was back at her cubicle by 8:00am and reviewing real estate contracts. She eyed a photo of herself and two female friends: The Démener Divas.

7 days…

Amy went for some coffee and snacks in the breakroom and saw the story about Lannie above the fold in *Variety* and that brought her joy as well. Ten minutes later Zabéla tweeted out: 'Thrilled about next project lined up, Paying Allegiance, from fabulist writer Lannie Telfair.'

Amy laughed to herself, "Fabulist writer, Lannie Telfair."

****

Late Saturday night Amy met up with Lannie at Klub Kaboodle and teased her about being so 'fabulist.'

They partied until 4am. She dared not go back to the Microscope and crashed at the Clubhouse.

Amy allowed herself to sleep in until 10:30. It was a luxury only afforded once a week, sometimes only twice a month. She had coffee and read the

Sunday *New York Times.* She then worked out in the building's gym to get the cobwebs out. After that it was lunch and back to reading legal stuff.

****

On Monday morning Amy sent a text cheering on Lannie as she was heading off to L.A. She then returned to reviewing and proofing a six-inch thick legal file in her cubicle. Amy reminded herself this was the week The Divas would be reunited. Gabby Gonzales, Abby Albright and Amy Arrington had been a tight trio for 14 years. She recalled the unlikely confluence of happenstance that made their meeting possible. All three were enamored with the album *Spiderland.* They had met at a Slint concert at the Brown Theatre in Louisville on Feb 22, 2005.

Amy had just returned from spending several years away at a boarding school. Abby and Gabby were already students at the Brown School in downtown Louisville, where Amy was about to enroll.

Abby was the positive one, always keeping their spirits up. She rarely took chances, but if she did, she was talked into it by the other Divas.

Amy was the sensible one, always thinking events through and understanding the angles and ramifications, but had a wild streak.

Gabby was the adventurous one, never satisfied, always pushing forward. She was plugged into the local scene from a very young age. Gabby was friends with one of Slint's guitarists, Brian McMahan and the drummer, Britt Walford, who both had graduated from the Brown School.

Amy recalled she learned of the bands Maurice and Squirrel Bait through Gabby and took a deep dive on what Math Rock was.

Gabby came up with the name 'The Démener Divas.' Démener was French for 'thrashing,' or 'exerting oneself.' It stuck. From then on, they were The DDs. Their friendship endured all the way through high school and college, with them attending different universities and into adulthood. This weekend was Abby's birthday; the three had vowed to make it an event to remember.

Amy recalled the itinerary in her mind: *Friday, at 5:05pm, whisked to the airport. Flight from NYC to Louisville two and a half hours.*

7:30 flight arriving in Louisville at 10:30. Be picked up and check into Brown Hotel. Party at hotel for Abby. Then next day, spa day and eating and partying later at 4th Street Live, while toasting Abby.

Amy hadn't looked forward to something so much since her high school trip to Washington D.C.

The week grinded on for Amy. She kept glancing at the DD pic for a boost. *Friday, at 5:05pm, whisked to the airport...*

Friday came and it was just after the tuna sandwich on wheat toast that she had for lunch, when she was summoned into the inner splendor of Peyton Padmore's office. Several of the senior partners were present, Harold, her 'mentor,' was not.

Peyton was gloomy, "Amy, we're in a pickle. A very big client of ours is having trouble moving forward with a project. The financing has been held up by a nuisance lawsuit. The judge is giving his decision Monday morning and we're wondering if you could review the case over the weekend and be on the team that makes an appearance."

"On Monday?" asked Amy, her mind convulsing on how this request of her was even possible. She subtly glanced around, hoping Harold was somewhere in this large, cavernous space, ready to step forward and defend her time off.

"Yes," said a voice she barely comprehended. "Monday."

"A month ago," Amy gathered her wits to make her case, "I asked for and received permission from Harold to go on—"

Peyton seemed to show genuine concern, "Yes, yes, we are well aware and we wouldn't ask if this wasn't extremely important. We are approaching the 30-day window on this action."

"I see." Amy felt numb.

"And the client personally requested you. The CEO of Dig Noble Holdings. He read something about you and wanted you to check out the problem and see if you could find a fix. If you do, we'll let you take a two-week paid vacation."

"Serious?" Amy was shocked by that.

"Yes," mumbled Peyton. "Seems our client was impressed with your skill-set."

****

Amy trudged back to her cubicle and sat for several minutes. An intern delivered a thumb drive and the physical case file to her. It was a thick collection of legal file folders and jackets along with several expandable file pockets, all stuffed with things Amy had to learn about. She stared at this with amazement and mumbled: "If I don't pull a rabbit out of the hat, a live one, I probably won't get the time off either."

Amy began digesting this substantial collection and stopped.

She then sent the text: a new case has been dropped in my lap, need to be ready Monday morning. My heart is breaking, I cannot be at Démener Diva reunion. I will make it up to you two!

She received sad broken heart emojis from Gabby and Abby.

Tiago texted her: have a blast back home!

Amy ignored him and started to turn off her phone, but received an alert. "Big Manolo Blahnik price drop…" She clicked to purchase.

****

It was Friday night and Amy was grinding. The only thing she had eaten was her ticket home. By late that evening she had digested the statements, pleadings, complaints and responses, cross complaints and answers to cross complaints, claims, counterclaims and the replies to counterclaims, reports and responses to the reports—all very stimulating reading. And then a video screen chimed and popped on showing the front door of her townhouse. The correct code had been punched in and they entered. Amy eyed the couple in the foyer on the screen and was confused—then she recognized the male and mumbled to herself.

"Tiago…what's he…?"

Tiago used a key to get in the security door. The female grabbed his butt and they kissed with some vigor.

Amy stared at this and frowned. She carefully took a samurai sword off the wall.

Tiago then opened the front door and entered with the rather attractive female.

Amy raised the sword up, "Intruder alert!"

"Amy! You're supposed to be in Louisville! You know, the reunion of The DDs!"

She lowered the sword. "Change of plans. I thought you were sick and went home to Long Island to recuperate."

"I'm recouping, still."

"And this must be your nurse."

"Incorrect. This is Sandy, she's in my acting class. We're going to run lines."

"Not here you aren't."

"This is Amy, your cousin?" asked Sandy. "This is her place?"

Tiago was sweating.

Amy frowned and then nodded. "Yes."

"We could go to my sister's apartment. But we have to be quiet, you know, running our lines." Sandy had a lascivious smirk and playfully pinched Tiago on his derriere.

"Yes, shoo-shoo, you crazy kids, because I have my own lines to learn. See ya, Cuz."

Tiago unfurled one of his gregarious grins, "Amy, come on, I feel better, I can stay."

Amy reared back with the sword and they scurried back out.

****

Saturday morning, after her workout, Amy was back under the Microscope. Later that afternoon she took a break and turned on her phone. She saw the two texts she got from The Two DDs: where's the 3rd?' There were a couple pics of them at the Brown Hotel living it up.

Lannie grumbled, turned off her phone and turned another page on the brief.

By late Saturday night Amy was nearly through the entire file. She easily dozed off. On Sunday, after coffee and the *New York Times*, Amy was back studying the case, for the rest of the day.

****

Amy arrived at work right at 7am. She had a quick meeting with the group that recruited her on Friday and informed them of her findings. They read her Demurrer and Motion to Strike and approved.

The team arrived together at the courthouse in a dark, armor-plated SUV. They got out with their game faces on.

Once inside, Amy stepped off to a side lounge and tried calling her dad.

The recording on the phone started: "You've reached Alexander, please share your thoughts with me. When I have time, I may or may not get back to you. But have a sensational day either way. *BEEP*."

"Hi, Dad. I'm about to go into court. I just wanted to check in with you." She hung up as Bert Snyder, a portly, middle-aged senior partner of the firm, the lead counsel on this case, came up next to her.

"Morning, Amy," said Bert, his cherubic face sporting a wide grin. He held up copies of the two filings. "Good job."

"That was my weekend."

"We are very appreciative that you stepped in here. Dig Noble needed this project to go forward." Bert moved on.

Amy got an alert on her phone. The price had dropped on some Jimmy Choo pumps, she clicked add to cart. "Sweet."

The Manhattan courtroom was filled and the hearing was in session. The clerk delivered a copy of the filings to the judge and the opposing counsel, Mr. Sullivan, a man approaching 60, who was ruffled and a bit rumpled. He read it and then slumped.

Bert stood, "Your Honor, if it would please the court, with the addendum filed this morning, we request that the case be dismissed."

The judge's brow was furrowing as he continued scanning the new information, "I can read, counselor."

Mrs. Mary Chambers, the plaintiff, a frail woman stared straight ahead.

Mr. Sullivan stood and buttoned his suit jacket, "Your Honor, my client, citing Local Law 1 of 2004, for years complained that the building wasn't safe with no response from the owners. Even though she has no children, she took it upon herself to pay for the paint to be analyzed and found it did not comply with the lead-based paint standards and was toxic to the children in the building. This was ignored by the management. Yet frequent mysterious 'renovations' go on at all hours disturbing the tenants. Drilling, pounding and hammering that shake the apartments scattering dust and debris about. After being ignored again by the management, only then did she go public and complain to the media and learn how to use social media to post her concerns. Mary stood up to them."

"Your Honor," Bert countered, "we were told the plaintiff moved out on her own volition."

"I moved out on my own?" asked Mary.

"When she was told it was an illegal apartment," Bert added.

The frail elderly woman was now quite agitated, "We lived in an illegal apartment??"

"Mr. Sullivan," the judge said softly.

"Sorry, Your Honor." Mr. Sullivan gently calmed his client.

Amy eyed the woman and wondered if her indignation was for real.

Mr. Sullivan braced himself, "Your Honor, three large gentlemen arrived and physically removed Mary from the apartment she had lived in for 31 years. They dumped all of her stuff into trash bags. We have been able to locate some of the items at the sanitation department, but it's mostly broken glasses and plates, broken pictures. Her furniture has been trashed. And there's an expensive watch from her dead husband that's missing and a pair of silver candlesticks, as well as most of her personal records."

Amy was stunned and thought, *really?*

The judge flinched at this.

"And Mrs. Chambers was physically removed on a Friday in the rain."

"Your Honor, our client knew nothing of this," Bert replied. "Not sure if this is passing the smell test."

The judge pondered, "I would agree with you, counselor, this does smell. Didn't your client put homeless people in the hallways to harass the residents?"

"I believe that was a security lapse."

The judge wasn't pleased, "It certainly was."

Amy was shocked, she turned to one of the co-counsels and whispered, "None of this was in the case file."

The lawyer just shrugged at her.

"Your Honor," Mr. Sullivan interjected. "When this happens to tenants, landlords know there are little penalties. As for the legality of the dwelling..." He sat and conferred with his client.

"I didn't know," said the confused woman.

Mr. Sullivan stood, "We contend that the management knew or should have known this was an illegal apartment. Dig Noble Holdings has been in control of this rent-stabilized building for nearly 4 years and they had no problem collecting rent from my client that was never late. The company allowed, even enabled, the decay of their property. For the last several years the owner just ignored safety and sanitation laws, didn't do repairs, ignored the mold and left garbage strewn about to force my client, as well as others, many who are elderly and sick, to move out."

"Your Honor," said Bert, "no credible evidence of that intention has been entered. It's simply hearsay."

"Your Honor," countered Mr. Sullivan, "this isn't the first time Dig Noble has been accused of such underhanded tactics. To side with Dig Noble, after what they did in this illegal eviction, it's just...crummy!"

"Your Honor," pleaded Bert, "again, we are under the impression the plaintiff, after learning the apartment was illegal, had voluntarily vacated the dwelling and now has second thoughts and is using the courts to regain possession."

Amy continued to be surprised by this.

Mrs. Chambers was stunned, she just shook her head slowly.

Mr. Sullivan groaned, "Your Honor..."

"How did you get the impression she moved out on her own?" asked the judge.

Bert considered that, "Your Honor, we heard that—"

"Hearsay??"

Bert felt the judge's wrath, "It's the best we have, Your Honor."

The judge sat back and sighed. He glumly glanced around the courtroom and settled on the team of lawyers representing Dig Noble Holdings and focused on Amy.

"I didn't see you here on Friday. Who are you, counselor?"

Amy stood, "Amy Arrington, Your Honor. I came in on this trial sort of in the 9th inning. And—"

"You found this?"

Amy blinked, not enjoying this attention. "Yes, Your Honor. I spent the weekend reading and cross-checking the entire court record of the case."

The judge lowered his glasses, "That must be over 20,000 pages."

"21,361 to be exact, Your Honor. Then I did some checking of the building and the Certificate of Occupancy and that's where I discovered the discrepancy."

"Again, Your Honor," Bert quickly added, "to reiterate, it only confirmed what we had heard that the occupant had already come to understand and acted upon."

"By 'voluntarily' moving out," groused the judge.

"Yes, Your Honor," said Bert, with no hesitation.

Amy grinded at that.

The judge gave Bert an icy stare. He then turned back to Amy. "You're what they used to call in baseball, the Fireman. You come in and put out the fire. Hugo, when did the big leagues drop that term, Fireman?"

"The 2000 season, Your Honor," responded the court clerk.

"Then you would be the Firewoman."

The other lawyers were checking notes, looking busy.

The judge slumped, "Up to this point I was leaning towards... But...with this new information, I cannot grant the stay and reinstate you, Mrs. Chambers. You can appeal this dismissal or refile. Court adjourned." The judge reluctantly banged his gavel.

Mrs. Chambers looked confused, "I was living in an illegal apartment for 31 years?"

Mr. Sullivan, heartbroken, crossed over to his client, explained what happened and apologized. She hugged him and thanked him for his effort.

Amy was awestruck at her reaction and oblivious to the congratulations from her legal team and corporate reps. "You rock! The Firewoman!"

Amy was irritated with Bert, "I didn't read anything about the movers just throwing her stuff away and carting her out of her apartment."

"That wasn't in the file?"

"No," said Amy.

"An oversight and it was only hearsay, it doesn't matter, you won the case for us. She's been staying with a neighbor down the hallway. Finally, this busy-body can now be barred from the property and will lose standing in any future litigation."

As the judge stepped off the bench, he whispered to the bailiff.

The bailiff crossed to Amy. "The judge would like a word."

Amy continued to focus on the elderly woman, who patted Mr. Sullivan on the back, who was very depressed over this.

Amy slowly crossed to the judge. "Yes, Your Honor?"

"I was just told your father is Alexander Aloysius Arrington. Is that true?"

Amy brightened with the recognition. "Yes, Your Honor."

"I knew him back when we clerked for the same judge on the D.C. Circuit. He got me to go water skiing on the Potomac River!"

Amy grinned.

"What a character he was," laughed the judge.

"He still is, Your Honor. He practices in Louisville, Kentucky."

"Your dad would do the craziest things. And he always fought for the underdog. He was a real stand-up guy. I have the greatest respect for him. Please give him my deepest regards."

Amy appreciated this, "I will, Your Honor."

"I do know one thing, Counselor."

"Yes, Your Honor?"

"Alexander was a very decent fellow. He would never work as a mouthpiece for the likes of Dig Noble Holdings." The judge cleared his throat in disgust and retreated to his chambers.

Amy was stung by this. She looked over to the small group of elites celebrating the win.

Then she again glanced at the lonely old lady now sitting alone and looking very lost.

Mr. Sullivan approached and stuck out his hand to Amy and they shook.

"Congratulations, counselor. Don't worry about her, she's staying with friends, but she has terminal cancer. She only has another year or so to live.

Of course, we'll need to find homes for her pets, three cats, which most likely will be sent to the pound..."

The sound of his voice just blended into a garbled stream of noise for Amy as she processed this.

****

Amy booked a ride to the address in Queens where Mrs. Chambers had been evicted. It was an older building that was in decline. Trash was strewn about. There was little security. The lock on the front door wasn't functioning. She entered and stepped around an informal group shooting up in the hallway. Loud pounding and drilling were heard. The walls shook. She found the name of the person who took in Mary and knocked. The drilling ceased for a moment. An elderly man cracked the door open, but kept the chain on.

"Yeah? What do you want?"

"I'm trying to find out about Mary, the person you helped."

He was wary and didn't let her in, "Who are you? The press? From the owners?"

"No, I'm just here to find out what really happened with Mary."

"What happened? What happened was three guys came and tossed her and her belongings out in the rain."

"Seriously, it wasn't her choice?"

"Hardly. They've wanted us all out of this rent stabilized building for some time. She has a lawyer and has been fighting them in court for years. In fact, she's been able to tie them up with some litigation, you should see all the legal documents."

"Huh," Amy said.

"She kept saying she was protected by the law. It was on her side. After that she was thrown into the street. Then she sued them. But I just got a call from her. The owners got some really powerful lawyers, the big dogs and you can guess what happened. They won."

"Oh."

"I can't put up with the harassment anymore. The power being cut, no hot water, the physical threats, constantly meeting intimidating people in the hallway." The heavy pounding and drilling started up again. "And that. It almost never ends. Now that her lawsuit has been dismissed, I'm moving too."

"Once the building is empty, it frees Dig Noble to do whatever," said Amy.

"Say, how do you know Mary?"

Amy pulled out her wallet and gave him a $100 bill.

He accepted it with gratitude, "Thank you."

****

That evening Amy was sitting alone and ruminating in the Microscope. She wanted to call someone and talk, but she didn't have any of those friends available at this moment. There was Abby and Gabby, but she felt bad about standing them up and having this result wasn't something she wanted to share with them. There was her mother, April, but they didn't have that kind of relationship. There was her father, Alexander. He would take the time to listen, but she didn't want to share with him the details leading up to this moment.

Amy heard the judge's comments, "*Alexander was a very decent fellow. He would never work as a mouthpiece for the likes of Dig Noble Holdings.*"

Then she heard Mr. Sullivan talking, "*But don't worry about her, she has*

terminal cancer. She only has another year or so to live. Of course, we'll need to find homes for her pets, only three cats."

Amy glanced around at the walls and whispered ever so quietly to herself, "They lied to me..." She grabbed the remote, turned on the 75-inch HDTV and angrily flipped through channels catching snippets of various commercials and TV shows. After twenty minutes of this she was getting drowsy, but still managed to keep pushing the channel selector:

--"You've waited for it and now it's here. Available for download, 6D: Delilah's Delightfully Delicious Downtown Digital Dungeon 7.0 Rule the ruins!"

--"Be the beast of your party, bring Balthazar's Boffo Barley Pops and win the day and the night!"

--"Brodie Bannister drops back to throw. Southwestern State needs to pick up this first down!"

--"Tonight on *Current Cross-Currents,* John Tenorio brings you the tragedy of the eviction of a sickly, elderly woman over a technicality the tenant was clueless to, coming up on this evening's edition of *Triple C*!"

Amy was jolted by this and now fully alert seeing the picture of Mrs. Chambers.

John Tenorio gazed into the camera, "I want to share with you the outrage that occurred today in a Midtown Manhattan courtroom against a Mrs. Chambers, by Amy Arrington, known as 'The Firewoman.' Crush, kill, destroy."

Ominous music played, as a hideously distorted picture of Amy was seen.

Even Amy herself was frightened by it.

Lightning bolts crackled and fire roared from her eyes. The giant firewoman monster ran amuck torching the village.

John had his pious face on, "I agree with the poor woman's attorney, this is 'crummy.' These blood sucking lawyers are so scummy! The only way to stop them is by pounding a steak into their hearts. And don't forget it has to be wooden!"

Amy stood at the window feeling a little lonely, but mostly numb. She thought back over the memories of her life growing up in Louisville, back to her childhood and playing in a creek, laughing and singing. The great times.

Amy picked up her tablet and went to a travel site. She booked a flight to Louisville Muhammad Ali International Airport.

****

The next morning Amy entered the glittering and gleaming edifice in lower Manhattan that housed Padmore, Pearce and Payne and definitely caused a stir, as no one had ever seen her dressed casually. She was wearing a Louisville Cardinal cap, jeans, a black t-shirt and Chuck Taylors, with a backpack slung over her shoulder. She picked up a couple things from her cubicle and then knocked on Harold's door.

Harold and Peyton were surprised by her appearance. They waved her in.

"Amy!" said Harold cheerily. "Or I should say, FIREWOMAN!"

"Just watch the flame in here!" Peyton joked.

Amy smiled just enough, "My favorite so far was pounding a wooden steak into my heart."

"Ignore that blowhard Tenorio," spouted Peyton.

"I know I promised you last weekend off for your reunion, but thanks for stepping in," said Harold.

"No worries," said Amy.

Peyton was pouring himself a drink. He held up the glass and savored the amber liquid within, "DSR. Dulsett Special Reserve Bourbon. One of the very special perks of being a partner, Amy. You'll see someday, I'm sure of it."

"Pate, she got us that bottle. It's from Louisville."

Peyton frowned, "Huh, well cheers to you."

Harold, a handsome and very fit man of 55, was in a fighting stance, harkening back, "As I recall, didn't you dislocate two of Tenorio's fingers last year at some nightclub?"

Amy thought back: *Sitting at a table, a hand wandered up her inner thigh.*

Amy took hold of the index and middle finger and snapped them backwards.

"Ahhhh!!!" John Tenorio recoiled in great pain.

"His hand went where it shouldn't. I should've dislocated his jaw."

"And now he's getting back at you," stated Peyton.

Amy rubbed her chin, "You know, I read that entire voluminous case file and there was no reference to any thugs going in and carting her to the curb."

"We didn't know that," said Harold.

Amy didn't respond.

"Uh, taking a trip?" asked Peyton.

"Yes, taking the two-week vacation you promised and going back home for a bit, see the family. It's been a while."

"You got it. Especially after that tomahawk slam dunk you threw down yesterday in court. You schooled those fools! Wooo!" Peyton declared.

The guys high-fived. Harold and Peyton raised their hands to her. Amy paused, then gave them both the obligatory high-five.

****

A car was navigating down a street in Queens. It stopped. Amy exited the back door carrying her pack and stared at the sign. LEGAL AID SOCIETY

It was crowded inside.

Amy squeezed in, "Excuse me, sorry." She made it over to the rather frazzled receptionist.

"Hi, I'd like to see Mr. Sullivan."

"Do you have an appointment?"

"No, but—"

"Take a number."

The number 287 was available.

"What number is he on?"

The receptionist pointed to an electronic sign that stated: 36

Amy frowned at that. She glanced at all of the people waiting and could feel the worry in them. "Actually, I just want to talk to Mr. Sullivan for a sec."

"So does everybody here. You got about a six hour wait, sugar."

"I have a plane to catch," said Amy.

A woman and a man overheard this and glanced at each other.

"I'm late for beers with Eli Manning," said the man.

"And I can't be tardy as I'm having tea with Michael Bloomberg," the woman announced.

There were some chuckles in the room.

Amy stepped up onto a chair, "May I have your attention?"

There was no response, people ignored her.

"Hello?" Still nothing. "Excuse me!!!"

This got their attention.

"You really don't have to be so rude," said a woman.

"I was wondering, if I buy 10 pizzas and sodas, can I skip to the front of the line and have just 10 minutes of Mr. Sullivan's time?"

There was little interest in this proposal.

Amy grumbled, "How about 20 pizza pies??"

The group now nodded at that.

"And cappuccinos and cake?" a voice called out.

Amy nodded as she pulled out her phone and credit card.

"But I was next," a big guy lamented. Amy slipped him a $50 bill and he was cool.

****

Everyone in the waiting room feasted on pizzas, soda, cappuccinos and cake, while Amy and Mr. Sullivan had a slice in his tiny, cluttered office.

"Here you are, in this little office, fighting the good fight."

"You think I'm tilting at windmills?"

"There are many to tilt at."

"Maybe I am delusional, you think?"

Amy could see the people waiting, "No."

"Feels like there was some internal debate there."

"I think you're trying to swim fast enough so you won't drown."

"Did I hear you say to the judge, your dad is Alexander Arrington?"

"Yes. Do you know him?"

"No, not really. I once traveled to Louisville to watch a case he tried and I follow his blog: Torts and Just Desserts. I love Alexander the Antithetical Owl."

"You're kidding me, right?"

"No, he actually inspired me to go to law school."

"The owl?" asked Amy, confused.

"No, Alexander."

"No offense, but you look a bit older than my dad."

"I was 36, working as an assistant in OMB in a government services position in Washington, D.C. Very secure, but dreadfully boring and really unfulfilling. I went with a friend to a lunchtime lecture. Alexander was 27, he had just finished clerking for a federal judge and was going back home to Louisville. He was sitting on the panel. I can still remember, clear as day, the topic: Frontiers of the Fourth Amendment. The way he used the language, it was mesmerizing. It changed my life. I introduced myself to him and he was very nice. I told him that I was interested in the law, but said I was too old to go to law school. You know what he did? He locked onto me and told me to follow my dream, and don't worry about the age thing. It was like a jolt of electricity went through me. I went to night school after that and eventually got my law degree. And, I think I've had a pretty good run, mostly filled with joy, few regrets. I helped some people—won a few, lost a few."

"And his daughter just crushed you," sighed Amy.

"Look, I watched you compete online in the National Criminal Moot Court Competition. When I heard you were brought on the team, I knew I was in for a battle."

Amy again viewed the hectic waiting room munching the grub. "You have a lot of people waiting."

"For most of them, our office is their last hope. Ironically, it gives *me* hope to be here and purpose. Maybe I'm crazy for doing this, or crazy *from* doing this. Who knows? I do know that I just lost this one."

"Look, that wasn't on you."

Mr. Sullivan nodded, "They did bring in the big gun."

Amy felt uncomfortable.

"Hey, if it wasn't you, they would have delayed and appealed. Dig Noble's philosophy is never back down, never apologize, never explain."

"Yes, my team is good at running out the clock and running up the bill."

He laughed at that.

"Mr. Sullivan, you've done good work. My dad would approve. You're not crazy. Here's your legal fee for the Dig Noble case." She handed him an envelope.

He opened it and stared at a check. His eyes bugged out and he gagged on the pizza.

"Careful, chew your food."

"I can't accept this."

"Why not?"

Mr. Sullivan's eyes were getting moist, "This is the most money I've ever been paid to practice law and you're my opponent."

"You deserve it. And one more thing." She pulled out a set of house keys that rattled.

****

Amy exited the building on a high. She put in her earbuds and found "One Big Holiday" by My Morning Jacket on her phone and started listening. The driving drum beat and fast paced guitar had her skipping down the sidewalk. She came up on two kids skateboarding and noticed they couldn't pull off a certain jump.

"Add more torque on the liftoff," Amy advised.

"Whatever, old lady!"

"Old? Want me to show you?"

The kids laughed. She produced a twenty-dollar note that she separated revealing two bills.

They were interested. One handed her his skateboard and she handed over the money.

She did a quick preflight check. "You need new bearings, dude."

The kids glanced at each other wondering.

Amy backed up, started sprinting and dropped the board. She hopped on and started with a 360-kickflip over the jump and then put on a show.

The guys were stunned. "360 kickflip!? Monster Walk!"

"Impossible Ollie!! Yo Yo plant!!!"

The weight of the world was lifted off her shoulders. Amy gave back the skateboard. The lads were quite awed. The music continued and she booked a ride.

****

Amy sat in the airport lounge at JFK and sipped bottled water. She was checking out the Louisville Eccentric Observer at leoweekly.com and getting caught up on her hometown.

Just when she was starting to relax, a child holding hands with her mother saw Amy and was scared. She pointed, "Look Mommy, Firewoman."

The little girl hid behind her mother, who was troubled.

Amy put on sunglasses and turned away as she continued reading from her tablet. Twenty minutes later she boarded her flight and turned off her phone.

****

After an extended session of imbibing at an Irish pub on the Upper East Side, Tiago had finally garnered the required courage. He sent her a text on his phone.

TIAGO: hi, Amy, can we talk?

Tiago waited and didn't get a response. He tried again.

TIAGO: can I come by, even just for a moment?

Still nothing. He chugged his Barley Pop, exited the bar and began the 17-block trek to her place. After a minute he realized he was going the wrong way. He turned around and started the 20 blocks to the clubhouse.

Tiago arrived and rang the doorbell.

A female voice was heard on the speaker. "Yes?"

"Hi, I was wondering if Amy was home?"

"She's not here. Is your name Tiago?"

"Yes, yes it is."

"I was told to tell you to ring the manager next door."

Tiago was dumbfounded. He punched the access code in and was denied. He grumbled, "Great, she changed the code." Tiago wandered next door.

The manager checked his I.D. and then gave him a box with his things in it. Tiago was in shock. He aimlessly searched his possessions and couldn't find a certain item.

He trudged back to Amy's place and rang the doorbell again.

"Yes?" was again heard on the speaker.

"Hi, it's me again. I got the box. But I'm missing a scarlet red Hermès dip-dyed silk scarf. It should be right around the corner there."

The door opened. "Oh dear..." Mrs. Chambers handed him the shredded scarf. "Daisey may have gotten to it."

They both smelled the foul odor.

"And that wee-wee is definitely from Mr. Chips, sorry. He is such a bad boy."

Two cats were heard screeching inside.

"Let's behave, Kiddies! No more scratching on the furniture or other things...and let's please use the box. I'm sorry, gotta run."

The door shut and Tiago grunted, quite disgruntled.

****

Tiago sat on the curb in front of the townhouse for a good bit and growled with gusto. "Now where am I going to stay in the city?"

A limo pulled up. The driver got out and opened the back door. An elegant looking lady in her late 40s stepped out.

Tiago sat up, he recognized the woman as Amy's mother, April.

April and the driver, carrying her luggage, crossed to the front door of the townhouse and she entered the access code. It didn't allow her in.

"What's this?" asked April.

"Amy changed the code," remarked Tiago.

"Really?" April groaned, "I see. And you are?"

"I'm Tiago, 'which means holder of the wheel' or 'may God protect.'"

"You don't say," April was finding him to her liking.

"I used to stay here, until Amy saw fit to kick me to the curb for no reason. Total misunderstanding. I was trying to improve my craft. She's moved a cat lady in there now."

"Really?"

Tiago held up his shredded scarf that flittered in the breeze.

April gasped, "An Hermès dip-dyed silk scarf."

"Yes. You have such a cultured eye."

"Well…" April was taken a bit by this compliment.

"You're April Arrington. I saw your picture inside. Amy and I have chatted about you. I admire the charitable work you do that actually makes a difference."

"That's kind of you to say."

"I live out on Long Island. Amy used to let me stay here in the city."

"And now she changed the code?"

"Yes."

"What if I would have showed up with the Sultan?"

"I don't know..." Tiago shrugged and nodded, "You know Amy. Ah, I mean, you *really* know Amy."

"Indeed, I do." April grumbled and wanted to unload, but held back.

Tiago was dramatic, "*Give sorrow words; the grief that does not speak knits up the o'er wrought heart and bids it break.*"

"She can be so difficult!" April thought for a moment, "That was from *Macbeth.*"

"I guess I'm being a bit over dramatic. I am an actor by trade."

"An actor?"

"At the moment I'm in an off-off Broadway show."

"Have I seen you in anything?"

"I don't know, what have you seen?"

"A lot."

"Any Shakespeare in The Park?"

"Yes. Wait, of course, at the Delacorte."

"*Midsummer Night's Dream*, a couple seasons ago."

"You were Lysander."

"Guilty."

"You were so good."

"Thank you."

"I loved that production," said April. "Puck, such a trickster."

"Everyone falling in love with each other," said Tiago.

"And switching partners," April added.

They both laughed.

April pulled out her phone and made a call.

The recording started and Amy's voice was heard: "Hi, I'm unavailable at the moment. Please leave a message or text me. Your choice."

"Ambrosia, this is your mother."

It was the first time Tiago heard that name and repeated it to himself.

"I just so happen to be in New York City as I'm meeting the Sultan for some consultations and I thought I might stay at my place, which I haven't seen in months and what do I find? You've changed the code, thrown a poor fellow, a gifted artist, onto the street and installed a cat lady. You know I'm a dog person. Whatever, please call, don't text me, when you receive this message."

****

The flight landed in Louisville and for the first time in nearly three years Amy Arrington was back in the Commonwealth of Kentucky. She checked her messages. She saw the pleadings from Tiago and groaned. "So glad to be rid of him." She then heard the message from her mother and groaned louder.

Amy called and April answered, as Tiago was under the sheets applying his versatile tongue to her lower extremities, "Yes, Amy?"

"You instructed me to call you, Mother. I'm complying."

"Oh, yes..." April trailed off, drifting blissfully.

"Mother? Are you okay?"

"Yes, I'm fine."

"As for the 'cat lady,' I'll find her a place, soon."

"Fineee..." April's voice kicked up two octaves.

"Are you sure you're okay, Mother?"

Tiago paused and played to the phone: "As Puck says, '*Cupid is a knavish lad thus to make poor females mad.*'"

April giggled with abandon and then transitioned to a sensuous moan, "Yes he is."

Amy was stunned, "Tiago..."

Tiago continued, "*Shall I compare thee to a summer's day? Thou art more lovely and more temperate: rough winds do shake the darling buds of May.*"

April cooed at that.

Amy mumbled, "Shakespeare sonnets... No..."

"Ambrosia, I'm okay with the cat lady for a month or two. I'll indulge you on that and you need to indulge me on this. Bye, darling." April hung up.

Amy's eyes widened even wider.

3

TORTS and Just Desserts from the mind of Alexander Arrington

The owl appeared wearing a Louisville t-shirt and spoke:

"Louisville is a place that has and continues to produce great patriots, great artists, great thinkers, great writers and great athletes who have made and continue to leave a lasting mark on this country's fabric. Louisville is a place firmly rooted in the past, remembering those who sacrificed for the country, carrying on the traditions and honoring the tenets on which this 'Great American Experiment' was based: 'All Men Being Equal' being front and center. And Louisville is a place squarely at the forefront on how we as a country, a nation, proceed in the future on the diverse and complex challenges we face."

~ ~ ~

"When I'm a very good boy I reward myself with a Lemon Raspberry Tart from the Blue Dog Café."

The owl faded out.

****

The sounds were slightly muffled. The images a bit blurred. Amy was going through the motions as she filled out the paperwork for the rental at the airport. She fought the urge to let her mind run wild. *There's no way she could have hooked up with Tiago.*

But it was her mother…

Amy searched on the car radio until she heard a creepy voice: "This is WooLoo 86FM. Rockin' the Ville day and night 'til you're 80 miles out and 6 feet under. You've been 86'd!"

This brought a smile to Amy, "I'm home."

Classic rock thumped out of the Mustang as she drove north on I-65 to the Park Hill section of town. Her mind couldn't help but drift back. Tiago could be quite kinky. She cringed and pushed back on the images attempting to seep into her imagination of any erotic proclivities involving Tiago with her mother.

Amy exited the freeway and traveled a few minutes before pulling into the parking lot of an apartment complex. Amy climbed up a flight of steps and knocked on the door. Abby, carrying 3-month-old Roxanne, opened it.

"Amy!"

"Abby."

"You're late by a week."

"I know, I'm sorry." They hugged.

The living room was partitioned into thirds. It was a modest 2-bedroom unit. One part was a small corner, the work space where Abby was employed as a remote medical biller; another was the nursery, where she tended to Roxanne—and the front third, which was the 'parlor,' as Abby described it, where they received their guests, played games, watched movies and sports.

"I know you're in demand."

"I guess. And here she is."

Abby turned the baby's face to Amy, "Roxanne, I want you to meet your Aunt Amy."

"Hello, Roxanne." Amy put down the stuff she brought in on the kitchen table. Abby handed her over and Amy held little Roxy, "She is so precious. Check the table." Amy pointed to a small gift box.

Abby hesitated. Amy urged her on. Abby opened it and found a pair of emerald earrings.

"Didn't I always say emerald earrings would go well with your auburn hair?"

Abby was overcome, she cried and they hugged. "Thank you, Amy."

"Try them on."

Abby put them in her earlobes and looked in the mirror. "They're fabulous."

"How's Mitch?"

"He's good. He's been managing the restaurant for over a year. He runs breakfast and lunch and he's getting back into shape at the Y."

"Good for him. Good for you, too."

"He's playing on a basketball team."

"Mitchell was a pretty good player as I recall."

Marcus, her 8-year-old son, came in, ignoring everyone.

"Marcus, look who's here."

The kid stopped, "Hey."

Amy tried to be friendly, "Hey, Marcus."

The little kid was sullen and distant. He retreated to his bedroom.

Abby was glum, "His grades are horrible and he spends all of his time in his room."

"What's he into?"

"*Star Wars.*"

"What's his favorite character, Luke, Hans Solo, Obi Wan, Yoda...?"

"Darth Vader."

"Oh..." They were quiet for a moment.

"He needs a friend."

Abby shook her head, "He doesn't have any." She checked her watch, "Mitch should be getting home from work, soon."

Moments later the front door was heard opening in the living room.

Abby grinned, "Right on time."

Mitch entered the kitchen and kissed Abby, "Hey, Babe." Then eyed their guest. "Amy."

"Hi, Mitch."

They hugged.

"Welcome back, it's been forever."

"It's good to be back."

"And you missed last week."

"Work, as usual, controlled everything. But I hear you're working out. You were always a good athlete."

"Yes, trying."

And then Abby blurted out, "And Bobby's on the team."

Amy was quiet.

Mitch hesitated, "Um, yes, he is."

"And they're playing tonight. Mitch, you should tell Bobby that Amy's back in town."

Mitch paused, "Uh…I'm sure he's probably already aware."

"That's okay, we haven't kept in touch."

****

Amy told them she would be home for several days at least and they should all have dinner.

After Amy left, Mitch let out a big sigh. "Why did you want me to let him know that Amy Arrington is back in town?"

"Why not? They did date back in high school. He's single, she's single."

"He's dating Nevada."

"That's not what I heard."

"Don't you remember the last time Bobby and Amy were involved? It cost us the state championship."

Abby rolled her eyes at that, "Uh-huh…"

Mitch's eyes narrowed, "And tonight is a big showdown. We need him on top of his game if we're going to make the playoffs."

"He's Bobby Dulsett."

"And Amy is his kryptonite."

****

Amy drove downtown near the waterfront. She loved seeing the big bat out front of the Louisville Slugger Museum and the Muhammad Ali Center. She then spotted the Galt House and once again wondered if she was conceived here. Neither of her parents would confirm or deny this fact. Alexander considered himself too much of a gentleman to hash over such matters; but her mother had made hints. These cryptic quips were usually made after a couple Mint Juleps, only to later claim ignorance on any conclusions or notions implied or inferred. It was maddening for Amy. Just more rubble added to the giant pile of frustration between her and her mother. She pulled into the parking lot of the small radio station and a large WooLoo 86FM sign was seen.

Cindy, the program director and resident Mama Bear was walking near the front and spotted her. "Amy Arrington, welcome back."

"Thanks Cindy. Good to be here." They hugged and she brought Amy past the security station.

The door to the studio opened and Gabby the DJ pointed, "You, Amy Arrington, enter."

"No...I don't think so..."

"Now."

Cindy motioned her in, "You heard the girl."

Amy braced herself and entered the studio.

The song "Love is Melancholy" was playing.

"Did you get the dates mixed up?"

"Yeah, that was it. I love Vandaveer. By the way, don't bring up the fire thing."

"Come on, Aim, I have to or they'll drum me out of the industry."

Amy grumbled.

Gabby filled right after the last chord, "That was Vandaveer. 'Love is Melancholy.' Drink it in, my miscreants. Now since you've been so bad, I've got a special guest for you. Welcome back, Amy Arrington. We are honored to have a local girl that has become a lawyer and works for one of the top New York law firms. And is the daughter of famed local attorney Alexander Arrington."

"I guess being known as his daughter will be my epitaph."

Bobby Dulsett was in his office at the distillery reviewing a report, with the radio playing in the background. Hearing this he used the remote to turn it down. He paused, drummed his fingers and then turned it up to listen.

Also at this moment Nevada Nash, a very attractive 26-year-old female, stylishly attired, in her pink Lexus coupe was cruising down Muhammad Ali Boulevard. Her phone rang. She clicked the call onto her headset, "This is Nevada."

"Girl, I know you said you and Bobby are taking a timeout. But you need to put on WooLoo 86."

Nevada put on 86FM and listened: "Not at all," laughed Gabby. "We always expected fantastic things from you, Amy. And now you've achieved a bit of fame from this Firewoman thing."

"More like infamy. Thank you for bringing that up. I was directed by my 'superiors' to research the merits of a legal case. I'm just one of the cogs."

"What you're saying is the label of Firewoman is unfair as you're just a small part of the brain of the Frankenstein monster unleashed on the average Joe."

Amy had a moment of clarity, "Exactly."

Gabby and then Amy laughed at that.

"How long will you be in town?"

"A week."

Bobby was quiet.

Nevada was pensive.

"Now, since I've come on as your guest. Do I get to make a request?"

"Sure. Who?"

"TORTs."

"The Ohio River Ticks?" Gabby asked, with her side-eye.

Bobby was amused.

Nevada wasn't.

"Yes."

"I think we have a bootleg copy from one of their concerts down in the vault."

Abby and Mitch were listening in their living room. She thought it was entertaining, but he slowly shook his head.

****

Gabby and Amy exited the station into the parking lot. She put a book in her backpack and Amy noticed.

"What's that, Gab?"

"A book by Hannah Drake. I love her. She lives here. She's a truth teller."

"I'll check her out."

"Aim, I ran into your E-S the other day."

"E-S?" Amy wasn't sure she wanted to know what this was.

"Eventual Soulmate," Gabby explained. "The one you're meant for, but is still a ways off."

"That is not a thing."

"Yes, it is. And I think we know who we're talking about."

"My, E-S?"

"Bobby! You're known as the girl that dumped Bobby Dulsett."

"Thank you for not mentioning that on the air."

"Everyone remembers. Crashed out of the state tournament way too early."

"That wasn't because of me. And you don't have soulmates in high school," Amy stated in her friendly—yet authoritative—tone.

"Let's recap. In your junior year you dated Bobby for two semesters and part of a summer. It was full of...what did you call the experience back then? Let's check the record. Oh yes, 'bountiful bliss.' Then you dumped him."

"It was like dating Elvis. Could you put up with that?"

"With those hips?"

"We were at different schools. When we got together, I got tired of all the dirty looks from the other contestants."

"And one of the greatest shooters in Kentucky history lost his shooting touch, at the worst time."

Amy groaned at that.

A car pulled up. Gabby advised, "Leave your rental, take your bag. You can pick it up tomorrow."

The car cruised down Bardstown Road in the Highlands section of Louisville. Amy and Gabby sat in the back.

"Have you missed the place?"

"The Ville? Hell ya."

Gabby opened a silver case and pulled out a fat joint and lit it up.

Amy was concerned, she glanced at the driver.

"Don't worry about Josie, I book rides with her all the time."

Josie looked in the rearview mirror, "No worries."

"This is the dank shit. I went to Illinois for this." Gabby took a hit.

Amy shrugged and took a puff. It had been nearly two years since she last indulged. She exhaled and coughed.

Gabby grinned, "It's been a while, eh?"

They soon arrived at the Hideaway Saloon and entered through the narrow entrance from the street. For both of them it had become one of their favorite places. They drank Barley Pops, ate chicken tacos and played Mario Kart on Nintendo 64.

"Have you seen your mom lately?"

Amy paused and contemplated on how to respond. "I just missed her in New York. She showed up right after I left."

"You two didn't coordinate?"

"She wanted it to be a surprise."

"Any luck in the romance department? I mean, New York is a pretty big place. Lots of variety."

"I don't have time. What about you?"

"I mostly get hit on by lunatics and freaks," Gabby laughed sadly and stared off.

Amy studied her face and again saw that melancholy she knew so well in her friend.

"Are you happy in New York?"

"Am I happy? I don't know if I know any one that's happy. It's more like a test, an endurance challenge."

"Last associate left on the island gets to be a partner?"

"Pretty much. But it's good to have a place to come back to, to call home. You happy being a star here in Louisville?"

"I love my job. But..."

"But what?"

"I've directed some videos for bands and a PSA on pollution. Hoping there's more to my career than just spinning records."

"They still do that? Spin them?"

"Or tapping computer keys that play the audio files."

"Why aren't you going for what you want?"

"See that's the thing, you have to know what you want to do, to go for it."

"Wow, Gab, that is deep."

"How's your dad doing?"

"As far as I know just fine. You know, being Alexander Arrington. I just got here. You were my second stop, after Abby, to patch things up."

****

Mitch stepped into the gym and started warming up with the seven other guys on the team. Bobby arrived and was enthusiastically greeted by his teammates. He warmed up and felt good. And then proceeded to have a terrible night shooting. He missed shots he normally would drill in his sleep. They lost.

Mitch took Bobby aside.

"Sorry, Mitch, I had an off night."

"No, Bobby, you fell off the cliff. Did you happen to listen to Gabby's show this afternoon?"

Bobby scoffed at that with indignation and marched off.

Mitch watched him stride away in a huff and groaned to himself, "I'll take that as a yes."

****

Gabby and Amy played a couple games of ping pong while still at the Hideaway Saloon, stopping several times by fans of Gabby, who had her sign a bar napkin and take selfies with her.

Amy tried to blend into the background, but was failing, as being the Firewoman had brought her way too much unwanted notoriety.

They didn't stay much longer. Amy lived a few minutes away and was dropped off first, then Gabby was delivered to her place in the 'hip and trendy' NuLu section of town.

After the mending of the fences mission with The DDs, Amy finally made it home to Casa Arrington just before 9pm.

Amy entered the gate and maneuvered down the tropical walkway. An elegant silky cream-colored long-haired cat came up and rubbed against Amy's leg.

"Hello there, Miss Sassy."

A sign stated: **Alexander Arrington Attorney at Law.**

Amy arrived at the door, used her key and entered. Various animals that resided in CA greeted her. Amy was thrilled to see her old pals. Duke, Duchess and Diva were Beagles. Nutmeg, an orange kitty and Cantankerous Cat, a thick old gray tom, were formerly feral felines that had found their way into the fold. Luminary the Legendary Lizard, lumbered up. Regis the 'Rascible Rabbit and Hamlet the Hammy Hamster took a break from their cardio in their large looping enclosures and joyfully pressed their noses up against the glass. All the creatures were happy to see Amy back, except Rudy and Ronda, a rodent couple that were quite blasé about it. Almost all had been saved from the pound or were adopted after being abandoned on the roadside, or left to die at the vet.

Then she saw Henry Clay, an Irish Setter with a deep, rich, red chestnut coat. They had a special bond.

"Henry Clay. Do you forgive me for being away for so long?"

He forgave her and came up and she petted him and he loved it.

She proceeded to the kitchen to find Mrs. Simmons, a Black woman of 55, the legal secretary, paralegal and house manager of Casa Arrington and mother to all the four legged and two legged critters in CA.

"Amy?"

"Hi, Mrs. Simmons."

"Hello, child." They hugged.

Her granddad, Arthur Arrington, in his late 70s, was in the living room on a stationary bike wearing VR goggles going at a good pace. A screen showed what he was seeing. It displayed the bucolic hills and a rider, a female character on a bike.

"I'm going to catch you on this hill," boasted Granddad.

"Try it!" yelled the female avatar back at him.

"Granddad and his friend are racing in the English countryside," said Mrs. Simmons. "They meet virtually and cycle together."

After another twenty minutes they finally finished peddling, gave each a virtual wave and logged off. Granddad took off his VR goggles and saw his granddaughter. "Amy!"

"Hi, Granddad." They hugged.

He checked his results, "Hey, 81 watts created. Not bad. I took it easy on her."

"Where is your cycling friend?"

"England."

"I love England, which part, Granddad?"

"North London, the Highgate area. It's beautiful."

"Waterlow Park is a favorite of mine," said Amy.

"Mine too. I get to go back, but virtually." He held up his goggles.

"Nice."

"I thought you were going to be here physically last week?"

"Me too, Granddad. A change of plans. 'Be like water making its way through cracks.'"

Granddad reflected on that, "Quoting Bruce Lee. Your father's big on that one."

"I didn't say anything about me coming this weekend, I wanted it to be a big surprise."

"Trust me, it's going to be that, for sure," said Mrs. Simmons.

"Where is the fearless defender of the people?" asked Amy.

Mrs. Simmons cleared her throat, like she always did around prickly subjects.

Granddad picked up a twenty-pound dumb bell and started doing curls. "At the moment, your father, Alexander, is in the hoosegow, the big house. Jail."

"Surprise," exclaimed Mrs. Simmons.

Amy's jaw dropped and her good vibrations twanged out of phase.

4

Amy called the jail and was told that visitation hours ended at 6pm. She attempted to find out what was going on, but the clerk didn't give out any information. Amy pondered who she could contact that could shed some light. It came to her, but she hesitated—then made the call.

"Hello, Amy?"

"Hi, Reston."

"Yes, hello. I heard you were back in town."

"News travels very fast in your world, Reston."

"It's all data and when you have access to it. How are you? How's New York? I love that town, have you had dinner at Restaurant Daniel?"

"I'm good, New York is great and yes, I have dined at that restaurant."

"Have you experienced the Maine Sea Scallops layered with Black Truffle in Golden Puff Pastry?"

"No."

"You should also try the Lobster, Asparagus and Artichoke salad with Fresh Hearts of Palm and Meyer Lemon Dressing."

"I did have that. The reason I'm—"

"How was it?"

"It was excellent. The reason I'm calling is to find out about my father."

"Alexander has been incarcerated. This afternoon in the Louisville Metro Department of Corrections."

Amy could sense the smugness, "Why?"

"Contempt of court."

"How?"

"I'll pick you up tomorrow and take you to see him."

"But—"

"I'm sorry, Amy, please understand, I'm on a business call right now to Asia. I have a meeting in the morning. I'll be around to pick you up tomorrow at 1pm. Great to have you back. Cheers."

The line went dead.

She wished she knew what this was about. Amy recalled her father had spent time behind bars for social justice, but she really didn't pay attention or understand his motivation. She turned off her phone and compartmentalized it into tomorrow's business and concentrated on decompressing.

Granddad had turned in for the night and Mrs. Simmons had retreated to her section of the compound.

Amy began to relax. She glanced around at the eclectic collection of art. She was familiar with some of the pieces, but there were new additions. Some were paintings from her granddad, others were local artists Alexander followed. There was one from Mark Priest on the UGRR, the Underground Railroad.

The house phone rang and she just blankly answered, "Hello?"

"Ambrosia."

"Yes, Mother?" The calmness dissipated.

"I wanted to state for the record that John Tenorio is a cad. May I remind you back in the day when he grabbed my derriere at the Derby and what ensued."

"I know that story."

"My point here, dear, is he has an agenda and a grudge and you've been swept up in that."

"I understand."

"I'll be home late tomorrow. When can we have lunch?"

"How about the day after tomorrow?"

"Let's see..." April was checking her book. "How long are you staying?"

"A week."

"The Buechel Area Historical and Preservation luncheon is then."

"By the way, Reston is picking me up tomorrow at 1."

"Reston? You talked to him?"

"Just did."

"Why?" April was a bit concerned.

"It was the only place I could get information on Daddy. Haven't you preached to me about using connections, Mother?"

"Alexander's been locked up for his big mouth. It's a wonder it hasn't happened sooner."

"Reston is taking me to see Daddy at the jail."

"I believe there is some malevolence between Reston and yourself."

"That's not true, Mother."

"Really?"

"Not like Alexander and Reston. Why is that?"

"Two rivals vying for my affection."

"I sense it's more than that, Mother."

"It started steamrolling about 10 years or so ago. There was a federal settlement with Purdue Pharma over their opioid exposure. But Kentucky opted out and went to court, which caused others to also sue. Alexander was on the legal team. Reston took a bit of a haircut over that."

"And he blames Daddy?"

"That and Alexander taunted Reston about being a *narco trafficante*, claiming oxycodone drug stocks were like the cartels, hugely profitable, while destroying lives. He said only the little guys were punished. The big honchos, the financiers, like Reston, were almost never held accountable."

"What happened?"

"Reston took a swing at Alexander, but missed. Reston considered filing a defamation lawsuit. I think Alexander wanted him to go for it, but Reston didn't want any more publicity and he knew Alexander would have gone to town over this. But it's simmered down now. They behave, mostly."

"Reston is such a..." Amy caught herself.

"I rather doubt you've liked any of my suitors since your father."

"Other than that sketchy Russian oligarch...Igor, I'm cool."

"*Ivan* wasn't sketchy. It was my Dr. Zhivago moment."

"Mother, they said he fell out of a plane. Explain that."

"It was Russian made."

"Right..." Amy shook her head in immense disbelief.

"The problem was Ivan had a big mouth too, like your father."

"Mother, I'm sorry I brought this up. I would strongly advise you not to discuss stuff, *any kind of stuff* about Ivan on an unsecured line, or, on *any* line."

"Fine. And I can continue to rely on your discretion about..."

"Hey, what happens in Manhattan..."

"I've raised you well. I would hate for the cat lady to be evicted twice."

"Mother, what you do in your private life is of no concern to me. Even if he's one of my castoffs."

"I declare!"

"Declare all you want, Mother."

April gasped, "Well, holler fire and save the matches!"

"Yelling fire isn't protected speech. Be careful, the northern Yankees up there don't understand that southern colloquialism."

"I... you are...grrr..." April continued to huff, exasperated with her daughter.

"Calm yourself, Mother. You're getting the vapors."

"Tiago may have left your island, darling, but there are other destinations, with just as appealing fruit and vegetation on them, if not more so."

"Whoa, now, you're giving *me* the vapors."

"Good. How about a late lunch Friday?"

"Fine," replied Amy.

"Hold on, there's the Waverly Hills Society Board meeting. What about on Saturday?"

"Mother, I'll have my people coordinate with your people and see what we can squeeze in."

"Honey, I have another call, it's the governor and you're right, we're going to work this out. Tell Granddad I said hi. Tootles."

The line went dead.

Amy pondered, "The governor?"

Casa Arrington was located in the north Highlands area of Louisville, just south of Irish Hill. It was a sprawling two-story Victorian house nestled on a large wooded corner lot. It hosted an eclectic collection of family and friends, which were plentiful. There were six bedrooms and several more nooks where they could stick a visiting ambassador or traveling minstrel for the night.

A sign inside welcomed visitors: **Thank You for Contributing to Our Power.**

Casa Arrington was off the grid. A diagram explained how kinetic energy was gathered from people walking on the floors. On average five watts of electricity was generated for every step taken. A real-time scoreboard displayed captured energy from outside and inside, using the stationary bikes and treadmills. A collection of solar panels were aesthetically attached on the roof and embedded into the structure. Vertical helix maglev wind turbines intertwined seamlessly with the property. They had plenty of power to run all of the appliances in C.A., two electric vehicles and a wide array of e-devices.

Amy opened a closet in the hallway and found a metal rack that had a velvet cover over it. She removed the cloth which revealed four stacked skateboards. She pulled out the second one down, hers, and checked it. It was in good working order.

She flipped on the lights to the backyard. There was a serious garden and a vertical greenhouse that blended casually into this very green home. But the main feature was the 12-foot-tall half-pipe.

Amy put on a helmet and jumped on with her board. She started slow and tried to banish her thoughts, but events continued to swirl in her brain. Her momentum increased. She was now skating angry, grabbing some big air, until she caught the lip at the top and lost control of her board. She landed with a thud mid-pipe and slowly slid the rest of the way down the curved smooth wood to the bottom. She stared up at the sky and a quiet groan emanated from her.

"Why is he so frustrating?"

****

Action pics of a young Rodney Mullins, Shawn White, Tony Hawk and Lizzie Armanto were on the wall of Amy's bedroom. It was a secret fantasy of hers to give up the law and have Tony Hawk beg her to join the Birdhouse skate team. A poster for the band TORTs was on the side wall.

Amy slept until almost 10am and felt remarkably rested, but a bit sore on her side where she landed. And then she recalled her Dad's situation and grumbled. Amy got up, came downstairs and greeted Cantankerous Cat, Nutmeg and the gang.

Granddad grunted by doing lunges holding two twenty-pound kettle bells.

"Morning, Granddad."

"Morning, Sunshine. How'd you sleep on your first night back?"

"So-so, just worried about..."

"Yeah. He can be such a nitwit at times, but your daddy has a method to his madness, usually..."

Amy cocked her head, "Contempt of court?"

Granddad continued his workout, "He must have really riled one of the judges over there."

"Reston is picking me up this afternoon and taking me to see him."

Mrs. Simmons arrived from the kitchen carrying a plate with a bowl of oatmeal and fruit, along with green tea for herself. "Good morning, Amy."

"Morning, Mrs. Simmons."

"Can I get you anything?"

"Don't worry, I'll fix myself some kind of smoothie."

"There's yogurt, bananas and blueberries, some apples and nuts, seeds, spinach and kale."

Amy was already sorting, "All my favorites."

"When you get some time, you might take a look at some of the cases Alexander is handling at the moment. They're stacked on the table. I've prioritized the responses and filings needed on the most pressing matters."

"Uh, sure."

"The case Alexander is currently 'dealing' with, in his own unique style, is on the top. It's about the planting or not planting of some Bonsai Trees."

Amy fixed her smoothie, sat, slid the pile of legalities over, drew a deep breath and took a deep dive in.

****

Over at Dulsett Distilleries. Bobby and Cassidy Dulsett were ensconced in his office diligently studying a marketing proposal. An animated Kerry the Caiman was being presented as a possible celebrity endorser for their brand. They read the pitch sheet as they each held a foot-tall plastic action figure of a grinning Kerry the Caiman, wearing a Dulsett Distilleries t-shirt, with his little belly hanging out over a speedo.

Cassidy cringed at this hideous creature and politely put the action figure on the floor away from her chair and wiped off her hands. "Bobby, have you seen the ads with Kerry the Caiman selling Balthazar's Boffo Barley Pop?"

"Yeah."

"They royally suck," said Cassidy.

"Yeah."

"This reptile will not be good for us. I vote no." Cassidy got up and left his office.

Bobby took a moment and made sure she was gone. He slid over to his closet and dug through some stuff. He pulled out his skateboard. It wasn't in good working order. He placed it on the carpet of his office and carefully stepped on. He slowly and steadily advanced.

Cassidy knocked and reentered the room, "Bobby, I also needed to talk to you about—"

Bobby was startled and lost his balance. The skateboard shot out from him and he fell back onto the carpet on his backside, right smack dab onto the toothy grinning caiman. "Ahhh!!!"

****

"I told you Kerry was bad for us, especially you," Cassidy quipped, as she checked out one of the young doctors in the ER.

Bobby—in a hospital gown—was laying on his front in a side examination room, he snarled at her.

Mitch blew into their examination room, "Bobby, I'm here for you, man!"

Cassidy looked up from her phone, "Mitch, how'd you get in here?"

"If anyone asks, I'm Bobby's cousin. Are you alright??"

"This isn't life threatening," Bobby grunted. "Only life humiliating."

Mitch was checking his phone, "I got a text that Bobby Dulsett can barely walk and was taken to the ER with a bruised… How do you pronounce this word? Coc…"

"It's coccyx," said Cassidy. "He has a bruised coccyx!"

Mitch cringed at that and subtly covered his own groin.

Bobby growled, "Not everyone heard you on the first floor, Sis."

"How did this happen?"

Cassidy looked to Bobby who nodded back to her. "Dulsett Distilleries is considering a new marketing push, with Kerry the Caiman."

"I love Kerry!" Mitch gave two thumbs up. "He is one cool caiman. Can't go wrong with that reptile. But, how do you bruise your…?"

"I fell on my butt on the plastic caiman action figure."

Mitch was confused, "Your coccyx is on your…*backside*?" He moved his hand from his groin area around to his rear. "Ah, gotcha."

Cassidy closed her eyes, quietly shook her head and then was back scrolling through the screen on her phone.

"Are you injured, Bobby??"

"Mitch, chill, it's just a bruise."

"Were you indulging in your product a little early?"

Cassidy didn't look up from her phone, "He was up on his skateboard."

"What?? Why in the… Wait…" Mitch paused. "Amy Arrington is into skateboarding."

Cassidy nodded, "Yep."

"Is she?" Bobby innocently inquired.

Cassidy scoffed, "Dang, that's such an awful impression of an honest person."

"With our recent loss…" Mitch was sputtering. "After Amy returned…and you with a very strange and severe dip in your shooting ability… And now falling on your coc… If we don't win this next game, we're *out* of the playoffs!"

"I'm fine!"

Mitch turned to Cassidy, "Please remove all skateboards, skates, bikes, make it anything you can get on with wheels."

****

Amy had read and reread the Bonsai Tree case trying to make sense of it. It had achieved priority status on the docket, proceeding rapidly as the defendant contested nothing and ignored everything. In Kentucky civil cases 'personal jurisdiction' is required before a monetary judgment. This happens when the defendant is deemed to have notice of the lawsuit. However, Amy did some more digging and learned no 'officer' or 'managing agent' of the property could be located. No process server was successful. No correspondence returned. No signature for certified mail recorded. Only at the 11th hour before a default judgment was awarded, an attorney was retained, filed an answer and made an appearance at an evidentiary hearing. He challenged the photos taken by the plaintiff and was successful in having this evidence excluded. Alexander went beyond the pale and was jailed. Amy then received word the defendant had hired a new attorney of record. She thought this was bonkers.

It was just after 10:45am. Amy decided she had plenty of time before Reston picked her up. A burgundy electric vehicle was plugged into the wall in the garage. She untethered it and drove a short distance to the east.

Alexander was representing a small landscaper who claimed he hadn't been paid. The homeowner was asserting he never planted the trees in the first place. Amy questioned why her father was going to such lengths. He had sacrificed for great causes. *But now, going to jail for a single client?*

Cherokee Triangle neighborhood had a historic feel to it. Since 1975 it had been designated a preservation district. This significantly slowed development and the encroachment of modern apartment complexes and kept many of the grand old houses.

She slowed to get a good view of the estate. The area was very nice, well maintained. The location of the disagreement was a stone house on what looked to be a quarter acre lot. Amy checked it online and found it to have four bedrooms, three baths, wonderful parquet floors and a fantastic gourmet kitchen. There was a gentle slope to the front yard and she could see where the trees were or were not planted and uprooted with the turned over dirt. It also looked like the blinds moved on a window in the far corner of the home. Amy had a creepy feeling she was being watched and drove on.

****

Amy was back at CA by 11:30. She skated on the pipe. Midway through the session she couldn't resist and checked out the website of Dulsett Distillery. Bobby was listed as president of operations. Amy studied his smiling picture.

Predictable and reliable, Reston was on time. Exactly at 1pm. Amy entered his Mercedes. It was smooth and quiet and oozing power, just like Reston.

"Have you seen your mother?"

"Funny you say that, we just missed each other. She arrived at her townhouse after I was on the plane here."

"Your mother said she's doing some consulting for the Sultan and having a good time in New York. Taking in the drama and the cultural stuff. We usually see a play or two when we're there."

"Mom's a sucker for Shakespeare."

"She said she's coming home sometime later today."

"Yes, that's what she said."

"Did your mother say what flight she was taking?"

"No. Now please tell me about my father."

"He's in the drunk tank."

"He was intoxicated?"

"No, it was just the safest place to put him."

****

Reston contacted an officer who took Amy back to a 25'x 25' holding pen with a dozen men of various ages and social status.

"You've got 10 minutes, ma'am," said the officer.

"Thank you."

Alexander Aloysius Arrington. Almost 50, he was attired in a seersucker suit; his formerly athletic body had slid gracefully into a middle age spread around his waist. He sported longish graying hair that curled about; a quite stylish mustache and goatee complimented the rest of his face. He spoke with a subtle southern accent that he modified for the setting. On an acoustic guitar he was strumming an ominous chord pattern and telling one of his tall tales to the captured and enraptured sharing the lock-up with him.

Alexander's strumming began to build, "Finally, after enduring two typhoons, a broken mast, those nasty piranha and nearly capsizing after fighting off that killer whale, we were approaching the island."

His audience vibrated with excitement and anticipation.

With crashing chords, Alexander's face went white as a ghost, "But then, off the starboard bow I caught sight of the beast."

The guys leaned in with intense interest.

"It was a giant sea monster that rose up from the depths and it was coming right at us!" The music screeched to a halt.

The group gasped with dread and distress.

Alexander noticed his daughter and grinned, "Ambrosia! Darling, what are you doing here?!"

The group moaned, "Come on, Alexander, what happened next??"

He waved them off, "I'll get to it."

Amy was calm, "I never expected to find you here."

"*Expectation is the root of all heartache,*" quoted her father.

"Daddy, just for a moment, please, quit throwing Shakespeare at me. And how are you allowed to have a guitar in here?"

"*Music is the wine that fills the cup of silence.*"

Amy groaned.

"Not Shakespeare, dear, Robert Fripp."

"Oh."

"Let me tell you why I'm in here."

"Is this you being like water?"

Alexander paused at that, "In a way, yes."

A voice bellowed out, "He called Judge Winslow a 'boneheaded buffoon!'"

Alexander shrugged and nodded and the place went up for grabs.

Amy was getting annoyed and about to pitch a bitch, but she controlled herself. "I made a phone call. If you apologize by close of business hours today, he'll drop the contempt of court order."

"I already apologized."

"Really?"

"I humbly apologized to every boneheaded buffoon in here for comparing them to that doofus on the bench. Sorry guys!"

The prisoners all busted up laughing again; even some of the guards were snickering.

Amy glanced around and finally laughed to herself and then she didn't. She snarled, "Grrr, enough!!!"

An inmate was alarmed, "I thought that was her, she's the Firewoman!"

The prisoners stepped back from the bars with concern.

Alexander was impressed. Amy was stressed.

****

Amy had taken a walk to rebalance herself, something she would have to do occasionally dealing with her father. She had a late lunch and booked a ride to the radio station where she picked up her rental. Then she drove to the St. James Court section of town in the old historic Louisville. Beautiful brick homes were situated between stunning Victorian mansions, all surrounded by lush greenery.

Judge Wilbur Winslow was in his 74th year, he was a small man in physical stature, but had an imposing presence. Willodean Winslow, his wife of 44 years, was a year younger, with a more welcoming personality.

It was early evening and they both sat on the porch drinking iced tea. Katydids had yet to make their appearance, it was still very early in the summer, though the crickets could be heard.

The judge read the *Courier-Journal* and the Mrs. knitted as Amy strolled up and stopped in front of their residence.

"Lordy, look who's here!" exclaimed a cheerful Willodean. "Amy!"

Amy had a warm smile, "Hi, Ms. Winslow. Hello, Judge."

"Hey there, kiddo. How's old New York?" asked the judge with a wry grin.

"It has its charms."

"I noticed close of business has come and gone and I didn't get a call," replied the Judge, now with some bite.

"You know about old dogs learning new tricks."

The judge lowered the newspaper and leaned forward, "It can happen. Oh, it can happen all right, just depends on the teaching method."

"I suppose," said Amy.

"We are at a standstill. I'm going to train that old dog not to wiz on the court's carpet." The Judge leaned back, raised up the C-J and went back to reading.

Mrs. Winslow shrugged and offered her warm smile.

****

After that encounter Amy was, as she would describe it, 'in a most certifiable funk.' The frustrations of the day had drained her. And then Amy had a craving and realized the solution was very close. It was a very pleasant recollection of her father, back in the day, whisking her away in the early evening, brushing off any negativity, banishing the problems and they would arrive at Dairy Del. As a child she loved the neon sign. The line was usually long, but so many friends were also there, it didn't matter. They could catch up. She and her father would sometimes get chili dogs, but always order a banana split—and they would talk about their day, which always made it better.

Amy arrived, but it was out of reach. Reliving this memory wasn't available at the moment. The business was closed for the day.

She slumped and returned to familiar adult territory that she knew would be open, Heine Brothers Coffee in the Highlands. She had a hot Salty Turtle Mocha, with dark chocolate and sweet caramel, with a touch of sea salt and stewed royally.

Just when she began to rebound, she noticed him enter: Randolph 'Chip' Richardson, son of Reston. He was 28, handsome and well dressed.

"I see you. Hey, Amy."

Amy was cautious with him, but friendly. "Hi, Chip."

"I talked to my Dad and I'm sorry to hear how he had to take you behind the scenes to see Alexander."

"Yeah, well..." There was quite the awkward pause. "So, Chip, how are things with you?"

"It's going great. I made partner."

"At your family's law firm?"

"Yes."

"Congratulations. I always knew you had the chops to be a very good lawyer."

"Thank you. It's been a long time, Amy. How's it going with you?"

"Living the dream in the Big Apple."

"I should congratulate you as well, I saw you on *Current Cross Currents*. You snatching victory from the jaws of their defeat. The Firewoman. Crush, kill, destroy. Impressive."

"You watch that...show? Really?"

"*Triple C!* I love it. John Tenorio brings it, every time. Did you see today's offering? It was just broadcast."

"No... And I don't want to—"

Chip instantly brought the show up on his tablet.

John Tenorio was at his desk, working on his laptop, searching tirelessly: "We're learning more about the infamous 'Firewoman.'"

Shots of Amy in a club were seen. She was dancing with a girl, they kissed on the lips and laughed.

John eyed the camera, "This girl has some tales to tell after years of practicing law in the New York courts AND her moves in the New York clubs! That is hot!"

Amy was momentarily stunned. She tapped it off. "Thanks for that."

Chip fanned himself, "That *is* hot. Is this the real reason we broke up?"

Amy cringed, "There was no 'we,' ever. We were never going out. I had a momentary lapse of judgment, a regrettable six-minute slip-and-fall."

Chip motioned to the tablet, "After this, I don't think I can get you hired at our law firm."

"That's a real shame. But you guys aren't usually on the side of my team."

"Your Big Apple firm, Padmore, represents the same people we do. You guys just jack up the price a bit more, I guess you have to cover that Manhattan overhead."

"I'm talking about my dad."

"Alexander has a lot of passion and he fights for the little...poor...guy."

"That he does."

Chip preened, "This Bonsai Tree case has no merit. Your guy didn't do the work. We're going to prove it. It's what we do."

"Wait, *you're* the new opposing counsel??"

Chip grinned, "Just came on board."

5

Amy returned to CA and wasn't ready to enter. She plopped down on a chair on the porch and just vegged. A circus clown shuffled by and Amy mumbled to herself, "That's odd even for this place..."

And then jugglers appeared and passed bowling pins by her nose and double-jointed performers maneuvered through them.

Amy glared at them.

Mrs. Simmons stepped out and looked up checking the weather. "Oh, hi, Amy."

"Hi, Mrs. Simmons."

"Is your father still in jail?"

"Yes, I'm working on that."

"Good."

"You know...I just saw a couple circus acts."

"The Khrakistan National Circus and some dignitaries are staying with us. Alexander did give me a heads up on that and I forgot to mention it to you."

Two emperor penguins majestically waddled by with their noses in the air.

"You know how your father always dreamed about running away to join the circus?"

Amy glanced around at the performers, "I do indeed..."

"Instead, Alexander had them come to him."

"The circus moved in?"

"They say it's only for a week."

Amy and Mrs. Simmons entered and strolled through the house where other acts were rehearsing.

"Who's in charge of these circus animals?" Amy asked.

"There's a wrangler around here somewhere," said Mrs. Simmons. "I saw him a little while ago."

Amy noticed something missing, "Did you safely secure the Ming vase..." A miniature pony trotted by, followed by a ducking 7-foot giant. "...to avoid any accidents before our guests arrived?"

"Didn't have to. Let me tell you why. Alexander has a new hobby. Can you guess?"

"Axe throwing?"

"No, blowing fire."

Amy hung her head and sighed.

"When Alexander saw your Firewoman episode, he immediately went on the internet to learn fire breathing. Later that night, after he became 'an expert,' he was practicing blowing 'small fire,' as he called it, in the kitchen. Granddad yelled at him saying breathing fire in the house was against the rules and to take it outside. And he did, where he blew 'big fire' and accidentally set alight a painting Granddad was working on and it burned to a crisp."

"Oh no..."

"Oh yes. Alexander apologized profusely, but Granddad chased your father around swinging that steel whip he has."

"Daddy escaped bodily harm?"

"Alexander got on his skateboard and was just about to get away when he wiped out and knocked the Ming vase off its 'secured' pedestal and it fell to the floor and smashed into a million pieces."

Amy was stunned by this, "That was Jihong porcelain..."

"He didn't insure it. Therefore, the need to protect it from the circus is moot."

Amy lamented, "The normal daily chaos already took it out. We had planned to pass it down through the generations."

"Alexander singed his goatee. I believe his fire breathing days are over."

"If only," muttered Amy.

"Watch out for Deveraux the Llama."

"A llama?" asked Amy, realizing she had never seen one up close.

"Yes. He's really moody."

"Duly noted. Deveraux is moody," Amy grumbled, not in a great mood herself. "Where's Henry Clay? Duke, Duchess and Diva?"

"Ever since the circus showed up with Sven, they've made themselves scarce."

"Sven?"

"He's their Siberian tiger."

"Siberian tiger?" Amy knew for sure she had never seen one of these up close.

Mrs. Simmons groused, "You should see the kitty litter now."

Around the corner in the living room Sven had hopped up on the couch.

"There he is!" Mrs. Simmons rolled up a newspaper and entered snarling, "Sven! Get off the couch! You heard me, you overgrown alley cat!"

The tiger growled, then whimpered, then jumped off and sat on the floor.

Amy made her way out back and came face-to-face with the llama. "Hi, Deveraux."

Deveraux just stared at her with his threatening and accusatorial eyes and slowly moved on.

Amy gave him a wide berth. She maneuvered around to a corner where Granddad was working.

"You think you can take me??" Granddad was yelling out to the street.

Old Man Miller was strolling by on the sidewalk towards the street corner. "I know I can, you overrated house painter!"

"You wouldn't know talent if it punched you in the nose, which I have a good mind to do!"

"Just try it, Artie. I'll clean your clock like I did with that haymaker back at the Haymarket!"

"That was a sucker punch you got me with!"

"Keep telling yourself that, Artie!"

Granddad was ready to rumble. He threw down his paintbrush and started for the street, until he noticed his granddaughter. "Ambrosia! How are you?"

Amy glanced out to see their neighbor shuffling on, "Chatting with Old Man Miller?"

"He's just a big bag of gas."

"Hey, the circus is here." Amy took a look at what he was painting and it was a happy and a sad clown.

"Yes, Alexander made friends with them when he visited Khrakistan."

"This is very interesting. I like it."

"Thank you. Later today they're going to teach me the saw-a-person-in-half trick. I'm going to practice on your father."

"I'm sorry to hear about your other painting."

"Nothing is permanent."

"And the vase. Holy smokes..."

Granddad sighed and shook his head regretfully, "Oh well... Is your Daddy still in the slammer?"

"Yes, he insulted Judge Winslow and hasn't apologized for it. I thought owls were supposed to have some wisdom."

"Alexander may be an idiot, but he's no fool. He's up to something."

Amy went back out front and sat. She closed her eyes and shook her head.

At that moment Chip arrived and came face to face with Deveraux. The llama was on patrol and not feeling neighborly. Chip was frozen in fear. Deveraux stared him down.

Chip slowly moved around him and saw Amy on the porch. "Amy, you have the biggest, ugliest dog I've ever seen."

"Chip, I'd be careful. Deveraux, being a llama, might take offense to that."

Deveraux wandered close and continued with the evil eye. Chip jumped up onto the porch. And then a monkey strolled by.

"And you have a monkey."

"That's Merlin."

Chip squinted and frowned as jugglers and acrobats traversed around him.

"The circus is visiting. What can I do for you, Chip?"

"Yes, well, our client, the father, was unaware of the Bonsai Tree lawsuit as he's been out of the country for some time. Currently there's an aunt and his son living there and that's where the breakdown in communication has been."

"Hmmm...I see. That could explain a lot."

"The owner wants it over. What will it take to end this?"

"Come in."

Amy led Chip into the house and right into their house guest, the 'dignitary' she had yet to encounter: President Ibragimov, the heavily mustached, balding, short and stout leader of the oil and mineral rich country Khrakistan.

"This is the one!" exclaimed the excited president. "Is your lucky day, pretty girl, because you are to experience the bountiful rod of love! You will remember this night until you go into grave because of the great joy I will bestow you!"

Amy was clueless on who he was. He grabbed Amy's firm butt.

Amy grabbed his soft throat and slammed the pudgy president against the wall.

His four bodyguards instantly pulled their weapons, HK MP5s, and trained them on her and Chip, who almost fainted.

Amy increased the pressure, "Lower your weapons or I'll snap his neck like a Pignut Hickory twig."

President Ibragimov twitched his bushy mustache, "Ah! I not like pig nuts!"

They lowered their weapons and she let go of his neck.

His assistant whispered into the president's ear.

President Ibragimov was annoyed, "She not one of the girls?"

Two young American beauties flitted by. Amy frowned.

The assistant inquired, "Woman, who are you that you would touch our great president in such a way?"

"This is my family's house. Who are you??"

The president bowed to her, "5 million and one pardons! I thought you were one of the…"

Another very attractive female smiled at the president and joined the others.

Chip was now working the room as he slid each of the ladies, as well as the security team, his business card.

President Ibragimov righted himself and regained his decorum. "Sorry, please, I make introduction."

"We've met, how can I forget?"

"Please. I am Grigory Mukhamedova Ibragimov, the president of Khrakistan on Caspian. Is pleasure for me to make acquaintance with you."

A large Burmese Python slithered over Chip's foot. "Ahhh!!!" He fled the room to another across the hall.

Amy knew the tiger was resting in that locale. "Chip, don't run that way! Watch out for Sven…"

Chip shrieked. A ferocious roar rang out. And then Chip screamed again.

Amy could see Mrs. Simmons run into the room and then heard the *CRASH* of shattering glass. Merlin covered his eyes.

Amy bolted around the corner to see Mrs. Simmons and Sven staring at a broken bay window.

"Lordy, that boy jumped clean through that window and just kept on running."

Amy glanced at the president observing and then back to their fleeing guest, "I feel like joining him. We'll talk later, Chip!"

Mrs. Simmons and Amy huddled, "The snake on the floor got here last week. The snake calling himself president slithered in an hour ago."

Amy noticed Sven had been listening in. She then noticed there was blood on his claw. The tiger seemed surprised by this and then embarrassed. Sven covered up his paw and looked away innocently.

Merlin shook his head, as he'd seen this before.

Amy frowned, "This isn't good…" She went back to the other room. The security team kept the president guarded.

"Sven is really pussycat. He just try to get screaming guy to quiet," declared the president. "Some people think I am bad guy, but really, I am sweet guy. Like Sven."

Amy was getting irked, "I'm thinking some don't think so."

The president waved that away, "To those that think this way, I say too much thinking."

"Right, watch out for too much of that," Amy said warily.

"Your father is great man! We made brotherhood together in my country!"

The assistant pulled out a tablet and displayed various pics of Alexander.

"That's Daddy alright. Ugh, I didn't need to see that one."

"And here is his invite for me to visit. And picture of him signing it."

"Sorry, but he's not here."

The president was confused, "I sent him news of my coming arrival and I watch his owl cartoons."

One of the president's assistants spoke, "Many pardons, Your Excellency. But..." He whispered into the president's ear.

"What?" The assistant whispered it again. "Ah."

"I am presently aware that Alexander has been put into chains for a most unfortunate comment."

Amy thought about that, "Actually, chains might work."

"He call judge..." He glanced at the assistant who again whispered it in the ear of his boss. "For calling judge, 'Buffoon with Boner!'"

"No! No!" cried Amy. "That's not what he said! And don't give him any ideas, he'd use that one."

"If is your persuasion," the President leaned in and whispered. "I will make phone call and problem is over. Difficulty will disappear. He is only judge."

"No. No. No. I'm dealing with it." Amy turned away wide-eyed and met up with Mrs. Simmons.

"I learned a fun fact," said Mrs. Simmons. "He's been in power for over 25 years. One of his titles is President for Life."

"Those lucky dogs." The phone rang. Amy removed Luminary the Legendary Lizard draped on it. "Excuse me, Luminary. You haven't seen Henry Clay, have you?" The lizard had nothing. She answered the phone. "Hello, you've reached the Casa Arrington circus."

"Yes, we're trying to reach Alexander Arrington. This is the State Department."

"Sorry, he's on a retreat right now, out of reach. Working on his music. I'm his daughter. What has he done now?"

"Please hold for the Under Secretary."

"Who?" Amy waited.

"Hello. Miss Arrington?"

"Yes?"

"I'm Miles Montgomery, Under Secretary for Diplomatic Affairs at the State Department. I was hoping to talk to your father about a houseguest there, the President of Khrakistan."

"Soon to be ex-houseguest," responded Amy, curtly.

"I'm aware the President can be a bit forward at times."

"When we first met he assumed I was a part of his harem and it was my lucky night."

"Miss Arrington, I'm urging you to put up with President Ibragimov for just a little while longer. Please, for your country."

"What's this about?"

"Khrakistan is vital to our national interests, strategically with their location and economically, with their oil and gas reserves."

"Then if he tries to slip me the rod of love, again, you prefer I not break it off and stuff it in his ear?"

"This is a time of great flux in that area of the world. And the situation with Khrakistan is fluid. Until now they've been a solid rock in our corner."

"And like a rock on his own people."

"The Secretary has tasked me with keeping him happy, while ascertaining the real reason why he's traveled to Louisville."

"I have a question," said Amy. "How does one become President for Life? Shouldn't we be encouraging their own democratic awakening?"

"We shall be in touch, soon, Miss Arrington." The line went dead.

Amy entered the next room to find the president yelling on his phone.

"$$%%^^^@@#$*$%!!!! Titter!%$#@^#&%!!!" He noticed Amy. "I apologize for these words, slight problem at home."

"Only caught 'Titter.' Of course that does sound like a porn site."

The assistant quickly corrected her, "Porno sites are banned in our country."

"I'm curious, how does one become "President for Life?"

"Permission from plebiscite by our people, 99.4% say should be this."

"No elections for over 25 years?"

"Correct."

"He's that beloved?" asked Amy.

"Yes! And this has saved tons of money. President is fiscal conservative."

"I always save money," boasted the president, as he ended his phone call. "Which is why I here."

"Why *are* you here?" asked Amy.

"We have negotiations with people who have what I need. I came here to get help from my brother Alexander to close deal. I need Alexander to be free. Offer still stands to make magic trick, abracadabra and judge disappears. Poof."

Amy gave him a very odd stare, "Are you mental?"

The president was stumped.

The assistant responded, "I believe she mean mental, as in mental powers."

The president didn't hesitate, "I have heavy powers, yes to your question. I am very mental."

Amy's own mental abilities were churning, "If you close this deal, would you then bestow your great joy to other parts of this vast globe?"

"Yes, and deal must close quick. I have situation gurgling at home."

Amy entered the office. She shut and locked the door behind her and sat at the desk. She then did a search on the computer: "President of

Khrakistan." She clicked and horrific images, human rights abuses and torture, appeared on the screen.

Amy began to learn about the President of Khrakistan, serious alarm set in. "Oh…my…God… Oh My God!"

****

The jarring images connected to their house guests disturbed her far into the evening. It didn't help that it was quite a stormy night.

Early the next morning Amy was in the kitchen drinking coffee.

The circus was slowly emerging. Merlin was still groggy. Deveraux didn't want to deal with anyone at this hour, though he didn't want to deal with most people at any hour.

Mrs. Simmons entered, "Morning, Amy."

"Good morning, Mrs. Simmons. Did you sleep well?"

"Like a log. You think Alexander will get out today?"

"I'm going to see him. I wanted to get out of here before…"

"The presidential rod of love arose?"

Two security agents burst into the kitchen and secured it.

President Ibragimov marched in behind them, "It is glorious morning!"

"Too late," grumbled Amy.

"Hello to you young ladies."

"And it's getting deep," said Mrs. Simmons.

"My team will cook breakfast for me. With food we brought, not to impose on you."

"Go for it," said Mrs. Simmons.

"Some people can't be too careful," Amy added.

"I have special diet." The president sat at the table as his team cooked eggs and bacon. "Amy, how are you today? Did you sleep well?"

"No. Not at all. I was researching mysterious deaths in the world."

"Yes, yes, death is a mystery," agreed the president.

"But usually, we can determine who caused the death. Don't you love the whodunnits?" asked Amy, with some enthusiasm.

"I'm sorry, the what?"

"No, who. As in who has blood on their hands for the murder, the mystery."

"Ah, yes, Agatha Christie. Hercule Poirot."

"Exactly," replied Amy. "Take for example Vitaly Shishov."

"Does not ring my bell."

"He ran a group that helped people escape your repression at home. He was found hanging from a tree."

"And?"

"Care to share anything, Mr. President? You know, unburden yourself."

"My security forces did not kill him. He was nobody."

Amy gave this some thought, "And then there was Nikita Krivtsov. Another activist, another thorn in your side. Also strung up."

"It is very sad when people take their own life."

Amy saw the cold disconnect in him, "Yes, it is and when life is *taken* from them for trying to improve it."

The president wiggled his gray mustache and sloughed it away.

Amy checked the time and chose not to go to battle, as she had more pressing business to attend to.

****

Amy drove past the office for Dulsett Distilleries and slowed the car. She was tempted to pull in, but moved on. She called Chip at his family's law firm and left a message: "Hi, Chip, it's Amy, sorry about Sven, that big cat. Hope all is well. Call me about the case." Some time went by and she heard nothing. Amy then tried Reston and he wasn't answering his phone. "Hi

Reston, this is Amy, just wanted to follow up on what Chip said about your client wanting to settle. Please call me back at your earliest convenience."

Amy surmised the radio silence may have something to do with a large Siberian tiger with blood on his claw and crashing through a bay window and she was right.

Amy parked, approached the jail and received a call, "Hello, Mother."

"You want to tell me what happened with Chip?"

"Daddy has some guests that may have been a bit naughty."

"You mean the circus and Sven?"

"You know more than me, what's going on?"

"Chip went to the ER requiring medical attention, after paying a call to Casa Arrington."

"How serious is it, Mother? Is Chip alright?"

"He'll live. You better let me handle this."

As Amy arrived at the jail, she received a text.

GABBY: Aim, I've got two tickets for the sold-out Bats game tonight. You in?

Amy really wasn't up for this.

AMY: not feeling so good.

GABBY: feeling guilty about Chip?

AMY: you know?

GABBY: everyone knows. You need a diversion. Doctor's orders.

AMY: okay doc.

GABBY: pick you up at 6

AMY: sounds good

Amy was led back to the lockup. Alexander was napping on a bench.

Another inmate greeted her, "Can I help you?"

"I would like to talk to my dad."

"He's indisposed at the moment, but might be available later after his chess match, but then there's Story Time. And it's a good one today. I could probably fit you in there."

Amy was in no mood. She threw a metal cup on the floor that clanked loudly.

The greeter backed away with a fright, "It's the Firewoman." The inmates were actually a bit intimidated by her.

Alexander woke and slowly got his wits, "Huh? Ambrosia? You getting riled up again? There's no need, honey."

"Gee, I was looking for that Ming vase."

"The Ming vase?"

"The highly valued, uninsured Ming vase, you shattered when you were blowing fire out of whatever end it was coming from."

"Honey, was it really Ming? Really?"

"*Get your facts first, then you can distort them as you please.*"

Alexander chuckled, "Throwing Mark Twain at me, deadly."

"Thought you'd appreciate that. Now record an apology on my phone to Judge Winslow, so you'll get out."

Alexander was reluctant.

"Daddy, did you know the president of Khrakistan has set up camp in our house?"

"Uh...who?"

"He said he sent news of his 'coming arrival.' And there was an invitation for him to visit. And a picture of you two signing it. Apparently, you two made 'brotherhood' when you were there."

"Sounds sort of familiar."

"Why is he here? He'll only divulge that to you."

"Is that a fact?"

"It is. And he brought the Khrakistan National Circus with him."

"Did Deveraux come?"

"Deveraux the Llama?"

"Yes."

"Deveraux's here."

"He's really shy," said Alexander.

"Sven sure isn't," Amy added.

"Sure, Sven can be a smidge forward, but he's really a pussycat."

"Ever since Sven the 'pussycat' has arrived, Henry Clay, Duke, Duchess and Diva have gone into the witness protection program, along with Cantankerous Cat and Nutmeg."

Alexander frowned, "That's not good."

"Are you going to record an apology for the judge?"

Alexander was still reluctant.

"Okeydokey, I'll let you get back to your nap and your story time. I hear it's a good one today. And I just realized that you might miss the 4th of July fireworks. That's a shame."

Alexander flinched at that thought.

"Oh, and your Bonsai Tree lawsuit. Chip told me they want to settle."

"He's the new opposing counsel? And they want to settle?"

"Yes, for the first question and not actually sure at the moment on your second inquiry. I can't seem to reach him or Reston after Sven mauled Chip."

"Sven would never do that."

"Daddy, Chip crashed through the bay window and went to the ER. I've seen the bloody claw."

"Is that so?" Alexander wondered about this.

"Mom said she would handle it."

Alexander came to terms with the situation. "How long is he staying?"

"Sven?"

"No, the president of Crack Land."

"He's not leaving until he sees you. He says he needs your help in closing a deal. He'll tell only you, his brother."

Alexander let out a deep groan, "He's so annoying. That pompous piece of…"

"Golly, you do remember him, rather accurately."

Alexander sighed at the memory and nodded.

"Make an apology to the judge." Amy pulled out her phone and started recording. "And action," whispered Amy.

"Your Honor, I am sincerely sorry, from the bottom of my heart, that you are a bone-headed buffoon." Alexander snickered.

"Cut!" Amy turned and walked off.

"Okay, Okay, I'll be serious."

Amy stopped, turned around and again put up her phone to record him. "Take 2."

"Your Honor, I apologize for insulting you, I was way out of line. I'm sorry."

"Cut. That's a keeper."

****

It was late afternoon and Amy was waiting in her car on a green, leafy street in the St. James Court neighborhood by the fountain.

Down the way a dark sedan pulled up and let the judge out. He walked up to his residence and entered.

Amy waited 10 minutes, enough time for him to do any personal business, but not enough time to sit down for a meal.

Willodean came to the door, "Amy, hello."

"Hello, Ms. Winslow. I was hoping to speak to the judge for just a moment."

"Certainly. Sit here and I'll bring out refreshments."

The judge came out and the three sipped lemonade. Willodean worked on her embroidery of a cardinal. The judge wanted to chat about Louisville basketball. Amy knew the history fairly well. Alexander had instilled that in her at an early age, but she wasn't close to the knowledge of the judge. He reminisced about Coach Bernard "Peck" Hickman who passed away in 2000.

"I was just 21 when I met him. I was in awe. Coach Hickman was a great player. When he was at Central High their winning percentage was 85%. When he played in college at Western Kentucky their winning percentage was just a tad under 77%. And he was a great coach. When he was at Hodgenville and Valley High Schools, he had a winning percentage of 81%. When he coached the University of Louisville, his winning percentage was right at 71% and in 23 years as the Cardinals skipper, he never once had a losing season."

Amy nodded, "Those are seriously impressive numbers."

"You betcha they are. And I am honored to be a friend of Coach Denny Crum," the judge proudly stated. "He's a fine man and a terrific coach. He really was Cool Hand Luke."

"His 2-2-1 zone press," Amy said.

"That transitioned to man-to-man at half court," added the judge.

"And the Doctors of Dunk!" Willodean exclaimed, having to calm herself, though not missing a feather stitch. "They were my favorite."

The three laughed and settled down and took another sip of lemonade.

"Judge, may I show you Alexander's apology now?"

The judge nodded.

Amy played the recording on her phone: "Your Honor, I apologize for insulting you, I was way out of line. I'm sorry."

"He was so humble and contrite today sitting in his cell," reported Amy.

"Was he now?"

"Yes, Your Honor. Would this satisfy your requirements for dropping the contempt order?"

"I'd like to tell you a story about Freedom Hall."

Amy wondered where this was going, "Okay."

"I saw Muhammad Ali's first fight there, when he was Cassius Clay. He showed up in a pink Cadillac and won a six-round decision over Tunney Hunsaker. And the Mrs. and I, right when we got married, my father, as a wedding present, gave us season tickets right behind home bench in Freedom Hall. Coach Hickman was there at the time. And then we had them through Coach Dromo, a loyal assistant for 17 seasons. He was the one that recruited Wes Unseld and Butch Beard, great Black players. They ushered in a new golden era. And then Coach Dromo has to retire after only four seasons because of a heart attack."

"That was a real shame," lamented Willodean.

"And then through Coach Crum. And then Rick Pitino…" The judge steadied himself and cleared his throat.

"Great men have great flaws, dear," reminded Willodean.

The judge harkened back fondly, "We had those wonderful seats from 1965 to 2010. And then, when the new place, the Yum Center opened up we lost those seats."

"It was quite a substantial disappointment," lamented Willodean.

"The point I'm trying to make here, Amy, is that for 45 seasons my wife and I always sat right behind our home team, directly behind the coach. "It's now 2019 and we haven't felt right since watching the Cards from our new, different seats, it's contemptible."

"I'm sorry to hear that." The shock and dread were settling in for Amy realizing where Alexander's seats were located in the Yum Center. "I've sat in those seats, right behind the coach, lots of times, yes? Alexander has those seats."

"Yes," said the old judge. "Look, I know Alexander pulled this stunt in my courtroom to buy time. And, maybe it worked, but in my mind he cheated."

"He was clearly out of line and disrespectful, Your Honor."

"Let me tell you a possible scenario, no quid pro quo mind you, but if I were to get those seats back, I would be in such a good mood that any contempt order would simply blow away."

Amy was stunned at this.

The judge stood. "He's lucky I don't have him disbarred. As for myself, if you want to lodge a complaint, go for it. Report me for misconduct, I'm ready for retirement. I'll go down in Cardinal history. It's been lovely seeing you again, Amy. Have a nice evening."

Amy returned to the car, slowly got in and screamed.

6

Amy returned home stunned and bummed. She then recalled that Gabby would be by in an hour to pick her up for the game, *do I really need this?* She flipped on ESPN on the flatscreen in her room.

SportsCenter was on, "You're right, Trey, the eyes of the baseball world will be on the Bats, Louisville's Triple A team tonight."

Amy froze and then pivoted to the screen in amazement.

"I'm sure most of you have heard by now the tale of Russell Cormack."

Amy shook her head, "No…"

"Right, Trey, the once rising flamethrower has reinvented himself as a finesse player and become a household name in one evening. His last outing, he pitched 5 scoreless innings, gave up one hit and gave the other batters a headache with a near unhittable knuckleball. Well, we can report he has reported to the Bats and will be the starter for tonight's game."

Amy was intrigued, she took her shower and was now really looking forward to the game.

****

The game was over. Gabby and Amy had a couple rounds and Amy was let off back at Casa Arrington near midnight. As she opened the door, the llama was checking her out.

"Hi, Deveraux," whispered Amy. She was tired and ready for bed.

Mrs. Simmons stepped into the room, "That was some game."

"Sure was, a no-hitter," said Amy. "Well, Mrs. Simmons, I'll see you in the—"

"And speaking of that no-hitter, we have clients that need help."

Amy froze, she could see that it was now past midnight.

"They're waiting in the den."

In the den were Theodore Snodgrass and Wei Wei Chen, a male and female, both in their early 20s. They were nervous for a good many reasons. After seeing the jugglers and clowns and circus animals, they wondered where they were.

The door opened and Amy strode in. "Hello, I'm sorry that you had to wait."

"That's okay," mumbled Theo.

"Can I get you any refreshments?"

"No," said Wei Wei. "But is this really an attorney's office?" She eyed Merlin giving her the eye.

"Yes, yes, it is. This is a traveling circus, friends of my father. What can we do for you?"

Theo and Wei Wei glanced at each other. She decided to speak.

"We are with a sports management company, our client pitched tonight, Russell Cormack."

"I was at the game, congratulations. That was the first no-hitter I've seen. I hear Russell's been called up to the Show." Amy was desperately trying not to yawn in front of them. Her eyelids were getting heavy.

"That is fantastic," said Theo. "But, the senior agent, Max Hoogaboom… Actually, something from his past came out tonight on *Current Cross Currents.*"

"John Tenorio?" Amy was hit with a jolt of adrenaline. She was now wide awake and locked on.

"Yes," Theo responded.

"And now," said Wei Wei, "Russell's parents are forbidding Russell to be repped by Max."

"All of this because of something broadcast on *Current Cross Currents*?" asked Amy?

"Yes, but it wasn't Max's fault," implored Theo. "He was tricked and fell into an awkward situation and John Tenorio embellished and ridiculed Max."

Amy was squeezing a tennis ball for some release.

"While Max was the only one who would give Russell a chance!" said Wei Wei. "He was the *only* one that believed in the guy and now Max is being tossed aside!"

"When Max heard he'd been fired by Russell, or Russell's parents," Theo said, bitterly, "He went off the deep end. He must have really gone gonzo because..."

"We saw Max running with no clothes," Wei Wei mumbled, in a daze. "...naked... down by the riverfront."

Theo was rocked, "Max is one of the good guys. He's worked so hard, put in the time, went the extra mile and now, to have it all taken away. It's just so cruel."

****

Amy promised to look into Max's situation first thing in the morning. But she couldn't sleep. Amy read several articles about Russell and Max. It was just after 4am. Her mind was troubled learning about Max and his struggles to reach his dream and have it blow up right in front of him and John Tenorio lighting the fuse.

Amy grabbed her pack and rode her bike to the waterfront. She stopped at one of her favorite places, the Lincoln Memorial. 'A House Divided Cannot Stand.'

She then rode over to Dave Armstrong Extreme Park, a 24-hour skatepark with steep ramps, large bowls and a giant half pipe. The lighting was excellent. There were challenges for everyone, at all skill levels. Amy pulled her skateboard out of her pack and was back at it. After an hour or so, Amy was regaining her near elite status.

****

Amy returned home and freshened up for the day. She drove to Quills to get caffeinated; after that remembered a recommendation she read in her father's blog and traversed over to Market Street and Lueberry Acai & Superfoods. She ordered the Power Green Smoothie, made of spinach, almond milk, banana, strawberry, peanut butter, pea protein, turmeric, ginger and spirulina. It instantly became one of Amy's favorites.

Amy arrived at the jail at fortified and ready to confront her father.

When informed of the situation Alexander was amazed.

"It's been nine seasons! I haven't heard a peep. Has the judge been gnawing on this all along?"

"Apparently so. Now he has leverage on you. What's your move?"

"I'm taking this national. He's not going to play me like this."

"Daddy, please. This has gone far enough."

"That old goat thinks he can push me around, well…"

"And we have a new client. Max Hoogaboom, a sports agent. He was picked up last night about midnight, he's on a psych hold."

****

Alexander, being quite friendly with the guards, was able to find out about a 'crazy naked tripping white dude' that was booked just after midnight and be transferred over to his holding cell.

Max currently had county issued clothing on. He was coming down off the insane LSD trip he accidentally had taken and it was a major bummer. Max just sat in the corner of the dingy holding cell trying to reconstruct events and realized he mistook some sugar cubes he gulped down at a '60s Theme Party the night before, which sent his brain off the psychedelic edge and imploded his world.

Max avoided his fellow cellmates and just stared at the wall. Having regained enough of his sane brain, he recalled snippets, shards of memory through his acid experience, on how he arrived at this place and realized that life was over for him. A deep depression descended upon Max. Dark thoughts filled his mind.

The guard escorted Alexander to the cell. Several of the detainees knew Alexander and greeted him warmly. Max continued wallowing, quietly.

Alexander went to the corner and sat. "Your guy, Russell, really showed up last night for the Bats, Max."

Max's gaze was broken, he glanced over and focused on Alexander. "You know who I am? You want to laugh too?"

"No."

"It's all down the tubes. End of story," Max stared off into the abyss.

"Let's not tear up the ticket before the final results. I've been retained by Wei Wei and Theo to be your attorney."

"Really?"

"Yes, Max. Alexander Arrington, at your service."

"Wow, you have incredible access here in the jail."

****

There was a definite buzz in the air. The local media had gathered at Bowman Field. The word was out that a very important guest was arriving in town from the Middle East.

The Royal Sultania Airway Boeing 777 landed in Louisville and pulled up to the tarmac. A truck with portable stairs arrived with a limo trailing it. The front door of the airliner opened and porters brought several suitcases and bags down.

"Who do you think it is?" asked a bystander.

"Rumor has it that it's the Sultan of Sultania. That's his jet."

After that only one person, a female, quite well dressed emerged. She stood at the top of the stairs and looked surprised at the fuss being made.

They zoomed in and could now identify the person. They took her picture.

"That's not the Sultan. That's April Arrington," someone said.

They took her picture anyway as she descended the stairs and entered the limo.

****

Alexander contacted Amy and added a stipulation to the season ticket transfer. The judge agreed and Alexander was soon released.

Amy was waiting in the parking lot.

Alexander strolled out of the Metro Detention Center donning his seersucker suit jacket. "I've been talking to some of my friends on the Force and I'm contemplating filing a lawsuit against the city."

"Another one?"

"LMPD police officers have been asked to sign liability waivers to work in buildings with code violations."

"Really?"

"Yes. If they don't have professional facilities, if they're not respected professionally, how can we expect the authorities to act in a professional manner?"

"This would dove-tail on earlier legal action, Daddy?"

"If you expect police officers to deal with the mentally ill, they need more training and they should be compensated for it."

"Agreed."

"But for now, I'm free. Ambrosia, how are you, darling daughter?"

They embraced.

"Hello, Daddy."

"Welcome home."

"Good to be back, even with this."

"Let's take care of Max Hoogaboom first and then talk tree settlement with Reston."

Amy had a steely glare, "Yes, let's do that."

Alexander noticed her focus. He pulled out his phone and started working.

****

Settlement was being talked about, but it was at the Richardson estate and it was an entirely different legal matter. Chip had several bandages on his face and arms.

"There was an actual tiger inside their house?" asked Reston. "I mean, I know Alexander is kookie, but a tiger?"

"I ran into it getting away from the giant snake!"

"A giant snake?"

"And it growled and lunged at me!"

"The snake?" asked Reston.

"The tiger!"

"Ah, yes, we should file, son," said Reston. "Ask for $40 million, settle on 10 or take over that zoo over there and kick Alexander to the curb."

"I agree," said Chip.

"And I'm advising our client to change his mind on the tree thing and not settle. I don't want to give Alexander any easy lay-ups."

"Also agreed, Dad."

Reston picked up his cell phone and made a call.

Alexander's phone rang. He checked the number. "Here comes the white flag." He answered, "Reston! How goes it, you old fox?"

"Alexander, I thought cell phones weren't allowed in jail."

"Just broke out. I hear you want to talk settlement."

"I was, but not now after the most appalling display of hospitality offered at your residence by your rude daughter towards my son! Not to mention the wild animals that populate your jungle compound! He's injured and upset."

Alexander snarled, "Chip is such a wuss. And so are you! I'm sending you a bill for the broken window!"

"FYI, Alexander, I've convinced our client not to settle and to fight you and beat you! And then we're going to file our own suit against you."

"Then so be it, you dopey old dork!"

"Alexander, I'm going to lop off your head and place it on a stick for the rest of the villagers to gawk at!"

"Bring it, bitch," Alexander hung up and snarled.

"How are the settlement talks going, Daddy?" Amy asked innocently.

"We'll crush them! I'm 5-0 against him. Reston and his firm have never beaten me."

"Actually," said Amy, "Chip may have a valid and substantial claim on you, me and the estate over Sven."

Alexander considered that and didn't show any concern, outwardly. The TV was on and a clip was run showing the Sultan's jet pulling up and April getting out.

Alexander squinted at the screen trying to make sense of it.

"That's mom getting a ride on the Sultan's jet."

Now Alexander exhibited his frustration, "In a country where women have almost zero rights, where people get prosecuted for speaking out. Seriously, people are being jailed decades for sending out some offending tweets. Or just made to disappear if they criticize the ruler. What is she doing with that creep?"

Amy was thinking this through and not enjoying it. "Mom's consulting on some remodeling. She does make appearances with him at public events. He's a very good client."

"Does she scrub his back doing all this greenwashing?"

****

Reston was driving his Jaguar and in a very good mood. He practiced the speech he was going to say when he gave Alexander and his crew the boot. "So long. Hit the road. Alexander, you've been gonged!"

Reston arrived at Silver Horse Sanctuary and parked. He was welcomed by the butler and entered the main house.

"Reston, darling," April greeted him in the foyer. "I missed you so much."

"Hi, sweetie." They kissed. "You stayed a couple extra days in New York?"

April walked him into the living room, "Yes, I consulted with the Sultan on the make-over of his apartment. It's going to be marvelous."

"How was the art opening you went to? I read about it."

"Divine."

"Did you tell the Sultan I said hi?"

"I did and he sends his best."

"Fabulous. And your arrival on his jet was on the news."

"It was being dispatched to L.A., so he had it drop me on the way."

"I see."

"And I hear you've been busy, darling. Dueling Alexander over a lawsuit concerning some Bonsai Trees."

"That's right," Reston said, with his swagger. "He's going down."

"And you're also considering filing suit against him for the scratch Chip got."

"Yes! And it was more than a scratch. That tiger mauled my boy. This is a slam dunk."

"Sven?"

"Who?"

"The tiger."

"You know the tiger?"

"He's a pussycat."

Reston frowned, "Pussycat?"

"The litigation over the trees, you and Alexander can go at it hammer and tong. But you're not filing a lawsuit against the estate or anyone personally. That'll impact Amy and Granddad and Mrs. Simmons. I'll make it up to Chip myself."

Reston was crestfallen, "But..."

"No," said April, as she fluffed up the flowers and then whispered in his ear.

Reston went white as a ghost. He pulled out his phone and made a call. "Chip, we're going to put the legalities on hold against Casa Arrington."

Chip could be heard screaming at that, "What?? NO! Not acceptable. We have to—"

April came up and kissed Reston's cheek. He ended the call as Chip was heard still fuming.

****

The media sharks were circling in the waiting room of the jail.

Alexander put a knit cap and shades on Max.

Amy checked her watch, "Diversion should be arriving...now."

A stack of pizzas were delivered in the waiting room. "For you guys," said the pizza boy. The reporters chowed down.

Alexander and Amy took a disguised Max out a side door. They met up with Theo and Wei Wei waiting by a van.

Max shook their hands. "Thanks for your help, Alexander, Amy."

"Next time, be careful how much, and what, you consume," Alexander advised.

Max nodded gratefully, but he was down.

Wei Wei hated to see Max like this. He looked like a beaten man, *don't be broken...* "There's always a next time, come on, Max."

Theo was worried, "Max…"

Max shook his head. He felt a bit dizzy and didn't see a point to continuing on. Everything had collapsed into a pile of crap, like it usually did.

Wei Wei and Theo saw how Max had lost his fire and any will to live. They desperately searched for a way to make it better, but they had nothing. They felt helpless and hopeless.

"Max, I talked to the judge," said Alexander. "Everything's been dropped and the record sealed."

"What? Really?" asked Max, with some hope.

"Yes," said Amy. "My dad, Alexander, pulled another rabbit out of his hat."

"I had some leverage with the judge over something he wanted."

"Thank you," said Max. "Thank you, very much."

Alexander shrugged, "I read your story, Max. You gave someone a second chance. You deserve one as well."

Max's eyes filled with tears and he hugged him, with enthusiasm.

Alexander's eyes bugged out from the pressure. Amy was amused, she snapped a picture on her phone.

Russell arrived and stepped into Max's line of sight.

"Russell? What are you doing here?" asked Max.

"It's what the great teacher Master Li said. 'When you have Max Hoogaboom as a friend. You have a loyal friend.' I can't turn my back on that loyalty. It's too valuable and precious to me."

Alexander and Amy were taken by that. She bumped him to second that. He savored this.

"What about your father?" asked Theo.

Russell thought about that, "He always told me growing up to 'stand up for myself.' And so, I stood up to him and made my choice."

"What about Shayne the Pain?" asked Wei Wei.

"I don't need that pain. I told him Max was my guy."

Max now hugged Russell with vigor who also grimaced from the force.

The group laughed.

Max turned to Alexander and Amy, "You saved my life. What do I owe you?"

"Nothing," said Alexander. "Maybe tickets the next time the Reds are home."

Russell shook their hands, "For sure! I'll see to that." Then he put his arm around Max, "Can my agent give me a ride to the airport? I have to catch a plane to Chicago. My teammates are taking on the Cubbies."

Max nodded, "I think that can be arranged."

Wei Wei addressed Amy, "We'll send a check when we get back to L.A."

Theo and Wei Wei glanced at each other. They prized the look in Max's eyes. The fire was back. He wasn't broken, just bruised and roughed up a bit.

Max was deeply grateful. He nodded in appreciation. He started to get emotional, again, until they heard a voice call out: "There he is! There's Max Hoogaboom!" The media came running over.

"Go!" yelled Alexander.

The four jumped in the van and waved to each other. Wei Wei started it up and they roared off. The horde of media arrived and cornered Alexander and Amy.

"Alexander, are you representing Max Hoogaboom?"

At this moment Judge Winslow was in his chambers watching on live local TV.

"I am indeed representing Mr. Hoogaboom."

"What was he picked up for?"

"Merely a misunderstanding. Max can confuse a signal or two, as you might have heard."

The reporters were amused.

"But Max is a fine man. We should all be rooting for Max and all the Maxes and Maxines and Russells of the world, who have so much to give and only need a second chance."

"Alexander, did you apologize to Judge Winslow?"

"I did. Let me say this about the situation by quoting the great Justice Louis D. Brandeis who said, 'If we desire respect for the law, we must first make the law respectable.' I have argued more than a dozen cases in front of Judge Winslow and although I haven't always agreed with his decisions, he's always been fair, reasoned, learned and compassionate. I believe Judge Winslow to be a jurist who makes the law respectable. He too is a fine man. I'm thankful he's forgiven me for my boorish and contemptible behavior. I am determined to work on myself and strive for improvement, as you folks might be aware, my emotions at times may bubble over a wee bit."

The reporters laughed harder.

"The judge and I are both passionate supporters of the University of Louisville business, science, arts and the law school, and sports, especially the basketball program." Alexander wagged his finger, "It's when they face off in the Old Rivalry, Manual versus Male High School, that's when the judge and I are on opposite sides."

The entire crowd cracked up laughing and cheered.

The judge frowned and leaned back in his nice old leather wingback chair. He turned off the TV and ruminated—and then had a small grin.

7

It was early afternoon on this bright, sunny day in late June. They were strolling off from the kerfuffle at the courthouse.

"There's a Blue Jay! I do enjoy the Kentucky summers!" Alexander declared. "And right over there an awesome patch of *Rudbeckia Hirta*. Love them."

Amy noticed the bright yellow flowers. "Yes, the Black-Eyed Susans, I love them too."

"They say the flower represents justice," opined Alexander. "Storms come and then the cold of winter, but with the spring they always return. The bright yellow leaves shining in on the dark center."

"Changing the subject, Daddy, but does Reston really blame you for the state of Kentucky suing Big Pharma and tanking his drug stocks?"

"You're not changing the subject at all. It's about justice." Alexander harkened back, "As I recall, the first time was five, six years ago. The commonwealth rejected the opioid settlement. The drug company offer $500K for the damage they did here?? Seriously?? Parts of this state have a prescription drug overdose rate that's almost twice as high as the rest of the nation. Why? Big Pharma flooded the market and didn't tell the truth about their product. Over a thousand Kentuckians are dying from opioid overdoses every year now. Kentucky sued and won a much bigger settlement and continues to win against those pill pushing vultures. But I was just a small cog in that fight."

"I see."

"And don't worry about Reston. He did fine."

"I'm not."

"Like a good cartel member, he still made money, then cut bait, took his profits and ran before the Feds came a knocking."

"Reston took a swing at you for calling him that, a narco."

"A swing and a miss." Alexander bobbed and weaved, "I did my Muhammad Ali lean back." He imitated the champ and danced, "I'm so pretty, he can't touch me."

Amy slowly rolled her eyes, downplaying how amused she was.

Alexander paused flitting around like a butterfly, "He's upset over his Mallinckrodt holdings. Kentucky sued the St. Louis company for their deceptive marketing tactics pushing oxy here and it killed off the rally. He did lose some serious money there. The stock now trades for pennies."

"Mallinckrodt? St. Louis? That sounds familiar," Amy said.

Alexander effected his thick Irish brogue, "Lass, six years ago Mallinckrodt became an inverted domestic corporation and avoided U.S. taxes by legging it to Ireland for the ultra-low leprechaun rate, while still doing grand business here, scooping up a pot of gold in this country."

"I remember that. No, something else, Lannie wrote about it."

"I believe," said Alexander, "you're referring to Lannie's piece about the co-founders of Just Moms STL, Dawn Chapman and Karen Nickel. They're a group that's been fighting for years for a toxic dump to be removed in North St. Louis. Dawn and Karen are true heroes in their dogged determination."

"Yes, that's it," said Amy.

"Mallinckrodt," Alexander reminded her, "enriched the uranium in St. Louis for the atomic bombs developed in the Manhattan Project that were dropped on Japan. 47,000 tons of radioactive waste, Uranium 238, Thorium 230 and Radium 226 with half-lives of thousands of years, were illegally dumped on some Missourians. That toxic brew sat in metal drums and was tossed into an unlined pit and covered over for 40 years."

"Right," said Amy, "the radiation contaminated the area through the air, and the dump was next to a creek it leached into and it was on the floodplain of the Missouri River. Lots of sickness in the area. Like Lupus. 15 people on just one street died of rare cancers, there were birth defects, babies born without eyes. This is the same company Kentucky sued over oxycodone and Reston lost big on??"

"The very one," Alexander stated.

Amy shook her head in disbelief, "Amazing."

"Reston and I have had some dust-ups. But we always play fair. We discuss issues. I listen to what he has to say and then comment and vice versa. We have several ongoing issues we debate."

"Like what? Is there a list?"

"I'll give you our top 5 greatest hits: 1) Mountaintop Removal, he's for it, I'm against it. 2) When a mining company declares bankruptcy, I'm against the worker's health and pension obligations placed last in line for judges granting 'relief.' Reston is for it. 3) I'm against the companies walking away from the workforce that made the business viable, enabling lavish executive compensation and creating shareholder wealth, then starting fresh with a clean balance sheet, ready to prosper again free of those pesky obligations to the former workers. Rinse and repeat. Reston thinks that's just fine. He called me a communist for my criticism of this practice. 4) In 2011 to save money in the Kentucky state budget, Reston supported and even called for the elimination of juvenile drug courts, which provided an alternative to prison, for kids that still have a chance. I argued that it cost more to incarcerate than to rehabilitate and was less effective. I presented facts, laid out all of the costs and all of the benefits, short and long-term. Reston ignored the data and research and accused me of being soft on crime. I called him an idiot. *That* he paid attention to. And 5) we continue to argue over the Persistent Felony Offender law they have on the books here in Kentucky. A non-violent addict can have an extra 10 years added to their sentence if they're busted again with at least 10 oxy pills. Once a felony drug possession is on your record, Damocles Sword is hanging above your head. It was the Ryan Troxler case that finally did it for me."

"I read the arrest complaint. Ryan was a repeat offender," said Amy.

"He ended up getting 15 years for selling 10 pills. Because he had a record. And as Reston's friend Rush Limbaugh said, 'If people are violating the law by doing drugs, they ought to be sent to jail.' Is that so? What 'people' does he refer to?"

"Hmmm..." Amy didn't comment.

"In the great state of Florida, there's a law declaring that possession or obtaining a controlled substance is a 3rd Degree Felony, punishable with up to five years in the pen. I understand Rush Limbaugh has to act a certain way and say certain things to entertain a certain audience. But according to the arrest complaint for Rush, when he was busted, he bought 2,000 OxyContin pills over four months doctor shopping and then finally just ended up forging prescriptions. He was doing 30 pills a day. Calculate how many repeat violations for forgery and possession of controlled substances that is. Reston didn't like that comparison."

Amy sighed, "I'm sure he didn't."

They arrived at a hot dog vendor and got in line.

"For the record, I don't want or think Rush should have been prosecuted, or at least put in that position. Clearly, he had pain problems, like many of us do. It was a medical issue. He got hooked on pain pills and was finally cut off from his primary care physician, but he was addicted. But is it fair that Rush pays a small fine for his 2,000 oxy pills, Reston makes a big healthy return on his Big Pharma investment that peddled hundreds of millions, even billions, of oxy pills and Ryan or Rick or Rasheeda is caught selling 10 or 15 oxy pills and gets locked up for 15 years?"

"No."

"And after pointing it out this time, questioning if this is really justice, presenting data to back it up and calling for change, Reston said I was a dangerous radical."

"Seems you two do have quite a history, besides mom."

"Yes." Alexander was quiet, being reminded that April was with Reston. "I would prefer just to avoid him."

Amy was sorry she brought it up. "Your friend, the Khrakistan president, will be thrilled to see you, Daddy."

Alexander cringed, "Terrific." He grumbled at the thought of again dealing with this character. "Tell me what happened with Chip."

"When he came to talk settlement…"

"Yes?"

"He was greeted with automatic weapons from the Khrakistan's security team, a love starved python AND scratched by that very persnickety Siberian tiger. He escaped by crashing through the window in the den."

"I missed all that fun?"

Amy began to join him in the frivolity but paused it, "Daddy, this is serious."

"It'll work out. And darlin,' I don't believe for a second what that slime bucket Tenorio said about you on that horrible show."

"Daddy, I'm so glad to see you."

"Me too, sugar."

Amy was amused, "Did you really punch John Tenorio?"

"Darn tootin,' that was years ago at the Derby. He was way out of line with your mama. I'm the only one allowed to touch her, well, *was* the only one, at that time… Enough of that, what's going on with you?"

"I want to hang out with you for a little while, maybe a week or two."

"That's a splendid notion!" It was their turn with the hotdog guy. "Care for anything?"

"That's okay, Daddy."

"Hey, Barney. The usual."

"Here you go, Alexander. You are one lucky dog. It's on the house."

Alexander was given a to-go container.

"Thanks, B."

They walked off.

"Why does he think you're lucky?"

Alexander opened the container and there was a hot dog with mustard and relish and an envelope. He opened it and saw it was filled with cash.

"What's that?"

"The reason he said I was lucky. I had a 3-team parlay that hit. Loving the Reds, Dodgers and the Cubbies right now."

"Huh."

"If we skedaddle, we can just make a weekly gathering I attend."

Alexander pulled out a deck of cards and did a couple of fancy one-handed cuts.

Amy frowned, "I got you out of the pokey in time for some poker?"

****

Amy was driving, "Isn't wagering on humans illegal in this state, Daddy?"

"Presently, at this moment in time, in our history. It will change back in due course."

"Check back later?" asked Amy.

Alexander was irked, "I must use some offshore online sportsbook or cross the state line to Indiana or Illinois."

Amy gasped, "No, you mean, Union territory?"

"I have to gamble my money somewhere else, go North, allowing someone else to profit off it, but not here, where it could help the kids."

"I know. You're all about the kids and getting better odds."

Alexander directed her to pull in and park.

Amy glanced at the sign, "Helen's Happy Homestead?"

"We're here."

"This looks like a retirement home."

"Very astute."

They entered the board and care facility. A group of elderly residents were sitting together.

"Daddy, don't tell me you've resorted to fleecing old people."

He snickered diabolically, "They're so easy."

Amy groaned.

Alexander was spotted and the place went up for grabs. They were all so glad to see him.

"Alexander is here!"

Some imitated an owl hooting.

Ester, an elderly lady stood. The place quieted and she pronounced it properly with passion: "It's Alexander the Antithetical Owl!"

The place cheered. Amy was amazed.

"My son has returned!" cried out another elderly woman.

"More like a grandson to you," teased her friend. There was plenty of frivolity.

"This is my daughter Amy. Don't hold it against her, but she's a lawyer too!"

The room busted up laughing. Alexander did two card tricks for the group that entertained them. They applauded with gusto.

"Let's check the board, who's our first victim?" asked Alexander.

A long list was on a blackboard.

"Mrs. McCubbins, hello, what kind of legal problem is giving you fits?" inquired Alexander, as he helped her sit.

"It's a Social Security question, but I first wanted to tell you, Alexander, that you have a lovely daughter. She looks so much better and friendlier, in person!"

"Yes, thank you for noticing. She is a lovely, intelligent person who brings me unbridled joy."

Amy was embarrassed by that praise and could only grin. Alexander motioned to the blackboard.

Amy nodded, "Mr. Peppers? How can we help you?"

Mr. Peppers rolled his wheelchair forward. "Hi! I have a question about some charges on my credit card that I know I didn't make."

"Sure, I can help you with that." Amy relaxed and felt at home.

Alexander and Amy took their time helping them all wade through their legal conundrums.

After about 90 minutes they were finished and made their way out. Alexander teased the gents and flirted with the ladies, and they loved it.

They said their goodbyes and he promised to return next week.

They drove away, around the corner and Amy stopped the car. "I need you to shine some light on what's really going on with you."

"Not sure what you're referring to."

"Daddy, why did you force the judge to put you in lock-up?"

"Here's the situation. I'm shocked that it's gotten this far, I mean it's a measly $10K. It should have been settled by now. I filed a mechanic's lien against the property for nonpayment for services rendered to the contractor. They ignored everything. Since it's over five grand, I filed a civil suit in the circuit court. At the last minute they hired a lawyer who showed up and was successful in barring photographs of the finished work. Without this proof, we were cooked. If he wouldn't have thrown me in jail, the case would have been tossed right then and there."

"You were buying time."

"I had faith something would arrive and there you were."

"And perhaps it was also to avoid your 'brother,' the president of Khrakistan and let your father, Granddad, get over his intense anger at you for torching his work. Killing three birds with one contempt of court, eh, Daddy?"

Alexander was quiet and then sported a goofy grin. "You got me. Granddad was madder than a wet hen and that president, Greg, is such a pompous ass. I just can't stand him."

"I understand."

"Last year I was in Rome at some legal conference with a bunch of old gasbags. And we got so polluted. We ended up partying on the presidential jet back to Crackland."

"Daddy, it's 'Khrakistan.'"

"I still can't find it on the map," griped Alexander.

"Khrakistan on the Caspian, full of crude and a crude leader," chimed Amy.

"As I recall he was certainly interested in equus caballus."

"He knows about more stuff than horses," Amy said. "Like peddling weapons around the world to whoever can come up with the ducats. He's the preferred jailer in the spook world. His secret prisons hold suspects for years while being tortured by various intelligence agencies that shall remain redacted to keep my security clearance."

Alexander thought back and stroked his goatee, "We were drinking Krambambulas and they kicked my ass, but what I remember, and it's not much, is that it was related to 'powerful ponies' and it was non copasetic. I was excited about the circus coming, but really wanted to avoid him. I made a mistake. I was ignorant of the situation there. I wasn't aware of his notorious activities. And again, you have to remember, I was there with a bunch of imbibing attorneys, ooh, it got fuzzy."

"Your 'brother' the president, caught my derriere with his hand, assuming I was part of his harem."

Alexander let out a whistle, "Whoa, Nellie, I'll bet big dollars on that being severely unpleasant for ol' Greg."

"Almost made the international news cycle."

"Kracky president cracked by Kentucky Filly."

"Daddy, I always thought you'd have made a great newspaper man."

"Me too. And I'll kick president crackpot out when we get home. Nobody inappropriately touches my girl."

"There's been a recent development on that. The Secretary instructed the Under Secretary to ask us to put up with his B.S. for a bit longer."

"What? Who's secretary? His?"

"Ours. For the United States. The Secretary of State. The Under Secretary called."

Alexander perked up hearing this, his fatherly pride beaming. "Uh-huh. My little girl has been advising the Secretary of State. Is he seeking your input on foreign policy?"

"Daddy, with your imagination, I always thought you should be a novelist."

"We are lawyers, darling, we spin yarns all the time. The advantage we have is that our audience, the jury, is a captive one."

"The Secretary also asked that we find out why he's really here in Louisville, on behalf of the country."

"A secret mission! Spy versus spy! Shh..."

"He's only going to give up the intel to you, his brother. But could we try waterboarding him first?"

Alexander had a deep belly laugh at that.

8

Granddad and Mrs. Simmons were invited, but both declined as he was deep into creating his latest work and she was 'updating files,' a general term she used when she didn't feel like going out and socializing.

Alexander took Amy to lunch at Jack Fry's on Bardstown Road on the Highlands/Cherokee Triangle border. A normal person would have needed a reservation, but Alexander wasn't normal.

When they arrived, they both said hello to several friends who were dining. They passed a picture of Jack Fry and his wife Flossie and then another photo of Granddad and Grandmother, Eunice, Alexander's mother and father. They both were smiling and having a good time and were friends with Jack and Flossie.

Alexander and Amy admired the image. 'Arthur and Eunice Arrington 1965' was written under the picture.

"Grandmother Eunice was so beautiful," said Amy.

"Mom passed that down to you and her smarts and the ability to understand logic and necessity," replied Alexander, who then pointed to the back. "That's where Jack used to take Granddad's bets on horses and *humans.*"

Amy nodded slowly and sighed. They were shown to their tables and sat.

"Granddad sure was a handsome man back then," said Amy. "And he's still dashing."

Alexander was checking his phone. "Uh-huh…"

"Especially when he's dashing after someone who torches his creations."

Alexander put down his phone, "Duly noted. And I'm working on myself."

"What kind of work?"

"Oh, you know…"

Amy could see that look in her father's eye, when his brain was searching for just the right fact or retort or shot from half court and then—

"Alexander and Amy!" It was the current owner, Stephanie Meeks.

"Stephanie! How are you, darlin'?" asked Alexander, really glad to see her.

"I'm feeling fabulous."

"And you look it, as well," added Alexander. She padded his arm.

"Hi, Steph," said Amy, smiling.

"It's good to see you back in town, Amy. It'll make Alexander behave."

"Still a longshot," Amy quipped. "But he's 'working' on himself."

All three laughed at that.

"Enjoy your meals."

"Thank you."

Stephanie moved on.

"I remember when Steph started working here in 1996," said Alexander. "She was quickly the general manager."

"And then she bought the place in 2008," Amy remarked. "I remember the party."

"So do I. Your mama and I were still together." Alexander had a moment of melancholy at this memory. Amy squeezed his hand and he smiled.

They shared some spicy fried oysters. Amy had the goat cheese salad and Alexander ordered the roasted beet salad. They both had the salmon croquettes that were pan-seared and toasted with a nut medley, baby arugula and basil pesto.

It was all delicious, as usual. At the end of the meal Alexander received a text.

"Good, just what I'm waiting for. Our investigator." Alexander texted him back. "He's got something, we're going to meet back at the casa."

Amy began to finish up her lunch.

"Take your time," said Alexander, "he's still playing 6D at Heroes Comics."

****

They rendezvoused a little later at CA. Gabriel Jonson, 21, Black and bookish, thin as a rail, wiry and wired into the city, was wearing a leather jacket and a helmet, as he rode up on a moped.

"Hey, Miss Sassy," Gabe petted their greeter and entered CA.

Alexander introduced the two, "Gabe, this is my daughter, Amy. Amy, this is Gabe."

They exchanged pleasantries.

"You play 6D?" asked Amy.

"Yes, I do. Yourself?"

"I have. And D&D."

"Cool!"

"I go to Heroes to use the TARDIS."

Gabe laughed.

"What the…?" Alexander was clueless.

"It's a time machine, Daddy."

"Of course," replied Alexander.

Gabe glanced over his glasses, "And I'm assuming you really can't shoot out lightning bolts from your eyes."

"No."

"But you can really nail a kickflip 50-50?"

"I can certainly do a kickflip 50-50."

"Awesome. I've been trying, but I'll get it. You know, I feel like I know you already. Alexander brags about you all the time!"

Amy glanced at her dad.

Alexander shook his head and shrugged, "I don't know what he's talking about."

Granddad had emerged from his studio with a paint brush. "I brag about her too."

Amy grunted, amused. "Thanks, Granddad." She gave him a hug.

"What have you got, Gabe?"

"Okay, Alexander, I've been checking out some rumors."

"About?"

"Rubén. This isn't the first time he's been accused of not doing the work and trying to get paid for it."

"Oh?" asked Alexander, very interested in this.

"Some are saying he's scamming the Wellington family and it wouldn't be the first time someone has tried."

"I wonder why when the trees were gone the next day, they didn't file a police report," asked Alexander.

"Has there been any depositions?" Amy asked.

"I've tried. They didn't have representation until a week ago."

"That's hard to believe," said Amy.

"And there's another thing that's hard to believe," said Gabe. "I found this photo taken near the site. People are saying this is a picture of the thief."

Alexander gave it a look and shook his head.

"What is it, Daddy?"

"I can't tell, it's too dark and blurry."

Granddad put on his glasses and checked it out. "That's either Old Man Miller next door...or the Pope Lick Monster."

"Pretty sure it isn't our neighbor. Who or What is the Pope Lick...?" asked Amy. She moved closer to see for herself.

"Pope Lick Monster. It's supposed to be some kind of part-man, part-goat creature that lures victims onto the railway bridge in the Fisherville area of Louisville," said Alexander.

"I remember you kids used to look for him when you were youngsters," laughed Granddad.

"But we never found him, luckily," added Alexander.

Amy studied the image, "Part man, with hooves... Wait, he has a flute. It looks like Pan the demi-god."

"Pan?" asked Alexander. "Yes, it does. There's a statue of him in Cherokee Park."

Alexander, Amy and Granddad drove on Alexander Drive—which always pleased Alexander—to the Scenic Loop in Cherokee Park. They swung by the statue of Daniel Boone guarding the south entrance.

"This really is a beautiful park," observed Amy.

Alexander gazed at the foliage, "It is a treasure."

They drove some more.

"The fountain is right across from where I sometimes play hoops," remarked Alexander.

They went up a small hill that bent right. Amy pulled over and parked at the Hogan Family Pavilion. There was a large gazebo which resembled a witch's hat, next to the basketball court. They crossed the road to Hogan's Fountain. Water trickled from the mouths of turtles at the base of the statue. Pan was on top, with his goat legs and feet, holding his flute.

"It was built as a drinking fountain for dogs and horses," Granddad said. "The troughs on the ground for the pooches and the granite bowl holds water for the horses. Enid Yandell sculpted both the Daniel Boone and Pan statue in1905."

"She was very talented," remarked Alexander, admiring her work. "It's cast in bronze."

The three studied the Pan sculpture closer.

Granddad glanced around, "This used to be a big gathering place for teenagers drinking beer at night."

"Including you, Granddad?"

"Guilty. Old Man Miller and I almost had it out here once."

"What were you fighting over?" asked Alexander.

"I don't rightly remember. It was probably over a girl."

Amy searched 'Pan statue Cherokee Park' on her phone and found some information. "The statue is supposed to come alive at midnight during a full moon."

"Right," Granddad had a twinkle in his eye, "They say during a full moon Pan supposedly causes great mischief."

Alexander did a check on his phone. "Rubén told me that he was ordered to plant the trees on that specific date, which according to the calendar, was a full moon."

"Then," Amy mused, "Pan is one of the suspects. He was greedy. The six trees were worth well over a grand a piece."

"No, no," said Granddad. "Pan is the defender of the forests."

"Maybe he didn't like the Bonsai Trees being planted," Alexander suggested. "Some people object to them."

Granddad nodded, "True."

"They're so cute, why?" asked Amy.

"I've been told," Alexander said, stroking his goatee, "their growth is artificially stunted by holding back water and an excessive amount of pruning. And they use wires for bonding, manipulating the direction of growth of the little branches."

"Daddy, are you saying the statue may have actually done this?"

"We have an image. We have motive. We have means, it's next door to this location and it happened the night of the full moon, opportunity."

Granddad whistled at that and looked away.

Amy didn't have a response, she hadn't considered this, and wasn't going to.

"Hold on," Alexander said, checking his phone. "Gabe sent a video this time." He watched and his eyes widened. He gave his phone to her.

Amy and Granddad viewed black and white CCTV footage of what resembled the hooved creature clomping up with his flute and spraying over the security camera with whipped cream.

"Is that Pan in action?" asked Amy.

Granddad, Amy and Alexander watched again in stunned silence.

9

Granddad, Amy and Alexander had returned to CA, with little said. They watched the Pan video several more times, each viewing just as befuddling.

"I need to work," Granddad said, as he made sketches of what he saw.

Later that afternoon Alexander's phone rang. He put it on speaker: "Yeah, Gabe, what's up?"

"I've heard a rumor from a friend of a friend, that a woman at the location in question—"

"The Wellington estate?"

"Yes. I heard she has a very expensive cocaine habit. And gets a regular delivery."

"A friend of a friend told you this?" Alexander inquired, curiously.

"You told me to turn over some rocks."

"I did. Keep digging." Alexander ended the call. "That must be Sienna, the sister. We should pay a visit."

"Daddy, do you think it's wise for the plaintiff's attorney to communicate ex parte with the defendant? There could be sanctions or—"

"Look, the judge has already thrown me in jail. If he tosses the case, it's on me. I'll reimburse our client personally for his losses."

"Really?"

"I've never had a case like this. I really can't get my brain around it," groused Alexander.

They parked in front of the Wellington house, walked onto the property, arrived at the area and stared down at the turned over dirt. Alexander then sauntered up to the front door and rang the doorbell.

"Daddy, I protest, this is highly improper."

"Once more, duly noted." Alexander noticed the curtain in a front window move ever so slightly. "They wanted to settle. I have to go around that horse's ass, Reston, and his bruised ego, to get anything done here." He rang the doorbell once more, again with no response. He raised his voice, "Until you come to this door, I'll be reciting verbatim, *The Tragedy of Richard III.* Don't worry, as you know, it's only Shakespeare's second longest play!"

There was still no response. Alexander cleared his throat. "*Now is the winter of our discontent! Made glorious summer by this son of York! And all the clouds that lour'd upon our house*!"

He continued on for a bit.

"*Cheated of feature of dissembling nature, deformed, unfinished...*"

The door opened.

Amy sighed with relief, "Thank you."

Alexander looked hurt, taking this as a criticism.

"Gee," said Amy, "for a second, I swear I thought it was Olivier at the Old Vic."

Alexander, ever the ham, enjoyed that one.

"What do you want?" said a nervous, middle-aged woman. "You're on private property."

"We'd like to talk to Mr. Sidney Sneijder."

"He's out of the country."

"Hi, Sienna, actually, we just wanted to again check out the location where the Bonsai Trees were taken from," said Alexander. "I still can't figure out why you didn't file a police report."

"I was going to, but—"

"Why?" asked a male voice from outside and behind them. "If there's no proof they were there in the first place."

Sienna gratefully retreated back into her refuge. Alexander and Amy turned their attention to Sean, a young man of 19-years-of-age, at the other end of the large house.

"Why are you here?"

"You must be Sean," said Alexander, redirecting his charm.

"Are you bothering my aunt?"

"I would never bother anyone's aunt. May I introduce my daughter, Amy Arrington."

Amy nodded to Sean, "Hello."

Sean looked away.

"We're simply trying to understand what happened," said Alexander, he then curled his lip, "Being that it was a full moon, perhaps Pan the demi-god disabled your security camera and dug them up himself."

There was an awkward moment of silence.

"I'll be honest," said Sean, "I was blown away when I saw that video. Damn."

"It's from your CCTV system."

"Yes, and I'm quite angry. It's a defect in the design that someone could just spray whipped cream over the lens of the camera and then do what they wanted. And I'm really pissed at our ISP for allowing this breach into our system."

"You didn't release that footage?"

"No way, dude. We're the suckers, the victims."

"There's no footage of the trees being planted or being there?" asked Amy.

"No, we were hacked. It was shut down. We pay a premium for what we thought was protection! We were assaulted not once, not twice, but three times! Someone is coming after us! I'm making them raise the camera mount, at their cost and to raise their game on security cyberwise. My aunt and I feel quite vulnerable after this incident. It could happen again."

Alexander shrugged, "Like the next full moon."

"Don't be ridiculous," said Sean.

"Do you think someone dressed up as Pan and stole the trees?" asked Amy.

"Who knows? It's a crazy world. I don't know if they were dressed up or if it was the real thing. When I left that morning there weren't any trees and when I came back, late that night, there weren't any trees. Just turned over dirt. I'm getting tired of all this distraction."

"What time did you come back?" asked Alexander.

"It was around 1am."

"I was wondering," said Amy. "Why would anyone plant such valuable trees out front in such a vulnerable place?"

"That's the way my dad is. He has to show off his big bucks. You know how alpha males are. But that leads to haters, because people get resentful and jealous."

"I get you, I know a few alphas," Amy said.

"Obviously you know alphas! That's all you hang with, the Chads," hissed Sean.

"You think? Why would you say that?"

"Right, Stacey."

"Stacey?" asked Alexander.

"Just go away," snarled Sean, "I've had enough of the act." He retreated back inside.

Amy and Alexander drove back home.

"He called you Stacey and said you hang out with Chads. What in blue blazes was that boy blathering about?"

"I'm not sure, but there's a group, mostly young males, late teens, in their 20s and some in their 30s, that define themselves as Incels."

"Incels? I've heard of that," said Alexander. "But don't remember."

"Incels, or involuntarily celibate, believe they are ignored by women they desire. These women, they label as 'Staceys,' only have relationships with physically attractive males they call Chads."

"Huh." Alexander mulled this over, "I never was a Chad. But you could be a Stacey."

Amy growled, "Daddy!"

Alexander snickered, pulled out his phone and made a call.

"Hello, Rubén, I'd like to come by and chat just for a sec, say in half an hour?"

****

On the way Alexander and Amy stopped by the dollar store. Amy was amused seeing Alexander be a kid picking out stuff he liked, lots of little trinkets and candy.

They drove to the neighborhood, parked and got out. Dogs could be heard barking. Amy glanced around at the rundown area.

Her father's voice was calm, "Don't worry, I know this turf."

It was a house, behind a slightly bigger house, just next to the railroad tracks where Alexander and Amy were headed. Amy thought the building might not be up to code or completely illegal all together, but she didn't raise the issue.

They arrived in the backyard and Alexander yelled, "*Hola, mi niños*!"

"Alexander!" a bunch of kids ran up to them. Amy and Alexander both gave out toys and candy from their bags and kids squealed with delight.

Rubén Sanchez, at 40, was trim, with a warm face that was aged well beyond his years. "Welcome, Alexander."

"Thank you, Rubén."

Ines, Rubén's wife, a friendly woman in her late 30's, joined them. "Hello, Alexander."

"Ines, it's nice to see you." They hugged.

"This is my daughter, Amy. She's assisting on the case."

"Hello, nice to meet you, Miss Arrington," said Ines.

Amy put her hand out to shake, "It's Amy. Nice to meet you, Ines and Rubén."

They shook hands and all smiled.

"Alexander, are you okay, my friend?"

"I'm good, you?"

"I heard you were in jail."

"Wasn't the first time, I'm sure it won't be the last." They laughed. "It was a technical issue. The judge got up on the wrong side of the bed that day."

"My dad was protesting, in his way."

"I know it was on my account."

"It's part of my job."

"I have not heard of many attorneys that would do this. It demonstrates your passion and commitment. Thank you."

"I appreciate that, amigo."

"What's next for my case?"

"I heard they wanted to settle," Alexander reported. "But then egos got involved. You originally talked with a woman, she's the sister of the owner?"

"That's who hired me. She paid 10%."

"I thought you're supposed to get half up front," Amy said.

"I still took the job, needed the work."

"Rubén has his green card and is applying for citizenship."

"They said I was volunteering to do the work."

The children went running by circling them.

"Look at those kids!" Amy was pleased to see them having such fun.

"We had two and when my sister passed away, I adopted her three, one has special needs. Yes, my wife and I are busy."

Amy had an urge to join them, "That's wonderful."

"We struggle and can't give them everything they need, but we try."

"In life," opined Alexander, "one either creates wonder or foments foul. I have dealt with many fomenters, but amigo, you are one of the certified creators of wonder."

A little girl, 5-years-of-age, hugged Amy's leg. She looked down at the smiling child and was surprised how affected she was by this.

"That's Naomi," said Alexander.

"Hi, Naomi, I'm Amy."

Naomi waved up to her and Amy waved back.

"Several months ago," said Alexander, "Rubén imported the very rare Bonsai Trees and planted them on the Wellington estate. He has pictures of the work. However, when the estate manager showed up in the morning, well you saw."

"Here," said Rubén, as he showed the picture he took of a professional, very beautiful and expensive garden with eight Bonsai Trees. The next picture was an image of the bare land. The trees were gone.

Alexander stated, "This was the evidence that was excluded. Judge Winslow claimed no 'judicial context.' The time/date stamp proves when it was taken, just not where."

"I can't see the house," said Amy.

"It was stupid of me not to get the house in the pictures. But I've never had something like this happen and I've been doing this for some time."

"What's next with the lawsuit, Alexander?" asked Ines.

"Horse trading. But, you two relax, let us worry about that. Rubén, I need to ask you about something."

"Yes?"

Alexander lowered his voice to a whisper, "This isn't the first time you're being accused of not doing the work, is it?"

"What are you saying?" asked Rubén.

"Look, I need you to be honest and forthcoming with me."

Ines took Naomi to the other side of the yard to play in a sandbox.

"Years ago, I was working as a day laborer, without papers and I only spoke Spanish. One time I worked three days in the hot sun digging trenches. It was very hard. When it was time to pay us, they told us to just go. They say, 'Go to hell!'"

"What'd you do?" asked Amy.

"What could we do with our status? They call us criminals. I was powerless. I work in the fields picking, work bussing tables and washing dishes for years. And then a window opened. Through my church I learned English, finished high school. I got a work permit. A green card. All of this was on my way to get my citizenship. I studied at night-school for several years. And Ines is with me in the process."

Ines returned, "Rubén and I have put in a lot of time studying U.S. history and civics. We have taken several practice tests."

"What are some of the questions?" inquired Alexander.

"What document was written in 1787?"

"The Constitution," replied Amy.

"Why were the Federalist Papers important?"

"They supported passing of the U.S. Constitution," Alexander said.

"Name an important event that occurred during the American Revolution," asked Rubén.

"Battle of Bunker Hill and Battle of Saratoga," replied Alexander.

"The Declaration of Independence," Amy added.

"Name five original states," asked Ines.

"New Hampshire, Massachusetts, Rhode Island, Connecticut and New York," stated Alexander.

"New Jersey, Pennsylvania, Delaware, Maryland, Virginia, North Carolina, South Carolina and Georgia," added Amy.

"Why did the United States enter the Persian Gulf War?" asked Rubén.

"Really?" asked Alexander. "They ask that question?"

"It's on the practice test."

"Well..." Alexander stroked his goatee. "The first invasion was to restore the Emir to his golden throne and keep the oil flowing. The second invasion was to remove Saddam from his golden throne and keep the oil flowing."

Amy quickly intervened, "When you take the test, I would leave out the 'golden' reference and the oil part. Just say for 'freedom.' That always works."

Rubén and Ines nodded.

"Give us two more," said Alexander.

"James Madison is famous for many things. Name one," said Ines.

"One of the writers of the Federalist Papers," said Amy.

"He was the fourth president of the United States," Alexander added.

"And, Benjamin Franklin is famous for many things. Name one," said Rubén.

"First postmaster general and one of the writers of the Declaration of Independence," answered Amy.

Alexander used his French accent, "In 1778 he was appointed the Ambassador to France, and *oui, oui,* he was said to be very popular with French ladies."

Amy cleared her throat, "Daddy, I'm glad you're not actually tutoring them on the test."

"That's okay," said Rubén. "I think we know what part to leave out."

"Amy and Alexander," announced Ines, "please come in and allow us to offer some food and refreshments."

Alexander grinned, "This is the best part of the job."

****

Back at the courthouse Judge Winslow finished his final hearing of the day. He entered his chambers, which had the usual various pictures and diplomas hanging on the wall as well as a banner for the University of Louisville prominently displayed.

Grace, one of his clerks, knocked and poked her head in. “Your Honor?”

“Yes, Grace?”

“I’m heading home, but I wanted to show you a video. It involves something on social media that concerns a case you’re hearing. You did tell me to keep an eye out for trending subjects you were ruling on.”

“Social media… Well, if everyone’s viewed it. Bring it up on my computer, please.”

Grace clicked it on. A video started and a voice asked: “Who or what really happened to the missing Bonsai Trees?” It was the same CCTV footage Alexander and Amy viewed, only this time there was a narrator and a spooky soundtrack. “Is it a coincidence that the trees went missing at midnight during a full moon? If you notice the time stamp, you will see this footage was obtained at midnight on a full moon. It shows what looks to be Pan on the scene and disabling the camera. I’m only presenting the facts, you decide.” The video ended.

Judge Winslow stared at the screen and finally turned to his clerk with a blank stare, “Should I order a bench warrant for Pan?”

****

They had wrapped up the meeting and lunch with the Sanchez family and were driving back to Casa Arrington when Amy got a text. “Mom’s inviting me over for a ride. I need to go home to change.”

“Okay, then I’ll drop you.”

Amy looked for any sign of emotion on his face but there was none.

****

Alexander waited in the car as Amy pulled on jeans, threw on some well-worn Western boots, donned a t-shirt and grabbed a cowboy hat.

When she emerged, Alexander was amused at the sight. "You always did tease your mother so."

Amy jumped in with a grin, "Isn't this riding gear?"

Alexander knew all the shortcuts to her place and they were there promptly. He turned into the long blacktop driveway.

April observed from the front window. Alexander noticed her and Amy noticed this. Alexander also noticed Reston's Jaguar. Instead of pulling up to the front, he parked by the stables.

Alexander got out with a big grin as the stable boss approached, "Gus, my old friend!"

Gus, a hearty soul with just a bit of a hitch in his giddyup, was 80, but looked 90. He was a trainer for decades, but now managed the horses here at SHS.

"Alexander! You old hound dog."

Alexander howled like a hound dog causing a couple dogs in the vicinity to join in. They embraced.

April laughed to herself and then she noticed Amy getting out of the car, dressed in her cowgirl look. April, adorned in very stylish English equine attire, shook her head and groaned.

"Amy! It's lovely to see you, ma'am."

"Good to see you too, Gus."

Alexander put his arm around his shoulder. "How's the world treating you, Gus?"

"The world keeps throwing me left hooks, but Ms. Arrington, she's treating me right. Putting an old mule like me in charge of a bunch of thoroughbreds."

"You're better with horses than anyone I know. She's lucky to have you."

"I appreciate that."

Alexander spotted a group of a half dozen young men in their 20s gathered over the way around some horses in a barn.

"What's going on over there, Gus?"

"Ms. Arrington is bringing in veterans from Iraq and Afghanistan with PTSD and having them interact with the horses for therapy. It's a beautiful thing."

Alexander saw the grizzled faces of these damaged warriors bonding with these magnificent, magical, giving creatures. He got choked up and turned away, "I'll see you later, honey."

Amy touched her father's shoulder. He patted her hand.

April, even from the front window, saw how Alexander was moved by this. She continued to observe and only looked away when she realized Reston had entered the room. "Amy's here."

"Yes," said Reston, now avoiding staring outside. "I can see that."

Alexander fist-bumped Gus, hugged Amy, got in and drove off.

Gus gave Amy the once over, "I like your outfit, though I'm not sure how the boss lady will feel about it."

"Is that so?" asked Amy, innocently.

Gus had a wry grin and shook his head as he went back to work, "Family..."

Amy looked forward to her mother's reaction as she traveled up to the main house and stepped inside.

"Ambrosia, you look like you're ready to ride into Tombstone with Wyatt Earp."

"Mother, you look like you're ready for the fox hunt with the Earl of Grantham. Will you be riding side-saddle as well?"

April was amused by her teasing.

They hugged. "Mother, it's so good to see you. I'm sorry we missed each other in New York."

"So am I."

Amy glanced around to check her audience and the usual scripted encounter between them commenced.

"Hello, Reston."

"Hi, Amy. Good to see you again. How are you?"

"Good. And you, Reston?"

"Very good."

"Great."

"How did you two ever miss each other in New York?"

Amy looked bewildered, "I'm confused about that. Did some situation spring up, Mother?"

"I had to deal with the Sultan."

"Before that, Mother."

"I had to tie up some loose ends and there was a snafu."

"A snafu?" asked Reston.

"The security code was changed. It was a glitch."

"Is the software suspect?" asked Reston.

"No, it was definitely hardware. It was a deliberate action."

"Deliberate?" asked Amy. "I hope those that deserved to be punished, were...punished properly."

"Agreed," said Reston. "Maintaining discipline is key."

"It's fine, my darlings. It all worked out."

He checked his watch, "Hon, I have a golf game. Those balls aren't going to hit themselves."

Reston and April kissed.

"Again, it's great to see you back, Amy."

"Thank you, Reston."

"And I'm happy Alexander is out of jail."

"Yes. I hope Chip is feeling better," said Amy.

"Me too," said Reston, avoiding eye contact as he picked up his car keys and was off.

Amy made sure he was gone. "Off to hit some balls, is he? Gee Mother, haven't you been doing that for the last couple of days in the Big Apple?"

April stood her ground, "Got several holes in one, actually, darling."

Amy had a slight cringe at her attempt of a witty retort.

****

The sun hung low on this early summer late afternoon day. April and Amy were riding their horses at a slow trot.

"I'm having a formal dinner tomorrow night. I'm sending you an invite."

"What about Reston?"

"Reston? He'll be there."

"I mean, aren't you two a couple?"

"Yes, we're going steady and he's asked me to the prom."

"Nice. Has he pinned you yet?"

"How old do you think I am?"

"I don't know, Mother, you always hid that fact from me growing up."

"Did I?"

"I heard that the local media was tipped off that a royal visit from the Sultan of Sultania was happening. A phalanx of reporters showed up at the airport. Except that his extremely elevated highness wasn't on board. Only one person, deplaned, you. How were they tricked into thinking royalty was arriving?"

"They weren't tricked, royalty *did* arrive." April fluffed her hair with a wry grin.

"Other than a big fat bank account and a big jet, why do you hang out with that big scumbag?"

"He hasn't been a scumbag to me. He's been a gentleman and invited me to several social events as his guest."

"Mother, I have no doubt he loves seeing you with him and having others see you with him."

"And you know how I keep the Sultan attentive?"

"I thought it was your keen design and fashion sense."

"I'm talking the other way."

"Not sure if I want to hear this, Mother."

"The Sultan has multiple wives and a hefty harem."

"Tell me the G-rated version, Mother."

"He gets all the action he wants. As long as I keep making him think that he has a chance with me, whilst not giving up the goods. His fantasies of me are…"

Amy groaned softly and closed her eyes.

"Unattainable. He's a great client that I consult with on his interior design. Once I give in on that carnality, I lose that mental advantage."

"But didn't you give in with Tiago?"

"That piece of eye-candy? I just used him for a sugar rush, honey."

Amy braced herself, "Here we go…"

"Oh shush, I've done my duty. I bore you, raised you and educated you. And I was a very good, faithful wife. But now, I'm a free woman. Deal with it."

"No issues here."

"Reston and I are a power couple. We see each other, but keep separate residences. I don't want him to find out about me reaching into the cookie jar at the clubhouse on the Upper East Side. Don't forget the cat lady."

"Not saying a word."

"Reston frequently prattles on what a great politician he would be."

"He's thinking about running for office?"

"Definitely. And I know he's had flings and a couple from his wild side, his Oscar Wilde side."

"Oh?" Amy was surprised at this.

"He has baggage and some of it's stored in the closet. No biggie with me. I like a man who's adventurous."

"How did you learn of this?"

"Someone sent me some photos."

"Someone?"

"I don't know who, nor care. And up until very recently I didn't use this intel. But he was eased back into his proper lane."

"Is that how you got him not to sue Daddy and me and the estate over Chip's scratches from Sven?"

"His curious wanderings are to be top secret, only between you and me. If it gets known—"

"You lose your leverage. But how much leverage on him is it really, Mother?"

"In some locations you're lionized and in other places the lion eats you. He's had several private polls done that show he has a chance if he runs for congress, as long as he's not eaten up."

"Why would Reston run for Congress?"

"He likes to complain," April mused. "But he usually doesn't understand what he's crabbing about, but that doesn't stop him. He's not very curious about the world. He has an enemies list of people he thinks have wronged him. And he likes to get his picture taken. You have to admit he's quite handsome."

"Uh-huh..." responded Amy, reluctantly.

"Reston has posted thousands of pictures of himself on social media, at least three times as many as me."

Amy nodded, "That is an important qualification for Congress. Shows his dedication to the higher office. He must really put the time in."

"Reston does and he likes to raise money. He's very good at that."

"Therefore, the platform he's offering is ego, ignorance, avarice and rage?"

April pondered that, "That just about covers it. And by the way, that was a mauling. Reston could have ended up owning CA."

"I realize that. Thank you for derailing those legalities that were chugging our way."

"When you eventually settle down and have kids, my grandchildren, they'll need a place to go, to stay. That is, if you ever intend to have grandchildren, one wonders."

"Why would 'one' wonder?"

"I saw those pictures from the club in New York that are circulating. *Your* Oscar Wilde side. I understand you want to explore and all that, just don't be so out front."

"Mother, I'm not gay."

"Bi? Curious? Or questioning? What do the kids call it these days?"

"I had a lot of tequila and we were out late at a club. We were goofing. She's a friend. It was the end of a 90-hour work week."

"Is this why you broke up with Tiago?"

"We were never an item. I ended the tryst with Tiago because he bored me and obviously he's a cad that will shag almost any—"

"Fine! Understand, I'm just looking forward to grandchildren."

"Don't worry, Mother, I've frozen some of my eggs just in case it takes longer than expected to find the right partner to make a life and nurture a child in this hurly burly world."

April considered that and finally had a slight cringe, "I see… Thinking about hiring a womb as well? Why not go to the sperm bank and open an account??"

"The way things are working out for me, this might be the way to go."

"Amy, why do you make everything so complicated?"

"Actually, it's been simplified."

April pondered that, "Therefore, tomorrow if you get struck by lightning, hit by a bus, or fall off a cliff, I can go make a withdrawal?"

"Mother..."

"Seriously, you need to tell me what freezer they're stored at and the password to get in."

Amy gave her mother the side-eye.

10

The judge was being transported home from the court. He had his driver cruise through Cherokee Park. At Hogan's Fountain they slowed and he focused on the statue of Pan with his flute for more than a moment and then had him drive on.

As usual, dinner was at 5:15. Spaghetti with meatballs with a nice green salad with plenty of croutons.

The judge was curious, "Willodean?"

"Yes, dear?"

"You know the fountain in Cherokee Park?"

"You mean the dragon-headed Viking ship. I love that one. Dedicated to the teacher Paulina Keofoed Christensen. She was so good to animals."

"That's very nice, but I'm referring to the one at Hogan's Fountain. With Pan the demi-god on top."

"Gosh, I like that one as well. It's a remarkable sculpture."

"Did you know the legend about Pan's statue coming to life at midnight on a full moon?"

"Of course," said Willodean, as she corralled a meatball onto her plate. "Everyone knows that one, dear."

The judge frowned, "I didn't."

****

It was nearing 5:30pm. Amy told her mother that she had already made dinner plans with Alexander and Granddad. She booked a ride and texted her dad that she was on the way home.

Alexander had stopped off at the Irish Rover Pub on Franklin, a stone's throw from CA, and asked her to pick him up.

Amy could hear the merriment before she entered the building. Alexander was with several pals and the owners, Siobhan and Michael Reidy, singing old Irish tunes.

Amy too was friendly with the proprietors. She had a Guinness and joined the music making. Amy knew maybe two dozen of the old songs; Alexander knew more than a hundred. "Lament for Owen Roe O'Neill," "Jack the Jolly Ploughboy," "Her Brow is Like the Lily," "Emer's Farewell to Cucullain," and on and on.

Her father was full of melancholy as they rode in the back seat of a Prius being driven home. Alexander looked at old pictures on his phone of April and himself.

It pained Amy to see him like this. She wished he could move on.

However, when they arrived back home Alexander's mood quickly elevated as he joined in with the circus acts rehearsing. He juggled a little and he mimicked the clowns running around. Merlin the Monkey mimicked Alexander and he laughed.

Amy was pleased to see his spirit rebound.

"It's great having your own circus!"

The monkey danced around.

"See, Merlin agrees with me. That's off the bucket list now," Alexander said, as they reached the front door.

Mrs. Simmons greeted them, "Hello, you two. Nice to see Alexander back."

"Good evening, Mrs. Simmons, it is nice to see you as well. Say, where is that Sven?"

"The Siberian Tiger?"

"Yeah," said Alexander, affectionately. "He's such a big ol' pussycat."

"He's around and by the way, that big ol' pussycat got ahold of your basketballs in the den."

Alexander was alarmed to hear that, "N,N,N, Not my autographed 1980 and 1986 University of Louisville national championship basketballs?"

"Yep. He shredded both your balls."

"Ahh!" Alexander ran into his den.

Amy and Mrs. Simmons followed him.

"I found Darrell Griffith's autograph on one of the shreds and part of Pervis' name on the other. 'Kenny Pa' was only left on another strip.

Alexander was grieving, "Doctor Dunkenstein? Never Nervous Pervis? Kenny Payne?"

Amy shrugged, "I guess that's just part of the fun of having the circus around."

****

Alexander was in such shock from losing his balls he took a nap—but he usually did that after his pub crawling anyway. Amy went to visit Granddad in his studio and knocked on the door.

"Come in," Granddad called out.

Amy entered, "Hi, Granddad."

"Ambrosia." Granddad was working on a portrait.

Henry Clay greeted Amy by moving closer to get some love.

"There's my buddy, Henry Clay." They reconnected. "And there's Duke, Duchess and Diva." Amy petted the Beagles.

Granddad put his brush down, "How are you, my child?"

"Better. Dad's out of lockup and you were right, he was up to something and it looks to be working out."

"When it comes to the law, your father is a cunning fox. When it comes to life, he can be more circus clown."

Amy now noticed a naked mannequin with blonde hair sitting on a chair.

"Granddad, I see you're busy."

"This is Miranda, she's a model."

"I see. Hello, Miranda."

"This is my granddaughter, Amy."

"Nice to meet you, Miranda. I'd shake your hand, but—"

"No, don't move, dear," implored Granddad, as he picked up his brush and continued working. "In my modest attempt to capture the essence of the elusive and eternal feminine allure, I apply pigments and oils to this linen canvas, the golden light is just right at this moment, but it's ephemeral."

"*Art can never exist without naked beauty displayed*," Amy remarked.

"Quoting the poet William Blake! Spectacular!" cheered Granddad.

"I see you have the naked and the beauty part. I'll see you at dinner."

Amy kissed him on the cheek. "Daddy's cooking dinner tonight. It should be ready in one hour."

"Smashing. Dinner in one hour." Granddad was back creating. "I need to capture these perceptions in this light that will soon be gone."

Amy nodded and waved to Miranda.

****

Mrs. Simmons was at the table preparing to dine. Sitting with her were two of the circus clowns. Miranda—now garbed—was also at the table.

The two clowns played to Miranda and created a happy little silent scene.

Mrs. Simmons was slowly shaking her head, "Llamas, tigers, clowns and now a mannequin. At least it won't be leaving boulder-sized surprises around the place."

The clowns shook their heads no at that.

Amy and Alexander came in from the kitchen carrying a large kettle of stew, a big bowl of pasta and a plate full of steaks.

"We've got just enough steaks that everyone gets one," said Alexander.

The clowns applauded. The food was passed out.

Granddad arrived at the table and sat next to Miranda. "Don't mind, Miranda, she's a little shy."

Alexander put down his fork and was serious, "Dad, what's going on?"

Granddad covered Miranda's ears, "I'm using a new technique. Projection Painting. I imagine Miranda to be the most alluring woman in the world. I mean, obviously she isn't. But I have to remain totally in character during the process, like a Jared Leto thing. Do you understand?" He took his hands off Miranda's ears.

The three gave him a wary look and nodded. The atmosphere was again cheery as they dined.

Sven then entered and like a humble pet, put his head on Alexander's lap and asked for forgiveness. Alexander froze.

His wrangler entered and explained, "He knows he upset you, Alexander. Sven is asking for forgiveness for shredding your balls."

Sven nuzzled Alexander's crotch and purred.

"Ahhhh," said Alexander, more than a bit on edge. "It's okay, Sven."

Amy and Granddad were also a bit concerned.

"Sven is very happy that you have forgiven him," said the wrangler.

"Yes," said Alexander. "We want Sven to be happy."

The room giggled nervously at that.

The wrangler gave a command in Russian. Sven raised up, but then wolfed Alexander's steak down right off his plate, smiled at Alexander, licked his chops and then retreated.

The wrangler yelled, "Bad cat! Sorry, sorry, he can be so rude!"

Alexander was stunned, he glanced at his empty plate with sadness.

The well-armed 4-person security detail burst upon the scene, followed by the Khrakistan president.

"Hello, everyone! Hello, all! Hello, Alexander, my brother!"

"He's your brother??" demanded Granddad. "Is this yet another product from one my past legendary romances coming back to bite us on the—"

"No, Daddy! He's not my real brother, really."

President Ibragimov faced Granddad, "You are for sure blood relative of Alexander—slightly older handsome brother?" the president inquired with a silly grin.

"You really suck up well!" quipped Granddad.

"Thank you! Thank you. I do suck well. Please to tell, how old you are?"

"Just about 80."

The President was stunned, "You joke, yes?"

"No."

"You are in very good shape, pumping and grunting do good for you."

"Daddy eats well, is active physically and mentally," beamed Alexander.

"I hope to be like you, sir."

Alexander motioned to a chair, "Greg, sit, have dinner and then we'll discuss your situation."

The president sat and pointed to the exercise bicycles. "This house! You peddle and make power. Sun shine down on your solar panels and make electricity! Every time you step on floor in here or skate on giant halfpipe, you make electricity! Wind blows you make electricity. You are totally off electrical grid and you drive electric cars! While my country sells oil... You know, you really scare me!"

Alexander snorted at that, "Hell, you really scare me too!"

They all laughed.

"I love your city. Very nice."

"Thank you," said Alexander. "We're quite proud of it."

"I have good times today! At place called 4th Street Live. Too much fun! I may open new franchise there of my very popular restaurant chain: FRIEDGOS: FRIED-GOAT-ON-STICK!"

Alexander and Amy were concerned.

"Greg, it's…it's such a long way from your home!"

"I would be close to my brother!"

Amy began to gag. Mrs. Simmons patted her on the back.

"You have here American Dream!"

Alexander contemplated him putting down roots here and felt the stomach acid churning in his gut.

"My Brother, how you get this house?"

"I'll let my father tell this story," Alexander said, looking for some Tums.

Granddad did a little strutting and took the stage, "In 1967 I put a thousand dollar bet on Proud Clarion at 30-1 to win the Derby."

"That's how he built this house," Alexander boasted proudly.

"Great story!" said the president.

Granddad cleared his throat, "Even better. I was doing a painting in a meadow, it was the essence of nature I was attempting to capture and I took a nap, it came to me in that dream."

"Name of horse winner?"

"Yes."

"Tell me if more dreams come to you for this upcoming Kentucky Derby!"

Grandad gave the president the okay sign. Almost all of them laughed.

Three of the bodyguards were peddling and sweating on stationary bikes and a treadmill.

Alexander observed, "You know, Greg, they've done enough."

"Is okay, I give you plenty of power." He signaled and they sped up.

Alexander, Amy and President Ibragimov moved into the den, followed by one bodyguard. Amy shut the door.

Into three snifters, Alexander poured three shots of Dulsett Reserve. "May I offer you something from a local distillery. It's run by a family that has been friends with our family for many years. And I've heard it's a big hit from London, Cairo and even Beijing!"

"Indeed it is," agreed Amy.

Alexander offered a cigar, the President accepted.

"My daughter lacks this bad habit."

"I have other bad habits."

All three sat in big leather chairs. A guard stood close.

"Now what can we do for you?" asked Alexander.

"My family, horse people for centuries in Central Asia. Grandfather grew fast horses. He race and win many times but never come here. My father, grew race horses, many wins, but never come here. I tried to breed top racehorse with so-so success. It is my dream to come here and win biggest race in world, Kentucky Derby! I have plan, not just outside of box, is outside of barn! A Plan of boldness."

He signaled to the bodyguard, who gave him a folder.

"We have negotiation with owner, cut price in half," boasted the president. "Presently, only $50,000."

The president handed the printout to Alexander and Amy of a Craigslist ad: Frozen Sperm of Race Horse Secretariat For Sale $100,000

Alexander and Amy had a look of bewilderment.

"Craigslist?" asked Amy.

"Now, Alexander, brother, please consummate deal!"

Alexander considered this, "Secretariat passed in 1989. But, let's pretend here for a second."

"I am very good at that," the president proudly stated.

"Splendid. Now you say you want to create a horse that would be eligible to enter and be victorious in the Kentucky Derby. Am I correct, sir?"

"There goes highly trained legal mind shifting into gear. Yes!"

"To be eligible to run in the Derby you have to be registered with the Jockey Club. And to be registered there must be a Live Foal Report, there's genetic typing AND, this is a biggie, no artificial insemination. Which would eliminate any creation from your 'plan of boldness,' sir."

"You can, how you say, 'smooth things over.' 'Fix it' for me."

"I will do no such thing! I have standards, sir!"

"You lawyer, standards are for sale!"

Alexander was enraged, he grabbed a sword mounted on the wall.

The bodyguard pulled out his HK MP5 and aimed.

Alexander pointed his sword, "Out! Out of my house!"

"Alexander, I beg you. Do this deal tonight and I will leave tomorrow! If can't race here, other places possible. And I make generous donation to your favorite charity."

****

They were waiting in Tom Sawyer Park. It was located east of downtown about 10 miles and very dark at this time of night.

The black SUV held the president and his security team. Gabe's banged-up white van was next to it. Amy and Alexander were sitting in the back.

Gabe was in the driver's seat researching stuff on his phone, "Fun fact, Tom Sawyer Park is named for Diane Sawyer's dad, not Huck Finn's buddy."

Alexander scoff-snarled, "Judge Sawyer was killed in a car crash, right before I was born. How fun was that?"

Gabe scrunched his face, "Too soon?"

"I'm a big fan of Diane Sawyer," Amy stated. "She's quite a journalist."

"She still worked with Nixon. Tricky Dick," grumbled Alexander.

"Daddy, you and Hunter never got over the Nixon thing."

Alexander became serious, "Diane has matured well. She has done some outstanding work. She was young back in the early 70s."

Amy thought back, "Yes, we all did things when we were young."

Alexander lashed out, "The President of Krackland isn't young and he's doing stupid things! I'm still trying to figure out why I'm going along for the ride."

"He's a client that actually pays, Daddy. And Uncle Sam wants you to keep an eye on him for national security reasons. And you always do your patriotic duty."

"This exchange isn't illegal," Alexander reminded himself.

"Taxes aren't owed for sales outside the state," Amy declared with her 'I know the code better than anyone tone.' "But if the mare owner takes possession of the semen in Kentucky it's subject to Kentucky sales tax."

"I'll insist he pay that," announced Alexander.

The three had looks of doubt on that one coming to fruition.

"This is really a plan?" Gabe asked, amazed.

"The ironic part," Alexander mused, "is that he probably has enough money to do it right, do it fair, and to be competitive."

"Naw," Gabe responded. "Cheaters never believe that. That dude's been alpha dog for over two decades. He doesn't want to be competitive."

Down range a car light flashed twice.

"There's the signal. Put on the night goggles, circle around and get the license plate."

"Got it, boss." Gabriel put on the goggles and exited.

"Stay here, I'll make the exchange."

"You think I came all the way from New York to sit in the car?"

Amy pulled out her Glock and loaded a clip.

Alexander was surprised, "Packing heat?"

"You're going to need backup besides his bozo security team. I have my CWP."

"Concealed Weapons Permit in New York City? That's a tough nut to crack. How'd you get one of those?"

"Daddy, you don't want to know."

"Tell me."

"So many people wanted to kill the lawyers of our 'unpopular clients' that our firm offered to acquire the CWP for us and I accepted."

"You're right, I don't want to know."

"Thought so."

"It's your journey, I'm not going to judge you. Just love you, which is easy and support you, which at times can be sort of challenging."

Amy and Alexander exited the vehicle with the briefcase containing the $50K.

A dark figure with a bright light appeared and used a voice synthesizer. "Put the money down and walk away."

Alexander blocked his eyes from the glare of the light. "Are you sure you want to do this?"

"I do. What about you?"

"Our client is a dangerous man," said Amy. "If the goods aren't for real, you'll be in serious trouble."

"Drop the money and we'll switch."

Alexander put the briefcase down and the dark figure put down a bag.

And then from the side a twig snapped and it spooked the dark figure. He grabbed the money and ran.

The president's bodyguard fired off several bursts of automatic weapon fire into the air.

The president emerged, ran over and snatched the bag.

"Stop!!! Stop shooting!!!" screamed Alexander.

The dark figure jumped in a car and roared away.

The president jumped up and down with joy, "I have it! I create super horse!!!"

Alexander was scouting around nervously. "I suggest we relocate with haste."

The president shouted, "But this now calls for celebration!"

"Automatic weapon fire might be 'whatever' in Khrakistan, you know, woo hoo! I covered the spread, but here, it tends to draw...attention." Alexander noticed two Louisville Metro Police cars rapidly arriving with their lightbars fully activated. "Like this..."

Four officers emerged and drew their weapons on them.

"LMPD! Drop your weapons and put your face on the ground, NOW!"

Everyone but the president complied.

The bodyguards were all down. One gently urged, "Excellency, it would be wise if—"

"I am President Grigory Ibragimov of great and glorious country of Khrakistan, I not put my face on foreign soil!"

"Louisville Metro Police Department. Get on the ground! This is your last warning."

"Call Embassy, we work this out."

Alexander, prone on the ground, was next to Amy. "This is going to be interesting."

"I have Ambassador's private number here. He loves me like brother!"

LMPD tased him. The president collapsed and convulsed on the ground in front of Alexander and Amy.

"*The common curse of mankind, folly and ignorance*," said Amy.

Alexander grinned, "The perfect Shakespeare quote! *Troilus and Cressida*, Act II, Scene 3, you really are my daughter!"

Amy treasured his compliment as the president continued to twitch next to them.

11

Mrs. Simmons was mid-way through a crossword puzzle and keeping an eye on Granddad. She knew his mind was troubled. He shuffled around checking the many solar panels and mini-wind turbines that surrounded the compound. He then did a diagnostic check of the entire system. It was all good, they had plenty of power. He wasn't worried about that. Granddad had a strange feeling. He checked his watch. It was past midnight.

"Everything will be alright, Arthur."

"They didn't answer the phones. I've got this feeling in my bones…"

"They're probably still… I don't know what they're doing." Her mind now began to worry.

Finally, Amy and Gabe entered.

Amy called out, "Mrs. Simmons."

"I'm glad you're back," Mrs. Simmons declared with some relief.

"The circus is gone?" asked Gabe.

"They're still here," Mrs. Simmons reported as she could now fully concentrate on her crossword puzzle.

Granddad came back in from the back and called from the living room, "There you are!"

"Granddad, you still up?" asked Amy.

Gabe greeted them, "Sir, Ma'am."

"Gabriel," said Mrs. Simmons nodding to him and then glancing over to Granddad, "I said everything would be fine."

Granddad acknowledged that.

"Hi, Daddy," replied Alexander, on the way in.

"Fess up, what happened, Alexander?" asked Granddad.

"Uh, nothing much."

Granddad harrumphed, "Ha! Whenever he says 'uh, nothing much' that way, I know it's something."

"We were detained," mumbled Amy.

Mrs. Simmons paused at that, "Huh, Granddad did have a bad feeling."

"I knew it!" growled Granddad. "Again?! My jailbird son! Which prison gang have you joined?"

"Daddy, I have *not* joined any prison gangs."

Granddad was alarmed at that, "That's even crazier! You know what it's like to go solo in there?!"

"Everything is fine."

"How is everything fine?"

Alexander settled into his chair, "The local authorities got a call from Washington. They ordered the release of the foreign leader and to hand over the item purchased by Greg and his boys."

"Which they had no problem complying with," remarked Amy.

Alexander rubbed his hands together, "Okay great. I have the Bats baseball game recorded. I want us to relax and watch, luckily nobody has told me the score so—"

Granddad raised up his arms in triumph, "The Louisville Bats won 3-2 in the bottom of the 9th over those feisty Toledo Mud Hens! A great game!"

"Shhh!" Mrs. Simmons tried in vain to shush him, but it was too late.

"Daddy! Grrrr...I guess I'll save that electricity."

"What?! Uh, sorry! I keep forgetting to forget the results when you record games."

"Only for the last 30 years..." sighed Alexander.

"I have to remember to remember not to remember. I should go write that down."

Amy commented, "I've always wondered what it's like to have diplomatic immunity."

"It's the moral hazard of international relations," lamented Alexander.

Amy nodded at that, "Having a get out of jail free card would skew your perceptions and actions."

"Damn, his boy gets to rip a fully-automatic MP5 whenever he feels like it," Gabe gushed. "And it's like it didn't happen. No paperwork!"

"Being an officer of the court," said Alexander, "I would normally be compelled to hand over the evidence Gabe retrieved, the license plate of the cab that was there."

Gabe was amazed, astonished and mystified all at once, "They didn't want information from us. Have you ever had an apology, been served tea and offered to be driven home after being arrested? Should I expect a mint on my pillow? I've never been treated so well inside a cop shop."

Alexander contemplated, "The diplomatic immunity would cover the Khraky president and his security team, but not us. That came from our guardian angel."

Alexander turned to Amy sporting a slight grin.

Gabe noticed, "What's up with this guardian angel? Come on, give."

Alexander explained, "The Secretary of State called and had Amy Arrington and her associates released, along with the Khraky president."

Gabe was highly impressed, "Whoa."

"You're welcome," Amy said, nonchalantly.

The Khrakistan security team entered. The low man in seniority placed the container in the freezer.

The president was on the phone in great distress as he marched through. "%%&*#$@%%^!!!!"

Granddad was observing, "Heavens to Betsy! This is the essence of RPB."

Alexander was curious, "RPB? Daddy, is that a new syndrome we need to ask our doctors about? I mean, they keep coming up with stuff and I fall behind."

"RPB! Rampant Paranoid Bloviation!" announced Granddad. "Extraordinary, I've never ever seen a better example! Where's my sketch pad!? I must create!"

Amy was concerned, "Granddad, that could take some time."

"Only a week, 2, tops! You see the potential of the brush strokes? The veins are bulging in his neck!"

Amy held her own neck at such a prospect.

President Ibragimov had a splitting headache. The tase still lingered, he twitched a bit as he screamed into his phone, "Turn off internet! Turn off, presently!" He ended the call and calmed himself and turned around. "My people, they do not know the sacrifices I make for them!"

Alexander took a drink, "They all have big crosses to bear."

Amy nodded slowly with conviction at that.

The president bowed to them, "I must go. I have something to do and get back home."

"What? No!" Granddad was quite disturbed, "I want to paint you!"

"I am very honored. Perhaps next visit."

"Yes, you are welcome any time!"

"Thank you! Come to Khrakistan with my brother, Alexander."

"It's a date!" Granddad was thrilled.

"Most excellent. I make our farewells now."

"Be sure you don't forget your new acquisition in the freezer," reminded Alexander.

"But of course, my brother! And I pay Kentucky sales tax."

"Great. And next time, call first again. Just to make sure I'm in this hemisphere."

"Yes, my brother, I will accomplish this."

The president turned to Amy. "I wish for you to know that I have no hard feelings for you..." He kissed her hand then whispered in her ear. "Maybe a little hard."

Amy cringed and groaned, "Eeeoww."

"Good night all and good bye!" He exited.

Amy and Alexander took a deep, welcomed breath. Amy put up her right fist for a bump.

Alexander paused, "That's the one he kissed."

Amy put up her left hand, they bumped and she washed her hands.

****

Gabe had gone home and Granddad had turned in. Amy sauntered in on a cloud and joined Mrs. Simmons, who knitted and Alexander, who practiced throwing his darts.

"He's finally gone!" trilled Amy. "I've scrubbed my hands. Yet, I still feel the need to shower to get the rest of the 'ick' off."

"I'll be exfoliating quite a bit extra this weekend," declared Mrs. Simmons.

"They asked and I said the circus could stay one more day," said Alexander.

A framed picture on the mantel caught Amy's attention. It was Alexander with another gentleman, William McMurry. "I really like this picture. It was the Klan case you worked on ten years ago, yes?"

"I was only assisting. Morris and Bill were the first chairs."

"As I recall late one night several years ago, you told me Bill McMurry was your hero."

"I might have said that."

"You took me to Bill's Kentucky Civil Rights Hall of Fame ceremony in Bowling Green in 2014."

"That was a great honor. Bill well deserved it," Alexander said, fondly recalling the event.

"That was quite a distinguished class. Judge Karem was included and Linda McCray," said Mrs. Simmons. "And as I recollect, your friend Shelby Lanier was inducted as well."

Alexander grinned at that memory, "Yes, yes he was."

Amy put the picture down and opened her laptop. "You worked with Bill on that Diageo lawsuit over the whisky fungus."

"The Angel's Share," said Alexander. "That case was dismissed."

Mrs. Simmons recalled, "That's when Alexander got into it with old man Dulsett."

"I regret the words we had between us before he passed. I'm sorry if it caused problems between you and Bobby."

"Daddy, we had long broken up before that was an issue."

"In retrospect," said Mrs. Simmons, "I believe that lawsuit caused the breakup of the TORTs band."

Alexander sadly shrugged, "Bobby took it personally. You know how sensitive he is. When you broke up with him in high school, it triggered that terrible shooting slump, which knocked his team out of the state tournament."

Amy waved that off, "That is such malarky."

Mrs. Simmons hummed at that, with a nod to Alexander's notion.

"We didn't even go to the same school. It was so awkward."

"That's why they said you didn't care."

"Daddy, it was 10 years ago! A decade!"

"Yet, you seem to have the same effect now. I heard Bobby, who has been killing it in the Y league, had a terrible outing the other night. On the same day you came into town and was interviewed on the radio."

Mrs. Simmons nodded.

Amy pooh-poohed that. Her attention was then captured by problems on her laptop. "Ugh. What's wrong with my computer?"

"Computers..." mused Alexander. "They can open the world and they can open a can of worms."

Amy's phone rang, she checked it and sighed, "Hello, mother."

"It's past midnight, you should be sleeping, honey. Is he making you run on the treadmill to charge up your alarm clock?"

"No, Mother, we have plenty of power. I just had a busy day."

"I heard. I was calling to make sure you're coming tomorrow night, or I guess it's tonight now."

"To what?"

"I told you about it. It's the social event of the season at Silver Horse Sanctuary. Formal attire required."

"Is Daddy invited too?"

Alexander closed his eyes and shook his head no.

"Sweetie Pie," said April, "allow me to take you back to the previous encounter. Last fall we had a small gathering here with your father in attendance."

"Mother, I'm going to put you on speaker."

"Please do. We had some friends who were interested in the law. There was a Mrs. Kilbride, who considers herself somewhat of a scholar on the U.S. Constitution, even though she never formally studied the law. She usually makes her thoughts known to the world."

"Go on," Amy was staring at Alexander who was trying to ignore this.

"And she was in a discussion with your father. Where she shared the fact that she was a strict originalist and was in agreement with Justice Clarence Thomas of the Supreme Court on his interpretation of the U.S. Constitution. She said it was written by our Founding Fathers and should not be tinkered with in any way."

"Uh-huh..." replied Amy, wondering how this played out.

"Your father said that was an interesting opinion. And she thanked him thinking that was a compliment. And then he said, 'Let us consider this. In the original constitution, Article I, Section 2, said slaves count as 3/5 persons. If it was still like that today, we wouldn't have Justice Thomas and his rulings, would we?'"

Amy's eyes widened, "I have a feeling this didn't end well."

"It gets better, dear. Mrs. Kilbride was stung by this. And then Alexander reminded her that the Founding Fathers didn't think the ladies should vote and it wasn't until 1920 when the 19th Amendment was passed that gave voting rights to women. Alexander said we had federal elections for 128 years in the country and did just fine and then we had to go and make changes."

Amy was now trying to suppress a grin.

"Alexander then reminded Mrs. Kilbride who the first president was that women were able to vote for: Warren G. Harding. The more handsome candidate, who won with the women's vote, but who's generally acclaimed by historians as one of the dumbest and most corrupt presidents ever. He ended it by saying, 'Thanks for the contribution, ladies!'"

"In my defense," replied Alexander, "I was teasing the woman. It was a joke. An attempt at irony. That election was decided over the League of Nations and Wilson's invasions, not—"

"Whatever!" Amy was now snickering, "Mother, what happened after that?"

"Mrs. Kilbride splashed her full glass of red wine in his face."

Amy was stunned and curtailed her amusement, slightly, "That's...surprising."

Alexander agreed, "It certainly was surprising, because it really was a rather garden-variety vintage."

"Right," scoffed April. "I serve 'garden-variety' vintages. And then she dumped a bowl of salsa on his head."

"It was savory and quite picante," remarked Alexander. "That was top notch."

"I'm thrilled you approved of my salsa. Especially since it mixed with the wine and dripped down your face and onto my white rug."

Amy held her laugh, "Daddy being Daddy."

"Well, the agent provocateur can just be himself elsewhere. By the by, I was thinking I could set you up with someone."

"Got a date, mom!"

"Wonderful. Ta. See you tonight!" The call was over.

Alexander gathered his thoughts and pulled out some large historical texts. "The Founding Fathers, in their wisdom, created a mechanism to amend their original vision. Women can now vote. Minorities can now vote and you don't have to own property to vote. Justice Antonin Scalia was once asked about the difference between him and Justice Thomas. He said, 'I'm an originalist too, but I'm not a nut.'" Alexander crossed to the front window and gazed out. "When I'm on the University of Louisville's campus, where do I always make a point to visit?"

"Your alma mater. The Louis D. Brandeis School of Law, named after your idol and where his ashes are interred in the law school's portico."

Alexander eyed a portrait of Justice Brandeis on his wall, "Justice Brandeis said, 'Our constitution is not a straitjacket. It is a living organism. As such it is capable of growth, of expansion and of adaptation to new conditions.'"

"Did quoting Justice Brandeis help your case with Mrs. Kilbride?"

"The fur and food and drink were flying well before that. Yet I'm the one that was insulted! It was offensive that Mrs. Kilbride believed that I actually believed that!"

Alexander began turning to images of the people he described.

"With the history of the Arringtons in Louisville! My great-great-grandfather aided John Parker, a major conductor on the Underground Railroad, Delia Ann Webster, the 'petticoat' abolitionist and Elijah

Anderson, dubbed the 'General Superintendent' of the Underground Railroad. Louisville was known as Grand Central Station on the way to freedom. The Arringtons helped them get across the river to free territory. My great-grandmother was present when the first Women's Club of Louisville was started in 1881. She supported and assisted the great work of suffragettes Susan Look Avery and Emma Dolfinger. When Mrs. Avery hosted Lucy Stone and Henry Blackwell, outspoken activists for women's voting rights, for a visit and to exchange ideas, there were some in polite society here that were shocked and quite angry. The Arringtons applauded and donated more to the cause. In the early 1960s, demonstrations were happening in Louisville to end segregation in white-owned businesses. My mother and father were right in the middle of that helping to organize boycotts and voter registration and supporting the sit-ins at Stewart's Dry Goods and the Blue Boar Café."

Alexander points to a newspaper headline.

"My parents were at the signing of the law on May 14th, 1963. It made it unlawful for anyone in Louisville to refuse service in a public place because of race, color, religion or national origin. I declare! With this history and my beliefs that human rights are my cornerstone, for all people, whatever sex, race, creed, persuasion or religion. I've crusaded for equal rights and equal pay! And I received death threats for representing Black clients."

"Death threats?" asked Mrs. Simmons.

"Amy was too young and her mother for sure didn't need to have her feathers ruffled over this."

"What happened, Daddy?"

"I had two clients that were accused of a robbery. But they were found not guilty. Some folks at the time didn't like that I was representing them. Either way, if you believe in the system, these gentlemen, like everyone, deserved to be defended to the hilt, so I took it on. Why? The 14th Amendment, Section 1: No state shall make or enforce—"

Amy jumped in, "Any law which shall abridge the privileges or immunities of citizens of the United States;"

"Nor," said Alexander, "shall any State deprive any person of life, liberty, or property, without due process of law; nor deny to any person, and that means *any person,* within its jurisdiction the equal protection under the law."

Mrs. Simmons was moved by this and reminded why she worked for this man, while Amy was reminded how in awe she was of her father.

"Seems she didn't grasp your 'modest proposal' at satire, Daddy. It happens."

"Yes, Jonathan Swift, he had the same conundrum. I doubt though he ever had a white linen suit ruined by a very pedestrian Cabernet Sauvignon and tangy pico de gallo. Enough of that. Now, do you have the owner of that cab company?"

Amy handed him a piece of paper, "Here it is."

Alexander perused the information, "I sued this guy twice for gross negligence. No love here for me."

They pondered. Time passed. Each went through their idiosyncratic tics.

Alexander got an idea. He made a call.

Sally Messenger, a 45-year-old, well-put-together full-figured dominatrix with shocking pink hair, was between clients. Her phone rang, she checked and then smiled seeing who it was.

"Hello, wild man."

Alexander was quite proper and business-like, "Hello, Sally, how are you?"

Sally was in control, "Shut up, Alexander, I'll bet you've been bad."

"I've been good. It's nice to talk to you."

"Understand. You're with someone. Alexander, are you finally ready for some?" She rattled some handcuffs.

"Golly, thanks for asking. I've been really busy." Alexander was trying to keep his cool as Amy and Mrs. Simmons observed, wondering why he had become so antsy.

Sally purred, "I know, 'the law is a jealous mistress,' but so am I."

"Sally, I need a favor."

"Name it," she selected a heavy chain.

"What I need…is this evening's GPS trail for cab number 18 from Herbie's company."

"No problem, I'll get out my feather tipped whip. He loves that one."

Alexander covered the phone and reported to the ladies, "She said she would inquire."

12

Torts and Just Desserts from the mind of Alexander Arrington

The owl appeared and spoke:

"Angel's Share is the part of the bourbon that evaporates when aging the spirit in the oak barrels. It escapes as a gas and reforms into the black, sticky stuff coating buildings in the surrounding area. It's also being inhaled. Imagine that in our lungs. The industry says it isn't harmful. *Baudoinia* has no known adverse health effects, but public health officials recommend people not inhale spores that come free during washing. How can the industry claim it's benign if there are no long-term studies of acetaldehyde or 'flying sugar,' on humans to back these assertions? Long-term inhalation studies of acetaldehyde on rats and hamsters revealed laryngeal cancers. It meets the criteria of the Occupational Safety and Health Administration for potential carcinogens and recommends that worker exposure be reduced to the lowest feasible concentration. I would assume that also was the advice for those that live in the area.

Like Dr. Stockman in Ibsen's *Enemy of the People*, who revealed the famous and profitable therapeutic water in his town was not so healthy and earned the wrath of the locals, speaking out on this topic has brought scorn from those who are in the bourbon business and cost me some friends—one who I thought was very close.

Look, I love drinking bourbon. It's part of the fiber of Kentucky. It's popular the world over and getting more so, with distilleries expanding by a whopping 250% in the last decade. I just don't want to put what could be a carcinogenic byproduct into my, or anyone else's, lungs.

It survives the coldest winters and hottest summers. Do the math on this. Every couple of months the folks living around the distilleries and warehouses involved with bourbon production either do it themselves, with water and bleach, goggles, holding their breath with mouths shut and noses clamped—they've been thoroughly warned—or pay a couple hundred bucks to someone else to power-wash the sticky, gummy gunk off their homes and cars. You can't power-wash your lungs. Workers and residents in and around the distilleries and warehouses—up to a mile away—that age the bourbon face this reality on a daily basis. If they don't clean up the dark sticky stuff, they can be fined by local government's code enforcement.

Bill McMurray had the cajones to take on the $9-billion spirits industry over Angel's Share. I understand the fungus, *baudoinia compniacensis*, wasn't even identified until 2007. We live in a modern world. There is a solution. Either Scotch Bonnets, wraps, modified warehouses or something else. Yes, it will for sure cost some money in the short run, but could be very profitable down the line if that 2 to 5 or 10 percent or more of the Angel's Share is saved or diverted—which can be up to as much as 1,000 tons of ethanol emissions every year, per distiller. It would be like a large tax break for the local residents not having to power-wash as much. Hundreds of thousands of barrels of bourbon are filled and aged in this state every year. All efforts must be employed to maintain the fine world-class product produced here in Kentucky and the producer's bottom lines. With leadership, partnerships and some creative thinking, I'm betting it can be solved. It's being done in other places, why not here?"

~ ~ ~

"My dessert of the day: Cappuccino Chocolate Cheesecake from Rawnaissance on Bardstown Road. I'm already a fan of the Derby Pie and the Lavender Dark Chocolate Cake. And now the Cappuccino Chocolate Cheesecake has been added to my list. All dishes are made with natural ingredients and organic sweeteners. No GMO, dairy, gluten, soy or refined sugar. A delicious dive into decadent raw delights that will tantalize your taste buds without the guilt or bloat."

The owl faded out.

****

Amy didn't get any sleep, couldn't drop off. Events were still swirling in her mind on the great exchange in Tom Sawyer Park. She was thankful the foreign 'dignitary' had left. She jumped on doc review for her firm and billed several hours. She knew Abby would be up by 7am and texted her if Mitch had mentioned anything about Bobby having an off night the other night playing ball. Abby didn't have to ask. Mitch had been grumbling about it since he came home, how their 'once dominant team was on the verge of failing to make the playoffs.' Mitch kept muttering about 'history repeating itself with Bobby.'

Abby didn't include that last part in her reply.

****

Being Alexander's legal secretary and the house manager, Mrs. Simmons was the actual captain of this ship. Even though a cleaning team came in twice a week, Mrs. Simmons was dusting and straightening pictures on the wall. She delivered sustenance to the various winged, fuzzy, furry, four-legged residents of Casa Arrington.

A local kid came in early and walked the dogs. Lately he was showing up extra early to get this out of the way, so Duke, Duchess, Diva and Henry Clay could go back into hiding before Sven, Deveraux, Merlin and the clowns arose.

Mrs. Simmons entered the kitchen. She filled the teapot while proofing a motion for an appeal that Alexander had to file.

He was soon up, though still half asleep when he entered the half-pipe with his board. Alexander became fully awake and began to get some air and sing out a song.

Amy emerged with her board, "I believe that's a TORTs tune!"

"Yes, ma'am!"

"Ticks Rule!" Amy yelled, as they skated together.

The clowns and circus animals mixed with the braver of the pets in CA and observed with interest and curiosity. The birds chirped. Even with the upheaval and stress, there was a balance to Casa Arrington the way nature was woven in.

Sven and Deveraux were well behaved.

They had breakfast together. The animals and the pets got their needed attention. Alexander received the information he requested from Sally.

They reviewed the travels of cab 18.

"Look how close the pickup spot is to the Wellington estate," said Amy.

Alexander studied the record, "And it looks to be a regular fare from that location, Friday and Saturday nights."

"Interesting repeating pattern," remarked Mrs. Simmons, as she checked farther back in the record.

"Tonight," said Alexander, "if you're up to it, after the dinner with mom, we have a stakeout."

"I'll be up to it, except I need some sleep now. It's been a while."

"Good, go. I'll see you this afternoon when you get up." Alexander picked up a book and approached his father's studio. He saw a green light and knocked.

"Come in." Granddad was painting alone.

The door opened and Alexander entered reading Mark Twain's, *Life on The Mississippi.* "Morning, Daddy."

Granddad paused working and checked Alexander's book, "Morning, son, reading Mark Twain? Still going for your riverboat pilot's license?"

"Haven't you always said, 'don't let go of your dreams.' What are you working on?"

"I'm painting a portrait of Ambrosia. I know it's only for a moment, but it's sure nice having her around."

"She's a ray of sunshine," Alexander put his arm around his father. "And so are you."

Amy entered her room and collapsed on her bed bone tired. She checked her phone and answered the texts sent by Gabby and Abby, mentioning that she was on vacation, but she had been roped into a legal case with her dad. Amy then contemplated sending a message to Bobby, but declined. She quickly was asleep and had a dream about playing in a creek when she was 17, with Bobby Dulsett.

****

It was just after 10am. Amy was up from her nap. Living with a circus rarely allowed for peaceful siestas. Deveraux was clomping around shrieking and having a general meltdown like he was prone to do at times. Sven was roaring in vain trying to get him to shut up. Merlin was wailing for them all to be quiet.

Amy then received a call back from the State Department asking for any intel she had gathered. She reported the president had flown all the way from Khrakistan to purchase a jar of frozen horse jizz allegedly from Secretariat.

After a rather uncomfortable moment of silence, she was thanked and the call ended.

Amy downed some coffee, donned her helmet and was back skating on the half-pipe trying to wake up.

Sven had gone the extra effort and made friends with Duke, Duchess and Diva; while running off Nutmeg and Cantankerous Cat, who were hiding God knows where. Merlin and a couple clowns were fascinated with Amy's skateboarding. Henry Clay was still MIA, only to appear early for the morning walk and meal and then again disappear for the day.

Deveraux stepped forward, allowing Amy the esteemed privilege of giving him some attention.

"Deveraux, I don't want to talk to you," growled Amy. "Your screeching woke me up."

Even Sven was irked by this. He thought the llama was crazy.

Merlin believed Deveraux was a drama queen and didn't have the time of day for him.

Several of the other of CA's animal inhabitants, including Luminary the Legendary Lizard, were in agreement; but kept their opinions to themselves at a considerable distance, as they had never encountered such a creature with such an attitude.

Deveraux was unconcerned with Amy's or anybody's crabbings and preened off his reflection in a window.

"Did you get any shuteye?" Alexander asked, grabbing his helmet and board and joining her.

After years of skating together they had a natural rhythm.

"I got a couple winks." She gave a quick dart of the eye to Deveraux, who looked away, acting uninterested.

Father and daughter challenged each other and both were getting some air. The clowns clapped, Sven was thrilled, Merlin approved and even Deveraux was impressed, but he kept his cool.

Amy's phone rang. She pulled up, checked and picked it up, "Hello, Mother?"

"Yes, dear, I just wanted to make sure your invitation made it to you. It was sent by registered and bonded courier and delivered about an hour ago."

"An invite, delivered an hour ago?" Amy looked up.

A clown put up his index finger to get her attention. He then unbuttoned his backside, pulled out the invitation, administered a dusting and presented it to her.

Amy frowned, "Yes…I got it."

"It's high security."

Amy stared at the clown, "Yes, Mother, I can see that." The clown nodded.

"There's a barcode and a hologram on the invite that needs to be scanned at the entrance."

"Why so hi-tech?"

"The mayor and the governor are also coming tonight, along with a ton of VIPs. You better allow some extra time to clear the heavy security."

"Understand."

"And you have a date, right?"

"Yeah. Gotta go."

"See you tonight!"

Amy stored the invitation in a drawer in the living room table. There was a knock at the door.

Amy answered it, "Hello?"

A delivery guy was standing there with a package. He checked his clipboard, "I have a delivery from Bobby Dulsett for the Arrington house."

"I can sign for it." Amy signed.

"Is that *the* Bobby Dulsett?" asked the guy.

"Who's Bobby Dulsett?" asked Amy.

The guy laughed, "Good one. It says handle with care."

"Thank you." Amy brought the box inside, opened it and found an LP. An album from the band The Ohio River Ticks. Bobby Dulsett was one of the musicians. Alexander was at the side playing guitar.

"This is so groovy!" Amy carried the record into the den and opened up her dad's turntable.

Merlin came from the other side and quietly liberated April's invitation in the drawer of the living room table and scooted off.

Alexander entered reading the morning *Louisville Courier Journal* newspaper, "What's going on?"

"Bobby just sent this. Let me spin a little vinyl at you." She put on the record. The TORTs' style of blues came wafting out of the speakers.

Alexander was pleased, he started to move and get in the groove. "Lordy, that sounds good."

Mrs. Simmons came in and was digging this, "It sure does."

Alexander and Mrs. Simmons danced together to these funky beats.

Granddad came in with his version of the Electric Slide, credit and apologies to Ric Silver, and he was soon dancing with Amy.

The animals were getting into it. Even Cantankerous had appeared and was digging the tunes and twitching his tail.

Amy showed the album cover and they all roared with laughter.

Alexander pulled out his phone and made a call.

It was Saturday and Bobby Dulsett was in the offices of their family distillery reading reports and catching up on paperwork. His phone rang. He checked, grinned and picked up. "Hey, Alexander."

"I appreciate your gift, sir."

"You like it?"

"I love it. We haven't had a jam session in a while."

"I hear you, Alexander."

"We can play here. The circus is leaving someday, soon…"

"Circus?" asked Bobby.

"It's a long story."

"Yeah, uh, is Amy around, I heard she was in town."

"Amy?"

Amy glanced over, her eyes widened.

"She is in town. Let me see if she's at home."

Alexander stepped up next to Amy and yelled upstairs. "Amy? Are you home? Bobby's on the line." He turned to her and she nodded. "Here she comes." He handed her the phone.

"Bobby?"

"Hi, Amy. I heard you were back."

"I'm on a short vacation."

"How's New York?"

"It's quite a place."

There was a pause.

"How long are you going to be here?"

"At least a week. Remember when we were kids and you granted me a wish?"

"That's my superpower, the ability to grant people one true wish."

"You never gave me my wish."

"You never asked for anything."

"My mom is having a dinner party tonight. I wish that you would...accompany me."

"Save your wish, I'd go anyway."

"Really?"

"You sound surprised. What time?"

"8 pm? Formal dress."

Bobby paused, "Formal?"

"Is that okay?"

"Yes, sure. 8pm."

"Great. And are you saying I still have my wish?"

"Your wish is solidly intact. So, I'll pick you up at 7:30?"

"Perfect. Wait. My mom said there would be security to clear. How about 7:15?"

"It's a date! I, uh, mean that'll work."

****

Bobby wrapped up work early and was quickly at his place in Butchertown searching through his closets. The hunt was getting desperate. He checked the time: 3:05pm and sent a text to his sister.

BOBBY: do I have a tux at the house?

CASS: new dress code at the sports bar?

BOBBY: yes or no

CASS: yes, mothballed. I'll pull it out

BOBBY: I'll be there in 20 minutes

****

The family home was situated in the Crescent Hill section of town. A nice upper middle-class neighborhood filled with trees and families with kids. It was in the eastern part of Louisville, about five miles from downtown. A lawnmower could be heard, some kids attempted to skateboard and a pickup game of basketball was being played on a driveway down the street. The residences were nice homes with well-kept lawns. A dog barked.

At the end of a cul-de-sac was the Dulsett family home. It wasn't a showpiece, just very comfortable with four bedrooms and solidly middle class. Although they could have lived in the really upscale and luxurious parts of Louisville—farther east—Bobby's father kept the house his parents had owned. It was a way to keep his children grounded. The backyard had plenty of room for a swing, horseshoes, BBQ set and a basketball court.

Cassidy didn't want to sell the family home and decided to live in it.

Bobby pulled up in the driveway. He was pushed for time, but he heard a basketball being bounced. He headed around back and found a 9-year-old boy shooting around.

"Hey, there," said Bobby. "What's your name?"

"My name is Braxton Barns. Cassidy said I could play, is it okay?"

"Sure."

"My family just moved here from Lexington. I saw the court, introduced myself to Cassidy and she gave me permission."

"It's quite alright, Braxton."

"It's not really alright. I'm having a hard time. I thought I was a better shooter. My shot isn't falling."

"I'll let you in on a little secret. Most basketball rims are 18-inches in diameter. This one is 15-inches."

"Why is that?"

"Ervin Stepp."

"Who?"

"One of the greatest high school shooters in the history of Kentucky, even the nation. Ervin's dad was a welder who made the rim smaller for him." Bobby drilled a 3-pointer.

"Wow," said Braxton.

Cassidy stepped out back, "Hi, Braxton."

"Hi, Cassidy. You can call me Brax, all my friends do."

"Okay, Brax. You can call me Cass."

"I now know why I can't hit a shot, it's too small."

"Very little margin of error," commented Cassidy. "The ball, at 9.5-inches in diameter, must enter the cylinder almost exactly in the center. It really sharpens your accuracy."

"That's interesting," remarked Braxton.

"Have you ever heard of Bobby Dulsett?" asked Cassidy.

Braxton gave it some thought, "I think I know that name. One of my uncles, Uncle Craig, said Bobby Dulsett was a great player. But Grandpa said Bobby Dulsett couldn't carry King Coleman's jock strap."

Bobby grunted at that.

Braxton shrugged, "That's what he said. But I don't know what it means. I don't know who they are. I can't say for myself."

Cassidy muttered, "Isn't there anything on YouTube?"

Braxton took another shot and missed. "Drat. That's tough."

Bobby picked up the ball and drilled a 3-pointer.

"Whoa," said Braxton. "How do you do that?"

"First search for a better option among your teammates and feed them the ball where they want it, moving in the flow. If the cupboard is bare and time is running down and you have a decent look, take the shot. Spot the target at the back of the rim, lock-on, line up the elbow, always have the same light feel with your palm and fingertips on the ball, get the hops from your legs and follow through with your wrist."

Bobby buried another 3-pointer.

"Ha! Cool."

"Brax, meet my older brother, Bobby Dulsett."

"Hi," said Bobby.

"Huh? For real? You're this guy Bobby Dulsett?"

"Yes."

"Can I ask you a question?"

"Of course," said Bobby.

Braxton inquired innocently, "Grandpa said you couldn't do it. But are you actually forbidden from carrying King Coleman's jock strap?"

****

Cassidy and Bobby entered the house.

"Kids are so cute, eh?"

"Yeah…" said Bobby, wanting to move on.

"Bobby, I want to see you play horse with Whitney Creech, Caitlin Clark and Hailey Van Lith. We could do a Pay-Per-View."

"No way I'm taking on those three. They're deadly."

Cassidy brought the tux out of the closet. "I was thinking, Bobby. Where do you need to dress formally? Then I remembered that April Arrington is having a big swanky formal to-do tonight at her ranch. Some bigwigs."

"Yes, I'm going. Amy called me today and asked me to accompany her."

Cassidy couldn't contain her glee, "A date!"

"No, I didn't say that."

"With Amy Arrington."

"Just an accompaniment…"

"Face facts. If you're dressing up formally and taking her to a party thrown by her high society mother, it's a date, dork. What happened with you and Nevada?"

"We're taking a break. She has her career, I have mine. We're just so busy."

"I always said you and Amy were destined together. Maybe this will get them from suing us again. Get them on our side."

"Stop. And like Dad would always say, I would ask you to please bridle your tongue, little sis."

Cassidy snickered, "You said, 'bridal.' So freakin Freudian."

Bobby grabbed the tux and took a quick shower. And then he tried on the formal wear and let loose a cry of agony, "Ahhh!!!"

Cassidy came running in, "What happened?? Are you alright??"

"Ahhh! It doesn't fit!" It was literally bursting at the seams.

"Bobby, did you get a dad bod without becoming a dad?"

Bobby groaned and grumbled, "What happened??"

Cassidy was trying not to laugh, "Jocks always put on a few pounds when they retire."

"I play on a league team at the Y."

"Uh-huh and then reward yourself with a burger and some Barley Pops."

"What now??"

Cassidy picked up her phone, "I know a tailor at Sam Meyers, in the Mall St. Matthews and they're open."

****

His dress shirt needed a collar button extender and to be let out around the middle, as well as the jacket and pants. Bobby was sweating. It was accomplished with time to spare. It helped to be Bobby Dulsett; he of course was asked to be in a selfie.

Bobby's BMW pulled up and parked in front of Casa Arrington with a few minutes to spare. He relaxed a bit in his tux and then glanced in the mirror and bummed that at 27 he was still dealing with the occasional zit and or blemish and yet he noticed his first gray hair, *whoa…how can they converge?*

Bobby got out of his car, walked through the gate into CA and came face-to-face with Deveraux the Llama. Both froze, not sure about the other.

While inside Amy descended into the living room in her formal wear. She was wearing an off-the-shoulder black evening dress with a pearl necklace and black stiletto heels—simple, but with Amy wearing it, stunning.

Granddad and Alexander stared.

Amy put the TORTs album on. "Well? What?"

"Magnificent," said Granddad, as he snapped a few pics with his phone.

"Thank you, Granddad."

Alexander took some of his own on his phone. Amy made a goofy face.

"You're as pretty as a peach, Darlin'."

"You mean, one of those mushy ones in the marked down bin, about to go bad?"

"Yes, one of those," he rolled his eyes. She swatted him playfully.

Bobby arrived on the porch and rang the doorbell.

"That must be Bobby," said Amy.

"I'll get it," said Alexander. "One moment." He made a side trip to the den and stowed away the open bottle of Old Forester Classic bourbon at the bar and replaced it with a bottle of Dulsett Reserve bourbon.

Amy observed and rolled her eyes, "We all have our secrets."

Alexander put his finger to his lips signaling to keep that secret. Then he crossed to the front door and opened it. "Bobby, welcome, lad. Come on in."

"Good evening, Alexander."

"You look swell in that tux."

"Thanks."

Amy was dancing to the rhythm. "I like these guys."

"Amy, you look fantastic."

"Why thank you, Bobby. You look quite dashing yourself."

"There he is, Bobby 'sweet shot' Dulsett," Granddad announced. "In the same class as King Kelly and King Rex."

"Sir, please," Bobby said, embarrassed. "Not even close to Kelly Coleman, or Rex Chapman, or Darrell Griffith, or Richie Farmer or Manuel Forrest or Winston Bennet or Chris Lofton."

"Close enough!" exclaimed Alexander.

"I hear some music!" said Bobby.

"When did you make that album, 1977?" teased Alexander.

"I wasn't alive in '77."

They all laughed.

"You even aged the album cover!"

"We made ten LPs. This one is for the Arrington household. I'm glad you guys have a turntable."

"I played Chuck Berry and Little Richard on that turntable," Granddad announced.

"And the Beatles and Stones!" Alexander added.

"And," said Amy, "the Clash, the Boss, My Morning Jacket and now The Ohio River Ticks!"

"Without a doubt, vinyl rules!" declared Alexander emphatically.

"You got that right," said Granddad.

"Would you be interested...in...getting the band back together?" asked Bobby.

"The Ticks?" replied Alexander, with glee. "Yeah, I would."

"We'd need to do some rehearsing," Bobby said. "You know, knock the cobwebs out."

"Definitely," Alexander said, with a look to Amy.

This idea pleased her, "I need one last pit stop before we go. I'll be back ready to go in five minutes." Amy was off.

"That really means 10 minutes," remarked Alexander.

Bobby smiled at that, "Alexander, I've been meaning to ask this, why did you go so far to get a contempt citation and get thrown in jail?"

Alexander stroked his goatee, "You know when you're playing a basketball game and you get a bad call that really puts you behind?"

"Sure," said Bobby.

"Right and then fouling at the right moment where it still gives you a chance instead of letting the clock run out and lose."

Bobby understood, "Intentional fouls at the end to preserve time."

"Exactly. And sometimes it gets you sent to the bench. But it's what you have to do for the team. It takes sacrifices. And we came from behind and won, with the help of Amy."

"I see."

Amy returned promptly, "See, five minutes means five minutes, not ten."

Alexander checked his watch, "You two better get going, you don't want to irritate the hostess."

Amy was looking around, "Except, I can't find the invite, and security is going to be tight."

"I have a feeling your mama's going to let you two in," said Alexander. "Now git."

Amy kissed Granddad and her daddy. Bobby shook their hands. They were off.

"They make a nice-looking couple, don't ya think, son?"

"Daddy, you're preaching to the choir on that subject."

"Gotta go," Granddad got on his bike and put his VR goggles back on.

"Where to?" asked Alexander.

"We're cycling the French Alps. Hello, my dear."

A female voice was heard, "Hello, my sweet."

Alexander stared, not quite into this tech yet; he entered the kitchen, retrieved a barley pop from the fridge, stepped out back and noticed Merlin. The monkey was lounging in a chair, slowly rotating April's invitation, totally fascinated by the hologram.

****

Bobby and Amy arrived at Silver Horse Sanctuary and stopped at a security checkpoint.

Amy recognized one of the security guards, "Hi, Wayne."

"Hello, Miss Amy. And...Bobby Dulsett??"

Bobby nodded, "Hi."

"This is Wayne. He's part of my mom's private security."

"Oh man...Bobby. Wow..." Wayne was having a fanboy moment. "Whoa."

"Breathe, Wayne and give me your phone," Amy advised him. Wayne handed it over. "Scrunch down and I'll take a pic."

"For sure!" Wayne put his face next to Bobby's and they grinned together.

Amy captured the image.

"I appreciate that, Amy. Nice meeting you, Bobby."

"Same here, Wayne."

"My mom sent me an invite and I misplaced it at home."

"That's okay, Miss Amy, go on up."

"Thanks."

They drove down the long winding road to the main house.

"I really admire what your mom does, taking in so many thoroughbreds that aren't wanted anymore. She's an angel."

"Uh-huh," Amy agreed.

They pulled up to the front and a valet took his keys. They approached the house and noticed the front door was open. They entered.

April—formally attired, fabulously coiffed and dripping in diamonds—fidgeted frantically, as she fretted over the messages on her phone. President Ibragimov—formally attired, fit to be tied, a mess over the stress—was checking his messages as well. They paced off each other.

"I can't believe this is happening!" April exclaimed. "They're just turning around and leaving!"

The president was dealing with his own crisis as he screamed into his phone. "Why is internet still on there?? Turn off presently!" He ended the call and growled.

April approached them, "Amy, Bobby, thank God you two are here! Everyone is canceling!"

"Mother, what is *he* doing here?"

"President Ibragimov? The dinner is for him."

"Why didn't you warn me?"

"His name is on the invitation delivered to you. I thought I sent you to law school. Don't you read? He's a legitimate head of state."

"Mother, don't *you* read? How legitimate is he? The man is evil. Why are you honoring him??"

President Ibragimov was not happy with this, he harrumphed.

"Amy, you're just using this to start another fight."

"No, Mother."

Reston stepped into the room and the discussion. "President Ibra...game-off, is one tough cookie. You should see how his staff cowers when he addresses them. It's so cool."

"Reston and I have made brotherhood."

Amy processed this, "Seriously, Reston?"

"I mean, he's never said bad things about me."

"I would never."

Reston shrugged, "And they say he's done all these terrible things. I've never seen any of it. And I don't trust the news."

"I would never do bad things," swore the president.

"I believe him," Reston was smitten.

The president put his arm around Reston, "He is handsome man, with brilliant mind. We will do much business in my country!"

Reston was brimming, "Greg's a great leader!"

A security guard gave the president a phone and whispered in his ear.

"What?? I say turn off internet!" The president paused, "I need to take this." He was back yelling orders into the cell phone on the way to another room, "Turn off electricity presently!"

Alexander strolled in, "You're dancing with the devil, sweet pea."

April stiffened, "Are you behind this social sabotage?"

Alexander folded his arms, "Guilty as charged."

April let it rip, "You've been quite productive, Alexander; you've managed to ruin yet another one of my dinner parties!"

"I read who you're honoring on your invite. You may know everything that happens here in Derby City and the salons of New York, Paris and Milan, but not in the rest of the world. You can thank me later."

"I will thank you to depart the premises or I'll have your presence removed without regard to your dignity."

"Sugar pie, one thing I've adapted to over the years is you not having any regard for my dignity."

April was hurt, "You must be quite pleased with yourself. This dinner was with the A-List of Louisville."

Alexander eyed Reston, "I see some of the C-List made it."

Reston was riled, "I should have known this was your spiteful little stunt. You felt the need to burn all of that electricity to come over and throw a hissy fit?"

"The A-List of Louisville doesn't want to break bread with this tyrant!" stated Alexander. "He's a killer. No friend of this country. April, these Sultans and despots, they're using you to gain some respectability." Alexander pulled out his phone and showed April a story posted on Politico:

Alexander Arrington Hosted Bloodthirsty Fascist Dictator

Alexander pleaded with her, "April, imagine when it got out that you held a dinner honoring this scoundrel and tainted all your friends. It would be the end of your socializing days. You'd be radioactive, darlin.'" He turned to Reston. "You, I don't care."

April's brain was spinning. Amy searched on her phone and showed her mother images of the oppression. April looked to Reston, who realized he lost a great business opportunity and just grunted and shook his head.

April's phone rang and she answered. "Hello? Yes? What? You're from the *Courier-Journal*? Yes, I did cancel the dinner! Why?" She glanced at Amy and then Alexander, "Because after becoming more fully aware of the situation, I realized someone had to stand up to this scalawag! Yes, you certainly may quote me on that!"

She hung up in a huff. Alexander and Reston eyed each other.

Reston went to April's side and rubbed her shoulders. She leaned into him for comfort.

Alexander was jealous and hurt, he still had strong feelings for her. Reston knew it and gloated.

Amy saw the sadness in her dad.

But Alexander put his game face back on with a cocky grin. "My work is done here, for now."

Reston saw Alexander's swagger return and it bugged him. "One second, dear, I'll be right back." Reston zipped in front of Alexander and faced him down. "Don't think you scored any points here. Because, let me tell you—"

"Condor's Claw! Condor's Claw!" yelled Alexander.

Reston stopped and immediately left the room.

April groaned, "I wish you'd stop doing that!"

Bobby turned to Amy and wondered what that was about.

"It's from Reston's college days," replied Amy. "If you're a member of the super-secret organization Claw of the Condor, you're required to shut up and immediately leave the room whenever 'Condor's Claw' is mentioned in public."

"And Alexander has weaponized it," observed Bobby, subtly amused.

President Ibragimov reentered the room, "Alexander."

"Why didn't you tell me she was having a dinner for you?"

"I thought very awkward, she being ex of you. But is true what you do to me? It is you who send out messages tonight and ruin dinner of honor for me?"

"Yes, I just found out at the last minute or I would have sent the warnings out a lot earlier."

"I must announce, our brotherhood is over, presently."

Alexander threw up his arms, "Dang, is that all it took?"

The president announced cryptically, "Maybe I go owl hunting. This time with big gun."

"Just go back under the slimy oily rock you crawled out from," said Amy.

The president chuckled at that, "Your country needs me. Addicted to my product! And yet, still you look down nose at me! Even after I do many things for you people in shining democracy on hill, who wish not to get own hands dirty when you play world like chessboard. Install leader, me, a hero! Then later warranty expires, replace with new friendlier strongman that continues to supply oil you cannot do without! Well, I will not go so easy."

There was silence.

The president now got in Amy's face, "But you know what is huge ironic thing here, Miss Amy? You and I are 'birds of a feather.' The same."

"Hardly! What a joke!"

"You Firewoman! Crush, kill, destroy and eliminate opponents like I do, with efficiency and enjoyment. Much enjoyment."

"Wrong! I do it in the courtroom. *You* do it in a dungeon or on some killing field in a war zone you supplied. There's a huge difference."

The president looked her over with a sneer, "Is only small step up to my league. You will enjoy rush of taking life, taste blood. We are same."

"That's so sick! Shut up!" yelled Amy.

Alexander moved to stop this, but Bobby was there first. "Okay that's enough, pal," said Bobby, leaning into him. "Move on."

The president's security team didn't let him get any closer.

Amy was disgusted, but held everything in check.

Alexander didn't and was about to explode, "'*Oh, let me not be mad, not mad, sweet heaven, keep me in temper...*'"

"After quit with the talking funny, we settle this man facing man, with fists, yes? Be mad."

"Whoa!" said Amy. "You're 10 years younger and at least 30 pounds heavier."

"Not to mention twice as rude and three times as ugly!" declared Alexander.

Amy surveyed his security team, "And you've got your boys as back up."

"I forbid my boys, any boys from jumping in! Is that good enough for deal? Or maybe you have your owl step in, speak *and* fight for you too."

His boys laughed at that.

Alexander snorted, "Deal." He glanced at Bobby. "No boys or bird participation and then snarled at the president: '*When the blast of war blows in our ears, then imitate the action of the tiger: Stiffen the sinews, summon up the blood.*'"

"More with funny talk!"

"Enough Shakespeare," stated Amy. "Perhaps we don't go to the breach and step back and let this pass. Daddy, is this really a good thing?"

"It is indeed." Alexander threw some practice jabs to warm up. He set himself and they began to spar.

"Someone please play music of Rocky!" yelled the jolly president as he put up his dukes.

His security team laughed.

Alex punched him solidly on the nose. "I declare! That's for inappropriately touching my daughter's derrière, you cad!"

The president, as well as his security team, were surprised by this.

Alexander landed another shot to his jaw. "That's for wanting me to do something underhanded at the sacred grounds of Churchill Downs!"

This rattled the bear of a man. He recovered, swooped in, grabbed Alexander and slammed him violently to the ground.

"Daddy! You, okay??" asked Amy, quite nervously.

Alexander was dazed, he groaned.

The president reared back. Bobby again moved in, but two security guards waylaid him to the ground.

The president saw, grinned and followed through on the coup de grace—until a thud was heard. He froze. From the president's backside, Amy had kicked with substantial upward force smashing into the president's groin. He was stupefied. Time stopped. Little squeaks emitted from his mouth. He tipped over in a catatonic state.

Amy sheepishly turned to his stunned security team, "In the agreement, boys and owls were barred. Technically there was no stipulation limiting 'girls' from jumping in." She shrugged, "Loopholes. I'm a lawyer."

One bodyguard moved to get Amy, but Bobby sprang up and tackled the guy to the floor.

Alexander regained his wits and heard something, "Stop…stop, listen!"

Everyone froze. Merlin walked in carrying a radio: "We repeat the breaking news, reacting to the severe and punitive crackdown by government troops, rebel forces in the northwestern Asian country of Khrakistan, have succeeded in overthrowing President Ibragimov who has held power for over 25 years."

Alexander stood and tried to jump for joy, but was in no condition. He did a half cheer, "Yay! Give me liberty or give me death!" He grimaced in pain.

The now ex-president, flopping on the ground, straining from the groin shot, moaned with confusion. "But how? How is possible? I am president for life."

13

It was 11:08pm when Bobby got Amy back to Casa Arrington. He parked and walked her to the front door.

"I had a great time, thanks for inviting me."

"Bobby, I'm sorry how it turned out."

"No, I'm serious. I really had a great time tonight. I mean, because I was with you."

Amy smiled at that and nodded. "I feel the same, being with you."

They moved closer and kissed.

Inside CA, Alexander was quiet, smoking a cigar and waiting with Gabe in the parlor—they were dressed in black.

Amy entered, "Where's the circus?"

"Pulled up stakes," reported Gabe.

Alexander had a hint of melancholy, "The jugglers, the clowns, Deveraux, Merlin and Sven are gone."

"Daddy, you recall a wise man once told you, 'I have to leave, in order to make my return.'"

Alexander smiled at that memory, "Dann."

"Daddy, I have a feeling that's not the last we're going to see of Merlin, Deveraux and Sven, as long as it's just them."

"How was the party?" asked Gabe. "I can't get anything from Alexander."

Amy stared at her father, "Quite a memorable time."

Gabe was reading off his phone, "There's a bunch of negative stuff being posted about Alexander and the bloodthirsty dictator at Casa Arrington."

Amy thought about that, "But not about mom or SHS."

Alexander puffed away on his stogie nonchalantly, "Someone's always taking a poke at me."

"I'll be ready for the stakeout in a jiff," said Amy, as she zipped into her room and changed into black sportswear and black Chuck Taylors. She pulled her hair back and donned a black University of Louisville baseball cap.

They were out the door by 11:38pm.

****

Sienna locked the house up and turned on the alarm for the night knowing she was being observed. Sean dropped the surveillance from behind a pillar and retreated back to his room filled with high-tech toys. He tapped on some tunes: Rad Ransom's "Return to Domination Station." Through Rad's thunderous cascading guitar riffs, Sean now assumed his alter-ego: Gokuro Gangsta. He garbed himself in green, slicked his hair back with gel and stepped into his silver cowboy boots. He used his phone to reroute the alarm system around the far corner of his room. He opened his bedroom window in that area and slipped out into the night.

****

The van was parked, away from any street lights, almost completely in the dark. Amy, Alexander and Gabe were inside.

Alexander read some material on his phone, "Pan is said to be very strong and can run for a long period of time. He wouldn't have to go far, he's pretty close to Sean's house."

"Pan's still our number one suspect, Daddy?"

"The other gods ridiculed Pan for his appearance," Alexander reasoned. "Which caused him to withdraw. Pan is said to be really horny and chases nymphs around who have no inclination to hook up with him."

"Probably just a bunch of Staceys," cracked Amy. "Maybe Pan is the god of the Incels."

They waited a few minutes and then a car rolled up. A colorful figure appeared from the shadows and stepped under the streetlight and got in.

They observed from the van.

"I think that was Sean," Amy stated. "He's in a green jacket, in silver cowboy boots and his hair is slicked back."

"It looks like he's dressed up as Gokuro Gangsta," said Gabe.

"Who?" asked Alexander.

"Yeah, who?" Amy also asked.

Gabe searched on his phone and showed them an image of Gokuro Gangsta wearing a green outfit, silver cowboy boots, shades with slicked back hair.

"The character is from the video game 6D. Delilah's Delightfully Delicious Downtown Digital Dungeon. I've played it a couple times. The description of the Gokuro Gangsta avatar is: 'Behold a gambling man, with a killa' grin, the ladies latch on 'cause he's in for the win. All can plainly see that GG is royalty! Sports silver kicks, green drawers, with a green jacket, 'cause greenbacks this dog's racket.'"

Alexander and Amy stared at him blankly.

The cab took off and drove for about 15 minutes and dropped off Gokuro Gangsta.

Gabe, Amy and Alexander watched as he strolled up, pressed the buzzer to the house, spoke into a mic and was clicked in.

"I think that's the Riverboat," Gabe surmised. "A rolling high-stakes match of Texas Hold 'em. You need the unique friendly phrase that gets you past the guard dogs, that bite, hard."

Alexander pondered, then made a call. "Hey, Stu. I need to know something..."

****

Inside the location five players were sitting around the table in the middle of a hand. In the reception area a buzzer was heard. The security team glanced at the screen. Alexander, Amy and Gabe were there.

Alexander leaned into the microphone, "Humpty Dumpty sat on the wall."

The door buzzed and they went in. The bouncers ran a wand over them scanning for weapons. The lead guy was Dante, an imposing well-built 35-year-old Black gentleman, dressed in an expensive dark suit. He brightened when he recognized his friend, "Alexander!"

"Dante!"

They hugged.

"Welcome to the Riverboat." Dante turned to the other security guards. "They're cool."

The other guys stopped checking them.

Alexander admired his suit, "Nice threads."

"Thanks."

Alexander felt his bulging arms, "Where did you get the alterations done, big man?"

"Cavalier."

"Sergey?"

"Yes."

"He does good work. He lets *your* arms out and *my* waist." They laughed. "This is my daughter Amy."

"Hi, Amy, I've heard a lot about you," said Dante.

"I'm not sure if that's good," Amy remarked, as they shook hands.

"All I've heard is great things."

"You're not getting the whole story," said Amy.

Dante laughed.

Alexander motioned over, "And our essential associate, Gabriel." He nodded.

"You folks want to try some wine? We're having a tasting here tonight."

Alexander shook his head, "I don't think so..."

"We have some Bourbon Barrel Red, from the Old 502 winery."

Alexander's eyes perked up and he tilted his head, "Bourbon Barrel Red?"

"From right around the corner." Dante snapped his fingers. An assistant arrived with a platter of cheese and several glasses of red wine.

Alexander sipped, "Excellent."

Amy took a glass, tasted and nodded in agreement.

"I'm driving," said Gabe, begging off.

Dante put his arm around Alexander, "They were trying to evict my grandmother for not paying rent, but the landlord wouldn't make the repairs so she was refusing to pay. Alexander stepped in, got the place cleaned up, the repairs made and had better security installed."

Amy was struck by this and pleased at the outcome. She patted her father's shoulder, "That's my Dad."

"It was my pleasure," said a smiling Alexander. "Just to get some of her sweet potato pie is more than I deserve. How's she doing?"

"Much better, thanks to you. I am very appreciative."

"That's great. Tell her I said hi."

"I will."

Alexander rubbed his hands together in anticipation. "Okay gang, let's play some poker."

"That'll be $25,000, each."

They paused, not expecting it to be so high.

"25 large buy-in. I'm sorry, Alexander, but they're tight with the books here."

"I understand, Dante."

The three huddled off to the side.

"That's a bit steep," said Alexander. "Let's wait this one out."

"Daddy, have another glass and you and Gabriel sample some more hors d'oeuvres. I'll go." She pulled out a credit card.

"American Express Black Card," Gabe swooned, totally stoked. "I've never actually seen one of these in person. No limit. Boom."

"Just have a big fat trust fund and it's yours," quipped Amy.

Gabe glanced at Alexander.

"It didn't come from me."

Amy handed the card to Dante. "One, please."

He ran the charges and it was approved. "Welcome and good luck."

"Thank you." Amy noticed his sunglasses on a table. "How much for your shades?"

"They're yours for being Alexander's daughter," Dante happily exclaimed.

Amy—now wearing the shades, with her hair pulled back and wearing the U of L baseball cap—joined the game.

Sean, with his Gokuro Gangsta threads, slicked back hair and shades, didn't recognize her. He was too focused on his cards and dwindling stake.

Time passed. Amy had won a nice pile of chips. Sean leered at her and she smirked at him. More time passed. Amy was up more. Sean had nearly run through his stack and was getting really frustrated.

Gabe and Alexander ate pie and followed closely.

"You taught her to skateboard and also play poker?"

"Skateboarding enhances her balance and grace. Poker is helpful in life and essential in the law."

They noticed Dante step into the room and whisper in Sean's ear. He was led out of the main room and down a back hallway.

"I need a break," said Amy. She pulled out a scarf, scooped up her chips and stuffed them into her pocket. She joined Alexander and Gabe, "What's going on with Sean?"

"We need to find out," responded Alexander. "You two hang here."

Dante led Sean to a back room and had him sit at a small steel table. A large mirror was on the wall. Dante exited down the hallway where Alexander was waiting.

"Alexander, why are you back here?"

"That kid owes my client a large chunk of cash."

"Your client isn't the only one."

"I need a little favor. Could you make some inquiries on our behalf?

****

Amy, Alexander and Gabe entered a side room and could see through the two-way mirror that showed the interrogation space. Sean, in his silver kicks, green drawers and jacket and slicked back hair, sat nervously on the rather uncomfortable steel chair and fidgeted. He snuck glimpses of himself in the large mirror on the wall.

Ralfie, a brute of a man in a cheap suit, entered, sat at a corner desk and began cracking walnuts. Sean flinched.

"You two will want to film this," said Alexander.

Amy and Gabe got out their phones and began capturing the scene.

Ralfie casually crunched a couple more nuts before pausing, "Kid, why should I extend even more credit to you? You're back up to 40 large in the hole here."

"Yo dog," said Sean, still attempting to be in character. "You know I'm good for it."

Ralfie thought about that, "Dog?"

Sean quickly humbled himself, "I mean, sir."

Ralfie pulled his chair around and sat right in front of Sean. "There has to be a way for you to scrounge up some more money."

"I can get more. I have an amount transferred to me every month."

"An allowance from your parents? You need to pay the kitty now, she's hungry."

"Come on, I laid $50,000 on you today, didn't I?"

"How'd you get that chunk of change?"

"I had this scam set up to sell the sperm of Secretariat and—"

"Wait, some bozo paid you $50K for this?"

"Yes."

"What a dumb ass," snorted Ralfie.

Amy snickered.

"It was sperm," smirked Sean, "but it wasn't from Secretariat, or any horse."

Ralfie frowned.

Amy cringed, "Eeoow... That was in our freezer."

Alexander and Gabe tried to contain their grimaces and grins.

"Why don't you scam one of your dad's employees! Don't you have a Mexican or two working for you?"

"I've already done that! That was the $10K I gave you a month ago."

"And how'd you pull that off?"

"That's it, I pulled them out! I yanked out the eight Bonsai Trees that were planted on a full moon. Got dressed up as Pan and blamed it on him."

Alexander, Amy and Gabe nodded with big grins.

"Isn't the contractor suing you?"

"Yeah, I kept hiding the letters from the lawyer that came to the house. But they finally found my dad, who's not in the country, and he wanted it over with and then I heard they're going to fight."

Alexander grumbled, "Reston."

Ralfie leaned in with a scowl, "Go home, Gokuro Gangsta. You need to break open your piggy bank and bring more greenbacks to the table, dog. And don't forget, we know where you live."

****

Amy spent a good bit of the night and early morning, immersing herself in the strategy and lore of Delilah's Delightfully Delicious Downtown Digital Dungeon.

It was early the next morning when Alexander and Amy paid their visit. She wore the same hat and sunglasses. Sean came to the door and recognized her from the game. Amy took off her disguise.

Sean's face fell as he realized he'd been tricked. "It was you last night, at the game…"

Amy showed him her phone and played the scene of Sean bragging: "That's it, I pulled them out! I yanked out the eight Bonsai Trees that were planted on a full moon. Got dressed up as Pan and blamed it on him."

Sean was stunned. "That can't be admissible in court."

Alexander's eyebrows raised up, "Excellent, Master Sean wants to debate the finer points of jurisprudence. This will be a great episode for my blog."

"That's right, Daddy, you do have a blog. And a lot of people subscribe to it."

"Torts and Just Desserts. It's where I comment, through Alexander the Antithetical Owl, on criminality, culture and custard. It's becoming very popular." Alexander turned back to Sean, "Perhaps this video might not be admissible in a court of law, but in the court of public opinion, as content for social media, how might that play?"

"Fine. Hold off posting it. I'll settle the problem," said Sean. "Let me talk to my lawyer. I'll be back to you shortly."

****

9 miles to the east of downtown Louisville was the town of Lyndon, a home-rule city that was part of the Louisville metro government. Alexander

took Amy to lunch at one of their favorite eating establishments: Joe's Older Than Dirt. They were both happy to see the moose statue again out front. Alexander had taken little Amy to the old Joe's Older Than Dirt and then it became the Red Barn Kitchen, which banished the moose and now it was the new Joe's Older Than Dirt, with the moose back on duty welcoming the hungry patrons.

It was a lovely summer day and they sat outside on the patio. Both had seen several bands perform in this location, including TORTs, which had played here twice a couple years ago. Alexander did show up at Joe's on a few Mondays for trivia night.

Amy pulled out her phone. "Let's see...Torts and Just Desserts..."

"Don't read it now, sweetie, later."

"That's cool. Phones off."

They both disconnected and stowed their exterior communication devices and focused on in-person interchange.

"I have some very pertinent questions," Alexander mused. "It's been nearly two years, where has the moose been all this time? What tales does he have to tell?"

Amy was snickering at that, "He's not talking."

"I've heard rumors that it's an entirely new moose," stated Alexander. "But I believe it's the same one. Just had some work done. Little nip and tuck and now he's looking fabulous."

"You go right on believing that, Daddy."

"It gives me hope for myself!"

"You're just getting more distinguished, while I'm getting wrinkles."

"You're the fairest lass in all these parts."

"You're already talking gibberish and you haven't even started imbibing."

Alexander knew better than to pry any further into her social life—she got enough of that from her mother. If she wanted to share anything, he would listen.

Alexander ordered his usual Fried Green Tomato BLT and Amy got the Veggie Wrap.

He took a bite of his sandwich and looked down his nose at her, "I just wanted to pass along the news that U.S. News ranked my Manual the number one academic high school in Kentucky ahead of your Brown School, in second place."

"Where did Male High School place?"

"8th."

"You didn't tease Judge Winslow, did you?"

"Of course I did."

"That probably wasn't so pleasant."

"No, it wasn't. He told me, 'There's 538 high schools in the state. The academic differences in the top ten is almost a rounding error. The Old Rivalry between Male and Manual football teams started in 1893, Male beat Manual then. The current ledger has Male at 85 wins and Manual 45. And Male High School has won the last 5 in a row. That's more than a rounding error.'"

"Ouch," laughed Amy, with a sardonic grin.

"I have learned in the many years walking and talking on this earth, one should take care and definitely think twice, even thrice, debating or dueling an opponent that's so better armed than one's self. And if you tell the judge I said that, I'll deny it."

Amy and Alexander both had a pleasant lunch chatting about a number of things. They discussed the Louisville City FC club in the United Soccer League. They had won two USL championships in a row. It was the final season at Slugger Field, a converted baseball park, where they had season tickets. LouCity would be moving to their own place, designed for their game, in Butchertown—and Alexander had secured much better seats. He had from the start been pushing for a soccer-specific stadium. Alexander loved going to the Bats games in their baseball park, but it didn't really work for other sports. And although he liked the USL, he was pushing for Louisville FC to join Major League Soccer.

Alexander was also a political junkie, so local, state, national and international maneuverings and machinations were discussed as they chowed down—at least in between the frequent flatterings from his fan club that moseyed up for a chat and a pic. And as always Alexander made his daughter laugh, at times uncontrollably, with reports and recollections of his antics in and out of the courtroom.

Finally, as they were finishing, Alexander pulled out his phone and turned it on. "I'm going to check with Mrs. Simmons and see if there's anything we can bring home."

Mrs. Simmons was heard answering her phone and things were a miss, "Alexander? I've been trying to get a hold of you."

"Yes? What's wrong?"

"You better get home. We have a situation like never before! Deep-fried crickets with powdered sugar??"

Alexander's eyes widened with concern, "Say, what?"

Amy saw, "What? What's going on?

****

Arriving back at CA they found quite a gathering. Alexander and Amy had to push through an eclectic and spirited collection of individuals—more than a few offering deep-fried crickets with powdered sugar on them.

Mrs. Simmons was mystified, "The phone has been ringing off the hook by people wanting to enlist."

"Enlist in what?" asked Alexander.

Amy was reading on her phone, "I just found today's offering on Torts and Just Desserts."

"I haven't posted anything in a couple days."

Amy played the post on her tablet. Instead of an owl, a hideous neon green lizardman creature appeared and began to speak:

"I, Alexander Arrington, now having a blog, Torts and Just Desserts, believe it is the right time for me to come forward and confess to being one of the lizard people that you've all heard about. It's happening. The takeover has begun. I am putting out the call for volunteers for the Lizard Brigade that will be the security force that will be in charge. I ask only the serious to respond and show up. Here is my phone number and the address of my home. Call or come by."

~ ~ ~

"As for my dessert choice, who could go wrong with some deep-fried crickets with powdered sugar drizzled over them. That sounds yummy!"

Alexander was stunned.

"Daddy did you get drunk and do this as a prank?"

"No!" Alexander flipped open a laptop and was furiously tapping away on the keyboard. After several attempts, he sat back, quite concerned. "I'm trying to access the site now and I'm locked out." He paused and considered the ramifications. "Someone is communicating in my name and I have no say over it." Alexander had a rare moment where he felt powerless.

The phone continued to ring. Amy picked it up, "Hello?"

"Would you please tell Alexander I'm ready to join up! And I'm sending over some deep-fried crickets!" The voice cackled with laughter and hung up.

"How do I get the blog taken down?" asked a very glum Alexander.

"Give me your login password and your recovery email and phone number."

"I'll be right back." Alexander blankly trudged into his den, pulled out a sheet of paper hidden among a mountain of files and gave her the information.

"Daddy, it's not the end of the world. People get hacked all the time."

Amy tapped away and then paused. "They've changed the password, recovery email and phone number."

Alexander grimaced, held his head and shuffled off out of the room.

****

A little bit later Amy found Alexander sitting out back, slumped in a chair.

"Daddy, I did some basic computer forensics and found out some stuff. The hack took place earlier this morning, right after we confronted Sean with the incriminating video."

Alexander was furious, "I want to march back over right now and have the confrontation!"

"I don't think so. You're already skating on very thin ice with the Kentucky Bar."

Alexander stewed, "Could this be an attempt to get my law license suspended or worse?"

Amy wondered what kind of rabbit hole her father had descended into this time.

****

That evening Amy secretly promised Mitch Bats baseball tickets if he volunteered to watch the kids. The DDs reunited at another of their haunts, the Garage Bar, a former auto service garage that was true to its roots on Market. It was a lovely summer eve and they were sitting out on the patio, sipping Barley Pops. Amy was sullen over the lizard blowback they were dealing with at CA. Being with The DDs smoothed things over for this brief moment. They were soon laughing about earlier encounters: partying with the ghosts in Sauerkraut Cave, skinny dipping in the neighbor's pool at midnight, and the time they climbed the Maker's Mark water tower in Lebanon. In a small town, an hour south in Kentucky, was located what The DDs deemed the coolest water tower in the country. Muralist Eric Henn painted a giant bottle of Maker's Mark on the side of the structure doing a long pour down to the base.

After The DDs made it to the top of the structure, they were arrested for trespassing when they returned to the bottom.

Alexander made a phone call and got the charges dropped. They breathed easier until they found out Alexander committed The DDs to volunteering the full seven days of the Marion County Fair. They were to work the animal clean-up crew from 7am to 10pm.

At the time it was quite challenging. They quickly became familiar with bulls, cows, steers and heifers. They busted up laughing recalling the prolific output, regularity and variety of dung, as well as the various 'scents' emanating from the large gathering of livestock on the scene.

"Smelled Straight," claimed Gabby. "It cured me of doing any really goofy-crazy stuff. Now I only do 'sort of' goofy things."

Abby and Amy shared looks of doubt over this.

"Try being a mother," said Abby. "You should see or smell some of those laundry encounters."

Amy and Gabby cringed and howled with laughter at that.

****

The DDs were next let off on Bardstown Road at the Bambi Bar, considered one of Louisville's best dives. It was a Démener Diva tradition to consume the 'almost famous' Bambi Burger.

Amy was chewing on her sandwich and the problem, "You still a gamer, Gab?"

"Yep, still going at it."

"I don't play," said Abby. "But my kids will no doubt be into it soon."

"What do you play?" asked Amy.

"Some Fortnight and 6D."

"We have a problem. Someone is bullying my Dad. I believe he's using the Gokuro Gangsta avatar in 6D."

"You don't say," commented Gabby. "We can't have that."

"Do you know many players of the game?"

"Honey, I have an entire battalion that follows me."

Amy mulled that over, “Gab, I have an idea.”

14

It was just after dawn on the 4th of July. Amy was up and gazing out the window at the first streaks of light in the sky. It was going to be a nice day. And then she saw her father in the shadows below, quietly exiting his side door. She thought he might be going off to a workout.

She got into a tracksuit, got a power smoothie stored in the fridge and got out on this cool summer morning. She checked in with Gabby and learned what a productive evening it was for her and her followers.

Amy started with a brisk stroll and then shifted to a slow jog. Her body was warming up and she eased into a longer stride. Finally, she pushed it and entered Cherokee Triangle, ran up to Sean's place and banged on his side door.

He answered, dazed and disoriented.

Amy was trying to catch her breath, "Morning, Sean. Happy 4th."

"Hi, Stacey, same to you."

"Sorry to interrupt your blogging… But you're probably dying to hear about my date with Chad."

"Did he bend you over the hood of his still hot car?"

Amy was finally recovering from her run, "Hmm, that sounds interesting. I want to get a handle on this. You're angry because a chick like me isn't interested in you. Suppose I told you that I've had it with the players and I was seeking something solid. Are you ready to settle down, commit to one person, me? Are you ready to be a provider?"

"What?"

"I'm wasting my time if you're not thinking the same way. You mention how upset you are, how society has changed with women becoming liberated. Are you able to go out into the workplace and earn enough cheddar for your family to live a comfortable life? We'll need our own place.

And a vacation home. A traditional 'Stacey' of my status would demand that."

Sean was considering, "I don't want any of that."

"Ah, then it's only a momentary exchange of bodily fluids and then...?"

"You're gross."

"But that's what you want. The free will of females set aside to satisfy your desires. However, after reading your many comments while playing 6D, I find it odd that you slut-shame women that are submitting to *other's* desires."

Sean growled, "We should go back to a more conservative society. Women have changed!"

"You're angry that we've become too open. Too independent."

"Yes!"

"Too liberal."

"Yes!!!"

"And you're angry at hot girls for not having sex with you."

"Yeah! I hate these bitches! They're so stupid and shallow," Sean grabbed his belly. "I'm too fat and ugly for them. I always have been. They laughed at me all through high school."

"Genetics is a cruel game," agreed Amy. "Teenage girls for the most part *are* shallow. Guilty as charged. I sure was."

Sean shook his head, genuinely mystified, "There are dudes that have killed and maimed people, but they look handsome and cute. And girls are pleading and crying that he's too beautiful to be put away for 24 years. If he was a schlub, a schmuck, a wimp or a pathetic geek, he'd be locked away and ignored, like he already was in life."

"But, Sean, with women, there's a maturation process that occurs and we want different things."

"I'm still a virgin. Nothing's changed."

"If you just want to have sex, there are places you can go. But it's not free. Like anything in this life. Just set up an account and show up twice, three times a week. Problem solved."

"I don't want a hooker."

"You want a relationship."

"I want a girlfriend."

"Have you worked on yourself to make yourself attractive to someone?"

"I'm not a Chad."

"Let me tell you, a lot of Chads are too self-centered to be a decent partner. I'm just saying we all can improve ourselves somehow, no one is perfect."

"And hope to be beta-buxxed?"

Amy pondered, "I don't know that one."

"Look, I'm a Blackpiller. I'm too tired and it won't work anyway."

"That I know. I'm aware of Blackpill philosophy. You see what's going on, you understand the ramifications and it's all crap, nothing can be done, just deal with it."

"There you go, Stacey."

"Sean, you're 20. You've barely started, giving up already? And do you even know about what you so crave? When you have a girlfriend, and you're in a relationship, you help each other to survive and hopefully thrive. And there's a required give and take. Some don't like to compromise and that leads to problems, on both sides."

"First off, I don't want a woman my age. By now she's had a thousand relationships and she's been screwed over and messed up by multiple Chads."

"Let me get this straight, you want someone naïve, subservient, innocent, adoring and hot with the mental development of a 17-year-old. That will service you in bed, not ask any questions and still have the morals from the 1950s. That sounds like some mythical unicorn."

"It's always ridicule from the Staceys. You're annoying and talk way too much. That's why I'm into the young bitches."

"It makes you just want to retreat to your safe space. But what happens when you can't get there? Must not feel too good, eh, GG?"

Sean was rattled by this. "You… You did this? You went after me in 6D??"

"Having some problems in your cyberplace?"

"A vicious velvet vegan vigilante squad jumped me from some secret portal. I've been captured and locked in some dungeon. I don't even know what level…"

"It's Subterranean Level 137. Boy, that's pretty deep," Amy said. "One of those places where the sun doesn't shine."

Sean was stunned and then angry and then frustrated.

Amy smirked, "I took out my 36-ounce Louisville Slugger and gave you a whack, virtually."

Fear was creeping into Sean's eyes.

"But that was only my first swing." Amy moved closer, "After my second swing you're out for a month. And then at three strikes you're banned from 6D, for life."

Sean was mortified at the thought of losing his world. "What do you want?"

"You know what I want. Drop the complaint you made, the harassment online and make it right for our client on his invoice."

"Just cut him a check for ten thousand dollars? Just like that?"

"You lost, what, triple that the other night? Am I right, Gokuro Gangsta?"

Amy leaned in, "Behold a gambling man, with a killa' grin, the ladies latch on 'cause he's in for the win.' Are you winning? Or whining? Ladies don't like that."

This struck a nerve, "Fine. I get it. I'll have the complaint withdrawn."

"And for hacking into my father's blog. I think we should sue you for 10 million and settle for this house."

"I won't do it again and the thing I posted was just a simple prank."

"A simple prank? The lizard post. Doxxing my father. I think the courts would see this as a sophisticated attack."

"Hardly. I'm not that tech oriented, really. I just went looking on Black Fungus on the Darknet. Some vendors will even walk you through the hack, like with me."

"You defamed my father and his client."

"Look, any reasonable person would not believe what I said, so do you think it'll hold up in court?"

Amy mulled that over and had some trouble with it. "That's your excuse? Only the nutty are on board with you?"

Sean had a sweet smile.

Amy matched his grin, "You know, after all the crap you pulled, I think 25 grand should cover things."

Sean transitioned to a sour frown, "I can pay you in Vidarcoin."

"Cryptocurrency?"

Sean nodded, "It's all I have left."

Amy pondered, "Okay, this is what you're going to do…"

****

Amy came back from her run, took a shower and helped Mrs. Simmons and Granddad feed the animals and plants. A little while later Alexander exited his room fresh from a shower, dressed smartly in tan slacks and a University of Louisville Cardinal Colosseum Red Santry Polo shirt. "Morning all. Happy 4th of July!"

"Morning, Daddy. Same to you. You look nice."

"Thank you."

"Good morning, Alexander. Yes, Happy 4th to you," Mrs. Simmons said, with her warm smile.

"Glad you could join us, it's 12 noon," Granddad groused.

"Apologies, long nights," Alexander replied, now checking messages on his phone.

"You've been sleeping in a lot lately, son. You can bet George Washington's men didn't sleep in when they were fighting the British!"

Alexander paused and politely stated, "And Daddy, we're saluting them today for allowing us that freedom."

Amy declined to cross-examine after witnessing him leave the premises around 5am this morning.

Alexander found a message that quite surprised him: "150,000,000 in cryptocurrency?"

Amy was reading the LEO Weekly on her tablet, "Say what, Daddy?"

"Is this serious? I just got an email from Sean. He bypassed Reston and sent me Vidarcoin, 150,000,000 of it."

"Very serious," said Amy. "It converts to 25,000 in dollars. 12 for Rubén plus an extra 5 grand as a punitive hand slap and 8 grand for your fee. I believe you went above and beyond on this one. When it was only for a..."

"A small amount?"

"Well, yeah."

"It wasn't a small amount to Rubén. And his reputation was on the line here."

Amy reflected on that and nodded, "I understand."

"I have been doing this for some time and what I don't understand is the offer to settle is *always* lower than the amount tussled over, not higher. Which is what just occurred here. Would you be so kind as to diagram the play you ran that got us to this point."

"Certainly. Allow me to allay your fears concerning the corpus delicti. I can emphatically state for the record, in no uncertain terms, assure you prima facie…"

Alexander whistled, "Hoo-doggy, I reckon that's some mighty fine, high-priced, smooth New York polished, legal yammering."

"No local, state or federal laws were broken."

"Good. Great!" exclaimed Alexander.

"But…"

"What?"

"Daddy, you are the attorney of record and being an officer of the court in the Commonwealth of Kentucky, you are bound by ethics and certain boundaries, that you—*mostly*—follow. I'm not a member of the bar here. I needed to color outside the lines—*a smidge*—to make the picture right."

"Uh-huh…"

"In the gray area."

"Oh..."

"At times we go places and do things we don't always share with others, right?"

"Fruit of the poisoned tree?" asked Alexander, delicately.

"No, no poison," Amy assured. "The video has been released of Sean confessing, proving Rubén's honesty, hopefully restoring some goodwill to his business and payment has been transferred. Plus, you have control over your blog again and a statement explaining the 'slightly unusual content' that was posted was due to a massive hack."

"You did all that, Amy?"

"Don't worry, you won't have to make any phone calls to get me out of trouble or volunteer me for anything."

"No volunteering?"

"I might volunteer on my own, though. The fair is coming up."

"For the livestock clean-up crew?"

"I had so much fun I might do it again. But maybe not the entire seven days."

Alexander grinned at that and all she had accomplished. "Good work, kiddo." He got a chime on his phone and checked it. "What? No… I don't believe this."

"What, Daddy?"

"Rubén is taking the oath of citizenship this afternoon."

"Yes?"

"He just got picked up by ICE agents a few moments ago."

"No way." Amy received a text and read it. "I just got a message from Sean, he said he couldn't stop it."

Alexander growled, "Sean did this??" He grabbed his keys, "Rubén has to make the swearing in."

"Daddy, where are you going?"

"I have a tee-time," Alexander said, out the door.

Amy joined Mrs. Simmons and Granddad who were equally confused, "Since when does Alexander play golf?"

****

The sun was up in the Eastern sky, the temperature rose and the humidity hung thick on this bright Fourth of July morning. Alexander's EV flew south on Robin Road. He loved the lush landscape of the area and the substantial collection of American Flags lining the houses celebrating the country's birth. It was one of his favorite times of the year. But he really couldn't savor it, he was on a mission.

He pulled into the Audubon Country Club and found a place to park in the visitor's lot. He wasn't a member, but knew several arriving for early golf games and tennis lessons—and a couple of the custodial and maintenance guys greeted him as well. He helped several get jobs and assisted others with the legal system.

Alexander was pleasant and friendly, but he needed to make it out to the pro shop. He arrived with a few minutes to spare and checked in with a buddy, the caddy master.

"Royce!"

"Alexander!"

They fist bumped.

"How are things here in paradise, Royce?"

"Things are good."

"How's the shoulder?"

"Better. My putting has been primo."

"Staying away from—"

"Alexander, I promise you I haven't been back to that place. It was all a misunderstanding. I went with my brother-in-law. I didn't know that it was…"

"That it was the bar for the notorious biker gang Odin's Enablers."

"Right. I mean, I did see some women there in leather at first and this one babe was so friendly. I thought it was a fetish club, not where Odin's Enablers hang out."

"I talked to Sigi."

"Sigi?"

Two women in golf outfits strolled by. Alexander nodded to them with his charm and they smiled back. "Local Chieftain of OE."

Royce whispered, "Really, I didn't know she was his girlfriend."

"No. It was Warthog's woman. Seriously, I can tell you some stories about that dude."

"Warthog?" Royce quietly repeated.

"One of the enforcers of OE."

Royce held his chest, "Alexander, I swear, she was hitting on me."

"I believe you. Anyhoo… I convinced Sigi to order Warthog not to burn down your house, as long as you stay out of Indiana."

"Got it. Thank you, Alexander."

"Now, is Judge Winslow's tee-time at 10:30?"

Royce checked the book, "Yes, in just a few minutes."

"And he's playing with Judge Ramsey?"

Royce double checked and nodded.

Alexander glanced around and saw golfers warming up their swing and putting on a practice tee. He liked the game of golf, but didn't play. Alexander took it up in his college days and then retched his lower back, which caused him to suffer for weeks. After he recovered, he tried the sport again, which had the same torturous result. He stuck to something he had been doing since he was 5-years-old and much safer for him: skateboarding.

Alexander kept a sharp eye peeled and then caught sight of Judge Winslow.

"Happy 4th, Your Honor."

"Same to you, Alexander. You know, I just got a call. A video's been posted on the internet of Sean Wellington confessing to ripping off your client. It has over 50,000 hits already."

"Your Honor, I believe the phrase is 'it's gone viral.'"

"I thought the demi-god Pan was responsible for the pilferage."

"Yes, Your Honor, my thoughts exactly. But Pan has an alibi; apparently, he was on the base of his statue in Cherokee Park."

"Why are you here?"

"I need to ask you a favor."

"Which is?"

"It's not for me, Your Honor. It's for my client, Rubén Sanchez. A family man about to get his citizenship, picked up on a bogus warrant, that's been withdrawn. He's being held right now and it'll take a day or two to process him through."

"Then it's a federal matter."

"You're going to play a round with Judge Ramsey. He has jurisdiction. It would be so sad if Rubén missed his swearing in on the 4th of July over the 'slow as molasses grind of bureaucracy in today's blink of an eye world.'"

The judge straightened up, "You're quoting me from an earlier opinion I wrote."

"Yes, Your Honor, I read all of your opinions."

The judge nodded to himself, it felt good.

"The swearing-in ceremony for new citizens will be at the Waterfront Park Great Lawn today at 5pm."

"You came all the way out here for this?"

"And to wish you a Happy 4th."

The judge considered this and gave Alexander a look. Deep down they had long respected each other. "If I ever get caught running afoul of the law, I'm calling you, Alexander."

"Seriously, Judge, I doubt you'll ever be caught."

****

Alexander, Amy, Bobby, Gabe and Granddad had a spot on the Great Lawn at the waterfront of the Ohio River. There was a blanket rolled out. Several picnic baskets, with various goodies, surrounded by folding chairs, were in a circle.

Amy noticed how nervous her father was. He kept checking his watch and the several dozen people gathered off to the side. Rubén's kids were playing. He noticed Ines, she too looked concerned. They made eye contact and Alexander nodded to her in support. It was 5pm, on the nose.

Judge Sherrilyn 'Sherri' Daniels, in her black robe, was also checking her watch. She glanced over to Alexander, who signaled her to wait just a little bit longer. Sherri nodded.

Amy noticed their interaction.

A few minutes later a van pulled up and ICE agents delivered Rubén. He was reunited with his family. He hugged Ines.

"Here's Rubén! Yes!" cheered Alexander, he nodded gratefully to the federal agents and the magistrate. Judge Daniels nodded back to Alexander.

"I'm so proud of you Daddy," said Amy.

Rubén joined the swearing in ceremony: "I hereby declare, on oath, that I absolutely and entirely renounce and abjure all allegiance and fidelity to any foreign prince, potentate, state or sovereignty of whom or which I have heretofore been subject or citizen; that I will support and defend the Constitution and laws of the United States of America against all enemies, foreign and domestic; that I will bear arms on behalf of the United States when required by the law; that I will perform work of national importance under civilian direction freely without any mental reservation or purpose of evasion; so help me God."

Judge Daniels posed for pictures with the new citizens. Alexander was pulled into the frame by Judge Daniels and smiled with her and Rubén, who became quite choked up and hugged Alexander. Ines then embraced and thanked Alexander. Their family went off together.

Amy watched and savored this sight. She then noticed her father easing over to the federal judge that just swore them in and she moved closer as well.

Alexander greeted the judge, "Sherri, it's so good to see you again."

"Sherri?" mumbled Amy to herself.

Sherri and Alexander hugged.

She removed her black robe and an assistant took it. "It's been forever, Alexander, how are you?"

"I'm feeling super. And you are looking quite fit."

"I do Pilates."

"It shows."

"And you're still the cat's meow, Alexander."

Amy mumbled, "Cat's meow?"

"You were always so kind." He pivoted and waved her over, "Sherri, this is my daughter, Amy."

"Amy, nice to meet you."

"Nice to meet you too, Your Honor."

"Please, when I'm out of my robe, it's Sherri. I have followed your career so far. Very impressive."

"You must not be keeping up."

Sherri waved that off, "If you're referring to John Tenorio, he's a man who panders to whatever he thinks his audience wants to hear and has admitted under oath to lying on various occasions. I'm rather mystified how he has any credibility at all."

Amy glanced at the people milling about, "It must be a thrill to swear in new citizens."

"It is my most favorite part of the job." She checked her watch, "I'm sorry, I have to run. Amy, I hope to see more of you." Amy nodded at that. "Alexander, same for you, outside of my courtroom." They all laughed.

"Yes, ma'am," said Alexander.

The judge strolled off.

Amy shifted closer to her father, "You two seemed friendly."

"Sherri and I went out a few times when we were in high school."

"You never mentioned her before."

"We lost track. Our paths didn't cross, until this swearing in."

"I want to hear more about the 'going out' a few times."

"That was forever ago. Your mama and Sherri were not on the best of terms."

"I'm not going to wave any red hankies in front of my mother."

Alexander seemed quizzical, "Sherri and I are both divorced and empty nesters."

"I thought you lost track of her."

"We hadn't communicated for years before this moment. I may have seen something about her online."

"And Daddy, just for the record, 'empty nester' means there's only one or two left in the home. Casa Arrington is filled with people and animals that live there in actual nests."

Alexander was distracted by Sherri walking off, "Excellent point, Counselor." He continued to watch her and Amy could see something in his gaze.

Bobby came up to Amy. They smiled and plopped down on the blanket.

"It's like a decade just melted away," said Bobby. "We were here, together, watching fireworks on July 4th, 10 years ago."

Amy nodded and reflected back on that, "A special time."

Alexander heard the music starting, "Joslyn & the Sweet Compression! One of my favorite bands." He jammed and he moved to the beats.

Amy got up and enticed Bobby to join in. The three danced together, with everyone else.

Later there was a spectacular firework show launched from a barge on the Ohio River that lit up the night sky.

****

An actor dressed like Pan clomped up and stood before the Judge and Willodean sitting on their porch on their couch watching the fireworks.

"Good evening, Your Honor and ma'am."

Willodean was a bit concerned, but the judge touched her hand and calmed her.

"You look like Pan," declared the judge. "Got your flute?"

Pan pulled it out and bowed to him.

"Can you play anything?"

The actor blew into the flute, alas the notes were sour.

"That was lovely."

"Thank you, sir. I have a delivery for you." He handed him an envelope.

The judge opened it and found the season tickets. "We've got Daddy's present back, Cookie!"

"That's wonderful!" exclaimed Willodean.

"Once again, right behind home bench!" They held each other with joy. "Can't wait for the season," said the jubilant judge. He turned to Pan and pulled out his wallet.

"That's fine. I was well compensated."

"I insist on tipping you and I'm the judge." He handed the young man a $20 bill.

"Thank you, sir. Good night, folks." Pan continued clumsily clomping off into the night.

"Bye," they waved him off.

"That Alexander," Willodean affectionately stated.

The judge grunted, "Really. He's such a card." They watched more explosions in the sky and he couldn't help grinning. "Actually, I knew right away that wasn't the real Pan."

"Did you now, dear."

"It wasn't midnight."

"And the full moon is a week away," quipped Willodean.

"Exactly! And he really was awful on that flute," the judge added. He held up the tickets and they both laughed like the kids who were gifted them way back when.

****

The fireworks continued as Amy got an alert on her phone. It was a news report. She put in her ear-piece and played the video: "Reports have been confirmed that outside forces have intervened and returned President

Ibragimov to power in the country of Khrakistan. Opposition forces are being routed."

Amy was horrified, "No! NO!! NOOO!!!" She was devastated to see President Ibragimov back in the saddle and being cheered by his supporters from his presidential balcony.

Amy was nearly seething, "I wish someone would just take him out!"

The fireworks continued for a bit. Amy wandered around and finally joined her group enjoying the pyrotechnics. Her phone buzzed. The ID was blocked.

"Hello?"

"Miss Arrington, this is the Undersecretary."

"Oh, hi, Miles."

"I wanted to thank you for going the extra effort and just wanted to bring you up to speed on President Ibragimov."

"I saw on the news. He's back in power. He bragged to me that he was President for Life. I guess he is."

"Or was. 20 minutes ago, after he returned to the palace, one of his guards turned on him and President Ibragimov was shot and killed. Again, Miss Arrington, your country thanks you for your assistance and wishes you a Happy 4th."

The call ended and she recalled Bobby assuring her: "*Your wish is solidly intact.*"

Amy then recalled herself saying: "*I wish someone would just take him out.*" She pondered this with a subtle grin, "The wicked witch is dead." She savored the moment. Amy was stoked. The adrenaline was pumping in her. Then the words of the president came back to haunt her: "*You know what is huge ironic thing here, Miss Amy? You and I are birds of a feather. The same. Is only small step up to my league. You will enjoy rush when you take life, taste blood. We are same, we are same.*"

Amy was stung by this memory. She heard his laugh and now was quite troubled by his prediction.

Bobby joined her. "Is everything okay?"

Amy moved close, "Hold me, Bobby. Please, just hold me."

Bobby put his arms around her.

Alexander, along with Mrs. Simmons, Granddad and Gabe were pleased with this possible romantic development.

Fireworks continued to explode above them. Alexander cheered like a little boy and pumped his fist.

"Hold me closer." Bobby hugged Amy closer as she sorted through her emotions.

Above, the fireworks crackled and boomed, illuminating Louisville's dark sultry summer sky.

****

The four had returned to Casa Arrington. Granddad announced he had generated enough power for the day and retired for the evening. Mrs. Simmons also turned in.

"It's quite surreal, Greg being dead after just being here."

"Yeah," agreed Amy. She was distant.

"What?"

"I wished him dead and he became dead."

"Big deal. I had similar thoughts, but we didn't act on them. What I want to know is how you fixed things with Sean. Tell me."

"We took away his happy space."

"What's that?"

"6D, Delilah's Delightfully Delicious Downtown Digital Dungeon."

"Where might this be found?"

Amy brought up a website describing 6D. "In cyberspace. Online. I agreed to let him back in if he fixed what he broke—and he did. But I'll do it in the morning. Let him stew in his electronic juices a little longer."

"Space Invaders sure has changed," remarked Alexander.

"They still roughly have the same objectives."

"Well played." Alexander kissed the top of his daughter's head. "'*We are such stuff as dreams are made on; and our little life is rounded with a sleep.*' Which I'm off to now."

"Good night, Daddy." Amy went out back and gazed up at the night sky. Then her phone rang and she answered.

"This is Scott Wellington returning your call about the legal matter."

"Oh, yes… Can I Facetime with you?"

"Sure. One second." Scott's face was now seen from the camera on his laptop. It was in a home office during the day.

"I'm consulting on a case involving your son."

"God, what has he done now?"

"I'm sorry, may I ask where you are located?"

"I'm based in Singapore. I'm a fund manager."

"Can I ask why Sean isn't living with either you or the mother?"

"Cindy? That's a good one. I met Cindy when I was working in New York and we had a good thing. And then she got pregnant and neither one of us wanted to get married and especially raise a kid at the time. After the birth, she left for Europe. I was relocated to Asia. I bought a house in Louisville where my sister was renting a small apartment. She moved in and took custody of him. I cover all the expenses and offer plenty of support."

"How much support? When was the last time you were here?"

"You need to tell me what this is in regards to."

"Why isn't Sean living with you?"

At that moment a small child came running into the room laughing.

His Singaporean wife came in after him and smiled, embarrassed, "I'm sorry."

"That's okay, hon." She herded the little guy out. Scott turned back to the camera. "It wouldn't work for him to be here. And, well, as you may have derived, he's a handful. Sean has a criminal juvenile record."

"Does he know about your situation there?"

"Yes. What is going on there?"

"Actually, the situation here has been rectified. Good day, sir." Amy hung up and thought for a bit and then texted Gabby: don't wait until the morning, please let Gokuro Gangsta out of his cage now.

****

It was very early, just after dawn and the air was still relatively cool. Amy was jogging and wondering how a parent could divorce a child. She had her own issues on this subject, but realized they were minuscule and manageable compared to what Sean was dealing with. She couldn't imagine the damage that had been done and wondered how this would play out. Amy ran the Louisville Loop by the river. She still had a week left in her vacation, but was already thinking about her return to New York.

Amy spent some time at the Waterfront Botanical Gardens, a place she had viewed before the opening and fallen in love with. She then jogged east on River Road to the Patriots Peace Memorial. She was with her 4th grade class at the unveiling of the memorial in 2002 and returned frequently over the years. On that day they learned about Louisville native Brice M. Simpson, a U.S. Air Force 1st Lieutenant, who died in a training accident in Japan in 1998 when his F-16 crashed and burned. The memorial was inspired by his sacrifice and it was dedicated to all service members that died under circumstances other than declared hostile military action. Over 400 were recognized here.

Amy sat on the bank of a pond on the south end. The building was lit up. Her view caught the memorial reflected in the water. She spent some time there reflecting on their sacrifices. It always humbled her to visit this place.

Running back to CA her brain was fixating on what her legacy was to be. Scenes from her still early legal career were flashing through her mind. Amy stopped on a small hill that gave her a view of the river and pondered where she wanted to be 10 years from now and then 20. She pulled out her phone and made a call.

"Hello, Amy."

"Hello, Harold."

"Ready to get back in the fight?"

"I need some more time to consider my long-term plan."

"We need you back here."

"Then, maybe I should resign."

"Whoa, hold on here. Some go through this. Take a breath and take that time. We have a five-month pause that we offer our most promising 3rd year associates if they need it. If after five months you feel the same way, well good luck. But some want back in and we let them. Think about it. We'd hate to lose you. Let's just hit the pause button and talk in December."

"Fine, let's do that."

Amy jogged back home and sat on the front porch. She pulled out her phone and made a call.

Bobby was in the office early reading more reports. He was in a funk. He brought up a picture on his phone of him and Amy laughing together. He then got a call, checked the number and answered.

"Good morning."

"Hey, Bobby. Did I catch you at a bad time?"

"You have never caught me at a bad time. How are you?"

"I'm pretty good. I just wanted to call you to tell you that I've been granted a 5-month sabbatical."

"What does that mean?"

"I'll be here until Christmas."

Bobby was quiet for a moment, his attitude took an upswing. "That's some very interesting news. We should get together over lunch, or dinner."

"I agree. I'll let you get back to work. See you soon."

Later in the day Cassidy noticed Bobby had an extra spring in his step and wondered.

****

Amy and Alexander were on their half-pipe together. He wiped out and laid back.

"You okay?"

Alexander shrugged, "I'm alright. Just getting old. It sneaks up on you."

"Daddy, you're like a fine wine."

Alexander appreciated the sentiment, but didn't believe her.

"I talked to my firm in New York."

"Your vacation is coming to an end."

"They have a program for their 3rd year associates where they can take a 5-month sabbatical and still get back in. And I took it."

"You're going to be here for 5 months?" Alexander was hopeful, but tried not to show it, too much.

"If you'll have me."

"I think that can be arranged."

Amy was pleased at that, "Thanks. I'll try to behave."

"Don't change course on my account," groused Alexander.

"Daddy, the other day, the 4th of July."

"Yes?"

"The judge."

"Sherri?"

"It was the way you watched her leave."

"What?"

****

Amy was alone, waiting in the salon of Silver Horse Sanctuary. She picked up a book on the history of the family. She browsed the hundreds of pictures.

April left a meeting she had with her staff and entered. "I could have put the Sultan off. The real reason I made a special trip back from Europe, dear, was to take you to Amanda Burden's gathering the next night. It was quite an event. She had some young Earl and a Viscount she wanted to introduce you two."

"Sorry, I'm holding out for a Baron."

"Crafty."

"You still have this *Downton Abbey* fantasy that I'll marry some English aristocrat. Eh, Mother?"

"Heavens no!"

"It's okay, you're not under oath."

"It just gave me a very good reason to see you. When you go back, there will be plenty of time for socializing."

Amy nodded, but was distracted.

April always knew, "What's going on?" Amy shook it off. "Come on, honey. What is it?"

Amy ignored her and pointed to a picture in one of the books, "Who's that?"

April put on her glasses and took a look. "That's a picture of your great-great grandfather at a party that was held at the Cuthbert Bullitt house where Fourth Street is. They had a great view of the river. Amanthis Bullitt inherited the land. Here's a picture of your great-great uncle attending the marriage of George Weissinger. They would have grand gatherings at the farm, which is now Central Park."

"Those are great stories to have," said Amy. "It centers one."

"Good, now I have a question, dear, shouldn't you be getting back to Padmore, Pearce and Payne? Are associates allowed to take so much time off?"

"I have a 5-month sabbatical."

"They told you this? It doesn't sound good. Did you screw up?"

"I requested it."

"What? Why? You're five lengths from the finish line."

"What's the finish line?"

"You know, becoming a partner in the firm and then named partner."

"Dangling that or maybe I'll be used up in another 3 or 4 years and tossed out in favor of a younger, hungrier contestant."

"That's not what I heard."

"Mother… Maybe I don't like defending really horrible people."

"Mother Teresa doesn't need legal representation."

"I work over a hundred hours a week in a cubicle. I live, albeit quite comfortably, in company barracks, the Microscope. I have almost no social life. Instead I read thousands and thousands of pages of legal documents, hunting for actionable intelligence."

"Did you not understand what a lawyer does and who seeks their services when you took the LSAT?"

Amy groaned and hung her head. "In five months I'll have to choose and give my final decision."

"In the meantime, you're going to work with your father?"

"I plan to. But you shouldn't worry, in five months I'll probably be itching to get back to my cramped little cubical, drowning in the tsunami of documents looking to shank our opponents. And you can continue to brag to your friends how your daughter works for one of the top firms in New York."

"Amy, dear, Padmore isn't just 'one' of the best, it's at the top of the heap; it's *the* white-shoe firm in the Big Apple."

"I was at the Patriots Peace Memorial and I was thinking about legacies, a lot. Like, my legacy."

"Honey, you're not even 30. You're a bit young to have your mid-life crisis."

"Mother, I look at your life and you have lots of accomplishments."

"Such as?"

"You might be the only person ever on the boards of the Louisville Downtown Management District, the Louisville Downtown Development Corporation, Kentuckiana Works, Actors Theatre of Louisville, the Kentucky Derby Museum and you know, back in the day, in Louisville, if you wanted to go to the river, you had to literally trespass over scrap yards, fill pits and landfills. Now Waterfront Park is a treasure, you worked on that."

"That was David Karem's vision with Marlene Grissom, they did the heavy lifting and kept pushing. They got it done."

"Mother, you don't give yourself enough credit for your legacy."

"My legacy? It's just another run of the mill story. I'm a woman who fell madly in love with a silver tongue dreamer. But I got out, stepped off of Mr. Toad's Wild Ride and invested my money wisely in some start-ups and earned a very good return. I had some wise advice and planning and a bit of luck. And now I'm trying to give some back. Your father, to be fair, is frequently brilliant and always passionate, when he isn't being a complete jackass."

15

It was that time of the year and one of the two festivals in the summer that Alexander never missed was upon them and he saw a press release:

Forecastle Festival 2019: Music. Art. Activism.

July 12, 13, 14, 12:00pm - 11:00pm – Forecastle Festival represents a place where people come together for a good time. Founded in 2002, Forecastle Festival has grown from a small community event to one of the most anticipated summer events in the USA. The festival annually draws in tens of thousands of fans from across the world to the scenic waterfront park in Louisville, Kentucky. In addition to showcasing the hottest musical acts, the festival consistently promotes local talent and focuses on environmental activism and outdoor recreation.

Forecastle was also an event that The DDs attended. Mitch was working late, so Alexander agreed to babysit the first night. He would be attending the next two days. Abby came by at 6:00pm with Roxanne and Marcus. Gabby and Amy were waiting.

"I want to thank you for watching Roxanne and Marcus," said Abby.

"I want The DDs to get their groove back!" declared Alexander.

They all busted up laughing. Marcus eased forward.

"Hey, Marcus," welcomed Alexander.

"Hi," Marcus quietly replied.

Alexander handed him a card, "Here's the wifi passcode."

"Cool."

"We have so many guests coming through we print up cards. And," Alexander pointed to the kitchen, "help yourself to anything you see in the fridge, except for the Barley Pops."

They all laughed, except Marcus. He found a seat in the corner of the room, pulled out his tablet, put on his headphones, connected to CA's internet and was back playing a game in his world, walled off. The animals didn't know what to make of him and stayed away.

Abby sighed, "I just wish he had one friend."

The rest of the group observed, shrugged and nodded.

Granddad eased into the living room wearing his VR goggles. He was oblivious to any of the humans in the room, he was in the middle of a contest in virtual reality.

Amy smiled, "There's Granddad, off somewhere."

Marcus also noticed and was utterly fascinated. He took off his headphones, put down his tablet and walked over to Granddad.

Amy crossed over and put her hand on Granddad's shoulder. He took off his goggles.

"Amy, hello. Gosh, we have guests, sorry."

"This is Marcus. This is Granddad."

"Hi, Marcus!"

"Hi. Should I call you Granddad?"

"Everyone does."

"I don't have a granddad."

"That's what I'm for."

Marcus was intrigued by that, "Uh-huh."

"I was in the middle of a craterball match."

"Craterball?" asked Marcus.

"It's a sport you play in domes on the moon in near zero gravity. 7 on 7. You pass the rock around and try to throw it or jam it into a crater at each end the opponent defends."

"They play it on the moon?" asked Marcus.

"In the future. But right now, I'm playing it in virtual reality. You know we could use a player. You want to be on my team?" Granddad pulled out another pair of VR goggles.

Marcus gazed at them and his face lit up. He looked to his mom, who nodded. Marcus put on the goggles. Granddad did a quick tutorial and how to maneuver and soon Marcus was zooming around in a dome on the moon playing craterball. The virtual action was actually intense.

"Talk to your teammates, Marcus. Let them know what's going on."

"I'm coming up on your side, Granddad."

"That's a good move."

"Granddad, watch out for that defender!"

Granddad changed vectors and avoided the collision, "Thanks, Marcus! Okay, let's do it, give and go."

"Sounds good."

"I've cleared a lane," barked Granddad. "Take the rock and rocket!"

"I've got it, Granddad!"

Marcus saw himself flying towards the crater with the rock.

Meanwhile, back in actual reality, her mother was gawking at this. She watched her son, with the VR goggles, gyrating around, avoiding the opposition and getting an advantage.

"Almost there, Marcus! Just two more bogies!" yelled Granddad.

"I see them."

Marcus faked one out and hurled the rock past the last defender into the crater. It lit up. *KABOOM!*

"You scored!" Granddad yelled.

"Yes!" exclaimed Marcus.

Granddad and Marcus danced around and celebrated together.

"Great pass, Granddad!"

Abby and the rest of the group were happily stunned.

"Marcus, no time. Next rock is up."

"Okay, okay, I'm on it." The craterball match continued on.

Gabby declared, "Alexander, it's so nice what you're doing. I'd like to put forward a motion. I nominate Alexander to be an honorary Démener Diva."

Alexander touched his heart, filled with emotion at this notion.

Amy, Gabby and Abby voted thumbs up.

"I am truly honored." Alexander stroked his goatee, "I remember the first time Amy wanted to go to Forecastle. 2002, the year it started. It was in Tyler Park. Amy was 11 and wanted to see the band Blue Goat War. She first asked her mama and April put her foot down and refused to let her go see blue goats warring with each other. She didn't believe in animals fighting."

The four broke up laughing.

"Then I went to ask Dad," said Amy. "I offered to do double chores for a month."

"Little did she know I was already planning on attending and see a band I knew called Fire the Saddle and I was going to ask Amy to go. But she made me the offer and I took her up on it. She did the double chores."

"Daddy taught me a valuable lesson in law that day. Don't offer so much to start when you're negotiating."

"Soon after that The DDs were formed and we went ten years in a row," Gabby added.

"And who was your favorite band?" asked Alexander. "Gabby?"

"That's a tough one. If I'm made to pick..."

"Which I'm forcing you to do."

"Sleater Kinney."

"I like them too. Abby, you?" inquired Alexander.

"Hmmm...White Reaper."

Alexander nodded, "From Louisville. Great rockers."

"Abby's favorite band to crowd surf to," Gabby added.

"And my daughter, what is your favorite band ever at Forecastle?"

"My Morning Jacket," said Amy.

"Another Louisville band. Those talented lads, Jim, Tom, Patrick, Bo and Carl have jammed here at Casa Arrington," bragged Alexander.

"Halftime!" announced Granddad. They both took off their goggles. "Follow me, teammate, we need some ice cream sandwiches to fortify ourselves for the second half."

"Sounds great," said Marcus.

"Better yet, can you go dig them out in the kitchen? They're in the bottom freezer."

"Roger that, Granddad." He was off.

Abby was thrilled, "Thanks, Granddad."

"Marcus is a good kid. And another good kid you were just talking about, Jim, Jim James of My Morning Jacket. I met Jim's great aunt Betty Cheeseman, also a musician, in the early '60s. I was working as an intern at the Brown Theatre. Betty was so talented. The story goes, after the great flood of 1937 that walloped us, Dann Byck Sr. and some of the other city leaders thought we all needed a lift and they started the Louisville Orchestra. And Betty was there at the beginning and played the upright bass for 28 years."

"And we're going to see the conductor of the Louisville Orchestra, Teddy Abrams, tomorrow," opined Alexander. "It's all connected, sewn together in our wide and long tapestry, the rich fabric of life."

****

The ride picked them up and The DDs were on their way.

Gabby was still contemplating the earlier exchange, "Really, My Morning Jacket is your favorite band?"

"Yes," said Amy.

"Cool guys," Gabby replied. "But you'd think it would be the other way around with you and Abby."

"How so?" asked Amy.

"You, a ruthless lawyer, likes a band that sings 'Love, Love, Love,' and Abby, an innocent stay-at-home mom, who does medical billing, likes White Reaper, who sings 'You Make Me Wanna Die.'"

Abby frowned, "I'm not so innocent."

Amy too thought this through, "Really? Ruthless?"

"Said with love and mad respect for both of you," assured Gabby.

****

Things had gone rather well. Alexander made his pizza special in their outside oven. Roxanne was a joy. They kept her engaged so she would sleep at least partly through the night for Abby and Mitch.

Granddad and Marcus were out back by the half-pipe. They had entered an international craterball tournament and had advanced to the third round.

It was just about 8:30pm and Mrs. Simmons and Alexander were settling in for the evening in front of the ginormous large flatscreen.

"Reds are two games back of the Rockies," declared Mrs. Simmons with some spice. "Showdown is at Coors Field. Boy have I been looking forward to this."

"First game after the All-Star break," mused Alexander.

"There's been some time away and this is the first test back," said Mrs. Simmons. "These encounters are often a bellwether for the rest of the season. Can the team come together? Do they have the stuff to make it over the finish line?"

"Exactly," agreed Alexander. "I wonder if this is the first time two guys with the same last names faced each other in a major league game."

"You don't say," exclaimed Mrs. Simmons.

"I do say. The starting pitchers are Gray versus Gray. No relation. Sonny against Jon. I have no idea about Jon, but I am excited about Sonny Gray and his terrific curve ball. The Reds have gone 8-2 in his last 10 outings."

"Then bring it on," stated Mrs. Simmons in anticipation. They were ready.

There was a knock at the door.

Mrs. Simmons answered it and found April standing there. "Good evening, Ms. Arrington."

"Hello, Mrs. Simmons, how are you?"

"Very well, thank you. And you?"

"I'm okay. I came by to see Amy."

"She's not here, please come in."

April entered CA, the first time in several years, and took in the familiar nooks. Many things were the same, she noticed a few new critters eyeing her from various vantage points. She entered the main living room and stepped out back to eye Granddad and Marcus wearing their VR goggles.

Granddad had just taken the rock, when he smelled a scent. "Perfect from Marc Jacobs...." He grinned, "April's here."

April heard him and was amused, she went back inside.

"You have the point, Marcus, I have to attend to something."

"10-4, Granddad."

Granddad took off his VR goggles and went back inside. He welcomed her warmly, "April, it's good to see you."

"Granddad," April was thrilled to see him and they hugged. She kissed him on the cheek. "You look great."

"No, April, you're the one that looks great."

"You are such a flatterer."

Alexander entered the room and was happy to see her, "April, how are you?"

"Hello, Alexander. I'm fine. Yourself?" They didn't move to embrace.

"I'm good. Is everything alright?"

"I came by to talk to Amy."

"She's at the Forecastle Festival."

"I see. Has Deveraux and Sven moved on?"

"They have. If it's important that you speak to Ambrosia, you can call her."

"That's okay, it was a spur of the moment thing. I had a free evening and came by to see what my, *our* daughter, was doing. It was presumptuous."

Alexander stared at her for a moment remembering times past with them.

"Are you on babysitting duty here?"

Alexander's attention was snapped back, "Yes. This is Roxanne, Abby's daughter. And Marcus, her son, is out back defending the virtual universe with Granddad. Mitch had to work at his restaurant. I'm doing this so Gabby, Abby and Amy can go to the event."

"The Démener Divas," April said, fondly reminiscing. She laughed.

"Yes," Alexander laughed along with her.

Mrs. Simmons seemingly became tired, "I think I'm turning in."

Alexander was surprised, "What?? The game just started."

"Mrs. Arrington, nice to see you, ma'am."

"Thank you, Mrs. Simmons, same to you."

"And I need to get back to the tournament, we've made it to the third round" proclaimed Granddad. "Good night, all. April, you remain a treasure. I hope to paint you someday."

She smiled at him, "Someday, soon."

Granddad joined Marcus in the back. They gave each other a thumbs up, put their VR goggles back on and were back at it.

"You've been charged with the care of this child, Alexander?"

"Yes. Until midnight, at the very latest."

"3 ½ hours?"

"Correct."

April furrowed her brow, "I don't know if my conscience can allow me to let you be alone with no support for this child."

"I'm fine. We're fine.'"

"Just shush and put the kettle on."

****

First night and The DDs arrived at Forecastle. Amy handed out their VIP wristbands with the RFID chips she had already purchased. They were loaded with $200 on each for food and drinks inside. Amy refused to be paid back and closed any further discussion on the matter.

"Sorry if I'm being difficult," said Amy.

"We forgive you," Gabby assured her. "But we'll get even."

"I know the first thing we need…" They said it together, "Froggy's Popcorn!"

The Forecastle Festival was held at Louisville's 85-acre Waterfront Park on the Ohio River. 75,000 tickets were sold daily. It was a nautical theme for the event. There was the Mast, which was the main stage and three additional stages, Boom, Ocean and Port. Chairs were shaped like waves. To the right of the Ferris wheel lay the legendary Party Cove, from which giant plastic squid tentacles emanated. Mermaids lured you in with lifeguards shooting water out keeping attendees cool, while DJs blasted out beats on a stage on a boat parked inside.

Attendees were free to move between the venues experiencing the different genres. Jazz, hip-hop, indie rock, folk and bluegrass music was on the menu.

The DDs voted with their thumbs, up or down, and if it was 2-1 against, the odd one got a minute to convince the other two why they should switch. Of course, after the first two songs, a reconsideration was allowable if two voted for it. They would then wander to another stage, to another band and another experience.

They realized they had already missed The Band Camino and Waax. They took in the scene. It was a gigantic gathering of cool people. First things first. Gabby took Abby and Amy to meet Liz Cooper backstage of the Port Stage before her show.

All The DDs loved her song "Motions" and had already danced along to "Mountain Man" several times and they would dance again.

After Liz's show The DDs checked the Forecastle app on who was performing and ventured towards the river and the Mast Stage where they caught the last chunk of Portugal. The Man. They were pleasantly surprised when local rapper Jack Harlow appeared for his cover of "Sundown."

The final song from them was, of course, "Feel it Still." Amy quietly hummed along. She contemplated the lyrics of being a rebel just for kicks. It was about someone past their prime, but still having fuel in the tank and raring to go. She thought of her dad, who would be irritated at the comparison, as he declared his prime was still approaching.

They hustled over to the Boom Stage and caught the last half of Judah & The Lion and dug the energy.

After this show they checked out the dozens of booths dealing with environmental issues. There were also local artists, paintings, crafts, designers of jewelry and clothes, tie-dyed t-shirts and other accessories.

They were getting hungry. They found a tent selling "Nonna" slices from Pizza Lupo. It was Sicilian pan pizza made with a generous amount of olive oil.

They fortified themselves for the climax brewing on the Mast Stage: The Killers.

Lightning flashed in the dark brooding sky in the distance. While below, the Killer's delivered a pulse-pounding, surging rock-and-roll performance.

The DDs had powered through to this point on caffeine, adrenaline took over now.

Nearly halfway through the set, the lead singer, Brandon Flowers, called up two guys holding up signs advertising their drum and bass abilities.

Amy was amazed, "He's putting these fans on stage. They look like twins."

As they walked up the stairs, Abby recognized them, "That's Sam and Nick Wilkerson, from White Reaper!"

"Abby, that's your band," said Amy.

"Yes, and I heard they just shot the video for 'Real Long Time' at Joe Ley Antiques. And guess who directed it, Lance Bangs."

Amy thought for a second, "That name sounds familiar."

Gabby grinned, "He's the guy that did *Breadcrumb Trail,* the Slint documentary."

Abby pumped her fist, "Yes! The DDs' band!"

"Way cool!" yelled Amy.

Nick took over drums. Sam picked up the bass and they played the Killer's tune "For Reasons Unknown" from the album *Sam's Town* and they killed it.

"White Reaper!" yelled Abby.

"That's amazing," said Amy. "They know this song really well!"

Abby laughed, "The Killers and White Reaper have been touring together for the last couple months."

Gabby nodded at that. Amy laughed at the goof.

The Killer's 15th song "When You Were Young," was again from their second album *Sam's Town.* It's about a woman who was married to a man who cheated on her. She was shocked and saddened, but goes back and forgives him. Amy always shook her head at this when she watched the video.

Their 90-minute set had seemingly ended and it was a release, the festival goers were nearly drained, but not satiated.

A chant started up "One More Song, One More Song, One More Song."

The Killer's first encore was from *Day & Age*. "Human" questioned if we as humans were petrified to step out of the expected norm. Amy was struck by that, as she had up to this point toed the line.

The second song was "Mr. Brightside." The crowd erupted with joy. Amy knew the lyrics well. It described a naïve sucker looking for love who blindly puts up with their partner sleeping around— then was consumed by jealousy and destined to do it again. Amy bought the album *Hot Fuss* and bought what she thought was the message of "Mr. Brightside." She laughed at this fool and how silly they were. Her defenses had been solidly erected. She wasn't about to be vulnerable enough to be tricked by anyone for going on 13 years. But presently, nearing the end of her 20's, she began to feel like she might take a chance.

****

It was 11:34pm. Granddad had headed off to bed. April and Alexander were in the living room with Roxanne in the cradle. Marcus, exhausted from the craterball encounter, was asleep on the couch.

"I appreciate your concern. But you know, April, looking back, when Ambrosia was an infant, I did the majority of the changings and the 2ams. You really had no cause for worry."

"I did the pumping for late night feedings and I did my share of changing dirty nappies as well."

"Certainly. And you did it well and with style."

"I tried to be a good mother. I really did."

"And you were. I'm the last person you have to convince."

April appreciated that. She pulled out her phone and sent a text. "I have to go."

Alexander stood and offered his hand to assist her.

"Thank you, Alexander." She stood and thought how Reston never did that.

"And thank you for your help tonight."

"You're welcome. It brought back some good times."

"April, you've really done a terrific job with Ambrosia."

"I hope so. But Alexander, it's you she takes after."

He patted her on the arm, "Our daughter has a lot of her mother in her. Which makes her so interesting."

They gave each other a smile and a nod and she was gone before the clock struck midnight. April's car picked her up and whisked her away. The DDs were soon back and Abby took parental control of Roxanne and Marcus, who had the time of his life. In fact, they all had a great time. Abby thanked them and Marcus found a piece of paper and wrote, 'Granddad, thanks for the craterball game. Marcus.'

"Could you give this to him?" asked Marcus.

"Sure," said Amy.

"Thank you." Marcus turned to Alexander, "Thank you, sir, for tonight."

Abby was thunderstruck how her child, normally sullen and withdrawn, was quite sociable and respectful.

The animals now approached him. Nutmeg trotted up and rubbed against his leg.

Marcus was thrilled, "Hi!"

"That's Nutmeg," said Abby. "She's a sweetie. And here comes ol' Cantankerous Cat waddling over for some love." Abby spotted a bunny, "I don't know who that is?"

Amy was impressed, "Here's our unicorn. Regis the 'Rascible Rabbit. He hides from everyone."

Marcus was tickled by that, "And he is coming to see me?"

Regis hopped over in front of him and Marcus lightly stroked the bunny.

Cantankerous Cat felt like he was being ignored. He gave Marcus a nudge to remind him of his presence on the other side.

"I see you, Cantankerous Cat," Marcus petted him too.

Cantankerous Cat purred and the room broke up laughing.

Alexander announced, "Looks like you're going to have to come back, Marcus. By order of Cantankerous Cat."

"Really? I can come back?" Marcus was quite taken by that.

Cantankerous Cat meowed at him and the room erupted. Marcus petted him, reassuring the old cat and then their ride arrived.

"Thank you, Amy and Alexander, tell Mrs. Simmons and Granddad, especially Granddad, how grateful I am." Abby got Marcus in and she slipped in carrying Roxanne and the car drove off.

Back inside CA Amy sensed her father was a bit unsettled, "Daddy, are you okay?"

"I'm fine. Just thinking back on some things. I'm glad you had a good time. Get some rest. Tomorrow is *our* day."

"Yes, sir," grinned Amy. "Can't wait."

****

It was Saturday, very early, just after 5am. Amy was awake. She looked up at the sky and it was clear. She then again spied her father down below slipping out in work clothes.

By 11:45am Alexander emerged from his bedroom wearing his number 35 Louisville Cardinal basketball jersey.

Amy read news on her tablet, "Sleep well, Daddy?"

"Sure did, looking forward to today."

"Then I'm glad you're well rested."

Alexander, Amy, Mrs. Simmons and Granddad arrived on the 2nd day of the festival in the early afternoon. A giant blue octopus was draped over the welcoming Forecastle sign at general admission with the message: Music – Art – Activism.

Amy again cut everyone off and purchased four VIP bracelets for the day. They thanked her and joined the merrymakers. There was plenty to do and see. Alexander loved the vibe here and he was collecting free swag. Certainly, the music was the main draw with 55 bands scheduled to perform on the multiple stages, but it was so much more. It was a gathering of artists, artisans, poets and good souls. From the culinary and spirits world, to striking and captivating art and activists defending and supporting rights and protecting the God-given land. Believe in the Ship.

Alexander joked around with the giant fish people on stilts, pirates and the dancing lifeguards about. Plastic wasn't the word around here; none to gum up the oceans and suffocate the sea life, containers were aluminum.

The temperature was approaching 90 degrees with the humidity ever present; it was to be the hottest day in Kentucky so far this year.

"Stay hydrated," Alexander reminded, as he bought everyone canned water. He grabbed a Super American Premium Lager from local brewer Against the Grain, often his approach to life.

Alexander met up with the founder of the Forecastle Festival, JK McKnight. JK remembered that Alexander and Amy were at the very first Forecastle with six bands and just a couple artists 17 years ago.

Amy remarked, "It was quite memorable as I did double chores just for the privilege of attending."

Alexander held JK in high regard and complimented him on producing another grand event. He also gave props to the Forecastle Foundation, the activist arm of the festival, for donating over half a million dollars to local and global conservation projects since 2010. Their stated goal: 'On a mission to protect and connect the world's natural awesome. We do so by shining a light on biodiversity hotspots – the richest reservoirs of life.'

Alexander bought into JK's philosophy of 'partying with a purpose.'

'Believe in the Ship,' a phrase seen and heard at the gathering. *It's the only one we have*, Alexander would think.

After fortifying themselves with deep fried Oreos, the four of them made it over to the Port Stage, sat under some shade trees and people-watched. Artists had set up shop there. Granddad made a point to take in their work and some knew of him and his creations.

Teddy Abrams, conductor of the Louisville Orchestra, came by and sat with them. His group, Teddy Abrams & Friends would be performing a little later. Alexander and Teddy had become pals over the years. They both firmly believed there was 'something special in the water of Louisville.'

Alexander loved that the orchestra was commissioning new works, cutting new fields.

LO encountered some difficult times in 2013. Alexander and the community would always be grateful that Teddy came in and brought a jolt of electricity that revived the orchestra. Teddy's drive, talent, boundless creativity and his charm were used in his mission to bring music—not just in the concert halls—but to the streets. He had on occasion set up his piano and performed impromptu concerts on sidewalks, in hospitals and processing centers for arriving refugees.

Whatever the future held for Teddy, Alexander and the community had a special place in their hearts for him.

****

After they caught Israel Nash's melodic, soulful late afternoon set on the Port Stage, they headed over to the Holy Molé Taco Truck and met up with Max, the owner and buddy of Alexander.

Granddad, Mrs. Simmons and Amy chowed on a couple of vegetarian tofu and kimchi tacos. Alexander got the pulled pork.

After refueling they were then back to the Port Stage to catch Teddy Abrams and Friends starting at 7:45pm. There were about 30 in the group from classical musicians to electric guitars. They played Beethoven's "Symphony No. 5" and they rocked out with it. They performed until 9pm and received a standing ovation.

Mrs. Simmons and Granddad had grown a bit tired and they booked a ride home.

Alexander and Amy kicked it up a notch. They stopped by the Gonzo Bar. It was a sloping tent that resembled a fun house with bright colors and a large selection of bourbon to behold.

"Hunter would have tolerated this well," remarked Alexander.

With a VIP ticket came a membership to the Bourbon Lodge. This was a 16,000-square-foot bourbon retreat. Representatives from Heaven Hill, Four Roses, Old Forester and Dulsett Distilleries were there. It was air conditioned. The decibels were somewhat lower in this more intimate setting. Alexander felt an infusion of energy when he fully absorbed the rapid temperature shift south. Amy too felt relief. She glanced around but didn't see Bobby, he said he would be there.

"I'm going to use the facilities, Daddy."

Alexander navigated to a bar that was lit up with what looked like Christmas lights.

"Alexander!"

Alexander recognized them both, "Justin!" He shook his hand. "And Justin," Alexander shook his hand as well. They were Justin Sloan and Justin Thompson, co-owners of Justin's House of Bourbon "I see the House of Bourbon is again hosting the Rarities Bar."

"That's correct," said Justin.

"That means some of the 'dusties' have been brought out, yes?" Alexander inquired.

"Yes. A couple from pre-prohibition," Justin said.

"We have some really old Old Crow you might be interested in," said the other Justin.

"Boys, you've got my undivided attention."

Amy meanwhile casually searched around but still didn't see Bobby. She ventured out to the lodge's patio.

Cassidy Dulsett was leading a tasting. There were about a dozen people sitting in the Dulsett corner of the Bourbon Lodge.

"Folks, do me a favor and pause your first impression, put it aside, bourbon is at least 40% alcohol," Cassidy advised. "It's all about the tongue. It needs to be acclimatized to the warmth. Then the next several slow sips should be the determining factor of your acceptance level of the spirit. File away those flavors and aromas you experience, how your mouth reacts and the after taste. You may experience fruit and floral flavors such as pears or apples, or citrus and rose. And sweet aromatic flavors such as honey, vanilla, caramel or butterscotch. Or spice flavors such as nutmeg, cinnamon or black pepper."

Alexander joined her on the patio with his drink, "That's Cassidy Dulsett."

Amy studied the speaker, "She's changed since the last time I saw her."

"We're talking, what, a decade?"

"About."

The people in attendance sipped the glass in front of them.

"Is bourbon…whisky?" asked a taster.

"Yes," replied Cassidy. "All bourbon is whisky, but not all whisky is bourbon. To be a bourbon, the mash, the mixture of grains, must be at least 51% corn. Bourbon must be distilled to more than 160 proof, which is 80% alcohol by volume. Bourbon must be aged in new, charred oak barrels. No artificial colorings or flavoring can be added. It cannot be introduced to the barrel at higher than 125 proof, 62.5% alcohol by volume and it has to be produced in the good ol' USA to be called bourbon."

"How are bourbon brands different?" asked another taster.

"51% is corn. The other 49% and the aging process, that's where the distinctions are. It's usually a combination of malted barley and either rye or wheat and years."

Cassidy noticed Amy and Alexander. She continued, "In the 1800's distillers messed around quite a bit with their whiskies. That's why you didn't know what you were getting. That all changed in 1897, the Bottle in Bond Act that set some standards. To be bonded, the spirit must be the product of one distillation season and one distiller, at one distillery. It must be stored in warehouses guarded by Uncle Sam for no less than 4 years. At the end of the 90s, the 1990s, the G-men weren't required to watch over the warehouses anymore. But they still have very strict security and high standards."

"Is all bourbon made in Kentucky?" asked yet another.

"Not all. Only about 95%."

The group laughed. "Why's that?"

"It's not required that bourbon be distilled here, but we are blessed with limestone-rich riverbeds that create acid levels that are advantageous to the mash cooking, fermentation and aging process—and the greatest master distillers live here. I mean, is there a better place to reside? Really? I don't think so."

The audience was charmed. They laughed and applauded.

Another guy inquired, "According to the 1964 law, bourbon can only be made in the USA. But they don't limit foreign ownership in the companies."

"That is true," said Cassidy. "But if you think I'm going to actually comment on that here at this moment, then you've been hitting the sauce a bit early."

The group had another laugh. Amy and Alexander were now fans of hers.

Bobby eased forward and joined them, "She's pretty impressive, huh."

"She is!" Alexander exclaimed.

"I agree," said Amy. She and Bobby had a sly grin for each other.

Bobby shook his hand, "How are you, Alexander?"

"I'm floating along on a very cool festival vibe. Where have you been?"

"I've learned how to find nooks to hide in."

Cassidy arrived, "Amy Arrington, it's so nice to see you again."

"Cassidy, it's good to see you too. Have you met my father, Alexander?"

"No, but I know who he is. It's a pleasure to make your acquaintance, sir," Cassidy replied, respectfully.

"As it is for me, ma'am. I was quite impressed with your presentation."

"Thank you. It's the family business. It's in my blood. And I do my utmost to defend our company and industry."

There was a moment of silence.

"And I applaud you for your passion, ma'am," said Alexander. "And I do the same on my side."

"As you should," said Cassidy. "You have an enviable record, sir. Excuse me." Cass moved on.

Bobby sighed, "Excuse me for a second."

"Do you think she's still mad about the lawsuit?" asked Alexander.

Cassidy and Bobby sat off to the side of the Bourbon Lodge.

"You know they did sue us," said Cassidy.

"Alexander was one of the lawyers, but that's his business."

"His business was coming after our business."

"Wasn't personal."

"Uh-huh."

"But, sis, you know, if we could capture a higher percentage of the Angel's Share, it could be a substantial profit upgrade. Have you checked out his blog?"

"You mean the talking owl?"

"Yes."

"No."

"I'll send you a link for a post you should see."

Amy took her dad to the Mast Stage to check out Anderson .Paak and the Free Nationals. They experienced the soul and funk inspired hip-hop. Alexander got into it.

The final song Saturday night from .Paak was a tribute to Mac Miller, who passed away the year before. He performed "Dang it." It was a touching moment. .Paak's voice was filled with emotion. Photos of Mac filled the screens around the stage.

At 11:35pm Alexander and Amy boarded the iconic paddle boat Belle of Louisville for the Moon Taxi midnight show.

Amy subtly observed her father closely studying and admiring the exterior and then the interior of the vessel with a sharp eye.

"Can we expect you to be captaining the Belle someday, Daddy?"

"Maybe, someday in the future. I have been doing some studying. Need to do some more." Alexander checked his phone before turning it off. There was a picture of him with April. Amy pretended not to notice.

Alexander glanced at the image for a moment. It had been some time since their break up. Years had gone by. Things began to settle, but last night, when they were together taking care of little Roxanne, something dislodged in Alexander's already tenuous equilibrium.

Bobby arrived on the Belle just before midnight and caused a bit of a stir. Amy was quite surprised and pleased. The guy next to her only asked for a selfie with Bobby and for him to autograph his program and he gladly moved four rows over to let Bobby Dulsett sit next to Amy and Alexander.

"Still got the mojo," Alexander mumbled, with a grin.

Bobby just rolled his eyes. As the music started, Amy and Bobby slyly held hands.

Alexander pretended not to notice.

Moon Taxi played their first song, "Not Too Late." It was about a man hoping to hear a relationship wasn't too late to be saved after many years had gone by.

It was like a punch to the gut. Alexander's eyes began to tear up. He glanced away. Amy pretended not to notice that either.

****

It was Sunday. Alexander had over indulged way too much and had way too little sleep and was paying for it. He attempted to be a sentient life form, but suspected an attempt was made on his life as his skull felt like a dagger had been shoved into one of his lobes. Even attempting to think about it triggered a dull throbbing pain that washed over his cranium.

"Daddy, are you sure you don't want to attend the last day of the festival with Gabby and me?"

"I think I caught a bug or something."

Amy locked on, "A bug...or something?"

"I just hesitate to go. You two run on. Maybe I can get Mrs. Simmons to make me some chicken soup."

Mrs. Simmons entered reading the Sunday morning C-J, "Menudo works better on a hangover. But I'm not making that."

"Hangover? Me?"

Amy tapped her chin deep in thought, "I know. Odd. You, a veteran festival goer, a man quite familiar and comfortable with spirits, usually you don't take it to the limit."

Granddad trudged through, "I heard him up and about most of the night. Really affected my work."

"Sorry..." grunted Alexander.

Mrs. Simmons checked the freezer, "Did you finish off the rest of the ice cream last night?"

"Maybe," Alexander's eyes darted back and forth.

"It was two scoops short of a gallon. And I see a jumbo burrito was microwaved in here last night. It's like a crime scene."

"I'll clean that up later, don't worry about it," Alexander said, trying to find an ounce of comfort.

"Daddy, you sure you're staying in?"

He held his stomach, "I just hesitate to go..."

****

LouCity FC was on the road, north of the border playing the Ottawa Fury. Alexander could relate, there was some fury going on in his brain and stomach at the moment. He would spend the day on his couch recovering. He watched their match, a 1-1 tie. He then went channel surfing, sipping water, nibbling on sardines, crackers, various stinky cheeses and drinking matcha tea.

****

Amy and Gabby returned to the festival and immediately caught Sunflower Bean at 2pm on the Mast Stage and totally rocked out there. They both agreed, singer/bassist Julia Cumming was fully in charge.

Then they took in Evan Giia's show on the Ocean Stage and it was upbeat and inspiring. Plenty of energy—lot's of girl power.

Gabby then took Amy into the VIP lounge to the left of the Mast Stage and introduced her to Carly Johnson, a long-time friend. Amy was thrilled to meet Carly and confessed she absolutely loved her sultry voice ever since seeing her with Liberation Prophecy. Gabby mentioned she bought two copies of the vinyl pressing of "Hit the Ground Running" at Matt Anthony's Record Shop and sent one to Amy in New York.

There was big disappointment when Denzel Curry canceled due to an injury, so they looked into Big Frieda at 4:30 on the Ocean Stage. The Queen of Bounce and her crew did not disappoint. She invited volunteers from the crowd onstage for a twerk contest. Gabby and Amy thought about it, but passed.

Next Gabby took Amy back to the VIP Lounge and introduced her to another pal, Tyler Childers. Tyler was a country star on the rise, yet quite humble. They talked for a bit. Laughed and joked around. Gabby wished him well on his new album and commented the video for "Country Squire" was one of the funniest videos she'd ever seen and the one for "All Your'n" was just about the trippiest video she had ever seen in all of her 15 years of paying attention to such things. Tyler thanked her.

His set ended just after 8:30. Amy and Gabby were highly entertained. They both enjoyed Tyler's performance and agreed that his talent was extraordinary and his songs quite catchy.

As they were leaving the Mast Stage after Tyler's show, Gabby caught sight of another friend and introduced Amy to artist, actor and musician Will Oldham, one of the legends of Louisville.

They scooted over to the Boom Stage to Chvrches and totally dug their pop-synth sounds and Lauren Mayberry's voice. This was the real discovery for Amy and Gabby at the festival.

At their finish Gabby and Amy shifted back to the Mast Stage and the folksy, melodic, soulful sounds of the Avett Brothers.

2019 Forecastle was coming to an end and many had great memories, The DDs included—but others missed out somewhat.

****

It was Monday morning and Alexander was feeling himself again. He got out on the half-pipe early and really leaned into it. He was feeling it.

Amy heard him and joined him.

"Daddy, Saturday night, why did you go so overboard?"

"It's my one big party day/night of the year."

"No. There's something else."

Alexander sighed, almost expecting this from his bloodhound daughter. "Your mother came over Friday night to help me take care of Roxanne. Anyway, it just got me thinking late Saturday night after we got home from the festival and I stayed up late, way past my bedtime and it ended with me drowning my sorrows."

"Wait. Hold on, this is news to me and very surprising news. My mother helped you babysit an infant?"

"Your mother was a good mother, in her own way."

"This is not in her nature."

"Maybe it's a dry run for when she has grandchildren."

"Thanks for that input, Dad."

Alexander shrugged, "Just looking through her lens."

"Right, only her perspective. I see why you went off the deep end."

Alexander just grunted and shook his head. "Did you enjoy the festival?"

"I did, very much so. It was a great time."

"And Sunday?"

"Carly Johnson was fantastic."

"I love her voice," said Alexander.

"And you'll be interested to know that she's really nice and interesting to talk to."

"You talked to her?"

"Yes. Then I met Tyler Childers."

"Wait, what?? You met Tyler Childers?"

"Yes, Daddy, we hung out with him."

"No..."

"Yes." Amy showed several pics on her phone of Carly, Tyler and Amy and Gabby.

Alexander grimaced at this, "How?"

Amy boasted, "Gabby is pretty darn connected."

Alexander was still unpacking this, "You hung out with Tyler?"

"Yes. Really intelligent and talented. And funny too."

"Yesterday?"

"Correct. The last day of the festival, Daddy, when you 'hesitated' on going. And as you know, quote, 'Hesitation of any kind is a sign of mental decay in the young, and a physical weakness in the old.' Oscar Wilde said, in *The Importance of Being Earnest.*"

Alexander was not amused, "Throwing quotes at me! How is this helping??"

"Exactly," said Amy."

Alexander frowned at her counter jab.

"And I chatted with Will Oldham."

"You met Will Oldham??" Alexander's jaw dropped open.

"Yesterday, at the festival. Is the dreaded FOMO creeping up on you? Because I was thinking, isn't meeting and jamming with Carly, Tyler and Will on your bucket list somewhere? Actually, I think it's right at the top."

Alexander sat and silently stewed.

16

It was mid-week before Alexander's funk cleared up. To his delight, Abby thanked him again for babysitting with three bottles of Old 502 Bourbon Barrel Red wine. The other festival he rarely missed was also coming right up. Alexander regarded *Fear and Loathing in Las Vegas* and *Fear and Loathing on the Campaign Trail* as classics.

Hunter Thompson and Alexander Arrington both held Richard Nixon in the same regard and had discussions on the subject on various occasions. Alexander deeply regretted Hunter departing this mortal coil so early, as presently there were subjects that needed the bite of his analysis.

Alexander read a press release:

Thursday, July 18, 2019

6:00 PM - 8:00 PM

Frazier History Museum

Join us for a Gonzo Birthday Bash to celebrate Louisville's Hunter S. Thompson on what would have been his 82nd birthday. Friends, fans, and special guests will gather to toast him and eat cake in his honor at the Frazier History Museum.

Food provided by Adrienne & Co. Bakery, Another Place Sandwich Shop, and Jimmy Can't Dance. Each guest will receive a ticket for one complimentary Flying Dog Brewery beer. Other drinks are available for purchase.

Freak Power, Thompson's bid for Sheriff in Aspen, is currently on exhibit at the Frazier.

Alexander, Amy and Granddad attended.

On Friday, July 19th, from 5-10pm, Alexander and Amy visited the Speed Museum for the monthly after-hours party. Hunter's son, Juan, was there to tell some stories, as well as Thompson scholar Dr. Rory Feehan.

Alexander wondered what Hunter would think about having scholars study his work.

Another press release described the next night:

GonzoFest Louisville returns in 2019 on Saturday, July 20, the Saturday after Hunter S. Thompson's birthday, to the Louisville Free Public Library!

GonzoFest Louisville is a literary and music festival honoring the legacy of Hunter S. Thompson through spoken word, poetry, art, panel discussions, live music, and more.

****

It was Saturday and Alexander and Amy were in the back of a car riding to the library.

"What happened with Granddad and Mrs. Simmons?" asked Alexander.

"He was working and she was doing something," said Amy. "She said it was a personal day."

They rode some more.

"The mayor has proclaimed 2019 to be the Year of Gonzo," stated Alexander.

"Daddy, does that mean swilling copious amounts of amber liquor, smoking green bud and digesting purple microdot?"

Alexander scoffed, "Come on now, some of it sure, I saw it, but Hunter didn't do *all of that stuff*, really..."

They arrived at the Louisville Free Public Library and settled in to hear some speakers. They both enjoyed listening to some of those tales. Hunter's editorial assistant, Cheryl Della Pietra, wrote in *Gonzo Girl* that Chivas and water was his all-day drink—and that he actually did all the drugs he bragged about: cocaine, LSD, mescaline, magic mushrooms and still was able to function and even write.

One speaker talked about the feud Hunter was having with his 'jerk of a neighbor' next to his place in Woody Creek, Colorado. One night, drunk and coked out of his gourd, Hunter drove onto the neighbor's estate and 'lit it up' by blasting a shotgun, shooting a pistol and firing off a burst or two from an automatic rifle. He hightailed it back to his place and when the authorities paid him a call, Hunter claimed he was attacked by a giant porcupine and was defending himself. No charges were filed.

On the way home from the library Amy was giggling, "Next time I'm in Colorado I'm going to be alert for those giant porcupines."

Alexander had a laugh that morphed into a frustrated groan.

"What, Daddy?"

"You know I've been nominated twice to be a Kentucky Colonel."

"I'm aware. You weren't interested when you were younger."

"A man lives his life, gets older and learns things; his perspective changes or it should. A child rarely really understands the world they're in."

"Now you want it."

"Indeed. It is a high honor."

"It is a high honor. But perhaps, Daddy, let me describe them as your 'quirky characteristics,' that prevent you from being accepted into their selective club."

Alexander was glum, "Hunter S. Thompson was a Kentucky Colonel."

"Huh." Amy didn't know how to respond to that.

****

It was a couple of days after Gonzo. Alexander and Amy were skating together on the half-pipe.

"Daddy, since Hunter S. Thompson ran for sheriff in Aspen, would you ever consider it?"

"Running for sheriff of Aspen?"

Amy rolled her eyes.

"Honey, he wasn't victorious and I wouldn't be either. I doubt I could be elected dogcatcher, since I'd probably let all the mutts go."

"Hunter didn't take it seriously. It was for publicity. What about you getting serious with your lawyering?"

Alexander was taken aback, "I am quite serious about the law."

"I talk not of the practice, but the promotion."

"I have a billboard. You should hear the compliments I get from it."

"That's not enough. You should do a commercial."

"A commercial?"

"Yes. You'd be great. We can run it on local TV and online. I'll produce it and Gabby will direct it. She's done several already. I've seen her reel, she's good."

Alexander thought about it and shook his head. "No. I don't think so."

****

Amy and Gabby met the next day. They watched commercials from several different styles of lawyers. First the nice ones, then the pushy ones and then the scary ones that smashed stuff. They hashed out ideas and got a script for a 30-second ad.

Alexander read the copy and was won over. Two days later Gabby's six-person crew had set up lights and two HD digital cameras on tripods in Alexander's den pointed at his desk.

"How are we doing?" asked Gabby, as she entered surveying the location.

"We're good," said one of the PAs.

Alexander was studying the script. One PA did his makeup and another mic'd him. The light readings and sound levels were checked.

Amy came in and looked at Gabby who appeared positive.

Alexander had memorized the lines. He rattled the words off to himself. He was ready.

The crew manned the lights and cameras and signaled they were set. Amy stood off to the side.

"Alexander, do you want to rehearse?" asked Gabby.

"I got it down. Ready for my close up."

"Okay, great… And action," Gabby said.

Alexander stared into the lens and froze.

Gabby was gentle, "Alexander?"

"Yes, sorry."

"Whenever, you're ready."

"Right… Hello, I'm Alexander Arrington. I've been an attorney in Louisville and the surrounding areas in the Commonwealth of Kentucky for going on 25 years…" Alexander paused. Beads of sweat appeared on his brow. His heart was racing and his mouth was getting dry. "Sorry." He gulped some water.

"You want to touch him up," Gabby directed.

The PA brushed on some more makeup powder.

"Okay, let's take it from the top. Now that we got the rehearsal in, let's go for it. Mark it." A PA did the slate. "And action."

"Hello, I'm Alexander Arrington. I've been an attorney in Louisville and the surrounding areas in the Commonwealth of Kentucky for going on 25 years. If it's business litigation, civil trials…" Alexander paused. "I'm sorry. I'm just not myself today. Let's put this on hold. I'll pay you all for a full day's work."

Alexander took off the mic and promptly exited the room. Gabby and Amy stared at each other.

****

Amy gave him some time. She started skating the pipe. Alexander joined her.

"I don't want to talk about it."

"I didn't ask," replied Amy, then hearing an alert on her phone. She skated up onto the lip and checked.

"What's that?" Alexander continued skating.

Amy read the article. "My Zabéla alert. I'm now following her. Since Lannie is out there."

"Zabéla Z?" Alexander lost his balance and had to catch himself.

Amy hesitated and gave her dad a grim look, "Yes, she's going to be on *Current Cross Currents* this evening."

Alexander mumbled, "Ugh, John Tenorio..." He sulked.

Amy brooded as well, "John Tenorio..."

Alexander finally rebounded, "We need some BBQ."

"Sure..." Amy needed a diversion.

"Ambrosia, prepare yourself for the best BBQ you'll ever sink your teeth into."

"That's a high bar to get over, Daddy."

"You've been advised, darling."

They were soon on the west side. 26th Street and Broadway. Alexander took Amy to YaYa's BBQ Shack. It was a popular BBQ stand in the neighborhood.

Alexander and David hugged as they arrived. He was a bear of a man, in good spirits.

"Alexander, always good to see you, my brother."

"David McAtee, or YaYa. It's just that I knew you before."

"Perfectly understandable, Alexander and we both are getting older."

"True. I want to introduce you to my daughter, Amy."

"Hello, Amy. Welcome to YaYa's."

"Nice to meet you, YaYa."

Alexander was eyeing the menu, "How's your mama Odessa?"

"She's fine. Keeping everyone in line."

"Good. Tell her I said hello."

"Will do."

"We're hungry," said Alexander.

YaYa grinned, "Luckily you've come to the right place."

Alexander and Amy went in and were each served an order of his ribs and dug in.

"You're right, Daddy. These are the best I've ever had."

"David or YaYa, is a fixture in the community."

"YaYa?" asked Amy.

"That's the name he took when he became a Rastafarian."

"Ah."

"He's a protector. Cops eat here. They try to pay but he rarely accepts payment from them. He'll also feed a lost soul that's down on their luck."

Amy watched YaYa interact with his customers. He knew everyone by name and joked around with them.

****

When Alexander and Amy returned home, they learned from Mrs. Simmons that Granddad was deep into a creative spurt and was not to be disturbed. Alexander needed to do some reading and excused himself.

"How was YaYa's?" asked Mrs. Simmons.

"Loved it. However, the rest of the day not so great."

Mrs. Simmons was responding to an email on her phone, "The commercial didn't work out."

"No."

Mrs. Simmons sent the correspondence, "In my many years I've learned there is usually more than one path to get to a destination. Just keep your eyes and ears open for the signposts."

Amy nodded and pondered that and then noticed how busy she was. "What are you doing, Mrs. Simmons?"

"Other than the Kentucky Seedlings Dinner, we're hosting a charity fundraiser coming up."

"We are? For what?"

"The Summer Shakespeare Festival and the Bekki Jo Schneider internship program. Alexander didn't tell you?"

Amy shook her head, "He has other things on his mind."

"Bekki Jo died last year. She was an actress, writer and producer. Such a dear person. She owned the Derby Dinner Playhouse. We saw several shows there. It was a great place. It's such a loss to the local theater family. This weekend Casa Arrington is having a fund-raising dinner for the Bekki Jo Schneider Internship Program. 100 tickets at $100 were available and we sold out. Dulsett Distilleries donated 10 bottles of their finest bourbon."

"They did? Nice."

"And then we're going to the park to watch *King Lear*."

"Sounds fun," said Amy, who really was looking forward to this.

Amy retreated to her room and sent a text.

AMY: thanks for the high class hootch

BOBBY: you're welcome, save some for the auction.

AMY: would you be interested in being my date this Saturday?

BOBBY: what would this require?

AMY: come to a dinner and bring sparkling conversation

BOBBY: I can do that

AMY: And watch *King Lear* in the park after that

BOBBY: I would be interested

Bobby recalled the last time he delved into this drama was in high school. He put off a distribution meeting he was dreading anyway and immediately went online and began reading the play on his laptop—halfway through he went Cliff Notes.

****

It was a lovely Saturday afternoon and the cast of *King Lear* for the Summer Shakespeare Festival mingled with the guests at Casa Arrington and would be performing later that evening at Central Park. April sent a nice check, but she didn't show up at CA. It was a lively crowd and everyone was enjoying themselves.

Alexander stood on a platform and addressed the gathered. "I believe I'm safe in saying Bekki Jo touched every one of our lives here. Up until her death last year, on May 4th, 2018, she had been the friend, confidant, coach, shoulder to cry on and mother to us all. She helped so many. And then there was her immense talents: writer, director, performer and manager. Bekki Jo had a prolific career, won many honors, yet remained relatively humble. I miss her. I miss her energy. I miss her love. But her spirit remains. Let's raise a toast to Bekki Jo."

The group raised their glasses and drank. There wasn't a dry eye after that.

Gabby turned to Amy, next to Bobby, and whispered, "Why can't he do that on camera?"

Amy could only shake her head.

****

Oscar Sanderson, 'Oz,' a 28-year-old tall Black man, was named for the all-time great hoopster Oscar Robertson, who his mother and father admired.

Alexander had known Oz ever since he noticed him at 12-years-of-age sneaking into a movie theater and recalled he did the exact same thing at his age. When Oz was caught, Alexander paid his way in. Later Oz confessed that although he liked basketball, he didn't want to be a point guard. Alexander paid for what he wanted: theater camp.

At first his parents weren't too keen on this, but were on board now. After directing several theatrical productions and a couple videos of local bands, Oz was getting interest from New York and Hollywood. At the moment he was doing what he dreamed about growing up: directing a production at the Louisville Summer Shakespeare Festival.

Alexander and Oz were alone on a side porch of CA.

"Oz, how have you found *King Lear*?"

"Hmm... The themes Shakespeare explored continue to be universal. Can the poor and forgotten find meaning and a purpose?"

"True," agreed Alexander. "Lear doubts life would be bearable without the wealth to acquire things, the creature comforts and status which goes with it. He certainly didn't listen to the Buddha's audiobook."

"Directing this play has made me realize the essence of power."

"Which is?"

"It's transitory. If people are getting run over and getting the run around... When someone has very little to lose, no dignity, no respect and little hope, that's when it becomes dangerous to all and change will be quicker. It only takes a spark."

"How many times have we seen that rerun?" asked Alexander, who couldn't help but think of a certain recent house guest at CA.

"The transition is often tragic and regretful, but in many cases," mused Oz, "it's necessary in the search for—"

"A wise and benevolent ruler," said Alexander.

"True," agreed Oz. "Tis a noble ideal. However, I know a world where not having your door kicked in and robbed or violated by the state is good enough." They eyed the people having a good time. "Alexander, since you know the play even better than me, what do you think?"

"Oh boy... Lear has many problems. First, all that wealth and no real retirement plan. Did he really think he could spend the rest of his days bouncing around to the different places he's bestowed to his daughters? And they would accommodate him at a moment's notice, for months on end, with the dozens of horndog knights that were his security team? And Lear's take on power, did he want to walk away from it all or not? He divides his kingdom, retires and then acts like he's still the alpha dog controlling everything. He physically abuses those he sees as lesser. He insults one by calling him a mongrel and another a fool. He's a vain and shallow man, silly and stupid who can't or won't see reality. His vision is clouded by his ravenous ego and vicious nature. Tossing the true, loyal, daughter and favoring the ones that best buttered his chops. If a leader is so delusional, or their self-esteem so fragile, that they don't or can't have that one person that isn't afraid to sugarcoat it and say the real shit, then that leader is also doomed to a transition much sooner, rather than later, only to rage off into the night."

****

Bobby found a former teammate and they were getting caught up.

Alexander and Amy were sipping their drinks, when a male friend in his early 30's walked up.

"Hi, Amy."

"Daddy, this is Conner. Conner, this is Alexander Arrington."

"I am well aware of you, sir."

Alexander chuckled, "Sounds like a Fed giving me a warning."

Conner laughed nervously, "No, no, sir."

"Call me Alexander and it's nice to meet you, Conner."

"Conner is in *King Lear* tonight."

"Marvelous! What part?"

"I play Kent."

Alexander came to life, "Kent, oh Kent is perhaps the most loyal of all the Bard's characters. He stood by Lear when others didn't. I'm looking at you, Goneril and Regan." Alexander glared at the two actresses playing the parts of the bad daughters. They were amused by his teasing.

Conner was surprised, "You know this play?"

"He does," Amy boasted. "He's memorized it and several more."

"Say what?" Conner was now amazed.

Alexander shrugged and then nodded. "I use it as a mental exercise."

Conner thought he was being played, "Naw… Really?"

Alexander took this as a challenge and started to run lines as King Lear.

KING LEAR

"What art thou?"

KENT

"A very honest-hearted fellow, and as poor as the king."

KING LEAR

"If thou be as poor for a subject as he is for a

king, thou art poor enough. What wouldst thou?"

KENT

"Service."

KING LEAR

"Who wouldst thou serve?"

KENT

"You."

KING LEAR

"Dost thou know me, fellow?"

KENT

"No, sir; but you have that in your countenance

which I would fain call master."

KING LEAR

"What's that?"

KENT

"Authority."

KING LEAR

"What services canst thou do?"

KENT

"I can keep honest counsel, ride, run, mar a curious

tale in telling it, and deliver a plain message

bluntly: that which ordinary men are fit for, I am

qualified in; and the best of me is diligence."

KING LEAR

"How old art thou?"

KENT

"Not so young, sir, to love a woman for singing, nor

so old to dote on her for any thing: I have years

on my back forty-eight."

KING LEAR

"Follow me; thou shalt serve me: if I like thee no

worse after dinner, I will not part from thee yet.

Dinner, ho, dinner! Where's my knave? My fool?

Go you, and call my fool hither."

The crowd had gathered around, applauded and cheered Alexander, who took a bow.

Oz was impressed, but not surprised. Mrs. Simmons just smiled.

Gabby threw up her arms and turned to Amy who had a quizzical look of amusement.

****

Soon after arriving back stage in Central Park for their call times, half the cast had food poisoning and were upchucking.

Meanwhile the audience was settling in. Alexander noticed April and Reston a few seats over and smiled politely at them. Mrs. Simmons, Amy and Bobby went over to chat.

Oz was devastated. He was about to make the announcement, until he had an idea—actually more of a Hail Mary.

With Amy and Bobby currently visiting April and Reston over at their seats, Oz sat next to Alexander.

"Hey, Oz. Shouldn't you be prepping the troops?"

Oz appeared to be in deep thought. "You know the story about the 12th Man at Texas A&M?"

"Yes, a student is brought in from the stands to play for the home team."

"Correct. 1922."

Alexander added, "But he didn't actually play."

"Don't ruin a good legend. I'm here to ask you to consider something. You see all these people here tonight, anticipating the drama, ready for the magic that is theater, especially when it's from the Bard."

"I gotcha, Oz. The play's the thing."

"Alexander, a bunch of the cast got sick on something they ate at your party."

"What? You're joking."

"Dead serious."

Alexander was shocked to hear that.

"Maybe I shouldn't say it like that. No one died."

"We used two catering companies… I didn't have any of the food."

"Neither did I," said Oz. "We both were nursing our bourbon."

"What about tonight?"

"Half the cast is fine. It's rep, we have others that can step in. Two can double up, but the first, second and third string Lear performers, even the taxi squad, are down. If we don't have someone step in and play Lear, we'll have to cancel."

It took just a moment and then Alexander frowned with disbelief, "Hold on…are you asking *me* to step in?"

"As I said, you know the play better than me."

"But I've never played the role on stage. The last time I was in a play was high school and I had four lines."

"You perform every day on your job."

Alexander gave it some thought and it wasn't gaining any traction.

"Alexander, weren't you the one who encouraged me to follow my dream? You got me a scholarship to theater camp, that you actually paid for yourself."

Alexander was too stunned at the moment to respond to that.

"You thought I didn't know. Your investment is paying off. This is a big moment for me."

Alexander was still rocked, but getting his wits about him, "And you want me to come in from the stands and play quarterback, without knowing the signals."

"But you're familiar with the playbook. You know the text forwards and backwards."

Alexander glanced around at all the people happily waiting in their seats filled with anticipation.

Oz locked on, "The show must go on."

Alexander saw April and Reston talking to Amy and Bobby. He turned and nodded to Oz, "Okay…once more unto the breach."

Oz patted him on the back and forced a grin, "Good, good, but that's from *Henry V*."

Alexander was hustled backstage, garbed and had makeup applied as he was getting a crash course from Oz on the blocking in the first act. The other performers gave Alexander encouragement, while trying to make themselves believe he could actually pull this off.

Conner gave him a thumbs up that did bolster him, luckily Alexander didn't see him grimace over what was unfolding.

They returned to the seats and Amy sighed, "I wonder where Daddy went?"

Bobby glanced around, "I don't see him."

"Me neither," said Mrs. Simmons.

Gabby arrived, "Hey."

"Gab, have you seen my dad?"

"Nope, I just got here."

Amy groaned, "Don't tell me, he saw Reston and mom and he bailed."

The lights soon dimmed and the play began. When Alexander appeared as King Lear, Amy and April were stunned, they made eye contact.

Reston whispered, "What's he doing now?"

Bobby leaned over to Amy, "Alexander is playing King Lear?"

"After years of hearing him quote the Bard," said Mrs. Simmons, "I'm ready for this."

Gabby turned around with a confused glare.

Amy just shrugged, wide-eyed seeing the same look in her mother; who was demanding some clarification, but getting nothing.

Mrs. Simmons sat up with some anticipation, "After hearing him quote the Bard forever, I'm reading for this."

At every scene change and act break Oz was giving him direction on where to be, at what line. There had only been a few miscues that only a Shakespeare scholar would have noticed. After a bit of a shaky start, Alexander had gotten his sea legs and the crowd was on board and along for the ride.

Finally, it was nearing the end:

KING LEAR

"Howl, howl, howl, howl! O, you are men of stones:

Had I your tongues and eyes, I'd use them so

That heaven's vault should crack. She's gone forever!

I know when one is dead, and when one lives;

She's dead as earth. Lend me a looking-glass;

If that her breath will mist or stain the stone,

Why, then she lives."

KENT

"Is this the promised end."

EDGAR

"Or image of that horror?"

ALBANY

"Fall, and cease!"

KING LEAR

"This feather stirs; she lives! if it be so,

It is a chance which does redeem all sorrows

That ever I have felt."

KENT

[Kneeling] "O my good master!"

KING LEAR

"Prithee, away."

EDGAR

"'Tis noble Kent, your friend."

KING LEAR

"A plague upon you, murderers, traitors all!

I might have saved her; now she's gone forever!"

Alexander stared out at April, thinking that she was gone forever. April was transfixed by his performance. Reston, not so. Amy couldn't believe what she was seeing.

KING LEAR

"Cordelia, Cordelia! Stay a little. Ha!

What is't thou say'st? Her voice was ever soft,

Gentle, and low, an excellent thing in a woman.

I kill'd the slave that was a-hanging thee."

CAPTAIN

"'Tis true, my lords, he did."

KING LEAR

"Did I not, fellow?

I have seen the day, with my good biting falchion

I would have made them skip: I am old now,

And these same crosses spoil me. Who are you?

Mine eyes are not o' the best: I'll tell you straight...

"And my poor fool is hang'd! No, no, no life!

Why should a dog, a horse, a rat, have life,

And thou no breath at all? Thou'lt come no more,

Never, never, never, never, never!

Pray you, undo this button: thank you, sir.

Do you see this? Look on her, look, her lips,

Look there, look there!"

King Lear died. Alexander slid down into his chair.

The play ended a few moments later followed by a thunderous standing ovation.

April applauded loudly. Reston clapped his hands.

Mrs. Simmons, Bobby, Amy and Gabby enthusiastically cheered him.

There was a huge sigh of relief, mixed with jubilation among the participants in the production. A couple of the crew hoisted Alexander up and carried him around on their shoulders as everyone patted Alexander on the back.

Oz called out, "Bekki Jo is smiling down on this performance and your portrayal, Alexander."

"Hear! Hear!" rang out.

Gabby was blown away by what she just experienced.

Alexander was toted over by Bobby, Amy and Gabby, who clapped and yelled.

Alexander nodded to them. He was then brought by April who was thrilled for him.

Alexander nodded to her. Reston applauded politely. Alexander nodded to him.

Judge Wilbur and Willodean Winslow, also in attendance, were up and cheering him as well. "Way to go, Alexander! Bravo!"

Alexander nodded to them.

When he was carried to the other side of the crowd Alexander was pleasantly surprised to find Sherri, smiling, standing and clapping, with vigor.

Alexander nodded to her.

April noticed. She lost her smile and her eyes narrowed.

Reston spied April's reaction to her old rival's response to her ex.

While Bobby and Gabby gathered themselves to leave, Amy noticed her mother's sour reaction to her father enjoying Sherri's enthusiastic applause and Reston's silent seething over it all.

Alexander was carried off backstage.

April continued to glare at Sherri, who sensed something. She turned and realized April was focused on her, but only for a moment. The two turned away from each other, bad blood still simmering after all of these years.

Amy just shook her head at this and joined Mrs. Simmons, Bobby and Gabby on the way out.

****

It was the next day. Amy and Gabby met at Derby City Pizza on Brownsboro Road on the east side and shared a large vegetarian pizza.

Gabby pondered, "I think it's because he can see the audience. It's immediate. They're in it together and he's controlling the room."

Amy thought that through, "When you're staring into the lens, you relinquish control."

Gabby added, "You have no idea where the performance goes, who sees it or how it's manipulated."

They sat and ruminated.

"I tried prodding, a bit of encouragement, some coaxing," Gabby groused. "I know he doesn't have glossophobia."

"Fear of public speaking. No, my dad thrives there."

Gabby sighed, "This must be why he uses the owl avatar, instead of appearing as himself on camera."

Amy had a brainstorm, "I think we should try again with the commercial."

"Have the owl appear for him?" asked Gabby.

"No. Let's go a different route. A new path," said Amy. "I think I know how to do it."

****

The next morning Alexander was focused as he digested Corn Flakes and Joe Gerth's latest column in the *Louisville Courier-Journal.*

"Morning, Daddy."

Alexander stopped reading and smiled, "Good morning, honey. How are you?"

"Super," said Amy. "You?"

"Couldn't be better," he went back to reading and nodding slowly.

"Great, then you'll be up for my idea. We make another go at shooting your commercial."

Alexander paused, squinted at the notion and shook his head no.

****

Two days later Gabby and Amy filmed Alexander petting a horse and at several iconic Louisville locations listening to people, strolling in Waterfront Park, listening to people, in a coffee shop, listening to people, in front of the court house, listening to more people and finally crossing Four Corners

Bridge over the Ohio River—just as the Belle of Louisville chugged under him.

"Cut!" yelled Gabby. "That's great Alexander, you're a natural."

Alexander did a little jig, "Thank you."

"Let's go back to your casa."

When they arrived back at CA, Gabby and Amy brought Alexander into the den, where Abby was sitting on a chair wearing glasses.

"You remember the lines we had for you?" asked Gabby.

"Yes."

"Can you say them to Abby?"

"You said I didn't have to perform in front of a camera."

Gabby glanced around, "Do you see a camera in here?"

Alexander checked the brightly lit room. He peeked behind a curtain, as a goof.

"Think of her as the jury," said Gabby. "A jury of one and you're selling yourself with that script. You're the defendant on trial."

"I can do that," said Alexander, as he composed himself and turned towards Abby. "Hello, I'm Alexander Arrington..." He finished saying the lines.

"Is that the best you can do?" asked Gabby.

Alexander frowned at that and delivered the script again, perfectly.

Gabby nodded.

"I'm hungry!" declared Amy.

"Me too," said Abby.

Gabby was gathering her stuff, "I'll take a rain check. I need to get to work."

"Okay, Gabby, see you later," said Amy. "Daddy, I'm grilling steaks, you in?"

"Yeah, sure..." Alexander observed Gabby.

"Could you go ask Granddad?" Amy inquired easing into his line of sight.

"Okay..." Alexander said, as he leaned around her and witnessed Abby hand the glasses off to Gabby, who slyly pocketed them. He nodded to himself, "AVI? HD 1080p?"

"In the glasses? Yes, Daddy."

"Thought so."

"Did you now?"

Alexander gave her the side-eye, "Tell Gabby to be careful with that micro memory card, really easy to lose when you pop it out of the frames."

"Thanks. Good to know," Amy said.

****

The next morning Amy was coming back from a run and found Granddad and Old Man Miller mid-encounter out front.

"And Artie, I heard about the kerfuffle with your big theater party," laughed Old Man Miller, from the sidewalk, pointing his cane.

Granddad was checking some of his plants in the front yard. "Yes, we had a case of food poisoning."

"I heard half were blowing chunks, what a sight that must have been!"

"You want to take credit?"

"I wasn't there. It was probably your potato salad. Positively boring."

"My potato salad is excellent!"

"Artie, you are so stupid!"

"Melvin, I may be *ignorant* of many things, like why is it *Generally* Accepted Accounting Rules? Do some people have a different rule book? I'm also ignorant on how you ever graduated from the University of Kentucky—but I am *not* stupid. I am able to process information and make an informed decision."

"You're just a moron, Artie. Have a nice day," Old Man Miller turned to Amy and noticed her. "Good morning, Amy."

"Mr. Miller," Amy replied, cordially. "Yes, good morning. Is everything okay?"

"Your granddad just needed to get his trash talking in."

"No, *you* were trash talking," countered Granddad. "I was just *taking out* the trash."

Old Man Miller laughed, "Since you're not actually in possession of a garbage bag and just came out of the house, that qualifies as 'trash talking' as well. Res ipsa loquitur. Ask your granddaughter to explain it to you."

"I know what it means, fool."

Old Man Miller tipped his cap to Amy, "Good day, ma'am."

"Mr. Miller." Amy joined her granddad and watched the elderly man hobble on his cane across the street to his place. "You never told me who bought their house first. You or him?"

"I bought first and then the one across the street became available and he took it. At the time I suspected it was just to pester me, over the years I came to realize it was more than a suspicion."

"How did this all start?"

"How did the feud start between Old Man Miller and myself? We first met back in the Haymarket."

"That sounds familiar."

"The Haymarket was a giant gathering area of commerce near downtown. It had been on-going since the 1890s and lasted into the early 60's."

"They sold hay?"

"Not much, really. It was the ultimate farmer's market for people. A giant distribution zone for food and other stuff. Heading north on Interstate-65, it was located where the freeway jogs to the right at Liberty Street before crossing the Ohio River. Oh brother, this tightly confined space was capitalism in its purest form. Success required persistence, guile and sharp elbows. When we were kids just starting out, Old Man Miller and I worked for competing vendors."

"Is that when the bad blood started?"

"More or less."

"I'm trying to get a handle on this conflict between you two. What caused it?"

"I don't rightly remember. It was business related, or it might have been over a girl."

"Seriously? You don't even know the genesis of this decades long battle?"

Granddad waved that away and went off as he continued to attend to his plants.

Amy took a look at Old Man Miller before he entered his residence. He turned around to observe CA and noticed that Amy was watching him. He sported a wicked grin. She entered and for a second wondered if he was responsible for the food poisoning.

When Granddad saw her clear the area, he did a search on his phone: 'res ipsa loquitor.'

****

After lunch Granddad was on his stationary bike and not wearing his VR goggles at the moment. Amy stopped by.

"Hey, sugar."

"Hi, Granddad. I'm still curious about what happened between you two after the Haymarket."

He got off the bike and they both went to the front window.

Granddad glanced out and sighed, "We both turned 18, he joined the Army and I joined the Navy. By the early 1960s we were both out, back in Louisville and starting families. I had yearnings to be an artist, but needed to make a living."

"What'd you do?" asked Amy.

"Luckily, I had met three guys who were merging two theater groups that would become the Actors Theatre of Louisville: Richard Block, Ewell Cornett and Dann Byck Jr. I applied and was hired. I learned all the jobs. I worked over the years as a set, lighting and sound designer at Actors Theatre of Louisville. When Jon Jory started the Humana Festival in 1976, I worked the production crew. I went to night school at the University of Louisville and studied design and landscaping and graduated with a BA in art."

"And Mr. Melvin Miller?"

"Old Man Miller went to the University of Kentucky and graduated from their College of Business with a degree in accountancy. From there he became a CIA, Certified Internal Auditor. When I saw him he always had some crack about the sets or the lighting of the productions I was involved with."

"I see."

"You know, for him I think one of the great things about accounting forensics in his view is there's way less human interaction. Mel was feared by executives during his time as a financial overseer. He was married, had a boy and a girl and was soon divorced. They all moved far away."

"Oh," said Amy, trying to imagine this.

Alexander joined them and also glanced out the window.

Granddad stared at his house, "Melvin retired with quite a large nest egg and now gets his jollies by betting on sports and competing with me over who could put on the best holiday presentation for Easter, July 4th, Halloween, Thanksgiving and Christmas—the majors."

"I've seen some of his efforts, they're pretty good," said Amy.

"They're excellent," announced Alexander. "He gets what he pays for."

Granddad groused, "He hires big name designers to help his cause."

Amy was impressed, "This is a pretty intense rivalry."

"I would say so," said Alexander.

Amy asked, "Do you think he would ever use some of that large nest egg to sabotage one of the gatherings here to make you look bad?"

Alexander and Granddad both frowned and then thought about it.

Amy observed Old Man Miller observing Casa Arrington through his front window.

Amy stepped back from her front window, but caught sight of Sean across the street. He was sitting on a motorcycle and staring at the house. "It's Sean." Amy ran outside.

"Sean??" Alexander followed.

Sean started his bike and quickly rode off.

Amy saw this, ran to the garage, jumped into the car and pulled out before her father could get in. He huffed at that.

Sean was rushing to get back home. They raced through the streets and he scooted onto his property. Amy pulled up, got out of the car and strode up to him as he made it to his door.

"Scoping out our house? Preparing for the next attack?"

Sean snickered, "What do you want, Stacey? Feeling ill?"

"Yeah, someone wrecked a party we had at my family's house. Messed with the hors d'oeuvres."

"Zowie, Stacy, did you hire some dumb Chad for security?"

"Know anything about the incident, Sean?"

"I heard it was awful. Why would anyone want to have another party at your place again?"

"Did you get some payback with that food poisoning, Sean?"

"Did someone embarrass you, Stacey? Ruin your day?"

"Sean, maybe you need to be really punished."

"Maybe *you* were punished, Stacey."

"I could have you dropped so deep in Delilah's dungeon you aren't found, ever."

"Try it." Sean sported a subtle smirk.

It chilled her to see his joy.

"Get off the property or I'll call the cops, 'cause your trespassing, Stacey." He slammed the door in her face.

Amy stood there for a second emotionless. She walked back to the car and made a call, "Hi, Kelly, could you check on Gokuro Gangsta? Something's changed. Thanks."

Amy went back home and 20 minutes later she got a text.

KELLY: can you talk?

AMY: yes

Amy's phone rang and she answered it, "Hey, Kel."

"GG is offline. He either quit playing or is using a different avatar."

Amy pondered that, "He's still playing. Can you find out his new name?"

"I'll look, but he knows you're after him. Pretty sure he's covered his tracks."

17

The days were long, warm and a bit sticky, with the occasional welcomed downpour. It was August 2nd, the first Friday of the month. NuLu time. Amy and Gabby strolled on Main St. They went right past Dulsett Distilleries. Gabby stopped and glanced at the business, while Amy kept moving on.

They jumped on one of the trollies deployed on the First Friday Trolly Hop. They got off farther down on Main, wandered through several art galleries, did some shopping and saw some old friends.

"I'm nearly done editing Alexander's commercial."

"Great."

"I noticed we didn't go into Dulsett Distilleries on the tour."

"Right, we didn't go in," said Amy.

"Have you been in since you've been back?"

"No. But we've connected."

"How's Bobby been?"

"I thought I had stress in New York. He has problems with distribution and his Master Distiller is being difficult. Plus, he needs to hedge foreign currencies, in the countries they do business in and not be drowned in the wake of the whales."

"That's some pressure. I was more asking how you and Bobby are?"

"It's low key. I know what it's like to have serious demands on your time."

"Are there still some embers burning between you two?"

"A bit. What about you? How are you, Gab?"

"I'm cool. I have a chill gig and this town rocks."

"But you, personally?"

"I sometimes miss the overnight shift. You get the lunatic fringe calling in."

"Probably more interesting."

"The shields are lowered. You really can connect on a deeper level."

"Easier to form a bond then?"

"Yeah."

"You haven't been able to make connections in the daylight?"

"It's harder."

"I know."

They jumped on another trolly.

"Aim, you seem troubled by something."

"The food poisoning at the event."

"You think it was sabotage?"

"I don't know. I looked into it and I can't make connections there, either, to anything deliberate."

"Do you have a suspect?"

"Yes."

****

Cassidy was a vice-president at Dulsett Distilleries. Currently she was in one of their warehouses. She interacted with the workers, knowing each and every one by name. They stored and rotated the stock. Then she checked in with their Master Distiller to see what she could do about his issues. She listened and calmed him and then promised to take care of his concerns. She drove back to the office, had a quick sandwich and read a report on quality control. She glanced at a picture on her desk of a smiling woman with dark hair. It was Peggy Noe Stevens. One of her heroes. Besides founding multiple companies, creating the popular Kentucky Bourbon Trail, encouraging and mentoring women into leadership positions in the spirits industry, Peggy was the first woman to become a Master Bourbon Taster. She had mentored Cassidy since her Louisville Cardinal undergrad days with sage advice about the industry and life. Cassidy admired how Peggy described herself being 'underestimated,' and using that as her superpower to excel. This was a scenario familiar to Cass. The book Peggy co-wrote, *Which Fork Do I Use with My Bourbon* was now one of her favorites. Cass was lucky enough to get Peggy and the other co-author, Susan Reigler, to both sign it.

Cassidy was in a hurry to prove herself. She knew she wanted to be in the family business. From about 13-years-of-age, Cassidy had been learning the trade. It would be years before she could legally sample her work, which she was doing now some 12 years later. By her mid-teens she knew many secrets of the Master Distiller. Cassidy graduated early, got her MBA, became certified as an Executive Bourbon Steward and returned to Dulsett Distilleries. She was then all of 24 and had been on the job for a year. Being a Dulsett obviously gave her a huge advantage for her career in the industry, but she worked twice as hard to prove she belonged. Her friends always asked Cassidy how she stayed sober with all the tasting. She said she did a lot of spitting, a skill she refined playing softball in high school. Cassidy crossed the hallway and knocked on the CEO's office.

Bobby was at his desk watching Louisville Cardinal basketball highlights on his computer. He clicked to a spreadsheet. "Yes?"

Cassidy entered, "Hey, Bobby. I pulled a dozen samples and tagged these barrels this morning." She dropped a folder with some results she had compiled onto his desk.

"You work too hard, sis," said Bobby. "You should downshift for a bit."

"Someday, soon. Need to check some more quality control. Text me if you need me." Cassidy exited down the stairs and was out the side door.

****

Gabby and Amy jumped off the trolly and shopped some more. Gabby soon had to get to the station for her shift. Amy pondered what to do for just a moment and then started on Louisville's Urban Bourbon Trail. This time when she was in front of Dulsett Distilleries she entered. It was situated in the eastern zone of the world-famous Bourbon District on East Main, bordering NuLu and Butchertown. The back of the complex opened up to Billy Goat Strut Lane. A fact they took great pride in; especially during the annual goat races.

Bobby switched back to the highlights and then checked the time.

Currently on the first floor Amy was among the group of 20 excitedly anticipating the event. This was the 2:30 tour. She overheard more than one hoping Bobby Dulsett would appear.

And there he was, "Hello, folks, welcome to Dulsett Distilleries. I'm Bobby Dulsett."

"We know," someone cried out. They all laughed. Almost all in the group used their phones to take pictures, Amy included, but she was taking pictures of the crowd taking pictures of Bobby.

"I'm happy to tell you about the spirits we produce." Bobby walked the group through the distillation process and didn't skip a beat when he recognized Amy. He gave a summary referencing pictures on the wall of the history of the business. There were samples, which were popular. Taking selfies with Bobby were also popular.

After he made time for everyone in the group Bobby turned to the last person on the tour, Amy. "What about you, ma'am? Care to take a selfie with me?"

"Naw, you don't impress me much, whoever you are."

Some in the group were surprised that Amy was so clueless. They laughed among themselves, "She doesn't know who Bobby is."

The tour was over and Bobby took Amy's hand and led her up to his office on the second floor. They were surrounded by distinguished portraits of several generations of the Dulsett family looking stuffy, stern and accomplished.

"How'd you like my trained seal act?"

"Pretty good."

"Coffee?"

"Yes. Please."

Bobby fixed it just like she wanted and then for himself.

"Honey and cream. You remembered how I liked it."

"Sure," said Bobby. "It's only been what, 10 years?"

Amy was taking in the ambiance, "You know, this is the first time I've been in here."

"Welcome to the nerve center." Bobby motioned for her to sit. They sat in two big leather chairs that faced each other.

They shared summaries of what had transpired professionally for themselves over the decade they had been out of touch.

Bobby finally motioned to the dozen or so portraits around them. "Five generations of Dulsetts, all staring down, reminding me not to dribble the ball off my foot with the family business."

"Especially when dribbling wasn't your strong point. That's some pressure. Shooting was your forte."

"I had a lot of assists too. Can I assist you with some lunch?"

"I'm open, pass me the chow," said Amy.

"Proof on Main?"

"Definitely." Amy checked her watch, "Wait, I think it's closed. Brunch is over and dinner doesn't start until 5pm."

"Not for me."

"Right. You're Bobby Dulsett."

They walked down to Bobby's favorite restaurant. It was closed, but they let Bobby and Amy in. He introduced Amy to Chef Jeff Dailey, who personally cooked a Proof Bison Burger and Amy had the Farm Egg Frittata.

They had the place to themselves as they dined on their food.

"This is a good assist, Bobby. And sure, you were a good passer, but it was your scoring that has Louisville fans naming their sons after you."

"Hardly… How are you doing being back home?"

"It's been good. Really good."

"What will happen in five months?"

"If I want to go back, I can go back. If I don't, then that door is then closed and I move on."

"I see. What do you miss from Manhattan? Culinary? Culture? The clubs? The pro teams? Friends?"

"There are very good restaurants in New York and here too in Louisville." She motioned to where they were. "Culture? The LO, the Louisville Orchestra, 'the most interesting orchestra on the planet.' Thank you, Teddy Abrams. We have top quality theater and the Speed Art Museum is a treasure. Clubs? Not an authority, I don't go to them much, but Louisville has all the nightlife you can handle. The pro teams? I enjoyed a couple Mets games and one trip to the Bronx. But I love the Louisville Bats and the stadium here. I've been to several Knicks games, two Jets games and four Giants games, but my heart is here with the University of Louisville Cardinals hoops and football teams."

"Okay."

"And how's this? I never went to a soccer match in New York, but I was in the stands here at Slugger Field choking on the purple smoke in 2015, when LouCity FC played their first game and won 2-0, with goals from Magnus Rasmussen and Charlie Adams!"

Bobby held back laughing, "Wow, impressive."

"I cheer for the Hoyas, as I graduated from Georgetown, but I grew up rooting for the Cardinals. And while I do have friends in New York, I have friends here, too. Much closer friends."

"What about the buzz of the Big Apple?"

"There is a buzz, but I mostly missed it, too busy working as an associate in a large law firm."

"That must be interesting."

"It's kind of like a giant Pac-Man game. Instead of pellets, you try to gobble as many billable hours as you can, while being chased by ghosts or the Turk."

"The Turk? You mean, like in the training camps of the NFL, the guy that tells you that you're cut from the team?"

"Right. Padmore has an office manager that lets you know that you've been let go because you billed too low, didn't gobble fast enough, too many quarters in a row. It's the Natural Selection process on the way to partnership. If you bill large and maneuver just right, you survive, avoid the Turk and move on to the next level."

"That sounds like serious stress."

"But I don't have the legacy of multiple generations riding on my shoulders."

"True. I'll bet you don't miss the hours you put in."

"I get almost enough sleep I need here."

"Almost?"

"You may recall that I bunk at Casa Arrington."

"Ah. Right. Hmm..."

"What?"

"It's Friday. Do you have any important legal showdowns later today?"

"My daddy always said, lawyers and judges have an agreement. Friday afternoons are to be reserved for debates over Old Forester."

"Ouch."

"And Dulsett Reserve," purred Amy.

"Damn straight. Counselor, I propose we blow this pop stand and take the rest of the day off."

"What do you have in mind, Bobby Dulsett?"

"Something impulsive. Let's go, right now."

"Where?"

"An overnighter. Like we used to do."

"Just take off, right now..."

"I'll show you how I chill out and I'll have you back at Casa Arrington by tomorrow afternoon. Scouts honor."

"You were in the Scouts?"

"No."

"My daddy always warned me to never trust an Ohio River Tick."

"Yet, Alexander is one himself."

"The contradictions and contrasts in my father are really quite fascinating."

"Yes..." Bobby and Amy both gazed into each other's eyes and were taken back ten years, hormones again firing wildly. "And of course," assured Bobby, "I shall be honorable and discrete as to not sullen your reputation in polite society."

"I think that train has *long* left the station. Won't they miss their trained seal here?"

"If they complain, we'll give them a refund."

****

After traveling south on I-65 for about twenty minutes, they passed the city of Shepherdsville. Bobby took the Clermont exit and traveled west for a minute and pulled into the Bullitt County Store. They loaded up on supplies. Amy was able to get service and send a text to Alexander that she was doing an overnighter and turned off her phone.

They drove on Clermont for a moment, pulled into Forest Edge Winery and walked out with three bottles of Forest Edge Old Vine Zinfandel.

"This goes great with pizza," Amy said, with a hint.

Bobby pulled out his phone and sent a text. They drove east on Clermont for a moment until they passed a turn off to the left.

Amy was quite familiar with the area, "There's your rival."

"I know, they have a road named after them: Jim Beam Way."

"Big company," remarked Amy.

"Yeah," said Bobby. "And one poll had them voted number one bourbon in the world. They are challenging to compete against. The Bullitt County Pipeline is being built just north of them and will be supplying them with plenty of liquid natural gas. You think that's a coincidence?"

"That's power," stated Amy.

"LNG is a relatively clean burning fuel. Which leads me to a secret confession."

"What?"

"If I divulge, you won't tell a soul."

"What is it, Bobby?"

"Every now and then I take a taste of Jim Beam's Knob Creek 12."

"Zowie."

"I kind of like the cherry and dark chocolate flavor."

"And this is a big secret?"

"If my father had ever known, or my uncles…it would have been ugly. Even Cassidy. I would never share this with my family."

"That is so sweet you would share this with me. I guess I should reciprocate." Amy thought for a second. "Hmm…even though I'm a lass with Irish blood surging through me, every now and then I don't mind a taste of Glendronach."

"That's a Scottish whisky," intoned Bobby.

"It is."

"And another competitor with Dulsett Distilleries."

"Don't tell the CEO Dulsett Distilleries."

"Thanks for sharing that."

"You're welcome."

Bobby scrunched his face at that and continued driving and then finally announced: "This is what we need. Bernheim Arboretum and Research Forest."

"I absolutely love Bernheim," said Amy. "So does my dad."

****

They continued driving until it was getting dark. Amy had never been here. Tall trees surrounded them. Bobby pulled onto the property. It was a small cabin with a garage. He got out, opened the garage door, got back in and pulled in.

Amy emerged and surveyed the surroundings, "Nice. Remote."

"The way I like it," said Bobby. He opened the cabin door and they entered the sparse interior.

Amy stepped in and glanced around, "There's no basketball stuff. No trophies, sports pictures or awards."

"This is another world. I keep it simple. No landline. No internet. Spotty cell service. No satellite dish. Completely off the grid. There's a wood-burning stove and we do have solar power."

"Totally off the grid? Just like Casa Arrington."

"CA is off the grid with all the modern conveniences. We don't have such distractions here."

Amy moved closer, "How interesting. To have this world that's so simple. To concentrate on what's really important." They kissed.

Bobby said, "I have a DVD player and a library with books I've always wanted to read, but never had the time; when I come here, I have the time."

"Nice."

"It's almost dark, tomorrow we can go for a hike in Bernheim."

"Sounds like a plan."

Bobby checked his watch, "I'm going to do my manly responsibility and go out and hunt and gather food for us."

"Hunt and gather?"

"Yes, ma'am." Bobby said, as he flipped on the outside light and exited. "Now where's my hunting rifle?"

Amy peaked through the curtains and wondered what he had up his sleeve. Two minutes later a car pulled up and delivered a pizza. Bobby paid for it and tipped well. He entered with the pizza box.

"You did a good job hunting and gathering," complimented Amy.

"That was the text I sent on the way down."

"Forward thinking, a trait I admire." Amy opened the pizza box. "What's this?"

"The Mama Bearno's Special. Sausage, pepperoni, onions, green peppers, mushrooms, black and green olives and fresh mozzarella cheese."

They both took a slice and munched away.

Amy chewed and hummed with delight, "I got into a debate over someone on Louisville-style pizza. I mean New York has thin crust and Chicago has deep dish. But Louisville-style is a hybrid between them. It's thin crust with the ample toppings, which makes it seem like deep dish, without the extra dough."

"Exactly," Bobby said, covering his full mouth. "I have a surprise."

Amy scrunched her face at that, "A surprise? Like on a fast break, one of your no-look passes that bounces off the face of your unsuspecting teammate?"

"With you, I promise, no no-looks. Too much respect."

"Or fakes?"

"You can't handcuff my game that much." He pulled out a small sack from his backpack. It contained a DVD. "Something from your past. 65 Mighty Mouse cartoons."

"How did you know I used to watch them, when even I forgot?"

"I asked Alexander what you really liked as a kid. He sent me this."

Amy was pleased with the extra effort. They sipped on the wine and woofed the pizza, while watching Mighty Mouse come to the rescue several times. They again heard the theme song "Here I Come to Save the Day." Amy thought about her dad.

After two episodes they had enough food and drink. Amy turned off the DVD player and they kissed again…

****

It was early the next day. They woke and kissed and it got steamier, until they heard the front door open and someone enter. Bobby put his finger up to her mouth for quiet. He slowly reached for a Glock semi-automatic pistol he kept in the headboard. The front door was heard closing.

"Who's there?" asked Bobby.

Cassidy walked in, "Bobby? Ah!"

Bobby lowered the weapon, "Cass, I said who's there, not come in."

"I didn't see your ride."

"It's parked in the garage."

"Huh. Hi, Amy."

"Hey, Cassidy."

"Uh, sis, we'll be right out, give us a minute."

"Sure."

A few minutes later Bobby and Amy emerged as Cassidy was cooking up eggs and breakfast sausage, had bread toasting, along with freshly squeezed orange juice.

"Look, you two, I'm sorry. Bobby was the one that said I should downshift for a bit. I agreed with him and said it would be soon."

"Did you give me a head's up you were coming, like I always instructed you to?"

"Bobby, I sent you a text, but you were radio silent."

"My phone is off. Besides, you remember how it is with your communicator here."

Cassidy pulled out her phone, "Yeah, still not getting service. How can you handle it?"

"It's kind of nice. Except for moments like these."

Cassidy scooped out some eggs and put them on a large serving plate. "Next time I'll send a smoke signal, though maybe not a good idea so close to a forest." She eyed the DVD case, "Mighty Mouse, wow, I read about people who like to get dressed up in animal costumes. Mighty Mouse is a favorite, along with furry and—"

"No! That's not it, dear sister."

Amy snickered and picked up the case, "I used to love watching this as a kid. Bobby asked my dad and he sent over the DVD."

"I see. You really did this, Bobby?"

"10-4. Did the intel gathering, total black ops."

Cassidy was impressed, "That is really cool. Wait, is this some replicant? I'm not fooled, my brother is not this sensitive."

Bobby scoffed. Amy and Cassidy instantly bonded.

"How did we miss each other when we were younger?" asked Amy.

"You were almost 18 and I was just hitting 15 when you two first dated, no chance for us having any serious friendship."

"Then we will have lunch and catch up," Amy proclaimed.

"I would love that. We have so much in common."

"Whoa," this was rocking Bobby. "Time out. What do you two have in common?"

"You, for one," pronounced Amy.

Cassidy goofed on that, "Girl, I could tell you some stories of him growing up."

"I've hit the motherlode." Amy's eyes bulged with delight.

Bobby's eyes bulged with alarm.

****

The three were walking through the forest on this early summer day awed by the natural splendor.

"This is my pressure release," whispered Bobby, as they took in their surroundings.

"Bernheim Forest is a treasure," said Amy. The giant wooden sculptures in the park were so striking, so hypnotic and so welcoming, among the many trees surrounding them. Amy, Cassidy and Bobby didn't say much, didn't need to. The serenity of the place was so soothing.

****

Meanwhile back at CA, the investigator, Bruno, was giving Alexander an unsettling update on the food poisoning inquiry. Epidemiological, traceback and food and environmental testing had been done. The data showed the outbreak was contained at Casa Arrington. They examined the chain of food production, processing, transportation, handling and preparation, but they couldn't pinpoint the entry point.

"We haven't identified the contaminant or who was behind it," Bruno reported. "Both catering companies denied knowing anything about it. I do know you've received several threats over some of your legal actions."

Alexander waved that away, "Threats are one thing. I've got a trunk full of them. Actions are different."

"And, Alexander, I'm pretty sure Sean Wellington is not over his snit."

"Tell me something I don't know."

****

Amy was back by late Saturday afternoon mentally and spiritually bolstered from the nature field trip. Alexander joined her in the living room.

"Just did an overnighter with Bobby at his cabin by Bernheim."

"I got your text. That must have been nice," Alexander said, his attention trailing off.

"What's wrong, Daddy?"

"Bruno, our investigator was here and said Sean might be active again. The matter I shouldn't know all the details about."

"Yes."

"What should I know or not know about what's being hidden from me?"

"How I was able to get Sean to behave."

"And…"

Her serenity had been drained, "He's off the leash, bitter and I don't know how to contain him anymore."

Alexander sensed her heightened concern.

****

It was very late on this early August summer evening. The annual cicadas had arrived and were making their presence well known. Sitting out back of Casa Arrington was Alexander, in his pajamas, and his friend Shelby Lanier Jr., a Black gentleman just a few years his senior, in a dark suit. They were drinking Dulsett bourbon and smoking cigars.

"Shelby, of all the people I know, you've made the biggest impact. 27 years on the force."

Shelby reflected back, "It's been quite a run."

"A little while ago Amy and I were talking about you being inducted into the Kentucky Civil Rights Hall of Fame."

"That was a special night," said Shelby.

"It was an honor you well deserved," said Alexander. "You know what they say about the squeaky wheel. Shelby, you were squeaky in your career. You spoke out and brought change."

"That's how you get the grease, Alexander."

They both laughed.

"All trailblazers and reformers are called trouble makers," Alexander opined. "But someone has to take the heat to make it better for others. A lot of Black officers on the force today owe their careers to you, Shelby. Your class-action lawsuit in 1974 was a game changer."

Shelby was modest about it, but he nodded in agreement. "Qualified Black candidates were taking the police exam, but not getting accepted. Just as an example: In 1977 one Black officer was recruited, while 38 White officers were welcomed into the Louisville police department. A lot of talent was ignored and passed over for promotion."

"Your legal action brought the consent decree ordering the Louisville Metro Police Department to hire one black officer for every two white officers."

"It felt good."

"I'll bet it didn't feel good when you were fired."

"No. But it did when I won my defamation suit and got my job back."

"LMPD wasn't the only place you had an impact. You championed equal education for Black children and into higher education."

Shelby mused, "You can't deprive our kids of knowledge, then criticize them for not knowing their lessons and punish them as an adult for not fitting in. Some things needed changing."

"That kind of talk ruffled some feathers," remarked Alexander.

"That needed to be ruffled!" replied Shelby. "Discrimination is not what this country is based on."

"No sir, it sure isn't," agreed Alexander.

"Your family also knew about discrimination, right, Alexander? Bloody Monday."

Alexander pondered that, "True. The anniversary is coming up, tomorrow."

"All men are created equal. And you know, Alexander, sometimes it takes fresh eyes, that can see things, point them out and actually do something."

Alexander raised his glass, "And you made it happen, Shelby. Cheers, my friend."

Amy and Mrs. Simmons were observing Alexander, sitting alone, from the side.

"Shelby Lanier passed last March," Mrs. Simmons said, quietly. "Alexander, Granddad and myself attended Shelby's funeral at Emmanuel Baptist Church. He was buried at Green Meadows Cemetery with full military honors."

Amy came in and sat next to her father, alone.

Alexander lowered his glass, "Hello, my darling child."

"It's time for bed, Dad. It's late."

"Yes, it is indeed late. Later than we think..."

Amy assisted Alexander to his room and tucked him in.

****

It was nearing 7pm the following day. Reston was half in the bag as he raged around his big house, "Why do we have to keep bringing this up?? I hate this day... She's there with him." Reston played out the scene, "'Hello, April... Hello, Alexander.' No doubt he's making cracks, 'Hope you understand that Reston and his family are direct descendants of the Know-Nothings.' 'I know, Alexander.'" Reston stewed some more and poured himself another drink. "I hate this day."

Alexander and April were actually on opposite sides of the gathering. Even after they split up, she continued to come. A group of about 40 or so assembled at the sign on West Main between 10th and 11th Streets. Candles were handed out to those that didn't bring their own and were being lit by each other.

Amy took one and was pleasantly surprised to see Bobby arrive. He took one too and joined her. Alexander and April both took notice.

Alexander stepped up on a small platform by the sign noting Bloody Monday. "For those that are new to this group, we meet here every year on this date, the 6th of August. It happened here in the year of 1855. A row of frame houses owned by an Irishman, Patrick Quinn, was burned to the ground. Several were shot trying to flee the fire and were thrown back into the flames. The nativist Know-Nothings, a group of Protestant men, feared their way of life would be undermined. It was election day. They guarded the polling stations and intimidated those they deemed foreign and undesirable. Hundreds were deterred from voting. There was arson and looting. A hundred businesses were damaged. Protestant mobs slaughtered immigrant Irish Catholics and German Lutherans with ropes, clubs, pitchforks and guns, in an effort to suppress their votes, and preserve their version of the 'American Way.' 22 officially perished, there were reports of entire families being consumed in the fires, with perhaps a hundred dead as the unofficial count. The irony in all of this is the original surveys of the land that would become Louisville were made by the Irishmen John Campbell and John Connolly. The first European settlers to the area were the Irish families of Coomes, Doherty, McManis and Hart. As a society, as a country, as a city and as a commonwealth, we have made great strides since 1855. I believe we gather here and light candles to keep the memory alive of those lost in this barbarism. Not for any kind of vengeance, but to remind ourselves how precious life and liberty is, which is the right to vote. And how we should all strive to not let these actions of suppression be repeated. Because, it can easily be snuffed out."

Alexander blew out his candle and so did the rest of the crowd. There was a moment of silence.

Amy and Bobby hugged and then he had to get back to work.

April and Amy separated themselves from the group.

"Your father is such an eloquent speaker."

"Try putting him in front of a camera lens."

"Alexander still has that problem?"

"Did he always have this issue, in the past?"

Amy and April walked arm-in-arm, "Yes. But when you think about it, the past, it really isn't in the—"

"Mother, if you're going to quote the line from *Requiem for a Nun,* about the past, be advised Faulkner's estate sued Sony Pictures and a hundred people for using that line and profiting without permission and mangling it to boot."

"If someone mangles it, or rephrased it, wouldn't that allow it?"

"The estate sued for copyright infringement and asked for damages, disgorgement of profits, costs and attorney fees."

"You're joking," said April.

"Serious. It was about five or six years ago. A judge dismissed it as frivolous."

"And presto, lots of lawyers were paid."

"You should see the conjuring Padmore, Pearce and Payne does."

"Such as?"

"I'd tell you, Mother, but I signed a big, scary NDA."

"You can tell me other things. I saw Bobby."

"He came for a moment and then had to get back to the office."

"Let's have lunch, soon. Bring Bobby."

"Lunch with the mother, that's a big step," said Amy.

"Oh fiddle, I know Bobby. I'm going to have some things for him to autograph." April glanced over to Alexander and Granddad who both gave a respectful nod. She smiled back at them, signaled, her car arrived and whisked her back to her world.

Amy rejoined Granddad and her father.

"There goes the great lady," Granddad remarked, with all sincerity.

"Indeed," said Alexander, trying to hide his wistfulness.

Amy put her arm around him, "I'm proud of you, Daddy."

"See," said Alexander, "I can behave. I didn't say anything bad about April's know-nothing friend."

****

TORTS and Just Desserts from the mind of Alexander Arrington

The owl appeared and spoke:

"George Prentice was not naïve or stupid—quite the opposite—he was extremely intelligent, having mastered Latin and Greek by the time he was 14 and then graduated at the top of his class at Brown University. Mr. Prentice became a newspaper editor, writer and poet who built the *Louisville Journal* into a major publication. He used his abundance of gifts to preach hate to his barely educated followers. 1855. New people moving in with new ideas. The Irish and Germans were said to be for women's suffrage and the abolition of slavery. A lot of the local folks didn't appreciate these new perspectives. George Prentice didn't like the numbers. The biggest patriots of democracy can become tyrants when the demographics start to cut against them. He whipped these poor dumb bastards into a fever pitch. And he wasn't the only voice freaking out over immigration. There were Know-Nothings in several cities, with their own cheerleaders, but George Prentice was one of the loudest and most persistent. Leading up to election day he filled his Louisville paper with statements such as: 'Strike a glorious blow for our glorious Republic,' and 'Buckle on your armor.' On election day he wrote, 'Americans, are you ready? We think we hear you shout ready. Well, fire! And may heaven have mercy on the foe.'"

Those that were deemed the 'true' Americans were given a code and allowed to vote. Others were turned away and that's when it hit the fan. By dusk parts of the city were a blaze and dozens were dead and hundreds brutalized and disenfranchised. The Know-Nothings carried Old Glory with them as they beat and killed their fellow Americans, while burning down their homes and businesses. They didn't like these progressive ideas being presented in the land of freedom and democracy and they did something about it. 1855 doesn't seem so far back."

~ ~ ~

"Occasionally, when the à la mode craving consumes me, I saunter over to Louisville's Homemade Ice Cream and Pie Kitchen and get the Caramel Apple Pie with Vanilla Ice Cream. Oh my."

The owl faded out.

18

Two days later there was a small private gathering at Casa Arrington. Mrs. Simmons insisted she would be doing the cooking, as they were still paranoid about outside food.

Alexander was nervous, he fidgeted.

"Daddy, you're not performing. This is the Fine Cut."

"I know. Out of my control."

"No. You can still give notes and you had the opportunity to review up till now. This is to get picture lock, so we don't need any more edits."

"Let's get the post mortem over with," grumbled Alexander.

Precisely at 8pm Gabby pulled out a thumb drive and handed it over to Amy. She inserted it into the USB port on the TV. The commercial started. Different scenes from around Louisville were seen. Alexander appeared at various places and listened to people. Then a voice over was heard: "Hello, I'm Alexander Arrington. I have been an attorney in Louisville and the surrounding areas in the great Commonwealth of Kentucky for over 25 years." Alexander gazed into the camera. "If it's business litigation, criminal or civil trials, discrimination, harassment or if you've been wronged, come see me. If you're facing a storm and you need competent, passionate representation, consider our firm, consider the best. Allow us to be your defender. Alexander Arrington, at your service."

The commercial ended and everyone erupted with joy. It was very good. Gabby had pulled it off. The voice, the images and message were clear and heartfelt.

"Alexander, you're a natural!" someone cried out from the group.

Alexander motioned to Gabby, "Here's the maestro."

The room applauded. Gabby bowed.

Amy whispered to Gabby, "Nice job."

****

The next night Alexander took Bobby, Amy, Gabby and Cassidy out to his favorite restaurant: 610 Magnolia. They were met and seated by the general manager and director of wines, Lindsey Ofcacek. Alexander introduced everyone around. Cassidy was a fan of Lindsey and they had met earlier. She admired Lindsey's efforts to mentor female chefs. Lindsey was the co-founder of the LEE initiative which aimed to level the playing field for women in the industry. The culinary world, like other places, had some bad actors who had been called to account by the MeToo movement.

Bobby didn't have to be introduced, a signed picture of him with Lindsey and Edward was on the wall. And then the owner, the celebrated chef himself, Edward Lee, came in from the kitchen.

Edward and Alexander had been pals since 2014 when Alexander met Edward at the Youth Build and IDEAS 40203. This was the zip code of Smoketown. It was a program to train youth that wouldn't be able to afford to attend and be taught by a world class chef. Alexander was all in on this and enthusiastic about what the LEE Initiative was doing. It was a week-long mentorship program that paired five Kentucky-based cooks with a respected chef from restaurants around the country. It was an opportunity to shadow a mentor and learn the ropes of the industry.

Edward warmly welcomed the group and gave the bro hug to Alexander, who then congratulated Edward on winning the James Beard Award for Best Book of the Year in Writing. He promised Edward he was going to read *Buttermilk Graffiti* very soon.

It was a tasting menu at 610 Magnolia. Inspired by the French term *degustation*, described as the careful sampling of various foods with a focus on the senses and culinary art. It consisted of several bite-sized dishes served over a single meal. When done correctly, it was quite a gastronomic experience. 610 did it right.

Near the end of the Third Course, Sherri Daniels arrived with another friend. This was an intimate place. Sherri made eye contact with Alexander.

They smiled at each other and Alexander nodded. Amy saw a spark in him and pondered the meaning.

****

Later that evening Amy cornered her father, "How did you feel about seeing Sherri?"

"She looked well."

"She did," agreed Amy, searching for any clue he gave off, "Alright, good night, Daddy."

"Good night, sweet pea." Alexander smiled at her walking off and went into his den. He sat and thought about what he was feeling. He pulled out an old high school yearbook and found a picture of Sherri.

Amy came back to his den and stopped at the open door. She could see him gazing at the picture of Sherri.

****

Along with the cicadas came the long, hot, dog days of August. Amy assisted Alexander on several cases that were settled by his charm and gentle—and on one occasion not so gentle—persuasion. When required, Alexander could be tenacious and play hardball with the best, but still be what he would describe as 'cleanish.' Normally he rarely set foot in a courtroom. He did appear in a couple of administrative hearing rooms on a personal injury case and a wrongful termination, batting .750.

As for entertainment, Alexander really liked Actors Theatre of Louisville's production of *Ring of Fire* about Johnny Cash. He was a fan of Johnny before, but became obsessed for a bit after that. He immediately tried to learn some of his songs on the guitar, wore black and Amy even detected her father picking up a smidgen of the Man in Black's cadence.

Alexander, Amy, Mrs. Simmons and Granddad attended the Louisville Bats games, who were having a down year. Alexander grumbled whenever a player started to produce, he was sure to be called up and across the river to the Cincinnati Reds. Granddad shut him down by saying all AAA franchises had this challenge and it was up to the manager to adapt.

They also had their season tickets to LouCity soccer matches who were attempting to win the hat-trick, 3 titles in a row in the United Soccer League.

****

When it became really hot and they were wilting a bit, the four got up early and drove several hours southeast to Black Mountain in Harlan County. It was cooler in the higher elevation.

Once there, Alexander, Amy, Granddad and even Mrs. Simmons were being fitted with a harness and a helmet, while she muttered about losing her sanity. She really didn't fully believe this was actually happening. But she was finally going to do it, Mrs. Simmons was going to take the 2-hour zip-line canopy tour.

Alexander and Amy held her hand.

All four zipped down the mountain over the treetops, by themselves. At first Mrs. Simmons was terrified, but she soon began to enjoy the ride, as this was as close as she would ever get to flying. She pulled out her phone and started filming. Her spirit soared. They took pics of her coming in. At the end she was thrilled and happily added her name to the list of those that took the ride and wondered why they made such a fuss over it.

They had a picnic. Alexander and Amy rode horses later that afternoon. Granddad set up shop and attempted to capture the essence of the Appalachian landscape around them. Mrs. Simmons was happy to sit in the shade, sip on iced tea, listen to the breeze through the trees and the birds singing their songs. She filled in another crossword puzzle and then sent out emails to several friends. She attached a picture of herself on the zip-line and the video she captured zipping along. Mrs. Simmons humble-bragged that she was 'only doing 55-mph.'

She heard a bird chirp, "I was up there flying with you, birdie. I really was!"

Late that afternoon they drove a few minutes north to the town of Lynch and checked into a Bed and Breakfast. They had reserved two rooms. The four went out on the town, had dinner and sampled some of the nightlife.

Later that evening they returned to the B&B. Alexander and Granddad bunked together and were out like a light right away; while Mrs. Simmons and Amy had their own pajama party, staying up late chatting about this and that and telling secrets that wouldn't get past these walls.

The host couple at the place was very friendly and the four checked out of the B&B. Alexander drove them to the visitor's center for the very curvy Highway 160, aka the Dragon Slayer. Alexander bought them all t-shirts with dragons on them. They signed the wall and Alexander drove them up to near the summit of Black Mountain, which was just about the highest point they could reach in the Commonwealth of Kentucky. It took around 20 minutes.

The reason this area remained relatively pristine, was thanks to a group Alexander had been involved with since the 1990's: Kentuckians for the Commonwealth. This group fought hard and was successful in protecting the area. There was no mountaintop removal mining here. Alexander felt immense relief and satisfaction that the view of Harlan County from this vantage point had remained exquisite and awe inspiring—he hoped for many generations to come.

This area had been through some very trying times. Most notably in the 1930's with the miners and the mine owners going to war. It didn't help that there was a depression. Coal was a major factor in the building of modern industrial America. Today, the area was struggling to adapt in a carbon sensitive world. The economy of Appalachia was being forced to transition. Alexander knew the hardships they endured and challenges that still lay ahead of them, but gazing out over the majesty of the land he felt very positive for their future.

They retraced their route back down the mountain. Amy did most of the driving back to Louisville. The four were home that evening. It was a nice two-day state staycation that recharged their batteries.

****

It was a late Saturday afternoon in August. Cassidy Dulsett sat on a panel at the Bourbon Women 2019 SIPosium and did well, as usual. She shared her thoughts, observations and a couple predictions. Cassidy wanted Bobby to go with her that evening. They both had been invited. Monica Wolf, the founder and managing partner of the Spirits Group, was hosting 'an immersive dining experience steeped in classic Kentucky hospitality and Derby tradition,' in her restored 1850's brick home, which Bobby loved. He knew Churchill Downs Turf Club's Head Chef Nick Sullivan would be preparing a four-course meal. But the problem was when Bobby went anywhere, he was well aware that he just sucked all of the oxygen out of the room, even if he didn't mean to. He told Monica and Cassidy that he didn't feel well. He wanted his very talented sister to shine. Cassidy had been on the panel earlier and now he wanted her to interact and step forward.

Cassidy was able to attend Southern Hospitality at Monica's house; then Soiree and Sip, with Louisville writer Susan Reigler, at her home on the veranda and got caught up with Heather Greene, New York City's first female whiskey sommelier. Heather was CEO of Milam and Greene Whiskeys. Heather was also an author and the first American woman to serve on the Scotch Malt Whiskey Society. All notable honors and Cassidy thought Heather was really cool, but what really impressed Cass was that Susan Reigler and Heather Greene had both been inducted into Kentucky's Esteemed Order of the Writ as a keeper of Bourbon Whiskey and someone who upholds honesty and authenticity in the industry. It was a very high honor that must have a unanimous vote for acceptance by The Fifteen, the Order of the Writ's founding members.

Cassidy was then able to finish the night with her idol, Peggy Noe Stevens, on her patio. Britt Kulsveen, the President and Chief Whiskey Officer of Willett Distillery, was the special guest. It was a magical night for Cass. At each event she posted pics with the various notables. Sitting down with Marianne Barnes, Kentucky's first female master distiller since prohibition, was quite memorable.

Bobby was getting the reports from the field and loving them.

****

With the daily sessions and trips to the skatepark, Amy's skills had risen to a level she had never experienced before.

Alexander was amazed at her progression. "My awesome child. You look so much like your mother. She was so beautiful." He allowed a moment of clarity, perhaps too honest. "I just wasn't good enough for her."

"Dad…" Amy didn't know how to deal with this.

"Be careful who you fall for, sugar." Alexander laughed at himself. "It can mess you up…" He went back to skating.

Amy's mind flash back 10 years ago to the moment Amy broke up with Bobby:

"Why are you doing this??" demanded Bobby.

"It's not working," said Amy.

"You're doing this now?"

"I can't stand all of this attention. I don't even really like basketball!"

Bobby was doubly stunned.

She walked away, but looked back and saw how devastated he was.

Amy then remembered watching Bobby on TV have a terrible game and Manual High, an overwhelming favorite, get bounced out of the state basketball tournament in a shocking upset. Amy received calls, letters, emails, texts and DMs; direct messages, direct as in a sign with a message pounded into CA's front yard. All communiqués finding fault with her for Bobby's shooting woes, mixed in with a couple of anonymous threats that were just ambiguous enough not to stick legally, but linger mentally.

"Daddy, would you consider doing another babysitting shift?"

Alexander continued skating, "I would, but this time don't tell your mother."

****

It was the second game of the night at the gym. Abby and Amy were sitting in the upper corner of the stands, laying low. Abby was in black jeans, a dark gray Squirrel Bait band t-shirt and a black beret. Amy had on black sportswear, cross-trainers and a dark Cardinals Basketball cap. There were two dozen watching and spread out in the viewing section.

"Hopes are high, it's a new season," said Abby.

"I know," Amy mumbled. "They missed the playoffs last go around."

"I usually don't watch Mitch's games. Can't really bring an infant here, unless we get some protective headphones. I'm grateful that Alexander is doing this."

"I think my dad is just as grateful. This is satisfying a deep parental yearning lying dormant in his psyche. I know Granddad is happy to have Marcus as a craterball teammate."

"Marcus wants to be a professional craterball player."

Amy considered that, "That sport should arrive by 2050. He has a shot."

A 14-year-old boy and girl stepped up and stared at Amy in the stands. "You look like the Firewoman," said the boy, holding up his tablet with an image of Amy shooting fire out of her mouth and eyes.

Amy groaned quietly, put on her shades and ignored them. "Kids are just so precious..."

"Firewoman!" The two adolescents ran off.

Amy groused, "Yelling Firewoman in a crowded gym, starting young..."

"Aim, you've become famous," marveled Abby.

"You mean, *infamous*, a subset I was attempting to avoid. Tenorio has run that a couple times on his show. It's become a meme, with NFT status soon, I suspect."

The stands were beginning to fill up.

Abby was scoping around, "Their game is next, we should see them arrive any minute to warm up. Bobby pays for everyone's Uber ride to the game and the after-game chalk-talk."

And a few minutes later Mitch was spotted with several other guys coming into the gym.

"There's Mitch," whispered Abby. "I'm going to blend in now."

"Right, blend in with your beret."

"I'm doing better than you, Firewoman."

The players warmed up, stretched and shot around. Then Bobby arrived. It caused a stir in the gym. He stretched, flexed his knees, jogged, took a couple shots and was ready.

The Dulsett Distillers took the court and the game started. The crowd was anticipating a show.

Amy enjoyed seeing him in his element. She noticed he was still wearing number 7, but his game wasn't the same. He displayed flashes, but after several knee and ankle operations, along with the Achilles, his explosiveness had faded somewhat. Bobby was patient and directed players around and dutifully dished off to his teammates, drawn from his buddies. They hit some shots. Mitch held his own and made the max effort.

When there was an absolute need for a bucket, Bobby took control and either buried a three or drove in and drained a near-certain mid-range, while still having in reserve the hops for an occasional dunk at 6'2".

The crowd would jump to their feet and cheer like it was 10 years ago.

Dulsett Distillers won by 9 points.

Abby walked down to the courtside. "Mitch."

Mitch looked up from his gym bag, "Abby? What are you doing here?"

"I came to see you play."

"What about the kids?"

"Alexander is taking care of them. I came with Amy. She wanted to see Bobby play. And I wanted to see you play too."

"Amy's here. Good… Great. We're uh, going to…"

Abby pointed at her shirt, "That's why I wore my old Squirrel Bait tee."

As Bobby signed several autographs, Amy eased forward until he noticed her.

He tried to contain his grin. "Who'd you cheer for?"

"I always cheer for the underdog," assured Amy.

"You were rooting against the Distillers?"

"Wait, you guys were the favorites? Seriously?"

Bobby hummed at that with a wry grin. "Wanna go have a beer with the team? It's our chalk talk."

"And where would that be?"

"The Blind Squirrel."

Amy smiled and nodded.

"You can ride with me."

From across the court, Mitch glanced over and noticed.

****

The Blind Squirrel was a large sports bar, filled with people enjoying themselves. The inside had plenty of room and there was a multilevel outside area and patio. Numerous big screen TVs were playing different major league baseball games and pre-season NFL games in progress. Bobby encouraged everyone to order whatever they wanted, wives and girlfriends, even kids included: all the wings, burgers and brew they desired.

People joked about Abby's t-shirt, "Squirrel Bait? What kind of bait is that?"

The guys laughed. Mitch too, but he felt kind of weird about it.

Bobby and Amy were sitting out by the volleyball courts.

"You pay for your teammates and their plus ones, to the game and for the food and entertainment afterwards."

"I have an expense account that would otherwise be ignored."

"And you still have your skills out on the basketball court."

"Phooey, I play old man-ball now," said Bobby. "Little elevation and lots of jump shots, which cuts down on the running, the wear and tear."

"You dominate here."

"It isn't exactly the NBA."

"No."

"I had my chances with the Heat and the Hornets, but my bum knee and ankle didn't cooperate."

"That was tragic. But you played in Europe, some interesting places."

"Yes, Liga Endesa."

"In Spain," said Amy. "I totally love that country. And I learned that Liga Endesa is their top basketball league. Lots of talent. Very competitive."

"You looked it up?"

"I did. You played for Real Madrid."

"For a bit. I still could shoot, just not jump and run up and down the court three or four times a week, for seven or eight months on end. Once a week, limited minutes, that I can handle."

"Were you ever going to invite me to see one of your games?"

"As I recall, you said you really didn't like basketball."

"Was I under oath?"

"I didn't think a sweaty gym was your cup of tea."

"Don't assume you know what tea I drink. Maybe you're worried I might cause you another slump."

"Amy, I don't blame you for—"

"Missing the playoffs last week or losing in the state tournament 10 years ago? How could I have that effect on you?"

"Exactly. It's ridiculous."

"You may not blame me. But some of your fan base still does."

"Look, I just hit a patch of bad luck in my junior year and went cold. And then the next year, I was a 5-star recruit who blew out my knee and tore my Achilles right before the tournament. I sat out for two seasons. I always wanted to play for the Louisville Cardinals, that was my dream. I used to wear their t-shirt under my shirt in high school."

"When was that?"

"Not when I was with you."

"I'll just have to take your word on that."

"It would have been really nerdy wearing two shirts on a date."

"Wouldn't matter. When I think Bobby Dulsett, I think nerd."

"That is one of the nicest things you've said to me."

"You ended up in idyllic Bardstown College. Lots of ivory on the towers down there."

"It's a wonderful school, its own world."

"The Bardstown Woodchucks play at the D2 level."

"My knee and Achilles took a long time to get back into playing shape and even then, it was just a touch slow. Bardstown gave me a chance to play my way back and I rehabbed pretty much all the way back and found my shooting touch."

People came up and wanted autographs and selfies.

"Bobby! Could we get one picture?"

"Can you sign this?" Napkins and hats appeared.

Bobby was a bit embarrassed in front of Amy. She finally had just accepted it. His white-hot celebrity status had dimmed, but it was still beaming bright in some corners; which she could deal with. She pulled out her phone and searched Amazon for some reading material and ordered some books.

Mitch noticed them from a distance and continued to have mixed emotions.

****

Granddad and Marcus logged off and took off their VR glasses.

Mitch, Abby, Mrs. Simmons, Alexander and Amy were watching.

"Great game, Marcus. You had 4 goals and 8 assists," Granddad announced.

Marcus had some swagger, "Thanks, Granddad. You had some great assists yourself."

Mitch and Abby expressed their gratitude to Granddad, Mrs. Simmons and Alexander for their help and were driven home.

Abby sensed her husband was irked at something. "What is it?"

"The kids are out too late."

Abby suspected something else triggered this, "I rarely do this. I guess I won't do it again, you happy?"

Mitch wasn't happy.

Marcus just didn't want them to fight again.

****

At CA the next morning started with a drenching and Granddad in the middle of a dry spell, artistically, which made him unusually cranky about all sorts of stuff. Mrs. Simmons immediately knew to stay clear. She locked herself in her office and got caught up on paperwork.

Alexander chose another path. As Granddad snarled over some triviality, Alexander made barnyard animal noises to serenade him.

The sounds emanating from this encounter prevented Amy from capturing the last winks she desired. She was wide-eyed hearing the farm animal range her father possessed. She arose, garbed herself in her workout gear and emerged from her room. There was a package waiting for her. Amy opened it and was delighted. Her books had arrived. She came into the kitchen holding one book and studying the other.

"Morning, Daddy."

"Good morning, sweetie. You got your delivery. What are you reading?"

She slid the one she was holding over to him.

"The biography of Dr. Naismith. The inventor of basketball."

"His students wanted to name the new sport Naismith Ball," Amy remarked. "How catchy was that?"

Alexander stroked his goatee, "Truly great men keep their egos in check."

"In the original rules of the game, in order to make it fair," said Amy, "every time they managed to make it into the peach basket, they would get the ladder, fish out the ball and then have a jump ball at center court."

"I believe that would fall under the rule of unintended consequences," remarked Alexander. "If you have a really tall guy, you could shut out the other team. How fair or entertaining would that be?"

Amy recalled more, "Another original rule said three fouls in a row and the ref can penalize a team a point."

Alexander gulped at that, "You think the fans already yell at the officials. Imagine having games decided by that. Hoo-doggie."

Amy showed him the cover of the book she was reading. "This one is a manual for basketball coaches on the finer points of the Triangle Offense."

"Not such light reading, is it?"

"It's way more complicated than I realized."

"Like certain things. Why are you taking this deep dive?"

"When Bobby and I agreed not to see each other 10 years ago, cease and desist ..."

"Golly, it sounds like you drafted a separation agreement for the petitioner and respondent. What kind of legal mumbo-jumbo is that?"

"When I dumped Bobby, I told him I really didn't like basketball."

Alexander was aghast, "You...you...told Bobby Dulsett you didn't like basketball??"

"Being in the eye of the hurricane of attention constantly swirling around us *every single time* we went anywhere drove me crazy. I was just trying to make a clean break."

"It's like telling Rembrandt you don't like art." Alexander was holding his head.

"I wasn't serious, Daddy!"

"I applaud your effort to fill in the gaps of your pursuit."

"My pursuit?"

"The Triangle Offense is like a lot of things in life, it's all about spacing and then knowing when to rotate your attack angle. Which begs the question: when will the commercial be done and ready to run?"

"Gabby is on the color grade now and will be doing the full rendering soon. Then she says they have to examine every frame on multiple devices, TVs, tablets, phones and laptops and upload a test copy to the web to check the compression and make sure there isn't any artifacting."

"Got it…whatever that is."

"I don't know what it means either. Still nervous?"

"No. The commercial was a good idea."

"Gabby said it'll be done very soon."

"Fine."

"Do you need anything?"

"No."

"I'm going to take a run, Daddy."

"Great idea."

Amy ran along the riverfront. The thick humidity hung in the air. Soaking wet from perspiration, she sprinted up the spiral ramp and jogged across the Big Four pedestrian bridge that spanned the Ohio River, entered Indiana and then ran back across into Kentucky again. She then jogged back up to Casa Arrington and read a text from her mother saying she had a young man she wanted to introduce to her. Amy groaned and used the side entrance to the kitchen. In the living room she could hear her father and grandfather squabbling or 'debating with vigor' as they would describe such exchanges of opinions.

She picked up a file, took a gulp of water and started a legal brief concerning a property dispute. The yelling continued. Amy paused at the ferocity. It was while maneuvering through the menagerie of plants and pets in Casa Arrington on the way to the shower, she received the text.

LANNIE: can you talk?

Amy took a quick detour into her room, shut the door and called her back. "Lannie, how's Hollywood?"

"They don't call it the dream factory for nothing."

"Things are good out there?"

"Yes, how are things back in your hometown, Aim?"

Amy paused and considered that. "Things are...interesting."

"I would love to hear about it. You got a moment?"

"Sure, Lannie, for you. How long of a moment?"

"How about a weekend?"

"Road trip?"

"You up for that? Zabéla's big end of summer party. This weekend. Malibu."

"Malibu, as on the coast of Southern California?"

"Correct."

"This weekend."

"Correct."

"I'm available."

"I'll pick you up."

"Pick me up, in what?"

"Zabéla's chariot."

Amy wondered what that meant, "Huh?"

"Just be ready to go in two days. Await further instructions."

"Okay."

Amy hung up, opened her door and again heard the squabbling, only this time it was amped up. This spirited disagreement erupted between her father and grandfather over who was the greatest Irish writer, W. B. Yeats or G. B. Shaw.

Amy grimaced at this cacophony and held back from yelling James Joyce! She relaxed as she reminded herself, "I'm going to Malibu." She bounced into the shower.

****

Alexander drove his EV to Bowman Field and parked. They got out and walked over to the Art Deco administrative building.

"I took my first plane ride here," said Alexander. "Lannie is picking you up in a private jet?"

"Seems so," said Amy, checking her phone for any updates.

Alexander thought back, "Lannie... Wasn't she the one that got tipsy and..."

"Danced on mama's Steinway? Yes, like you've never done that."

"Um, checking...and that's a no."

"Daddy, if stories are to be believed, you've done far worse."

"Stories..."

Amy and Alexander looked at each other and then laughed.

"I like Lannie, we chatted about all sorts of subjects and boy, we debated the law and she can hold her own, being a non-lawyer."

"That's Lannie."

Alexander was amused, "She sure raised some hackles on how she got the Hawkwood story."

Amy mulled it over, "Lannie can be a smidge ruthless, but she's honest and true." She now noticed the pop-up hullabaloo happening around them.

Two busloads of people pulled up and were let out. Signs welcoming Zabéla Z were prominent.

"Zabéla Z is coming?" Alexander was intrigued by this.

"I didn't know Zabéla was traveling with her, Lannie didn't mention that."

"Zabéla Z..." Alexander's mind drifted to the power drill scene in *Kara Killer Luv Child.*

Amy could see he was daydreaming and didn't want to know about it.

Fifteen minutes later they would find out as a Gulfstream jet landed, pulled up and parked. The door opened and a security agent stepped out of the plane and walked up to the gate.

Amy and Alexander glanced at each other wondering.

There was a moment of hesitation and then Zabéla emerged. "Hello, Louisville! How's everyone doing?"

It was well covered by various local and national news gatherers.

"Za-bél-a!"

"Za-bél-a!"

"Za-bél-a!"

The crowd continued chanting. She calmed them. Her assistant, Rodney, whispered in Zabéla's ear and directed her over to a smartly dressed young woman.

"Hi, Felicity?"

"Yes, hi, Zabéla. Welcome to Louisville."

"Thank you, Felicity. I'm thrilled to be here. I'm also very happy to present a check from my foundation to MJ's Animal Sanctuary."

"Thank you, Zabéla. That's very generous," said Felicity.

Lannie slyly stepped out and looped around the media scrum. She caught Amy's eye and waved her over. As she arrived Zabéla swung around and put her arm around both Lannie and Amy and turned to the assembled media. Alexander faded back.

After Zabéla was done parading them about, Lannie and Amy returned.

"Hello, Alexander."

"Lannie. It's great to see you and congratulations on your success."

"Thank you, but it's still a long road."

Lannie then gave Amy an envelope with a check. "Here, I can pay you now on all of the accrued billable hours I owe you."

"Hollywood's been good for you," said Amy, as she pocketed it.

"A client that pays," Alexander beamed.

Zabéla joined them, "Alexander Arrington, I am aware of you, sir."

"Zabéla Z, I declare, welcome to Louisville."

"Thank you. I think we have room for another passenger. Would you like to go to Malibu for the weekend? You could sit next to me."

"You don't say." Alexander got a little weak in the knees, as he was more than a smidgen starstruck, but was able to maintain.

"I do say," purred Zabéla.

Alexander recovered, "I've done the Hollywood thing. And I'm done. I have a meeting with a client later regarding his bail and I certainly can't bail on that."

Zabéla ran her finger lightly down Alexander's nose, "I so admire those so dedicated to their craft. Ta."

Alexander was cool, barely. He fans himself.

Zabéla waved to her fans and sashayed back onto her jet.

Amy and Lannie were amused.

And then Chess appeared from the plane.

"This is Zabéla's attorney, Chester," said Lannie.

"Hello. Miss Arrington and Mr. Arrington. It's an honor, sir."

"Chess has read one of your books and attended one of your lectures, Alexander," teased Lannie. "He's a fanboy."

"Actually, a couple of your lectures."

"Ah, interesting," said Alexander.

"They *were* interesting, sir. *Very* interesting, I read your legal critique, which is a classic, Dear Jurisprudence Won't You Come Out to Stay."

Alexander was surprised and pleased.

"And, Mr. Arrington, I'm now a regular consumer of your blog, Torts and Just Desserts. Alexander the Antithetical Owl is a favorite of mine. Your post of the deconstruction of corpus linguistics and your selection of dark chocolate coconut mousse cake were both equally fascinating to me."

"You think so, Mr. Chandler?"

"It's Chess and I do indeed, sir."

"Huh. You, Chess, are good. Really good."

"Thank you, sir."

"I am in the presence of a master manipulator," Alexander said with a thud.

Chess looked confused, "I uh…am only here to administer the non-disclosure agreement, sir."

"It's like getting inoculated from spreading any bad bugs," Alexander quipped.

"For whoever gets on the plane, sir."

Lannie shrugged, "I had to sign one before getting on as well."

Amy gave it a quick read through and handed it to her dad.

Alexander did his own check, "I wonder what Hollywood is so scared of having to use these NDAs?"

"Creative types can be different," Lannie mused. "And in the business of creating illusions, reality, perception itself can be massaged and marketed. It's just who owns the content."

"And catch and kill," Alexander declared with some bite. "It's a device used by the powerful or those with deep pockets to keep stuff secret that's embarrassing or even injurious to the public. It's buried, shoved down through the cracks." He eyed Lannie and had a cynical laugh, "I can't believe someone I thought one of the top investigative journalists, is doing the Hollywood thing now. How's the Kool-Aid taste?"

"Excuse me?" Lannie was taken aback.

"How many days have you not been stoned and drifting on that beach in bliss?"

Amy shushed him with a wry grin, "Daddy, you are in no position to be preaching against the 'evil weed.' I believe we've smoked out together. Maybe you don't remember the Telluride Film Festival. Please. And you were friends with Hunter S. Thompson as I recall. I have a picture of you two gonzo bros, grinning, high as a kite."

Alexander waved all that off. "My time has passed, this child had great potential."

Lannie laughed that off, "Had..."

"We need you out slaying the dragons, or at least pointing out the toxic and radioactive ones that are threatening us--not doing lunch in the belly of the beast! The story will be focus-grouped, reconfigured, rethought, with the rough, embarrassing edges sanded down to a finish that will please the largest demographic and tell them nothing and avoid the theme of what that story is really about." Alexander turned and walked off. "Y'all have a good time out there. Nice meeting you, Chess."

The group was momentarily stunned.

"It was a pleasure to meet you too, sir," Chess called out.

Alexander waved back, got in his car and drove off.

"Thank you, Daddy." Amy rolled her eyes and signed the NDA.

"I meant what I said about your father, all of it. Maybe I didn't say it the right way."

"I know," said Amy.

"And, you know, normally that kind of flattery works on people."

"Not on my dad."

"Apparently not." The admiration Chess had of Alexander was bolstered by this outburst.

They boarded the jet and flew west.

Amy sent a text to Bobby:

AMY: going to L.A. for a few days

BOBBY: have fun

Bobby was in the middle of a budgetary meeting and wondered how much fun she would have.

Cass noticed his mind drifting, "What?"

"Nothing."

****

A middle-aged woman, smartly dressed, explained she really liked the commercial she had seen of Alexander during the 3am airing of the Judge Jodocus Jamison show. The way she batted her eyes and complimented his attire, Alexander wasn't sure if she was there to hire him or admire him. She said she would bring in a legal file concerning a case she would be back again to discuss. Since they didn't discuss it in the first place, he wasn't sure what she meant.

Alexander joined Mrs. Simmons and Granddad out back. He seemed confused, "There's a show called Judge Jodocus Jamison?"

Mrs. Simmons replied, "Judge JJ? Indeed there is. He claims he's fit, firm and fair."

"Not always," countered Granddad. "What about the ruling for the owner of that emu after it crapped in his neighbor's rose bed."

"True," said Mrs. Simmons. "Perhaps not the most sterling of judgments."

Granddad held on to his imaginary suspenders, "I believe it was a landmark decision. And your ad was on right after that."

Alexander mumbled to himself, "I'm sponsoring emu doo-doo precedents..."

"I was going to tell you, son, but I guess I forgot, I got distracted by the terrific manscaping laser commercial that ran right after yours."

Alexander groaned, "I don't believe this..."

Granddad happily exclaimed, "Neither did I. But it really works down there. I got one half-off."

Mrs. Simmons cleared her throat with disapproval, "You won't catch me using a laser in those parts."

Alexander was shaking his head in a daze, "Really, Daddy, I'd be careful about trusting anything being sold at that hour of the night."

"You mean like your services?"

****

Later that night, Bobby was working late when he got another text from Cass. He grinned wondering what luminary she had crossed paths with now, but this time it was footage from the TV show *TMZ*. It showed Zabéla Z landing in Louisville. Amy was clearly seen next to Zabéla and with Lannie on the other side. Zabéla presented the check for $100K and accepted the praise and adulation.

Bobby was surprised.

CASS: that was Amy hanging out with Zabéla Z.

BOBBY: she told me she was going to L.A.

Bobby thought about it and mumbled to himself, "She didn't say she was going with Zabéla Z..."

Abby and Gabby also both saw this on Facebook and were also surprised.

Bobby received another text

CASS: Z bragged to the paparazzi: "I'm hanging out with a great writer and a great legal mind."

****

It was Saturday of the Labor Day Weekend. Dulsett Distilleries was empty, all were off celebrating the holiday—except Bobby in his office reading reports and attending to other business required for running the company. He had turned off his cell phone and wasn't answering the office phone. He then heard a door open. He checked the security monitor and it was Cassidy. He came out of his office.

"Bobby, it's Labor Day Weekend, when you're not supposed to work, if at all possible."

"I need to get ready for the meeting on Tuesday."

"You're going to let me go alone to the picnic?"

"Cass, you have tons of friends."

"I guess I can help you here. What can I do?" She checked her phone. "Did you see these pics?"

Bobby grumbled. "Fine. I'll go, if you quit showing me scenes from Malibu."

"You mean the ones of the really hot looking guys that seem to be hitting on Amy?"

"Right. Because I don't care. It's not serious between us."

"Deal. And by the way, let me remind you that you're Bobby Dulsett. Don't forget that."

"Sometimes I remember and don't want to go out."

"Come on, let's go to the flea market and Worldfest. You can put on your Cards cap, shades and fake beard."

Bobby laughed and locked up and they walked over to Waterfront Park. Cassidy and Bobby both loved this annual market with multitudes of booths selling candles, which she stocked up on, and clothes, jewelry and antiques.

Bobby was carrying a few items as they ran into Alexander, Granddad and Mrs. Simmons out strolling through the market from the other direction.

Alexander spotted him, "Hey there…" He whispered, "Bobby."

He kept a low profile, "I'm merely a sherpa here."

"Hello, Cassidy."

"Good afternoon, Mr. Arrington."

"It's Alexander, and this is my dad, you can call him Granddad, everyone does."

"Because I'm older than most everyone, but can still do twice as many push-ups as my boy here."

"Whoa, don't use me as a benchmark, that's quite a low bar," huffed Alexander. "It's more like three times as many."

The group chuckled.

"And of course, this lady here is my right arm, my legal secretary, who keeps me afloat, the manager of my business and life, Mrs. Simmons."

"It's not my fault," quipped Mrs. Simmons.

More laughter.

"Amy said she was going to L.A. for a bit," said Bobby.

"And I saw her on *TMZ*," Cassidy said. "When she was picked up by Zabéla Z and her jet and then in Malibu."

"Yes," said Alexander. "She's there with a friend and client working on a project for Zabéla."

Bobby was spotted and people started to gather, "She didn't say how long she'll be gone for?"

"No," said Alexander. "She didn't. I'm not sure when she's coming back. Probably in a couple days."

Voices were murmuring around them, "It's him."

"No, it isn't."

"It is. You're him, right, you're Bobby Dulsett. Aren't you?"

Bobby eyed Cassidy with the 'I was trying to avoid this' look and turned to the gathering crowd and forced a smile. "Yes."

The people were thrilled. "Can I get a picture?"

"And me!"

"Would you please sign this?"

"Can I have just one selfie?"

Alexander patted Bobby on the back, gave a nod to Cassidy and moved on with Mrs. Simmons and Granddad, who were shaking their heads at what he had to put up with.

19

There was a cool ocean breeze. The sun was setting over the Pacific. Rad Ransom's, "Late for the Expiration Date" was heard thundering inside. Amy was sitting with Lannie on the patio at Zabéla Z's Malibu beach mansion drinking Margaritas. A large social gathering was in progress.

"I turned in the rewrites and I'm waiting for the reaction," commented Lannie.

"Do they have a director yet?" asked Amy.

"I thought they did, but it was for another project she's developing. I heard from my agent it's likely down to three choices. Zabéla said she's going to make a decision soon."

Amy glanced over the crowd and recognized a few celebrities.

"Aim, if I told you something really bizarre, would you keep an open mind?"

"Of course," said Amy.

"It's really out there."

Amy gazed at the sky above them, "*There are more things in heaven and earth, Horatio…*"

"Exactly."

"Okay, Lan, what is it?"

"A party or two ago, I felt this incredible attraction to someone, a connection that was strong...deep. It was almost spiritual."

"I think we're all striving for something like that," Amy said.

"And then I started daydreaming and when I snapped out of it, he was gone."

"That's too bad."

"But then I saw him again and followed him out onto the beach, right over there. He smiled at me and then vanished before my eyes."

"Into thin air?"

"Became invisible."

"How?"

"That's the question. He disappeared, but he was still there. Cloaked. I saw the footprints in the sand as he walked off and then he got into some kind of craft."

"What? What kind of...?"

"It was some sort of vertical takeoff vehicle, also cloaked."

"Like Harry Potter."

"I don't know. Maybe he is a wizard. He didn't have an English accent."

"You were smoking out..."

"Yes, but I wasn't doing shrooms or acid or coke and I wasn't drunk and I've never tripped on weed."

Dr. Trainer approached from the side, "Maybe it was a dream."

"Maybe it was real, because there you are, just who we were discussing. The elusive Dr. Trainer," Lannie said cheerily.

He stepped up and shook her hand. "Lannie, nice to see you again."

"This is my friend—"

"No introduction is needed," said Dr. Trainer. "Amy Arrington, it is a sincere pleasure to make your acquaintance."

"Dr. Trainer, nice to meet you, too."

"I think all that stuff in New York about being the 'Fire Woman' was entirely unjust and unfair."

"Oh," said Amy, thrown a bit.

Lannie paused, "What? What is that about?"

Amy shrugged to Lannie, "It was just an incident."

"I have been living under a rock scribbling away."

"Nothing big," said Amy wishing this hadn't been brought up.

Lannie searched on her phone and saw it. "Amy Arrington, Fire Woman. Uh…"

"It was big enough that she left her big fancy New York law firm and returned home," teased Dr. Trainer.

"I'm on sabbatical from my firm."

Lannie kept reading, "How did I miss all of this?"

"As a story creator, Miss Telfair, you are very good at blocking out distractions; only living in the world you're working on, rarely coming up to see what the rest of us are doing."

Lannie took a pause at how accurate he was.

"It's okay," Amy tried to change things up. "What's your doctorate in?"

"Physics."

"Are you theoretical or experimental?"

"Both."

"I thought you had to choose," said Amy.

"True, almost all do."

"But you?"

"Correct. I dream at night and prove it during the day."

"Wait...I recall a story about...dark matter."

"This is an area I work in. Something that takes up so much space and is all around us and so little is known of it."

Lannie was confused, "I thought you were a movie producer."

"I do that too. Among other things."

"Like...your magic tricks or special effects?"

"You're referring to my disappearance last time."

Lannie and Amy gave each other a look.

"I tutored David Copperfield on that trick."

****

It was late, Saturday Night of the Labor Day holiday. There were plenty of pictures in the Dulsett home of the family together. Bobby, with his number 7 jersey playing basketball and Cassidy playing tennis. At the moment they were both engaged in a different contest.

Thuds. Clanks of swords. Groans. *Blood splattering.* Bobby and Cassidy were facing off in 6D on Xbox. He was the mighty Pulsar Parallax and she the undersized Nimble True. The action was intense and didn't let up as they pounded and pelted each other with punches and projectiles.

"Watch out, Pulsar! You're going down," Amy stated.

Bobby barked, "Nimble True is wrong!"

Pulsar Parallax was proficient in numerous weapons, which he unleashed in a steady stream, but Nimble True was lightning quick and scary lethal when she pounced on her opponent's mistakes.

Pulsar focused his forces and mounted a major assault, but Nimble True countered with an inverted portal entry giving her the opportunity to disable his power source. With Pulsar Parallax's shield down, Nimble True slipped through his defenses and delivered a stream of antimatter charges that obliterated Pulsar.

'Pink Mist' flashed on the screen.

"Ouch!" yelled Bobby. He dropped his controller.

"The mighty Pulsar Parallax is defeated!"

"Nimble True for the win," said Bobby, with a bow to her.

"When is Pulsar Parallax going to learn? Always protect your power source. Did you hear me? Always protect your power source."

"Gotcha," grunted Bobby.

"And never underestimate me, big brother."

"I've never underestimated you, sis. Ever."

"Or me to you," responded Cassidy, as she picked up a picture of Bobby on the court. "I still think you should have been Mr. Basketball your senior year."

Bobby shook his head, "Over 'The Bullet'? No, Elisha Justice was an excellent choice. He had mad talent. He took Shelby Valley to the state title."

"True. And the next year he was voted Hottest Male Athlete in the World."

Bobby sighed and shook his head, "I wasn't even nominated…"

"Maybe he was one of the hot guys on *TMZ* out in L.A. hitting on Amy. But it doesn't matter because you don't care because nothing serious is happening between you and Amy."

"Correct. Nothing serious is happening."

"Uh-huh. Okey-doke."

"And I talked to Elisha a little while ago." Bobby's voice trailed off. "He's coaching now."

"You know, Bobby, Mom and Dad are looking down, smiling, that you gave up your career and took over the helm here."

He nodded at that.

Cassidy patted him on the back, "Good night." As she went up to her room she yelled out, "Survey says: Bobby Dulsett is still hotter than The Bullet!"

"Check your eyesight!" laughed Bobby. He sank into the couch and reflected back:

THREE YEARS AGO

Bobby was playing basketball overseas. Injuries had robbed him of his lightning first step and explosive leaping ability that allowed him to create space to shoot his silky-smooth jumpshot. Without this advantage he became a good, mostly just average, player. But he could still drill a couple three-pointers. His name was chanted "BOB-BEE" by the half-filled arena.

Bobby was in Riga, Latvia. He had a small fan club and was dating a local celeb, the weather girl of one of the TV stations. They barely could communicate, she spoke some English and he struggled to learn Latvian, as it somewhat resembled Lithuanian, which he learned a bit as he played the year before in Vilnius. The year before that he played in Spain.

He recalled receiving the call from Cassidy that both of their parents died in a plane crash.

Bobby pulled an afghan over himself, turned off the light and stretched out on the couch. He wondered what Amy was up to in L.A.

****

September 2. A Monday Night. The first football game on the schedule. The Cardinals were hosting the Notre Dame Fighting Irish. Fans in The Ville had been highly anticipating this encounter for some time. Alexander, Granddad and Mrs. Simmons had on their Cardinal red in Cardinal Alley. They were members of Cardinal Tailg8ters, founded in 2006 by Vince Tyra, son of Cardinal great Charlie Tyra, which incorporated Charlie's number 8 into their Tailg8ting name. Charlie was Louisville's first All-American and that was in the sport of basketball. Granddad remembered him well, especially since he was on the 1956 team that won the NIT, which was the college championship.

Tonight's game was not only a sell-out, but would set a new attendance record at Cardinal Stadium at 58,187. The NFL season had yet to kick off. Lots of potential high school players would be tuning in. The entire football world would be watching this internationally televised game. The best line Alexander could find was Louisville +17. The Vegas line at one point was +20.5, he couldn't lock into that, as he was forced to take the less attractive number from his guy in Kentucky. Alexander took the points and wagered $500.

Many Cardinal fans were yearning for the second coming of Heisman Trophy winner Lamar Jackson. Lamar had spoiled them with blazing speed, lightning quick moves in a fastbreak offense; but he had long matriculated to the NFL.

Alexander thought Lamar was a once in a generation or two talent, he had a more realistic hope for a breakout player the likes of a Jeff Brohm or Teddy Bridgewater 2.0. Granddad was still hoping for another Johnny Unitas. He would always be grateful to fellow Irishman, and coach of the Notre Dame Irish, Frank Leahy, who told a 145-pound Unitas he was just too skinny and would "get murdered" if he was put on the field. Johnny U. came to U of L after that. At the University of Louisville Unitas played quarterback and for some time was playing safety and linebacker as well as returning kicks.

The Cardinals went up 14-7 late in the first quarter. But that would be the last TD they would score. They lost 35-17. The passing was the difference. Notre Dame was more effective. It surely didn't help with recruiting. Alexander lost his bet because he couldn't get the Vegas points. His money would be swallowed up into the vast pools of dark, unregulated, untaxed black market money.

****

Amy soon arrived back in Louisville from Malibu needing a rest from her 'vacation.' She felt like some blitzed out, wrecked character Hunter Thompson dreamed up. She had seen the decadence and debauchery he so eloquently opined on. Malibu was like a Ralph Steadman sketch to her. Amy had escaped in the dead of night and merely left a thank you note for Zabéla and a text to Lannie with a pretext of having to get back to work. She needed to detox and considered a cleanse. Attempting to get a final ruling in her mind on the Southern California adventure she mumbled, "Truly bizarre..." And quoted Thompson, "Well, 'When the going gets weird, the weird turn pro.' Indeedly so..."

Riding in from the airport her phone buzzed, it was her mother. "Hello, Mother."

"Welcome back, darling."

"How is it you know the exact moment I touch down on Kentucky soil?"

"How was your jaunt out to the coast?"

"I survived."

"Marvelous. Why don't you be a dear and invite Bobby to lunch?"

"Gee, nailing down a time with you is—"

"Saturday, 12 noon after our ride."

****

Amy arrived home and greeted the menagerie.

Mrs. Simmons was working on her laptop in the dining room, "Welcome back, Amy."

"Thank you, Mrs. Simmons."

Alexander entered, "Welcome home, daughter." He sensed it, "Ambrosia? You look shaken."

Amy crossed over and gave him a hug, "No, Daddy, I'm quite fine. It's good to be home. I think we should have a skate-off later."

"You are on, little girl."

"Okay, old man."

They both grinned at each other.

Amy retreated to her room and sent a text to Bobby:

AMY: you free to talk for a sec?

The phone rang and Amy answered. "Hello."

"Welcome back to this time zone," said Bobby. "Did you have a good time?"

"Sure, did a lot of contractual work for my client, but I also had sand between my toes and some tequila and a bit of that legal herbal stuff."

"Oh, interesting."

"You want to hear something not really interesting? My mother has invited you and me to lunch on Saturday. The three of us. You're under no obligation to accept and if you can find any reason to decline, I would owe you."

"I'm checking and I'm free."

"Serious?"

"Having lunch with April Arrington is on my bucket list. What time?"

"Noon."

"Perfect."

"Okay... Huh."

"Can I pick you up?"

"I'll meet you there. My mom and I are going for a ride in the morning."

****

Later that day Amy and Alexander met and discussed several cases he was working on, now with her unofficial assistance. Alexander wanted them to work together, but wasn't going to tug her away from her dream. Amy had several helpful suggestions on how to approach two of his cases, which he appreciated.

"You know," said Alexander. "We should have a BBQ on Sunday. Invite Bobby if you want."

"Actually, I'm having lunch with him on Saturday."

"Good."

"With Mom."

"Ah...I see." Alexander's spirit dipped hearing that, but he offered a smile. "That's nice."

"She insisted that I invite him over to her place. I'd ask him about Sunday too, but that would seem a bit much. Would The DDs be okay?"

"That's a capital idea! And I am an honorary DD you know!"

"I know."

****

The DDs were all on board. Mitch was invited, but said he was busy. Abby would bring Roxanne and Marcus.

Amy had one other person she wanted to come. Friday morning. Amy was let off at the Omni Hotel on 2nd, down by the riverfront. She waited a few minutes and was at the door when the Heine Brothers Coffee Shop opened at 7am. Amy didn't want to take a chance of a swing and a miss. She got coffee, worked on her laptop and checked her phone, not for messages, but the time. She continued to wait—but not much longer. Sherri came in and picked up her order. She then noticed Amy working on her laptop.

"Amy?"

"Judge Daniels?"

"Please, it's Sherri. May I join you for a moment?"

"Yes. Please."

Sherri sat at Amy's table, "I needed to fortify myself as I have some really tedious stuff on the docket today." The judge put down her purse and satchel. "As I recall, your mother wanted you to go to Yale."

"Yes, she did."

Sherri was amused, "April knows where the power players gather. And Alexander said any place other than Yale!"

"Right. Georgetown Law was the compromise, but it's where I always wanted to go."

Sherri thought back, "I love Georgetown."

"I do too," Amy said. "And I had ideas about working in Washington. But the problem for me was seeing how the government worked up close; maybe too close."

"Seeing how all that legislative sausage was getting made there changed your mind?" Amy tilted her head for a half nod. "Is that why you took a job with one of the big boys on Wall Street?"

"Maybe—and now I've taken a leave from them."

"Take your time and really think about what you want. I know that's simple advice that can be really complicated to carry out."

"I've always known you and my mom and my dad were friends in high school."

"Friends? At DMHS? Frenemies would be more apt to describe my relationship with your mother."

"They both shy away from telling me any stories."

"Your mother and I kind of competed against each other. We were both on the debating team and ran cross country."

"My mother was on the track team?"

"You didn't see any pictures from that time when you were growing up?"

"None."

"April was a good athlete. Once we were on the same team for a JV track meet. It was the relay, and well, the baton was dropped on the hand-off between us and we lost because of that."

"Oh. Huh."

Sherri stirred the cup and took a sip of her Mayan Mocha. "There was other stuff. It went on and off between us until…"

"What?"

"The Heine Brothers Coffee Shop incident."

"What's that?? What happened?"

"It was at the Heine Brothers original location. I guess I like their coffee so I've kept up."

"When…what happened?"

Judge Daniels checked her watch and was on the move, "That story is way too long to tell here. I have to be in court."

"Judge, Sherri, would you like to come by our house on Sunday for a barbeque at 2pm? Maybe you would have time to tell me that story."

Sherri paused and smiled at that notion.

20

Saturday's weather was lovely. The car Amy was riding in turned into Silver Horse Sanctuary and drove down the long, well-manicured lane and caught the first sign of the sun rising for the day. Some of the OTTBs, the off the track thoroughbreds, were frolicking about in the cool morning air blanketing the pasture. She smiled and waved to them.

Amy was let out. She was dressed in very proper English equine riding attire.

Gus brought their horses out and was impressed with her outfit. "Well, a good morning to you, m'lady."

Amy grinned, "Thank you, Gus."

April emerged from the main house wearing jeans, western boots and a cowboy hat. "Howdy."

Amy and Gus were surprised and then broke up laughing, along with April.

****

April and Amy were riding on a trail.

"You had a boring time in L.A? It looked like fun, fun, fun from what I saw on *TMZ*."

"It was all right."

"How was Lannie?"

"She's doing well, navigating the choppy waters of Hollywood."

"I can still see her on the piano. See how laid back I can be?"

"I'm guessing she's the only one that got away with that."

April thought and agreed, "True."

"Lannie lives life to the fullest."

"I saw a documentary on Zabéla Z. She also lives a rather flamboyant life."

"She does. And in moderate doses, she's tolerable."

"Actually, I've really liked some of Zabéla Z's acting roles, other than her horror flicks. I mean we all have to start somewhere."

"Zabéla has several projects she's developing."

"Then I shall look forward to them," said April. She then harkened back, "You know I had a chance for a movie audition."

"You never told me this, Mother."

"A talent scout saw me in a college senior musical. He said he knew an agent in L.A. and offered to introduce me."

"What happened?"

"I didn't believe him. I turned him down."

"Perhaps preventing another Black Dahlia case."

"Or preventing an acting career and chasing a dream," April's voice trailed off in reflection. "And wearing this wild west outfit should be proof that I can act and that I'm willing to compromise, yes?"

"Yes, indeed, Mother."

"What about you?"

"What about me?"

"Think long and hard where you want to end up."

"Certainly."

"I was serious when I said I had someone to introduce you to. He's a vice president at Goldman Sachs."

"Mother, there are north of 12,000 vice presidents at that company."

"But it's Goldman."

"Haven't you read the studies done on pairing lawyers and non-lawyers? This sick cross-breeding should never be attempted."

"Then you're open to attorneys. I've got candidates at Skadden, Arps; Simpson Thacher; and Latham & Watkins."

"Mother…"

"Isn't Bobby a non-lawyer?"

"We were together before my legal career."

"Ah, the loophole you've devised. Well played. It's what you do. I know you've always held a torch for Bobby."

"Holding a torch? Careful, that sounds like it could get me put on the no-fly list. And just to update your file on me, Bobby and I are just good friends. I brought him so you wouldn't fix me up with someone."

"I read in the C-J, Maggie Menderski's column, that Bobby Dulsett is dating Nevada Nash."

"Nevada Nash?" asked Amy.

"No, she's not an exotic dancer."

"Actually, I was thinking more riverboat gambler, Mother, but now your image is planted in my brain—thank you very much."

"I've heard she has the moves."

"What moves?"

"She's a local real estate agent." April did a quick search on her phone, brought up one of her commercials and passed it over.

Amy watched an attractive 25-year-old blonde woman, dressed business-professional, gaze into the camera with a warm confidence: "In Indiana, Ohio or Kentucky, if you're looking for quality properties, or if you're ready to sell, come to me. I'm Nevada Nash. I've got what you're looking for and I have the buyers lined up. I'll make it work for you. I will close the deal and leave you with a smile."

Amy stared at it for a second and handed back the phone, "Lovely. She's promising happy endings."

"She moves a lot of property," said April, with a respectful tone. They rode some more.

"I know Sherri is coming tomorrow for the BBQ. Were you ever going to say anything?"

"Excuse me? Mother… How…how do you know this?"

"You do know that Sherri Daniels and I go back a long way."

"Everyone knows that. You two were on the relay team together. The baton handoff."

"She told you about that?" April had a belittling tone, "She probably said it was my fault."

"The judge did not rule on that. What about the incident at the coffee shop?"

"Heine Brothers? She mentioned that?? She has some nerve."

"What happened?"

April was still working through this, "It was nothing."

"No, Mother, this was, *is* a serious thing."

April considered it, "That subject isn't advised at the moment as I don't want to get worked up into a tizzy before our lunch with you and our guest."

Amy sighed, frustrated. They were silent and rode some more.

As they approached the house her mother inquired, "Speaking of serious. Were you serious when you said you froze some of your eggs?"

"But *this* is an apropos subject presently?"

"I would just like to know the address and the access code, you know, just in case."

"Just in case, what?"

They noticed Bobby's BMW arrive yonder in the parking lot.

"In case you're in a fiery crash in a fancy, really fast foreign sports car."

Bobby got out and waved and they waved back.

"Mother, I don't think this is the proper time, presently. You wouldn't want to see me worked into a tizzy. You know what that can be like."

April cringed, "Heaven preserve us from that." She dismounted and transformed into the charming hostess, "Hello Bobby, it's wonderful to see your handsome face again!"

****

Lunch at SHS was pleasant enough, until...

"Bobby?"

"Yes, Mrs. Arrington?"

"How's Nevada been?"

Amy squirmed, "Mother...you must be inquiring about the Silver State."

"No, what I read in Maggie's column."

"Nevada is fine, as far as I know and, well, I don't know much. A while back we were mentioned attending a charity event. But that was several months ago. We both were extremely busy and couldn't find the time to continue."

"Yet, you find time for my daughter. Huh. Lucky her."

"Yes," said Bobby, in jest. "Amy is very lucky."

Amy fawned with faux-appreciation, "So lucky."

They all chuckled.

April took a sip of tea, "I saw a documentary on you, Bobby. You injured your knee as a senior in high school, which is why you didn't get any scholarship offers from Louisville or Kentucky."

"I blew out my Achilles and my ACL. Anterior cruciate ligament. It stabilizes the knee. It was pretty significant. The doctors said my playing days were over."

"But they weren't, eh?"

"I rehabbed, played at Bardstown College, got my degree and then got an offer to play in Europe, professionally and jumped at it."

"How many countries have you played basketball in?"

"Counting the U.S., five."

"Besides injuring your knee and getting, correct me if I pronounce this incorrectly: Plantar Fasciitis."

"Yes, ma'am, that's correct."

"It's not contagious?"

"No, no it isn't."

"We dodged a bullet there," quipped Amy.

Bobby tried to contain his amusement with Amy's rib.

"Yes, Bobby, my daughter is very witty. But beware, that wit can be lethal."

"Permission to treat my mother as a hostile witness."

"It's just an injury on the bottom of my foot. And yes, injuries did plague my career."

"And you're healthy otherwise?"

"Pretty good."

"And you came home to take over the family business."

"It's something I grew up with. When I wasn't in the gym practicing."

"Because of the accident."

"Yes."

"Mother, must you?"

"It's fine," said Bobby. "I can talk about anything."

"How's business?"

Amy could see her mother's predatory mind kick in.

Bobby took it in stride, "It's very good. Kentucky bourbon, thanks to its smooth, unique taste, from the strict requirements, has become desired by the world over. And Dulsett Distilleries, with our secret sauce, has modernized, without losing what made the brand so special."

"This sounds like the speech for the roadshow."

"We are not considering going public."

"You mean, at this time," said April. "I'd be willing to get in on the mezzanine financing."

Bobby admired how charming and yet so probing April was. "Ma'am, there's no IPO on the horizon."

"Dearest Mother, please… I can't believe I'm saying this, but don't you have something for him to sign?"

****

Bobby drove Amy back into town.

"Your mother is so...interesting."

"She is. You signed a dozen things for her."

"Maybe she's going to unload them."

"Bobby, she's a shrewd investor. She'll turn a nice profit."

"Boss move on her part."

"That's what my mother is all about. When she stops inviting you to lunch, then you'll know something's up." Amy got an alert. "It's my Zabéla feed."

"Zabéla Z, your friend in Hollywood?"

"Hardly my friend." She read the text. "No…"

"What?"

"My friend Lannie, actually my client. The one I visited in L.A. Her movie deal has collapsed."

"That sucks."

Amy called her and it went to voicemail. "Lan, I just heard. Call me when you can. Hang in there." She hung up. "Lannie must be devastated." Amy tried to reach Lannie the rest of the day without success.

****

The next morning Amy woke to find a text from Lannie, who was bummed, but it wasn't the end of the world. Amy knew she never let on when she was really down and sent another text for her to call if she wanted to talk. Amy felt terrible for her as this wasn't the first time one of her deals fell apart. She wondered what kind of mindset would put up with walking a tightrope without a net, only to have it cut at any moment. Amy knew Lannie would take some time to recover.

It was Sunday. Amy focused on the BBQ.

The DDs arrived early and they had tea. The doorbell rang and Alexander answered it. Sherri Daniels was standing there.

Alexander was stunned for a moment, "Your Honor?"

"Hello, Alexander."

"Are you serving a warrant?"

"I have federal marshals for that."

"Good one, Dad," said Amy, as she came up behind him. "I invited her. Hi, Sherri. I'm glad you could make it. Please come in."

"Thank you, Amy."

Alexander cornered Amy in the kitchen, "How did you end up inviting her?"

"We just happen to run into each other getting our morning java," Amy reported. "Call it kismet with a sprinkle of serendipity."

And then the doorbell rang again and Amy answered it.

Bobby was standing there, "Hi."

"Bobby...?" asked Amy, surprised.

"Some of those serendipitous sprinkles must have magically spread," mumbled Alexander as he stepped past her and embraced him. "Bobby, welcome. I'm happy you accepted my invitation."

Amy cornered Bobby, "Since I dragged you to lunch yesterday with my mother, and how that went, I didn't want to do it again today with my father. That didn't seem fair."

"I'm honored that Alexander invited me."

"And," said Amy, "I didn't want to bore you with too much of me."

Bobby waved that off, "You're far too mysterious to ever be boring. I was worried it would be the other way around."

Amy looked surprised, "Who knew Bobby Dulsett was so modest?"

Alexander was soon at work grilling his King Louie BBQ Chicken special, with his own 'secret' spices. Bobby volunteered to be his sous-chef and assist. Granddad told everyone stories about Alexander misbehaving as a lad. Sherri loved learning these memories. Alexander seemed embarrassed, but he wasn't. He liked being with friends and family, and especially Sherri—and Amy noticed.

Later Amy and Sherri had a moment in the kitchen. Nutmeg and Cantankerous Cat were overseeing their meeting from different vantage points.

"You're in your third year as an associate at Padmore in New York?"

"Yes…"

"Have many dealings with Harold?"

"As a matter of fact, yes."

"We crossed swords in an earlier life," Sherri recalled.

"Really?"

"Padmore, Pearce and Payne is a juggernaut," exclaimed Sherri. "Do you think you'll be going back?"

Amy stirred her drink, "Padmore is like playing for the Yankees in the Big Leagues. People spend years trying to get to that level on that team. Who walks away from the Yankees?"

Amy and Sherri moved into the living room.

"The Heine Brothers Coffee Shop incident, spill the beans," prompted Amy.

"It had been brewing, all puns intended, before that. After school, all of us used to meet at Carmichael's Books on Bardstown Road in the Highlands, even when going to college." Sherri smiled and shook her head, "And then the Heine Brothers opened up their coffee shop next to

Carmichael's in '94 and we all hung out there as well. We became friends with Mike and Gary. Now look at them. 17 or 18 locations, I think. Then I went to Brandeis Law School."

"Yes, Dad was a year ahead of you."

"Correct. And the place I camped out to study was at that Heine Brothers Coffee Shop."

"Okay, okay, the incident."

"I remember that April was telling everyone that she broke up with Alexander. Which was the only reason, when Alexander asked me to meet him, I agreed to at Heine Brothers to study and only study. And we were just talking and your mother came by. It was quite a scene."

"Really? What happened?"

Sherri's eyes went wide, "Huh, well..."

"Lunch is served, ladies!" Alexander announced, using his spatula as his fencing foil. "Parry and thrust!"

Sherri was amused at his antics, "*En garde*!"

Amy, foiled again, grimaced with grace at this.

As they sat down to eat Bobby apologized, saying he received a message on a 'serious problem' at one of the warehouses. He gave a respectful nod to Amy and made his departure.

Amy waved him off, but was troubled.

****

Later that week Amy got a text that settled some of her concerns. Lannie sent word that she had another gig. She had left L.A. and was heading to New Orleans to interview artist and influencer Raven Laveau for Prod Magazine.

Amy marveled how Lannie was able to land on her feet no matter what may come.

Amy wanted to talk to Bobby, but he seemed aloof. She sent a text to Cassidy:

AMY: care to play some tennis?

CASS: how about tomorrow, noon?

****

Cassidy was a member of the Louisville Indoor Racquet Club on Westport Road. They met out there and played two sets. Amy's game was fairly sharp, but Cassidy was number 1 on her high school team and number 3 on the Louisville Cardinals. Cassidy won 6-3 6-4.

"Awesome match, Cass."

"You play very well, Amy."

"My mother insisted I have proper golf and tennis lessons. Anything less would have been child neglect in her eyes."

They both laughed at that.

"Being an associate in a big firm, you must not have a lot of time to play."

"My game has suffered some in the last couple of years practicing law. But even at my best, I couldn't have beaten you."

"I was okay in my day," said Cassidy. "Not good enough to go pro, like Bobby. He had the skills, but the ball didn't bounce his way, a couple bad breaks."

"He's seemed distant the last couple of days. Of course, it started after he had lunch with my mom Saturday. She can be a bit intimidating as she probes. Sunday, right as we sat down to eat, he left the barbeque saying there was a serious issue at one of the warehouses. I hope everything's okay."

Cassidy paused, "Sure, that was taken care of..."

****

Freshly showered, Cassidy came back to the office and knocked on Bobby's opened door.

"Guess what I just did?"

Bobby stopped reading a report and noticed her wet hair, "Swam across the Ohio River."

"No. I played some tennis."

"I'll bet you didn't drop a set."

"I didn't, but in two sets I lost 7 games."

"You had some competition."

"I did. Amy is really good."

Bobby frowned, "Amy?"

"Arrington."

Bobby went back to reading the report, "You're hanging out with her now?"

"Since you aren't. Are you avoiding her?"

"I've been busy."

"Is it her mother, did she freak you out?"

Bobby grunted at that.

"I heard you bugged out at Alexander's BBQ before chowing down saying there was a serious issue at one of the warehouses."

"Yes."

"What was the issue?"

"Some of the braces. But it was a false alarm." Bobby went back to work.

Cassidy suspected there was an issue, but not with the building.

****

April and Amy were attending the opening of Christy's Garden in the Paristown Pointe section of Louisville. The Louisville Orchestra and Teddy Abrams were performing outdoors.

"What's going on with you and Bobby?" asked April.

"I don't know."

"Crash and burn?"

"Thanks for the analysis, Mother."

Later April and Amy watched one of the great ladies of Louisville, Christy Brown, play ping-pong with the mayor. The media filmed them.

"Christy's Garden." April glanced around and admired the end result. "You know this area used to be so rundown, a dump, and now it's been revitalized. This is a place where the community can come together. It's from her efforts. Christy worked in an office for 15 years nearby and envisioned what this space could be. And now look at it."

"It's impressive," said Amy.

"You just need to stick to your original plan and follow through, darling."

Amy was surprised by this insight from her, as she knew her original plan and it didn't sync with her mother's. She wondered if she actually meant it.

****

It was time for the annual St. James Court Art Show. It was a large 3-day open-air festival celebrating all that was art. The event started in 1957. It was held in the St. James-Belgravia Historic District, 'Old Louisville,' just south of Central Park and around the corner from the Judge and Willodean's residence.

It was a big deal. There would be over 700 artists displaying paintings, photography, glasswork, gems, ceramics and more. Well over a hundred thousand patrons of the arts would be attending over the three days.

Amy had promised to assist Granddad on one of his biggest weekends of the year.

It was just past dawn as Granddad arose in his room and immediately poked his head out of the window and up at the sky. It was clear. He stepped out back and the morning air was crisp. He checked his phone for the forecast. "Good, no rain. Right at 70 degrees. Perfect."

He then saw Old Man Miller walking his dog.

"Morning to you, Artie."

"Good morning, Melvin."

"I suppose you'll be setting up at the fair."

"I suppose I will."

"Good luck to you," Old Man Miller had a slight sneer as he continued on.

Granddad grumbled and mumbled, "Does he think I need luck to sell my work?" He continued to consider what paintings to take and leave behind—and after he decided, he made some changes. Switched some in and out. Some items he didn't feel were completed, others were too personal, some sketchings he didn't want to unload.

Several workers soon arrived. They carefully loaded the pieces he finally settled on into a van and transported them to his location. Amy helped him set up his booth. There was excitement in the air. Granddad waved to and was friendly with other artists.

The other DDs came by and sat with them on Saturday. Mitch was watching Roxanne and college football with some friends. Marcus stayed in his room.

When Old Man Miller came by Sunday afternoon, Granddad flashed the sales invoices on the paintings he sold.

"You've had a successful festival, Artie."

"My Granddad's done very well, Mr. Miller."

"You know what..." Old Man Miller pointed at a canvas with a stark landscape of a river and a forest that surrounded it. "I'd like to purchase this painting."

"Really?" Granddad was quite surprised.

"Yes. How much?" He put on his spectacles, "Five thousand dollars??"

"That's the price. But I don't think I want to sell to you."

"No?"

"No."

"Why not?"

"You're too stupid to appreciate the art."

"Great. I've got a discrimination suit against you now."

Amy pondered this, "You'll admit under oath to being too stupid to appreciate art and claim he has a bias against your class of people?"

"Yes." He leaned in on Granddad, "I can have my attorney depose your Granddaughter and use her against you. Hee hee!"

Amy sighed and shook her head, "This is why everyone hates lawyers."

"I want to buy this as an investment because it's sure to double in value. Because a fossil like you won't be living much longer."

"It'll triple in value! And I'm still not selling to you. Go ahead and sue me, you old goat!"

"Then I'll see you in court!"

"You realize that investing in my work is pretty shrewd. You just admitted you're *not* stupid, which means you just lost your standing in the lawsuit!" crowed Granddad. "How stupid is that!"

Old Man Miller waved that away. Alexander arrived in time to see him harrumph off.

"What'd I miss?"

Amy shrugged, "Two old friends, catching up."

****

A couple nights later Alexander Arrington was in his office at home and had just finished writing emails and returning phone calls. It was approaching 10pm in Louisville. There were various pictures on the wall. Alexander and Hunter S. Thompson. A smiling picture of Muhammad Ali was on one wall and opposite there was a fierce, warrior, Ali. His six core principles listed: Confidence. Conviction. Dedication. Giving. Respect. Spirituality.

Alexander reflected on this wisdom. He got up and entered the living room or 'arena,' where he viewed his sporting events.

He poured himself some Old Forester, flipped on his 70-inch TV and watched basketball highlights on *Sportscenter.* He changed channels and saw the promo for another TV show: "Tonight on *Current Cross Currents* John Tenorio will lay it out for you."

Alexander chuckled, "That blowhard."

John appeared, "I will break down the case against the disgraced writer, Lannie Telfair and her latest incident in New Orleans. Folks, you could not make this up. If you recall, I recently told you about Lannie Telfair, the loser writer. Well, the word is there's a video the police have in their possession proving her guilt as an arsonist and extortionist and they are preparing to arrest her in New Orleans. I mean after *Triple C* and your favorite journalist, me, brought you the still breaking story on how John Hawkwood, a national hero, a tough guy, was wronged. Tune in tonight for the latest on Trainwreck Telfair, still in freefall."

"What??" The bourbon splashed over the edge of the glass. "Ambrosia!"

****

Amy booked the next flight she could to New Orleans and sent word to Lannie that she was on her way. During the flight Amy was catching up on the requirements to get waived in. She also saw the story of the Voodoo Killer loose in the city.

A car picked her up from Louis Armstrong International and drove her to Raven Laveau's compound: Nichoir Noir.

"Amy, thank you for coming," said Lannie.

"Lannie, are you alright?" They hugged.

Raven entered.

"Raven, this is my friend and attorney, Amy Arrington. This is Raven Laveau."

They shook hands. "Miss Laveau, nice to meet you."

"Same here, call me Raven."

"Call me Amy."

Raven led them into the office area that opened up to a comfortable salon. There was a pot of tea and some cups waiting.

"Can I offer you some tea?"

Lannie and Amy readily agreed. Raven poured them all a cup and they sat.

"I guess I should expect to be arrested any time soon?"

"Not today."

"You're sure?"

Raven gave her a look of 'why are you asking that?'

Lannie relaxed.

"Amy, I deposited a $50,000 check with your law firm in Louisville and got you waived in."

"I can practice in this state? To do so, I'm required to—"

Raven rattled off the requirements in rapid fire style: "An out of state attorney is eligible for admission pro hac vice if 'the attorney acts in association with an attorney duly licensed to practice law by the Supreme Court of this state as required under Louisiana Revised Statute 37:214 and the out-of-state attorney: (a) lawfully practices solely on behalf of the attorney's employer and its commonly owned organizational affiliates, regardless of where such attorney may reside or work; or (b) neither resides nor is regularly employed at an office in this state; or (c) resides in this state but (i) lawfully practices from offices in one or more other states and (ii) practices no more than temporarily in this state, whether pursuant to admission pro hac vice or in other lawful ways.'"

Amy was impressed with her grasp of the issue. "I do practice lawfully in New York and I don't reside here. But I don't have an attorney to act—"

"To act in association with? You're working with my lawyer. He signed the agreement."

"Then I guess I'm working, temporarily, in this state for Lannie and you."

"Which gives us attorney-client privilege," stated Raven.

"Great," said Amy.

"Now let me tell you what happened with Lannie. She was set up..."

****

Alexander, Granddad and Mrs. Simmons were having breakfast the next day at CA.

"I feel like U of L will do really well this year," said Alexander.

"Son, you say that every year. We'll start to see in little over a month."

"I really feel it in my bones."

Mrs. Simmons and Granddad gave each other the look and agreed.

"When do you think Amy will be back?" asked Granddad.

"Raven put $50,000 on retainer for Amy," remarked Alexander. "Lannie's case must be complicated."

"Alexander, do you know who Raven is?" asked Mrs. Simmons.

"She's some kind of artist, right?"

"Raven Laveau is an artist, very talented," agreed Mrs. Simmons. "She's also the descendent of Marie Laveau, the former voodoo queen of New Orleans. And many say Raven's continued on in the family business."

Alexander frowned at that and then shrugged it off. Amy was going to do what she was going to do and he wasn't going to look over her shoulder, unless she asked for assistance.

There were legitimate legal cases generated from his commercial. A sexual harassment case he leveraged into a large settlement for a secretary and a juvenile who was caught boosting a Corvette and going for a joy ride. Alexander had pulled the same stunt at that age, once, in simpler times and didn't get caught. He made an extra effort on this one sorting out the genesis of such behavior and attempted to course correct this lad with the ability to get around the complexity of modern anti-theft protections.

After losing to Notre Dame in football the Cardinals beat Eastern Kentucky and Western Kentucky and then lost to Florida State: their 9th ACC loss in a row. The next week was a thriller, a 41-39 victory over Boston College. The week after that they beat Wake Forest on the road 62-59, with 4 TD passes—and then the offense went to sleep for the next 3 games and lost. Then they beat two losing teams NC State and Syracuse and then got pummeled on the road at Kentucky: 45-13. It devastated Alexander. It wasn't even a game.

Alexander was back to being in a major funk. He was also worried about Amy still down in New Orleans. They had talked, but Amy seemed vague and distant.

The Cardinals qualified for a post-season bowl because they won six games. They had a record of 7-5. The University of Louisville got on I-65 and traveled south to Nashville to face Mississippi State, who had a record of 6-6. Louisville was itching for some payback. The last time these two teams squared off against each other the Cardinals were slayed by the Bulldogs in the TaxSlayer Bowl. This time the Cardinals were in tune and played them 38-28 in the Music City Bowl. Alexander almost forgot to watch the game and napped through part of it. He was happy though. It was the first bowl game win in four years. It gave Alexander hope. There was something to build on.

****

It was now approaching the favorite time of the year for Alexander.

Basketball had been in his DNA since he was a young lad growing up in Louisville. Alexander knew all of the legends, not only of his hometown and university, but also the rich history of basketball in the Commonwealth of Kentucky, the NCAA and NBA.

Other than the use of the possession arrow in college basketball, his number one rant for years, his biggest pet peeve was how their rival, the University of Kentucky, had their Big Blue Madness to kick off the start of basketball practice. Several times—incognito—Alexander had traveled the 77 miles east to take in these extravaganzas at Rupp Arena in Lexington. At first it actually was 'midnight madness' as it kicked off at 12:01am and it was crazy; but in the following years the NCAA allowed the events to start earlier, which really brought out the fan base. It was a show. After waiting an entire off season, it was a massive explosion of joy between fan and team celebrating the return of basketball.

Alexander compared Louisville's start of practice to attending a chess match. It was just compounded for Alexander when he saw other schools with their own Midnight Madness that looked incredibly fun; yet for years the Cardinals just started early in the morning of the first day they were allowed to practice.

During gatherings, socials, BBQs, get-togethers and fundraisers, if there was anyone even remotely attached to the school, Alexander would bend their ear on creating their own Midnight Madness.

And then it finally started in 2018. Now in the year 2019 a half-court basketball rim was set up outside in the heart of the downtown social scene. Louisville Live on 4th Street Live, right in front of the Hard Rock Café.

Alexander, Granddad and Mrs. Simmons were waiting like the rest of the people ringing the stage on multiple levels. The place was rocking with Kid Rock blasting from the sound system. The lights dimmed. Lasers sliced through the darkness. The men's and women's teams appeared. First seen on a giant screen above, players were introduced individually as they burst out through the generated fog. They strutted down a runway surrounded by fans on the sides and in the balconies above shouting out their love and respect, while gathering content.

Louie the Cardinal or Cardinal Bird, U of L's bright red mascot was present and accounted for and stirring things up. Mrs. Simmons was thankful that it was too loud in the place for Granddad and Alexander to start debating what the proper or real name of the mascot was or should be.

Previously Old Man Miller had cracked a joke about Louie the Cardinal having teeth under his beak.

Granddad had told Old Man Miller it was to bite him on his ass.

On the women's team, Jazmine Jones told fans they expected to carry on what last season's team established: an Elite Eight appearance.

The Harlem Globetrotters made an appearance, there was a 3-point shooting contest between Cardinal great Luke Hancock and the school's AD, guess who won? There was a dunk contest that was judged by Donavan Mitchell, Jack Harlow and Darrell Griffith.

Alexander and Granddad were thrilled to see Denny Crum in the house.

Darrell Griffith saw a face in the crowd and walked over with a microphone. "And I'd like to thank one of our top fans who has been lobbying for this event for years. Boy has he been lobbying and I think he threatened a lawsuit if he didn't get his way!" The crowd laughed. "And now we have our own Midnight Madness! Let me introduce one of the loudest voices that kept pushing for this and at times the most irritating! Let's hear it for Alexander Arrington!" There were big cheers.

Alexander waved to the crowd. "Thank you, Dr. Dunkenstein for those kind words calling me irritating." More laughter. "All I can say now is...Let's Go Cards!" Alexander raised his right hand up with the Louisville 'L.'

The place erupted with joy. Basketball practice had begun and all was right.

****

TORTS and JUST DESSERTS from the mind of Alexander Arrington

The owl appeared holding a basketball and spoke:

"All right, hang onto your hats, grab a cup of Joe and settle in, because this rant rambles a bit, but trust me, it's significant.

Basketball season is fast approaching and I was quite pleased to learn of the court settlement reached last year, 2018, with the NCAA concerning several Louisville Cardinal basketball players. They won't have some irritable asterisk by their name in the record book for their individual achievements; however, they still have the 2013 NCAA title taken away, for only the second time in history, which for the players was a terrible injustice.

Life and sport. It's all really about timing and trust. One day something is permitted, and the next it's not, and then it is. Salaries for college players were prevalent in the early decades of the 20th Century. In 1939, freshmen football players at the University of Pittsburgh, went on strike over the fact they were compensated less than their upper-class teammates. In 1948 the Sanity Code began to put the kibosh on above-board payments to "student-athletes."

Looking back over the history of college basketball there have been some shocking events. The point shaving scandal of 1947-1950. Two Kentucky players were banned for life from the NBA and the NCAA suspended the entire Kentucky basketball program for the 1952-53 season. There have been other point shaving episodes: Northwestern, Tulane, Boston College, to name a few of the hallowed programs touched by such a stain.

But nothing like that has ever been linked to the University of Louisville.

There have been transgressions, embarrassments, some shocking and shockingly brief on a restaurant table—but nothing that threatened the credibility of the sport or the trust of the authenticity of the game. No sir.

We need rules, we need laws and we need the cop on the beat. But the authorities must be fair and open in the enforcement, for fear of losing the trust held by the players, coaches and fans.

Which calls to mind the denouement of the process engineered by the NCAA's Committee on Infractions. The COI event is usually held in a hotel conference room. There's high security. The public isn't allowed in, which is understandable with emotions running so high. Outbursts and demonstrations wouldn't be palatable; but it's not streamed on the internet, which is not understandable. All of the parties are present with counsel and statements are read. The Committee on Infractions lacks subpoena power. Witnesses are not compelled to show up, while their side of the story has been thrown into the mix. No cross-examination of those that read statements, confronting your accuser is forbidden—and none of it is under oath. You just have to look into their eyes and choose to trust them or not.

Trust. It's up to the 24 members of COI to ferret out the truth Colombo style. They ask their probing questions of those that do choose to attend this Star Chamber setting.

The inevitable result is some coach is sent packing, with full pockets. An AD has to switch jobs and a university president feels embarrassed. The school cuts a check to the committee, releases an apology, is barred from a bowl game or competing in March Madness. Scholarships are reduced. The athletes, almost all who did no wrong, are shamed and their record sullied. The fans feel cheated and are angry.

Trust. Five years after taking the national title back from the USC Trojan football team—the first time such a draconian punishment occurred—a court later ruled that the NCAA "reached a predetermined conclusion" and "ignored the truth," in the process.

The educational institutions in the Power 5 conferences rake in gobs of greenbacks from selling the viewing rights and compete for the elite coaches with fat 9-figure compensation packages.

Timing. Now the cogs in the machine that grind together to create such largesse, the 'student-athletes,' are allowed to profit off their Name, Image and Likeness. Because of NIL, at least future sanctions, shunning and shaming won't be coming for a basketball player from an economically challenged family that accepts help, or some poor slotback that puts in 40 plus hours a week practicing and studying for the team and gets a truck from a local dealer.

Though I see awkward future college settings where multi-millionaire players, point guards and QBs, share locker rooms with linemen and forwards that block and rebound for scraps. The NCAA has neatly placed the issue of having to again compensate anyone out of their own pocket back on the back burner.

The NCAA passed other new rules in 2018. Now all presidents and athletic staff members at Division I basketball schools, as conditions of their employment, contractually commit to providing full cooperation to the NCAA during any investigation or infraction process. This means that all university presidents and athletic staff members must report all violations, hand over all evidence requested, including all electronic devices and passwords to social media in a timely manner and be confidential.

Exactly what the University of Louisville did.

When the school became aware of the violations—unlike many other institutions that have been in their sights—the University of Louisville was open and upfront and cooperated completely with the NCAA. What was the result of not lawyering up and coming forward? They were punched in the beak and mugged. Besides the 2013 trophy, the NCAA clawed back a large chunk of change, $600,000 and 123 victories—Louisville got to keep the losses.

Other schools observed and have learned from these unfolding events.

Again, the most interesting change under these new rules is that university presidents and chancellors at Division I basketball schools *will be held 'personally accountable' for violations by their athletic programs.* Similar to Section 906 of the Sarbanes-Oxley Act, that requires CEOs and CFOs to substantially increase their role in disclosure by personally certifying the accuracy of the information presented in financial reports. The penalties from the NCAA may not be as harsh as a CEO facing up to 10 years of prison time for willfully certifying such a statement they knowingly didn't comply with; but why not?

It should at least be financially onerous enough to make the leaders of these schools actually make an effort to see what's really going on and not continue to play Captain Renault in *Casablanca* being shocked at such naughty behavior.

With these new rules the NCAA believes it finally has subpoena power.

So it really is about timing. Because if these rules making the administration and coaches actually toe the line would have been in place earlier at the University of Louisville with the NIL deals athletes are getting now, it's doubtful any of the wrongly timed violations or shocking lapses of judgment would have even occurred. Unfortunately, it slammed the athletes who worked hard, trusted and just had the bad timing to be on a team that should never have received such a harsh penalty as taking a national champions trophy away. A dastardly deed if there ever was one.

I will withhold any opinions on university presidents being held 'personally accountable,' or CEOs on Wall Street, until such events actually happen and are adjudicated in a transparent manner.

The evolution that has come to amateur athletics would shock and amaze Jim Thorpe. Many consider him the greatest athlete ever to compete and perhaps the most infamous case of bad timing in sports: his Olympic medals were taken away when he was alive, for playing professional baseball and returned when the rules changed and he was dead—really bad timing on his part.

Looking down the road you can see what area the bad timing will be in, just not who.

The NCAA has clearly stated NIL deals cannot be used as a recruiting tool to entice an athlete to enroll or transfer. No coordination between the school and the business looking to advertise is allowed. No coordination. But it looks like the NCAA has uncorked a gusher much like the Supreme Court through *Citizens United* allowing 501(c)(4) groups, the dark money pools of politics that can accept and spend unlimited amounts of cash in support of a candidate, as long as they don't coordinate with the candidate they support. No coordination. That may be the law in marketing political candidates for office and the rule for luring athletic candidates to the playing field, but seriously, folks, in the hyper-competitive worlds of politics and college sports, are we so naïve to believe there isn't some, even significant coordination?

I would advise the Committee on Infractions as they do their job, to carefully consider the collateral damage caught up in the coming crackdown on collusion and noncompliance. The players that had the bad timing of trusting the wrong school as this tsunami of NIL cash is swamping so many moral compasses.

However, hope springs eternal as the optimists say. There was quite an interesting development in 2015 concerning a very famous, or more appropriately *infamous* case. The NCAA decided to return the 112 wins it vacated back to Penn State and Joe Paterno. It was punishment over the absolutely shocking Sandusky sex scandal. If forgiveness, redemption and restitution can be found there, I believe the timing is right for those 123 victories and the 2013 national championship stripped from the University of Louisville basketball team to be reviewed and ultimately reinstated."

~ ~ ~

"Blackbird Pie. A most satisfying dish I know very well.

3 ½ cups self-rising flour.

1 cup very warm water.

25 crows.

Mix a little biscuit dough. Knead until dry. Roll with rolling pin until very thin and cut into 2-inch strips.

Clean birds, rinse.

Cover birds with water, cook until tender. (at least 2 hours) Season to taste.

When crows are tender, keep broth boiling and drop in pastry pieces.

Cover and cook for 10 more minutes. Let sit for 10 additional minutes.

Enjoy! You just feel better when you finally get around to this treat."

The owl faded out.

21

Amy soon returned from New Orleans and Alexander immediately cornered her and wanted to know what went down. For days she had been reluctant to report on the happenings. Alexander had been in the dark and quite on edge. Amy admitted it was another unique adventure that involved Lannie and this time included Raven Laveau. Amy confirmed the weird had made all-pro on this sojourn. Alexander wanted details. Again, Amy hesitated sharing events. Alexander insisted she come clean. Finally, Amy explained that Lannie, while profiling Raven, did some investigating on her own on the Voodoo Killer. Lannie had gotten so close she was linked to the slayings. Raven, using her gris-gris, her unique talent and special 'powers,' was able to fix things.

Alexander blankly stared at her and digested this summary. He was quiet for an extra moment and then asked her to hold off sharing these details with Granddad and Mrs. Simmons, for fear of triggering some medical event with them.

Amy had an invitation from Raven to return for Mardi Gras and ride on Krewe Morrigu's float. She vowed to recover first physically and mentally before accepting. Amy was sure of three things: 1) The weather was cool, which she liked. 2) Her relationship with Bobby was cold, which she didn't like. And 3) She was quite happy to be back home.

Abby couldn't help but pass on Mitch's rantings about Bobby shooting like it was '10 years ago.' Bobby turned down a chance to meet up as he was 'snowed under' with work and took an extra-long time to return her text.

Amy told herself that she was busy too.

****

Later in the week Amy was up early and ready. And sure enough, Alexander slipped out the side door and walked down the street. This time

Amy followed him on foot. Two blocks away a van came up, he got in and it drove away.

Amy groaned at losing him.

4 hours later, Alexander appeared from his bedroom and yawned.

Amy had been waiting patiently, with her curiosity nearly bubbling over, "Morning, Daddy."

"Morning, Sweetie."

"How'd you sleep?"

"Good. I just need to wake up." He poured some coffee and checked his phone.

"Daddy, can I ask you something? About where you go—"

Alexander finished reading a message and was concerned. "I just got an urgent text from your mother asking me to ask you to turn on your phone."

Amy stopped, went into her room and turned on her phone. There were several texts from April needing to talk. Her phone rang.

"Hello, Mother?"

"Ambrosia, we have a situation."

"What is it?"

"It's terrible! A tragedy! I'm on my way over!"

Amy was now concerned as she almost never heard her mother in such a state. She sat down at the table and opened the newspaper wondering what the crisis was. And then she saw the C-J headline above the fold and was stunned:

ZABÉLA Z CHOKES ON FIRM TOFU IN HER FINAL SCENE DEAD at 34

Amy was shocked, "Oh my God..."

"Everything okay with your mom?"

"She said it's terrible. It's a tragedy. She's upset and on the way over."

Alexander glanced at the newspaper, "You think it's because of Zabéla?"

"Mom was a big fan."

"Hmm... Say, what did you want to ask me?"

"It can wait, Daddy."

April arrived a few minutes later at the front door and fidgeted. Amy led her in.

"April."

"Alexander." They both were nervous.

"Mother, are you okay?"

April gathered her thoughts mumbling, "How could this happen?"

"Mother, you know, I liked Zabéla Z as well. No one could take a power drill to the gut and still let out a blood curdling scream with such authentic passion."

Alexander agreed, "Totally. And I think *Kara Killer Luv Child* is vastly underrated. It's a slasher classic in my book."

"And Zabéla was super nice when she flew Lannie and me out to her place in Malibu."

April broke from the deep state of self-pity, "What are you two talking about??"

"Zabéla Z, she just passed away, Mother. Weren't you a fan?"

April took her aside and whispered, "I need to talk to you about my, *our*, problem."

Amy led her off to the conference room. "Can Daddy be in on this?"

"What is it, April?" called out Alexander. He hadn't seen her so flustered in a great while.

"I need to talk with Amy for a moment and then, maybe."

Alexander couldn't stand seeing her like this. Amy shut the door.

April's eyes darted about checking the surroundings. "I have your word that this room isn't bugged?"

"You're that worried?"

Her mother nodded.

"Mother, give me your phone."

April gave up her phone.

"I have a friend who deals with this stuff," Amy said, as she took her own device and put them both in the mini fridge and shut it. "There's no recording going on in here. Full disclosure, we don't have any long-range sonic radar jamming devices on the windows."

"Ambrosia..." April was just holding on.

"Mother, what's going on?"

"There's a show that's on tour and it's playing here in town..."

"A show?" Amy waited for more. "Um, where?"

"At the Burnbury," April's mind was churning.

"I've seen several productions there, Mother. It's a nice theater."

"What?" April was on edge hunting for answers in her mind.

"It's in the Henry Clay building. It's a great space. You should go."

"No! For heaven's sakes no."

"Mother, calm down."

"I can't go. Tiago is in the cast."

This paused Amy for a moment, "Tiago, from New York?"

"Yes. That Tiago. How many Tiagos do you know?"

Amy groaned, "Mother, what's going on?"

"Tiago called me and told me that he has video from his phone of us, when, well, we were together. I met him here in town and he showed me."

"Mother, you're into filming your escapades now?"

"No! He surreptitiously recorded our interlude."

"Is he blackmailing you?"

"Yes. But...that's not the only thing. After he showed me the video of myself and him, he showed me a video with him and *you,* also in flagrante delicto. And I have to say it was *way more* kinkier!"

Amy shrieked, "WHAT???" He has that?? You watched it?"

"Not all of them. There were 4 or 5 on his phone."

"4 or 5? No, no, no…"

"Where did you learn that stuff?"

Amy erupted, "I never consented to any filming! Not once!!!"

"Neither did I. But that didn't stop him from capturing the moments on his phone for future revenue streams."

"Grrr!!!" Amy sat back with a deep sigh. "I knew I couldn't trust him… But he was just so…"

"Yes, I know."

That phrase finally stung Amy, "Future revenue streams?"

"He said he would make it go away for $25K."

Amy's jaw dropped open and hung there for an extra moment, "We need to bring in Dad."

"But that means he has to know."

"We have attorney-client privilege."

April groaned at the thought.

"Mother, he's going to be our attorney. I'm in on this now and despite your opinion of him, he's the best lawyer I know."

"I'm fully in agreement that he's a great barrister, it's just the baggage between us two."

"You need to stow that stuff away because this will be a bumpy ride."

Amy opened the door. Alexander came walking into the room. "Yes?"

"Daddy, we have a problem."

****

Alexander took what they shared with him under advisement and came up with something.

Amy went over to be with her mother at SHS and they waited.

"What if Reston comes over?"

"I told him that I was spending some quality time with my daughter."

"Good one."

They waited some more.

"I wonder what Daddy's going to do."

"Your father said he would take care of it. I am to make a call on this burner phone and convince Tiago to come outside."

"Outside, where?" asked Amy.

April recalled the many times he did the same sort of thing for other people over the years. "Your father is shielding us; being a gallant knight, dealing in the darkness, to make things right in the light."

Amy's apprehension was growing, "But what sort of dealing…in the darkness?"

****

It was Monday night. Alexander was cruising around downtown and checked his watch: 10:06pm. The performance had been over for about 15 minutes. He then got a text from one of the stagehands, a friend of his. The cast had relocated after the show to Merle's Whiskey Kitchen on West Main.

A few minutes later Alexander pulled into the parking lot and got out. He glanced around on the street and called the burner phone.

April answered, "Hello?"

"Tell him to meet you outside at the bus stop and it will be taken care of."

"Got it." April hung up and checked her phone for the number of Tiago and called him on the burner phone.

Tiago was with his fellow cast members. He saw the number and didn't recognize it. "Hello?"

"Tiago, it's April. I'm here."

"Where?"

"Come outside at the bus stop. I can't be seen."

"Are we going to settle this? It's a drop in the bucket for you."

"Yes, I know. It'll be taken care of. By the bus stop."

"Be right there." Tiago turned to a friend in the show, "When I get back, drinks are on me."

"Yeah, dude!"

Tiago exited and stepped out on the street. He saw a bus stop with a bench and crossed over to it. Alexander emerged and sat on the bench as Tiago arrived.

"Tiago!"

"Do I know you? Where's April? Wait, I know you. I saw your commercial. You're Alexander Arrington."

"Being a professional actor, Tiago, give me your opinion. Did you like it?"

"It was okay."

"The performance?"

"Good."

"The production quality?"

"Excellent. You're the father of Amy and you're April's ex."

"Correct on both. Let's sit down and settle this."

Tiago was hesitant.

"Come on, it's a nice public place. And you want to get what's coming to you."

Tiago sat.

"Before we start, I know who you are, Tiago."

"Are you trying to scare me?"

"I know all your credits. You did a *Law and Order.*"

"Yes, I did. Did you see it?"

"No. Every New York actor has done a *Law and Order*. I know who your agent is, Sheila and your manager, Denton. Which means, if you ever contact Amy or April again, ever make a threat again, I will bury you. I'll make your name dirt in Hollywood and New York. Your career will be over, just as it looks like it might be taking off."

"Understand. Let me see the money."

"Let me see the videos."

Tiago pulled out his phone and started to show him one of Amy. "Stop, that's my daughter."

"Right, sorry. Here's your ex." He showed another one with April.

Alexander cringed and then braced himself, "Enough. Here's the cash." He handed over a wad of money and took a couple of snaps with his phone of Tiago with the currency. "I doubt you'll be declaring this. I have friends in the government, too." Alexander captured another image of him.

"Hey, stop it."

"You don't like it when people invade your privacy?"

Tiago counted up the money. "There's only $1500 here."

"It'll cover the cost of a new phone."

Tiago was enraged, he pulled out a knife.

ZAP! Alexander used a stun gun to subdue him. Tiago flopped back on the bench. "That's for filming my daughter and her mother, you perve." Alexander took Tiago's phone and observed him convulsing. "Tiago...I'd say you're more Iago. Understand that this is merely a taste of what you'll get if I run into you again. Or I find out you've shared some pictures from some cloud. If so, take heed, not only will your acting career be trashed, it will rain down on you like some Biblical plague."

****

And just like that the problem went away. April texted her gratitude to Alexander. He had gone into a bit of a funk over the episode. Amy felt a bit awkward as well, but immensely grateful and relieved.

"I have two tickets to the Louisville Orchestra," said Alexander.

"Are you going with Granddad?"

"He's busy. He says the muses are yelling in his ear. Would you like to ask Bobby to go with you?"

"We're not in sync right now."

"Would you like to go with me? The program is called From the Sea. It's four different aquatic short programs from four composers. One of them is Claude Debussy's *La Mer*."

Amy sat at the piano and played the beginning of 'Claire de Lune.'

"*Bien sûr, je suis fan du plus grand compositeur Français*," Amy declared.

Alexander mumbled in his state of faux-confusion, "The best French composer ever? I believe Messieurs Bizet, Berlioz, Camille Saint-Saëns and Ravel may have something to say about that."

"Monsieur Debussy loved going against the grain, doing it his way. You might know a few things about that, eh, Daddy?"

"A wee bit. Debussy was fascinated by water ever since he was a small child."

"As you have been as well."

Alexander nodded at that.

"I'm still waiting for my first steamboat ride on the Belle of Louisville with you as captain."

"I'm getting there. This piece of music is hypnotizing. A dream that transcends my spirit to distant realms."

Amy always enjoyed her father's analysis of the law and the arts.

"Some critics, they complain that Debussy's music lacks form," explained Alexander. "Phooey, I say. They just don't get what he's really about, what he's going for." Alexander drew a Greek letter on a piece of paper: ϕ

"Phi?" asked Amy.

"Correct." Alexander started diagramming on flower petals and then on a seashell. "The Golden Ratio, 1:1.61, can be found all through nature in its design. They say it's the most pleasing to the eye. Perhaps it's also the most pleasing to the ear. It's found in Debussy's music. The Golden Ratio is there. I think we both need to go to rehab our moods."

Amy agreed, she did need something to sooth her ravaged spirit.

****

They had dinner downtown at Vincenzo's, which was always superb. They were pleased to catch up with the owners, brothers Vincenzo and Agostino and then strolled the block down to the location of the performance, Whitney Hall. It was filled. Amy always liked the design and acoustics of this interior. She started seeing the Golden Ratio around her in the layout of the building.

Teddy Abrams came out to enthusiastic applause. He turned to the audience and gave a short talk, an almost warning, on how this was an 'odd piece of music.'

The orchestra performed *The Oceanides* by Jean Sibelius. It was a tone poem about the mythological nymphs of the Mediterranean Sea. It began with flutes lightly flitting about. Soon the strings eased in and then the oboes arrived with their balm. Halfway through you were reminded there was a brass section. The piece built to multi-layers of sound waves crashing into each other, only to retreat with the oboes again calming things.

Alexander and Amy glanced at each other quite charmed by this.

Garth Neustadter's *Seaborne* was an interesting multimedia event. The Percussion Collective, six percussionists, backed by the strings in LO, performed with a film projected above. It showed scenes of the ocean, the beauty and power. The three movements were from above, on the surface and submerged into the depths. The xylophones were rocking. It was a thrilling performance.

After intermission Amy and Alexander settled in for John Luther Adams' *Become River*. After which they felt this was the piece Teddy was describing as 'odd.'

And then Debussy's *La Mer* began. It was a hypnotic experience for both of them. Alexander was totally into the music. It was just perfect and then he happened to catch sight of April and Reston across the way. He flinched.

"Daddy, what is it?" Amy said, quietly.

"Over there," whispered Alexander.

Amy noticed, "Oh."

April had already seen them. Mother and daughter locked on for a moment, smiled for each other and looked away.

Amy whispered, "Come on, Daddy, you are just going to have to learn to deal with that." Amy then laid eyes on Bobby with Nevada a few rows behind April and she flinched.

Alexander realized what she saw and was also wide-eyed.

Amy felt like the warning about it 'being odd' was meant for her. She wished she could morph into a sea nymph, submerge and swim away. Debussy's timeless masterwork being performed by these talented musicians was not soothing Alexander or Amy at the moment.

22

The days were shorter, the leaves had turned, the weather cooled further, and the wind whipped around in Louisville. The end of October was approaching. The large and diverse group of animals that lived in CA realized it was the spooky time of year and they were all a bit creeped out by it.

Alexander, Granddad and Amy did their annual drive through Iroquois Park and were marveling at the collection of creatively carved pumpkins in the Jack-O-Lantern Spectacular.

"There's quite a selection this year," Granddad exclaimed.

"Sure is," said Alexander. "Look at that scary one!"

"Is that it, son. You're scared?"

"Of the Jack-O-Lanterns?"

"No, women."

Amy—who had been a bit distant since the 'soothing' *La Mer* concert—cleared her throat in agreement.

Alexander frowned, "Dad, must we have this conversation in front of my daughter and your grandchild?"

"Actually," replied Granddad, "if I didn't have to pay ASCAP royalties, I'd sing a few bars of 'Desperado.' It's a great song. A classic from the Eagles. About that lonesome cowpoke that pines for someone he can't have."

"I'm not lonesome."

"You better let someone love you and by the way, time isn't on your side, son."

Alexander grumbled.

****

All Hallows' Eve had finally arrived. Alexander was reading notes on a case when he came around a corner in CA only to be confronted by a screeching neon apparition lurching out, "WAAA!!!"

"Ah!" Alexander stumbled back bouncing off a wall as green slime dripped down.

"Good one, eh, son?" Granddad was dressed as an evil scientist.

Alexander grinned and then grimaced, "One of your better ones, Dad."

"The slime was Amy's idea. That dopey old mule actually thinks he's going to beat me this year."

"We're going to bury Old Man Miller!" howled Amy, assisting him with the props in her very authentic zombie costume. "Bury him in an unmarked grave!"

Granddad and Amy both cackled at that thought.

"Boy, you two are really into your characters there," commented Alexander, wondering a bit.

Mrs. Simmons just sat in her chair and shook her head as she continued reading the *Louisville Defender*.

Casa Arrington was once again decorated with big black hairy undulating mechanical spiders, spooky skeletons clawing their way out of the ground and poltergeists patrolling above on wires. All of it in motion with haunting howls and scary screams to boot. Once again there was a not-so-friendly and highly competitive competition in the neighborhood on who could create the best Halloween experience.

And naturally, Alexander couldn't resist, "I walked by Old Man Miller's place. He has some good stuff, Dad. Really gory."

"I saw it." Granddad cogitated, "You think he has a chance?"

Alexander shrugged and attempted to hide his amusement.

"Son, I'm glad you mentioned this. You confirmed something for me."

"What?"

"I was holding something back. You know my friend Vern? He works at the funeral home that handled Felix. Vern and I both knew Felix well."

"You mean, your friend who died last week?"

"Yes."

"I was sorry to hear about that. You went to his funeral two days ago."

"We had some great times. Anyway, Felix is set to be cremated tomorrow, but Vern said he would look the other way if we wanted to sneak Felix out for one more round. He loved Halloween. I have a place for him right over here."

"Dad!" Alexander was thunderstruck and couldn't get his breath after hearing this because he knew his father was quite serious.

Granddad had a little laugh, "It would be like when Errol Flynn and the boys broke in and took John Barrymore's body from the funeral home for one more go around."

Mrs. Simmons grinned at the thought.

"I think Felix could help put me over the top with the contest and he'd want that. Maybe even extend his stay into the next day, *La Dia de Los Muertos.*"

Alexander was finally able to draw a breath, "NO!!! Do not bring actual human dead bodies onto this property. That's against the law!"

"Fine. Sure. But watch Old Man Miller walk away with the prize."

By late afternoon the trick-or-treaters began arriving and they had a steady flow into the early and later evening.

Alexander, Granddad, Mrs. Simmons and Amy treasured the many little goblins and ghosts ringing the doorbell to Casa Arrington; as well as more than a few grownups in the spirit of things. It was well known that CA gave out the best candy. But it was also understood that for the good stuff, CA required them to actually do a trick, as it was a house of lawyers.

It was always interesting to see what costume Alexander appeared in. This year he pulled out his classic giant cardinal outfit. It was on one condition that no debating on the name would be forthcoming. Most loved his bird calls, while some of the younger kids were a tad frightened of him.

Granddad won the design contest again, even without resorting to actual corpses. When he saw Old Man Miller out walking his dog the next day, he was humble, for about 15 seconds…

****

Alexander was skateboarding on the heated half-pipe out back.

Amy walked out drinking tea and reading the C-J. "I see the National Women's Soccer League is expanding into town here. They're going to be called the Racing Louisville Football Club."

Alexander pulled up and slid down the pipe, "The announcement was last week. I've already got season tickets for 2021."

"Wow. Cool."

"What are you up to today, darlin'?"

"I'm going riding with Mom."

"Ah, good." Alexander went back to skating.

****

It was the first Saturday in November. It would be the last time they rode together for the year. The air was crisp, they were bundled up.

"I saw Bobby…with Nevada."

"I did too, Mother."

"I told you she has the moves."

"I'm happy for them."

"What happened?"

"I don't know. You know how men are."

"He just broke it off with you for no reason?"

"There wasn't much to break off. I don't know the reason."

"There was that litigation over the Angel's Share."

"That's over."

"Is it? Attempting to reform a multibillion-dollar industry? For many that's a sacred cow. Did Alexander not expect some blowback? You might be caught in that wake."

Amy didn't want to debate this anymore.

April sensed this and inserted a thumb drive into a portable speaker in her saddlebag. Music started up.

Amy recognized the voice, "That's Jim James."

"Yes. *The Order of Nature*. This is the album Jim did with Teddy and the Louisville Orchestra on Decca," April said. "It's topping the U.S. Classical and Classical Crossover charts. I really like it. Say, would you be interested in going with me to the premier performance tonight of the Louisville Orchestra at the brand spanking new, state-of-the-art Old Forester Paristown Hall?"

"Right next to Christy's Garden?" asked Amy.

"Yes. The program is called Teddy's Soundcheck and I think Teddy asked me if you were going to be there."

"Did he?"

"And there's a post-show DJ party."

Amy went with her that evening and it was quite memorable. LO and Teddy were top notch, again. The new Old Forester facilities lived up to the hype. April knew everyone and introduced her to a lot of important and impressive people—but she was careful not to connect Amy with any of Louisville's most eligible. She didn't want to complicate things as the path seemed to be cleared for Amy's return to New York, April's original plan.

At the end of the evening Amy understood this was her mother's way of one-upping her father for him taking her earlier to the concert at the Whitney—and Amy didn't mind.

****

The basketball season opened up and games were being played. Casa Arrington gave equal support to the men and women. Three seasons ago the women's team made it to the Elite Eight. Two seasons ago the women's team made the Final Four, so the female hoopsters were elite. They were 9th in preseason rankings. Alexander had courtside tickets for the women, who blew out their first seven opponents on their schedule and then beat Oregon, the nation's number one ranked team in the U.S. Virgin Islands by 10. This led to a number 2 ranking. But then there was the letdown the very next game against the Buckeyes.

For the men, Sunday November 10th, was the opening home game against Youngstown St.

As usual Alexander stopped in the Troll Pub Under the Bridge, patting Louie the Troll on the nose for luck as he entered. The establishment was almost under the bridge, but for sure underground. It was jammed, but having done pro bono work for some of the struggling staff, allowed Alexander and Amy to slip in through the kitchen and head to the corner of the bar that was reserved for him on game days.

They both powered up on their usual pregame cuisine. He had the Fleur de Lis Dip sandwich, marinated roast beef on a hoagie with provolone, caramelized onions with brown sugar and Old Forester bourbon and she got the Louie's Club sandwich.

As they exited the Troll Pub, Alexander glanced up at the bridge above them. "George Rogers Clark Bridge, aka the Second Street Bridge, that connects Louisville to Indiana and is connected to a man I highly admire, not only for his physical skill, but his philosophy and political stances, the great Muhammad Ali. When he was Cassius Clay, I believe he threw his Olympic gold medal off here into the Ohio River."

"Is that really settled, Daddy? Is there a definitive history? Earlier this year I heard people still debating this. Still calling it a mystery."

"Well," said Alexander, "the story is that after he won the Olympic gold medal in boxing in 1960 in Rome, he was so proud of that gold medal he wore it all the time, even slept with it—and then it disappeared. And the reason, some said, was that when Cassius was turned away at several restaurants because of his race, he threw the medal into the river in disgust, as a protest. At the 1996 Olympic games in Atlanta the medal was replaced. Live on the air Bob Costas said throwing the medal in the river was 'a symbolic story, it could have happened, but definitely did not. Somehow the medal got misplaced.'"

"Some people say a ghost writer in an early biography made it up about throwing it into the water," remarked Amy. "And that Ali just went along with it. Ali's brother says he recalls vividly when Cassius lost the medal and was desperately looking for it. Many believe someone in his entourage pilfered it, including a championship belt and sold it off."

Alexander stroked his goatee giving that some thought, "I might put some stock in that, but in 2014, during one of the annual Ohio River Sweeps, where people pull junk and debris out of the river, a gentleman from Louisville, a Mr. Robert Bradbury, found the Olympic gold medal from 1960 stuck in some mud. He turned it into the Muhammad Ali Center. They authenticated it and gave him a check for $200K."

"It was found in the river?" asked Amy. This gave her some more to chew on.

****

When entering the Yum Center and experiencing the substantial atrium, one instantly realized this was big-time college basketball. They took it seriously here. It was high-tech, with food and drink for all tastes. Escalators took the fans up to their seat locations. At just over 22,000 seating capacity, it was the largest arena designed primarily for the sport of basketball in the country.

The Cards hit their first 11 shots and didn't look back. They won by 23. It was a good tune-up, but it was odd. A strange new world, as Alexander no longer had his choice seats. They were now back in the possession of Judge Wilbur and Willodean Winslow.

Afterwards Amy commented, "The Judge and Willodean looked like they had a really good time."

Alexander forced a smile, “Great.”

Amy patted him on the shoulder as they made their way out.

****

Amy agreed to have dinner with April, she assumed Reston would be there.

Arriving at SHS she noticed Chip’s Porsche and almost did a 180 and scooted out of there, but she wouldn’t make a scene in this way. April was trying to be a mother and peacemaker and Amy endured this.

The four of them got off to some pleasantries. The scars on Chip from Sven were almost unnoticeable, the chip on Chip’s shoulder was quite apparent.

Sports were safe, usually. As Amy worked in New York, Chip went out of his way to take a dig at the futility of the Jets, Giants, Knicks, Rangers, Nets and Mets recent and continuing troubles.

Hollywood was also normally a safe place to chat about, except Chip took the chance to dance on the ashes of Lannie’s deal imploding.

Amy was restrained, even when Chip made a snarky comment if the Firewoman was about to ignite.

Reston gave him the ‘cut it out scowl.’

“Amy, I’m just teasing you.” Chip still had yearnings for another shot with her. Amy made it crystal clear that there was zero chance; it annoyed him. He enjoyed giving her little jabs.

April smiled at him, “We know how provocative Chip is.”

“I do like to discuss the issues.”

“Chip, not now,” implored his father.

“What issue is on your mind right now?” asked Amy, sweetly.

“It’s the old story, why do I have to pay to have someone else’s child educated?” asked Chip,

Reston gave his son the look to pull back, but he ignored him.

"Why?" asked Amy. "Maybe to prevent an illiterate teenager from breaking into your house in 10 years."

"If he does, he'll encounter my state-of-the-art security. He'll be arrested, prosecuted and incarcerated. We have plenty of prisons for that. But thinking about the problem critically, maybe they end up in prison because of the public schools."

"Please share your thoughts on that," asked Amy.

"Little kids get along fine and then you teach them to read and then you teach them about slavery and the civil rights struggle and discrimination and they get uncomfortable and angry that they're made uncomfortable and others get upset and they get the idea they should hate each other and parents get chafed. They join a gang to get their 'reparations,' get busted trying to break into someone's house and are sent away."

"Chip, you sound like you have it all figured out."

April's mood fell, as well as Reston's.

But not Chip, he was primed for the fight. "I'm assuming you prefer to indoctrinate them early."

"If learning history in high school is your idea of indoctrination, then perhaps you should put the 17-year-old children in a bubble that you blow and fill it with butterflies and unicorns, so the little snowflakes won't be uncomfortable by what occurred, you know, reality, or be upset by accounts of slave holders like your own family."

Chip was riled, "You think so??"

"Yes, I do and I think the students *can* handle the truth. It's the parents that are having a hard time with it."

"Oh, well you can just go—"

"Condor's Claw! Condor's Claw!" yelled Amy.

Reston and Chip froze, then glanced at each other and quickly scurried out of the room.

April sighed, "You're doing that too?"

"Would you rather we continue to throw barbs at each other and take it to DEFCON 1?"

"I guess this is better, I heard Chip whispering to Reston that he was going to 'own' you."

Amy groaned, "I'm out of here. Goodnight, Mother."

"Goodnight, darling child." They hugged.

Amy strolled off, "Idiots…"

April shrugged with a diplomatic smile.

Amy left. After the front door was heard closing, the faces of Reston and Chip appeared from around the corner.

"She's gone," assured April.

****

Amy and Gabby went out. The subject of Bobby came up.

"Look, I contacted him, but he said he was really busy."

"And it was right after you had lunch with your mother."

"Yes… Some find her a bit intimidating. She grilled Bobby on his health, and the health of his company. I'm not an expert on securities law, but she may have come close to violating a couple of them and she then brought up the deaths of his parents."

"That sounds like it was a lovely time. Who wouldn't want more of that?" asked Gabby.

They went bar hopping and got some axe throwing in. Amy really felt she was getting the hang of this, just needed more practice and a target.

Amy was dropped off late and was very quiet coming home. But when she came into the compound, she heard classical music emanating from her father's den. The door was ajar. She whispered to herself, "The 9th Symphony."

Her father played Beethoven when he needed to contemplate deeply, or if his mood was sagging.

"Daddy?" There was no answer, she pushed the door open and found him concentrating on the article he was reading.

"Daddy?"

Alexander now heard her. He picked up the remote and lowered the sound level. "Ambrosia, darling. Welcome home. How was your night?"

"It was good. What are you up to?"

Before him on his desk were the contents of a file he had spread out.

Amy picked up a document, "Alberta Jones…"

"It's November 12th. It's Alberta's birthday."

Mrs. Simmons entered, "She would have been 89, if she wasn't murdered three months shy of turning 35."

Alexander poured three drinks from a bottle of Dulsett Reserve. "And her case is still unsolved, since 1965."

"So we drink a toast to Alberta on this day," said Mrs. Simmons.

"To Alberta," said Alexander.

They all held up their glasses and took a sip.

Mrs. Simmons thought back, "After passing the bar and becoming a lawyer Alberta was quoted as saying, 'A lot of people told me, 'You've got two strikes against you, you're a woman and you're a Negro.' Yeah, but I've got one strike left, and I've seen people get home runs when all they've got is one strike.'"

The three laughed.

Mrs. Simmons picked up a picture from the file, "I knew her when I was a child. I was in awe of her. She taught at my Sunday School."

"Alberta was murdered several years before I was born," said Alexander. "I really first got interested in her and her case after seeing her picture on the wall in the law school."

Mrs. Simmons marveled, "Alberta was a force to be reckoned with. She was the first female prosecutor, Black or White, in this city. She was so smart. Could have worked in Washington D.C. or New York, but chose to come home to Louisville to try to make it a better place."

"Alberta was a trailblazer for sure," agreed Alexander. "She was Muhammad Ali's first lawyer, when he was still Cassius Clay."

"And Alberta was in the march on Washington in 1963 and the protests here for civil rights," recalled Mrs. Simmons. "She got thousands of Black Kentuckians registered to vote and publicly pushed for a ban on racial discrimination by local theaters and lunch counters here in town."

Alexander picked up a printout, "Alberta wrote in an editorial, 'Exclusion because of race is a contradiction of democratic principles and a denial of a basic human right. It is most unfortunate that White Christians in Louisville and believers in America and its democracy have not found it necessary to extend democracy and its rights to all races.'"

All three were silent.

Amy tried to visualize, "I can't imagine what kind of world she lived in. I'll bet that ruffled some feathers."

"Feathers were indeed ruffled," agreed Alexander. "She was quite progressive and right in the middle of the civil rights protests. It's been 54 years. Her body was found in the Ohio River. Initially they thought she just drowned on her own. But it's now accepted that she was assaulted and thrown off the Milton Sherman Bridge."

"They found her purse hanging on that bridge," said Mrs. Simmons.

Alexander sifted through the papers, "Years ago, I got a copy of the police file, a portion of it. I very much admire and I'm loudly cheering on Professor Lee Remington's dogged persistence on this case. She is an esteemed fellow alumnus of mine from law school. And she has discovered several overlooked or ignored clues."

Mrs. Simmons agreed, "She's done very good work on this."

Alexander sat back and pondered, "Flora Shanklin, Alberta's sister says she was being harassed by a court officer at work. One day Alberta became enraged with him and hit him with her briefcase."

Mrs. Simmons considered that, "I've often wondered what that encounter was over."

Alexander motioned to the thick folder of documents, "I read this file every November 12th and will continue to do so, until they solve the case and justice is served, as long as I'm still able."

"Alberta is one of the Hometown Heroes," commented Amy. "Her picture is up on the River City Bank."

"Right. A Hometown Hero," said Alexander. "And the Louisville Police lost or misplaced almost all of the physical evidence they had gathered on the case. The photos, the fingerprints, the dirt and blood samples, all gone."

Mrs. Simmons sighed, well aware.

Amy was stunned, "What?"

"Yep," Alexander quipped, "Which takes us back to what Flora, her sister, said. And interestingly, in 2008, the FBI matched a fingerprint that was found inside Alberta's car to a man that was 17 at the time; but didn't pursue the case saying too much evidence had been lost."

****

It was still dark when Alexander's clock alarm went off. He was groggy as he shuffled over to a table with a banana and opened the small fridge in the corner. He pulled out a prepared smoothie, gulped it down, peeled the banana and munched it. He quietly slipped out his side door, walked down the street and hopped in the van as it came by.

Behind him a car followed, being driven by Amy—who now didn't feel good about this—as she really didn't want to catch her father in a delicate or embarrassing situation, some secret affair he was conducting sub-rosa.

Just as she decided to peel off, Amy noticed the van arrive at a construction site. Alexander got out. He was greeted by a couple workers gathering for a job.

Amy turned around and simultaneously felt worse because of what she had suspected and better because of what she now knew. A peculiar construct, she thought, her emotions swirling in a cauldron of cognitive dissidence.

Back home she brewed herself some tea, read the LEO Weekly and waited for Mrs. Simmons. About twenty minutes later she walked into the kitchen from her room to face the day.

"Good morning, Mrs. Simmons."

"Good morning, Amy. How are you today?"

"I'm quite fine, except..."

"Yes?"

"I was wondering if you can fill me in on something."

"What?"

"I've seen my dad slip out early several times and then later come out of his room near noon, like he just got up. I followed him this morning and he ended up at a construction site. I have a feeling in a couple hours he's going to emerge from his room like he's just getting up."

"It's Habitat for Humanity," replied Mrs. Simmons. "Alexander has been volunteering to work on other people's homes for years."

23

It was soon Thanksgiving morning. At the crack of dawn Alexander slipped out. Amy was waiting for him this time.

"Can I come along?"

"Ambrosia..."

Alexander drove his car. Amy was in the passenger's seat.

"I know about you volunteering at Habitat."

"Oh?"

"I've seen you leave several times before dawn since I've been back. Why didn't you ask me to go with you?"

"You never liked doing that stuff before. I took you to a couple things."

"Really, what?"

"One was a barn raising. You said it was boring."

"Right...I remember. It was out in the country. It was hot...and dusty."

"Another time I took you with me to a soup kitchen I volunteered in."

"Right...I told Mom on the phone I was scared of the people and said they smelled bad when she was over in London."

"It was Milan. She threatened to revoke my visitation rights."

"I shouldn't have been so stuck up."

"It's okay. My problem was years ago I failed to prevent the eviction of a client from her apartment. I fumbled the ball. And the next day, as penance for my screw up, I volunteered at Habitat for Humanity to help others gain home ownership. I didn't know squat about how to do it. I could swing a hammer, but that was about it."

"I never knew."

"You were away at school or over at your mother's."

Amy thought back, "And I usually wasn't up at that time."

"Today is Thanksgiving. No building. I'm going to help serve."

Alexander and Amy arrived at Feed Louisville with a donation. He had become friends with the co-founders Rhona Kamar and Donny Greene and was impressed with how they worked with the local farmers and the generosity of several local restaurants. Feed Louisville not only fed the homeless and the food insecure, but advocated for them in the areas of mental health and worked to get them off the street and back on their feet. Alexander and Amy went into their kitchen and joined a team that helped the chef prepare hundreds of Thanksgiving meals.

****

As they were driving back to CA, Alexander and Amy both had big grins.

He reflected on the morning. "I think Churchill said it best, 'We make a living by what we get; we make a life by what we give.'"

Amy nodded, "True."

Alexander was wistful, "If I wasn't an attorney, I think I would have been a farmer, working the land."

"Daddy, you earlier said if you weren't an attorney, you would have toured with Springsteen."

"Grow my crops during the week, tour with the Boss on the weekend. I met Bruce in '95 in D.C. during the Ghost of Tom Joad Tour and we had a few beers after the concert. We hit it off. He would have been flexible."

"There's only one person that's a bigger name dropper than you and you married her."

When they got back home, they found Mrs. Simmons cooking in the kitchen.

"My goodness, it smells scrumdiddlyumptious in here. What can I do?" inquired Alexander.

"Stay out of the kitchen and go watch some football, the Detroit Lions desperately need your support," ordered Mrs. Simmons. "Everything is under control here."

Alexander grabbed a brew from the fridge, "Happy Thanksgiving, Mrs. Simmons."

"Same to you, Alexander."

Amy stepped up next to her, "Do you need any help?"

"I've been cooking Thanksgiving dinner longer than you've been skateboarding in this world. Actually, twice as long."

Alexander and Amy both freshened up and met in the living room. He picked up his guitar and strummed away.

Amy sat and watched the game, "Daddy, did you invite anyone?"

"I did."

"And I'm not talking about the place you would set for Elvis."

"You never know." He strummed some more, "I invited Sherri."

"Good."

"There's a couple foreign exchange students that didn't go home. They're coming by."

"Interesting. I invited Gabby and Abby and Mitch, Roxanne and Marcus."

"Great. What about Bobby?"

"We aren't sharing our thoughts at the moment."

"What happened?"

"I really don't know."

The house quickly filled up. They gave great love to Miss Sassy.

Amy wished Bobby was there, but she put it out of her mind. Her 5-month grace period was coming to an end and she didn't want to complicate matters.

During dinner, one of the visiting students asked about a local landmark worth visiting that was off the beaten path.

Granddad stated, "The Lincliff estate. Situated on the Ohio River, it's a 30-acre Georgian Revival style home with incredible gardens built in 1911. Previously owned by the late hardware mogul, William Belknap, it had fallen into disrepair, until it was purchased by local author Sue Grafton and her husband Steve Humphrey."

Alexander bragged about his father, "Granddad consulted with Sue and Steve when they were remodeling the Lincliff estate."

"That's impressive," said Sherri. "I love that place."

"I wasn't a consultant. They didn't use any outside designers. They asked me my opinion on a few things as a courtesy. Not much. Steve and Sue deserve a ton of credit for bringing that classic old manor back to life."

The students were fired up and wanted to visit. "We must go!"

"However, I don't think it's open to the public," Mrs. Simmons stated diplomatically.

Granddad and Alexander paused, they didn't think about that part.

"I'll look into it," said Alexander.

"I'll make it happen," promised Granddad.

The students looked hopeful.

"It broke my heart when Sue died two years ago," Sherri lamented. "I really loved her Alphabet Mysteries. I heard she made her family swear an oath not to sell her books to Hollywood. And if they did, she would 'haunt them from the grave.'"

"We'll know soon on that front," said Amy.

"Did you hear something out in L.A.?" Alexander inquired.

Amy had indeed heard something. During one of Zabéla's soirees in Malibu a coked-up talent agent learned Amy was from Louisville and let her in on something still in the early stages.

Amy announced, "The Alphabet Series from Sue is going to be greenlit by A&E."

The room was surprised. "What? Really?"

"I wonder when the haunting will begin?" mused Sherri.

****

It was a most excellent dinner. The group had transitioned to the living room and sat in front of the fire.

Amy then got a text from her mom asking her to come outside.

"Mother? What's going on?"

"Could you ask your father to come out? I'd like to talk to him."

"It's terribly cold, Mother. You sure you don't want to come in?"

April was about to agree, but checked, "Is Sherri here?"

Amy groaned.

"That's okay, you don't have to ask him to come out."

"April?" Alexander stepped out.

"I'm going in, Mother." Amy kissed her on the cheek. "Happy Thanksgiving."

"Same to you, sweetheart." April touched Amy's face lovingly.

Amy turned and patted her father on the shoulder as she entered the house.

"Happy Thanksgiving, April."

"Happy Thanksgiving, Alexander. The day we're supposed to give thanks for our blessings." April glanced off at a distant street light, "I guess I have many reasons to be thankful."

"As do I," said Alexander.

"And I never thanked you properly for clearing up that mess with the videos."

"Not a big deal."

"It would have been. But you were there, Alexander, like always, solving problems."

"I had a guy break the encryption on the phone and he determined that the images weren't exported. They were contained on the device."

"And the device?"

"Dissolved in a vat of acid."

A very wide grin appeared on her face.

"I couldn't have my little girl and my lady, or my former lady, being played by that two-bit hustler. There will be no more threats from him."

"How can you be so sure?"

"He's an actor. I threatened to nuke his career in Hollywood if he does."

"I see."

"April, I never thanked you for shutting down the lawsuit Chip and Reston were planning against Casa Arrington over that tiger."

"Sven?" April pooh-poohed that, "Such a sweetheart. I couldn't have my daughter and my…former man facing that."

They gazed at each other, she kissed him on the cheek and then they locked lips.

Amy was watching from the window and was flabbergasted, "Huuuh???" At that exact moment Sherri joined Amy and she gasped.

"Amy, you look like you just saw the ghost of Thanksgiving past."

Amy guided her away from the window, "I still can't get over that trick play the Bills used to beat the Cowboys today."

"That was surprising," said the judge.

"Excuse me, Your Honor…Sherri. I need to check on the dessert in the kitchen. Would you like to accompany me? I would love your opinion. It's also a surprise. Just like today."

April's driver pulled up out front and she got in the car, glanced back at Alexander and they drove off.

Alexander wistfully observed the vehicle until it disappeared around the corner.

Amy ditched Sherri with some lemon meringue pie, slid around the outside of the house and spied her father sporting a goofy grin. "Psst! Psst!"

Alexander glanced around and noticed Amy off to the side. She waved him over.

"Daughter, what are you up to?"

"Father, what are *you up to*?"

"I uh…"

"I saw."

"Oh."

"And I saw Sherri inside."

"Did she see me, us?"

"I don't think so." Amy wiped her mother's lipstick off her father's cheek and lips.

"I didn't try anything. I mean, I didn't mean for that to happen. It just did."

"I know. Now go in. I wiped off the evidence, you wipe off the goofy grin."

"Right." Alexander reentered the front door.

Amy reentered the kitchen.

Later, Sherri sat with Alexander as he strummed his guitar.

"You know what's really ironic?" asked Alexander.

"Tell me."

"When you pitched in softball, I mean, you were very good. Fanned 10 batters against Western Hills."

"I had some skills, not a superstar."

"But you still crabbed at some of the calls by the umpire and now, Sherri, *you're* the umpire."

"Do you think I call a fair game?"

"You haven't been impeached or recalled."

"Great endorsement, counselor."

"Yet."

Sherri swatted him playfully.

Alexander flashed his mischievous grin. He then became serious, "I must confess that I admire how you handle your courtroom and get starry-eyed over your stare decisis."

"I believe that's probably the most romantic thing you've ever told me, Alexander."

It was a nice moment and then a wave of Alexander's friends started arriving. He welcomed Wendell Berry. Alexander considered Wendell a wise man that should be sought out and listened to. Alexander and Wendell had ongoing deep deliberations on the state of the world. Subjects included the death penalty, the curse of fossil-fuel dependency, the handling of toxic pollution, coal, soil degradation and the decline of rural communities. Alexander was greatly impressed with his essay "Solving for Pattern," where a 'ramifying set of solutions' was sought for multiple problems, improving the harmony and health of the entire system along the way.

While Alexander and Wendell were off discussing, Amy lured Sherri out of the house and out back by the half-pipe.

"Gosh, just like every kid I've known, a giant half-pipe in their backyard."

Amy was almost embarrassed, "True. I didn't grow up in the most normal of households."

"The daughter of Alexander and April Arrington? Of course not."

"Meanwhile, where we left off in the story about 'the incident' was that you regularly hung out at the Heine Brothers Coffee Shop in the Highlands. And you met my dad there and my mom came in."

"Yes."

"What happened?"

"She dumped my soda on me and my papers and notebook."

"Yikes!"

"I guess I was lucky because in those days we didn't have laptops or that would have been ruined."

"Wow. That is shocking."

Friends of Sherri and Amy spilled out into the back. Casa Arrington was like a magnet for those souls out seeking a connection and entertainment. People continued to arrive after their own family Thanksgiving gatherings. Music was in the air.

Various friends of Alexander were hanging out, some from out of town. All present were musicians contributing, at different levels, it was a giant karaoke/jam session all harmonizing together deep into the evening.

Sherri stayed late and thoroughly enjoyed the impromptu concert.

At 2am CA had nearly emptied out. Amy was sitting with Sherri.

"After all this time, I still don't understand the animosity between you and my mom."

"Amy, I don't think I should talk about this."

"Please. My curiosity is killing me."

"I really shouldn't..."

"I'll come over and mow your grass, Sherri."

"There you go!" laughed the judge. She took another drink and was quite relaxed.

Amy made a face of desperation, "I'm losing sleep over this. I need to know."

"All right... There's been so much water under the bridge I can say this now. There was a moment, where Alexander and I might have made a go of it, but I hesitated."

Amy was surprised to learn this. "Oh?"

"I think April saw how close I was getting with Alexander and she sabotaged me. When she has you in her sights…" Sherri pulled back and didn't want to continue.

"Please, tell me more."

"You know how she can turn a phrase. She called me 'a salacious and—"

Alexander arrived and finished it, "—and pernicious tramp on the prowl.'"

Amy gulped.

Alexander mused, "April's verbosity can veer into vitriol. I find it easier to delete such events in your memory."

"If only I could," said Sherri. "April claimed I swooped in on you when she went off to band camp."

"You make it sound like I was some sort of prey being hunted by seasoned predators."

Sherri laughed, "Alexander, you were always the best at summing things up." She then displayed her melancholy, "And I was on the losing end. I lost a life I should have had with you. I turned you down."

The air was sucked out of the room. It was really quiet. Sherri realized her tongue was too loose and confessed, "And now I need to go home."

Alexander walked her out to her car. She gave him a kiss and then they kissed longer and with passion. She got in her car and was driven off.

Amy watched from the front door, "And I was worried about him being alone…"

Granddad was currently at the other end of CA and didn't notice the lovebirds. He had his own concerns scouting across the street at Old Man Miller's property. He noticed a dull reflection from the second floor. Granddad picked up his binoculars and caught the moonlit glint from a pair of field glasses peering back at him and gave his rival a big confident grin.

There was no competition for Thanksgiving. Granddad and Old Man Miller were keeping their powder dry for the major showdown on their calendar. There was an arms control treaty between these neighborhood design superpowers. They agreed to hold off the start of Christmas decorations until Black Friday, which was hours away. Trucks, material and workers would soon be descending on both properties.

Bobby slowly drove by CA. He wanted to stop and come in, but he continued on.

Amy caught sight of his car. It froze her as she watched the auto disappear down the street and around the corner. She shook her head and gazed up at the night sky and stars above.

24

It was a spa day for April and Amy at SHS. A crew came in. A mani-pedi for both. Hard skin had been removed. They had been shaped, soaked, exfoliated, and were getting cuticle work done. They sipped on spicey pumpkin lattes.

"Is everything on schedule?"

"For?"

"For the Kentucky Seedlings Dinner," said April.

"I thought you and Daddy did that together."

"We hand it off every other year now. This year he's taking the lead."

"I saw him and Mrs. Simmons working on that."

"Thank God for her," exclaimed April.

"She's a treasure," Amy agreed.

"I've read all of the Final 50 and made my votes," said April. "It was tough to narrow them down."

"I've read several of the applications. There's a very promising list of young people to choose from."

"And I was told that you had quite a promising list of guests at the late-night after-party on Thanksgiving at Casa Arrington."

"Um, yes…"

"Sounds like it was a nice group, rock stars, film producers, actors, writers, professors, philanthropists, art curators and a former diplomat to the UK. We could have traded stories on the royals. I've got a real gobsmacker on Prince Andrew."

"Mother, everyone has one of those for Prince Andrew."

"I suppose…" April seemed quite out of sorts at missing such an event.

"You know how it is at Casa Arrington."

"Yes," April wistfully recalled. "We had such interesting people come through. I used to call it the Southern Algonquin Round Table."

"Mother, I did ask if you wanted to come in."

"But there was that certain federal judge."

"You're going to have to get used to that."

"I would, if she would just apologize to me."

"For what?"

"The Heine Brothers Coffee Shop incident."

"Sherri mentioned that."

"She ruined one of my blouses, not to mention me taking a direct hit to my dignity."

"Mother, what are you talking about?"

"The Heine Brothers Coffee Shop incident. I went to see Alexander in the Highlands. And I go up to his table and Sherri is sitting there. She takes her soda and dumps it on me. I declare! Can you imagine??"

Amy frowned at that and understood one of them was imagining something. "That is shocking."

"However, I have put that aside." April removed a piece of lint from her sleeve, "One of us has to be the adult here."

"Good."

"But the thing about Sherri is that when she goes after someone, it sticks and it's cruel. In high school she was the one that started 'April is an ammit!' It really caught on. April is an ammit! It was used to taunt and haunt me."

"It sounds...horrible?" Amy didn't understand.

"Do you know what that means? I looked it up. The ammit is the most destructive monster in Egyptian mythology. She's considered a goddess, but also a demoness that eats human hearts. With the head of a crocodile and a body that's part-lion and part-hippo. How dare she! Part-hippo??!"

"That's the part that upset you?"

"I am not upset, anymore. Just giving you some of the backstory."

"Thank you for that."

"I'm having lunch with the governor next week. Care to come along?"

"I'll clear my schedule. I would be honored." Amy sensed another attempt of her mother to stay competitive, after Thanksgiving.

****

Amy came home after 9pm. The exterior work had ceased for the day. There was a giant tarp put up around the front yard of Casa Arrington. The same could be said for Old Man Miller's place across the way. Other houses attempted to show their stuff. As most weren't that maniacal, they didn't worry about keeping their efforts top secret.

It was a critical time. There were 12 days to prepare. The unveiling would be on December 7th. The judges, the residents on the street, ages 5 to 95, had three days to vote by email. The winner was announced on December 15th on Facebook.

Old Man Miller had sunk a fortune into his designs over the years, with little to show for it. Granddad had also invested some cash, but he did way more with much less.

About a dozen of the homeowners in the neighborhood really participated; but everyone knew it was like the Big 10 Conference in football, there were two teams that dominated and one of them had been on a roll as of late.

Amy believed their design-arms race had gotten out of hand, but she just continued to observe and be in awe.

When Amy left earlier that day Granddad had been working on the animatronics and they were giving him fits—but that was then. Robot elves gathered and then stood at attention.

A mechanical reindeer appeared at the front door with a high-pitched voice. "Welcome to Casa Arrington, I'm Roderick the Reindeer!"

Amy nodded, "Wow."

Alexander and Granddad arrived from the living room.

"You like?" Granddad asked.

"Very impressive. Roderick the Reindeer," said Amy, with a cheery face.

"Old Man Miller thinks he has a chance this year. Roderick the Reindeer will vanquish that fool."

Alexander patted him on the back, "Glad to see you're really getting into the Christmas spirit, Dad."

"I'm all in. He's going down."

"You won at Halloween and now it looks like you have this in the bag."

"You don't sound like you mean it, son. Because I was thinking of bringing in several actual live reindeers."

"Wait… What?" Alexander gave this a quick thought and frowned.

"Come on, I gave in to you and didn't bring any live corpses."

"Live corpses?" asked Alexander, his indigestion returning.

"Don't worry, not the ones that can actually fly."

"Live corpses that can fly?"

"No, reindeers. I'm serious here."

Amy's eyes went wide.

"I know you're serious!" said Alexander. "That's what keeps me up at night."

"It's called bringing your A game, son."

"Dad…might real reindeer upset the delicate balance we have here? I mean Duke, Duchess and Diva and Henry Clay are still out of sorts and Nutmeg and Cantankerous Cat, well, he's always cranky, but Luminary the Legendary Lizard seems a bit melancholy and I think it's because they're all still recovering from Sven. It was such a disruption."

Granddad considered that, "You know, you may be right, son. He was a big cat. Hamlet the Hammy Hamster hasn't been himself lately, either."

"Imagine what that could do to their psyches by introducing some reindeers with their big honkin' antlers."

"Gotcha. I'll just bring in some baby reindeers. They're so cute. Always good for a few votes. Wait until Old Man Miller sees them frolicking about. He'll wet his whiskers." Granddad chuckled with joy as he strolled off scheming.

Alexander and Amy both sighed at this. They joined Mrs. Simmons in the living room working on her laptop.

"Baby reindeers now?" inquired Mrs. Simmons, blankly. "I wonder what they eat."

"I'll talk to him," Alexander reassured her.

"What are you two working on?" asked Amy.

"On the Kentucky Seedlings Dinner," replied Alexander.

"Can I do anything? Read any of the applications?"

"Sure."

"Let me change and freshen up. By the way, Daddy?"

"Yes?"

"Do you know about the Heine Brothers Coffee Shop incident?"

Mrs. Simmons paused and waited for the response.

Alexander was thrown by that, "That was a long time ago."

"Do you remember what happened?"

"Actually...I believe I had already left the premises before the event."

Mrs. Simmons didn't comment and went back to work.

"Just curious." Amy moved on wishing she could put all three under oath and depose them. "Rashomon in the Highlands," mumbled Amy.

Mrs. Simmons gave Alexander a look. He ignored her.

Amy crossed through the living room talking to herself, "April is an ammit. April is an ammit. Hmm, that is catchy." Amy passed behind a large wing-back chair where Granddad was working on his iPad.

He heard her and scrunched his face. "An ammit?"

****

Alexander continued to hope Amy would stay in town, but didn't want to push for it and promised himself he wouldn't bring it up. It was her choice and he wanted a natural outcome. A lobby-free decision. He supported her chasing after her dream and fulfilling her potential no matter what or where it was to be.

However, after putting this off for quite a significant time, Alexander believed it was the right moment to rent office space. He thought a change was needed, away from Casa Arrington and the eclectic collection of characters, both animal and human, that had been greeting prospective clients. He reminded himself that he was thinking about this before his daughter came back, so there was no deviation on the pact he made with himself. He headed to greener pastures. The only place that was actually greener than Casa Arrington: The Green Building.

Completed in 2008, it was located in NuLu, in the East Market district. The Green Building was the first LEED Platinum project in the city of Louisville and the first LEED certified adaptive re-use project in the state of Kentucky.

Alexander held this place in high regard, he loved visiting. He believed all interested in art and architecture would be wise to take a tour and do a deep dive on the nuts and bolts of this structure. The Green Building had led a renaissance of the neighborhood. It was a 115-year-old edifice. The planners kept the ornamental masonry shell and gutted much of the interior. They believed in the philosophy that sensible architecture emerged between 'spatial and programmatic relationships.' Design and sustainability were interlocked. One benefit was the many green plants of The Green Building used no city water. Rain water was absorbed by the roof and diverted to three large barrels or into the rain garden where toxins were removed. The Green Building used a high percentage of recycled materials: 100% of the flooring, 70% of the windows and 80% of the insulation, made from recycled blue jeans and stuff diverted from the landfill.

The Green Building had 81 solar panels and 12 geothermal wells 225 feet under the building. The result of all the energy efficiency was that The Green Building saved 30,000 pounds of CO2 a month, more than enough to offset the carbon footprint of all its employee's vehicles.

Alexander had a cup of coffee at the café in the front of the building. The first floor displayed local art that he always took time to take in. He mulled over what he was going to do and decided not to ask any favors from anyone he knew that had sway over this. Alexander inquired with the building manager who apologized that no office space was available. Alexander was put on a waiting list. He decided to stay put at Casa Arrington for the time being.

****

TORTS and Just Desserts from the mind of Alexander Arrington

The owl appeared holding a cup of coffee and spoke:

"I brewed myself a strong cup of coffee, sat and digested the entire Relocation Assistance Guidance Manual issued by the Commonwealth of Kentucky Transportation Cabinet. The RAG manual is quite thorough. As it states, 'It provides guidance on statewide policies and standards for relocation transactions.' It details eligibility criteria, moving expenses, move methods, required notices, claims for payment, reconsideration of claim denial... It goes on for some time. Kentucky follows the federal regulations established in the Uniform Act of 1970. A system was created for those who were collateral damage in the eminent domain process. It's obvious that a lot of thought has gone into people affected by 'the greater good' of urban renewal.

There is increased revenue from these areas to the state with the new businesses. Renters are considered transitory, vote sporadically and rarely donate politically, which means they're not given much consideration. There is no rent control, landlords can charge whatever they want and raise the rent by whatever they feel like and there are no caps on how much a landlord can charge in late fees. Rents will no-doubt rise significantly and tenants will be squeezed.

Kelo v. City of New London was a Supreme Court case that affirmed eminent domain transfer from one private owner to another to further economic development. It was permissible 'public use' under the Takings Clause of the Fifth Amendment. Which states, 'private property cannot be taken for public use, without just compensation.'

However, one class of people was overlooked in the taking: 'just compensation' is ignored for the homeowners that remain. Some will argue the property values will increase, but that's on paper; many in the zones of gentrification are geriatric on fixed incomes. More than a few will be hard pressed to pay the eye-watering property tax increases and face troubling decisions with their lives. Should they leave their neighborhood, their world and try to find some other place to live out their time? Or stay and face troubling decisions with their finances—some actually cutting back on food and/or medicine to pay the government.

In 1928 the great Justice Louis Brandeis delivered his famous dissent writing, 'The Founders conferred against the government, the right to be let alone—the most comprehensive right and the right most favored by civilized men.'

And now, nearly a century later, I submit that having the government give the stamp of approval, even push for some of these projects and then have property taxes shoot up, double or more, overnight, is not letting them alone. For those hiding behind precedents and stare decisis, Justice Brandeis also said, 'Knowledge of the decided cases and the rules of logic cannot make a great lawyer. The controlling force is the deep knowledge of the human necessities.'

I believe the necessities for many lay in some horse trading between urban and rural representatives in Frankfort and in other state capitals of this great country. The state is the landlord raising the rent here. Are their policies as cutthroat as the private sector?

The representatives need to construct a fair and equitable solution for those, through no fault of their own, who are caught on the wrong side of the tremendous revitalization sweeping the land. It's coming. It's a natural turn of events. But the question remains on how it's handled. Is it a government of the people or *over* the people?"

~ ~ ~

"I totally love Georgia's Sweet Potato Pie Company and their Pies With Purpose. They put positive books in the hands of kids that get in the habit of reading. And I love their caramel sweet potato pie."

The owl faded out.

****

Alexander, Granddad, Mrs. Simmons and Amy traveled to Lexington for the women hoopsters. It was boisterous and the Cardinals won 67-66. The ride home was lively.

****

April met up with Amy and they walked down the street checking out the houses decorated for the season. There were several very nice creations.

And then they came to Old Man Miller's lavish production. Over the top lights, lots of man-made snow and Santa swooping in and landing in the front yard. A robot Santa turned to the street and bellowed, "Ho, Ho, Ho, Merry Christmas!!!

"That'll scare the crap out of most kids," said April.

"Wait 'till you see Roderick the Reindeer," remarked Amy.

They went across the street and took in the show at Casa Arrington. Such detail. A whole bunch of robot creatures were moving about. Elves were busy.

April was enthralled and then she noticed one of the characters, "Look, there, the head of an alligator and the body of a lion and a hippo. That's an ammit, Damnit!"

"An ammit?" asked Amy.

"Yes! An ammit!" announced Granddad. "I believe in giving credit where it's due. I heard you Amy, talking about an ammit. I know a thing or two about the Egyptian religion and I went with it. Brilliant idea."

"Ahhh! April is an ammit!" snarled April bitterly.

"What's going on here?" asked Alexander.

April composed herself, "Our daughter told your father about how they put me down in high school and he's gone and recreated it!" April glared at Amy with anger and then hurt and then stormed off.

"Mother!" Amy watched her mother march away. "I didn't mean that or this or whatever happened...I'm not quite sure."

"I'm also confused," announced Granddad, "It's quite authentic. And she didn't like my ammit? I'm not changing it."

****

Sherri came by for a nightcap. She had heard about the dustup and had to see the ammit for herself. She cracked up laughing and captured an image of it. Sherri told Granddad that she loved his ammit. He appreciated it.

Amy saw and was amused.

Alexander and Sherri kissed.

Amy turned away, intrigued at that.

25

The weather had turned gray and chilly. It was December 17th and time for the annual Kentucky Seedlings Foundation Dinner. This was an organization that April and Alexander had created when they got married. Rather than honeymooning in Bali, they invested the money creating a group that would plant seeds in people. After April and Alexander split, KSF continued on. It was a low-key dinner with some high-powered people.

The Kentucky Seedlings Foundation had teachers from the different high schools in the expanded Louisville area and beyond in the state, send one confidential nomination. In 500 words or less, no more than one typed page, they were asked to explain why it should be their student who should be a Seedling—without the student even knowing they were being considered. No other lobbying was allowed. It was all kept under wraps.

The guidelines were informal. KSF sought young people who went out of their way to help their communities, their schools, their fellow students. Candidates might not have had such a great support system, be from a challenging environment, encountered difficult surroundings and yet volunteered to tutor or delivered food and spent time with shut-ins or were friends and defenders of special needs kids, or the ones that organized trash pick-ups and regularly cut the grass of the elderly lady on the corner. They had to be good students, not necessarily Honors Society, but someone dedicated, who put the effort in, showed potential, was curious of the world and wanted to learn.

Some needed college scholarships and financial aid, while others yearned to go to technical and trade schools. The board had the option to read all of the applications, usually several hundred, or just the 50 they voted on to get to 10.

The 10 received cards by special delivery congratulating them and inviting them to Casa Arrington for dinner, transportation provided.

On the evening of the dinner the board met for cocktails and caught up, while limos picked up the 10 recipients and delivered them to CA.

Over the years the anticipation grew annually on who the lucky 10 would be.

This was a big deal. Their arrivals at CA were covered by the local media and watched by the board. The students were ushered into the den where they eagerly waited.

Then at 7pm the board transitioned into the dining area. There was a long row of silver platters. The board members stepped up to the silver serving trays that were being kept warm by burners underneath. Each rolled up their sleeves and put on aprons with their names on it. A door was opened. The 10 students entered and the board of 20 applauded the 10 Kentucky Seedlings for 2020.

The young people each picked up a plate and the board members served them the food they requested. After dinner each of the applications were read and the scholarships and grants were given out to the 10.

April and Alexander kept a distance. Only twice did they make eye contact. They had polite smiles for each other, which Amy observed.

The night finally wrapped up. The board members had left the building and the Seedlings, so full of excitement, were driven back home.

Amy and Alexander watched the last vehicle depart.

"Quite a night," Amy said.

Alexander mused, "Just seeing the joy in their faces. I'm talking about the students *and* the mentors."

Amy grinned at that and then noticed someone across the street staring at their location. She recognized the face, "Sean…"

"Sean??" Alexander was stunned at that name.

Sean pretended to stick his finger down his throat and throw up.

Amy slowly turned away from the door and kicked off her pumps. She slyly slipped into her cross-trainers and made eye contact with Sean. He faked throwing up again and laughed.

Amy started running at him. Sean fled on foot. Alexander followed her.

They sprinted halfway down the block. Sean was speeding up, but Amy was accelerating as well. She was surprised he was so fast.

Alexander pulled up and gasped for air, "I'll cover this area if he doubles back..."

The moon was bright as they both ran south down Edwards Street. It was freezing cold. The air was hurting her lungs, but Amy was gaining on him. A stone wall was in front of them, topped with barbed wire. Sean pulled himself up onto the lip of the wall and then used a telephone pole to push off and clear the barbed wire.

Amy followed. She was so pumped she jumped up onto the front corner of the wall and then also used the telephone pole to vault over the barbed wire—but her evening gown was ensnared by the fence. She swung around and smacked the stone wall with a *thud.*

Amy dangled on the inside section of the wall to St. Louis Cemetery and moaned. "Uhhh... Crap..."

Amy limped back home with her cream-colored designer dress filthy and in tatters. She stopped by the bathroom for supplies. She then joined Alexander, sat by the fire and treated the cuts on her legs and elbow.

"You okay?"

"Yeah. And it was Sean. He was taunting us. He got away. I don't know what came over me. That was stupid."

"The incel idiot. I totally understand," assured Alexander.

****

It was now one week until Christmas. April took her usual trip to Hawaii with Reston. He brought Chip and April had brought up the notion of Amy coming along with them. Amy attempted to contain her laughter at the thought of her spending 10 days on Kauai with Chip. She bolstered her case for not going by sharing a bad dream she had about being stuck on a deserted island with Chip. It ended with her going *Lord of the Flies* on him, which looked worse than what Sven had done.

April was partially pleased, as she didn't want to endure the drama the two created.

Amy again secretly promised Mitch she would provide two tickets, this time for Cardinal hoops. Mitch then told Abby that he was more than happy to babysit the kids. The DDs went out on the town.

Abby bragged how Mitch really had turned around and become a real dad. She was so pleased and she was pleased that The DDs had reunited.

Amy insisted on taking both Abby and Gabby out and covering the costs as a double do-over for missing the first reunion. The DDs descended on Miracle on Market, a pop-up Christmas bar at The Green Building. Just stepping into the place put one in the Christmas mood. There were two sections: the front which was rather intimate and the back room which was larger and showing Christmas movies on a screen. They had a menu of Christmas-themed specialty drinks. Abby had the Gingerbread flip, an eggnog-bourbon drink, and Amy and Gabby had the Christmaspolitan, 1.5 oz vodka, 1oz St-Germain, 1oz spiced cranberry sauce, half an oz of lime juice and two dashes of fig bitters.

It was Wednesday, so it was Karaoke night. The DDs sang their little hearts out.

They regrouped for the next song. Abby had to inquire, "Still a no-go with Bobby?"

"He gave me the cold shoulder. He's now in the rearview mirror."

"Right." Abby stood, "I have to use the ladies' room. Talk among yourselves." She was off.

Gabby's grin faded quickly. Amy noticed, "What?"

Gabby was down in the dumps; she didn't want to talk about it.

"Gab, what's going on?"

"My dad found out about Leti and me. We had this huge fight."

"He just found out you have a girlfriend? First time?"

"He's basically disowned me." Gabby was crying, "Look at me..." She dabbed her eyes.

"I'm sorry, Gab." Amy was crestfallen over this news.

"Please don't tell Abby."

Amy nodded. A moment later Abby returned and could see that Gabby had been crying.

"Okay, what'd I miss?"

Gabby grinned, "I'm sorry, you two. I was just thinking about a relative that upset me."

"Gabby, we know how much you love your family," said Abby.

****

Bobby was finishing up a meeting with his managers. It was a good news/okay news sort of thing. Sales up, costs up. He did his bit and schmoozed with the right people. Finally, when it was his own time, he made a call.

"Mitch, let's play some ball. Round up the posse."

Mitch was glued to his computer screen, "Bobby, sorry man, but I volunteered to babysit so The DDs could do their thing tonight."

"You are the man! You volunteered?"

"Hell yeah."

"Mitch, I am impressed you stepped up to the plate on this."

"Thanks, Bobby. Spending the time. You know, it's about being a dad."

"Would you know where The DDs would be tonight?"

****

Bobby surfaced at Miracle on Market and spotted The DDs. He started to cross to them, but was cut off by several fans that recognized him and clamored to take selfies and group photos. One woman shrieked with joy.

Amy, Abby and Gabby heard the commotion and turned around.

"I've seen this rerun," said Amy.

Bobby was surrounded and captured. He patiently took pics and signed some stuff. After several minutes he turned around and The DDs were gone.

****

Christmas morning found Alexander up early and dressed like Santa, delivering little treats to the many critters that resided in Casa Arrington. Duke, Duchess and Diva and Henry Clay were in hog heaven.

Santa Alexander Claus delivered worms to Luminary the Legendary Lizard and catnip to Nutmeg and Cantankerous Cat who rolled around in their inebriated state.

****

Amy was in her room alone. She wondered how it would play out with Gabby's family. Abby wasn't aware, didn't suspect a thing, but Amy knew Gabby was gay, or at least bisexual in high school. Gabby never admitted anything, Amy never asked. Coming from a conservative Mexican-American family, she knew Gabby had to just play along and keep her head down. It wasn't until she got out of college before she actually explored these feelings and started dating. Gabby then confessed to Amy that she had a girlfriend. Amy assured her it wasn't a big surprise and kind of a yawner; both agreed to not let Abby in on this for the moment, which had become several years. The main reason was not having to burden her with keeping this from Mitch, who would almost certainly freak out and most likely cause a problem.

Amy knew Gabby always looked forward to Christmas with her big family; but this year was different. The tension was thick between her and her dad. For the sake of the family, they both had agreed to go to neutral corners to get through the holiday season.

****

It was early evening on Christmas day when Bobby parked his car. Cassidy observed the many lights flashing and twinkling in the night on the other side of the street. "Look at that."

"That's Old Man Miller's place," Bobby said. "There's a contest. He lost to Amy's granddad."

They walked up to the front door of CA bearing gifts. The elves stood at attention. "Welcome to Casa Arrington, I'm Roderick the Reindeer! Merry Christmas."

Cass and Bobby laughed at that.

The door opened and Amy was there, she tried to hide her look of surprise. "Hey, Bobby, Cassidy."

Alexander arrived right behind Amy, "Welcome, Merry Christmas, you two."

Bobby and Cass made their greetings and entered, "Thank you for inviting us, Alexander."

Amy gave her dad a look that he avoided.

****

Amy and Bobby were alone in the living room, well, except for Luminary.

"How's Nevada?" asked Amy.

"We went out again. I saw you at the concert. But…"

"What?"

Bobby eyed the lizard that seemed to be giving him the once over, "Look, I don't want to be the reason you stay or go."

"My dad is doing the same thing."

"I heard you talking at Thanksgiving that you were going back."

"I said that?"

"'Padmore is like playing for the Yankees. Who walks away from them?' After I heard you say that, I didn't want to cloud the issue."

"That's why you've been giving me the cold shoulder…"

"I figured you've already made your decision by now. The time is up." Bobby pulled a present out of his satchel. "For you."

Amy unwrapped it. It was a picture of them together back in high school, sitting and laughing. It was framed and in black and white.

Amy was quite taken by it. "Thank you." She reached under the tree and pulled out a present.

"Let me guess," said Bobby. "A sweater. I'm hoping for an ugly Christmas sweater." Bobby unwrapped his present. It was a framed picture of him playing basketball in the Spanish League.

Bobby was quite taken by it, "That's very nice. Thank you, Amy." They kissed and kissed again with some passion.

Cassidy entered the room, noticed, turned around and walked out approving of this.

Amy stopped and whispered, "Bobby, I'm going to make an announcement at dinner."

****

Everyone was sitting in the living room listening to the TORTs album where they covered the Christmas classics.

Alexander grooved to it, "We sounded good."

They were by the young tree in a wooden stand. It had been through three holiday seasons and would probably do a dime, 10 years, as the Arrington Christmas Tree.

Granddad thought back and had a laugh, "I remember as a wee lad, on Christmas, we fired our guns. It was for good fortune. An attempt to keep away the evil spirits. Maybe that's what we've been missing."

Alexander's eyes narrowed as he noticed his dad was actually working through this. "That was old Virginia and Kentucky. I'm betting we'd get angry spirits galloping up to our front door if we did that now in the city."

Granddad countered snidely and played to the audience, "More evidence of the decline."

The room laughed at that.

Alexander thought back, "You used to take me downtown shopping. The energy was amazing. People were in such high spirits and then we'd go watch a movie at the Brown Theatre. It was a magical time. Thank you for that."

"I admit I was a pretty good dad."

The room laughed again. Alexander hugged his father. They had a moment.

Mrs. Simmons was also affected by similar memories.

Alexander noticed, "Mrs. Simmons, are you okay?"

"Hearing about the Brown Theatre just took me back."

"Please tell us," Alexander said.

"I can tell you what my mama told me. This year makes it 60 years. 60 years ago today, she was with a group that wasn't allowed to buy tickets for *Porgy and Bess.* She was refused entry into the Brown Theatre because of her race."

The room was stunned silent.

Mrs. Simmons explained, "When my mama told me this as a youngster, I thought it was so very odd. Think about it. They were barring Black people from buying tickets to watch a movie with Black actors and a Black story."

Amy was trying to deal with this, "This was 1959?"

"Yes. My mama was part of the Youth Council of the NAACP. Raoul Cunningham was the leader. After that she set up a picket line in front of the theater. Finally, it changed in 1963 when discrimination was banned state wide with the Public Accommodations Ordinance. It makes me proud that Louisville was the first city south of the Mason-Dixon Line to do it."

Alexander toasted that.

They were all having Christmas dinner. Amy was pleased that Bobby and Sherri were there.

"I loved Roderick the Reindeer," Cassidy announced. "And the elves are amazing."

"Granddad won again," remarked Amy, with a faux yawn.

"Congratulations!"

"Thank you, Cassidy," said Granddad. "I had a lot of help."

"Granddad is becoming a dynasty," Bobby declared.

Nearing the end of the dinner, Amy cleared her throat and stood.

Bobby braced himself. Cassidy could see he was concerned.

Amy gazed over the gathering, "I just wanted to thank everyone for coming tonight and wish all of you a Merry Christmas. And I wanted to say that after the New Year's Eve event next week at Silver Horse Sanctuary, I'll be accepting an invitation and returning to New Orleans and helping the Morrigu Krewe prepare for Mardi Gras."

"I've been offered a seat on their float in the parade. Which should be memorable."

"That does sound cool," said Cass.

"And then after that I'll be back for the Speed Art Museum Ball, with Bobby, 'first Saturday in March,' and on the 9th of March I promised my firm I'd give my answer if I'm returning to New York or not."

Everyone was quiet. Amy sat and felt the room was a little deflated. "As you were." The room lightened a bit. "I didn't mean to bring anyone down. I just wanted to share this with the ones closest to me."

"We appreciate you being so candid, darling," remarked her father, earnestly. "We are all rooting for you."

They all agreed.

Alexander held up his glass, "To the future. The new year and whatever that'll bring." Alexander glanced around the room, but settled on Sherri. They all drank to that.

Cassidy saw Bobby trying not to look at Amy, who was also attempting not to gaze at him.

The rest of the night the group laughed among themselves as Bobby and Alexander dueled each other in banjos.

****

"Mother, I could have waited until your party in a couple of days to tell you, your intelligence network probably would have reported to you by then, but here I am calling you now. How's Kauai?"

"Kauai's perfect, as usual." April was sunning herself by the pool surrounded by lush vegetation. "When you go to Mardi Gras, will your friend Lannie be there?"

"Yes. She's working. Things are happening for her."

"And not happening. I heard she lost her Hollywood deal."

"Lannie was then hired to do a major profile on Raven in New Orleans."

"And then she was a suspect in a murder case, as I learned from the papers."

"Which she was cleared of, Mother."

"Therefore, let me get this straight, after my New Year's Eve party you're venturing off to the Crescent City and rubbing shoulders with the Queen of Voodoo. Then, after your sojourn south, you'll return for the Speed Ball and then announce your decision for the future?"

"Correct. Except Raven's ancestor was the Queen of Voodoo. Not her."

"Raven is a woman with many powers."

"Mother, how do you know so well?"

"I just do."

****

Alexander, Granddad, Mrs. Simmons, Amy and Gabby traveled to Lexington to watch the men play. Over the years, playing their own long game, Alexander could see acquaintances that went to UK games that had become friends, that were able to move their seats ever so closer to the court. There were no luxury suites in this gymnasium. When they weren't taking on the University of Louisville, Alexander rooted for the University of Kentucky. He admired the fans giving opposing players standing ovations for outstanding efforts. He thought it was a fabulous program, great traditions, but he kept that to himself.

Amy insisted Gab accompany them in an attempt to cheer her up. Amy and Gabby chatted privately. Amy wanted to know how it went with her family gathering for Christmas. Gabby was glum reporting there wasn't any bloodshed, but it was chilly. As hard as they tried to hide it, there were those that sensed the simmering anger her father harbored towards her.

Rupp Arena was packed and boisterous. The Cards were ahead by 3 with just over two minutes to go. It went into overtime and Kentucky won by 8 points. The ride home was gloomy, there would be no cheering up for anybody.

Alexander was seriously in the dumps. The game weighed heavily on him and Amy would soon be heading to New Orleans and from there, who knows where.

When they got to CA it was late. Alexander put up a brave face, said goodnight and trudged to his room.

Mrs. Simmons, Granddad and Amy could see it was more than a disappointing game that had him down.

26

Lannie picked up Amy at Louis Armstrong Airport and took her back to Nichoir Noir. And after several days her perceptions, assumptions and conclusions had almost all been once again challenged by entering the world of Raven Laveau.

On the 12th day of Christmas, January 6th, Epiphany, the carnival season commenced. The Krewe of Joan of Arc kicked things off. At the Joan of Arc statue, they sang "Happy Birthday." The parade concluded with a King Cake ceremony.

For the next six weeks around 50 parades would be held until March 25th, Fat Tuesday, where it all ended at midnight.

Krewe Morrigu's parade was on February 23rd. It was a Sunday and started at 8pm, after the conclusion of the Bacchus Krewe's parade.

Krewe Morrigu had two giant Ravens in front on their float. Lannie, Amy, Raven and her krewe, were throwing swag out to the multitudes.

And then a voice cried out, "Amy!"

Amy glanced out on the crowd and saw her father as he lowered his mask.

"Daddy!"

Alexander waved.

"That's your father?" asked Raven.

"Yes."

"Invite him aboard."

Alexander squeezed through the heavy crowd and was gently lifted up and onto the float by several very buffed friends of Raven.

"Thanks, guys," said Alexander.

Amy and Alexander hugged.

Raven shook his hand, "Welcome aboard, Mr. Arrington."

"Thank you, great to be here. Please call me Alexander."

"Have you attended Mardi Gras before, Alexander?"

"I have, but never ridden a float."

"Well then, you've got responsibilities," announced Raven. "Grab some swag and help us distribute it."

****

Late that evening Amy and Lannie both retreated to their rooms. Raven provided Alexander a place in Nichoir Noir, so he didn't return that night to his friend's house, the only lodgings he could find in the Big Easy. Raven and Alexander talked for several hours.

The next morning Alexander and Amy were sitting alone in Nichoir Noir having tea.

"I didn't come to check up on you."

"I know, Daddy."

"My curiosity got the better of me. I had been to Mardi Gras back when I was in school."

"Uh-huh."

"And Mrs. Simmons…"

"Yes?"

"She mentioned Marie Laveau and some of the stories…and Raven…and some of the stories. And your mother contacted me and went on about Marie Laveau and Raven and some of the stories. After that I wanted to meet her. And I also ran into Bobby downtown by his office and he asked about you."

"Daddy, after Tuesday, I'll be ready to go home."

"Sure. But until then…" They both grinned.

Alexander, Amy and Lannie enjoyed themselves until Fat Tuesday was over. Father and daughter joined the cloudy exodus leaving the city and returning to their homes elsewhere.

Father and daughter flew back to Louisville on February 28th.

During the flight Alexander was flipping through a magazine and remembered something, "Late one night, after much merriment, I overheard someone talking something about a Recompiler."

"That's a computer term. There's an I.T. guy at Raven's place."

"No, not this Recompiler. It was describing something else as I recall and it was used in a most creepy way."

"Daddy, I'm surprised you can recall anything from your holiday." Amy looked out the window at a fluffy cloud floating by and wondered if he had heard too much.

****

Alexander didn't want Amy involved with a long, drawn-out case, if she was headed back to New York.

Amy worked on her skateboarding and then felt like she needed to do something. There wasn't anything in the hopper she could help her dad with. But her time was soon taken up. Her mother called and wanted to do lunch. She offered to pick her up, but Amy said she'd meet her.

It was the elegant English Grill in the Brown Hotel. They ordered crab cakes for appetizers. April glanced around at the dark oak paneling and the tracery ceilings. Fine looking equestrian paintings adorned the walls.

"I told HRH I'd take her here the next time she got back to Kentucky."

"HRH?" asked Amy.

"But she's getting up there. It's a long trip."

"You mean, Her Royal Highness?"

"Yes, that's what it means; with her friends it's Liz—and that's between you and me."

"When did you tell her this?" Amy wondered if dropping this seemingly uncheckable nuke was a wily way of burying her father.

"Last year, when I was in London."

"Right. You said flippantly, with your dodgy English accent, 'the trip was nice and had a nice cuppa with her majesty.' As if you were joking. I recall."

"Why would I joke about that?" April pulled out her phone and showed pictures of several other ladies and one of them did look like the Queen of England, with April.

Amy's eyes widened.

"The Corgis are so adorable. I call them perky little low-riders."

Amy saw a picture of her mother sitting with the dogs.

They ordered Arugula Salads. April had the Verlasso Salmon and Amy got the Hot Brown.

"How was your trip to New Orleans?"

"It was…different."

"What happened with Raven?"

"What is it you have with this woman?"

"Nothing. You don't have to tell me. Have you come to a decision on your future?"

"No."

"Are you leaning one way."

"Yes."

"Towards the east, New York?" April didn't want to appear too eager. "It'll soon be the perfect time in the city."

"I do like springtime there."

"I talked to Harold and he said they're really quite busy. Mergers, takeovers, deal-making. What's your father doing?"

Amy didn't answer. She went home and got a call from Abby that Mitch had accepted an offer to move to Chicago and manage a restaurant on the southside. Abby was shocked by this. Amy was surprised, but if it was a move up, why not?

****

Over at SHS, April had been keeping a wary eye on the coronavirus situation. Her nerves were beginning to fray. Reston saw how jittery she was and took it upon himself to closely follow the news and keep her up to date on the situation.

Back on January 22nd, he told April, "Not to worry, it's one person coming in from China."

On February 24th he told her, "The Coronavirus is very much under control in the USA."

On February 26th he told her, "The 15 cases in the US, within a couple of days, is going to be down close to zero." The next day he assured her, "It's like a miracle. This virus will disappear."

On Friday March 6th, the day before the Speed Art Museum Ball, Reston assured her, "They're doing a really good job in this country at keeping the numbers down. A tremendous job."

****

The first Saturday in March arrived. Of all the places April had explored, this was her favorite museum and top two favorite social events. The Speed Museum was a modern state-of-the-art facility that displayed a wide variety of spectacular artistic creations.

Alexander used to attend this gathering, but since April was being escorted by Reston, he stayed home. Chip's date was Nevada.

They dressed formally and got informal with some very interesting people. Fabulous artwork surrounded the attendees. The hors d'oeuvres were provided by Wiltshire at the Speed and the cocktails by Brown Forman.

Amy and Bobby arrived. He signed some things and took some selfies.

Chip stepped up with his worship-tease, "OMG, it's the basketball legend, Bobby Dulsett."

"Chip, how's it going?" They shook hands.

Amy held Bobby's hand, "Hello, Chip."

"Hey, Amy."

Chip's date joined him, "Hi, Bobby."

"Hey, Nevada," Bobby was pleasant.

"You're Amy Arrington," announced Nevada. "I saw you on *Triple C.* That is a neat trick with the fire."

"It takes years of practice. You're Nevada Nash. I saw your commercial. Nice to meet you."

"We met already. I was a year behind you at the Brown School."

"Sorry, I don't remember you."

"My name in high school was Noreen. Noreen Nash."

"I'm sorry, I still don't remember you."

"I remember you and The Démener Divas. The DDs."

"I guess we were a bit rowdy."

Nevada demonstrated how she was one of the top wheeler-dealers in the 3-state area. "Amy, first, I think Alexander has something going there with the Antithetical Owl. Seriously. The owl has a zeitgeist feel to it. Second, and I'm not joking about this: you need to market The DDs merchandise. T-shirts, coffee mugs. I have the network and supply chain that can make it happen. I think The DDs could really catch on."

Amy was taken by that, "You know, Gabby mentioned something about doing that. But we just laughed it off, mostly because we didn't know what to do."

"And The DDs live on, right? You still hang out."

"We do."

"That's good," said Nevada. "We should get together and discuss."

"Sure," said Amy.

"Friendships that last are a fantastic thing," Nevada opined. "It's a shame when they don't."

Bobby's gaze was frozen on the floor. There was an awkward pause.

People then asked for his autograph and picture. Normally celebrities were left alone at this event, but this was Bobby Dulsett. Amy had to step back as she was in the way.

****

Amy and Bobby were walking together in the museum and taking in the exhibitions. They came up to a display of a 125-page novella written by Bret Hurley. They admired the illustrations Mr. Hurley did and read the information. Hurley, a resident of Louisville from 1898-1955, wrote a mystery, *Loose Nuts: A Rhapsody in Brown*, did the artwork and included himself as a character, as a hard-nose reporter for the West End Tatler operating in Louisville's West End in the 1930s.

Bobby pondered that, "Including himself in the story as he told it, sounds like an early form of Gonzo journalism."

Amy was amazed from a different angle, "And he included several real-life people living in Louisville at the time in his fictitious novel. That's bonkers. Just one defamation lawsuit from one of those real people would shut the project down today."

****

On the way home Amy kept thinking about Nevada and her idea—and her magnetic personality. She could see why Bobby dated her and how she would be good for him. Bobby was always a bit shy and Nevada drew him out of his shell with her charm. That evening Amy had witnessed Nevada chat about the big four sports: baseball, basketball, football and hockey, with authority. At one point she had a dozen guys hanging on her breakdown of basketball players from the U.S. versus Europe. Willie Loman knew the secret of success in sales was to be liked, and Nevada was.

****

It was late when their ride pulled up in front of CA.

"Thanks for escorting me to the Ball."

Bobby was wistful, "Now the clock is striking midnight. Is Cinderella going back to her other world?"

"Cinderella thought it was all a dream when she left the ball. And to be fair, returning to Manhattan and Padmore isn't quite comparable to what Cinderella faced."

"And Cinderella doesn't really need Prince Charming," said Bobby, beginning to feel like she was gone.

"And Prince Charming has a wide selection to choose from. Always had."

Bobby understood, "I see." He attempted to hide his disappointment.

"Bobby…I've put 3 years into that firm."

"That's a lot of time and sacrifice. I get it." Although he was crushed by this, he really did understand.

Amy kissed him on the cheek and got out. "I'll contact you later." She smiled at him. "Thanks for everything." Amy waved him off, like it was the last time.

That night when Gabby and Amy were chatting, Gab revealed she was considering taking a leave of absence from the radio station and checking out L.A. to see what she could see career wise. She had a friend she was going to stay with.

Amy felt like she was running away, not running *to* anything. "What about Leti?"

Gabby didn't have an answer.

Amy wished her well and hoped for the best for her dear friend, but slumped at the thought of Abby and Gabby leaving. It made the choice to return to Padmore, Pearce and Payne much easier.

Amy called a meeting with Alexander, Granddad and Mrs. Simmons. Even the house critters gathered around sensing something significant. Amy informed them that she was going back to New York.

They all had supportive smiles. They all really wanted the best for her, but the animals saw the sadness.

Amy went to her room and wrote the email. She had a response within ten minutes. She read it and returned to the living room.

"I just got a message from the firm. They welcomed me back and told me to work remotely because of this COVID-19 virus that's spreading."

"Then you're staying?" asked Alexander.

Alexander, Mrs. Simmons and Granddad had hope. The animals felt it.

"For now. The situation is getting worrisome. We may have to isolate here."

Gabby admitted things had changed and she wasn't traveling anywhere. Abby said Mitch informed her the Chicago offer was on hold. Amy said she would be working from home and isolating, as she lived with three other people who were at an elevated risk.

A dark cloud was now over everyone. People infected from COVID-19 were dying in China and Italy, especially the elderly and those with a compromised immune system. But it was a long way away. The sliver of a silver lining for Alexander was that his daughter was home and safe. He then held his breath, remembering that April had Type-1 diabetes.

Alexander cornered Amy, "Could you talk to your mother, in your own way, and advise her to be extra careful. Because of..."

Amy thought about that, "Being a diabetic, she has a compromised immune system. She's especially vulnerable. I will do that."

"Thank you." Alexander looked ashen, filled with worry.

Amy sent an email with medical evidence from three sources backing her up, pleading with her mother to be very careful.

She was touched and thanked her daughter for her concern, it was much appreciated—but April, with her medical condition, was already well aware of her situation and the perils she faced.

27

Amy was working virtually in New York, earning Big Apple bucks, living in her family's home in Louisville and not under the Microscope. She would get up, meditate, do yoga, skate, shower, have breakfast, read the *Louisville Courier-Journal* and the *New York Times* and go to her room where she would dress nicely. After a quick brush on her coif, she would sit in front of her laptop and patiently wait for the link to appear. After clicking on it, multiple small, silent video feeds from other associates would pop up on her screen in rows. They waved at each other from their various locations of isolation and sent text greetings that scrolled on the right side of the screen.

Amy knew just about all of them from the office on a friendly and sort of friendly basis. They had fought in the trenches together, put in the brutal hours together and had some rambunctious office parties together.

Since isolating, many had greatly increased their video gaming and online role-playing, or took it up for the first time. A disconnect from the physical world was unfolding. For more than a few their time at the law firm had morphed into a video game. The participants were clearly defined. They were seen every work day morning on everyone's video screen. The battle lines were drawn. They all understood of the 75 associates, the over/under to make partner was about 5, with the smart money taking the under.

It was sort of like playing baseball. If you made it to the minors, the chances of making it to the majors was about 10%; which was comparable, maybe even better odds than making partner in a BigLaw firm, especially at Padmore, Pearce and Payne.

Amy waved again at what was now nearly the 75 live feeds—pixels, waiting for the 9:15 daily call.

With the lockdown of schools, students had to learn remotely and it was a struggle for many. When businesses shut down many lost their livelihoods and were in desperate straits trapped at home. Others were able to transition to doing their work remotely, online, but it was a challenge. It was all still so clunky.

However, one class of those remote workers thrived: associates in law firms. The pandemic's toll was tragic and scary, but ironically for these associates it was a rare moment of mental relief.

The office closed until October 1. The associates could leave the Microscope if they preferred, as long as they had a good internet connection where they settled.

All of a sudden these workers weren't toiling away 9-9-6 or 7 in their cubicle, with someone always looking over their shoulder. A good percentage of her colleagues took advantage of this 6-month shutdown to return to their hometowns. Grunt work, proofreading, managing a database, reviewing discovery requirements, was still time consuming, but could be done from a distance. Without the hassle of the commute, having to stay late and going out for the occasional dinner and late drink. Quite a few of these associates, for the first time in the years of their paper chase and swimming in the alligator-infested law firms, had a bit of time on their hands.

Business slowed considerably. Many wondered about job security. A few reassessed if they were doing what they really wanted to be doing, or if they were at the place they wanted to be doing it. Some did leave and shift course.

Senior partners gave pep talks and sermons to the team imploring them not to be distressed or depressed. There was even a good-cop/bad-cop routine. One partner would be soothing and inspiring—usually on a yacht or at a beach house or from a calming garden—telling the online group to 'hang in there. There will be a better day.'

And then Reece Rockwell, a senior partner, crew cut, built like a rock, was seen in a gym and talked about being a Marine in Iraq. He pointed out what they were dealing with presently wasn't such a big deal. He then perhaps went on a bit too long spitballing, when he predicted food riots would only occur if it 'really went sideways and the shit hit the fan.' They got a different bad cop the next time.

After the morning general pep talk, the associates would break off into smaller groups and individually with the partner they were assigned.

Amy normally worked with Harold, but he was in the middle of a historically hellacious breakup to his marriage and wasn't practicing his trade at the moment. She was picked up by Peyton, who she actually worried about. He was at home and seemed lost. In his mid-50s, he looked older. Occasionally one of the 7-year-old twins or both—from his second marriage—would race through and jolt him. He would take it in good stride, but Amy could see Peyton was rattled.

She thought about his vaunted workspace at the firm. In the reception area, resembling Praetorian Guards, two administrative assistants filtered all the requests for his attention. After being granted permission to enter, one instantly realized this was a center of power. It was a spacious office. In the meeting area was a Chesterfield leather sofa and four Eames Lounge Chairs surrounding a Joanna dark brown walnut coffee table. Further in, past the JD and his other degrees hanging on the wall, was his imposing mahogany and oak desk and his Ekornes Stressless Magic Office Chair, which Peyton let her sit in, once.

Special sports memorabilia adorned the dark-paneled walls. They were sacred. Historical. Untouchable. Peyton would at times share the story of a certain treasured artifact.

During this morning's call Amy watched Peyton panic and gently take back a football the twins were kicking around, autographed by Vince Lombardi, Bart Starr, Jerry Kramer and Fuzzy Thurston.

Peyton had Amy doing document review, nothing difficult. She would receive her homework, finish the assignments and have time to spare.

Alexander had occasionally Facetimed and done video calls, though mostly avoiding them; but all of a sudden everyone was doing it and he had to do it too. He grumbled and had Amy set up Zoom for him.

However, the mute button was on, then off, then on, before the buffering issues took over—then the Wi-Fi went kaput.

Alexander left Mrs. Simmons alone and mostly avoided Amy, as she was working. He would see Granddad, with his goggles, chatting with his friends around the world in VR. Alexander would stare at him and just shake his head.

As mentioned, Amy spent most of her time in her room, in front of her computer, rocking out and throwing darts at the wall. Amy was thankful to live in an era when she didn't have to travel to different locations to root around for memos, letters, receipts and depositions in dozens of boxes or multiple file cabinets, to find and confirm what she was searching for. It was almost all just a few keystrokes away.

Amy took a break and walked outside. She opened up a package that had been delivered earlier and examined several throwing axes. Amy stepped out back and past the halfpipe. She set up a target area with an x on some wood.

"Time to practice."

She stood 12 feet back and started throwing these axes, sticking five in a row.

Alexander noticed and his eyes went wide, "Whoa."

She practiced for another 20 minutes before getting on the half-pipe and skating. Her skills here continued to improve. She spent at least an hour a day letting off steam this way.

Alexander joined her and they skated together.

"I see you have a new hobby."

"Yes, axe throwing."

"Good. You're trying new things. I support that."

"Could you help me out, Daddy?"

"Of course."

"Would you stand with an apple on your head as a target?"

"Sure!"

"I love you, Daddy."

"See how much I believe in you!" His eyes became filled with worry.

"I'm not serious about the target thing."

"I'm worried about this virus thing, it's getting out of control. We need to protect Granddad and Mrs. Simmons."

Amy agreed with that. As someone who followed the news, she was fairly aware of COVID-19. But to be fair, Amy was also aware of avian influenza, swine flu, Legionnaires' Disease, MERS, Ebola, drug resistant-TB, HPV, HIV, the list of STDs, Zika, dengue fever, malaria, West Nile and hantavirus and she didn't forget measles making a comeback—just to name the few she could remember off the top of her head. COVID-19, had broken from the pack and was becoming a major problem, a pandemic. It was time to understand everything she could about this new threat and began with some searches.

It was spread easily through droplets and tiny aerosol particles transmitted through the air.

In 2002 there was a severe acute respiratory syndrome, SARS-CoV, outbreak in China that eventually infected about 8,000 worldwide in 20 countries. 774 died over a two-year span. In Canada 251 were infected and 44 lost their lives. In the U.S. 8 people were infected, but they all survived.

Now a new virus was emerging from China. SARS-CoV-2, aka COVID-19. This SARS2 was similar to SARS1 in that they were both coronaviruses and used the same host cell receptors. The two viruses had a 79% genetic similarity. The viral proteins of each virus latched onto the host receptors with the same tightness.

It was true that COVID-19 was slightly less lethal than SARS1. But that was offset by COVID-19's ability to bind with those host receptors much easier.

With SARS1, carriers immediately displayed symptoms, fever, chills, body aches, diarrhea. As many as a third of those infected with SARS2, COVID-19, could be asymptomatic for some time and infect dozens or more, which also greatly facilitated the rapid spread.

The tolerance level was exposure to about 1,000 viral particles. Just talking and breathing over a few minutes a human exhaled hundreds of thousands of aerosol particles that could be suspended in the air for an extended period of time.

COVID-19 had made its way to the rest of the European Continent. It then jumped the pond and was in the U.S.

Back on February 28th the CDC had announced that the first American case of unknown origin was found stemming from community spread.

For the most part the world was now on pause. Late that night Amy read different blogs and watched various videos about preppers. Some, who had binge-watched weeks, years of *The Walking Dead* and *Fear the Walking Dead* believed this was the beginning of the zombie apocalypse and they were ready—locked and loaded. Others thought it was the Great Tribulation, the Great Judgment, *the* Apocalypse. They were prepared for the beginning of the End Times.

The courts pushed everything back. Stories were circulating on how the super-rich were boarding their private jets and flying to remote locales such as New Zealand.

Alexander was in isolation in a corner wing of Casa Arrington. He spent the day reading cases, but was dealing with some serious depression at what was happening to the world. Videos of morgues running out of room and storing bodies in refrigerated trucks in NYC were seen on the news and online, along with massive pits serving as graves for other victims.

The large urban areas now began to empty out. Those that could retreated to a remote and rural area.

Amy talked to several friends back in New York and they were afraid. At that moment it was one of the epicenters of the world for the spread of the virus.

New Orleans was hit very hard as well. Amy and Alexander hoped they didn't bring anything back from there, but 10 days had passed and they hadn't gotten sick or had any of the basic symptoms.

People did not want to be around other people. The arcane term 'social distancing' became well-known. Amy and Alexander locked down Mrs. Simmons and Granddad, who both were vulnerable. Amy toggled between the two on things they needed. She ordered take-out from several of the restaurants, had it delivered and tipped well.

On March 11th the World Health Organization declared the coronavirus a pandemic. Almost immediately after that the NCAA announced that all Division I men's and women's basketball tournament games would be played in arenas without fans and with 'essential staff and limited family' allowed to attend.

Soon after that Alexander got an alert on his phone and checked, "March Madness has been canceled completely." He shook his head, "How much worse can it get??"

****

The Kentucky Derby was officially postponed until September 5. April retreated to Silver Horse Sanctuary and put everything on hold. She had once thought all of these disaster/horror movies about such events—that were unfolding in front of her—were silly. Not anymore. She recalled stories being passed down in her family from her great-great-grandmother to great-grandmother and great aunts, describing the Spanish Flu of 1918.

April didn't trust Reston on many things, especially living up to the quarantine rules. He was talking like this wasn't real. Like it was some giant hoax being played on everyone. April told Reston that she was cutting herself off from the world until there was a better understanding of this.

The reality was she didn't want to be stuck with him. He remained in his place. Chip was with him.

April had her dogs and horses. She thought about how her animals would help her get through this and then she read animals were also catching and spreading the virus. This really freaked her out.

****

Alexander was getting better with Zoom; but again, there was the time his microphone was on mute when he was objecting. More than a few of his colleagues wished they could do that to him in person.

Even when he had pushed all the right keys the audio was frequently choppy. Other people at times weren't speaking close enough to the microphone.

Alexander really didn't like being cut off from being there, the personal touch.

But on the other side of the slate, life was simplified. Distractions were stripped away. More people began to look inwardly and contemplate their existence.

Late Thursday night Alexander was in a funk and he was a bit drunk. He was relitigating earlier battles. It struck midnight. He missed being around other people and again wondered how much worse it could get. He fought that thought. His better angel whispered into his ear not to despair and he drifted off in his chair smiling at that notion.

It was around 1:30am when his phone rang. It jolted Alexander awake. The caller informed him of a botched police raid where a woman was killed at 12:40am on Friday the 13th. The more Alexander learned, the more he feared the fallout. He knew it was going to be significant. The woman's name was Breonna Taylor.

28

Later in the morning on Friday most didn't think much of the shooting. It was reported as just another drug raid, with a fatality and an officer wounded in the leg with gunfire.

The problem was a pandemic was hitting the United States for the first time in a century and nothing else seemed to matter at the moment.

Reston called April with an update. His voice quivered ever so slightly: "The virus is now a National Emergency."

"Is it?" April didn't call him out on this drastic revision to what he had been telling her for the last six weeks. She knew Reston was at best, full of puffery, and at worst a prolific liar who frequently just made stuff up and then denied ever saying it in the first place. April, of course, did her own fact checking and was actually aware of the calamity that was unfolding. It was useless to get into a debate with Reston as his facts were shaped and shifted to where and what he believed was the most advantageous position for himself and his brand, at that moment. Accuracy was an approximation. The few times she pressed the issue he raged like the spoiled, ignorant, narcissistic, arrogant buffoon he was. April learned early on she could only tell him things that would appeal to his fragile ego that constantly had to be fed and stroked. Yet, April still kept Reston around because he had his own money, played a good game of golf and tennis, was in fairly good shape, had great hair, a perpetual tan, could be charming and looked spectacular on her arm at social gatherings. It was manageable if the rest of the time she kept him at arms-length.

"Reston, honey, thank you for keeping me up to date all this time with your news."

****

The globe was facing an existential threat not seen in several generations. Cases continued to rise. There were over 2,000 deaths in the U.S. already.

By the following Monday the killing was well known locally. People were advised to stay in and avoid crowds, but they showed up anyway. Almost all had masks. They had to gather. Monday evening people congregated in front of the location of the event on Springfield. The anger was simmering, frustrations were flowing and the sadness was overwhelming.

At a news conference the police announced the arrest of Kenneth Walker for attempted murder of a police officer and first-degree assault. The deceased was only described as "an unresponsive woman who was later pronounced dead."

Then it came out: Breonna Taylor, a 26-year-old Emergency Medical Technician, trained to save lives, was gunned down, shot five times.

For some time now Alexander had advocated for law enforcement to get body cameras to protect the police as well as the public. Yet, even when the money was allocated by the city council, the equipment purchased and distributed to the force, there was no footage. Alexander was livid.

People reassembled in front of the mayor's house, chanting, demanding the cops involved be fired and prosecuted.

****

A couple nights later Alexander and Amy were sitting together in CA.

"What are you working on, Daddy?"

Alexander glanced up from his laptop, "I used several sources to do a deep dive into the death of Miss Taylor."

"What did you find?"

"The cops were targeting her former boyfriend."

"Okay."

"I learned five no-knock warrants were issued that night and then the Springfield location, Breonna's place, was changed to a 'knock and announce' midway through the operation."

"That sounds odd."

"At the Springfield location the police say they knocked and announced themselves: 'Police! We have a warrant!' Six times over 45 seconds. A dozen neighbors in the apartment complex, when interviewed, said they didn't hear the police identify themselves before forcing entry into the apartment. A couple of them heard the banging on the door. One gentleman lived in the apartment directly above Breonna's place and was ordered to go back inside by the LMPD right before the raid. He complied and was asked by investigators, 'Did you ever hear anyone identify themselves as police?' He replied, 'No. Nobody identified themselves.'"

"Really?" asked Amy.

"Kenneth Walker had a legally registered firearm. He stated he didn't hear them knock and announce themselves and thought they were being robbed. Under Kentucky's Stand Your Ground law he fired a shot at the intruders. He hit one of the three narcotics officers in the leg. 32 rounds were returned and two other apartments were hit in the barrage. The officer that killed Breonna accounted for half of the shots fired, without identifying a target and firing in three different directions. Another officer blindly fired 10 shots into the apartment. Images of the scene showed immense destruction."

****

The next day Alexander came to breakfast with a blank look.

"What is it, Daddy?"

"I just learned that Mr. Walker called Breonna's mother and told her about the shooting. She rushed to the apartment and the police told her that her daughter was at the hospital. She went to the hospital and waited for two hours before she learned that Breonna wasn't even there. When she returned to the apartment an officer said Taylor was still inside. Like she was being detained, when she had been dead for over two hours."

Amy was quite angry, "That's horrible."

"It is. And brings up the question the officers on the raid have claimed. After the forced entry and shooting, they didn't do the search."

"They just quit?" asked Amy. "That doesn't make sense."

"It's not clear. One officer says they tried later to complete the search and they were denied," said Alexander.

"The police have stated no drugs or significant cash were found," said Amy.

Alexander considered this, "The authorities were there for several hours. They did the search, they had to. If only for justification for this action, which they didn't find."

****

TORTS and Just Desserts from the mind of Alexander Arrington

The owl appeared and spoke:

"It's a lot like the soldiers that were deployed to Vietnam. All they wanted to do was make it home to their family. These conscripts, 'grunts' were sent off to a foreign land to maintain control, while not understanding the territory. The war planners called for dropping bombs and mounting midnight raids.

One could argue the drug war planners are operating from a similar playbook. They send grunts in to maintain control, while not understanding the territory. These midnight raids are Pyrrhic victories at best and horrific screw ups at worst.

The drug war planners should not be deploying assets into these areas, at these times, in this manner. The soldiers that went to Southeast Asia were doing their jobs, they should have never been disrespected—same with police. Certainly, if a person in authority abuses their position, commits a crime, the proper discipline should be applied. However, little scholarly effort is brought forth examining why these frontline soldiers/police are deployed or the strategy employed in these maneuvers, or alternative approaches.

The foray into Southeast Asia was marketed as an attempt to stop communism. Yet, the reality is, after the brutal losses of humanity on all sides of the Vietnam conflict, the environmental catastrophe, the billions of U.S. taxpayer funds down the rathole and the VC winning: this communist country has Most Favored Nation trading status with the United States. It exports tons of cheap stuff into America with their low-wage workforce.

The drug war on the American citizens today echoes so much of that war in the 1960s and early '70s. The U.S. is marketed as the 'Land of the Free and the Home of the Brave.' But the reality is that it's the paranoid puritanical land of the surveilled.

The drug war planners are pushed to get results, with the grunts in the line of fire and getting the blowback. Statewide legislation in Kentucky was passed after the Breonna Taylor debacle and the protests, setting the bar higher to mount no-knocks and knock-and-announce raids.

I would like to remind the drug war planners that never before in the history of the world has there been a society with such easy access to such high-powered firearms, with such little hesitation to use them.

The police sent in on these raids really just want to make it home to their families. Their lives, as well as the neighbors in the area and even the low-level targets, should never be put in such peril, so drug war planners can take credit for another hill taken."

~ ~ ~

"At the top of my list for all-time favorite desserts is the Kentucky Jam Cake. It's an old-fashioned cake made with flour, sugar, eggs, vanilla, buttermilk, raisins, blackberry jam, chopped walnuts or pecans, baking soda and baking powder. Then it's spiced with nutmeg, cloves, allspice and cinnamon. It's a favorite at Christmas, but I like it anytime of the year. I seriously love pairing it with Graeter's Madagascar Vanilla Bean ice cream. OMG!"

The owl faded out.

****

As March passed Alexander kept inquiring into what was going on with the Breonna Taylor case. It was as if the world had stopped spinning. Countries closed their borders. Infections continued to rise, along with the deaths. A collective dread was descending over many.

However, on April 30, 2020. President Trump cut through red-tape and promised he would deliver a vaccine. He announced the title: Operation Warp Speed. It gave people hope and he delivered on that promise—but that was still in the future.

The pandemic took almost all of the attention of the country. The shooting continued to stay out of the national news.

The NBA suspended its season, followed by the NHL, USL and Major League Soccer.

It was one shocking shutdown after another. They didn't want the games to be super-spreader events. Alexander hoped it wasn't passing in the protests. The images he saw were of people mostly wearing protective masks.

Major League Baseball delayed spring training and then the opening of the season; finally allowing the games, but with no fans in attendance.

The courts continued to be shut and Zoom a much lower caseload. Cases that would normally be pleaded out, were dropped outright. Low-risk prisoners were being released from incarceration.

Alexander appeared by Zoom several times. Either the judge, or opposing counsel or Alexander himself, again had difficulty connecting, staying connected and even keeping unmuted. But they were beginning to get the hang of it and that terrified Alexander: remote lawyering becoming the norm.

The DDs would also Zoom, but it wasn't the same. Gabby was hosting her radio show from home. Abby continued working as a medical biller; but she was worried about Mitch. He had lost his job managing the restaurant and was mumbling about 'it being the end of the world.'

Amy spent long hours by herself, reflecting on her place in the world. There were some dark dips where she wondered if there even was a place for her. She thought about what she wanted to do, where she wanted to go and what kind of future there would be. Several times she ignored the alerts on her phone to items she once yearned for that had big price-drops—she deleted the app.

Forecastle was canceled due to the pandemic. Alexander would normally be quite bummed out about this news. It didn't faze him. He was fixated on Breonna Taylor's death and couldn't believe there wasn't more attention on this.

On April 27, challenging the police narrative, Taylor's family filed a wrongful death lawsuit against the police department and city. Alexander wished there was bodycam footage.

****

A local newspaper in southern Georgia was the first to mention the Ahmaud Arbery incident in an online article on April 2nd. The police weren't sharing much information about a Black man who was shot on the street of a sleepy neighborhood on a Sunday afternoon. A local journalist, Larry Hobbs, had to file a public records request to find out what actually went down. The Brunswick News published details from the police report stating Arbery began to 'violently attack' and he 'started fighting over the shotgun, at which point he was shot and then a second later there was a second shot.'

Then on May 5th a video was uploaded to Twitter and YouTube showing a Black male being chased down by three White men with guns. He ended up dead. It was shocking to most Whites, but not most Blacks.

It just added gasoline to the fire. People were calling it a modern-day lynching and it was hard to argue against that. If it hadn't been filmed by the neighbor—who helped block Ahmaud's escape—there would be no clear evidence on what really happened.

Within a couple hours of this release the Atlantic District DA announced a grand jury would be reviewing this event to decide if charges were to be brought.

Alexander called down to Georgia to a lawyer friend, Buster T. Balkins. Buster was wired into events in the state. He practiced law on the Isle of Hope, which was close to where it occurred.

"Alexander, I have been made aware of these most despicable events. Ahmaud Arbery was shot dead on February 23rd."

"Six weeks ago?"

"Correct. The Georgia Bureau of Investigation is looking into the case as we speak. And let me say—"

Alexander interrupted, "Only because everyone has seen the video."

"Yes, from the neighbor. I venture to say that is correct, Alexander. Mr. Arbery was out for a jog and mistaken for a thief. A White father and son got in their truck and went into action. Mr. Arbery, a Black man, tried to get away, but after a four-minute hunt they cornered him with a shotgun and a Magnum .357. He fought back and was killed by the son with the shotgun. On February 27th the first prosecutor recused himself and a second prosecutor stepped back on April 3rd because he saw no reason to bring charges."

"This is unbelievable..." Alexander was stunned even further. "How can this happen today, in this day and age??"

"Just to put things in context, the truck that chased Mr. Arbery down had the old Georgia license plate with the emblem of a Confederate Flag."

"Geezee..." moaned Alexander, as he held his head.

"And one more thing. When Mr. Arbery lay dying with three gunshot wounds, the son was heard to say, 'Fucking Nigger.'"

Alexander let out a quiet sigh, he closed his eyes. "Oh God..."

****

Alexander and Amy were watching the news. It was announced that famed attorney Benjamin Crump, who was also representing Ahmaud Arbery's family in Georgia, was now the attorney of record for the lawsuit filed by the family of Breonna Taylor in Louisville.

Alexander nodded at that, "He's brilliant, tenacious and fearless."

Two days later Alexander was sitting alone in the dark. Amy came in and turned on the lights, she didn't expect to see him there.

"Daddy, what are you doing here in the dark?"

"Today's May 13th, exactly two months after Breonna's killing."

"Yes."

"The governor appointed the attorney general to be special prosecutor."

"I heard. That's good. Right?"

Alexander nodded and was quiet for most of the rest of the night.

With Mr. Crump and the Kentucky AG both involved, it alerted the national media. It was now news in their eyes.

A week later, after visiting Mrs. Simmons and Granddad in the backyard, at a distance, Alexander and Amy skated together.

"I heard from a friend in Washington," Alexander said. "The FBI is opening an investigation."

"Really?" asked Amy.

"Yeah, things are starting to happen."

****

May 16, 2020

Alexander and Amy were having brunch when he got a text. He picked up his tablet and read: "The Louisville postal inspector is asserting that the LMPD did not use his office to verify that a drug suspect delivered packages to Breonna Taylor's address, which directly contradicts what the police stated in the affidavit to secure a no-knock warrant for the home."

Alexander and Amy glanced at each other and shook their heads in amazement.

****

The owl appeared and spoke:

"I kindly ask for your patience, this one is going to be another doozy; so find your safe space and hold on. Shively, Kentucky, about 5 miles southwest of Louisville as the crow or owl flies, hadn't really been much in the news since 1954 when it was then a Whites-only neighborhood. Back then a Black Korean War veteran, Andrew Wade IV and his wife Charlotte, were unable to purchase a house due to Jim Crow housing discrimination. White activists Carl and Anne Braden, doing an end around on the locals, bought the house and the Wades moved in. Their neighbors were soon there and welcomed them with rocks and rifle shots smashing through the windows and regular cross burnings on the adjacent lot, demonstrating what good Christians they were. And then one night when the Wades were out, someone partially blew up the house with dynamite.

After all of this abuse and disrespect to a U.S. war veteran, people were outraged. How in the devil was a Black family able to move into this White neighborhood? Investigators started the investigating right off the bat and quickly came to the conclusion that this underhanded trickeration was clearly a despicable 'communist plot.' The authorities didn't bother to convict any of the inconvenienced and irate neighbors for expressing their displeasure with the shootings or the bombing. The authorities went after the troublemakers that originally pulled this prank. The Bradens were charged with sedition. Carl was convicted and sentenced to 15 years for his malfeasance. Anne McCarthy Braden was from Louisville, a journalist and she was a provocateur indeed, who pushed for equality and justice. And so did her husband, Carl, also a journalist that abhorred racism, discrimination and environmental degradation and did something about it. Seven months later the U.S. Supreme Court overturned Carl's conviction, surely adding to the consternation of those inconvenienced and irate neighbors.

Shively presently has a 30% Black population, which is higher than Louisville and in town there's Wade Braden Park, a small park honoring the two couples that had the courage to take a stand in 1954.

Since then, Shively has pretty much stayed out of the national news. But with the Breonna Taylor killing, they popped up on the screen once again.

Follow along on the twists and turns of this event. A Louisville detective went to a judge with a request for five no-knock warrants. It was granted and then one was changed to a knock-and-announce.

The knock-and-announce raid on Springfield Street went off and went off the rails.

Local SWAT wasn't even aware they were doing this raid. Body camera footage from SWAT showed them surprised something was even happening on Springfield.

LMPD's intel on the raid at Springfield wasn't aware there was a male companion at that address.

In the aftermath it was revealed that Breonna Taylor had a relationship in the past with someone LMPD was targeting at another address.

In the warrant request LMPD presented to the judge, it stated that a US postal inspector in Louisville had 'verified' packages were being sent to the suspect at the Springfield address. But Louisville's postal inspector didn't meet or even speak to the Louisville Metro Police Department detectives. Why? Simple, there was 'bad blood.' Seriously. I kid you not. The LMPD was feuding with the post office. I have heard suggestions as to why, but I'm not one to share things with you that I cannot prove in a court of law.

I mean, there may be shocking and disheartening rumors concerning actions undertaken by a subset of people I hold in high regard; a lucrative tax-free side hustle, that has been ongoing for an extended period of time, in the dark, with little oversight, that ranges from questionable and disgraceful to downright illegal. Whispers of significant amounts of missing money. I may listen to such gossip, and other stories of snapchat stalkers sending dozens of snaps of their junk and using their power to extort sex from vulnerable women with charges pending, you know, 'the deal,' by writing it up and not turning the ticket in. I won't share such salacious talk. But if I were to see some solid evidence, I may consider taking action down the road. Until then, it appears karma seems to have made a move and a prolific dealmaker was sent packing after Springfield. Pardon my digression, I needed to get that off my chest, as that stuff was really burning my bottom and it's hard enough to keep this straight.

Now getting back to the original kerfuffle I was hooting about. I have not yet ascertained exactly what the bad blood was, but something or someone in the LMPD had alienated the Louisville postal inspectors to the point they weren't speaking; I imagine words were exchanged, they unfriended each other and then argued who did it first. The fallout of this tiff being the Louisville detectives had to get creative and contact a guy at the Shively PD for a favor. LMPD asked really polite if the Shively boys would do some investigating and check with the United States Postal Service inspectors in Louisville to see if there were any packages addressed to their male suspect being sent to Breonna Taylor's address—and do it on the sly, not letting the postal guys in Louisville know where this was coming from or they could blow the whole thing. Shhh!

The LMPD detectives were told by two Shively detectives, who inquired with the postal service in Louisville, that no packages were being sent to that location addressed to the male suspect.

That settled it. The officer wrote on the warrant the USPS had 'verified' that packages were being sent to the Springfield address for the male suspect.

The LMPD officer who filled out the warrant request was fired. And naturally he filed a lawsuit. He admitted he could have worded it differently, but he claimed the captain of the LMPD that terminated him for his untruthfulness didn't understand 'collective knowledge.' The LMPD officer didn't have to actually speak directly to the USPS inspector; because – as you've been advised of – he knew this LMPD detective that knew a guy in Shively and he and his partner did some asking around with the USPS and these officers in Shively reported back to one of the LMPD detectives, who passed it on to the officer who used it on the warrant.

Simple. Duh.

But the LMPD captain stated her understanding of the collective knowledge was that the two Shively officers told the LMPD detective that no packages were being sent to that address on Springfield.

Here's where it starts to get murky—well, murkier—the LMPD detective claims, under oath, that he told his colleague, the LMPD officer, there were no packages. As far as I know, the fired LMPD officer who wrote the warrant to get the probable cause, still claims he was informed packages were being sent to the address on Springfield by the LMPD detective, who continues to deny this. Before they both packed up their stuff, it must have really set up an awkward moment around the water cooler, as this is a he said, he said, he said, he said, she said, dilemma, I think... Hell's bells, that's complicated! I need a cookie."

~ ~ ~

"I love navigating over to Bae where I harpoon a Salty Beach, a fudge brownie cookie swirled with butterscotch and chocolate chips, crushed salty pretzel, caramel bits, and shoved full of caramel buttercream. I return to port, drop anchor and in the middle of the chaos unfolding in this topsy-turvy world, I enjoy my Salty Beach in a hammock, under my palm tree and have a moment—and it's good and needed."

The owl faded out.

29

The overwhelming urge for most was to step back and wait to see how the virus would unfold. But for those who had years of pent-up frustrations, these latest social injustices were so blatant they couldn't hold back. People marched in the streets wearing masks. It was a nightly gathering for the two weeks up to Memorial Day.

Alexander wondered how long the tension would remain at such a heightened level.

Reston was at first surprised at the anger and then he became enraged himself. Three times he had to drive around protests. This caused him to lose his tee time for the all-important golf date and two massage appointments.

On May 25th in Minneapolis, video was recorded of a White law enforcement officer with his knee on the neck of a Black man, who perished. George Floyd Jr. was being detained. There was a struggle. Law enforcement was able to get their suspect restrained and face down on the pavement. It was here that the officer put his knee on Mr. Floyd's neck for over 9 minutes. Mr. Floyd said he couldn't breathe 20 times and that he loved his mom and his kids and then he died.

They were sitting outside at a distance. Alexander, Amy and Granddad were speechless after seeing this.

Mrs. Simmons thought back, "That's exactly what Eric Garner said 6 years ago before he was killed by the police: 'I can't breathe.'"

They were all deeply saddened.

"There will be more upheaval over this. People can only take so much." Mrs. Simmons turned and slowly retreated to her room.

Alexander, Amy and Granddad glanced at each other, fearing the coming tribulation.

****

May 28, 2020. The U.S. COVID-19 death toll surpassed 100,000.

It was a shocking moment, but the protests continued.

After several weeks many realized things were not going back to 'normal' any time soon.

In order to see if there was a bias in where these operations were carried out, Alexander tried to research no-knock warrants. He wanted to see where they were used and where they weren't. But he found he was unable, as they weren't tracked. In this era of big data it was laughable, if it wasn't so troubling.

In May the Chief of Police told the city council that the LMPD served 8 no-knocks in 2018 and 2019 each and 4 in 2020 so far.

When Alexander heard that he was quite surprised at these numbers and he wasn't the only one.

The chief later amended his remarks stating that there were 21 in 2018, 22 in 2019 and 6 so far this year.

****

Kenneth Walker was charged with attempted murder. Recordings of several 911 calls were released. Multiple neighbors called in after hearing the shots and receiving the bullets in their apartments. Windows and glass doors were shattered and pots and pans hit. One mother was scared for her 5-year-old in an apartment that received fire. And the 911 call from Miss Taylor's boyfriend was chilling and heart breaking. He cried out saying someone busted in their door. The police claimed they knocked and identified themselves 6 times. Mr. Walker said he didn't hear anyone identifying themselves as law enforcement. He thought they were being robbed and Kentucky being a Stand Your Ground state, did just that.

****

These images and recordings of the raid had rattled Amy. She realized she never had to deal with these issues before living in her very secure environment, even in New York. Breonna was her age. It shuddered her to imagine armed authorities bursting into her place in the middle of the night.

****

Pundits pontificated since there was no video of the Breonna Taylor raid, it was one reason it was kept local for so long. Others argued it was because she was a Black woman, which meant she was an 'afterthought.' Be that as it may, the attention was now rapidly growing on what happened to Breonna and what was going to happen.

On May 22nd the Commonwealth's Attorney announced that a grand jury did not have sufficient evidence to indict Mr. Walker on charges of attempted murder of a police officer and assault. He was let go.

Protests in Louisville over this latest raid really began to gain steam. The anger was palpable. People were out in the streets, not only locally, but protesting across the nation, even around the globe. Years, generations of frustration and anger that simmered over similar treatment boiled over. The world was now paying attention. Almost everyone protested peacefully, respectfully.

"Fuck the cops!" was heard.

"Defund the police!" shouted another.

"Get rid of the cops!" yelled someone else.

Some people cheered. Alexander listened and understood someone being mistreated, handled unfairly, different from other races or other social classes being angry—but thought, *they're the sheriff. The alternative is having war lords and vigilantes deliver their own form of justice with their own set of laws.*

"Reform the police!" shouted Alexander.

Some people gave him a funny look, a couple others nodded to him in agreement.

"It's our only hope," he added.

And then some began to break windows and loot stores.

Alexander saw this and shouted, "Stop! Stop! This is not helping! This is hurting the cause!"

Some heeded his authoritarian tone, some didn't. He headed home grumbling.

****

On the back deck at SHS, there was plexiglass separating them, with heaters.

They both watched their own TVs, synced to the same station, on the continuing protests.

Reston turned to make a point, "I don't like this upheaval."

April glanced at an article she was reading, "I read that Kenneth Walker nor Breonna Taylor had a criminal record."

"He shot at the cops," said Reston.

"Did he know who they were?" asked April.

"Come on."

April was feeling down, "Breonna's future looked so bright. I read she had turned her life around. That was the phrasing, turned it around."

Reston suggested, "Could this be a case of past relationships causing problems in the present? The cops were pointed to her address. I heard her old boyfriend used it in a jail booking."

"If there were illegal activities going on there," wondered April, "why would he let the cops know where to look?"

"I don't know," responded Reston. "Most criminals aren't that bright."

"Dear, they didn't find any money or drugs. No person, or people, or neighbor, should ever have to deal with what she and her neighbors had to endure—ever."

"Look, April, all I'm saying is one should be very careful who they associate with."

April took a long look at Reston, "Yes, one should."

****

Alexander had been avoiding everyone in his family. He didn't want them to know he was out demonstrating.

It was the third night of serious protesting. Amy had contacted Gabby who said she was going out to express her outrage over the killing. Amy felt the urge as well.

Abby's husband refused to let her go, fearing for her safety. Gabby didn't have to get permission from anyone and Amy, though she didn't need permission either, chose not to tell Mrs. Simmons, Granddad or her father. She quietly slipped out the side door.

The officers involved with the shooting had been transferred out of narcotics, but many called for them to be fired and prosecuted. It was a wide range of folks gathering: young and old, Black, White, Asian, Hispanic and Native Americans. People used different colors of chalk to write messages on the pavement remembering Breonna Taylor, George Floyd and Ahmaud Arbery. There was a plethora of signs with Breonna's picture, with, 'Say Her Name.' Other signs stated: 'No More,' 'I can't breathe' and 'I run with Maud.'

People chanted "No Justice, No Peace." Amy and Gabby masked up and joined in. Almost all marched peacefully, but some continued to elevate this confrontation with an agenda other than forcing reform. A statue of the King of France, Louie XVI, the town's namesake, who lost his head in the French Revolution, lost his hand during these protests. Windows on stores that weren't boarded up were smashed, including a police station. Red paint was splashed around and American flags were burned.

Gabby and Amy shamed those they saw doing this and yelled at them to stop. "You're not helping!"

And then just after 11:30pm shots rang out. The protesters shrieked and scattered. It was chaos. People panicked. Amy saw a young guy that was hit in the stomach and was on the ground bleeding. He was quickly attended to.

Tear gas was launched into the crowd. Amy's eyes and throat were burning. She lost track of Gabby.

"Gabby??"

The screams were deafening. She tried to move away, but didn't know which way to go in the melee and could barely see. Her eyes burned worse and she coughed like crazy. Tears streamed down her face. Someone grabbed her and guided her to a guy with a carton of milk ready to flush out her eyes.

"Don't use milk on the eyes!"

Amy recognized the voice, "Daddy?"

"Yes." Alexander was suffering himself, but he took control of flushing Amy's eyes out and then others using only water.

Amy was able to regain some vision. There was the sound of flesh impacted by a projectile. Amy cried out in pain, "Ahh!!!"

Alexander saw her drop to the ground, "Ambrosia!!!"

****

The mayor of Atlanta went on the air and she called for the end of the destruction, the burning of cars and the arson attacks on buildings. She urged people to 'go home.' It was directed at what was happening in Atlanta, but resonated across the land. She accused the rioters and looters of disgracing the legacy of Martin Luther King and distracting the narrative. They were doing it wrong. She mentioned that she was a mother and like all mothers, was worried for her children. She also called for people to register and vote if they wanted change.

Political pundit Van Jones stated, "When you call people out with pejorative names, you lose your audience. She was calling people up to a higher standard and you could feel the love underneath the mayor of Atlanta's anger. She said the protesters were better than this." Jones attempted to explain the uproar by saying, "If people see injustice and say something and are ignored, they yell. If they're again ignored, they might shout and if again they aren't heard, they might scream. And then if again you're ignored you might throw something." He went on to say you can't continue to put people down and expect them to rise. He summed it up by stating, "Hurt people holler. When something is desperately wrong and no one in authority will listen, people will go to more extreme measures. If people didn't want lawlessness in their communities, there can't be lawlessness in the police departments. That is the challenge." Van Jones wanted to hold young people to high standards and grownups to higher standards. The problem was that critics were quick to raise the standards on young desperate people, some acting stupid, some being true to the struggle for change and to lower the standards of adult law enforcement. That was how you get anarchy. And Van Jones asked the question, "When did it become radical to say the police should obey the law?"

****

Amy's arm was throbbing in pain. Blood was oozing out from the wound. Mucus gushed from her nose and mouth. Her eyesight was still sketchy.

"Daddy, I think they were rubber bullets."

He quickly guided her away from the plume of cayenne pepper mist. They both hacked and coughed. "No, you were hit by a pepper ball."

Alexander took her to the nearby Unitarian Church. It was a sanctuary. They treated her wound. Amy was feeling much better. They spoke to Reverend Lori Kyle. Alexander introduced her to Amy and commented that Reverend Kyle had only been in Louisville for 8 months.

Alexander was involved with the justice ministry of the church. They discussed the happenings in CLOUT, Citizens of Louisville Organized and United Together, which worked on policy changes within government.

Amy was trying to remember all of the things her father was involved with.

Alexander then introduced her to Pam Middleton. After talking for a bit, Pam reflected back, "I protested to end the Vietnam War and for women's rights, but never marched for racial equality. I felt the need to get involved, as a White American."

Amy was new to this struggle and Pam's story resonated with her.

Gabby and Amy texted each other. They were both safe. The welt on Amy's arm was the size of a grapefruit. Amy said she was okay, but Alexander called a doctor friend who made a house call late that night. He diagnosed it as a very bad bruise. It would be sore for a week or 10 days. She declined any pain pills.

Amy took a shot of Dulsett Reserve and slept some through the night. It was challenging.

The next day Amy watched the press conference on TV with her father. Seven people had been hit with live rounds at the protests. The mayor announced the shots did not come from the police and that all the victims were stable and recovering.

Amy had a faraway look, "It was the scariest I've ever been."

Alexander gently hugged her.

The mayor also announced a suspension of no-knock warrants, a dusk to dawn curfew that was starting and the Kentucky National Guard was being brought in.

Amy went back to bed. Alexander did more work and then saw footage from the previous night of a TV news crew—off to the side—filming the Louisville Metro Police Department on live TV deployed in response to the protests. Then an LMPD officer turned and pointed his pepper ball gun at the crew and fired multiple times at them. The crew was shocked as they were hit and took cover.

Alexander was stunned silent.

****

Statement from WAVE 3 News general manager:

"We strongly condemn the actions of the LMPD officer who tonight repeatedly fired at and hit our reporter and cameraman, both of whom were courageously and lawfully covering breaking news in their community. There is simply no justification for the Louisville police to wantonly open fire, even with pepper balls, on any journalist under any circumstances."

Statement from the president and co-CEO of the TV station's parent company:

"As colleagues and as citizens, we are indebted to the journalists who put themselves in harm's way on a daily basis to cover critical stories for their local communities, whether it's a pandemic, flooding, wildfires or a host of other dangerous situations. At no time, however, should journalists be fired upon by the police while peacefully exercising their constitutional rights to speak, assemble and report. We urge the LMPD to investigate fully and take all necessary actions to ensure that no journalist ever faces a situation like the WAVE 3 News team endured tonight."

The LMPD said they would investigate. The footage of the WAVE 3 news crew getting pepper balled continued to be stunning to Alexander. He thought, *this is how despots around the world operated to control things. Debase and attack the messenger.* The shock wore off and he was now furious that it could happen here.

After seeing the upheaval, Juniyah Palmer, Breonna Taylor's sister, posted on social media: "At this point ya'll are no longer doing this for my sister! You guys are just vandalizing stuff for no reason. I had a friend ask people why they were there and most didn't even know the protest was for my sister. What you guys started at the beginning was fine and correctly done, but once ya'll started vandalism you took my sister's name out of place! I honestly feel like you guys are disrespecting my family's wishes for a safe and non-violent protest!"

****

They met outside by the horse stables later that day. Amy and April kept their distances, it was a manifestation of their relationship over the years. Her eyes still had some residual stinging and her arm was quite sore.

"You were there protesting when the shooting happened." April tried to make sense of this.

Amy had a long sleeve shirt on. She had long given up trying to understand how her mother knew so many things, so quickly and accurately. "Yes…"

"How bad is your injury?"

"Just a bruise." Amy wasn't going to show her because it was seriously black and blue.

"Your eyes still sting a bit?"

"Yes…"

"I would like to discuss your earlier comment on storing your eggs. What's the password?"

Amy was irked, "Excuse me?" She flinched and the jabbing pain in her arm appeared again. "Mother, I believe you're being more than a bit rude here."

"I wasn't being rude, just prudent. This looks like Alexander's influence."

"No, Mother."

"Didn't your father encourage you to express yourself? Fight the man?"

"No. I never told him I was doing this. And I didn't know he was out protesting."

"Should have assumed that," April said wearily. "I was informed that he was out there as well. Alexander just goes on his way fighting the wrongs of the world."

"Someone should, Mother."

April went to her place of resignation. "Hmm."

"You seem to still harbor a good deal of anger towards him."

April was amused by that, "Not at all. He's in my rear-view mirror."

"I give you my word, Daddy didn't encourage me. I wasn't aware that he had already been to a couple protests. In fact…"

"What?"

"When I was tear gassed and couldn't see. That's when Gabby and I were separated, but luckily Daddy was there."

"You just happen to bump into each other in the middle of the bedlam and turmoil."

"Yes! And it's a good thing too. After I was hit with the tear gas, he stopped someone from washing my eyes out with milk, which is the last thing you should do."

"Milk? Not good when you're tear gassed. Good to know. That is something he would be familiar with. Such useful information. I'm pleased your father was there in the anarchy, being a dad."

"He didn't take me there. He saw me when everyone was running. He took me to safety. To the Unitarian Church." Amy added the location to get a reaction from her, which she did.

April held her head, "Oh, them..."

"They're doing great work."

"In light of your radical activities, this is the reason I bring up needing to know the password. I have our future generations to think about."

"That's the exact reason I'm doing this, Mother. For our future generations."

"Aren't you at least worried about being infected?"

"Almost everyone is masked up. It's outside and I don't get in the middle of the big crowds."

"Will you at least promise me you'll obey the curfew?"

"Yes."

****

The shock for Mitch being laid off had worn off. The restaurant business cratered with the pandemic and shutdown. He was now angry with the politicians and the Center for Disease Control. The CDC was late to declare an emergency and the masking policies were and would continue to be confusing. Mitch was panicking. The world he knew was dissolving in front of his eyes. He attempted to navigate the state's website to qualify for unemployment and was having a difficult time. Abby continued working and almost everyone else joined her working from home.

Mitch spent the first days in the bedroom hunched over his laptop listening to crypto evangelists and actors he really like challenge him to be bold. He had been really curious about Bitcoin, but missed out on the huge spike. He was searching for the next big thing. He had read a tip on a message board and found Vidarcoin—and it was beginning a historic run-up. Mitch got in fairly early and had bought 100 coins that were offered at $100 each. At first, he didn't think it was real or really happening. After a couple months the price had skyrocketed to over $22,000 a coin. He had been sitting on this secret for some time. But it finally burst forth: they were now multimillionaires. He took some profits and moved his family into a much nicer place. When Abby told Amy and Gabby, they were thrilled for her.

Mitch's family and friends were calling him the Crypto Kid. Mitch was flush with cash. He was now sporting a thick gold chain around his neck. He came by to visit Bobby, in his tricked out white Chrysler 300 with shaved inner fenders, front and rear lips that had been incorporated into the bumper. They socially distanced.

"Bobby, do you trade crypto?"

"No, Mitch. I have enough headaches hedging in the Forex markets."

"Bobby, you should check out Vidarcoin."

"A good bet?"

Mitch motioned to the ride and his chain.

Bobby nodded, "It appears so."

****

About an hour after Amy left, Reston visited SHS and they met the same distant way. He again assured April that he was willing to isolate with her, but she told him she might be already carrying something and to keep his distance. Having the compromised immune system and having two older friends—not by much—pass away from it, kept April focused.

Reston seemed to be on some sort of macho demonstration with his disregard for any preventative measures. He didn't think it was even a thing and would ridicule those who chose to wear a mask.

April thought about adding more plexiglass.

"Now the rioters are shooting each other. It's a 'Class A certified clusterfuck,' deadpanned Reston. "Six or seven cops were injured and went to the hospital. One got hit with a firecracker and has a concussion. This is outrageous! I'm tired of the protesting. Where's the respect for law enforcement? Why don't they just shoot the complainers in the legs?"

"Why not just go Tiananmen Square on them?" asked April.

"Why not? That got things ship-shape real quick."

April ignored him and watched some of the horses in the meadows and wanted to be with them.

"I wonder how Alexander lured Amy in."

"Reston, why do you do that? Amy has a mind of her own. I often think she doesn't listen to her father or me." April declined to share Alexander's participation and his helpful hint on milk.

****

TORTS and Just Desserts from the mind of Alexander Arrington

The owl appeared:

"The killing of Breonna Taylor is a tragedy. No doubt about it and shocking to some, who don't reside in areas where no-knock raids are carried out. With this notoriety and the other tragic events in Georgia and Minnesota, change can happen. Peaceful protests are called for and needed. Destruction of property should never be tolerated. Intelligent, socially responsible people know that takes the focus off of the injustice being protested. It is a self-inflicted wound on the needed reform—but how 'self' inflicted is it? Accelerationists and anarchists, hoping to speed up what they see as the inevitable race war, were doing their part and continue to foment.

The actions carried out on March 13th, 2020 by the Louisville Metro Police Department were clearly a violation of the 4th Amendment rights of Miss Taylor and Mr. Walker, if you believe in that sort of thing; accelerationists and anarchists don't. They want the law of the jungle. The Founders put in procedures and mechanisms to bring relief and reform is happening. Peaceful protests are called for and needed.

However, if one doesn't approve of their actions, inactions or time frame, it is outrageous and dangerous to show up at the home of a politician or judge or justice. The civil servant should not have to deal with this. Yet, every year the U.S. Marshals report thousands of threats and inappropriate communications against the judiciary and elected officials. Frequently other family members, children, become the collateral damage here and even victims. Would these protesters then be okay with a mob from their opponent showing up at their home? The accelerationists and anarchists would say yes. 'Bring it on.' Where does it end? When everything is burned to the ground?"

~ ~ ~

"As I mentioned, civil servants, I include the people that pick up your garbage and go out at night, in a storm to get the lights back on. For many, the ones that come to work in a pandemic, the 'essential workers' who work where you get your food, were sort of invisible before. I would ask you to recognize them for their service, a good word and maybe a little gratuity. It doesn't have to be much. This is where the thought actually does matter. Because we really are all in this together."

The owl faded out.

****

"I saw mom, remotely."

Alexander was perusing a motion he was preparing. He paused and glanced up, "Oh. How is she?"

"Fine. Being careful."

"Good." Alexander went back to reading.

"She knows you were protesting, but still doesn't understand why you get involved."

"When one is secure, with a big house and more money than they know what to do with, it can cause a separation from the reality that most endure."

"I think mom probably knows, but may not still understand. What about the death threats?"

"Oh please, I've lost track of how many death threats I've gotten. I'm not worried about those keyboard cowards, it's the ones that don't telegraph their moves you have to be ready for."

"How can you be ready for the unexpected?"

Alexander sat back in his chair and mused, "You can't, so just play the cards you're dealt, be aware and enjoy the ride, sugar."

****

It was the morning of the First of June. Alexander, Amy, Mrs. Simmons and Granddad were sitting out back of CA at a distance.

"Today the National Guard is arriving in Louisville," Alexander announced.

Mrs. Simmons thought back, "Mark Twain said it, 'The past doesn't repeat itself, but it rhymes."

"How so?" asked Amy.

"In early May of 1968, emotions were raw after Martin Luther King, another one of our leaders, was assassinated," recalled Mrs. Simmons. "We added him to the list. Soon after that the cops pulled over 31-year-old Charles Thompson, a Black driver on the west side. Not for a moving violation. They claimed he was driving a car that may or may not resemble one that might have been used in a burglary. It was always something like that. Well, his buddy, Manfred Reid, also 31, stopped and vouched for his friend. The cop didn't like his attitude. They were arrested and the anger grew. Mr. Reid stated they weren't in a White neighborhood. They were in their own area of town and still they were being harassed by the authorities and weren't left alone. This was a school teacher and a real estate agent.

These weren't the criminals, they were the Black middle class and they were treated no different. And then at the end of May... People just had enough of the harassment. If you've never lived under such circumstances, you can't really relate. Folks gathered at 28th and Greenwood and things got out of hand. Years of frustrations boiled over. There was confusion and anger and then there was a riot."

"And the governor called in the National Guard," said Alexander.

"What happened?" asked Amy, with some trepidation.

"There was burning and looting," recalled Mrs. Simmons. "I believe it was around 475 people that were arrested. There was a lot of property damage and two Black teenagers were dead."

They were quiet hearing this.

Granddad finally stated, "Which reminds us how important Shelby Lanier was. Shelby arrived in the '70s."

"True. Very true," said Mrs. Simmons, frustrated just reliving these memories.

"Yes." Alexander had a warm grin at the mention of his friend. "Shelby."

****

Amy and Alexander obeyed the curfew, they hung out at CA. They stayed on their side of the house and backyard. There wasn't any business to conduct. Granddad was working in his room. Mrs. Simmons was reading, listening to classical music, occasionally doing a snip or turn of dirt in the garden. Alexander and Amy skated on their half-pipe. With no pro or college basketball or pro or college or high school baseball games they contemplated stuff on their to-watch list and began to binge classic films.

****

Alexander and Amy were up late after watching several movies. Granddad had turned in and Mrs. Simmons was off with her crossword puzzles. There was a call. David McAtee, YaYa, had been shot and killed by the police at his barbecue restaurant.

Amy and Alexander were stunned and then heartbroken. "No…"

When the shock wore off, he became confused, this wasn't the guy Alexander knew. "YaYa was a calming influence, a rock in the community, loved by so many, from the economically challenged to the economically blessed."

The police announced that David McAtee had fired first—and they didn't have their body cameras operating. When Alexander heard this, he nearly blew a gasket. It was like some sick joke. When learning of this the mayor immediately fired the police chief.

There was CCTV security camera footage though. After looking at four separate video angles of the event, they saw a police officer fire pepper balls that shattered a bottle on an outdoor table. Another struck the doorway of the restaurant, almost hitting McAtee's niece in the head. Alexander and Amy watched the footage over and over and both came to the conclusion that YaYa and others in the kitchen of the restaurant, believed bullets were shot at her.

"He was the protector," said Alexander. "YaYa most likely thought they were under attack or being robbed."

They saw images of him instantly pulling his gun, crossing to the door, raising his arm and shooting to the sky.

"It looks like he didn't know who shot at them and fired two warning shots into the air for any attackers to back off," said Amy.

Alexander shook his head sadly, "It was the worst and last mistake of his life."

The National Guard fired back with live ammo until the threat was neutralized. YaYa was hit in the chest and died.

"Ironically," said Alexander, "it was his cop buddies who warned YaYa he should be armed if he was going to do business in that area. He knew LMPD policy is to fire pepper balls at the ground and not into a crowd of people or at a business; unless the individuals were creating a safety threat to the officer, another person, or engaging in arson or destruction of property. From the footage it shows his niece just standing there on private property."

In such a volatile situation Alexander wished he could have counseled YaYa not to be so quick to draw his weapon and fire, even if they were warning shots. LMPD and the National Guard troops armed with long guns were not to be messed with.

It then dawned on Alexander that YaYa died a couple blocks over from where Alberta Jones was last seen.

****

Alexander and Amy masked up and he took her to meet David's mother, Odessa. They paid their respects—from a distance—and cried together. They talked about what a wonderful person he had been.

****

June 5, 2020, would have been Breonna's 27th birthday. The DDs joined a thousand plus that showed up at Metro Hall in downtown. Two days later the mayor ordered a complete review of the Louisville Metro Police Department.

June 12, 2020, Louisville Metro Council unanimously passed "Breonna's Law" which banned the use of no-knock warrants.

The seal of Kentucky proclaimed: United We Stand, and Divided We Fall.

June 18, 2020, the Kentucky Attorney General stood before that seal of the commonwealth and stated: "I can assure you, at the end of our investigations we will do what is right. We will find the truth."

"Okay then, find it and do what is right," said Alexander as he turned off the TV and thought back to 2015 and the big changes the police department announced back then. The LMPD had updated their policies and overhauled its training. 21st Century Policing was the name. Alexander highly approved of the community-based approach. Get out of your squad car, walk around with a positive attitude, treat folks with respect—and the people welcomed it. Louisville was presented as a model city demonstrating to the world how to have public safety, while engaging with the community in a positive way that created trust. City leaders were honored at the White House in 2016 for these reforms.

Alexander was hopeful. There was progress and then as he described it, "Two steps forward, three steps back."

June 23, one of the police officers on the Breonna Taylor raid, who 'blindly' fired 10 rounds into Breonna's apartment and the unit next door, was officially fired. The current police chief added in his termination letter: 'that the officer showed extreme indifference to the value of human life.'

All eyes were now on the office of the Kentucky Attorney General. People wondered when the announcement would be on what charges would be brought. The Kentucky Attorney General said there was no timeline for the investigation. The protests continued. Jefferson Park was where folks gathered. It was a staging area and people were allowed to camp out in tents.

And then there were online posts and chatter about an armed counter-protest that would be marching into Louisville to 'restore order' happening on Saturday, June 27, the mayor tweeted out: 'We are aware of rumors suggesting that armed militia are coming to downtown Louisville this weekend. Our message is simple: We don't need you here. Our focus is on facilitating peaceful protest.'

The authorities closed several downtown streets and brought in bike rack barriers to keep the sides separated. Charlottesville was still fresh in everyone's mind. As the day went by there wasn't any counter-protest. There was a great sigh of relief and the city went into the early evening.

Then in Jefferson Park, there was a man who had been repeatedly asked to leave the area because of his odd behavior. The assembled group wanted him out, but in a bizarre turn of events this troubled homeless man grabbed a handgun from someone. People ran for cover. He fired it at no one in particular, but the fatal bullet hit Tyler Gerth.

****

Alexander and Amy were home when they heard the news late that night. Another senseless tragedy, against someone so decent. They learned that Tyler talked the talk and walked the walk. Alexander, Amy, Granddad and

Mrs. Simmons didn't know the young man, but they grieved for him. They deeply respected and admired him for sacrificing his time and energy to push for these reforms and ultimately sacrificing his life. It was well known to his family and friends, Tyler didn't hesitate in silence when he saw the wrongs of the world; he actually got involved in the struggle for social justice reform and he captured it on his camera to share with others—which was what he was doing at the time of his death.

The next day the Gerth family released a statement:

"Tyler Gerth, 27, was a beloved son, cherished little brother, adored uncle to seven nieces and nephews and a trusted friend. We are devastated that his life was taken from us far too soon. Tyler was incredibly kind, tender hearted and generous, holding deep convictions and faith. It was this sense of justice that drove Tyler to be part of the peaceful demonstrations advocating for the destruction of the systemic racism within our society's systems. This, combined with his passion for photography led to a strong need within him to be there, documenting the movement, capturing and communicating the messages of peace and justice. While we cannot fathom this life without our happy, inquisitive, hardworking, funny, precious Tyler, we pray that his death would be a turning point and catalyst for peace in the city he loved so much. We ask for your prayers and that the Lord would draw close in our sorrow, but we also ask that his death is not just another statistic of senseless violence. 'Darkness cannot drive out darkness; only light can do that. Hate cannot drive out hate; only light can do that.'"

More than a hundred people showed up for a vigil in Jefferson Square Park the next night for Tyler Gerth. Alexander, Amy, Mrs. Simmons and Granddad were in attendance and wearing masks, as were almost everyone else. Some lit candles, some burned sage and some placed flowers on the ground where Tyler died.

Chuck Gerth, Tyler's father, addressed the crowd: "He had good friends of all colors. He supported the cause, he saw the injustices with Breonna, and so many injustices throughout the world. He was here at the park because of a belief in racial justice and a desire to photograph an important moment in history. Tyler was driven to speak out against injustice, even as a young child."

30

April and Reston were sitting out back of Silver Horse Sanctuary, sipping pinot noir and watching the old thoroughbreds trot about in the late afternoon.

They both used voice-amps to get their message across to each other.

"Jefferson Park was cleared out after the death of Tyler Gerth," April informed Reston.

"I don't get it," said Reston. "I really don't. I read his story. He was a White kid, upper-middle class, talented photographer, had everything going for himself... Why would *he* be in the middle of these protests about injustices that he would never, ever face? It doesn't make sense. I just don't understand."

From the other side of the plexiglass, April watched him struggle with that notion and reflected on that herself.

Reston flailed his arms, "Hell, the family should be calling for some payback! But this statement from the Gerth family is...confusing."

"How so, Reston?"

"They're talking 'peace'? And that 'hate cannot drive out hate; only light can do that?' They aren't calling for a crackdown?"

April let him vent.

"And! Did you hear what Tyler's philosophy on human interaction was?"

"No."

"Be excellent to each other." Reston scoffed and shook his head, mystified. "What a bunch of warmed over love your brother bullshit. If I believed that I might as well grow my hair long, wear a robe and put on sandals."

"Reston, dear, you are a senior usher at church."

"What does that have to do with anything? What I'm saying is, if that happened to my boy, I'd kick some ass and remind them who Reston Richardson is. That's for damn sure!"

April ignored him and watched one of the horses in the meadow get up a gallop like the old days. Just to remind the others who he was once.

****

A radio was playing on a warm sunny day: "...and it's official. Louisville has canceled their annual 4th of July celebration due to the pandemic. Sorry, folks."

"Why can't they cancel the protests too??" yelled Reston, hammered, sitting alone by his pool with a drink in hand.

Over at Casa Arrington, Alexander was also listening to the radio, sitting alone out back on the half-pipe toking on a pipe.

"...and it's official. Louisville has canceled their annual 4th of July celebration due to the pandemic. Sorry, folks."

Alexander groused, "Oh man..."

****

Reston was on the way to a meeting in Southern Indiana the next day. As he entered the Clark Memorial Bridge that spanned the Ohio River, he was caught in a protest that closed the bridge down. Banners were unfurled. The police were quickly on the scene. Reston tried to turn around and get over to the Lincoln Bridge but he was blocked in by the cars. He was furious. When he calmed down, he postponed the meeting. 43 arrested and 20 cars were towed.

Five days later Reston was in NuLu for another meeting that would be held outside. But a protest erupted in the form of a block party that blocked Market Street and he couldn't get through. Reston just about had a meltdown. 76 people were arrested.

****

Alexander and Amy attended the funeral mass for Tyler Gerth on July 3. It was Tyler's birthday. He would have turned 28.

Tyler's older sisters, Brittany Loewen and Tiffany Hensley, began the ceremony by introducing Arnold the Football, Tyler's COVID buddy during the lockdown. It was a nice moment.

Brittany talked about their brother: "...Tyler was in most ways a pretty average guy. What was very special about Tyler was the perseverance he showed, no matter what life threw at him. The ability to reflect on himself, to grow, to change, to mature, to do better. But not just do better, to be *excellent* to each other. That was Tyler's mantra. Excellence is defined as the quality of being outstanding or extremely good. What does it mean to treat another human in an outstanding or extremely good way? Ask yourself, what does it look like for you to love others in an excellent way? And now, consider this. It does not say be excellent to those you love or be excellent to those you work with or those who you agree with politically. And it certainly doesn't say be excellent to those that look like you, who think like you, who talk like you or who believe in the exact same things that you do. Be excellent to each other. ...It's just that simple. It's just that ordinary. ...And our world has never needed us to exhibit that more than right now."

Later, Father Shayne Duvall said, "'*Amen, I say to you whatever you did to these least brothers of mine, you did for me.*' In a nutshell, that was Tyler and how he lived his life. He was a man of compassion and integrity and service."

****

The rest of the summer the protests continued against those who weren't being excellent, or even halfway decent. The pressure kept on. Voices were becoming strained.

During the first two months after Breonna Taylor's death there had been little interest or knowledge of this tragedy. The bright lights were on it now. At the end of the summer there was even an event billed BreonnaCon. Amy was surprised. She had been to ComicCon and was just amazed it had gotten to this level. This was a movement. For four days people showed up for workshops, training sessions on protesting peacefully and positively, help on food insecurity, school supply giveaways, along with an old fashion faith revival.

On the final day a large demonstration unfolded. It was called Good Trouble Tuesday. Playing off the term civil rights icon John Lewis said, 'Good trouble is getting in trouble you could be proud of, standing up for what you believe in.'

On Good Trouble Tuesday 400 people marched from South Central Park to the Louisville Metro Police Department training grounds. As it was located next to Churchill Downs and since the Kentucky Derby was running in 11 days, this got the attention of law enforcement. Many charged with providing security saw it as a dry run for disrupting the race.

Before getting to LMPD property, protests began blocking the road and by the end of the day, 64 more demonstrators were arrested.

****

The Kentucky Derby was the oldest continuous sporting event in North America. In 2020 it was 146 years in a row. It wasn't always run on the First Saturday in May, but it had never missed a calendar year since the inaugural Run for the Roses in 1875. April was in a group that had tea with the Queen of England in 2007 when she attended the race.

The 5th of September arrived. The Derby was a low-key affair. The usual celebrations were scuttled. Very few were let in and they were spread out. The infield was closed.

April was in her living room dressed up, wearing her fabulous hat and drinking a Mint Julep by herself watching the race coverage, with a disgruntled frown.

The mood wasn't much cheerier at CA.

The rumors of protesters disrupting the race were greatly exaggerated. There was a large crowd in front of Churchill Downs chanting "No justice, no Derby." There was plenty of security. The protesters weren't going to storm the castle, just yell at it. If you watched on TV, you wouldn't have even been aware it was going on.

****

September 15, 2020. On the 111th day of protests the city of Louisville settled the wrongful death lawsuit filed by the Taylor family for a record $12 million—a new series of reforms were coming to the LMPD. The city agreed to establish a housing credit program as an incentive for officers to live in the areas they serve. Social workers would provide support on certain police runs and commanders would now review and approve search warrants before seeking judicial approval. Alexander admitted it was some progress.

****

September 18, 2020. Musician Tyler Childers, a rising star of roots-music of the White working and underclass of the South, posted a video on YouTube talking about his perspectives on life. His video of the song "Long Violent History" had been released. The lyrics at the end of the song were:

could you imagine just constantly worrying kicking and fighting begging to breathe?

how many boys could they haul off this mountain

shoot full of holes, cuffed and laying in the streets

Till we come into town in a stark raving anger looking for answers and armed to the teeth

30-06s and papaw's old pistol

how many, you reckon, would it be?

four or five?

Or would that be the start of a long violent history of tucking our tails as we tried to abide?

Tyler then asked White Southerners, "What it would be like if the smallest interaction with a public servant led to being handcuffed, assaulted and possibly shot multiple times?"

Tyler continued on saying, "Chances are the people allowing this to happen are the same who keep opportunity out of reach for our own communities. That have watched jobs shipped out and drugs shipped in, eating up our communities and leaving people desperate. And we could stop being so taken aback by Black Lives Matter. If we didn't have to be reminded of it, there would be justice for Breonna Taylor, a Kentuckian like me and countless others."

Tyler ended the video by suggesting, "We need to preserve our heritage by getting back to the simple and rewarding things in life, growing food, learning a fiddle tune, sew a quilt, hunting, fishing, blacksmithing. Which would leave us less time to argue back and forth over things we really don't know. Backed by news we can't fully trust. Love each other. No exceptions. And remember: united we stand, divided we fall."

Alexander, Amy, Mrs. Simmons and Granddad saw his video and were amazed.

"That took some gumption," said Granddad.

"I don't think I've ever seen such a heartfelt and profound statement before," said Alexander. "It was quite remarkable."

Mrs. Simmons nodded, "It sure was. You have some of his music?"

"I do, on my phone," said Alexander.

"I think I'd like to listen to some of his stuff tonight," said Mrs. Simmons.

Amy had been introduced to Tyler at Forecastle, by Gabby. She saw him play live and was impressed at his musical talent, now she was awed by his insight.

At SHS, April was quite taken by this video. She had heard of Tyler, but only remotely. She was now very interested in him. She picked up her phone, went to his website, purchased and downloaded his album *Long Violent History.*

At Reston's house he was stunned by this video. He finally shook his head, picked up his phone and searched for any of Tyler Childers music on his device, "You are so gone, buddy boy. I'm done with you." Reston then realized he didn't have any of Tyler's music. He considered downloading one of his albums, maybe several, just to have the joy of deleting them all. He went on Tyler's website and shopped for merchandise he could purchase and destroy.

****

Simultaneously Louisville torch singer Carly Johnson released her song "Burn Your Fears." Amy was already drifting along, wondering where it was all headed. She listened to the song over and over. It captivated her. She went online and found out the story behind the ballad. A friend of Carly's, Marisa Wittebort, a 30-year-old non-smoker was diagnosed with an extremely rare form of lung cancer. Marisa embraced life and lived it to the fullest in her final four years.

It was only listening to the song a dozen times before she learned this. At first Amy was filled with melancholy, sad that such a beautiful soul was taken so early from this earth. It sledgehammered home to her how fleeting life could be and how little time we really had—and to quit wasting it. She was snapped out of her funk.

September 22, 2020, U.S. COVID-19 death toll surpassed 200,000.

It was on the same day that Alexander got an alert that LMPD was physically restricting access to the downtown area. A decision from the Kentucky Attorney General was imminent.

The mayor then issued an executive order restricting access to five parking garages and banning on-street parking.

September 23, a grand jury indicted one officer on three counts of felony wanton endangerment for firing bullets that went into an apartment next to Breonna's unit, where three people were present. No officers were indicted on Breonna's killing.

Alexander, Amy, Mrs. Simmons and Granddad were in the back of Casa Arrington watching on the screen.

Alexander shook his head, "Now they've invited the Justice Department back in. And it's going to be awkward in the state capitol when the federal boys return to do their own investigating. As for tonight, I think there's going to be some more righteous indignation."

"Dear Lord..." sighed Mrs. Simmons. "Batten down the hatches."

****

Mitch was out. Abby hired her cousin to babysit, she wasn't going to miss this. The DDs went out in full force to protest.

Around 8:45pm Gabby faced the other two, "You know we're going to violate the curfew."

"Not if we get to the church in time," said Amy. "Run."

At that moment flash-bang grenades went off nearby, they stumbled, disoriented. They helped Abby up and continued running.

The DDs made it to the Unitarian Church. The police were in riot gear and setting up as they scampered onto the property. The clock struck 9 and some outside were detained. The police, now geared up, surrounded the church.

People were then getting texts and alerts on social media that the LMPD was only pausing to get the go-ahead from their legal department.

The mood inside the place was tense. Paranoia was taking hold as a lot of them thought the authorities would storm the place.

At 9:32pm Alexander received a call from April.

"Alexander, our daughter is in trouble."

Alexander gave that a funny look, went up the stairs and knocked on her door. "Amy?" No response. "She's not in her room. Talk to me."

"She's in the Unitarian Church, which at the moment is surrounded by the police." April couldn't help but have an accusatorial tone, "You know, the place you took her before."

Alexander thought back, "She told me she was going to do some research."

"Did she tell you she was researching uprisings?"

"Let me get back to you."

****

At 9:35pm a speaker addressed the gathering in the church and warned them if they left the sanctuary of the church, they faced the possibility of arrest.

"You think we're going to get busted?" Abby asked, with some serious apprehension.

The group inside the church pulled together, supported each other and had faith it would work out.

Amy's phone buzzed, she checked it and answered, "Hi, Daddy."

"I've got the word you're trapped, really?"

"I'm going to put you on speaker, I'm with Gabby and Abby."

"Hello, DDs."

Hi, Mr. Arrington. Hello." Abby and Gabby were, as you might expect, a bit on edge.

"Are you all okay?"

"Uh. Yes... Fine... Sort of..." All three mumbled parts of that response.

"I got a call from your mother and she informed me. You guys need anything?" A helicopter roared overhead.

"Our own helicopter?" Gabby suggested.

"Sounds like a war zone there. Too bad they don't have any secret underground passageways. You'll just have to wait them out. You met Pam Middleton and Reverend Lori Kyle."

"Yes," said Amy.

"And Reverend Dawn Cooley is there too. You're in good hands."

"Daddy, we're seeing on social media that the police are getting legal advice on entering the church."

"Balderdash. Churches are part of the carve-out to the curfew. And sanctuary in a church goes back over two millennia. Even the Romans and Greeks recognized this. It was respected all through Europe and the Americas for hundreds of years. Though when one finally emerged, they were banished from the city for the rest of their life."

"You mean, we can't come back to Louisville?" asked a concerned Abby, not thinking clearly at the moment.

Amy and Gabby glanced at each other.

The helicopter buzzed over again.

"That's not going to happen. And they're not going to enter. Trust me," Alexander assured them.

"But they might just wait outside and pounce when we come out," said Gabby.

"We just got a warning about that," Abby added nervously.

"Let me make a call and I'll get back to you guys. It's going to be okay." Alexander hung up and faced Mrs. Simmons.

"Amy's in the church?"

"Yeah." Alexander got another call and learned that moments earlier LMPD officers approaching a protest downtown encountered gunfire. Two officers were shot and transported to the hospital.

Alexander was alarmed at this. Emotions were at a boiling point. Events were spiraling out of control. A state of emergency was called by the mayor.

April had moved out to the back deck.

Reston was now there, "This is crazy!"

Word spread in the church about the two law enforcement officers being shot. They wondered how this would weigh on the state of mind for the cops outside surrounding the place. The stress level inside shot up. Then they heard about the city-wide state of emergency declared.

April was watching this on TV and was back on the phone again. Her mic was on and her voice was being amplified over to Reston. "Alexander, can't you call one of your cop buddies? We used to have those big barbecues and feed half the police force!"

Reston rolled eyes.

Alexander thought back, "Yeah...remember the time Roland was chewing on that captain's leg?"

April paused and then had a quick laugh, "Roland..." She contained herself, "Please, Alexander, just do what you can."

"Sit tight. It'll all work out. I'll be in touch."

"Thank you." April ended the call.

Reston spoke into his voice-amp. "I think Amy spends too much time over there at Alexander's. Look where she's at now."

"Reston, please, shush on that. She chooses where she wants to stay."

"Who is this Roland?"

"It was a dog we had. He was chewing on the leg of a police captain."

"That's awful."

"Some of Alexander's special BBQ sauce dripped on the old captain's pant leg and Roland started licking, with a bit of gnawing."

"That's terrible."

"The old captain had a wooden leg."

"Huh."

"Alexander defended the mutt. He argued it had lost its mind as this was Alexander's very special secret sauce and no one could resist."

"Really?"

"Yep, the place went up for grabs laughing. But his sauce is really, really good."

"What's in his secret sauce?" asked Reston, trying not to reveal how interested he had become.

"It's a secret."

"It's a secret or you don't know?"

"I don't know."

"You were married to him."

"All couples have secrets. I'll bet you have a couple, eh, Reston."

"Bah. Phooey. What about Amy? She's boxed into a corner."

"Yes." April had calmed herself, "It'll work out."

"Because Alexander told you that?"

"Um, yes."

The DDs remained resolute. As did others. They supported each other.

At 10:35pm Alexander sent a text to Amy and April: there is an agreement.

"I've got something from my dad." Amy read it, relaxed and nodded to Gabby and Abby.

April was relieved to get the text. "He says there's an agreement."

Reston poured himself another drink, "That's a relief."

At 11pm they were allowed to exit the church and not be cited for the curfew violation. Amy, Gabby and Abby and another three dozen or so quietly walked by the riot police monitoring the situation.

****

It was the next day. Alexander and Amy watched the morning news.

The mayor announced the wounded officers would recover from their gunshot wounds.

Alexander sighed with relief, "Thank God."

Reverend Dawn Cooley of the Thomas Jefferson Unitarian Church was being interviewed: "This is what churches are supposed to be. They're supposed to be sanctuaries and havens for people who are in need. So this is absolutely what all the churches should be doing."

Alexander was in a very good mood and commented to Amy how he liked Reverend Dawn's style.

Amy agreed that she handled the standoff with courage and compassion.

At Reston's, he thought they all should have gone in, busted some heads, cleared out the place and jailed everyone. He also wondered on the side, *when the hell did female reverends appear*? He didn't like that.

****

At Casa Arrington, Granddad was reflecting on the situation, "The officers didn't get indicted by the Grand Jury for the actions concerning Breonna Taylor on any account, including how they got the warrant. Quite extraordinary."

"I agree," said Amy. "In a remarkable twist, we've learned the Grand Jury didn't have the option to indict on more serious charges."

"The Attorney General is a very clever politician," Alexander observed.

"Connect the dots for me, Daddy."

"He's having it both ways. He said wait for the Grand Jury to do their work. We waited. When the Grand Jury only indicted on the wanton endangerment charge, he said the people have spoken. It was 'ultimately in the Grand Jury's hands.' Usually that would be the end of it."

"This development is surprising," observed Amy.

"Very surprising," agreed Alexander. "To have members of the Grand Jury come forward and say the AG steered them away from having the opportunity to even discuss other charges. This way, when only wanton endangerment charges are filed on shooting up the neighborhood, the AG claims the people have spoken, so don't look at me. No blame here. He gets credit with important backers that he's a team player by not allowing any serious charges to even be considered. He'll be able to raise big dollars off this. Dang, I am impressed. He has skills."

"Amy mused, "I expect the AG didn't expect them to speak up. He then had to amend his comments on the situation."

"To be fair he did say he would 'find the truth and do the right thing.' He didn't say anything about sharing what that was or bringing any justice."

Amy sighed at that, "More stuff that Hunter S. Thompson should be skewering."

"Agreed, darlin,' this is right in his wheelhouse."

31

It was early November and the 2020 election season was here. There was a winner and there was a loser for the White House and the loser refused to accept it, even when it was certified by his own party and his own U.S. Attorney General—but he kept the rage up for some time and raked in mountains of moolah off this.

The pandemic loomed over everything. Granddad and Old Man Miller called a truce on the design wars and agreed to an extended suspension. It was that gloomy.

The holiday season had arrived. The Kentucky Seedlings received their scholarship awards remotely.

December 14, 2020: U.S. COVID-19 death toll surpasses 300,000. It was also on this day when vaccines began. April was at the front of the line.

New Year's Eve was again subdued. Alexander and Amy dueled on the half-pipe and played some table tennis.

January 1, 2021. Alexander wished all the humans a better new year, it had to be. He then visited all of the dogs, cats, rabbits, lizards, birds and hamsters and wished them a Happy New Year. He then read a press release that Darrell Griffith had been named as an ambassador for the University of Louisville in their anti-racism efforts. He sent a Happy New Year's greeting to Darrell and congratulations on his new position.

"Excellent, some good news," said Alexander, as he began breakfast.

****

It was when he began eating dinner on January 6, 2021 when he saw the footage. A riot hit Washington D.C. Hundreds of angry citizens tried to decertify the election and/or hang the Vice President for not overturning it. Neither occurred, but there was quite an effort. Over 100 capitol police were injured defending the capitol. Officer Brian Sicknick was sprayed by a chemical substance, taken to the ER and would pass away after two strokes. One of the invaders was shot and killed and four more Capitol officers would later die by suicide.

Reston was giddy as he watched it unfold on his gigantic UHD-TV from his home and cheered them on. "Fight like hell! Storm the capitol!"

There was a wave of people spraying more chemicals, smashing windows, punching, kicking, scratching, gouging and even bashing away with a crutch and a hockey stick. Reston just loved that one, he replayed it several times.

Over at Casa Arrington, Alexander watched in stunned silence.

"What the hell is going on?" asked Amy.

Alexander couldn't answer. He just stared at the wave of angry people smashing through the windows, overwhelming the security and beating the crap out of the police.

Amy was now completely blown away by this as well.

There was video of people roaming through the halls of the Capitol and picking up souvenirs.

The doors were barricaded by security, with their weapons drawn. Images were seen of politicians being hustled down hallways by Secret Service and running for safety.

Reston was rolling on the couch cackling, "Run for your lives!"

Then Reston saw a guy tatted up, with some crazy makeup and wearing horns. "You are the man!"

Over at CA the horn guy was on their screens as well.

"What the hell??" asked Alexander, blown away.

But truth be told, it would be the zip-tie guy, with a bunch of zip-ties in the House chamber that Alexander was most curious about.

****

Late that evening Reston was alone and not in a good place. From his back porch he stared out at the darkness of the night drunk and angry, "No one's going to cancel me. There will be no Great Reset. I can do and say whatever the hell I want. No one is replacing me. No Jew or nigger, or Mexican beaner, or Chink, or Mick or Wop, or any of the bitches that complained because I showed them some attention, or fags that wish I'd give it to them, lesbians that don't want or need me, or some confused transexual telling me how to use pronouns, or some smart-ass, over-educated woman that can't even define what a woman is, or some Indian from India writing code that makes no sense to me, or some Arab in a turban I can't understand, or some snooty Frenchman, or some stupid owl!, or the metrosexual assholes that look and smell so good, or the weak that have been abused...or have mental health issues...or the sensitive that can't take a joke. We had to put up with it! We had to put up with so much shit that was horrible and demeaning! What did we do? Go running to HR? Back to mommy? Post your hurt feelings on a blog? Tweet out your grievances? Hire a lawyer? Hell no! You either punched them in the jaw and kicked their ass or we sucked it up and took it in silence, no matter if it took something from you... Your dignity or respect... You took it! Endured it. Even if it fucked you up... And then...after all that, you turned around and gave it back to someone lower than you. The next ones coming up. Because you earned that right to lord it over them. Give it to them good. You have the right to mess with them, mess them up. That's the problem with this modern age. Now people claim they're working on their mental health. I say people don't know their place in the order of things. Instead of dutifully staying in their lanes, they're 'woke.' They've disengaged their auto-pilot and are looking around. Saying they're now seeing what's actually going on. They're changing lanes and I don't always see or understand the lane changing signals they give out. I don't like any of it! It's not the way the world works, it's not necessary. Woke. I hate that word. It disgusts me. What was wrong with the way it was? Everyone in their lanes..."

****

It was early and brisk. Amy was out walking the dogs. She waved to some of their neighbors, but still didn't see Old Man Miller. Amy came in, properly disposed of the dog doo-doo in the plastic bag and sat for the Zoom call set up with her mother. After a couple minutes they ran out of things to say.

"Hey there, Amy!" Reston yelled from the other end of the deck.

"Hi, Reston! How are you?"

"Good! Really Good. And you?"

"I'm fine. Stay safe, Reston."

"You too!"

"I'm glad to see you're socially distancing, Mother."

April mumbled, "Sometimes it has its advantages. When he's allowed over, he stays on that side of the deck and uses the facilities in the barn. He's not allowed in the main house."

Alexander sat next to Amy, "Hello, April, you look ravishing. Are you doing Pilates?"

"I have a new yoga instructor, she's in Sweden."

"It's working, darling."

April was amused, well aware of his blarney, but it was so full of charm.

"And I hope you're staying safe at Silver Horse Sanctuary."

"I am. Thank you."

Alexander could see behind her, "I see he's properly separated. Reston, hello!"

"Hello, Alexander. Have you gotten all the tear gas out of your nostrils?"

"All gone."

"When you march against the police," snapped Reston. "It's anti-cop."

"Reston, let me explain something to you. I support and champion proper constitutional law enforcement. I'm not marching against the police, I'm protesting against bad cops, unjust enforcement, dangerous policing and racist policies. If you just frame it as anti-cop, you can dismiss all of the protests and not have to look or think about it any further."

"It's anti-cop," repeated Reston.

"What about that beat-down of the Capitol Police on January 6?"

"What are you talking about?" asked Reston.

"The last time the Capitol was invaded was 1814, when the Brits got in and tried to burn it to the ground."

Reston scoffed, "January 6 looked like a normal visit by some tourists. They were well behaved. Quit making a mountain out of a molehill. Typical. What about the savages protesting and looting?"

"True," said Alexander, "there has been some looting, regrettably; which I agree is wrong. If one really is for positive social justice, this isn't the way. Those who damaged and destroyed private and public property should be brought to account. When there's actual equal protection under the law most of this will go away."

"Whatever…"

Alexander mused aloud, "Gee, in 1814, I wonder, did the Brits leave behind urine-stained carpets and fecal smeared on the walls like those tourists did on January 6?"

"What? You're making that part up."

"Fake news?" asked Alexander.

Reston sneered, "Just wait."

"Reston, seriously, don't you think encouraging this behavior, pushing to hang people, will bring more violence? You're giving them the green light. Think this through! What's the endgame?"

Reston marched off to the barn.

"Nice seeing you again, Reston!" called out Alexander. He then focused on April. "Whatever you're doing, keep doing it." They both smiled at each other.

"Thank you, Alexander." He left the room. "How is Alexander handling the isolation?"

Amy shrugged, "It's tough. He's a people person. He needs to circulate."

"He has you and Mrs. Simmons and Granddad at a distance. You probably are faring better than him, I assume."

"Why, Mother, because I'm cold and detached?"

"No, no, more independent. Ambrosia, you've never really needed people. Which is your strength. Maybe you get that from me."

"I didn't get it from Daddy."

"I would concur."

"What does Reston mean, 'just wait'?"

"He says that all the time now. Like some cryptic warning. He believes Sandy Hook was a false flag, a pizza place was trafficking kids, the Italians hacked our election and black helicopters with U.N. troops are going to attempt to take control of things in the near future, and it's all tied into 5G. Which is why Reston is adding to his arsenal and ammo stockpile, significantly."

"Mother... This is concerning."

"I used to laugh that I should pick up more aluminum foil for him. But after giving this some serious thought, the pandemic, with the long isolation, was a bad thing for Reston. And I just can't put up with any more bulletins from the lunatic fringe."

"Lunatic fringe?"

"Reston was never that interested in the news, other than the markets and the PGA and he rarely took the time to vote—but now he's consumed by politics. His news sources are from very far out areas of the internet, including the dark web. Reston's no longer witty and fun, he's dark and moody, mostly angry and fearful. He's cheerful when he uncovers fresh 'evidence.'"

****

Reston spent the rest of the day investigating and finally found what he was looking for. He was giddy. He forwarded it to April.

April was reading when she got an alert of a text. It was from Reston. He had just uncovered evidence that the people that smeared the poo and took a piss in the Capitol, were left-wing communist agitators, especially the guy with the horns.

April had earlier read that the horn guy was now in jail in Arizona. She learned some on the right were accusing him of being on the left. The horn guy was reportedly at first very angry and then felt hurt that anyone could ever think such an outlandish thing about him.

****

The next month when the vaccines were more widely available, Granddad and Mrs. Simmons got their shots. Alexander got his when he was eligible. Reston got the jab as well—but would deny it and continued to rail against it, sharing content that argued against getting vaxxed and calling those that did 'human pin cushions.'

Amy and Gabby and Abby all got the shot when it was their turn and Bobby too.

****

From one side of the deck, April put down her magazine and checked the email she just got. "I see you sent me more stuff to read, about the microchips in vaccines."

"I've done a deep dive on the issue."

"Yes, it's very deep."

"I'm really kind of an expert on all this stuff. I get it, I really do. People are amazed."

"I know, dear," April said, smiling from the other side of the deck, happily lost in her *New Yorker*.

****

Over at Casa Arrington, on the front porch were two heat lamps keeping the area nice and toasty. Mrs. Simmons was rocking in her chair. Alexander was on the other end of the porch, slumped, his face rumpled.

"Alexander, are you alright?"

"No. This world, this world is so messed up. Life had been rolling along, we were all making the most of every day and then we got stuck in the mud. For some it's quicksand. Events have overshadowed, overtaken our lives. Days and weeks pass that are a blur. Coronavirus cases continued to spread. Deaths are rising. Today U.S. deaths just topped 400,000. Life is so fragile."

"For some people…" responded Mrs. Simmons, "life has always been fragile. This is one of the few times we literally are *all* in the same boat. We haven't seen an example of this in a century."

"We may be in the same boat," said Alexander. "But some of us can work in our cabins, remotely, while others in steerage, the essential workers, can't."

It was true that most working-age Americans that died of COVID-19 during the first year of the pandemic, were those in service and retail, that require on-site attendance and multiple and extended contact with others.

Amy sat with Alexander and checked her phone.

"What are you doing, darlin'?"

"Doom scrolling, Daddy. The world has spun off its axis."

Alexander then noticed someone riding a bike on the street. He stopped and stared at their house.

"Hold on," said Alexander. "Is that…?"

Amy looked up, "It's Sean."

Sean pretended to eat and throw up—and then laugh.

Alexander was enraged by this, "That little… He's still taunting us about the food poisoning! I should go down there and…"

"Don't, Daddy."

Sean rode off.

Amy sighed, "I told you I couldn't control him anymore."

32

April hadn't gone to Hawaii. For several months it was closed to non-residents. Then the state imposed a two-week quarantine when arriving. Those that attempted to get around this were jailed.

April's attorney sent her an exception. One could avoid quarantine by presenting a negative nucleic acid amplification test from a qualified lab. She didn't know what that was and she wasn't going to any lab right now. Even when the island paradise reduced the period of isolation to 10 days, right before Christmas, she declined.

And normally, when the calendar month turned to February, April would be back from her annual trip, recharged and ready to go to work. It was a quick turn-around from September. The Derby was back to being the First Saturday in May. The season was upon them. April's mind would shift into gear as preparations would be kicking off. She was heavily involved with the Kentucky Oaks race, run the Friday before the Derby. The other event that would fill her time was the work done for the Royal Court of the Derby Festival Princesses. All of her involvement for both would be virtual and remote and indeed felt very remote.

She wanted to just fly away, forget about everything, then come back and it would be over. But the virus was everywhere, she couldn't outrun it and knew if she ventured out, the virus would find her compromised immune system.

The pandemic continued on. On February 21, 2021, the death count in the U.S. had surpassed 500,000.

It was announced that the Forecastle Festival was canceled for 2021.

Alexander sighed, dimmed the lights and put on "House Fire" by Tyler Childers. He sat back, sipped some Old Forester and recalled the memories from his youth.

****

Amy feeling grumpy, she was on a call to her mother and Reston. He was again downplaying the virus, wondering if it really, really was a thing.

Amy finally had enough, "Reston, a friend of mine I knew from New York, Ed Corbett, someone I really liked, a wonderful person, very talented, who lived here for a bit and acted at the Louisville Repertoire Theatre, died of COVID. Have some respect!"

That shut Reston up for the moment.

April was quiet, but she really liked when her daughter stepped forward and brought the hammer down.

****

At the end of March—just over a year after the killing of Breonna Taylor, on the last day of the legislative session—the Kentucky House of Representatives passed Senate Bill 4, which limited the use of no-knock warrants across the state.

It wasn't the legislation being sponsored in Breonna's name. However, the governor brought up Breonna's family when he signed the bill and gave the pen to Breonna's mom, Tamika Palmer. The governor and Mrs. Palmer were both quite emotional.

After watching the ceremony online Alexander read the bill, "Being a lawyer I was under the impression it was already perjury if an officer is untruthful on a warrant request. The person requesting the warrant is referred to as the 'affiant,' because he has signed an affidavit. But now I guess it's for real."

Amy continued reading, "And clearly visible insignia. I thought they did that already. If you go in looking like a ninja, who wouldn't take a shot?"

Alexander mused, "The ironic thing is that the Louisville Metro Council banned no-knocks for the LMPD 9 months ago. But reading the state bill, no-knocks are back in their tool kit; with an extra sign-off from the brass in the cop shop."

Amy finished reading and looked up, "Now no-knocks can only be carried out when a court finds clear and convincing evidence that the alleged crime involved is violent and leads to destruction of evidence."

"Only when the alleged crime involved is violent. Interesting how that will play out," observed Alexander.

"And it's limited from 6am to 10pm, hopefully taking away the chaos of being startled awake in the middle of the night and just shooting."

Alexander continued reading, "And bodycams are required. It's codified. Finally."

****

Reston and April were again sitting on the back deck with the giant plexiglass partition between them.

"The governor signed the no-knock bill," April remarked, not looking up from the article in the C-J.

Reston harrumphed, "You think that'll settle down the mob?"

"Reston, darling, have you ever been raided in the middle of the night by a SWAT team?"

"Heavens, no. I'm not a criminal."

"Yes, we know you're all about law and order."

"That's right, I am."

"You consider yourself a patriot."

"Hell yes, a patriot. Damn straight! Someone has to stand up for this country."

"Reston, darling, you've traded with inside information on Dig Noble Holdings, more than once. You've made several shady real estate deals. You bash illegal aliens, yet you illegally employ them at your businesses with below minimum wages. You consistently over inflate your assets for your bankers, while crying poor to the assessors, all the while having millions stashed in trusts that you've hidden from the tax man. You've been sued numerous times for unpaid bills. You've used the services of a sex worker.

You gamble large amounts of money in underground poker games. You frequently drive under the influence and you regularly disobey the speed limits."

"But I'm not a criminal."

"Darling, I'm sure you've got more nefarious activities you're holding back."

"They can't touch me, I'm bulletproof. I've got superior lawyers."

****

It was early in the month of April and the night of the Coronation Ceremony at the Galt House Hotel for the Kentucky Derby Festival Queen and April didn't go. She still didn't feel comfortable. The five princesses all nervously waited. April watched on her tablet. The Fillies president spun the wheel and a queen was chosen.

April toasted her from SHS and then gazed at a picture of herself as a young woman on the Royal Court of the Kentucky Derby Festival with four other women. Only the most civic-minded and academically achieving college students were chosen to be representatives for their community. These young women were elites.

April flashed back to that memory chiseled in her mind: *It was 30 years ago during the Fillies Derby Ball when they spun the wheel. April recalled how much she wanted it. But Sherri's name was selected and she was the Derby Queen. April applauded with a smile and a broken heart.*

****

Granddad and Mrs. Simmons were in their protective zone. Amy had walked the dogs. She joined Alexander.

"Daddy, what is your favorite part of the festival leading up to the Derby?"

Alexander straightened up in his seat, "You're asking me to choose? That's like telling me to pick my most favorite child."

"I was under the assumption that you only had one of those, unless you want to tell me something."

"Nothing to reveal and you're my favorite, by the way."

"Very reassuring."

"I would answer your inquiry with The Great Steamboat Race."

"I thought so."

"And you, my daughter? Your preference?"

"The Great Balloon Race."

"Right, you've always been fascinated by them."

"I have."

"I vote for Thunder Over Louisville," said Granddad.

"I agree with him," said Mrs. Simmons.

Alexander inquired, "What are some of your fondest memories of the Derby, Mrs. Simmons?"

"It was years ago when the cars cruised in West Louisville."

"We saw some of those machines," said Granddad. "There were some beauts."

"I remember that, Daddy," said Alexander. "You took me to see them."

Mrs. Simmons harkened back, "Everyone drove by real slow on Walnut Street. Later it shifted to Broadway. Calling out to each other. A reunion. You'd hear music, smell food cooking in the air. It was a celebration. It was called the Black Derby. Family and friends came back home and got caught up. Everyone from the neighborhood sat out front. We were a community. The motorcycle club, the Screaming Eagles would have a block party and it was such fun. It brought a lot of visitors and money into the neighborhood."

"They don't do that anymore on the west side, do they," said Amy.

"No. There was some violence—a shooting in 2005, someone was killed. The city shut it down. It left a bad taste with a lot of the local business owners with the loss of revenue and for the residents, it was a loss of joy. It created a disconnect in the area and a loss of enthusiasm for the Derby in general."

"I predict that cruising will come back," stated Alexander. "There will be a couple of hip and savvy sponsors, an official contest on coolest ride, funniest ride, with celebrity judges, with really good security and this will flourish again on the west side of Louisville celebrating the Derby and the neighborhood."

Mrs. Simmons stared at him and then smiled, "This is why I love working with you."

Alexander used his authoritative tone, "And we will get through this pandemic."

Granddad, Mrs. Simmons and Amy stopped wavering and believed.

****

The four of them bicycled to the banks of the Ohio River to watch the steamboats race. The weather was inclement that morning, but the rain held off as the race was run. Alexander was on his feet cheering the Belle of Louisville to victory from the land.

Thunder Over Louisville was not being held at the Waterfront, instead they would have 'three or five' secret locations where they would set off fireworks. The producers of the show suggested everyone watch it on TV or online or why not on your phone.

The airshow was trimmed to about two hours. A gigantic C-17 lumbered by in the sky and there were some aerobatics that impressed and several commercial carriers flew by. At nightfall there was a swarm of colorful choreographed drones putting on a delightful show and previewing what WWIII could resemble.

The fireworks were thrilling, as usual. Thunder always brought the thunder. The music pumping out over these images was positive and hopeful.

Granddad loved hearing Ray Charles sing "America the Beautiful."

Amy appreciated Katy Perry's "Not the End of the World."

Mrs. Simmons enjoyed hearing Celine Dion & Andrea Bocelli sing "The Prayer," and Kygo and Whitney Houston sing "Higher Love."

Alexander savored "Here Comes the Sun" sung by the Beatles.

And they all relished Tim McGraw and Tyler Hubbard's "Undivided." It was a fantastic song that was so needed and welcomed. It spoke a message of love and acceptance and rejected bullying and hate in this world.

****

The Kentucky Oaks was not at full capacity. As was the custom, everyone who attended wore pink in some fashion. It was a way of highlighting the effort to fight breast and ovarian cancer. And normally, April would be there supporting her friends, survivors, who paraded at the historic racetrack. But there was no parade. It would be a virtual format. April was at SHS, wearing pink.

The Oaks was run and it was a close race, but the favorite won, Malathaat.

****

The Kentucky Derby was run the next day. There was the pomp and circumstance, but again, attendance was limited. Reserved seats were only about 50% capacity and the infield was limited to 30%. April was at home wearing her new hat.

Chip was with Reston at his place. They both had been drinking since early in the day. Reston called in his bet.

Alexander, Amy, Mrs. Simmons and Granddad were watching out back of CA on a giant screen.

"My Old Kentucky Home" was played. Alexander always got a little choked up when he heard it.

The horses were loaded into the starting gate and off they went. Medina Spirit at 12-1 crossed the finish line first, which was a bit of a surprise. The bigger surprise was the next day when it was announced that Medina Spirit had tested positive for a banned drug.

Already mentally drained, April was devastated by this. Alexander was angry.

The famous trainer of Medina Spirit was indignant. In his career it was his 29th horse that failed a drug test, the 5th horse in the last 13 months; but there always was an excuse, yet the violations seemed to be increasing. The legend denied everything. He waved it all away claiming he was a victim of Cancel Culture.

When April heard this, she was furious.

Reston agreed with the trainer and thought they were all jealous and coming for him.

"Churchill Downs is woke?" Alexander was now laughing, nearly uncontrollably, "What's he smoking?? You know, it used to be religion, now Cancel Culture is the last refuge of a scoundrel!"

Reston continued to believe the famous trainer and thought he was a great guy who was being treated unfairly and he really liked his hair.

And then after the Derby binge, Reston sobered up and checked his ticket and realized he made a mistake. In his inebriated state, instead of betting on Hot Rod Charlie at 8-1, he bet a grand on Mandaloun to win. "With the disqualification…" Reston, in his joyous moment, did a little jig, "I won! I won! A thousand dollars at 26-1 to win! Ha-ha!"

And then Reston learned, nothing like this had happened since 1968 when Dancer's Image was disqualified for failing the post-race test and Forward Pass was declared the winner, officially, but not with the bettors.

Although Mandaloun was credited with the win and the owners of that horse would be getting the $1.8 million, it didn't affect the payout for the betters on the horse to win—they got bupkis.

Reston's opinion of the famous horse trainer, which he desperately wanted to have beers with for years, did a breakneck 180-degree reverse. He was so hot under the collar that he wanted the guy kicked out of racing, and he didn't like his hair anymore. Reston seriously considered joining a class action lawsuit that accused the trainer of violations of the federal Racketeer Influenced and Corrupt Organizations act—RICO—which was created to go after the most sophisticated and ongoing criminal organizations: meaning the mafia and drug cartels. The goal was to get the trainer to compensate the bettors that would have won, but—as the brief noted—for the 'illegal drug-induced win by Medina Spirit.'

****

Alexander was reading on his tablet. He recited some of the explanations put forth over the years: "A bagel containing poppy seeds may have been placed in the trainer's barn, causing a failure. An employee wearing a Salonpas pain relief patch on his back may have transferred lidocaine from the patch to the horses when the employee applied their tongue ties, causing a failure. A person in the barn on cough syrup took a whiz on some hay in a horse stall and then the horse ate the hay, causing a failure."

Amy was astonished.

In her refuge, Silver Horse Sanctuary, April was down. She didn't talk to anyone for three days after the race, she was that wounded. Considering the state of the world and now what this did to the Derby, made her horribly depressed.

April would only go out to be with her animals. She wasn't interested in talking to people at the moment. It was like her horses knew and understood the heartache, pain and disappointment hanging over the world and eating away in her. They would nicker and nuzzle April, attempting to sooth her and it would work.

April felt better the next day. The sun was shining and life was continuing. It was the first day of June. She saw her friends galloping about in the meadows, smiled and got a fresh perspective on things.

April had her coffee and oatmeal and opened the C-J. The Delta variant, which replicated quicker and generated more virus particles than other variants, had become the dominant variant in the U.S., kicking off a third wave of infections and death for the summer of 2021.

April slumped, let out a deep sigh that slowly transitioned and crescendoed to a shriek!

33

It was still dark. The clock turned to 6am. Alexander was already awake, he flipped off the alarm after the first two beeps. He gulped some water and ate a banana; then opened the little fridge in his room, pulled out a premixed breakfast shake and chugged it down.

Alexander brushed his teeth and splashed some water on his face. He grabbed his pack and quietly slid the door open to the outside and squinted up to the sky.

Amy was dressed, ready for work and reading the C-J newspaper on her tablet, while lounging on a chair in the garden. "An early summer's day in northern Kentucky, you can't beat it. Eh, Daddy?"

Alexander frowned and turned his gaze back down to earth. "Why don't you go back inside and write a poem about it."

"I'll write it in my mind, while I'm working with you this morning."

"You're really serious about this? I mean, seriously."

"I am and you don't have to skulk about any more, Daddy. I've walked the dogs and I'm tagging along."

They were the first to arrive at the work site. The frame of the house had been put up. They put on their masks and exited the car.

Alexander unlocked the door of the small trailer on the side of the property. He entered, sat at a desk and pulled out two bottles of water. He gave Amy one and read some paperwork.

Amy watched, "Can I do anything?"

"Sit." He pointed to a chair. "These are permits and inspections that were done. And paperwork that needs to be filed for stuff that will be inspected in the future as well as two mortgage applications. You can do some document review, if you want."

"I could do that. I just thought we'd be swinging a hammer."

"We will. The local ordinance allows construction noise between 7:00am and 9pm. But we're just being courteous. We wait until at least 8 or a bit later."

"And these people are volunteers," remembered Amy.

"Yes and it's customary that one volunteers from 8:30 to 3:30 for a service day. I've worked it out that from 7am to 8:30am I do legal work for them and answer questions. From 8:30 to 11:30 I'm swinging a hammer."

"And you're back home and rolling into the kitchen by noon, when it looks like you slept in."

****

At 8:30am there were half a dozen workers, all masked up. One of the topics of conversation was going over 600,000 deaths. It was now beyond surreal. Alexander introduced Amy to Patricia, the owner of this new house.

There were those that were very experienced in construction and they guided the ones with less knowledge, and soon new skills were learned.

Just before 9am a black SUV pulled up to the site and the back window rolled down.

Amy noticed and waved. Sherri waved back.

Amy then walked over to Alexander, "Daddy."

Alexander stopped drilling screws into the frame and took off his headphones, "Yeah?"

Amy pointed to the street.

Alexander walked up to the vehicle with a pleasant smile. "Good morning."

Sherri was quite serious, "Counsel, I just wanted to let you know how I admire a man who knows how to use tools."

Alexander controlled his growing smile and finally revved the drill.

"And I like the Antithetical Owl too."

"Hoo-Hoo and have a nice day, Your Honor."

"You too, Alexander." The window went up and the SUV drove off to the federal court building.

Alexander walked past Amy, "I wonder how she knew where I was."

"I forgot to tell you, Daddy. We're besties. We chat about fashion, food and federal 'man dates'."

"Ugg." Alexander cringed at the pun and went back to work.

About 10:30 Amy took a break, but Alexander continued working. He pounded nails and drilled in screws on the frame for three and a half hours straight at a good pace. Amy helped unload supplies and clear debris. She was impressed seeing her dad teaching others construction concepts and techniques.

And then Amy had the chance to pound some nails; she got better over time. It really sunk into Amy that they were creating a living space for someone.

At 11:45 a lunch wagon came and Alexander paid for all of their lunches. And then Sean rode his bike past the construction site. "Watch out! Don't get sick!

"Sean, again..." Alexander bolted after him.

"Daddy, stop!" Amy shook her head.

Sean was surprised at first and then amused as he easily peddled away.

Alexander came back completely out of breath. He got in the passenger's seat and they drove off.

"Daddy, it's the question I asked myself. What would you have done if you had actually caught him?"

"That...boy...is a menace. I would have..."

"What? You're like the dog chasing the car."

Alexander finally caught his breath and settled back down. But he had a steely gaze, "I will do something. He's not going to get away with this."

"Just let it go." They drove some. "I hope you don't mind I told Sherri where we were."

"No. Not really."

They drove some more and Amy reflected on the experience, "Daddy, Patricia, the recipient of this home, told me this would be the first time their family of three, her young daughter and son, had a home."

"Yes. Patricia had volunteered on a dozen earlier construction projects—and now it's her turn. She also works two jobs to put food on the table and a roof over their heads. She was always stressing about the rent. But now her payments are cut in half and she's building equity. It makes all the difference. Patricia and her family are getting a piece of the American dream and you are part of that too, Ambrosia."

Amy was fatigued from the work, but this gave her a jolt. She really felt a connection.

****

Alexander and Amy entered their side of the common area. Granddad was working in his studio. He had a green smoothie and gave orders not to be disturbed. Mrs. Simmons was updating files.

Alexander bought takeout from 610 Magnolia and had it delivered. The LEE Initiative, created to bring diversity and equality to the restaurant world, had transitioned during the pandemic to not only feeding food-insecure people that had the rug pulled out from under them, but to help fund kitchens to hire back workers to create these meals. The LEE Initiative bought from small farms, keeping them afloat as well and donated the food to the struggling restaurants. They then purchased thousands of meals every week from these establishments and handed them out.

Alexander and Amy were in back of CA and munching on chicken wraps, with a large salad.

Alexander chewed the green spinach leaves in his mouth, "See, I'm being good, eating healthy."

"Good for you. We want to keep you around for a while longer."

"I haven't caused enough trouble yet..."

"Daddy, I don't see you studying for your riverboat pilot's license anymore."

He grunted dismissively.

"Are you no longer interested in it?"

Alexander gave it some thought, "When I was a kid, I really was interested in piloting a steamboat, like Mark Twain. Being a riverboat captain was full of adventure. But the boats on the Ohio and Mississippi are computerized and the Army Corp of Engineers have smoothed things out."

"I see, less danger, less adrenaline, less appeal."

"No, darlin', less romance, less adventure."

"Society does that, you know, Daddy, tries to smooth things out. Like paving the roads, keeping highwaymen at bay when you go to the store. And now even delivering food to your doorstep."

Alexander mulled that over as he took another bite of his wrap.

Amy continued, "And in the early days of commercial aviation, some families when they traveled, flew separately, in case they crashed, so the entire lineage wouldn't be wiped out."

"I fully support refinement, safety measures, modernization, and especially takeout delivered, saving me that chore, but has the process taken away all of the thrills?"

Amy didn't know how to respond to that.

****

The next day Amy was having lunch on the back deck at Silver Horse Sanctuary.

April chewed her Cobb salad and stared through the plexiglass. "What was it like to work construction?"

Amy stopped chewing her tuna salad sandwich, "How did you know about that?"

"I just heard about it and I also heard Sherri stopped by your work site."

"Mother, do you have drones that just follow us?"

"People talk. I just wonder how she knew where and when to roll by."

"I told her when and where daddy was."

April was a bit irked, "Really?"

"Mother, he's a single man."

"You had to let the Queen of the Royal Court know where she could find him."

"The Queen of the Royal Court? You mean The Kentucky Derby Queen? Mother, they spin the wheel to choose the queen. Don't tell me you're still perturbed. How many decades ago was that?"

"Careful."

Amy groaned in frustration.

April griped, "*She's* a judge, a federal judge. Jeepers, I could tell you some pretty questionable things she did in her day."

"Gee, Mother, if she's picked for the Supreme Court, you can have all those stories ready in your hip pocket."

April was quite disturbed by that notion, "Have you heard something?? Is she on the short list?"

"No, Mother. I haven't heard anything. Calm yourself."

April fanned herself, "Oh fiddle. Just the thought is making my blood pressure rise."

"Why are you having such a hissy fit about Daddy and the judge seeing each other?"

April sighed and shook her head, "I guess…I don't really care."

"Good. I think he may be a little lonely."

"Your daddy is too busy saving the world to be lonely."

****

It was later that afternoon when Alexander got a call. Judge Wilbur Winslow had been infected with the coronavirus. Willodean got the shot, but the judge hesitated. He was admitted to the hospital and passed away.

Alexander and Amy drove by the house and it was overflowing with people. They decided not to go in. They sent flowers with a nice message.

The funeral was four days later.

People were streaming into the church, all wearing mourning attire and masks. Granddad stayed home, but Mrs. Simmons was determined to honor the old judge. They were let out of their ride, entered the church and observed the crowd.

"I'm glad to see such a turnout," said Alexander.

Mrs. Simmons nodded, "The Judge would have liked it, but wouldn't have admitted it."

Amy glanced around for Bobby, but didn't see him.

An usher came up to them, "I can seat you. But Mr. Arrington, I have a request for your presence."

Alexander was a bit irked, "Great, right before the service is starting. Tell whoever sent you it'll have to wait until after the—"

"It's from the widow of the Judge, Mrs. Winslow."

Alexander froze, then nodded and followed the gentleman to the door of a side room.

Alexander entered, "Willodean."

She was happy to see him, "Alexander."

He smiled at her, "How are you doing?"

"I'm holding up. The Judge would be disappointed if I didn't act the part."

"Is there anything I can do?"

"I would like for you to say a few words."

"I don't have anything prepared."

"The Judge and I always agreed. Alexander, there is no person we ever met who possessed a better gift of the gab than you."

Ten minutes later Alexander joined Amy and Mrs. Simmons near the front. He surveyed the room and it was packed.

Amy could see he was thinking about something, "Daddy, are you okay?"

Alexander broke from his mental prep and gave a nod.

Willodean was seated and the ceremony began. Alexander was soon signaled that it was his turn. He stood, buttoned his suit jacket and moved forward.

Amy and Mrs. Simmons were surprised.

Bobby slipped into the back of the church. He actually preferred wearing a mask as it sort of shielded his identity, but not really. They made room for him. He glanced around the front and spotted Amy and then he saw Alexander make his way to the lectern.

Alexander gathered his thoughts as he surveyed the gathering, "The Judge and I go back a few years. We had a three-sided relationship. We went to rival high schools. Manual and Male. We were a few years apart, but we had an instant bond of competition whenever they faced off. That was one side of our relationship. Another side was that we encountered each other in our chosen professions, the law."

Alexander noticed Sherri in attendance, masked, off in a corner.

"Pleading before Judge Winslow for more than a few years I found him to be more than fair. He was a learned and strict jurist who greatly respected the law. When he saw injustice, he wasn't afraid of making a controversial ruling. He was disciplined. Not an entertainer. He had a strong moral compass. And Judge Winslow made sure that others acted accordingly in the profession and he had the power to get what he wanted. There was a case I was recently handling where we didn't have enough evidence and needed more time and more resources, and I colored a little bit outside the lines to get more time."

The group assembled let out a chuckle.

"And it worked. The evidence emerged and I got the help, from my daughter, Amy, and my client won. But the Judge, correctly, wanted to punish me for twisting the rules. I mean, I would have sanctioned myself if I was the Judge, so he held me in contempt and I was detained. Actually, I was thrown in the slammer."

Alexander took a gulp from some bottled water as the gathered laughed heartily.

"Being held for contempt can be for some time. Depends on how contemptible the contempt is and the anger of the judge. What Judge Winslow required was that I record an apology and hand over my season tickets to him at Yum Arena for the University of Louisville Men's Basketball team. That was my penalty."

The group was surprised. Willodean was seen nodding around at that. There were some murmurs and muttering as the folks weren't quite sure how to process this. Amy was concerned and Sherri thought this was very interesting.

"If I may, a little backstory. When Yum Arena first opened in 2010, I used a geek I know to get me to the front of the line online and I bought the two seats right behind the home bench. Which leads me to the third side of my relationship with the Judge. I have had the honor and pleasure to be invited to their house and sample Willodean's marvelous cooking. It was during this time we would argue high school basketball, but come together over our love of college basketball. We both graduated from the University of Louisville and Brandeis School of Law, which means we are part of the close-nit Cardinal family. Many of you here are familiar with that tight bond as well."

Alexander glanced at Sherri and Amy noticed.

"When I was growing up and attending games in Freedom Hall, I dreamed about being in those seats right behind the home bench. I imagined hearing the strategy and advice being barked out by Denny Crum to the players. I idolized that man. I've had a good run in the legal profession so far. But I often wonder how my life would have been if I devoted myself to my first love of basketball. I only recently learned that the Judge's father gave them those two tickets for a wedding present in 1965. They had experienced Coach Peck Hickman, Coach John Dromo, as well as Coach Denny Crum at Freedom Hall. And after the year 2010, I took control of those seats when the new arena opened up. He never said a word about it over the years and I never gave it a second thought. I was wrong to jump the line and I willingly gave back those tickets they previously had for 45 seasons. But to my surprise and delight, Willodean just gave me the seats back. She said it was what the Judge wanted." Alexander was overcome with emotion, "That's just the kind of people Willodean is and the Judge was. I really miss him already. He was one who didn't stay on the sidelines. Wilbur Winslow got in the game and made a difference." Alexander put his mask back on and joined the others. There was hardly a dry eye in the church.

Willodean patted him on the back and Alexander nodded at her with affection.

Bobby was greatly affected as well, he slipped out the side entrance.

People exited the church and milled around the front. They thanked Alexander for his remarks.

A well-dressed and well-groomed Black gentleman in his mid-50's walked up, "Alexander, that really was an excellent talk."

"Thank you, sir. I apologize, have we had the pleasure of being introduced?"

"No," said the gentleman, who then turned to Mrs. Simmons. "But I do know Rose."

Mrs. Simmons, who was staring off in another direction, turned around and was shocked, "Ezekiel?"

Zeke nodded, "Yes."

"After all these years. What are you doing here?"

"I came back for the funeral."

"For the man that put you away," said Mrs. Simmons, her voice rising with emotion. "Why are you talking to me all of a sudden, after all of this time?"

Zeke was woeful, "Rose, I've thought about this moment over and over. This isn't how I planned it."

Mrs. Simmons was brusque, "I haven't thought about this moment at all. I will thank you to please stay away from me, sir."

Alexander was surprised by her anger.

****

They were in the car being driven back to CA. It was quiet.

Mrs. Simmons looked around and felt the awkwardness. They rode some more.

"I'll be the one to ask," said Alexander. "Is he one of your old boyfriends?"

"Yes. Ezekiel Williams. Zeke's nickname used to be, 'Billy Zee,' after Billy Dee Williams. Zeke was that handsome."

"He's still rather attractive," said Amy.

"And Zeke thought he was smarter than everyone. He was dealing weed. I told him he'd have to choose, dealing or me. He said he gave it up, but it was a lie. He got busted and sent away."

They were all quiet after that.

After several more moments, Alexander made conversation. "What'd you think of my eulogy?"

"You nailed it, Daddy."

"Thanks."

"I thought it was very nice," said Mrs. Simmons.

"But?"

Mrs. Simmons assured him, "No buts."

"But..." insisted Alexander.

"Daddy, you did cause quite a stir revealing how the Judge bullied you from his bench over those tickets. That was highly improper. There's going to be some tongues wagging over this. People are going to remember."

"Let the tongues wag and they better remember," Alexander announced. "That's the reason Willodean wanted to talk to me. She gave me those tickets back and said it was okay to tell that story, with a twinkle in her eye—which meant *he wanted it* to be told."

"Really, Daddy?"

"Sure, Judge Wilbur Winslow is now legendary in Cardinal lore. He won't be forgotten. What he always dreamed about."

Mrs. Simmons, Amy and Alexander were pleased and had a laugh.

****

July 4, 2021. Waterfront Park was once again opened to celebrate the country's founding. People had been waiting over a year for this. Some thought it was reckless to have this gathering, but others were relieved. People were weary of the pandemic. And most were vaccinated, so why not?

Teddy Abrams conducted a performance of the Louisville Orchestra. At 10pm a spectacular display of fireworks was unleashed.

Alexander, though he really wanted to be there, was in the back of Casa Arrington, along with Amy, keeping Granddad and Mrs. Simmons company. They all waved American flags and watched fireworks in the distance lighting up the sky.

Mrs. Simmons turned to Alexander and whispered, "You know, I'm kind of pleased Granddad and Old Man Miller don't compete on best fireworks display."

Alexander nodded slowly to that and put his index finger to his lips to make sure she didn't pass that idea on, as they observed Granddad cheering on the distant pyrotechnics.

****

The next day Granddad was in the front yard checking on the various plants, but he was really seeing if there was any life across the street at Old Man Miller's place.

Amy joined him, "Have you tried to contact Mr. Miller?"

"No."

Amy glanced across the way, "Life has shut down for a year and a half, while ending for some."

"I read the obits every day hoping I don't see that old goat as a casualty," mumbled Granddad. "Someone walks his dog. His mail is being picked up and people are delivering food to his house. The door opens up and it's pulled inside."

Amy walked across the street, knocked on his door and stepped back. He ignored her. She knocked again, with still no response.

"Hello, Mr. Miller. It's Amy Arrington. I'm just calling on you to see if you're okay and if you need anything."

After several moments she heard his voice, "I'm fine."

"I can go to the store for you or the pharmacy."

"All of that is delivered."

"If you ever do need anything, call over to the house."

"I understand. Thank you."

Amy came back across the street. "He says he's okay. Not very friendly, but surviving."

Granddad nodded at that. He went into his room and picked up a framed picture on a nightstand.

The next day, Old Man Miller got his mail and received a present. Granddad sent him the framed picture. It was signed by the old coaches of the University of Kentucky, Joe B. Hall and the University of Louisville, Denny Crum. Both were smiling, arm-in-arm. Once fierce rivals they had become close friends after they retired from coaching. It was a photograph of them in the studio doing their radio show.

Old Man Miller was greatly touched by this. He sent over an archived recording of the *Joe B. and Denny Show*, where they spent most of the time talking about their favorite fishing holes and Granddad loved it.

****

There were several developments at Padmore in New York. After two senior partners got infected and passed away, they extended the work-from-home order until the first of the year. And business had picked up. Amy was now piling up the billable hours. One afternoon she took off, went downtown and stopped in Dulsett Distilleries.

They had both been so incredibly busy and wary of interacting, they had kept their distance, but she had to see him. She asked the receptionist if Bobby was available for one second.

"I'm sorry, Miss Arrington, but he's in a meeting, his schedule is booked up and won't be available until tomorrow."

Cassidy spotted her, "Amy." She waved her into her office. It was low-key, but classy, with understated style. Cassidy oversaw the marketing and frequently ran meetings concerning production, distribution and keeping the peace with labor.

"Bobby's in a meeting?" asked Amy. "I just wanted to say hi. I know it's the middle of a business day and—"

"He's coaching youth basketball at the rec center."

"He's coaching?"

"He is Bobby Dulsett."

Amy nodded, "Yes. That he is."

****

"Come on, Clay, find the open man," yelled out Bobby to the little player who responded. "That's it, good pass! Keep it going." Bobby clapped his hands in approval.

A league game was in progress. 12-year-olds were trying to play the game of basketball.

"Come on, guys, move your feet," pressed Bobby, as he prowled the coach's box.

Amy had slid into the small gathering that were watching the game. The parents were cheering and chatting amongst themselves about Bobby Dulsett coaching their kids.

The game ended. Bobby took a couple of pictures with the players and the parents.

Bobby then gathered them around him, "I'm proud of you guys. This victory was a team effort. I'm pleased and you should be too. You're picking up the concepts I'm teaching you and putting them to use. I'll see you for practice on Saturday. Ready, 1-2-3 Team!" They all yelled it together.

And then he noticed Amy in the stands and wandered over.

"Hey, Coach. That was some pretty good coaching there."

"It's been a while. These are the first games back after the shutdown."

"You never told me you do this."

"It's just a hobby."

"You looked like you were really into it."

"I guess I know a little about the game."

"My dad has a theory. He says superstars don't make good coaches. Because they don't understand what the small cogs have to endure."

Bobby considered that, "What if the good player has faced adversity and was relegated to small cog status."

"A really good player like that would have valuable insight into the game. And by the way, that call you were arguing really was a charge on your player."

"I know that, I was just working the ref."

Amy projected faux righteous indignation at that, "Excuse me?"

"It's like a lawyer objecting to something they know is correct."

Amy was stopped in her tracks and gave a nod, "Touché."

****

On Thursday August 5, Alexander got up and stretched, he felt pretty good. He then got a phone call. Jefferson County Deputy Brendan Shirley, who was off-duty and working as a security guard, was killed overnight in Shively, Kentucky. Deputy Shirley had received the Medal of Valor from the department for his assistance in the fatal shooting of Tyler Gerth. This was another punch in the gut.

Alexander sat, did a search and read what a fine person Brendan Shirley was. Alexander shook his head and lamented how Shively again made national news.

****

During the dog days of August, Bobby and Amy returned to his cabin by Bernheim, twice. The second time was at the end of the month after they were both boosted. Amy and Bobby spent several days hiking and walking among the giants in the forest. They were mesmerized by nature and the large wooden sculptures that lived here.

They spent several nights playing Gin Rummy and Crazy Eights, and later in the evenings, Strip Poker—in which he had little success.

Amy would trash talk his skills after taking his remaining clothing, "Pathetic."

On the last night of the getaway for the month, Amy and Bobby were sitting together on the couch in front of the glowing fireplace, on their second bottle of Bourbon Barrel Red.

"I understand now when Cassidy told me you call this your Fortress of Solitude."

"Correct."

"You do know who also has one of these?"

"You mean my brother Kal-El?"

Amy snickered at that, "I wasn't aware Jor-El had another son."

"I was named Rob-El. But Jor-El wasn't impressed with me. I was slightly less talented than my older brother, Kal-El."

"You are so modest."

"It's my nature. I mean… I couldn't lead my high school basketball team to the state title in three tries."

Amy saw that it still nagged him after all this time. A part of him was trapped way back in three different state high school tournaments.

"Aww, Bobby. You are defined by so much more than that." Amy kissed him and soothed him.

The next day when they drove back, Amy had a big fat grin.

Bobby glanced over as he continued to drive, "What are you so happy about?"

"Um…"

"What?"

"After last night, I think Kal-El has some competition, Rob-El."

Bobby cleared his throat and took the praise in stride. "I did say I was only 'slightly' less talented."

They laughed and Bobby continued to drive wondering what would happen when her work-from-home order was rescinded.

34

It was Labor Day, early. Alexander was up and alone in his room still processing the fact that several days ago the University of Louisville had suspended the Cardinal head basketball coach for the first six games of the season. The coach was being punished for mishandling a termination and extortion attempt by a former assistant coach that triggered another NCAA investigation. The head coach recorded the encounter, which gave the proof to implicate the extorter. Alexander heard the secret recording that had been partly redacted. The assistant coach listed the violations in the program and wanted to be paid for another year and a couple months until he could collect social security or he would go public. The head coach then gave him his word he would make it happen, even if he had to pay him out of his "own money," because that's how much he "loved and respected him for all of his hard work." When the sentence was handed down: one year probation and a $10,000 fine, the judge added, "I remain puzzled why we are even here on a federal felony today. This is a strange felony prosecution in my observation."

It bugged Alexander as such questioning comments aimed at U.S. Attorneys from the bench weren't made that often, at least in public; but when they were, they meant something. But what really heated Alexander's sauce was the university's co-counsel, who did what was required of her being an officer of the court and alerted the authorities, would soon be gone and have to turn to the courts for redress.

Later Alexander barbecued out back for the four of them and fixated on the situation. It was so very sordid. He didn't like this feeling. Alexander felt it before, with a prior coach and his dodgy antics.

The college football season had just started. It's what he needed to divert his attention. The first game for the Louisville Football Cardinals was on the road at Mercedes-Benz Stadium in Atlanta, Georgia. They would face Ole

Miss on national TV. Labor Day Monday Night on ESPN. The NFL wouldn't be starting up until next week. Once again, the Cardinals would be showcased on the biggest stage. It was the only game being played. Lots of potential high school players would be tuning in. The entire football world would be watching. And to make it more interesting, Lane Kiffin, the Rebels' genius head coach, had tested positive for COVID-19 and didn't make the trip. Alexander pondered this and considered the Vegas line: Cardinals +9. He called his local guy, but could only get +8. He took the points and bet $500.

The offense and the defense were both outplayed. Ole Miss won 43-24. It would not be a positive on the recruiting front. Alexander grumbled. He lost, but was pleased the university shared the gate from that large arena in Atlanta and got a check from the cable broadcast.

****

TORTS and Just Desserts from the mind of Alexander Arrington

The owl appeared holding a rock:

"Basketball is a lot like a musical jam session. You only need a couple good players. They cover for the less talented. As long as the role players know how to accompany the leads, you can go far.

Football is an army. Lots of troops are needed, with lots of support. Feeding them, housing them, garbing them, training them, traveling with 70 or more bodies.

The NIL era has transformed college football significantly. The advantages schools have in bigger cities, with bigger businesses and wealthier fans is hard to overstate. It's a matter of accounting and physics. More money equals bigger, stronger, faster, more talented players and more dominant teams. These financial behemoths can stockpile prospects even more now, rather than have them competing against them. Even bigger Goliaths are coming. The only chance I see Louisville has now to compete nationally is to do what Cardinals and owls do: go up top. Nickname the coaching box Air Traffic Control. Become the premiere passing attack in the nation and start seriously flinging the rock. It's how David defeated his Goliath problem."

~ ~ ~

"I am in love with the Peach Cobbler Sundae at the Hip Hop Sweet Shop. There's other stuff I haven't gotten to so check back—soon to be delivered."

The owl faded out.

****

Alexander still wasn't that comfortable around crowds. He lent out his football season tickets.

It was the beginning of October and unseasonably warm for this time of year in Northern Kentucky. April really didn't notice as she felt dread learning the death count was now over 700,000.

Old Man Miller and Granddad had become friendlier, but they were still competitors. They again agreed to have a contest for Halloween, but it was low-key. They both had automatic candy dispensers for the few out trick-or-treating—and this time Old Man Miller was victorious.

Amy cornered Granddad and asked if he threw the fight and let Old Man Miller win. He denied everything and walked away with a smile, he was just sent a new recording of the *Joe B. and Denny Show* he had to get to.

****

Louisville Live, the Midnight Madness kicking off basketball practice for the men and women, had been moved to Churchill Downs to accommodate the popularity of the event. Alexander didn't attend.

November 9th was the tipoff of the new basketball season. Alexander was happy to get his old seats back, but used the surging COVID cases as an excuse not to go. If Alexander was honest—the real reason he wasn't attending the games was the same head coach Alexander heard on the secret recording, giving his word it would get done by offering payments out of his own pocket, to keep the latest scandal from getting out—was still running the show and Alexander had a bad taste in his mouth about it.

****

Thanksgiving was a subtle event. At CA the four of them were grateful they all had made it through so far. They donated to several organizations that fed those who were food insecure.

Alexander and Amy felt insecure themselves. They had been tested, but were negative. They continued to isolate together, away from Granddad and Mrs. Simmons.

The next day Amy went to SHS to spend the afternoon with her mother. They sat on the deck out back, plexiglass still in place. The heat lamps made it comfortable. They chatted about this and that and scanned the news on their tablets.

Amy saw it first and held her breath. Then April noticed the breaking news on her tablet.

The World Health Organization had classified a new variant in South Africa: Omicron. It was concerning as there were several mutations in the spike protein.

April's eyes widened and she let out a groan. After she settled down, Amy tried to talk her mother into not reading so much news.

****

Amy was thankful WHO waited until the day after Thanksgiving to make an announcement of the new variant. Black Friday. It was doubtful many noticed, as the hordes were fighting for the ultra-low deals. But this convinced April to cancel her travel plans once again for the holidays. The Kentucky Seedlings Ceremony was again virtual, like most everything in life. Remote. Clunky.

And on Saturday, to finish out the month of November, the Cards, a slight favorite, lost 52-21 to Kentucky in football. Alexander just shook his head.

And then on December 6, 2021, Medina Spirit, the disgraced Kentucky Derby winner disqualified for testing positive for illegal drugs, died while training in California.

April went into a tailspin. She didn't speak to anyone for two days. She read that he had a heart attack. Her heart ached for these animals and what they endured. She had pushed for something like HISA, the Horse Integrity and Safety Act, to bring some uniformity, better regulations and more safety to the sport. It was supposed to begin next year.

****

Alexander and Amy both had finished and put down their tablets.

"So that is the Horseracing Integrity and Safety Act," Alexander drawled.

"It's coming in July," said Amy.

Alexander predicted, "HISA may be pushed out a little farther as it's causing a dust up for some."

"It's a big overhaul," said Amy.

Alexander nodded, "The problem has always been horse racing is the only sport that doesn't have national uniform regulations. It's controlled by 38 jurisdictions, all with different rules. Trainers know how to run drugs through and clear the system by race day. Your mother has been pushing for reform like this for years."

"I'm having lunch with her today. Outside."

"Rather significant changes are coming in the horse racing industry. She must be at least pleased with that."

****

Amy was sitting with her mother separated by the plexiglass on the back deck of the house. Heat lamps surrounded them.

"I'm glad to see you, Mom. How are you doing?"

April forced a grin, "I'm hanging in there. Still thinking about Medina Spirit."

"Yes, that was tragic."

"Did you look into what I asked?"

"I did. I checked the details of HISA and there's some sharp teeth in the act. Evasion, tampering, administration of a primary substance, trafficking, complicity and retaliation can draw a sanction of up to two years. Failure to cooperate and administration of a secondary substance would be punished by a suspension of up to 30 days and a fine. Third violation of the anti-doping or safety protocols is a lifetime ban. It sets uniform standards in two areas to protect the horses and the jockeys. Lasix is prohibited on race day in all 2-year-olds and stakes races."

"Okay."

"Anabolic steroids and erythropoietin, which, as you know, increases red blood cells and boosts aerobic capacity, will be banned at all times."

"What about during training?"

"It will be against the rules to be out of reach for a snap test."

"I like that," said April. "Tell me the oversight being created."

"Two bodies. One called the Anti-Doping and Medication Control Standing Committee. They'll provide advice and guidance to the Board on the development and maintenance of the horse racing anti-doping medication control program. The other is the Race Track Safety Standing Committee. Which will provide advice and guidance to the Board on the development and maintenance of the racetrack safety program."

"How many on the committee?"

"Seven on each. On the Anti-Doping and Medication Control Standing Committee, the majority selected for each will be independent members from outside the equine industry. But they need to have significant, recent experience in anti-doping and medication rules. With the Race Track Safety Standing Committee, the majority will also be outside independent members, but the language is less specific on the qualifications."

April nodded at that, "Then it's the Race Track Safety Standing Committee for me."

"The nominating process is—"

April shushed her, "I'll take it from here."

****

Granddad and Old Man Miller met out front of CA.

"Artie, I don't like it. The sun has been down for nearly two hours. It's approaching 8pm and the temperature is still rising."

"And after today, it's mid-December and it was at least 15 degrees warmer than normal. I have that bad feeling too. You have your storm cellar stocked, Mel? You can come over here if you need."

"I'm good, Artie. Thanks. I'm going to go back in and monitor the weather. Stay safe."

"I will. You too, buddy."

They gave each other a look of support and retreated to their domiciles.

Granddad stopped and looked off into the southwestern sky. There were severe storm warnings put out for later that night. The air was unsettled, the wind began to swirl about and it made his skin crawl.

Tornado warnings were soon issued for the Southwest of the commonwealth, as multiple twisters were active over five states.

Alexander and Amy were monitoring events online and on the local TV stations. Supercells were lining up one after another in Arkansas and diverging into two directions. The northern path was leading into southern Missouri and Illinois, while the southern track, with much more energy, was traveling into western Tennessee and southwestern Kentucky. Louisville was advised it was in the danger zone.

At around 10:30pm they heard reports of damage to the town of Mayfield. At 11pm substantial gusts of rain began to fall. Louisville was issued a tornado warning and the residents braced themselves.

Alexander and Amy were herding and collecting animals and heading down. He told Mrs. Simmons and Granddad to get below.

Granddad didn't let on, but he was worried about Old Man Miller.

Alexander called Sherri and she was safe in her storm cellar. And he assured her he was fine. He then called April and she told him not to worry, she was safe and wished him well and hung up.

Alexander thought that was a bit abrupt, but knew her moods.

At the moment, April wasn't in her luxurious nuclear bunker, but in the stables with her horses. She was keeping them calm, even after the tornado warning. The animals knew a significant storm was coming. Gus saw April doing this. He helped and refused her order to go below, later justifying his actions by reminding her how iffy his hearing was.

Reston had a very good bunker. It was deep underground, with reinforced concrete and it was well-stocked. Chip was with him. They cooked a pizza, guzzled brew and played 6D.

At CA the wind continued to whip around. The many different animals taken below were remarkably well behaved, except Cantankerous Cat. The relentless band of storms and twisters kept inching towards the city. They waited and held their breath as the winds swirled harder and the rain continued to pour down. The intensity grew. The heavy winds gusted and buffeted the structure and hail was now battering the roof. And then it finally started to taper off. At 1:29am, the tornado warning for Louisville was lifted. There was a huge sigh of relief. They were able to get some sleep.

Early the next morning Alexander was watching the TV showing drone footage of the town of Mayfield, Kentucky. It was beyond shocking.

"Oh...my...God..." He pulled himself together and pulled out his phone and began sending texts.

Amy soon came out carrying her skateboard, "Morning, Daddy." She caught sight of the overhead video showing a town of 10,000 nearly completely flattened.

"Where's that?" asked Amy, flabbergasted.

"Mayfield, Kentucky."

"Do you know anyone there?"

"No. But I know they need help." Alexander continued to organize. He borrowed transportation. An RV pulled up with a trailer attached. Alexander and Amy loaded three chainsaws and several dozen blankets. Multiple trucks were delivering water, canned food and propane that was being transferred to the trailer.

Old Man Miller came out and saw the commotion. "What's going on?"

Amy smiled at him, "Hi, Mr. Miller. We're going to Mayfield."

"The tornado."

"Yes."

"I saw how bad it was." Mr. Miller turned around and went back inside.

Amy went back to loading the trailer.

Mr. Miller returned pulling a cart, "Amy?"

"Yes, Mr. Miller?"

"I have some canned food and some other stuff and I would like to donate money, but I don't know where."

"Perhaps the Red Cross."

"I wouldn't know where to go."

"Do a search online."

"I trust you, Amy. Here, please put it to good use."

Amy looked in the envelope and counted the money. "It's a thousand dollars."

"Please use it to help the recovery."

"I will. This is all very generous, Mr. Miller. How are *you* doing?"

"I'm fine, a few aches and pains. I haven't got sick. I heard about the judge."

"That was sad. I hope you're being careful. I'm glad you and my Granddad are on better terms."

"So am I. You take care down there, Amy."

"I will."

Mr. Miller waved and went back inside.

Gabriel arrived by Uber, "I'm here to help. If you're going there, so am I." He immediately assisted loading the trailer with supplies.

Alexander's phone buzzed. "Hello."

"Alexander."

Alexander paused, "April. Hi."

"Are you going down there?"

"Yeah."

"I figured that. Is Amy going too?"

"Yes."

"Watch out for her."

"Ambrosia lives in New York."

"She's not like you, Alexander, she hasn't been to any disaster zones."

"She'll be fine, April. Deep down, she can handle the pressure. She's just like her mother."

"Be careful. Text me the best place to make a donation and where you need supplies sent."

"I will. We'll talk soon." He hung up and immediately got another call. "Hello?"

"Alexander, are you going to help?" Bobby was watching the news.

"Bobby. Yes. I am, with Amy. We're leaving in about 90 minutes. I'm waiting for some more supplies." Alexander noticed Sherri exiting the back of a sedan. "Bobby, I've gotta go. We'll talk soon."

Sherri, in boots, jeans and a sweatshirt, strode up to Alexander. Her face was full of concern. "Alexander, are you going down to Mayfield?"

"Yes."

"How can I help?"

Alexander picked up a backpack. "Here's a bag full of satellite phones, you could double check they're fully charged and pass them out."

"Will do."

Bobby was in his garage loading stuff into his truck. His phone rang, he checked it. "Yes, Cass?"

"Bobby, have you seen the damage?"

"It's awful. I'm packing up now."

"What for?"

"I'm going down to Mayfield with Alexander and Amy to help."

"How long will you be gone?"

"Several days. You'll have to cover for me."

****

Bobby's vehicle was stuffed. He had 10 cases of water, a dozen blankets, two cases of canned mackerel, 10 large bags of pasta, a giant bag of AA and AAA batteries, 50 cases of protein bars, along with two tents packed in the bed of his truck. He pulled up in front of Casa Arrington as Alexander and Amy were loading the solar generators into the RV.

"I hope you're not leaving without me."

"Bobby? What are you doing here?" asked Alexander.

"I'm getting in the game."

Alexander and Amy gave each other a nod at this and to Bobby.

Finally, everything was loaded up. Sherri got in the RV with Alexander.

"Wait, Sherri, you're going with us?"

"Do you have room?"

"Yes, but—"

"Alexander, I have an uncle that farms right outside of Mayfield. I can't get in contact with him."

"We won't be back for a while."

"I've had my clerks trail all of the courts business for a day, two if necessary."

"Must be nice to just snap your fingers and things get done."

"Try being a federal judge."

"I just might."

Amy walked back to Bobby's vehicle with wide eyes and a worrisome sigh, "Alexander Arrington on the federal bench. Not sure if the world's ready for that."

Bobby's truck was so packed with supplies, in the bed and backseat, only one could ride with him up front.

Gabe inquired, "Hey, Bobby, you think I could ride with you?"

Bobby paused and didn't want to say no, but this wasn't what he had planned.

"Gabe?" asked Amy, gently.

"Right, sorry." He moped.

Amy diverted him to the RV and he trudged towards it.

Bobby called out, "Hey, Gabe?"

"Yes?"

"After things settle down, let's shoot some hoops."

"For real?"

"Seriously."

"You and me?"

"Yeah."

"Sure. Right on!" Gabe was pumped as he jumped in the RV.

Amy got in Bobby's truck and gave him the side-eye and nodded at his superpower. They were off by midday.

"You really filled up your ride with provisions."

"It's an emergency."

"Only one person could ride with you."

Bobby grinned and then suppressed it.

"It's filled with these cases of protein bars." Amy checked the wrapper, "Low in sugar. High in protein. They look pretty healthy."

"Give it a taste." He offered her one.

Amy opened it and took a bite and chewed and nodded.

"When I was playing in Lithuania, this was one of my endorsement deals. Part of the payment was in product. They still send me stuff. I've got cases and cases. All the nutrients required in that bar. It gives you natural energy. It's a meal replacement. Petra's Protein Punch."

"What a pitchman you are."

"*Labai ačiū.* That's 'thank you' in Lithuanian."

"You have led an interesting life, Bobby."

"Now I read reports and hold meetings about the quarter's ROI. You're the one with the interesting life. Living in New York, hanging out with Hollywood players in Malibu."

"With Zabéla Z? Look what happened to her."

Bobby thought back, "Who knew swallowing firm tofu could be so risky?"

"As for hanging out in Malibu, after a week I needed to get out before all of my brain melted."

"You partied that hard?"

"No, well, partied some, but I met this guy at one of Zabéla's social gatherings. He was a doctor. Dr. Trainer. He was the one that revived John Hawkwood, after he was clinically dead."

"It's amazing what modern medicine is doing."

"He made my skin tingle."

"Then you did have chemistry with him," teased Bobby.

"Not in a good way. And anyway, Lannie's deal collapsed."

"I read somewhere the project was scuttled because of John Hawkwood himself."

"That's what I heard too," said Amy. "He didn't approve and the man is a killing machine. You do know he was behind the D.C. massacre. 49 victims."

Bobby cringed at that number, "Yikes."

"And that's just one event. He's left a trail of death and destruction all through the Third World."

Bobby thought about it, "I read her article on Hawkwood. This is one of those stories that the powerful don't want discussed beyond this point."

"That's not the way Lannie operates. She'll find the financing to get it made and seen."

"And then you went to New Orleans."

"Lannie went back to her magazine and was assigned to do a profile of Raven Laveau and got into a little trouble when she got caught investigating a string of killings at the time. I went down there to represent her."

"She was cleared," said Bobby.

"Yes and then it got a bit weird, or weirder. Dr. Trainer was down there."

"He was?"

"He knows Raven."

"That is a really small world," said Bobby.

"And he was quite active there," Amy said.

Bobby didn't understand, but didn't pry, "I'm really looking forward to her New Orleans article."

"It's been held back because of the pandemic."

"That's too bad."

"The publisher wants to do an update and is going to send her back."

"That sounds intriguing," said Bobby. "New Orleans, Lannie Telfair, Amy Arrington and Raven Laveau. That is some spicy gumbo."

"I doubt Lannie could publish most of the stuff that went down."

"Too crazy?"

"Maybe."

"The voodoo princess," grinned Bobby.

"Raven's not a voodoo princess. I'm going back for next Mardi Gras—maybe you'll tag along and you can see for yourself."

"I've only been to New Orleans twice, once to play in a tournament and the other time I don't really remember."

"You will remember Raven."

"I look forward to meeting both Dr. Trainer and Raven Laveau."

"And finally, as for New York. The work-from-home order is over the first of the year."

"I heard that," said Bobby, as he squared his jaw and stared straight ahead.

"I'm not going back. At least to work. I'm going to ply my trade here. With my family and the people I care for."

"Really?"

"Yes, really. And that's between you and me. You're the first one who knows. I haven't even told my mom and dad."

"Gotcha." Bobby again worked to suppress a grin and continued to drive, with a new purpose. Amy sensed it.

They stopped in Dawson Springs. It was devastated.

Alexander gathered his troops, "Number one thing in a disaster zone, be on the lookout for any downed power lines. They can be fatal for you. And make sure there isn't any leaking gas. A spark could be fatal for a bunch of us. Watch what could fall *on* you or collapse *under* you."

They stopped at several places he knew to check on folks. They left food, water and a couple cases of Petra's Protein Punch bars. They came upon a small group.

Alexander moved to a small kid who was spooked. He pointed to a collapsed house.

"Let's check there," Alexander ordered.

They helped with what they could. Chainsaws were deployed, Bobby grabbed one and Alexander the other. They cut through the pile of splintered wood and pulled an elderly couple out.

By late that night they continued on. Alexander promised Sherri they would find her uncle. Reports from Mayfield had them in even worse shape. Alexander could see the worry in Sherri's eyes. She still couldn't reach him.

They continued southwest along the path of destruction. The tornado pretty much followed I-65 on its route. They had to move slowly as the roads were littered with refuse, shards of wood, downed power lines and the occasional former appliance. They listened to local radio stations. As expected, things were chaotic.

With the sunrise came a gloomy, overcast day. Coming up on Mayfield they were all stunned. The small town looked like it was carpet-bombed, there was near complete desolation. Trees had been completely ripped out of the ground or just sheared off. Cars had been tossed around and left cluttered on the ground, as if a child had played with them. Emergency vehicles were blaring.

Gabe was driving the RV as they headed just east of the town to Sherri's uncle's place.

"You're thinking about him," said Alexander. He held her hand and calmed her.

Sherri nodded, "Uncle Dwayne. He's lived in Mayfield for all of his life. He grew everything from asparagus to zucchini on 10 acres outside of town. I would do odd jobs on the farm during the summers and then go back to Louisville, the 'big city,' as he called it, for the school year."

"I remember. I wanted to come down here one summer with you."

"Why didn't you?"

Alexander thought back and shook his head. "I'm here now."

Sherri patted his hand.

The RV and Bobby's truck pulled onto the property. The buildings and structures lay in tatters. Sherri was horrified seeing this. She ran out of the RV and up to the pile that was her uncle's home.

"Uncle Dwayne??"

Everyone got out and looked around. Sherri was in shock.

All of a sudden, a pickup truck came roaring up the long driveway. It lurched to a stop by a pile off to the side. The driver, Dwayne Daniels, near 75 years on this earth, was bandaged up, covered in dirt and running on adrenaline. He got out and wondered who these people were.

Sherri moved to him, "Uncle Dwayne?"

"Sherri?" They hugged and they both cried.

"You're okay."

"Everything's gone. It was just blown away."

"I came with a group to help. This is Alexander Arrington, his daughter Amy, Gabe and Bobby."

"Thank you all for coming. But I can't talk. Jed Rawlings has some of his animals trapped. I came back here to get a chain out of the shed. Or, where the shed used to be. It should be on the ground somewhere."

Amy, Bobby and Gabe were searching on the ground and found the chain. They followed Uncle Dwayne next door to Jed's place and helped him free the trapped animals in the collapsed barn.

Alexander considered the situation, "If this was in the spring or fall, people's personal radar would have been on alert. As this was winter and it occurred at night, some may never have received the warning."

The search and rescue efforts centered on a candle factory that had collapsed on the outskirts of town and people were trapped in the rubble. Emergency crews were mounting a desperate effort to find them. When the storm was coming, workers that survived said they got the tornado warning, but were warned they would lose their jobs if they left.

When the tornado came through, 8 people died in the collapse of the factory. The company issued a statement that employees were allowed to leave that night and not be fired.

"Daddy, this is really bad."

"I know. I, we, are going to continue to clear the debris, hopefully finding more survivors and then concentrate on rehabbing and rebuilding their houses, while helping people fill out insurance claims and FEMA docs. I'm not handing out my business card. The coming class action is way too big for my shop. You'd need at least 10 associates, probably double that really, for the workload. It will take years. What about P3?"

Amy looked a bit disappointed, "Padmore doesn't do these lawsuits, at least from this side."

While every property was checked, Alexander's group set up camp in a vacant lot off 8th Street in town. This was once a main artery that wasn't recognizable. They gave out blankets and handed out bottled water and protein bars. The propane burners were quickly cooking vats of oatmeal and scrambled eggs. They put out various fruits, plums, bananas, apples, along with trail mix and beef jerky.

The next day Sherri hugged her uncle and thanked Bobby, Gabe and Amy for their help. Alexander walked her to her ride. They kissed and hugged. Sherri had to get back for court the next day.

"Thank you, Alexander. For this, for everything."

"My pleasure."

"How long will you be here?"

"For a little while."

"I'm coming back when I can free up some time."

They kissed again and she was driven back to Louisville.

****

The media had also set up camp and were looking for stories. Alexander didn't want to be interviewed and Bobby, wore a mask, goggles and a baseball cap hoping not to be recognized. Amy was thankful her 15 minutes had faded.

As the days passed, the shock began to wear off for the residents, but the realization of what had occurred overwhelmed some. The major long term relief efforts were now set up.

Alexander, Amy, Bobby and Gabe noticed a building that had been partially destroyed; but there was a wall that remained standing with a mural and the motto: 'Mayfield: More than a memory.'

Some residents needed to be transported to the giant Red Cross relief tent. Still others were staying in their damaged houses—even with ravaged roofs and collapsed walls. Alexander, Gabe, Bobby and Amy helped construct temporary coverings to keep the wind and rain out and offered to assist any claims, gratis.

That night after dinner, they were sitting around a fire. Alexander was next to Amy.

"Word on the street is that you've been called back to Manhattan."

"Not going back, Daddy. What would you say to adding a new partner to your shop?"

"Who could this be?"

"Me."

"Seriously?"

"I'm not going back to P3 and the Microscope."

"Sure, I'll take you on. This is great. You said as an associate?"

"Throwing the curveball early in the negotiations."

"You've lost your leverage, now that I know you're sticking around."

"Reston mentioned I had an open invitation at his firm, as a partner. They pay quite well. Significantly better than this shop."

"Welcome, Miss Arrington to Arrington and Arrington."

"Thank you. Name partner. I like the ring of that."

"Good bluff, partner."

"Thank you, Daddy. And you're still teaching me lessons this far down the road."

"You've just begun your journey."

****

Within 3 days the Mayfield-Graves County Tornado Relief Fund was founded. Alexander reviewed their setup. He approved of the people behind it and 100% of the proceeds would stay in the county. He mentioned this to April and she made a generous donation. Reston shook his head. He then called his accountant and realized he could be generous as up to half could be deductible. He was soon on board and making sure April knew of his altruism.

Mayfield was located in Graves County. There were 24 deaths and over 200 injured. 730 single family residences were destroyed and 1159 were damaged. There was a lot of cleaning up to do. For weeks Alexander, Amy, Gabe and Bobby helped clear lots of debris. Gabby and Sherri came down when they could.

Normal tornados show a path where some places were hit and some spared. The drone footage of the event revealed almost no one was spared.

Alexander had several bikes delivered. His crew rode around with baskets of food and water, looking for people that were staying in their homes. No one had power. They set up charging times for phones when they would come by with the solar charger. He then had a truck filled with solar chargers come in and he loaned them out.

****

December 15, 2021. April had made another donation to the relief efforts when she opened her newspaper and saw the COVID-19 death count in the U.S. had hit 800,000. The numbers continued to be jarring.

Alexander, Amy, and Bobby continued on in Mayfield. Gabby arrived with a trunk full of fruit and a backseat full of oatmeal and vegetables—and a friend sitting in the front seat.

Amy and Gabby hugged.

"Abby wanted to come, but..."

"I know. She's holding her own world together."

"This is Leticia, or 'Leti,' as she's known by," said Gabby.

"Nice to meet you, Leti." Amy could see she was a beautiful Hispanic young woman.

"This is Amy Arrington."

"Nice to meet you too," said Leti. "One of The DDs, I am honored and humbled."

"You two are seeing each other."

Gabby and Leti glanced at each other and nodded.

"Finally. Gabby, I knew you were gay or bi back in high school, probably even before you."

"Seriously?"

"Yeah, but it wasn't my business."

"Aim, I think your gaydar is better than mine."

"Maybe so. But I didn't say anything, it wasn't an issue."

"What about Abby?"

Amy rubbed her chin, "I'm pretty sure she has no clue. Just last week she asked me if I thought it was a good idea to set you up on a date with a guy her cousin knew. I told Abby it was my impression, that you were pretty busy at the moment, with work and your axe throwing."

Gabby felt bad that Amy had to do this. Later in the week Gabby met with Abby and came out to her. Abby didn't have a problem. Gabby asked as a favor to hold off saying anything to Mitch, as he might be uncomfortable with it. Abby agreed.

****

Alexander was currently using his chainsaw to clear the rest of a splintered tree in eastern Mayfield, while trying to deal with the news that the men's Cardinal basketball team had just lost to Western Kentucky for the first time in 13 years. Cody Smith, their letter carrier, delivered the C-J and Alexander learned that the Louisville Cardinal basketball team announced they were pausing all team-related activities due to multiple COVID-19 tests within the program. This canceled the Kentucky game. UK then substituted Western Kentucky, fresh off their upset victory. That made 31 games for the Wildcats, the limit. It would take a waiver from the NCAA to allow UK and U of L to reschedule. The odds were stacked against such a move. It was emblematic of the season the team was having. The Cards lost the last 14 out of 16 games.

Such news normally would have been devastating to Alexander, but at the moment, he had other things on his mind in Mayfield.

Alexander, Amy, Bobby and Gabe stayed through Christmas. Alexander dressed up as Santa and delivered presents to the kids in Mayfield, some of them still shell-shocked and depressed.

Granddad and Mrs. Simmons came down and visited for the holidays. Several legal matters were continued. Alexander promised to be back at CA soon.

****

It was New Year's Eve. They sat around a small fire. Alexander had several cases of Balthazar's Boffo Barley Pop delivered and people were relaxed and tongues loosened a bit. Alexander, Amy, Bobby and Gabe had been there for nearly three weeks. Gabby and Leti were there, as well as Sherri. Fireworks were going off in the night sky.

"Alexander, you know, you were the one that educated me about Mayfield," said Gabe.

"I don't recall."

"You mentioned that students today needed to learn their history to appreciate what the situation is today."

"Now I remember. I was ranting, as usual."

"You mentioned the Mayfield 10."

"I don't know this," said Amy.

"Mayfield High," recalled Sherri.

Gabe explained, "When integration was or wasn't happening in 1956. 10 Black students didn't go to Dunbar, the school for minorities that was grossly underfunded, but decided to go to the all-White, resource-rich Mayfield High School. It was a shocking event."

Alexander added, "The school administrators, to their credit, allowed them to attend."

"But some White students would get up and leave in protest," said Gabe. "And then when the school principal told them they had the choice to stay outside or come in, that really got them mad. Eventually they gave up and came in and joined the class."

"And the world didn't end," said Alexander. "Cheers to them for standing up and stepping forward. We should all be so bold trying to make the world a better place and celebrate those that actually do it. Like the Mayfield 10 and like Tyler Gerth."

"Agreed," said Sherri. The group nodded respectfully.

Gabe continued, "I learned quite a bit more history about Mayfield. I know the precise total of lynchings in the south isn't known, there were thousands. In Professor George Wright's book, *Racial Violence in Kentucky, 1865-1940,* he's documented 353 lynchings during this period. At least 6 were here in Graves County. I learned in 1896, during the Mayfield Race War, four Black men were lynched in one week."

The group was quiet at that.

Gabe stated, "To have such acrimony, to be that insecure that you have to use intimidation and violence, murder, to assert your superiority, reveals deep hatred and utter weakness. The way of the bully. And where does it stop? Do I get my homies and track down these guys, their relatives, for revenge? Or just ignore them now in their time of need? I see this disaster here as just people needing help. If after what I do to help them, they go back to hating me, disrespecting me, wanting to dominate me, I can't change that—only pity them being trapped by such a dark, narrow view."

The group continued their silence.

"Look," said Gabe, "I know all that and I want to help rebuild and help the healing. That's why I'm here."

Alexander held up his beer, "Cheers to that."

"Cheers!" said the group.

On New Year's Day it was warm, near 60 degrees. The volunteers took the afternoon off. About 30 people gathered around and watched a pickup game of basketball. Three-on-three, half court. Bobby, Amy and Gabe, versus two other guys and a girl.

Bobby was draining buckets, but also passing the ball off to Gabe, who hit a few shots and Amy who also made two.

The other side had a guy that was taunting Bobby about his high school days and how he didn't deliver a state title.

Bobby ignored him at first, but it finally got under his skin. To finish the game, Bobby drove past his defender and launched. The guy with the big mouth moved to defend. Bobby reared back and tomahawk slammed over the guy and the crowd went nuts.

But coming down Bobby was brushed off balance and landed at an odd angle, tweaking his knee.

When Amy saw his cringe she went right to him, "Bobby, are you okay?"

He nodded, with a grimace. Amy didn't like that.

Bobby tried to work that afternoon, but the pain in his knee forced him to knock off early.

Amy and then Alexander offered to drive him home. Bobby thanked them but refused. He said good-bye. As he drove off Bobby, Amy, Gabe and Alexander were worried sick he did more damage to his leg.

35

Bobby got home late. His knee was throbbing and he was chastising himself for screwing up the same way he did 10 years ago. He called his clinic and they stayed open late for him. He got an MRI on his knee. His orthopedic doctor confirmed there wasn't a tear, just a strain. Bobby was thankful. He was told to just take it easy for a week.

The next day Bobby was going back to work at the office on Main in downtown, but he froze and became lost in thought. Bobby reflected on his life and what he wanted to be doing 10 and 20 years from now and who he wanted to be doing it with. He got on I-65 and headed south. He transitioned to KY-245 and was at Bardstown College in just under an hour. He pulled into the parking lot and entered the athletic department. He walked down a hallway and paused by a display case that had his picture from five years ago and his number 7 uniform displayed.

"Bobby!" called out Cora Castillo, a 30-year-old Hispanic woman stepping out from her desk in the president's office.

"Cora, how are you?" They fist bumped.

"Still plugging along."

"How is Matías? He must be getting up there."

"He's 13. He plays basketball and his two favorite players are Bobby Dulsett and J.J. Barea."

"There's no way I could have ever covered J.J."

"But you shot better."

"Cora. How are things with you?"

"I'm good. Feel good."

"How's he doing in school?"

"He's great. He's a sophomore in high school already."

"What??"

"I know, how'd that happen?"

"I'm hearing you."

"Mind if I take a selfie with you, Bobby?"

"Of course."

Bobby moved close and she took the picture with her phone. "Thanks, Bobby. Matías plays guard and he said just the other day he was going to break your scoring records."

"Can I send him a message?"

"Sure." She handed him the phone.

Bobby began recording, "Hey, Matías, how are you? It's Bobby Dulsett. I've been a friend of your mom since I was playing here at Bardstown College like 7 years ago. She says you're a baller. Cool. But you know what's really cool? The guy that reads the defense and controls the game, the quarterback on the court dishing out passes to his receivers scoring buckets. That's J.J. Barea. You know what I'm talking about. I also love watching that dude play. His passes are sharp, quick, intuitive and accurate. Practice hard, but study harder. Good court awareness and good grades will take you far, my man. MC, I'll be watching." Bobby gave the peace sign and handed the phone back.

"Thank you, Bobby." Cora grinned at her favorite former Bardstown College player.

"My pleasure, Cora. Maybe my scoring records are safe now."

Cora laughed at that. Bobby turned and tweaked his knee. He felt a shooting pain.

"Are you okay, Bobby?"

"Just had my knee checked. Doing the same stupid stuff that got me in trouble before."

"You're posterizing people again?"

Bobby nodded, "I landed awkwardly."

"Bobby Dulsett, what were you doing flying so high?"

"I guess I was showing off."

"Who for?"

"Amy."

"Amy Arrington?"

"Yes."

"I can see you trying to impress her. High-priced New York lawyer."

"She's moving back home."

"Isn't that interesting."

"It is."

Cora locked on, "Any woman that you would do such a foolish thing for, has a special place in your heart."

Bobby considered that, "How's coach?"

"Same as always, just a little creakier. Still drawing up the x's and o's."

Bobby smiled at her, then slipped into the gymnasium and watched basketball practice being run by Coach Decker, Bardstown College's long-time skipper.

At 72-years-of-age the coach was still fully engaged and energized during practice. He demonstrated the proper technique on setting a screen and rolling off of it. Then he had them run wind sprints and hit the showers.

Bobby was recognized by some of the players and they asked for pics, he obliged.

The old coach strolled up, "Look who came back to visit. Hiya, Bobby."

"Hey, Coach. How are you doing?"

"I feel fine, what do my doctors know, anyways?"

They walked down the hallway to his office.

"Are the doctors saying something?"

"They're always saying something. I don't pay any mind to half of it. I'm still truckin' along. What about you, Bobby? How's the comfy executive life? CEO. I'll bet you have a lot of perks."

"Coach, I was thinking, maybe, I could come on as an assistant. I would take even an unpaid position. I would love to learn from you."

"What about Dulsett Distillery?"

"I'm leaving the spirits business. I want to get into coaching."

"I just lost my last assistant, gladly for him, to the Big East."

"You have an impressive coaching tree."

"Thank you, thank you… But the thing is…"

"Yes?" Bobby sensed reluctance in him.

"Let me call the school president in." The coach sent a text. A minute later a well-groomed 38-year-old gentleman arrived.

"Coach... Oh, Bobby, nice to see you."

They fist bumped.

"Nice to see you again, President Akerman."

"Please, call me Doug. We're not that much different in age. I was just out of graduate school when I watched you absolutely torch your opponents in high school."

Cora arrived at the door, "What you did to St. Xavier was unholy."

The old coach laughed, "I think you dropped a bunch on them, right?"

Bobby scrunched his face and shrugged, "I don't remember the exact number."

"It was 54," confirmed Cora. "I suffered through every point."

"Cora," said Bobby, "sorry, not sorry."

The room chuckled at that.

"Doug, you know I've been thinking about stepping down."

"Coach, you're the coach as long as you want to be."

"What if I put forward Bobby Dulsett as the new head coach?"

"Wait. What?" asked Bobby.

The president was equally surprised by this, "Really? Have you coached before, Bobby?"

"Uh yes, I have."

"Oh. Good. Where?"

"The Lakers."

"The Lakers?" The college president was surprised by this. "My goodness...L.A. That certainly is a very impressive—"

Bobby stopped him, "They're a team here at the Y."

The president paused and frowned at that, "The YMCA?"

Bobby nodded, "12-year-olds."

"That's a competitive league," said the coach. "I've seen some sharp elbows there."

Bobby nodded, again.

The president was digesting all of this, "I'm sure, but, really?"

The old coach groused, "Listen, Doug, I've been doing this longer than you've been alive. Coaching college basketball is 75% recruiting, 20% strategizing and 5% luck. He's Bobby Dulsett, he'll get you recruits."

The president continued to ponder, "What about the strategizing part?"

Cora questioned that question, "Did you forget? This is Bobby Dulsett."

****

It was agreed that the coach would finish the season. Bobby got them to hold back the announcement for 48 hours. He returned to Louisville and moved to secure Cassidy's transition to CEO.

Dulsett Distilleries was a private corporation that was closely held by five shareholders each having 20 percent.

Bobby knew he'd be drinking, so he booked a ride and was driven to the Riverwood section. It was a quiet tree-lined area in the east of town. The car let him out in the driveway of a roomy 5-bedroom ranch house.

Betty Huber, a friendly and spry 72-year-old, greeted Bobby at the door.

"Bobby!"

"Hi, Betty. I'd give you a big hug, but just to be safe I'll save it for the future."

"Understand. Nolan is around back by the pit."

It was in the low 40s. Bobby went around the house and sat outside with Nolan by the fire pit that was glowing.

"Goodness, if it isn't one of the legends of Kentucky coming to visit me."

"Hello, Nolan." Bobby sat a few feet away from him. "Thanks for seeing me."

Dylan, a 14-year-old, earbuds inserted, trudged by listening to Drake, while ignoring his granddad and his guest. Bobby could see the frustration and tension in Nolan's face.

"That's my grandson, Dylan. His parents are at a conference."

"Friendly, isn't he," remarked Bobby.

"We've been socially distancing from each other long before the virus hit. Can I offer you something?"

Bobby noticed the bottle, "I see you're a man of discriminating tastes. I'll have what you're having."

"Dulsett Reserve." Nolan poured him a drink and toasted: "To Dulsett Distilleries. They've been very good for me and my family."

"Mine too," Bobby added. They both had a laugh and clinked glasses.

Dylan walked back the other way still in his own world. Nolan wanted to say something to the kid, but backed down.

"It's a pleasure to see you, Nolan. I'm sorry, I haven't visited sooner. Of course, no one has hardly seen anyone in the last two years."

"I know. How has your work been down in Mayfield?"

"Slow, but steady. Those folks down there stick together. It'll take some time, but they'll come back."

"That twister was headed our way. It was 200 miles long. I thought it was going to be like 1974. You're too young to remember. What a mess that was. I don't mind that you're taking this time away from work to do this. We all support you. That tornado was a life changing event for lots of folks."

"Yes, it certainly was life changing. I've come to talk some business."

"About the distillery?"

"Yes."

"I'm coming to you to tell you I've accepted the head coaching job at Bardstown College and will be stepping down as CEO."

"Goodness! Bobby, congratulations. I wish you the best. I'm sure you'll be a great coach."

"Thank you, I hope to see you at some of our games."

"You just might."

"I'm here, because I want to back Cassidy to replace me."

Nolan frowned at that notion, "Bobby, you know I have nothing against her, but..."

"Look, she grew up in the business. She has an MBA. She handles the marketing. Cassidy is well connected in the industry. She's more qualified than me, when I took over."

"Listen, Bobby, I know someone we could bring in. Smart guy, he'll do a great job. Continue the winning streak we've had at Dulsett."

"Cassidy is the main reason we've had that winning streak, not me."

Nolan sat back, closed his eyes and rubbed his temples.

"Nolan, if you're recommending him, I'm sure this guy is great, but—"

"Cassidy is just so young! We bring this guy in, top of his field. 5-year contract, she'll be ready by then."

"She's ready now. I've got a big stake in this working as well."

Nolan grumbled, "I can't allow this. If you force my hand, I'll get Alice and Evan on my side and you'll be blocked."

Bobby now grumbled. "I know, they listen to you. That's why I came to you, first."

"Bobby, the old man set it up this way. To avoid making reckless or premature decisions and keeping a steady hand on the wheel."

"I'm telling you, Nolan, I don't know a more hard-working, dedicated, competent and talented executive than Cassidy. But if you make this move, she might walk."

Nolan waved that off, "I really doubt that. Look, this isn't personal, just business."

Bobby sighed.

Dylan traversed by once again.

"Dylan?" asked Nolan.

The teenager pretended to ignore him with the buds in his ear.

"Dylan??"

Dylan forced a sweet smile, paused the video on his phone and took out his earbuds. "Yes, Grandpa?"

"Dylan, this is Bobby Dulsett. I don't think you two have ever met."

Dylan wasn't really interested, "What's up?"

"Hey," said Bobby.

"Have you ever heard of him, Dylan?"

"Nope."

Bobby shrugged, "Oh well..."

Nolan laughed, "I guess it had to happen eventually. Your fame not reaching past two generations. Dylan, Google Bobby Dulsett."

Dylan did a search. "Huh. You played some basketball..." He was quite underwhelmed by this. "Wow..."

Dylan sat over on a chair, put his earbuds back in and continued watching the video.

"He wants to get into music production, shoot videos, start a band, rap, do all that, I think. I don't know what he's talking about half the time." Nolan regretfully shook his head, "I wish..."

"What do you wish for, Nolan?"

"That it wasn't some ordeal for our grandson when he's here. I wish I had some kind of connection with him. He puts up with his grandmother. But he ignores me, avoids me and I avoid him now. We isolate from each other and it's all so depressing to me. I even overheard him talking to his friend and he called Betty and me ancient and dusty."

"You want him to think you're cool."

"That's kind of a stretch. But, really, doesn't every grandfather want that?"

"Fine. Just play along."

"What?" Nolan's phone rang and he checked it. "Excuse me, Bobby, this is important. I have to take this. I'll only be a moment." He strode off and answered the call.

Bobby eased over to Dylan who continued watching the video and was irked by the interruption.

"What do you want?"

Bobby pulled out his phone, brought up an image and showed it to him.

Dylan focused on the screen and his eyes bugged out, "Dude, is that Jack?"

"Yep."

Dylan took a snap of that pic. "Way friggin cool! You guys hang out?"

"On occasion, when he's in town."

Dylan's jaw dropped.

"And guess what, last time when we were kickin' it, listening to some of his beats, he asked about your grandpa."

Dylan was thunderstruck, "Jack asked about my grandpa?"

"Yeah."

"Why?"

"We did some business. I told Jack I wondered if your grandpa was getting the proper respect."

"Whoa, what?? No way. From who?"

"You, bro. You may not know me, but I've been onto you for some time. Your attitude sucks and you have zero respect for your grandpa."

"Is that what you told Jack?"

"Yeah, and I also told him that you, Dylan, are blowing it, man."

"He knows my name now?"

"Not in a good way. Just think when your grandpa is gone and you missed out on the chance to learn from his vast wisdom. You have to reach out now, when you can. And it's not what *you want* to do all the time. What does *he* like? Take the time to listen and hear what he's saying. He really is a smart guy."

Dylan was bulldozed by this. Nolan came back from the call.

"Grandpa, I wanted to say I'm sorry if I've been a jerk. I've been in a rut about the whole state of things."

Nolan was surprised by this, "I understand, I get in a rut too."

Bobby showed Nolan the picture of himself and Jack. "I was just telling Dylan about the time I was hanging out with Jack and he asked about you. From the time we did that business thing."

Nolan paused for a moment, "Right. The business thing."

"It was a promotional thing. Your grandfather consulted on it," Bobby said, adding meat to the matter.

Nolan threw up his hands, "That Jack, he's one of a kind."

Dylan was pumped hearing this, "This is full-on wacked! I'm telling all my friends about it." He fist-bumped Bobby and his grandpa as he strutted away working on his phone.

Nolan was almost floating, "He's never fist-bumped me before."

"Huh."

"A promotional thing with Jack?" asked Nolan.

"Looks like your grandson thinks you're cool as shit."

Nolan was amused, "Alright, Bobby. I'm on board with Cassidy as CEO. Let's see what she can do."

Bobby smiled.

His next stop was a courtesy visit to Miss Alice, a kindly elderly lady and old Uncle Evan who both thought it was a smashing idea for Cassidy to take over.

****

Bobby arrived just after 8pm and knocked on the door.

Cassidy was working, of course, "Bobby, come in. I'm glad you're back. I've got a ton of questions for you."

"I'm sure you can figure them all out."

"No, only the boss can tackle these."

"Cassidy…"

"Uh-oh, I don't like this tone you have, it means something big is coming."

"I've accepted the head coaching job at Bardstown."

"Your alma mater??"

"Yes."

"That's fantastic! You're going to be a great coach."

"Thanks and you're going to be a great CEO."

"What?"

"On the way out the door, I held it open for you. CEO of Dulsett Distilleries is yours, if you want it."

"Bobby, quit playing. There's no way Nolan would go for that and he has influence over Alice and Evan."

"I went and saw Nolan this afternoon. He's on board. And I saw Alice and Evan and they're thrilled with the idea."

"You're serious?"

"Yes. I've protected your power source."

"Pulsar Parallax has learned his lesson," said Cass.

"He has. It's Nimble True for the win."

Cassidy let it sink in, "Huh."

"Just do your best. That's enough."

"Will do. I accept."

"Good."

Cassidy hugged him, "Thank you, Bobby, for believing in me."

"I told you I've never underestimated you. Ever."

Cassidy appreciated his support.

"Great. That's settled. Oh, and by the way, I'm going to ask Amy to marry me."

Cassidy was stunned, "What the fudge?? Again, you're serious?"

"I just picked up the ring today." Bobby pulled out a ring box.

Cassidy took the box, opened it and was floored, "Bobby, it's beautiful! But you know, you could have used mom's."

"That's saved for you, little sis." Bobby took the calendar off the wall. "Today is January 4." He checked the month of May. "I think May 14th would be perfect and it has to be at the Peterson-Dumesnil House."

"You are so romantic and so clueless. That's 4 months from now. You think the royal wedding of Bobby Dulsett and Amy Arrington can be pulled off by then?"

"Come on. It won't be that big a deal."

"Bobby, you are so lost in the wilderness on this. But if anyone can pull this off, it's April Arrington. First thing you need to know is if the Peterson-

Dumesnil House is available on May 14th. I would probably guess by now it's already booked."

Bobby pondered, "Can you check and if it is, find out who they are and how I contact them."

It took Cassidy twenty minutes to learn the future open dates, locate the bride-to-be and get her on the phone. "Phyllis Fielding has that date reserved and here are some alternative dates." She handed him a note and her phone. "She's on the line."

"Hello?"

"Is this really Bobby Dulsett?"

"It is. Is this Phyllis Fielding?"

"It is. What a pleasure. To what do I owe this honor?"

"Miss Fielding, I was—"

"Please call me Phyllis."

"Phyllis, I was wondering if I could possibly take over that date at the P-D House you have in May."

"On the 14th?"

"Yes, a friend of mine is having a party and asked if I could secure it."

"I don't think so."

"I'd really like to have it. I have some alternative later dates that are available."

The woman considered it, "Sign a bunch of stuff and come with us to a party and be our BFF."

"Seriously?"

"You want that calendar date?"

"How much stuff do I have to sign?"

"Three dozen items," said the bride.

The groom, Phil, was embarrassed by that, "Dear, really, three dozen?"

"It will pay for a nice chunk of the honeymoon."

The groom liked that idea.

"Fine," said Bobby. "Three dozen items and I'm your pal at this party. When?"

"Tonight. We'll pick you up at 8:00."

They were right on time. Bobby sat in the back of their Lexus. They photographed him signing the three dozen items. He smiled, smothering his grimace.

The groom turned around, "Hey there, Bobby."

"Hey, Phil," said Bobby, wondering what he had gotten himself into.

"What have you been doing?"

"At this moment, I work at my family's beverage company."

Phyllis, the bride-to-be, shushed her fiancé, "He's the CEO there."

"I forgot. But I remember some of your product and approve."

"Sometimes he approves too much," Phyllis added.

"You have to watch that," advised Bobby.

Phil checked a text on his phone, "Claude thinks I'm making things up again. Wait until they really see Bobby Dulsett in the flesh!"

Bobby forced another polite grin.

"You really want to have that date at Peterson-Dumesnil House," stated Phyllis.

"It's the perfect place at the perfect time, for my schedule, for my friend."

"Are you getting married?" asked Phil.

"That would be something!" exclaimed Phyllis.

Bobby could see his phone in his fingers at the ready. "It's just a little get together."

They arrived and the gathering all wanted pictures with Bobby. Phil was in Claude's face saying never to doubt him, as he was with his buddy Bobby Dulsett.

****

Amy was exhausted from another day of cleaning up and clearing out yet more debris. Before she nodded off, she saw a friend had forwarded her pictures on Facebook. She checked it and it was Bobby at some party with two friends that evening.

The next day, Bobby, hungover, loaded up supplies and headed back to Mayfield. During the drive at midday, he heard on the sports report on the radio that Bobby Dulsett was the new coach at Bardstown College. There was real excitement over this.

Bobby groaned, his hangover was now thumping, "Oh noo..." He wanted to let Amy know first, before it was announced.

Gabby arrived to help out and told Amy about the breaking news: Bobby Dulsett had signed a 5-year deal to be head basketball coach at Bardstown College.

Alexander also saw the report and was thrilled, "Bobby is coaching the Bardstown Woodchucks? Yeah! Go Chucks! We may have to see a couple games this year, that's a 40-minute ride down 65."

"Did you know anything about this?" asked Gabby.

"No. But I'm happy for him."

An hour later Bobby pulled into the work site and got out.

Alexander strolled up, "Welcome back, Coach. I'm so pleased for you, Bobby."

"Thanks, Alexander."

Some of his other friends hooted and hollered. He looked around and saw Amy off to the side.

"Amy."

"Hi, Bobby." He led her away to the side of the structure for some privacy.

"I'm pleased for you."

"I wanted to set things up and get back here and tell you and ask you before it became public."

"You've signed a 5-year deal to be head basketball coach at Bardstown College. What did you want to ask me?"

He pulled out a ring case and knelt down on his one good knee. "Amy Arrington, would you—"

"Stop, stop! If you're doing what I think you're doing..."

"Yes?" Bobby stood up and didn't like the sound of this.

"Look, all I'm asking you is, why are you doing this in private?"

"Because, well, I didn't want to put you on the spot and then if you turned me down, it would be awkward with the group."

Amy's eyes narrowed on him, "Get out there and let's do this in public."

Bobby grinned.

Amy walked out by the group and attempted to look casual. She tried to get her father's attention, but he was concentrating elsewhere.

Gabby noticed. She took out her phone and started filming. She signaled Alexander, who was now fully aware.

Bobby walked out and joined Amy by a pile of refuse. He pulled out a ring case and went down on bended knee before her, "Amy Arrington, will you marry me?"

"Yes, Bobby, I believe I will."

Alexander jumped for joy. "Yessiree!"

The group cheered.

Bobby looked uncertain, "Do you think it's possible that we can have the ceremony and reception on May 14?"

Amy thought about that, "A week after the Derby."

"We could then go on our honeymoon, wherever you want, and be back by May 24 or 25. You could then keep your streak alive with The DDs and Forecastle on the 27th. I know that's important to you." He glanced over to Gabby who grinned at that.

"Of course," said Amy. "And you need to begin recruiting, which is vital to you, for us. I understand."

Bobby smiled at her, "Thank you. And, I just happened to line up the P-D House on that date."

"The Peterson-Dumesnil House? How did you know?"

"How did I know that you've been dreaming of having your wedding there since you were a little girl? Alexander told me late one night some time ago. When I was gathering intel."

"I did?" Alexander frumpled his face trying to recall.

"It was a late night," Bobby explained.

Amy was working through this, "Bobby, does this have anything to do with the Facebook posts with your friends last night?"

"Facebook posts?"

"Someone forwarded me some pictures of you at a party last night. They were lively."

"I went to the couple that had the date reserved and they said they would let me have it, if I signed some stuff and went to a party and pretended to be their friend."

"You did this for me?"

"Yes."

Gabby was blown away, "That's so utterly exceptional."

"You are so thoughtful," said Amy. She curled his hair, "This is a good sign. I have spent time fantasizing about getting married there and eating cake under the Ginkgo tree. Yes, to getting married and yes to the time and place."

The group let out another hearty cheer.

Amy stepped off and called her mother.

"Hello, darling. So Bobby's the new basketball coach at Bardstown College."

"I think it's great, Mother."

"Taking a pay cut, leaving a cushy CEO position to get into the dog-eat-dog world of college coaching."

"He'll be challenged, but he'll be happy because it's where he wants to be."

"And you're sure about leaving Padmore and moving back here?"

"Yes, Mother. You have plenty of other friends in New York, for when you pass through there."

"It's not just that. You probably would have made partner."

"Maybe, in a couple years. But maybe not. That's a long and swervy road filled with late nights, potholes and no guard rails. Easy to land in the ditch and wonder what happened. But I have other news."

"Which is?"

"Bobby just proposed and I accepted."

"Congratulations, honey. I'm happy for you."

"Thank you, Mother."

"Have you set a date?"

The wedding is going to be held on May 14th."

That sounded odd to her, "What year?"

"This year."

"That's only 4 months! That's preposterous. I need more time than that to plan a tea party!"

"The date is May 14."

"Maybe in 9 months."

"Mother, that would put it right in the middle of basketball season. It's set. The date is May 14."

"He picked the date?"

"Yes."

April was nearly reeling from this, "I don't think I've ever heard of such a thing. The groom picking the date??"

"This date is after the Derby. Bobby needs to get out and start recruiting players as soon as possible. And it's going to be at the Peterson-Dumesnil House."

"Hold on, Ambrosia, I know when you were a little girl you dreamed of getting married there. But there's no way you could get that place on such short notice."

"Already done."

"Pardon me?"

"He's Bobby Dulsett."

"I see. Honestly, I love the P-D House. But they can only seat about 120 outside. I don't think you understand. This is the wedding of Amy Arrington and Bobby Dulsett. It will be the event of the season. We'd be lucky to keep the guest list under 750."

"Mother, on May 14th, of this year, I'm getting married to Bobby at the P-D House. And the guests will be limited to about 120. That's final!"

"Oh fiddle!" April shook her head and sighed. Then there was a truce between them. They went to their neutral corners.

"Oh dear, Ambrosia, the wife of a basketball coach."

Amy quipped, "Better than being married to a lawyer."

"That may be true." April thought back, "You expected this."

"I made sure to pay special attention during contract law class."

"Ambrosia, you are a determined and calculating young lady."

"Why does that sound dodgy?"

"Not at all. You knew what you wanted, strategized, was patient and you got it. These are admirable traits."

"I suppose you passed them on to me."

"Your father has a little of that himself. And I suppose I'm coming around to you working with him. Hopefully you'll temper some of his antics."

"That's a tall order."

“As for the wedding at the Peterson-Dumesnil House, in 4 months, it’ll be a challenge, but I guess, you, me and Steven can whip something together by then.”

Amy brightened, “I knew I could rely on his and your legendary skills, Mother.”

“There’s going to be a lot of angry people being left off the guest list.”

“We’ll be gentle.”

36

April was brought back to earth seeing that 900,000 had now perished from COVID-19. She was determined to get this wedding done and not get sick.

Alexander and Amy remained in Mayfield and continued with the repairing and rebuilding. They were now working with the Mennonite Disaster Services and their program, Homes and Hope for Kentucky, which didn't charge any fees.

He had suspended his law practice, until Amy got back from her honeymoon. Bobby began doing interviews for the two assistants he would be hiring. He also had to have a plan. What kind of offense? What style of defense? Who could they reasonably expect to come to a struggling Division II school? Bobby called around to his connections in the basketball world to get opinions and scouting reports. His name did open a few doors, but he had to then close the deal and he started out slow. Bobby hired an older and a younger coach. He relied on the old hand's experience and wisdom and the young gun's energy and tech-savvy with social media.

Still in Mayfield, Amy called Cassidy and asked her to be one of her bride's maids, and she accepted.

Amy continued working with her crew in Mayfield, she had promised to get a wall rebuilt for an old Marine veteran that was staying put.

April put her foot down, called Alexander and applied maximum pressure to get Amy back in town and planning her nuptials. Alexander came over and passed on the message.

When the Marine vet learned Amy was there helping him, instead of planning her wedding 'that was right around the corner,' he thanked her and ordered her home. Amy left, but promised to return after her honeymoon. Alexander remained and finished the job.

****

Amy arrived back home that evening. April called her and they chatted. Amy agreed to join her the next day for lunch.

Amy traveled out to SHS and April introduced her to a local designer. He was a stylish and attractive young man in his mid 20's. Amy recognized his name from a TV reality show she couldn't recall. April had several pieces he had designed for her. She asked him to present sketches of several wedding gown ideas for Amy to review. The designs were all very striking and chic. He presented multiple mood boards and talked fabric sourcing: lace from Calais, France and silk from the Lake Cuomo area of Italy.

Amy was impressed and made a choice. It wasn't as painful as she thought it was going to be. The three of them had a pleasant lunch. But now this local designer was under the gun. Normally a project like this took maybe ten months, with another two months for fittings. The wedding was just over three months away. It was that evening when he had the moment of 'wtf have I gotten myself into.' He braced himself and went all in on this monumental challenge.

****

<u>**TORTS and JUST DESSERTS** from the mind of Alexander Arrington</u>

The owl appeared:

"Mayfield, Kentucky. At this moment, when so much has been lost, after we've watched in horror and the shock has finally worn off, the question arises: 'How should we do this?'

Mayfield was devastated. Which means it now has immense potential. It's almost a clean slate. Construct sustainable, energy efficient, people-friendly buildings that would provide businesses with advantages in lowering overhead and help retain employees. Sustainable, energy efficient dwellings would attract residents and make home ownership more viable and landlords could offer more affordable rents.

The buildings that are coming should be revolutionary not only in their sustainability and affordability, but their durability to stand up to even larger tornados that are coming in the expanding and amped up tornado seasons to come.

If you happen to pick up the Kentucky Building Code and were curious about what was being done to improve buildings in this stark new reality, you would be hard pressed to even find the word 'tornado.' On page 21, 423.1.1 This section deals with the construction of storm shelters and safe rooms for tornadoes and hurricanes, but nothing on creating more advanced and safer residential buildings. We know how to do this. Homes must be nearly air-tight, constructed with a continuous load path with reinforcements that connect the entire structure and is bolted to the foundation. Will it cost money? Yes. Will it save money and lives down the line, most likely also yes. It is well worth the extra effort and needs to be codified, in not only the Kentucky building codes, but in all states for the residences in tornado and hurricane zones.

Mayfield has an opportunity to create green spaces, walking areas, people-friendly locales that will draw folks into town.

Mayfield will continue to be 'more than a memory' and perhaps a vision for a brighter future."

~ ~ ~

"I heard and read many great things about Wilma's Kountry Kitchen when I was in Mayfield. The restaurant took a big hit from the twister, but is building back. It has a remarkable fan base. I very much look forward to dining at Wilma's in the future and experiencing for myself the reasons for this loyalty."

The owl faded out.

****

It was in late January, after nearly 6 weeks in Mayfield, Alexander and Gabe were finally home. They both promised the folks they would return to Mayfield after events settled back down in Louisville.

Alexander dropped off Gabe, thanked him for all of his great work, made his way over to Casa Arrington and parked out front.

A male voice called out, "Hello, Alexander."

Alexander didn't recognize the voice, he looked around for the source and found it across the street. "Hello, Mr. Miller. Happy New Year to you, sir."

"Same to you. I admire what you're doing down in Mayfield."

"Thank you. And thank you for your donation, it helped buy food for some displaced people."

"I'm pleased." Mr. Miller smiled and reentered his house.

Alexander was surprised by this in a good way. He walked through the gate and was immediately greeted by their official ambassador, "Hello there, Miss Sassy."

Henry Clay, Duke, Diva and Duchess were front and center wagging their tails. Luminary the Legendary Lizard and Regis the 'Rascible Rabbit hustled to the front door. Hamlet the Hammy Hamster had his nose pressed to his glass. Nutmeg, no longer a kitten, was crouching eagerly and even Cantankerous Cat welcomed him home.

Rudy and Ronda, the rodents, still not that impressed.

Alexander greeted all of his little friends. And he greeted his big friends. Granddad, Mrs. Simmons and Amy. Life had returned, at least for the moment, to a modified normal.

It was Derby time and his little girl was getting married. Alexander had more than a little extra spring in his step.

Then he walked into his office and froze in horror, seeing how much paperwork had piled up. But then he heard a familiar sound. He stepped into the living room and saw Amy in the back area on the half-pipe. Alexander was drawn there. His eyes began to dance. However, when he searched for his skateboard, he couldn't find it. He glanced around but couldn't see anyone. "Mrs. Simmons?"

From the other room Mrs. Simmons announced: "When you make a significant dent in that mountain of paperwork on your desk, I'll give your skateboard back."

Alexander flinched and sighed, and trudged into his office.

****

On January 27 U of L fired the men's basketball coach. As previously mentioned, Alexander had lost enthusiasm. The school didn't even wait until the end of the dead-end season to hand him his walking papers.

Alexander would look back over the last 4 seasons on the men's basketball team and count up the losses. He compared the record to the women's basketball team and it would take 9 seasons to nearly match as many defeats. The men's program was wandering in the wilderness, while the women were residing at the top of their sport. They had been ranked in the top ten for 5 straight years.

Both programs were elite. And normally it would hurl Alexander into a funk that both were not there at the moment, but right now it wasn't going to bring him down. Things were going to get better and his daughter was getting married. He reminded Nutmeg and Cantankerous Cat twice and Luminary the Legendary Lizard thrice, who finally rolled his eyes being told yet again of the forthcoming nuptials.

It was early Sunday evening, when Alexander and Amy arrived back from the Yum Center in good spirits.

"How'd the ladies do?" asked Granddad, working on a clay sculpture in the corner of the room.

Alexander and Amy sat and relaxed.

"We just witnessed our number 5 ranked women take down number 21 Duke," said Alexander. "I love beating Duke. I love watching the Cardinals play and I love watching Hailey Van Lith play for the Cardinals. What game she has."

"You do know it's Sunday night, Alexander. Are you going to be making that call?" asked Mrs. Simmons.

"Thanks for reminding me, I have to make some calls," said Amy, off to her room.

Alexander picked up the remote and was scrolling through his recordings. "I'm well aware what day it is, Mrs. Simmons. I'm retrieving the NFC championship game I recorded this afternoon to see who will be playing my Bengals in the Super Bowl. Everything will have to be tabled until tomorrow as I will be settling back for two hours to watch, with no interruptions and lights out soon after that."

Granddad continued molding away on his glob of clay, "Whoo doggie, what a game! I can't believe the Rams pulled that one out!"

Alexander frowned and groaned, "Again?" He put the remote down.

Granddad paused and looked up, "Hold on, sorry. Strike that from the record."

"Can't unring that bell," grumbled Alexander.

"Hey now, Alexander," said Mrs. Simmons. "Since you have a moment, I wanted to tell you I heard that Sherri got an offer to go to the Speed Museum Ball."

Alexander was in no mood, "Was that your source in the cafeteria? In study hall? Out on the playground or was it in 5th period math? I'm having bad flashbacks of my rocky love life in high school."

Mrs. Simmons lowered her glasses, "You're fine with Sherri getting all dolled up and going with someone else to this swanky black-tie social extravaganza?"

Alexander mumbled, "Maybe she doesn't want to go with me."

Mrs. Simmons groused, "I saw her in 2nd period social studies and she said she was interested."

"She's not even taking that class," snarked Alexander, in his 'gotcha' moment.

Mrs. Simmons narrowed her eyes and ended the conversation, "You forget you already secured the tickets? And that's not lunch money." Alexander ignored her. "Are you still scared to run into April and Reston there?"

Alexander picked up his phone and called, "Hey, Sherri. Hi. How are you?" He listened. "Good. I'm glad you're well. Me? I've been just so out of sorts catching up. Stressed out."

Granddad mumbled, "More like stretched out."

Mrs. Simmons and Granddad both eyed him reclined with a beverage in one hand and the remote still nearby.

Alexander cleared his throat, "I apologize that it's so late for me to ask, but would you be interested in going to the Speed Ball as my date?" He listened and smiled, "That's great. I look forward to it. Talk soon. Bye." Alexander waved off both of them and started the game. "Don't tell me the score. I like the drama to see if I covered the spread."

Mrs. Simmons gave him the side-eye, "I sometimes wonder how this species survives."

****

Amy asked to be consulted on some of the more major decisions, but she relinquished control to April. She was the wedding planner. Amy believed her mother had been looking forward to this ceremony even more than herself. April envisioned this as an event that would be referenced for years in the bridal magazines. And since she was also funding it, there would be no dithering and decisions were forthcoming. Things couldn't just politely roll forward in the usual manner, the clock was ticking down quickly.

April had been approached by several media outlets that wanted to televise the extravaganza. Amy and Bobby both flatly turned that down. However, April did convince them to stream it online.

Alexander called her on the phone, "April, I plan to pay my fair share."

April paused studying the Excel spreadsheet on where money had already been spent and the projected future payments. "Poppycock."

"What?"

"Poppy Cock. It's already been arranged."

"I need to pay something. I'm the father of the bride."

April became very serious and almost sentimental, "Alexander, you've paid it forward so far already. Whatever you wanted to kick in, use it down in Mayfield."

Alexander was affected by that, "I will, April. Thank you."

"Thank you, for letting me have my way."

"April, you always get your way."

"And then all is right in the universe."

****

It was the beginning of February. Even though it was 10:30 in the evening and quite brisk out, Mrs. Simmons, Granddad, Alexander and Amy masked up and made it downtown to the Hyatt Regency Hotel for an annual event they almost never missed. It was a 35-year tradition that started back in 1987. The four sat in the lobby and waited. You could see the anticipation in the faces of those that showed up and others that had no idea what was about to happen. The hotel gave out earplugs, but almost nobody accepted. The lobby was at the bottom of a giant cone that rose up 20 floors. The balconies wrapped around and high school students were gathering on the various levels and waving to each other.

Every year the Kentucky Music Educators Association held the Kentucky State Choir Finals at this time and in Louisville. Around 600 high school singers participated. This was where they stayed.

Right before curfew at 11pm, it began. It was a hum. Someone started a pitch and then the "Star-Spangled Banner" began. It was described as a 'cylinder of sound.' No one planned this. It just happened every night of the finals. The acoustics were amazing. It sent a chill down the four and most likely everyone else that experienced it.

****

On March 5th the second annual Justice Fest took place. Gabby had attended the first one last year and told Amy. Gabby had never seen anything like it. She saw first-hand that it created hope in the community of color, which had faced immense challenges. This year they both attended

Justice Fest at the convention center. Gabby introduced Amy to NyRee Clayton-Taylor and Matt Kaufmann, Teachers of the Year award winners, who were behind the creation of this event. Gabby gave big props to them for their efforts creating this and getting the Kentucky Derby Festival and Humana to come on as sponsors. Students from the 3rd to 12th Grades presented their thoughts and perceptions on how they saw the world and pitched ideas 'Shark Tank style' to community and business leaders. These projects were seeking funding that could make a difference and be part of the solution to the challenges of the community.

The first two Justice Fests dealt with a whole range of issues: unfair practice of redlining, homelessness, improving trash collection, people living in food deserts, with grocery stores and fresh food a considerable distance away—and those that faced even basic food insecurity. Poems and spoken word were voiced describing the struggles and hopes and dreams of the young and vulnerable. Videos of under-represented and marginalized people were highlighted and even celebrated. Pleas to speak up, speak out and speak truth to power were voiced. Mighty Shades of Ebony shared their mission to train the next generation of storytellers, filmmakers and influencers that will fight for civil and human rights and against profiling and oppression. The youth-led social justice hip-hop group The Real Young Prodigys appeared and shared their passion for the state wide and eventually federal passage of the CROWN Act: Create a Respectful and Open World for Natural Hair. It reflected well on the city of Louisville that it had already passed such an anti-discrimination ordinance.

Through a video message, Lonnie Ali, the widow of Muhammad Ali, reminded everyone what her husband once said. "Injustice for anyone is injustice for everyone."

The president of Churchill Downs Race Track gave a video message telling the participants it was an honor to support their efforts for a more equitable world and praised them for being the champions of the future.

Abby and Gabby were really impressed by that. The kids put the time in preparing their presentations. On the way out they thanked NyRee and Matt, saying it was a fantastic idea that had become a terrific event. Gabby and Amy both thought it was a bright spot in the recent darkness. They would make donations to several projects and get Alexander, Bobby and April involved as well. They hoped Justice Fest would continue on and grow in the future.

****

That evening Bobby, Amy, Alexander and Sherri attended the formal Speed Museum Ball charity fundraiser. The newly engaged couple was showered with compliments and hints for invites. They directed those requests to April and Reston on the other side of the room. April hated being the Grinch and having to say no, but this power did give her a secret jolt.

Alexander and Sherri and Bobby and Amy had a grand time. Alexander was starting to believe that Sherri was actually attracted to an 'old dog' like himself.

Amy was pleased, she very much approved of Sherri and they had become real friends themselves.

It was cemented when they all went to the Bock and Wurst Fest in NuLu and they cheered the goat races, springtime and love.

And believe it or not, Reston and Alexander even had a moment of rapprochement to an earlier, less hostile time.

****

April couldn't devote as much time as she wanted. She sent a flood of flowers and good wishes to the Galt House Hotel Grand Ballroom for the Queen's Coronation and Dinner. April's mind again couldn't help but travel back to that night many moons ago, where she lost out to Sherri on the spin of that wheel. But she didn't dwell, she was too busy.

****

Alexander was at the Yum Center, as was the mayor, governor, Darrell Griffith, Russ Smith and Coach Denny Crum. The speculation had been snowballing for days on who the next head basketball coach of the men's team would be. And then he was introduced: Kenny Payne, someone well known to the Cardinal family and highly respected. He was an excellent recruiter and developer of talent. As a player he helped U of L win the national title in 1986. Currently he was an assistant for the New York Knicks. What made this even more interesting was that Coach Payne spent 10 seasons at the University of Kentucky learning from John Calipari where they won 6 SEC Championships and the national title in 2012.

Alexander was over the moon. He was thrilled at this new era beginning.

****

It was Thunder Over Louisville time again. Amy drove the gang down to the Waterfront Park and they spread out two big blankets, opened up the picnic containers and took in the show. This year, 2022, celebrated the 75th anniversary of the U.S. Air Force. It also returned as a Category 1 Aerobatic Box, which allowed for louder and faster aircraft and demo teams. Appearances were made by the advanced F-22 Raptor, classics such as the F-18, F-24, F-25, F-29, the workhorse C-130 Hercules and the massive C-17 Globemaster.

As dusk fell many anticipated one of the biggest fireworks displays in the nation. There was another drone display counting down to the show. Once again the Zambelli family didn't disappoint. The pyrotechnics were spectacular.

****

Meanwhile, the guest list to the 'social event of the century' had continued to mushroom. Amy had 40, Bobby had 30, Alexander 30, all holding steady—April now had 80. The demand was far outpacing the supply. It was quite the exclusive invite.

They met at SHS. Their intrepid designer was holding up fine with little sleep. They had the first fitting for the gown. Amy approved of the neckline, she wanted to shorten the train. April had envisioned one a bit longer, but that was fine.

****

And the détente was short-lived between Alexander and Reston.

In the back of CA Alexander had been building a bed frame on four wheels. After welding a push-bar to the foot of the frame, he sat at the front where the steering wheel was located. He gazed at a poster on the wall:

The Great Bed Race Monday May 2 – 6:00pm.

Alexander imagined zooming along and defeating all challengers.

This vision of glory was interrupted when he entered the house. Amy had her phone on speaker with her mother. They were discussing wedding details when April paused and groaned.

"What is it, Mother?"

"That Reston, he just went by again. He keeps boasting that he's going to win the Great Bed Race."

Amy was amused, "With Chip and some associates? They've never won."

Alexander eased closer to the phone.

"No, now Reston's hired some jocks from Lexington, went through a recruiter."

Amy thought this was odd, "He's doing this for the race?"

"It's a bit over the top," said April. "He claims they're going to break 34 seconds."

Alexander was spooked by that, "That would be a new record for the x formation."

"That's what he's saying, Alexander."

Alexander was concerned, his mind was racing. "Then I'm going to hire some blazing fast Cardinal football players for my team. How about that?"

"You little boys, still doing battle on the playground," quipped April.

****

Alexander and Reston were in Judge Beatrice Bonofiglio's chambers standing stiffly, staring straight ahead and ignoring each other.

Judge Bonofiglio entered carrying a takeout container with a salad, a tuna sandwich on whole wheat and a bottle of water. She sat at her desk. "Okay, gentlemen, I'm going to hear this matter in chambers, on my lunch hour, because I'm not going to take up the court's time on something I can't believe we're spending time on." She glanced at the paperwork, "Mr. Richardson has filed a motion to bar Mr. Arrington from hiring football players to be the bed pushers in the race tomorrow."

Reston jumped in, "Yes, Your Honor, we've filed this motion for a temporary injunction against Arrington and Arrington, as their actions would inflict irreparable loss before a final judgment could be reached."

The judge chewed on her garden salad and that statement, "You're talking about the bed races, right?"

"Yes, Your Honor and it's tomorrow. They are illegally using NCAA college football players as the bed pushers."

"Is this true, Mr. Arrington?"

"Your Honor, it's true we've retained the services of some of the players on the team. We've complied with all of the requirements with the university."

Reston pounced, "Your Honor, the defendant hasn't applied through proper procedures with the university or with Kentucky law. Student-athletes are to disclose and report all of their NIL activities, regardless of activity type, format, or compensation, within two business days of the NIL agreement being executed."

"I see, Reston. That's why you waited the extra day to file this against me."

"I believe you hired them three days ago, Alexander."

"Your Honor, that doesn't apply. This isn't a NIL deal. I'm not using their names, images or likenesses. I'm simply hiring them for their skill."

"You can't pay them for their performance," Reston retorted. "They'd lose their amateur status."

"As my opposing counsel knows, you can be an amateur in one sport and a professional in another."

The judge thought that through, "Professional bed pushers?"

"Yes, Your Honor. Why not?" Alexander asked.

"Your Honor," said Reston, "the NCAA regulation stipulates that any outside employment for the student-athlete must be compensated by the market rate."

The judge glanced over, "Mr. Arrington, what's the market rate for professional bed pushers?"

"Your Honor, we researched the matter with due diligence and were not able to come up with a figure. It's an emerging profession."

Reston wagged his finger at Alexander, "That may be so, but the NCAA regs forbid any remuneration for value that the student-athlete may have for the employer because of the publicity, reputation, fame or personal following that he or she has obtained because of their athletic ability. And didn't I hear you bragging about upping your game by hiring some blazing fast Cardinals."

"Is that true, Mr. Arrington?"

Alexander paused, "Your Honor, I may have said it in passing, in a private conversation."

"I heard it on the speaker phone at a location that's not my residence."

The judge was troubled by that. "I see."

Alexander saw he was sinking, but he wasn't going down alone. "Your Honor, then I would direct you to the rules about forming a team. It says grab four of your co-workers."

Reston countered, "Your Honor, that's not in the actual rules, but the introduction. Therefore, it doesn't apply. I would argue that there have been many teams that enter that aren't working at the same place. Just a bunch of friends that get together."

"Your Honor, the reason I recruited this top college athletic talent, was because my opposing counsel hired a mercenary team of bed pushers to chase after the title."

Judge Bonofiglio stopped chewing, "A mercenary team of bed pushers. Is that true?"

Reston hemmed and hawed at that. "Um... Uh..."

The judge leaned in, "Did you know any of these bed pushers before they committed to be on your team?"

****

They stood outside the courthouse both looking glum.

Reston turned to Alexander, "I guess that means your undefeated streak is over between us."

Alexander sneered, "That was a tie, she ruled we both were in violation of the spirit of the race and the Derby festivities. We *both* were barred from the race. I still haven't lost to you."

Reston puffed out his chest, "But you didn't beat me back there."

Alexander gave it some thought, "Your right, Reston. You argued a pretty strong case. We tied, fair and square." Alexander held out his hand and they shook.

Reston savored that, "Thank you, Alexander."

37

TORTS and Just Desserts from the mind of Alexander Arrington

The owl appeared and spoke:

I read the book *12 Seconds in the Dark* that was published in March 2022. It was written by a police officer that was on the Breonna Taylor raid presenting his version of events. In the book the officer writes about an encounter he was involved with a decade earlier in 2010. He describes it as 'remarkably similar to the night Breonna Taylor lost her life.' When the police officers tried to serve the warrant, a gunshot went off from inside the residence and a bullet whizzed within inches of the author's head. The shattered glass from the door cut his forearms. Even though he was bleeding and they had taken fire, the police didn't return fire, because they couldn't see who had shot through the door and couldn't identify a target. The encounter ended successfully with the suspects arrested.

Ten years later in 2020, when the officers tried to serve the warrant, a gunshot went off from inside the residence and the bullet made impact with a police officer's leg. This time the officers 'blindly' fired 32 rounds into that apartment killing Breonna Taylor. Three of those rounds went into an adjacent apartment, shattering the sliding glass door with a man, a pregnant woman and a 5-year-old child inside.

The author wrote that in 2010 the suspect claimed, (like Kenneth Walker in 2020) he didn't know they were the police and was scared. Then the officer laments 'it was years before body cameras.'

I'm not really sure why the author was making the comparison to this previous successful, deftly handled operation. It makes the chaotic and brutal response at Breonna Taylor's residence seem even worse.

As I am a supporter of law enforcement and a concerned citizen, I read the book hoping to find out more why the body cameras, which LMPD had, were not used. I learned from the book the main reason for not using body cameras was keeping informants anonymous. When they flip and become a snitch, it's a very dangerous path and their safety becomes the responsibility of the handler. I would agree. But that doesn't apply here on a raid. Another reason stated in the book is that body cameras would reveal tactics and be easily available to the defense attorneys. I submit *not* having the tactics available for the world to review has been a significant contributor to this disaster. The author further writes that he and his fellow officers don't like Big Brother looking over their shoulders. Who does? But law enforcement, with the ability to arrest, detain and use deadly force, has a special status in society that requires extra oversight. That's part of the deal. The author ends the book by commenting on the Breonna Taylor killing saying, 'I wish we, or at least I, had a body camera on that night.' And 'I would love for the world to see the truth and not just hear it.'

In the book I learned some of the officer's backstory. He was a person who once came to the aid of a young girl who was attacked. He didn't hesitate, he just ran to save her. In this heart-pumping rush of adrenaline, at this moment, he decided to be a cop. It takes a special person to put themselves in harm's way to protect and serve. And true-blue police officers deserve our admiration and utmost respect.

The author grew up in a diverse, impoverished area. His father was a Baptist preacher who ministered to Black, White and Hispanic members. After finishing the book, I don't think the author was racist and he seemed like a decent guy.

However, reading this account reinforced my strong belief he and others in law enforcement should never be put in such a situation, at this hour, in this country armed to the teeth, risking their lives on an extremely dangerous raid of this kind, against a woman they thought to be only peripherally connected to a target in some other neighborhood.

Shit goes sideways, people die, people lie and careers end. For what?

Even excluding the $12 million payment to Breonna Taylor's family, the cost of Louisville's legal settlements have tripled in the first two years of the 2020s. As of this writing the city's insurance company has canceled the policy. Louisville will need to find another insurer or face potential bankruptcy and that won't be cheap. Taxpayer money is being drained to cover the bad actors and bad actions at an alarming rate. A combination of services will need to be cut, or tax hikes enacted, if the situation isn't stabilized. In reality, this is a national problem.

After the killing of Breonna Taylor, all of the firings, the protests and penalty payouts, statewide legislation has been passed. The requirements to get a warrant have been increased and body cameras will be issued, worn and turned on—no excuses. It's a start."

~ ~ ~

"Let's say you line up a big scoop of vanilla ice cream to watch the game with and you don't feel like finishing it. It melts by halftime. If you put the pile of goop back in the freezer and expect it will be fine to consume when it firms up again for the next game, you're in for big trouble. It can really upset your system. With ice cream—and politicians—the melting process brings bacteria, like Listeria, that won't be killed off in the refreezing process. This bacteria can cause severe nausea, vomiting and diarrhea and lead to meningitis, an attack on the brain. Listeria can be passed on in sexual contact or from mother to child, with long term consequences such as severely curtailing mental development, blindness and deafness. Just a friendly reminder when you're making the choice for your next scoop!"

The owl faded out.

****

For as long as Granddad could remember the parade was on the Thursday before the first Saturday in May; now they were changing things. It was now the Sunday before the first Saturday, kicking off Derby week. Granddad embraced the change. More people could see the event. After a two-year wait, they were ready for it.

Granddad, Mrs. Simmons, Amy and Alexander picked up Old Man Miller and were dropped off on Broadway to watch the parade, with lawn chairs and a cooler full of supplies. The mayor and the governor rode by, they both yelled greetings to Alexander.

They all loved seeing the many big horses and mini-horses, several bands and classic cars. Shriners were in dune buggies, circus clowns in miniature cars and on tricycles.

Granddad and Old Man Miller saluted the Marine color guard.

****

After the parade the group was transported back to CA. Mrs. Simmons, Amy, Granddad and Old Man Miller came in and plopped down.

Mrs. Simmons fanned herself, "I loved seeing my alma mater march. The Central High Band and Dance Team. The Yellowjackets and they still got the mojo."

"They were excellent," Alexander agreed, on the way in. "The community was this year's Grand Marshal. And I loved Ethan the Dog as a representative."

"He was an excellent choice," declared Granddad. "The dog was abused by his former owner and when he was dying, they dumped him in the parking lot of the Kentucky Humane Society, where those folks nursed Ethan back to health. Now he goes into senior living facilities and cheers up the residents and brings joy to their lives."

"He's a cutie," quipped Amy. "Cruising in that green Corvette."

"I liked Virginia Moore as well," said Alexander. "Riding in that classic Vette. During the dark days, I looked forward to her sign language interpretations with the governor on his COVID updates."

"Do you sign?" ask Mrs. Simmons.

Alexander paused, "No. But I might take it up."

"Uh-huh," Mrs. Simmons tried to get up and help out in the kitchen, but Alexander waved her back down, as he was on the way to pull out a large plate of snacks and fruit for the group.

"Don't forget one of the other honorees in the parade, Sacred Heart Girl's Academy," stated Granddad.

"The Valkyries!" exclaimed Mrs. Simmons.

"They won the state title and were ranked 3rd in the nation," said Old Man Miller. "That's impressive."

Alexander entered with the food and offered him a Barley Pop.

"Thank you, Alexander."

"My pleasure, Mr. Miller. It's sure good to see you out and about. Thanks for going to the parade with us."

"Thanks for asking me. I've been going to the Pegasus Parade since the start in 1956."

"How long have you been collecting the Pegasus Pin?" Alexander asked.

"Since the first year they started issuing them to get into events. 1973."

"Same here," added Granddad. "Each year is totally unique. I've collected them all. Who did you like as Grand Marshals?"

Old Man Miller gave it some thought, "Fess Parker and John Wayne came that one year."

"The Duke was here in 1976," stated Granddad. "He grinned and waved right at me."

"And there was Joe B. Hall and Denny Crum," said Old Man Miller. "Our favorite radio guys."

"Right," chuckled Granddad. "Twice for them."

Amy was enjoying this, "What about you, Granddad, what were some of your favorites?"

Granddad sat up with a look of respect, "My favorite year was in 2011. The Grand Marshals were: World War II veteran Hershel 'Woody' Williams of West Virginia; Korean War veteran Ernie West of Russell, Kentucky; Vietnam War veteran Gary Littrell of Henderson, Kentucky; and Vietnam War veteran Don Jenkins of Quality, Kentucky."

"Excellent choices," said Alexander. "And I'd vote for Muhammad Ali, who appeared twice. And Teddy Bridgewater. I loved watching him play ball."

"What about you, Amy?" asked Old Man Miller.

"Growing up I admired Diane Sawyer," said Amy, "but she was Grand Marshal before I was born."

The room groaned and grimaced.

Alexander held up his Barley Pop in tribute, "Can't forget the 2013 University of Louisville Men's and Women's Basketball teams that *deserved* to be Grand Marshals."

The room nodded and sighed.

"Yes," said Granddad, "quite true. And I have to give some respect to Bellarmine University, when they were Grand Marshals. They moved up to the Division I level and in their first year won their conference. Before that, 11 straight D II postseason appearances. They were the Division II men's national champion basketball team in 2011."

Amy put up her hand, "A title Bardstown College hopes to also lay claim to, soon."

The group cheered and toasted that.

"What about you, Mrs. Simmons?" asked Amy. "Who were your favorites?

"I was excited to see Gladys Knight back in the day, plus there was Chubby Checker one year—and certainly Muhammad Ali."

Old Man Miller was thinking back, "And then there was 1967. Dale Robertson was set to be Grand Marshal. And they canceled the parade. I was so upset at the time. I really wanted to see him. I hated all that trouble."

"I was upset too," said Mrs. Simmons. "There was a lot of trouble. My family was living in a segregated world, that was separate and definitely not equal. Dr. King had come to town to support the struggle for fair and open housing. At a race leading up to the Derby, there were some protesters that ran onto the track."

"I was upset too," said Granddad. "And I did some protesting. I created some paintings that sold really well. I believed at the time—and still very much do—it's un-American to judge someone by the color of their skin, instead of the content of their character."

"That was the year Proud Clarion won for you," said Mrs. Simmons.

"Yes," Granddad fondly recalled. "And soon after that the Board of Aldermen of Louisville passed a fair housing law that inspired the statewide Kentucky Fair Housing Act, banning discrimination—so we both won."

Old Man Miller reflected on that, "Then...all of that protesting, and disruption, in the end, I guess, was worth it. It helped change things for the better."

****

Bobby and Amy strolled around the Great Balloon Glow that Friday night by the waterfront. Wearing a cap and glasses Bobby wasn't noticed. Everyone's attention was captured by the dozen lighter-than-air flying vehicles glowing in the night. Hot air balloons heated the air with propane that was compressed to a high pressure and dispensed as a liquid to the burner and ignited. And when this occurred you knew it, *everyone* knew it. And you never forgot the feeling when you first witnessed this ferocious blast. The burners aimed straight into the balloon envelope's center. After firing the burners, the heated air inside had less density than the air outside the balloon. With more heat came more differential density, allowing the craft to ascend.

The pilots were blasting the propane for show, as all the balloons were securely tethered to the ground. The real contest, the Great Balloon Race, would be bright and early the next day.

On the way home Bobby broached the subject with Amy on their future living situation: "What do you think about moving into my family's home after the wedding?"

"What about Cass?"

"She's taking over my bachelor pad in Butchertown. You could redecorate how you want. I'd commute to Bardstown, be home for a late dinner."

"Home for dinner, during the season? I know how coaching works. Let me look at the place."

"You've been there many times."

"Not as a prospective buyer."

****

It was a cold, gray day. You could barely tell the sun was up. The balloons had been trucked to Bowman Field, but there was doubt that the contest would even be held. The weather wasn't cooperating. It was overcast and blustery. The wind speeds were clocked at 50 knots at 3,000 feet. But they got the greenlight. The contestants fired up, filled up and the Great Balloon Race indeed kicked off. This was a Hare and Hound contest. The Hare launched first and then found a location in the open. The predetermined spot today would be Champions Park 10 miles north as the crow or balloon flies, right by the river. It was a wide-open grassy area.

The Hare set down and unfurled the target area. It was a tarp, 50-feet in diameter, with a large X in the middle. The Hounds then ascended to the sky. Alexander hadn't been victorious every year, but he had always bettered Reston—and he teased Reston about it, who casually laughed it off, but was grinding over this.

Chip was his co-pilot and they were determined. This was going to be the year they would bury the Arringtons.

Alexander and Amy flew early and he actually was off his game. His marker landed well off the bull's-eye. He groaned. Amy rubbed his shoulder. They landed their balloon and he shrugged. It was a successful flight, so the crew of six all toasted with the traditional champagne.

Reston was still in the sky and had been informed of Alexander's miscue. The closest marker was about a foot and three quarters. Reston and Chip realized it was theirs for the taking. Get within a foot and a half and get the win. Or just get it anywhere near the X, a virtual lay-up and he would vanquish Alexander for the first time and have bragging rights.

Reston dropped his marker and it was headed right for the center of the X. However, at this exact moment a pigeon was taking to the skies and was bonked on his beak by this falling projectile. The event not only stunned the animal, but Reston and Chip as well, as both the vector of the bird and the marker were modified. The pigeon flew on sideways for a bit and the marker landed completely outside the target area—once again preserving Alexander's personal winning streak against Reston.

Reston's team was aghast.

Alexander's team was elated.

Alexander toasted the pigeon as it continued on, now back on course.

"Yeah!!! That bird took one for the team!" The rest of the crew toasted and cheered the bird as well.

38

Amy went by the Dulsett family home and gave it an inspection. She had a key and checked out the interior. There were things she would change, around the edges, but she was happy with the house and could see starting a family here. She looked over the many happy family photos. Near the outline where the telephone used to be connected, she saw where the growth spurts of Bobby and Cassidy were documented by pencil on the wall.

Bobby showed up a half hour later, "You're right, Amy. Now that I'm a potential buyer, I'm looking at this place differently."

"You already own it, Bobby."

He eyed a small ding on the floor. "What's this? A deficiency. Who were these people, savages? How did that get there?"

Amy eyed the small crack, "I'm guessing you did that."

Bobby's eyes widened, "Guilty. That's where I dropped my bowling ball."

Amy glanced around the kitchen, "Just needs a little bit of work, some touch-ups."

"Have you seen upstairs?" Bobby moved closer to her and kissed her neck.

"As a matter of fact, I have."

"Right…" Bobby harkened back. "The night I snuck you into my room through the second story window."

Amy stated in her 'now hear this' mode, "First thing, we're installing security cameras, with motion-detection flood-lights covering that area."

"Agreed," said Bobby. "This is our advantage. We know all the secret passageways."

Amy took his hand and led him out the back door, "Instead of upstairs, let's check out back. Where the barbeques will be and the games of HORSE."

Amy eyed the setup, "It's a nice size basketball half-court, with the special practice rim."

Two 10-year-old boys carrying a basketball, shyly appeared from the shrubs from the far end of the backyard.

"Hey, there!" Amy called out, with her welcoming tone.

"Hi…" said the taller of the two. He turned to his friend, "See, I told you."

"Are you really Bobby Dulsett?"

Bobby grinned, "I am."

"This is cool. I've seen your burns on YouTube. Some nasty stuff."

Amy mumbled, "You nasty boy."

"Thank you!" Bobby then mumbled with satisfaction, "On to the third generation."

"We've been hearing the equipment here is smaller than regular size," said the smaller of the two.

Amy gave Bobby the sly once over, scrunched her face and whispered, "Wait a minute, your equipment is smaller than regular size?"

Bobby smirked at her, "Yes, the rim is just a bit smaller." He signaled and the guys passed him the ball. He took a shot and it rattled out. They rebounded the ball and passed it back. He took another shot and missed that.

Amy cleared her throat, "Where's the nastiness?"

The two kids were surprised. Bobby then loosened up, found his rhythm and began to bury the shots.

The kids were digging this. "Bobby, 'sweet shot,' Dulsett in the house!"

The other kid laughed, "In *his* house!"

A couple more boys and girls from the neighborhood filtered in.

"Bobby!" They cheered him. Bobby stopped. They applauded. He bowed and let them play on the Dulsett neighborhood court. Several of the kids were asking Bobby how he shot the ball. He was demonstrating the process.

At that moment Amy realized there would be many more scenes like this. Bobby was like the Pied Piper for kids. A great teacher. She realized he needed to do that now for 18 and 19-year-olds who played the game of basketball really well.

****

Back at CA, Alexander had been moping around. Amy then caught him out back eyeing the hot rod bed he had been constructing for the Great Bed Race. She could see that he still harbored some melancholy—but Amy had been formulating a plan that would soon be implemented that would mitigate such wistfulness.

On Wednesday of that week was the Great Steamboat Race. Amy, Alexander, Granddad and Mrs. Simmons were down at the dock where the Belle of Louisville was tied up and preparing for the race.

"There she is, the Belle of Louisville," said Alexander in awe.

Amy took in the view, "She's quite a sight."

Granddad thought back, "I took Alexander on her several times when he was a kid in the late 70s."

"The only steam-driven paddle wheel boat left," said Mrs. Simmons.

Granddad marveled, "It's like stepping back into history."

"All the equipment is original," stated Alexander. "The engine is from the 1880s."

Amy frowned, "I'm confused, I thought it was built in 1914."

"Yes, but the engines are from another vessel."

"That's old."

"That's classic," retorted Granddad.

"If you take good care of classic things," Alexander advised, "they'll hang around and still deliver."

"Just like you, Daddy. Except you don't always take good care."

"I'm working on it, Sugar Pie."

"Hmmm," hummed Mrs. Simmons, not that convinced.

Amy motioned them on, "All aboard."

"We're riding on the Belle during the race?" asked Alexander.

"Yes," said Amy.

"All right," stated Alexander, with some enthusiasm.

They reached the upper deck as the Belle blew its whistle. It maneuvered into place, fired the cannon and the race was on.

Amy led Alexander up the final flight of stairs.

"Where are we going?"

"Come on, Daddy, follow me."

They entered the wheel house. Amy introduced Alexander to the captain and he motioned Alexander to the wheel.

"Me?"

"If you would, sir," insisted the captain.

"Seriously?"

"Come on, Daddy, the race is on and you're the pilot, for the moment," said Amy. She pulled a Navy blue hat out of her bag and gave it to him. "This is what riverboat captains wore in the 19th century." She filmed him on her phone.

Alexander excitedly put on the hat. He was nearly giddy, but he maintained control and kept her on course. He piloted the Belle for only two of the 14-mile course—but it was enough, Alexander was thrilled.

As they left the wheelhouse, Alexander inquired, "You did this for me, Ambrosia?"

"It was a team effort between Mom and myself. Mostly Mom. She has the clout."

They rejoined Granddad and Mrs. Simmons and Amy pulled out her phone, "You two need to see this." She played the footage of Alexander at the wheel wearing his riverboat captain's hat.

"Very nice, Alexander," remarked Mrs. Simmons. "Look at the form he has at the wheel!"

"Way to go! You didn't hit any sandbars," teased Granddad.

Alexander was standing a little taller than when he boarded the vessel, "No I did not."

Granddad patted him on the arm, he knew what this meant to him. "I'm happy for you, son."

As the race ended under the Clark Memorial Bridge, it was clear the Belle was going to come in third behind the Belle of Cincinnati and the American Countess.

"Is this fair, really?" crabbed Alexander. "They aren't even steamboats!"

Alexander complained to the mayor, who tried to contain a grin. He was already 'consulting' with the judges, and after a battery of high-level discussions and some serious reviewing of the rulebook, the Belle of Louisville was declared the winner—as it was the only authentic steamboat in the Great Steamboat Race.

Amy put her arm around him, "Daddy, you helped pilot and argue the Belle to victory! A win on a technicality, it's a victory a lawyer can really appreciate."

Later, Amy got several pictures of Alexander proudly holding up the Silver Antlers, which went to the winners.

Amy printed out a picture of Alexander piloting the Belle of Louisville and put it on the wall. Alexander saw it and had a big sloppy grin. Amy eyed him staring at the image and had the satisfaction of her plan working.

****

Late that night Alexander and Amy decided to skate together on the half-pipe. After a few moments her father pulled his board and slid down to the bottom.

Amy joined him, "Daddy, you okay?"

"I'm going to miss these moments."

"We can still have these moments."

"Maybe, a few times. More I hope."

"Your little girl has grown up and she's about to get married."

Alexander was starting to tear up, "It was like yesterday. I remember you doing your first Ollie and now..."

"Yeah..."

They sat silent for a moment.

"Any last bit of advice?"

"Just enjoy the moment, Sugar."

Amy wiped away the tears, "Doing that already. And you always laugh about people giving generalities for advice -- 'Go for the gusto' 'Be happy' 'Give 110 percent' -- when they're looking for an actual strategy to make something work."

"Darlin,' you really know what it's going to be like married to a coach?"

"Yes. Long hours for him. Lots of travel. He'll need plenty of support. A coach's family should expect to move 4 to 5 times in his career or more. It's really rough on the kids. I know all that, Daddy. What can I do to help him succeed?"

Alexander stroked his goatee giving that serious thought, "Do a deep dive into NIL, Name, Image, Likeness. If you really want to help and support him, learn everything about NIL, because that's a major part of what drives recruits. The rules are complicated, about who can talk to whom and what can or can't be endorsed. Compliance will be the issue going forward. There will be coaches that break the rules and they will have the hammer come down on them. One of your jobs, as his partner and consulting lawyer, is to not let that happen to him; because he's going to have to go right up against that razor's edge. He'll need your informed guidance. He'll be tested. Bobby Dulsett likes to showboat at times and we've seen how that can end up."

Amy recalled such events, "Bobby has learned from earlier missteps."

"I hope he has."

39

The next day was 'Thurby at the Downs.' It was the official Derby Weekend kickoff. After two years Alexander especially looked forward to this Thursday. It was the day the locals claimed as their own and a tradition for Alexander and Amy to go together. It was a great way to get some early intel on how the track would run for the Oaks the next day and the Derby, the day after that—plus there was some pretty good music to listen to between races.

But this year, Amy told her dad she was skipping the event and getting a Multiplex Assay PCR test. It was a molecular COVID test and would take 24 hours for the results. Amy was isolating before and after the test, because her mother was making her first appearance in public and she wanted to be ultra-safe. Alexander understood. When Amy received the negative results, she emailed proof of it to her mother.

Alexander instead asked Sherri to go with him to Thurby. She had two hearings in the morning, but was free after lunch and accepted. When they arrived at the venue, Alexander mentioned he had seen Nathaniel Rateliff & The Night Sweats, the band playing that day, a couple of years before at the Highland Festival Grounds. He was introduced to Nate afterwards and they kept in touch. Alexander told Sherri about the Marigold Project that Nate had started. It supported community projects and non-profits. Their philosophy was that all people deserve to be treated with respect. They boosted civic engagement, pushed for gender and racial justice and helped those living in food deserts. All in Alexander's wheelhouse.

Alexander had been listening to Nate's song "Redemption" a lot lately—but also to another of his songs, "The Future." It asked if the future was indeed open and served a cautionary note about those who believed they were saved, yet were seeking vengeance and fire. The song warns others they were coming to steal and divide.

Later, Alexander met up with Nate again, introduced Sherri and they got caught up. He congratulated him on the excellent set and the good work in the Marigold Project. They laughed about his Rocky boxing workout in his video "Survivor."

As Alexander walked off, he didn't let on, but he believed Nathaniel Rateliff was one of the sages of our time, bringing some needed light to so much darkness.

He hummed what had become one of his favorites from Nathaniel Rateliff & The Night Sweats, "I Need Never Get Old."

"Alexander," purred Sherri, "*you* will never get old."

****

On Friday it was the 148th running of the Oaks, the premier and most lucrative event for 3-year-old thoroughbred fillies. The featured contest was a $1.25 Million Grade 1 stake race. A garland of lilies was awarded to the winning filly.

April wore a fabulous pink hat and dress, without a mask. Amy also had an awesome pink hat and a neon pink dress, without a mask. April said she was ready and she was relieved to be back at least part of the way; though she still felt leery indoors with a large crowd. April had her normal Winner's Circle Suite. It was an open-air covered lounge seating section right next to the track and close to the Winner's Circle.

And then it was the moment April had been waiting for. The Survivors Parade held every Oaks Day, had been paused for the last two years due to COVID, but not this year. The breast and ovarian cancer survivors were in high spirits as they gathered, thrilled to see each other after such a shutdown. Attendees to the race were encouraged to incorporate the color pink into their attire to show support. The grandstands were a sea of pink. 146 cancer survivors—warriors—marched for the first time in two years. The 100,000 in attendance cheered on the ones who went through the ordeal. April clapped and yelled out to friends as they strolled by. Amy could see her mother was getting emotional, it moved her too. It was a sisterhood. The survivors came together for a group photo.

April talked about Tricia Amburgey, an executive at Churchill Downs, who battled cancer for years. She came up with the idea for the parade in 2008. Tricia died in 2013. April's friends remembered and honored Tricia every year at this time. It was such a terrible loss, but her spirit lived on through all the love and support that was generated here.

****

Like Amy, Reston took the same molecular COVID test that Amy did. He was also negative. April was beginning to feel more at ease. They attended the Barnstable Brown Derby Eve Gala. It was a dazzling, celebrity-filled affair at the Barnstable mansion in the Highlands neighborhood. April was friends with twin sisters Patricia Barnstable Brown and Priscilla Barnstable. It was one of her favorite events. It supported the Barnstable Brown Diabetes Center at the University of Kentucky. Over the years they had raised millions for the cause.

****

Finally, it was the first Saturday in May. These two days, this weekend, was the Superbowl for April. For the first time in two years it felt nearly normal.

Right before heading out, just to be safer, Reston and April also both did a rapid antigen test that only took 15 minutes. With the good results they were on their way to Churchill Downs and the 148th running of the Kentucky Derby—the Run for the Roses.

A limo picked them up. April complimented Reston on his appearance. Over the years she had a few notes, but for the most part, he was always properly attired and impeccably groomed.

She reminisced and shook her head to herself thinking about Alexander's style. He was a work in progress for her—but there were times when Alexander dressed the part and was more than presentable. She wondered if they would run into him at the race; but he was yesterday's news.

****

Alexander had always looked forward to attending Churchill Downs and mixing with everyone, seeing old friends, reconnecting with old contacts. But he was indeed getting older, at least physically, the thought of watching the race on his big fat flatscreen appealed to him—and honestly, he really didn't want to run into April and Reston. It would have been a major buzz kill. He had moved on. Alexander went back to the way it used to be, when he threw legendary Kentucky Derby parties they still referenced in not so polite company.

At 10:20am the trumpet blared for the first 'call to post' for Race 1.

Alexander was reading a case file. He paused and watched the first contest. This process continued on for several more posts.

Currently Bobby and Amy were at his place in Butchertown. She was watching the TV coverage of the early races and he was watching film of a player on his laptop.

Amy shifted her attention over to what he was studying, "He's got good feet, stays balanced, plays good defense."

Bobby nodded in agreement, "He's so good he's either going to be a Louisville Cardinal or Kentucky Wildcat."

Amy pondered, "I would say to that, Bardstown College can't promise them great TV exposure, or even big NIL deals. But Bardstown College is a family, and families stick together. And you're going to push them to graduate with a degree and help them after leaving school."

Bobby thought about that, "Right, I do believe that and will do that."

"That has to be known and of course, you are Bobby Dulsett."

"Again, that may open some doors. But closing the deal is a high hurdle."

"Convincing the parents to trust you with their children and convincing players to trust you with their future, should be *very* challenging. When your first recruit gets his fairly good NIL deal, that'll help."

Bobby moved closer and put his hands around her waist, "If only there was someone I knew who knew legal stuff like this."

Amy gave that some thought, "Hmmm, I could give you a referral."

They kissed and he pulled her onto the couch and kissed her madly, "You can refer this!"

Amy howled with laughter.

****

It was early afternoon and guests started to arrive. Alexander welcomed one and all to CA, "Happy Derby! Happy Derby!"

Everyone was encouraged to dress the part. It was the Kentucky Derby after all!

In Derby days gone by, The DDs had ventured onto the infield at Churchill Downs and mixed with the other 80,000 merrymakers and lived to tell about it. Especially memorable was 2012, the second wettest Derby in history. The DDs were absolutely covered in mud and half in the bag. Amy then had the brilliant idea of them all sauntering over to have a Mint Julep with her mother sitting in Millionaire's Row—but was outvoted by the other mud-caked, less hammered DDs.

The infield was the Party Maximus zone of 'acceptable excess.' The DDs did and saw some interesting things. The race? All they could see was the grandstands and the legendary spires. They heard the distant thunder of the hooves and the yells of the crowd. They recorded the Derby and watched it at home later. In 2014 a jumbotron screen was installed that changed everything for the infield. However, this year The DDs would be at Casa Arrington and watching it live on TV.

By mid-afternoon Amy and Bobby arrived at Alexander's Derby party, already filled with about two dozen revelers. Granddad and Old Man Miller had started imbibing early and were telling jokes, some rather bawdy.

Old Man Miller and Granddad also teased Amy about sharing the Peterson-Dumesnil house on her wedding day, one week away, with the ghost who lived there, the 'Lady in White.'

Amy assured them, "I know all about her and heard the lady in white is very friendly and accommodating and even helped a little girl who was separated from her mother."

"Criminy," mumbled Alexander, as he rolled his eyes at this 'malarky,' wishing they wouldn't have brought this up. He didn't want to cause a scene so he instead studied yet another handicapper's opinion on the Derby.

Amy stepped out back. Dr. Trainer stepped forward, "Hello, Amy."

Amy was surprised, "Dr. Trainer."

"I was in town, so I took the liberty of coming by."

"Welcome to Casa Arrington, sir."

"Thank you. And I wanted to say how sad I am over Zabéla's untimely death."

"Yes," agreed Amy. "It was horrible and quite bizarre. And Dr. Trainer, Lannie told me that you were a great help to her in New Orleans. Thank you for that."

"My pleasure. But I defer to Raven, she orchestrated it."

"She orchestrates a lot," said Amy.

"As I recall you were quite fascinated by a piece of tech I had. The Holo-TV you saw at Zabéla's place in Malibu."

"I was interested." Amy thought back:

Zabéla pulled a black cube out of her pocket and put it down. It rang and Zabéla clicked it on.

A hologram appeared of Dr. Trainer. "James, lovely to see you."

The holographic image gave the look-see at several people, including Lannie and Amy. They marveled at how real he appeared. He turned around, "Nice to see you too, Zabéla."

"This is the famous Dr. James Trainer, everyone. Or at least a hologram of him."

The crowd applauded.

"Hello, everyone."

"I wanted to come by and show you the new thing I'm working on. I have my tech guy placing down four black cubes."

They watched a guy in a white lab coat place down the four black cubes and step to the side.

Amy then noticed her fiancé walking by, "Bobby, here's the gentleman I was telling you about. Dr. Trainer."

"He's here? It's great to meet you, sir. I've heard so much about you."

"Bobby Dulsett, it's an honor to meet such a successful basketball coach."

"I'm just starting."

"Your hard work is going to pay off."

"Thank you for the good wishes."

"They're more than good wishes, Coach Dulsett."

"I appreciate your confidence in me."

"And Congratulations on your nuptials."

"Thank you, sir." Bobby patted him on the back and gave Amy a look of semi-bewilderment and moved on.

"I wanted to come by and wish you all the best in person on your marriage next week."

"Thank you, Dr. Trainer. Do you know my dad?"

"Alexander? I only know of him."

"I'd like to introduce him to you."

"Terrific. But first I'd like to give you your wedding gift."

"You would?"

"It's a tip on this year's Kentucky Derby."

Amy quipped, "I've already made my bet. $10 on Mo Donegal at 10-1. I like the name."

"Put $200 on the Exacta. 21 and 3. Rich Strike to win and Epicenter to place."

Amy checked the odds. "That's crazy. Rich Strike is at 80-1."

Dr. Trainer locked onto her, "It's your wedding gift. You know how rude it is to turn down a gift. In fact, some people say if you do it brings bad luck."

Amy checked the odds on her screen again and then laughed.

Gabby came up to her, "What's so funny?"

"Gabby, I'm glad you're here. This is the gentleman I met in Malibu I told you about." Amy turned, but he was gone.

"Who?"

"That Dr. Trainer guy I told you about."

"He's here?"

"I was just talking to him. I introduced him to Bobby." Amy looked around but couldn't find him. She shrugged, "Don't want to bring any bad luck." She used her phone to access her sportsbook and bet the Exacta, 21-3, exactly like he told her.

****

April had on an even more flamboyant hat. When it came to head covering at the Derby, April brought her 'A' game every time. The feeling of joy after being pent up for two years continued on.

April and Reston strolled around Churchill Downs and people-watched. She was reminded of the term 'Dopamine Dressing' going around. It was more than how you presented yourself to the world, but how you were made to feel. There seemed to be even more brilliant neon and super bright colors this year. It was cathartic just being there and waving at friends.

At about 6:10pm the Derby contenders were led out by their connections, or team and paraded around the paddock area for several laps. People jammed in to see these magnificent animal athletes.

The attendees at CA were watching on a large flat-screen.

At 6:37pm the call rang out, "Riders Up." The jockeys were instructed to mount their horses and take to the track.

April and Reston were in their seats by the Winner Circle.

The tech guy activated the Holo-TV and a 3D rendering appeared before them. The group turned away from the flatscreen and stared. They were astonished at this image projected in front of them.

"What is this?" asked Bobby.

"I saw this tech in Malibu," said Amy. "Dr. Trainer wanted to show off the next generation of it."

Right around 6:39pm it was time to sing along to "My Old Kentucky Home" and Alexander again got a bit misty-eyed like a bunch of other Kentuckians. The riders were on their horses being led and loaded into the starting gate.

At 6:57pm they heard, "And they're off!" The gates flung open and the horses sprinted out. The Kentucky Derby had begun.

At Casa Arrington, the guests all gawked at this virtual 3D rendering of the broadcast of the race. Some followed the horses around the room and down the stretch. All were in awe.

Bobby was mesmerized. Amy was thunderstruck as Rich Strike pulled ahead right at the end and won it. The number 21 horse, Rich Strike, came in first and Epicenter, the number 3 horse placed, came in second.

At Churchill Downs, April and Reston were amazed at the results.

Bobby checked, "Dang, 80-1 on Rich Strike. I can't remember a horse winning with such long odds."

Amy heard a chirp and checked her voicemail. "You have one message."

"Hi, Amy. Dr. Trainer. I just wanted to tell you a little about your winner. The story of Rich Strike is absolutely amazing. Rich Strike had been on the bubble for several weeks to get into the Derby. This morning, at 8:45am the trainer was told they weren't going to be let in. The Rich Strike team was down, but right before 9am, because of a late scratch, they were able to get the horse entered at just about the last moment. He came from way back, stayed on the rails, weaved around a couple slower horses and out ran the rest to win the race. It's historic. An amazing performance. And it's my wedding gift to you. Proof that no matter how long the odds, you should never give up. Enjoy your winnings, Amy."

Amy was still in shock over what had transpired.

The spectators at the track were delirious as they pointed at the board and gawked at the odds of the payout.

The partiers at CA were nearly as speechless. Amy stared at the results in silence. She thought back to meeting Dr. Trainer in California:

"And there you are, the elusive Dr. Trainer," Lannie said cheerily.

He stepped up and shook her hand. "Lannie, nice to see you again."

"This is my friend--"

Dr. Trainer didn't need her introduction, "Amy Arrington, it is a sincere pleasure to make your acquaintance," he shook her hand.

"Dr. Trainer, nice to meet you, too. What's your doctorate in?"

"Physics."

"Oh. Are you theoretical or experimental?"

"Both."

"I thought you had to choose," said Amy.

"True, almost all do."

"But you."

"Correct. I dream at night and prove it during the day."

"Wait...I recall a story about...dark matter."

"This is an area I work in. Something that takes up so much space and is all around us and so little is known of it."

Lannie was confused, "I thought you were a movie producer."

"I do that too. Among other things."

"Like...your magic tricks or special effects?"

"You're referring to my disappearance last time."

Lannie and Amy gave each other a look.

"I tutored David Copperfield."

Amy checked her phone again to be sure of the results. She then slowly motioned Alexander, Bobby, Mrs. Simmons and Granddad out back away from the rest of the people.

"What is it, Amy?" asked Mrs. Simmons.

Amy gave the confirmation text to Alexander. "Could you check this because I think I just picked the Exacta. Rich Strike and Epicenter. 21-3."

Bobby checked his phone, "Well played, a two-dollar bet on the Exacta would pay out over four grand."

"No," said Alexander. "Amy bet $200. She just won $400,000."

Amy ran back into the house, but the black cubes and the tech guy were nowhere to be found. "He's gone!"

They were all mystified by this, by all of it.

Amy again heard his voice in her memory, *"I tutored David Copperfield."*

****

Later in the evening Amy got a call from her mother and she wanted to know how she made her picks.

"I got a tip."

"From who??"

"A magician. That's all I got."

April again wondered about her daughter.

Amy walked Bobby out of the house. It was still warm and a bit muggy.

"That was quite a race," said Bobby.

"Yes."

"And that was quite a bet you made."

Amy was still dealing with this, "It was something..."

"Kind of what happened to your Granddad those many years ago."

"Huh," said Amy.

At that moment a van rolled up. The door opened. Four guys in caps, shades and hoodies, grabbed Bobby and threw him into the van. Bobby glanced out at Amy and she didn't seem that concerned.

Mitch showed his face to Bobby, "Surprise."

"Mitch, Trent, Wyatt, Axel, did the River Ticks call a rehearsal?"

"Robert Dulsett, this is your bachelor party," barked Mitch. He issued Bobby a cap, shades and a hoodie.

Amy waved them off with a silly grin as the van roared off into the night.

Inside the van, Bobby was concerned, "Look, guys, I'm the new head coach at Bardstown College. I'm not going to be seen in a strip club."

"No clubs," assured Mitch. "No one's going to know, outside your buds. It's on the down-low, bro. Security Level-5."

The van pulled up to a closed garage. Trent got out and opened it and turned off the alarm.

"Bobby, you stay here, just for a moment."

Mitch led the three guys in. He pulled out a piece of paper.

"What's this?" asked Wyatt.

"This is an affidavit that you're all going to sign swearing what's about to happen will never be spoken of."

"Okay."

Mitch opened a small leather case. There were individually wrapped sewing needles. "Gentlemen, we are at Level-5 security. We're all signing with our blood."

"What??" cried Axel. "No way, dude."

"Prick your fingers with these sterile needles and use the blood to sign an X on this paper."

"I'm a diabetic, no biggie. I do it all the time," said Wyatt.

Axel cringed, "I'm not."

"Me either," stated Trent.

Mitch pricked his finger and signed an X in his blood. Wyatt chose his needle, pricked his finger and signed in blood. Trent and Axel grumbled, but followed suit.

Mitch swabbed their bleeding fingers with alcohol and gave each a band-aid. He then produced a bag. "Phones in here." The three complied.

Mitch then went out and brought in Bobby, in shades, a cap and hoodie. They all looked relatively similar. Mitch exited, checked his watch and right on time a sedan pulled up and three young ladies in trench coats got out.

Mitch welcomed them, "Hey girls, right on time. Phones please."

"Really?" asked Bunny.

"We don't normally give them up," said Pebbles.

"You'll get them back at the end of the event."

They reluctantly handed them over. He ushered them in, "May I introduce to you all, Bunny, Sunshine and Pebbles."

They dropped their coats and the three ladies, in lingerie, put on quite a show. And near the end, Bunny paused, "You're Bobby Dulsett."

"Bobby Dulsett??" All three of the strippers were giddy.

Mitch was alarmed, "Wrong! Totally wrong, Bunny,"

"Sure it is," Bunny insisted.

Mitch killed the music and moved in, "Party's over girls. You can collect your phones outside."

Bunny explained to the other girls, "I was in the marching band, when Bobby Dulsett came in and scored 48 points against our team and ended our home winning streak. I remember you taunting our fans."

Bobby was flabbergasted, "No I didn't."

"Yes, you did. I read you were getting married. Congratulations. You want a lap dance?"

Mitch swiftly had them out the door and was giving them their phones back. "Thank you, ladies, you got your payment. I expect your professionalism and discretion will prevail."

Mitch came back in with a sheepish look.

Bobby grunted, "On the down low, bro?"

"Bobby, I'm not sure that's possible with you," sighed Mitch.

****

The final fitting for the bridal gown was on Wednesday. It was the first time Amy felt any jitters, seeing the end product. The designer had done a fantastic job. The gown was spectacular and Amy took possession. The designer went home and with a sigh of relief, he took a long nap.

The DDs and the rest of the bridesmaids had their final fittings that evening.

April, while sorry that Bobby's parents were no longer among them, was pleased there wouldn't be the usual suggestions and requests from the groom's mother. She literally had free reign. April would let Amy think she was involved, which she was, to a point. April had been planning for this day for a quarter century. She had a guest list, files and files of her favorite food and floral designers, databases of all the other required vendors. Now that she knew it would be outside, April started monitoring the extended weather forecasts.

April, Amy and Steven, the manager at the P-D House, had meetings on the menu and the décor, the centerpieces and the fresh flowers that would be used. Everything had to be perfect and expedited. The staff at the place was professional and first rate and Steven had plenty of experience dealing with these situations and women like April.

****

On Thursday, Lannie Telfair flew in and met up with Amy just in time for the wedding rehearsal dinner. She was in the bridal party and had already sent her measurements in. Amy introduced her to Abby, Gabby, Bobby and Cassidy. Right before they sat down there was a bit of drama as Lannie tried on the gown—it fit.

It was a seven-course meal at the Brown Hotel. Amy handed out special gifts to her maids. The women received Longines Dolcevita watches. Bobby gifted the men Longines Hydroconquest watches. They were all very appreciative.

Toasts were made by Alexander and April. People were getting to know each other and they started to relax. The wedding party was full of good vibes and fun, but not for Alexander. He had previously handled a legal problem for one of the sous chefs and went into the kitchen to say hello, but was really on patrol. He continued checking around through the English Grill, onto the airy elegance of J. Graham's Café and the glamorous Lobby Bar. There was no time for fun, his eyes were darting about scanning for any problems, any sightings of Sean.

Meanwhile, back at the table, Amy and Bobby were talking privately.

"You didn't say anything about your bachelor party."

"Sure, just the thing a groom is going to chat about with his future wife."

"Did you have fun?"

Bobby grunted.

"What?"

"Mitch set it up that my identity would be hidden, but one of the ladies recognized me."

"Who?"

"We fooled Pebbles and Sunshine. But not Bunny."

"Bunny. Did she have a nice tail?"

"I'm glad *you* made that joke. I didn't notice."

"Eyesight starting to fail already. I hope Bardstown has a good health plan."

"Anyway, this 'dancer' had a grudge."

"Why?"

"She was in the marching band for a team I played against in high school."

"She remembered you."

"We won by 10 and ended their home winning streak. She remembered how many points I had and claimed I was taunting her fan base."

"Were you?"

"I don't remember. There were times…I was a bit full of myself."

"How many points did you score?"

"48."

"48??" Amy snickered at that, "I'd be mad as hell at you, too."

"Mad enough to post things?"

"First, if someone holds a grudge this long, *they're* the one with the problem. Second, it's a bachelor party. You were kidnapped and taken there by your Best Man and Third, when I learned this was going down, I made sure Mitch collected the phones, *all* of the phones in the room; which means there's no visual or audio evidence of the event."

"Of course. You did that. Thank you."

"You're the new coach at Bardstown College."

"I know. It's a steep learning curve. I'm glad you're going to be by my side and have my back." They hugged and he let out a big sigh of relief.

Amy had a laugh, "Mitch later told me he added 'Level 5 security.' With the affidavits signed in blood."

"That's why they had bandages," said Bobby.

"I advised him that wasn't necessary going forward," Amy said, with some incredulity. "You know, signing in blood…"

Bobby groaned, "Level 5 security. Dang."

"We won't be needing that type of security for my bachelorette party."

****

On Friday night The DDs, Lannie, Cassidy and a couple more friends had a stretch limo and they went out to dinner. Afterwards they traveled to a private location where a bar was set up. At that moment what looked to be an officer of the law entered. Music started and he tore off his shirt and pants and danced around in his briefs. The ladies were laughing wildly and getting into it. The male dancer finished up the song and faced Amy.

"Hey, are you the Firewoman?"

Amy's happy face became a frowny face.

40

You Are Cordially invited to the Wedding of Amy Arrington and Bobby Dulsett

The Peterson-Dumesnil House, designed in the Italian Villa style, was built in 1869 on 1.3 acres. The interior was striking with ornate furnishings and 14-foot-high ceilings.

It was surprising to no one, that April and Steven could put together such an extravaganza in such a condensed time frame. Everything looked fabulous. The guest list was now at 185. April studied the seating chart on her tablet and moved the places around like pieces on a chess board.

Elevated stands were brought in. Amy and Bobby wanted a nice simple wedding. April wanted one for the history books. It was to be a hybrid.

As the Peterson-Dumesnil House was nestled right in the middle of a neighborhood in Crescent Heights, April made sure to send generous gift certificates to the residents in the immediate area along South Galt Ave, Rowland Ave and South Peterson Blvd., as the circus would soon be descending. In fact, media trucks were already looking for locales to drop anchor. Some residents rented out their front lawns to them. The area was roped off. People began to camp out two days before the event to get close enough to see the bride and groom walk down the aisle.

April was studying her seating chart and texting with friends congratulating her on her daughter's nuptials, while continually scanning the weather forecast and checking in with Chef Jeff and Chef Broc. They were seasoned co-conductors of this orchestra of various sous chefs and pastry chefs preparing this symphonic gastronomic extravaganza.

Out front in the reception area limos arrived in the turn around and the guests got out.

Ezekiel Williams stepped out from his ride and had his invitation scanned. He cleared security and was being led to his seat.

Alexander was surprised, "Mr. Williams."

"It's Zeke, please."

"Call me Alexander. Pardon my curiosity, but may I ask how you were able to get an invite? Through Mrs. Simmons?"

"I tried to talk to her, but she's avoiding me. I called up Reston and asked for a favor."

"I see. Welcome."

"Congratulations to you, Alexander."

"Thank you." Zeke made it to his seat. He happened to make eye contact with Mrs. Simmons and gave her a nice smile.

Mrs. Simmons frowned, groaned and crossed over to Alexander. "How did Zeke get an invite?"

"I thought you'd about fly off the handle when you caught sight of him. He said he called up Reston and got the invite there, through April. Go complain to her."

Mrs. Simmons sighed.

Up in the bride's room, Gabby had her tablet out and was watching the pre-wedding stream. "Amy, you have paparazzi."

Another limo rolled up and a sharply dressed, very fit man with graying temples stepped out. He then helped out a young lady dressed quite fashionably.

Amy squinted at the screen and mumbled, "No way…"

"What?" asked Gabby.

"Who's that guy?" asked Cassidy.

"Harold Pearce. He's one of the partners at my old New York firm. He was my mentor."

Abby inquired, "Would that be his daughter?"

"No," Amy gazed at the screen trying to recall. "She was one of the cheerleaders."

"Cheerleaders?" asked Abby.

After searching on her phone, Lannie had a sly grin, "Harold's in the news."

Amy cringed and nodded, "An anonymous associate in the firm sends us updates."

Currently April was on her rounds checking last-minute details and still reviewing the seating chart. She got another text and read it. "What's this?? Tonight on *Triple C...*" April's eyes widened. She did a dramatic u-turn, marched up to the Bridal Room, didn't knock and strode right in.

"How is everyone? All is good?" Not waiting for the answer, "Good." She joined Amy at the mirror, "And you, my darling? Good? Good. There's a situation—"

"Yes, Mother, there is a situation. I have a question."

"Uh, yes?"

"Did you invite Harold Pearce to the wedding?"

"Harold?"

"I saw him on the video stream arriving with his guest."

"Yes, I did."

"How could you do that? And I'm not going back to New York to work."

"You say that now. I remember when I was a bride, not even close to thinking straight."

Amy had a low growl, "Mother...

"I'm just keeping that bridge open. You don't have to cross back over it. Just don't burn it down. And think of me, when I'm not here in my hometown, I'm probably in New York."

"Mother, have you read some of the tidbits that came out about the breakup of Harold's marriage? Multiple partners, 'hot oil' orgies, S&M?"

"Darling, he's a lawyer."

"What does that mean, Mother?"

April motioned over to the couch and they sat.

April's mind was churning with details, "What do you have that's old?"

"The pearl earrings from Grandma."

"Okay. Something new?"

"I just got Bobby's name tattooed on my arse."

"Okay, and what about something … Wait, what??"

"Joking. Lannie gave me a bracelet."

"Okay. Something blue?"

"I'm wearing one of Bobby's old blue wrist bands." Amy pulled up her sleeve to show her.

"And you laundered it before donning it?"

"No, it's all stinky."

April frowned.

"It's been properly laundered."

"And something borrowed."

"I was hoping you'd loan me something."

April was touched by that and pulled out a veil.

"You were ready."

"I was hoping you'd ask. This was my wedding veil."

Amy was pleased, "Thank you, Mother." They hugged.

"Give me your shoes."

Amy took them off and handed them over.

April pulled out some sand paper and began scuffing up the bottoms. "Just a little extra protection so you don't slip. And speaking of slipping, my dear, some reports have surfaced of your bachelorette party. I was just sent this." She handed Amy her tablet and kept sanding. "This is on tonight's show."

A clip from *Triple C* ran. John Tenorio spoke into the camera: "Sizzle sizzle my thizzle. We have footage of the Firewoman begging to be 'restrained' by an 'officer of the law' at her bachelorette party. You have the right to remain silent, but you won't!"

The male dancer displayed his skills, very close to Amy, who giggled and did some wiggling of her own.

"Hey, that guy stole my abs!" cracked John. "And look at her go!"

April paused the footage, "That's the first thing you get, the cellphones. Didn't I teach you that? Someone got footage of you and sold it."

"Why is he still coming after me? I'm nobody."

"I believe it's to get to me. I have that effect on men. At times they can't quit me."

"Ugg... Mother..."

"I can't help how I affect the male animal."

Amy ignored her and thought back, "After he groped me, I only dislocated a couple of his fingers, no breakage."

"This is why you have no standing criticizing me for inviting Harold."

"Say what??"

"There's some dirty laundry on the internet of both of you."

"Mother, I'm not judging, but comparing myself to Harold is like comparing an apple to an orange, if the orange, and I'll quote directly from the published divorce filing, 'was on Viagra, wearing a G-string, gagged, tied up in ropes and chains and getting flagellated in a leather harness by a squad of cheerleaders. His plus-one to my wedding is the captain of that cheerleading team.'"

April waved that off, "We all have our peccadillos."

Amy was quiet, she closed her eyes and rubbed her temples.

"Ambrosia, I am not going to have a tiff with you on your wedding day. I remember when I was a bride, emotions going haywire."

"Mother!!!" Amy's tone startled the room. She recalibrated and softly elucidated, "Dearest Mother. Thank you for all of your incredible efforts to bring this event to fruition. Now, please go and enjoy it."

April handed back the shoes, "No time to enjoy, a million things still need to be checked." April was off.

Lannie had a wry grin watching the screen showing Harold and his date being led to their seats. "So, Harold was your mentor."

"Only concerning matters of jurisprudence. His personal life was a mystery to me. I never had a problem with him. It's John Tenorio. That's the conundrum. He just won't quit me…"

Currently Alexander was ensconced behind a tall bush, slyly eyeing the people continuing to enter. Gabe, also on high alert, joined him.

Alexander stroked his goatee, "What's our number one threat?"

Gabe pulled a picture out of his pocket, "It's Sean. Sean Wellington."

"Good," muttered Alexander. "Be on the lookout for anything. Frogs raining from the sky, rabid rats or vampire bats. But seriously, he's taken payback to another level."

"Let that clown try," warned Gabe. "I'll take his punk ass down." He checked around over the well-heeled crowd, "With discretion."

"10-4, go on your rounds."

"Got it, boss." Gabe casually walked among the guests and warmly smiled.

Harold, his date and their usher, walked by.

Alexander stepped out from his nook, "Harold?"

Harold recognized the voice and stopped. He turned to his date, "You go and sit, sweetie." The usher continued to lead her to their seats.

Harold walked over and shook hands with Alexander.

"Congratulations, Alexander. This is a wonderful day."

"You aren't here with Kathy?"

Harold was a bit sheepish, "We divorced, a couple months ago."

"I'm sorry, I didn't know."

"I'm surprised, it was in the tabloids."

"I don't read the tabloids."

"That's a good thing. She took me for nine figures. I'm thinking about organizing a couple takeovers at those media companies and burning them to the ground. At the very least I'm filing against a couple of those rags for the crap they published."

"Was it true?"

"What?"

"What they published."

"What does that have to do with the cost of croutons in Khrakistan?"

"Not much, I'm guessing."

"That's what I thought," said Harold, puffing out his chest.

"Harold, your firm is still king of the mountain."

"For the moment. As long as we keep reloading with the top guns and hold onto that talent."

Alexander was silent for a moment. "You're right. Did Amy invite you?"

"No, I haven't heard from her. April did."

"Enjoy the ceremony and reception, Harold."

"Thanks, again, congrats, father of the bride." Harold punched him playfully on the arm.

Alexander smiled with gratitude. Harold found his seat next to his twenty-something friend. Alexander's smile faded.

Inside the house, April, two still photographers, a videographer and her bridesmaids, in their emerald gowns, were standing in the first-floor hallway capturing images of Amy descending the staircase.

"You look marvelous, darling!" April was beaming.

“Thank you, Mother,” Amy was beginning to feel it.

April barked, “Bridesmaids, get her to the starting gate. I need to do the final check.” April was off.

Back behind his shrub, Alexander was stewing at Harold being here and April inviting him.

April arrived holding the hand of an 8-year-old girl, “Alexander?”

He heard her voice, but chose to ignore it.

“Alexander? Are you there?”

Alexander finally responded, “Just lost in thought, sweet pea.”

“Are you okay?”

“I’m perfect. On this perfect day.”

“Good to hear. Alexander, this is Melody, she’s the flower girl.”

“Hellooo, Melody,” trilled Alexander.

“Hi,” giggled the cute little girl with flowers in her hair.

“Watch her for a second, I’ll be right back. I need to check on something.”

Alexander was civil to April, “Yes, ma’am.” He then had a goofy grin for Melody and she had an even goofier grin for him.

“Congratulations, Alexander!” One of his pals patted him on the back.

Alexander swung around, “Thanks, Lincoln. I’m glad you could be here, buddy.”

“Wouldn’t miss it for the world.”

“Get your seat, it’s about to start.” Alexander looked back and Melody was gone. “Ah…” He began to hunt around. When he immediately didn’t locate her, he was filled with serious concern.

April met up with him, “It’s showtime, Dad. I’m taking my seat.” She noticed Alexander was wide-eyed, “Where’s Melody?”

“I don’t know. I just took my eye off her for a second and she was gone.”

April was now nearly panicking, but she had to keep her cool. "We need to find her, like immediately."

Alexander and April greeted more friends as they subtly searched around, not wanting to cause a ruckus.

"I'll check out front," said Alexander. He went around to the front porch of the house and found Melody standing on the steps."

"Melody! Thank God."

A woman in a white dress was standing with her, holding her hand.

Alexander knelt down in front of Melody, she giggled again. He smiled at her and turned to the woman, "Thank you for watching her." But the woman in white was gone.

April came around the corner and found Alexander with Melody. "Where was she?"

Alexander was a bit rattled, "She was being looked after by a woman…in white."

April sighed with relief, "Good. Great."

Alexander looked around, "Who *was* this woman?"

"There are a lot of women in white here, Alexander."

"Her dress didn't look modern. Where'd she go?" He continued searching.

"Probably went back to her seat. Now, Alexander, you need to get over to your location. You're about to walk your daughter down the aisle."

Alexander blankly nodded and met up with Amy.

"Daddy?"

"Yes?"

"You look like you just saw a ghost."

Alexander opened his mouth to comment on the situation, but kept quiet. He grinned at his daughter. "You look so beautiful."

"Thank you, Daddy."

Bobby was standing at the altar with Mitch, his Best Man, and his groomsmen. He was nervous, naturally, way more than he ever was when he was on the court. He slowly looked out over the crowd, but it was a blur to him.

The ceremony was a couple minutes from starting. April AA1, checked her tablet and went over the seating chart. She observed Chip, CR1 and Nevada, NN1 settled in. Reston, RR1, was set. Alexander, AA2 was ready on his mark. April studied the crowd. She was thrilled to see the woman she most admired, CB1, with her daughter BBB1 and her husband MB1. They all had a friendly wave.

April saw Bobby's friends, four really tall guys in a row: LH1, DG1, PE1, RS1. She smiled at the most talented of all her guests: TA1. April said hello to her most favorite lawyer, other than Alexander, TB1. She was happy to see Alexander's idol had made it: WM1.

April greeted pals, GH1 & ABH1, arriving with JH1.

April was relieved to see their talented wedding gown designer, GD1, who hadn't gotten much shut eye for a couple months, had caught up on enough sleep to attend.

April saw and checked off Nolan Huber, NH1, Betty BH1 and Dylan, DH1. Harold Payne, HP1 and Harold's Guest, HPG1. She checked off Sherri, SD1 and grimaced.

April smiled at Max, MG2 and Granddad, AA3 and his new BFF, MM1.

April was pleased to see Alexander's guests, who he had gotten to know since the tragic death of Tyler Gerth. CG1 & GG1, JG1 & MAG1, BL1 & TH1.

610 EL & LO were settled in. April waved at GC1 and AC1.

April then spotted a friend, MG1, sitting with son PB1and CB2, who had flown in for the event. Daughter AB1 was also with them. The four of them had a friendly wave.

April smiled at Stephanie, SM1. She then waved to Chris and Maria, CG2 and MG3 and Brett Clay, BC1.

April then saw JH1 signal Bobby and they had a laugh together.

Dylan saw this as well and his jaw dropped.

April noticed Mrs. Simmons, RS1, seemed to be annoyed by the presence of ZW1.

April was honored to see DC1 who nodded to her.

April then spotted JL1 & CM1 off to the side, being inconspicuous. They grinned at each other with a subtle wave.

The usher then escorted April to her seat next to Reston. The music started.

Alexander gave Amy a kiss on the cheek and whispered, "Okay, sweetheart, here we go."

Amy had a big smile on her face as Alexander escorted her down the aisle and they met Bobby at the altar.

The priest faced the gathering, "Dearly beloved, we are gathered here in the sight of God, and in the face of this company of witnesses, that needed extra seating and media credentials, to join together this man and this woman in Holy Matrimony..."

There was some laughter at that.

"...Robert Dulsett, do you take Ambrosia Arrington to be your wife? Do you promise to be faithful to her in good times and in bad, in sickness and in health, to love her and to honor her all the days of your life?"

"I do."

"Ambrosia Arrington, do you take Robert Dulsett to be your husband? Do you promise to be faithful to him in good times and in bad, in sickness and in health, to love him and to honor him all the days of your life?"

"I do."

The two exchanged wedding rings, looked up and smiled at each other.

"By the power vested in me by God and the Commonwealth of Kentucky, I pronounce you husband and wife. What God has joined together, let no man put asunder. You may now kiss the bride."

The crowd cheered. Bobby raised the veil and kissed Amy.

The wedding location transitioned to a reception.

Several cases of Dulsett Reserve were at the ready, with plenty in reserve. Balthazar's Boffo Barley Pops continually rose through the ice and people snatched them.

Tables were quickly set up. Chef Jeff and Chef Broc and their crew produced and displayed a dazzling feast for the guests who ordered from an army of servers. There was a vast selection of sushi, seafood, prime cuts of meats, scalloped potatoes, roasted veggies, arugula and avocado roasted garlic salad, pasta Bolognese, linguine with shrimp scampi, buttered corn, BBQ ribs, fried chicken and wild rice, cupcakes and frosted brownies.

The curtain was now raised and the vision of their spectacular wedding cake was revealed. In honor of Bobby's number 7, it had seven tiers, with rustic textured buttercream frosting, adorned faux succulents and edible gold leaf.

Amy and Bobby fed each other a piece of wedding cake under the Ginkgo tree like she always fantasized about. The crowd cheered them again and the celebration began. My Morning Jacket serenaded them as Amy and Bobby had the traditional first dance.

Bobby had a big grin.

"What are you so happy about?" asked Amy.

"I didn't think I had a chance. Just like Rich Strike, I was the longshot and had to weave through a crowded field and then eek out a victory right at the end."

"Stay humble, Bobby. I was the one in the crowded field."

Amy then danced with her father.

"I don't think there has ever been a more beautiful bride."

"What about mom?"

"All right, a tie for first."

"We'll keep that between us, Daddy."

"I remember the first time you told me you were dating Bobby Dulsett."

"You thought I was joking."

"You have been known to kid around, kiddo." Alexander thought he saw something for a second.

"Daddy, relax. You're more nervous than I am."

"I'm good, just so happy." They continued to dance, but he subtly continued his watch.

Bobby was dancing with April.

"Let me say, welcome to the family, Bobby. I'm thrilled that you're my new son-in-law."

"Thank you, April. I will do my best to make her happy."

"After the honeymoon you're off to start recruiting?"

"Yes. Trying to get the best players to come play for me. Train them and then, hopefully, coach them to victory."

"I've been reading about this NIL thing, Name, Image and Likeness."

"Yes."

"I have some friends, business people, that may be interested in supporting Bardstown College, the players, through this NIL program."

Bobby let that sink in, "That's interesting. There could be no coordination between me, the school and these interested parties."

"Don't worry about that, Coach, I definitely know how 'not to' coordinate."

Bobby nodded and realized he needed to tread very carefully here.

April and Alexander were now dancing together.

"Darlin', the day's finally here. You really did a remarkable job putting this all together." Alexander's eyes were scanning about.

April thought back fondly, "I remember the first time they put Ambrosia in my arms."

"I remember the first time I held her," recalled Alexander.

"She spit up on you, as I recall," teased April.

"Great moment. Who knew we would end up here?" asked Alexander.

"She knew," said April. "10 years ago, Ambrosia told me she was going to marry Bobby. It was her original plan."

"She told me that too," said Alexander recalling. "She seems to be very good at making certain predictions. She also said she would one day sing with the band My Morning Jacket." They both observed Amy fulfilling that fantasy, as she was on stage crooning with the band.

"And...predicting the Kentucky Derby," said April.

"Yeah... That too..." They both had perplexed looks.

Thinking he saw Sean, his eyes darted to the side.

"What is it, Alexander?"

"Just worried about keeping this place safe."

"There's a ton of security here," April assured. "We're secure."

"We've had some threats," Alexander explained. "Not explicit, but connected to the food poisoning incident a couple summers ago."

"Really? You mean before the Shakespeare performance?"

"Yes. That's how terrorists work. Make a big mess and then threaten to make another big mess. You just never know when."

"Who's behind this?"

"I believe it's a kid we sued. We won and he can't get over it."

"A kid?"

"Sean isn't a child. Maybe mentally, he's in his early 20s. He's intelligent and twisted. He was stung and wanted to get back at me. Sean hacked my blog for starters and invited the crazies to the house. Then it looks like he got serious revenge for our takedown by somehow poisoning the food through one of the caterers at the gathering before the King Lear performance. He's been taunting us over it ever since. Multiple times. In front of the house and online, day and night."

"Your legal skills can't make him go away?"

"I've hired a guy to look behind the curtain. He's coming here later to the reception. He says he's got something. With that I'll be able to shut him down."

The song ended. Alexander escorted April to her table and then returned to his table. He led Sherri out and they started dancing with the next song.

"I say, you look quite handsome in your tux, sir."

"Thank you, ma'am. You are a vision to behold."

"Amy looks so beautiful in that dress," Sherri swooned. "I hope they are going to be very happy."

"I do too. Being married to a coach is going to be an experience."

"Amy is going to be working with you?"

"That's what she says."

"Alexander, you must be very pleased with that."

"I am. She's a blessing being in my life. As you are too, Sherri."

Sherri appreciated that, she smiled. Alexander's eyes darted off to something.

"Alexander, come on, chill out. That's your security team's job."

"You're right. I have a guy I hired to look into the matter. He's going to be here later."

"Sounds very cloak and dagger," Sherri stated in a stage whisper.

"Some of it might not be admissible," declared Alexander. "But reliable."

"Then I'm pleased there is still some mystery in our relationship."

"For your sake, I intend to keep it that way, Your Honor."

The song ended and Alexander escorted her back to their table. He touched her shoulder, "Excuse me. I'll be back in 15 minutes for another dance, I promise."

Alexander ducked into the security tent and joined Gabe. They both surveyed the bank of monitors covering the event. 185 people were enjoying themselves.

"We made it through the ceremony. Halfway there," stated Alexander. "Here's the real challenge. This is when he'll most likely make his move. Watch for spiking of the food, or someone releasing a toxin. I've got people monitoring the situation. Just be a floater, watch over the watchers."

"Got it, boss." Gabe again eased back into the crowd of people.

Alexander, still unable to enjoy the moment, on the day he always dreamed of, continued his vigil of events. He confirmed there were photos of Sean in front of the four security agents stationed at the monitors covering the reception. Multiple facial recognition scans were being done.

Alexander exited the security tent and climbed up on a perch where he could survey the gathering. He gazed over the guests enjoying themselves and then his efforts paid off. He spotted Sean in the crowd and they made eye contact. "There he is!"

Sean laughed and again simulated putting his finger down his throat and gagging.

Alexander pulled out his walkie-talkie, "Suspect has been spotted in the south section of premises."

The security team moved in and quickly surrounded him. Sean tried to run, but he was hit hard by a private security associate and slammed to the ground. The guy rubbed Sean's face in the grass as part of the punishment. The breath was knocked out of him and he struggled. They zip-tied and then yanked Sean to his feet.

Alexander strolled up with a satisfied grin, "May I see your invitation, Sean?"

"I ...left it...at home."

Alexander leaned into Sean's defiant face, "Then you're trespassing. I want to press charges. You hacked my blog and made me a laughingstock. You got away with the food poisoning at my house and you laughed about it. Now you're going to pay. We have security cameras everywhere. If you pulled something here, we'll have proof. And since you're such a nuisance, I'm going to have to swear out an affidavit on how many times you taunted us over the incident. You're not going to make bail. Enjoy lockup Gokuro Gangsta. It's an actual place where the sun really doesn't shine."

Sean's face turned ashen as he was led away.

Alexander fist-bumped the security team for their assistance.

Alexander told Granddad, Mrs. Simmons, April, Reston, Bobby, Amy and Sherri that the problem was taken care of. He was now able to relax.

"Amy, who was that guy?" asked Lannie.

"A pest that's been buzzing around. I'm glad that's over."

Alexander again danced with Sherri and they got close and kissed.

April was chatting with a friend and she noticed the smooch, her face sank in disappointment.

Reston was at the next table laughing with some of his buddies, but he spied her reaction to Alexander's kiss.

Old Man Miller and Granddad also saw the kiss and gave each other a sly look.

"I remember those days," said Old Man Miller.

"I remember them too," said Granddad. "Like, last Saturday night."

Mrs. Simmons cleared her throat at that and gave him a look.

Granddad corrected himself, "Or the Saturday before that."

Mrs. Simmons gave him a pity nod.

Granddad groused at her, "I believe I'm heading over to the dessert table for round 2 of that cherry pie."

"It would be round 3," Mrs. Simmons snapped back and then she lightened up with a twinkle in her eye, "Amy just got married, gentlemen, if you would, please bring me back one of those fancy pastries."

Old Man Miller and Granddad nodded, guffawed and shuffled off together. They passed through the gathering and greeted friends and joked around with others. They arrived at the bountiful table of pastries and other decadent goodies.

"What would you gentlemen like?" inquired pastry chef Jaclyn.

"They all look so inviting," said Old Man Miller, enamored by the sweets.

"Indeed," said Granddad. He then noticed movement off to the side. It was Marcus by himself, wearing the VR goggles, living in his virtual world. Granddad looked around at other kids the age of Marcus who were running around playing, and became very sad seeing this.

Back at the table Mrs. Simmons was people-watching when Mr. Williams came up, "May I join you, Rose?"

"Why?"

"To catch up."

"I don't think so. No need to."

Zeke stood there for another moment, "I'm sorry, Rose. I truly am. I wish things would have worked out differently." He walked on. Mrs. Simmons looked away, there were tears in her eyes.

The song had ended. Sherri and Alexander were headed back to the table, but Alexander had witnessed the scene and saw the pain Mrs. Simmons was feeling. Alexander felt like he was intruding by observing. He turned away and bumped into Bill, who congratulated Alexander. These two grizzled legal warriors, old friends, conversed. He was still amazed that Amy was just a kid like 'only a moment ago.' Alexander was with him on that sentiment and mystified as to where the years went to.

Abby and Mitch were sitting together and he was on edge.

"What is it, Mitch? You aren't enjoying the wedding?"

"It's fine."

"No, it's not. Tell me."

"Not at the wedding."

"Why not?"

"Not now."

"You're scaring me, Mitch."

"Remember I told you we were millionaires?"

"Yeah…"

"We were. And I was reading some analysts and they were saying it would double again. And I went all in. And…"

"What?"

"It crashed."

"That's fine, you diversified, right?"

"It was going to double again."

"How much did you lose?"

"I tried to get out. But they froze the withdrawals and now, they're under investigation for fraud."

"What about our investment?"

"Gone."

"What about the car?"

"Leased."

"We still have our savings."

"I threw that in. I did it for us. I wanted us to be able to do things."

"You emptied our savings?"

"It was going to double…" Mitch's voice trailed off into oblivion.

"We're wiped out?"

"We can get it back."

Abby was in shock, "I didn't give you permission to withdraw our savings."

Mitch, full of grief and guilt, got up and walked off.

On the opposite side of the reception and social orbit was April and Reston.

"Harold was a billionaire before the breakup. No prenup. Now he's only worth around $600 million," Reston stated.

"Poor dear, he's probably clipping coupons now," faux-lamented April. "Prenups. Very important."

Reston was reassuring, "Again, I have no problem signing a prenup with you, dear. I understand where you're coming from."

"I don't think we're at that place, yet, Reston. Don't worry I haven't had my attorneys prepare anything."

"Fine."

"Why are you so on edge, Reston?"

"My only problem at the moment is that I got you to give Zeke Williams one of the very exclusive invites and he's spending way too much time over at Alexander's table. I have some ideas for some potential deals and wanted to bounce them off him."

Meanwhile, across the way, Zeke was bouncing ideas off Alexander. "Why not recreate what happened in Northern California, Silicon Valley, and in Southern California, Silicon Beach, and do it here, Silicon...Meadow? You know, bluegrass and all that."

Alexander gave that some thought, "Hmm... Or maybe Silicon Ville."

"Whatever," said Zeke. "What we do is inject this area with a serious infusion of private/public investment in STEM, coding in kindergarten. Nurturing ideas from the students in grade schools through high school. Entrepreneurship and R and D gets ingrained in their DNA early. Silicon Meadow becomes a giant incubator nurturing a string of startups."

Alexander was running with this, "Silicon Ville becomes the point guard dishing off assists in a series of high-tech fastbreaks. I like it, Zeke."

"Thank you, Alexander. That means a lot coming from you."

Alexander sluffed that off, "Where's this coming from?"

"I was thinking about Judge Winslow. We used to write letters to each other when I was in prison. He said redemption was waiting for me. His wish was for me to exit incarceration, move forward, succeed and then reach back and help others. I exited incarceration, moved forward. He encouraged me to get my degree and into law school, for which he paid. When I tried to pay him back, he had me donate the amount to a charity."

Alexander chuckled, "That sounds like the judge."

"And I've had some success."

"I'll say," agreed Alexander. "I Googled you. You've been busy. You put together some significant deals in Silicon Valley."

"I was always good at making deals. I got on the right side of the law and things have worked out. But I'm getting on in years."

"Aren't we all."

"The judge also said he wanted me to reach back and help others."

"How's that coming along?" asked Alexander.

"I've been a bit slow on the reaching back, make that very slow. You know, I Googled you too, Alexander."

"Oh dear, there are some embarrassing pictures I cannot for the life of me get removed from the internet."

Zeke laughed, "I was referring to the cases that you have taken on."

"They are not in your wheelhouse, Billy Zee."

"Not as of yet. I'm going to be honest with you, I screwed up. My ex-wife and my daughter are angry with me. I was cheating and then she was cheating. She could prove her claim, I didn't try. I didn't want to make it ugly. The marriage was over a long time ago."

"That's too bad," said Alexander.

"I have a few regrets."

"But, you did it your way."

"I did...and there's some amends to make."

"I wish you well in your quest."

"Would you be interested in partnering up with me, Alexander?"

"We're only a small boutique firm."

"I have access to significant funding. This is how I want to reach back and help others. I want to work on these cases. Show that I can do more than make rich people richer. Fulfill my promise to the judge."

"Now Zeke, I would be open to this personally. But I need to run this by some people."

"You mean, Rose, Mrs. Simmons."

"I really can't get along without her. If she isn't on board, it won't work and there's my daughter as well."

"I understand. I'll be patient."

Alexander ambled to the bar and got another brew. He listened to the sly, clever beats of Flexy-P on the stage and then settled at the table where Mrs. Simmons was sitting.

"Can you believe your little girl, wild as she was, is finally hitched?"

"It's a wonderful feeling. Now I don't want to drown out the joy, but I need to ask you something and I'm giving you complete veto power over this. What would you say if Zeke Williams became a partner at Arrington and Arrington?"

"What does Amy think about this?"

"No, no, your opinion is the most important thing to get here first. If you can't work with him, no use even approaching Ambrosia. Your thoughts on this are paramount to me."

"You would function at a decidedly lower level of productivity if I walked, that's for sure."

"Precisely," pronounced Alexander. "I've witnessed the consternation between you two. It's complicated and deep, it goes back over time. I'm not going to create an uncomfortable work environment for you."

"I'm fine if Zeke comes on board. It's probably what this firm needs."

Alexander pondered that, "You think so?"

"I most certainly do. And since I'm so vital, I think a healthy raise should be in the offing."

"Already in the works."

"Ipso facto, do you see how beneficial Zeke is to the firm already?"

"My eyes have been opened, ma'am."

"Then my answer, Alexander, is let 'er rip."

Amy was alone for a moment at her table and her father sat down. "How are things going on your day?"

"Everything is perfect."

"Since you're going to be gone for 10 days, I'd like to run a piece of business by you before you jet off."

"Shoot."

"Zeke Williams has approached me about joining the firm."

"Really? Isn't he kind of a highflier to come down to our level?"

"He says he's getting up there in age and wants to fulfill the promise he made to Judge Winslow."

"A promise? To the judge?"

"The judge apparently saw something in young Ezekiel and offered him a path to redemption, but made Zeke promise to reach back. After he did his time, he got him into college and covered law school. Zeke then made a pot of gold in Silicon Valley. Zeke's now moving back to Louisville, his home and reaching back. What do you say?"

"What does Mrs. Simmons say? I saw the friction."

"She's willing to give it a go."

"Then I say yes."

"Arrington, Arrington & Williams?"

"Sounds good."

"Great. I'm kind of excited and I'm so happy for you, sweetie."

"Thanks, Daddy."

Bobby joined them.

"Here's my boy," chimed Alexander. "You two leaving for South Beach tomorrow for your honeymoon?"

"Yes, sir," Bobby answered.

Amy quipped, "There's going to be a high school all-star game in Miami that Bobby's going to attend in a couple days."

"Daughter, you are fitting in nicely as a coach's wife."

"I agree. I'm in awe," said Bobby.

"I'm just storing my chits in the bank for when I need them. And I will cash in."

"And there's the lawyer half of my child." He rubbed her back and kissed the top of her head.

Mitch, Trent, Wyatt and Axel now gathered around Alexander and Bobby.

Wyatt announced, "There's a rumor that TORTs is going to make an appearance."

"I haven't heard that," said Alexander. "Have you, Bobby?"

The crowd started chanting, "TORTs! TORTs! TORTs!"

Bobby stood, reached down, offered a hand and helped Alexander to his feet. The band made their way onto the stage.

"Bob-Bee! Bob-Bee! Bob-Bee!" was now chanted.

Bobby glanced around to his bandmates and they gave a thumbs up. He then eyed Alexander and he gave a nod.

The Ohio River Ticks began playing and they were surprisingly good.

Amy looked around and saw Gabby smiling at her. She was with Leti, who was chatting with another couple. Amy waved her over.

Gabby arrived, "You look so beautiful."

"And you too, Gab and so does Leti. Thank you for bringing her. I know this is the first time you've been out in public together."

"Right, we thought, let's start slow, something low-key."

Amy and Gabby laughed.

"Mitch was surprised, a bit wary, but cool with it."

"That's good."

Gabby eyed April and then Alexander, "And, it's so wonderful the relationship you have with your parents."

"We have our differences, but we do get along."

Gabby nodded at that and was becoming emotional, "Family is everything… And the way you are with your dad. I wish… I wish I could have that with…"

Amy was starting to tear up as well, "I know…"

The Ticks played one song and an encore and were cheered.

And then all of a sudden Amy was confronted by her bridesmaids, "It's time to toss the bouquet!" Amy and Gabby dried their eyes. Amy went out to the clearing on the lawn. She grabbed Lannie, who at first tried to resist, but lined up with the rest of the ladies. Amy set herself and tossed the flowers back. There were cheers and applause for the young lady who caught it.

Lannie applauded with everyone else and then was surprised to recognize her friend Kelly Davis, the high-priced gray-hat hacker, dressed in a suit and moving through the gathering. She mumbled to herself, "Kelly… What's he doing here?"

Kelly continued over to the side of the reception. Lannie subtly tracked him and saw that he met with Alexander at a table. She tried to get closer, but couldn't hear what they were saying.

"I'm glad you could make it, Kelly."

"Thanks for the invite, Alexander."

"Sit. Please."

"Sure."

"You said you had something. On the food poisoning."

"Yes. But it can wait. Until after your daughter's reception."

"I paid you enough to tell me. Besides, we already got him."

"Who?"

"Sean, the guy you've been checking. He was trespassing and has been arrested."

"Sean certainly has some issues."

"Someone could have died at my house. A bunch of people got sick and he continued taunting me and my family. But that has come to an end."

"You're right, Alexander, I saw evidence that he's for sure not over the takedown you pulled on him. It's going around in the manosphere how Gokuro Gangsta was played by a Stacey."

Alexander groaned, "Oh brother..."

"But Sean's piggybacking off the food poisoning incident. It's his way of reclaiming some cred."

Alexander was troubled by this, "What are you saying?"

"You see, it's like when a terror group takes responsibility for something they didn't do."

"What??"

"It's true Sean hacked you, has been stalking you and indeed taunting you. He's broken several laws that I can see, but he wasn't behind the food poisoning."

"Then who??"

"It was Reston."

Alexander was shocked and surprised he would go this far. "Whoa. Hold on, do you have proof?"

Kelly handed over an envelope. "He used Telegram to communicate with his accomplice and transferred $50K in Vidarcoin as payment."

"I thought the Telegram app was secure."

"It's very secure. To most. Reston mentioned he hated you getting so much attention with the theater group putting on *King Lear* and he was tired of April continuing to visit Casa Arrington. Does that ring a bell? He suspected something was going on as she had made several trips to your address."

Alexander found a picture, "What's this?"

"I got these off his phone."

The first image was of Alexander and April taken through CA's front window. She was holding an infant.

"This is my home when April and I babysat Abby's child during last time Forecastle was held, two years ago."

The second picture had Alexander and April outside his home embracing—and the third one was them kissing passionately.

Alexander thought back, "These are from Thanksgiving, two years ago."

"To his credit," said Kelly, "Reston wasn't trying to kill anyone with the food poisoning; just make you and your home what he called, 'radioactive.'"

Alexander was lost in thought, "Thank you, Kelly."

"Are you going to be alright?"

Alexander patted him on the shoulder. "I'm fine. Go enjoy the party."

"Thanks, I will." Kelly felt unease as he walked off.

After Kelly departed, Lannie was able to get closer. Alexander took a moment and reflected. He pulled out his phone and made a call. "Hello, that guy that was arrested for trespassing at the Dulsett-Arrington wedding, Sean Wellington. Let him go. Drive him home. I'm not pressing charges." Alexander hung up. He quietly seethed at Reston dancing with April, who were both oblivious to his glare and his wrath.

"*I will have such revenge on you, that all the world shall see. I will do such things. What they are, yet I know not: but they shall be the terrors of the earth.*"

Lannie was stunned to hear this. Alexander then calmly rejoined the reception and was his usual charming self.

Lannie slid over to the bar, "Kelly."

Kelly turned around. "Lannie. Good to see you."

"You're back in the states."

"Yes, for now."

"And you're here at the wedding. Not to be rude, Kel, but why are you here?"

"Alexander invited me."

"Why?"

"You'll have to ask him."

"Come on, Kelly. I know how you earn your ducats. What's going on?"

"You also know my policy. If you want to know why I'm really here, ask him. He hired me." Kelly moved on, "And I've already told you too much."

Lannie joined Amy, "Just wanted to let you know our friend Kelly, the hacker, is here."

"Really?"

"He is."

"Where is he?"

"He just met with your dad. That's who invited him and hired him."

"Hired him?" Amy had a look of concern, "Why?"

"He didn't say and I couldn't hear what they discussed. But after Kelly left your dad…"

"What?"

"Alexander was staring, I'm pretty sure at Reston, quoting from *King Lear.*"

Amy thought this was odd, "Quoting from the play?"

"Yes, the revenge scene where Lear swears to bring the terrors of the earth."

Amy was concerned, she glanced around, but couldn't see Kelly or her father, but did see her mother, "Excuse me for a moment."

Amy joined April, "Hello, dearest Mother."

"That salutation usually means trouble. What's going on?"

"Is Daddy okay? Is something bothering him?"

"Your Daddy? Oh, well, he almost caused a catastrophe before your wedding even started."

"How so?"

"I assigned him the simple task of watching the flower girl and she got away from him. He had no idea where she was and then he went around the front and said, now get this, 'a woman in white' was holding her hand and looking out for her. He said she fixed things."

Amy was stunned at this. "A woman in white?"

April was distracted by a friend wanting to chat.

Amy stood and was drawn around to the front. Through the crowd she noticed a woman in a white dress. Amy moved closer to her. People congregated and congratulated Amy on the way and she smiled and thanked everyone, but it caused her to lose sight of the woman in the white dress.

Amy then glanced out past the security checkpoint and noticed someone. She walked up as Gabby's father was walking away.

"Mr. Gonzales?"

He stopped and turned around.

"It's okay," said Amy, to the security guards. "Mr. Gonzales?"

"Yes? Hello, Amy. I came by just to congratulate you on your wedding."

"Thank you, sir. Would you like to come in and have some cake?"

"No, no, I'm not dressed right and this is a very exclusive event."

"I can let in who I want, it is my wedding reception."

"I don't know."

"Is it because of Gabby?"

"How long did you know?"

"How long have I known that Gabby's a wonderful person, a great friend and a loving daughter that literally idolizes her father?"

"How long did you know?"

Made in United States
Orlando, FL
18 November 2022

"A long time. And the reason you didn't, because she respected you and didn't want to upset you. She wasn't true to herself to please you and it tore her up. Because of her attempt to honor her father. She was very unhappy. Actually, she was quite miserable growing up."

Her father was heartbroken, "Because of me..."

"Please, Mr. Gonzales, come in, it's time to see your daughter."

Mr. Gonzales came in and saw Gabby. They faced each other and he finally reached out and they embraced. Amy watched her lead her father to where Leti was sitting. She stood. They were introduced. Leti put out her hand to shake and her father embraced her too.

Amy again saw the woman in white and she smiled at Amy, went back inside the Peterson-Dumesnil House and faded away. Amy was wide-eyed, but just went with it. She gazed over the crowd, Abby and Mitch were over in the corner having a heated discussion over something. Amy was thankful My Morning Jacket was drowning out the conversation.

Mrs. Simmons was sitting with Mr. Williams. "Zeke and Rose," mumbled Amy. "They must have been some duo. Who knows, maybe again."

Bobby's sister Cassidy was huddling with several investment bankers.

Harold was worn out from the dancing. His date was up grooving with a younger version of Harold.

Old Man Miller and Granddad were sitting together, laughing and telling stories.

Lannie was talking with Kelly at a table.

April and Reston were dancing together.

Sherri came up to Alexander and he let go of the animus he was feeling and danced with her.

Bobby came up and asked for this dance. Amy nodded to him and joined the others. The lights of the reception put a magical glow on this gathering and they celebrated late into the evening.

End of Book 1